Son of the Shadows

BOOKS BY JULIET MARILLIER

THE SEVENWATERS TRILOGY
Daughter of the Forest
Son of the Shadows
Child of the Prophecy

SAGA OF THE LIGHT ISLES
Wolfskin
Foxmask

THE BRIDEI CHRONICLES
The Dark Mirror
Blade of Fortriu
The Well of Shades*

*Forthcoming

Son of the Shadows

BOOK TWO OF THE SEVENWATERS TRILOGY

Juliet Marillier

TOR®
fantasy

A TOM DOHERTY ASSOCIATES BOOK
NEW YORK

This is a work of fiction. All the characters and events portrayed in this book are either products of the author's imagination or are used fictitiously.

SON OF THE SHADOWS

Edited by Claire Eddy

A Tor Book
Published by Tom Doherty Associates, LLC
175 Fifth Avenue
New York, NY 10010

www.tor.com

Tor® is a registered trademark of Tom Doherty Associates, LLC.

ISBN-13: 978-0-765-34326-0
ISBN-10: 0-765-34326-6
Library of Congress Catalog Card Number: 2001017387

First Edition: May 2001
First Mass Market Edition: June 2002

Printed in the United States of America

0 9 8 7 6 5 4

To Godric, voyager and
man of the earth;
and to Ben, a true son of
Manannán mac Lir

Acknowledgments

Grateful thanks to my fellow bard Paul Kelly, who provided invaluable help with Irish spellings and pronunciations. This project owes a great deal to the continuing confidence and support of Cate Paterson of Pan Macmillan and to the understanding and professionalism of my editor, Anna McFarlane. I am indebted to them both.

Author's Note

CELTIC DEITIES

This book contains many references to gods, goddesses, and heroes from Irish mythology. The reader may appreciate a brief introduction to them and a little help with the pronunciation of the Irish Gaelige, remembering that there may be several versions of the spelling and pronunciation of a certain name, all quite valid.

Tuatha Dé Danann   <u>too</u>-a-ha day <u>dann</u>-an
(The Fair Folk)
> The people of the goddess Dana or Danu, they were the last race of Otherworld beings to inhabit Ireland. They defeated two ancient races, the Fir Bolg and the Fomhóire, at the two battles of Moytirra, but were themselves relegated to hidden parts of the landscape, such as caves and barrows, with the coming of the first Gaels.

Fomhóire   fo-<u>vo</u>-reh
(The Old Ones)
> An ancient race that emerged from the sea to inhabit Ireland. Inaccurately described in later written accounts as misshapen and ugly. They were eventually defeated by the Tuatha Dé Danann and sent into exile.

Brighid   <u>bree</u>-yid
> A youthful spring goddess associated with fertility and nurture. In later Christian writings she became inextri-

cably identified with Saint Brigid, foundress of a convent in Kildare.

Dana (Danu)   dan-a, dan-u
    Mother goddess of the Tuatha Dé Danann and associated with the earth.

Morrigan   morri-gan
    A goddess of war and death. One of her favorite forms was that of a crow or raven.

Lugh   loo
    Celtic sun god. Lugh bore the blood of both Tuatha Dé and Fomhóire. A multitalented hero.

Dagda   dog-da
    A respected leader and chief of the Tuatha Dé.

Díancécht   dee-an kyecht
    God of healing, and chief physician of the Tuatha Dé. He constructed a silver hand for the smitten hero Nuada.

Manannán mac Lir   man-un-aun mac lear
    A sea god, mariner, and warrior, who also possessed powers of healing.

CELTIC FESTIVALS
Celtic deities are often associated with the major festivals that mark the turning points of the druidic year. These days not only have a ritual significance but are closely linked to the cycle of planting, growing, harvesting, and storing crops, and are paralleled in the life cycles of man and beast.

Samhain (1 November)   Sowan
    Marks the beginning of the Celtic New Year. The dark months begin; seed waits for new life to germinate. It is a time to take stock and reflect; a time to honor the dead,

when margins may be crossed more easily, allowing communication between human world and spirit world.

Imbolc (1 February)   Imulk, Imbulk
Festival of the lactating ewes, sacred to the goddess Brighid. A day of new beginnings, when the first plowing was often undertaken.

Beltaine (1 May)   Byaltena
On this day the bright half of the year begins. A deeply significant day, related to both fertility and death. The day on which the Túatha Dé Danann first set foot in Ireland. Many customs and practices grew up around Beltaine, including maypole and spiral dances, the setting out of gifts, such as milk, eggs, and cider, for Otherworld folk, and, as at Imbolc, the dousing and relighting of household fires.

Lugnasad (1 August)   Loonasa
A harvest festival sacred to the god Lugh, it developed from the funeral games he held in honor of his foster mother Tailtiu. The mother goddess Dana is also recognized at Lugnasad. Many practices are observed in order to ensure a good and safe harvest. These often include the ritual cutting of the last sheaf of grain. Games and competitions are also popular.

In addition to the four fire festivals outlined above, the solstices and equinoxes mark significant turning points in the year, and each has its own ritual celebration. These are:

Meán Geimhridh (21 December)   winter solstice
Meán Earraigh (21 March)   spring equinox
Meán Samhraidh (21 June)   summer solstice
Meán Fómhair (21 September)   autumn equinox

SOME OTHER NAMES AND TERMS USED
Aengus Og   eyn-gus ohg
Caer Ibormeith   kyre ee-vor-may

Cú Chulainn	Koo <u>khu</u>-linn
Scáthach	skaw-thuck
Aisling	<u>ash</u>-ling
Ciarán	<u>kee</u>-ur-aun
Fionn Uí Néill	fyunn ee <u>nay</u>-ill
Liadan	<u>lee</u>-a-dan
Niamh	<u>nee</u>-av
Sídhe Dubh	shee dove

bogle
A goblinlike creature

Bran mac Feabhail   bran mak <u>fev</u>-il
An eighth-century text describes this hero's voyage to distant and fantastic lands. On his return to Ireland, Bran discovered hundreds of years had passed in the earthly realm.

brithem
In old Irish brehon law, a maker of judgments.

clurichaun   <u>kloo</u>-ri-khaun
A small, mischievous spirit, something like a leprechaun.

deosil   <u>jesh</u>-il
Sunwise; clockwise.

fianna   <u>feen</u>-ya
Band of young hunter-warriors. One particular group of fianna was said to be led by the legendary hero Fionn mac Cumhaill. The term was used for roaming bands of fighters who lived in the wilds and operated under their own rules.

filidh   <u>fil</u>-lee
Ecstatic visionary poets and seers within the druid tradition.

grimoire
> Sorcerer's book of spells.

nemeton
> Sacred grove of the druids.

Ogham
> Secret alphabet of the druids, with twenty-five letters, each of which also indicates a particular plant, tree, or element. Ogham signs might be carved on a tree trunk or scratched on a stone, or indicated by gestures—the druids had no other written language.

riastradh   <u>ree</u>-a-strath
> Battle frenzy.

selkie
> This term can be used for a seal or for one of a race of seal folk who can shed their skins and become human for a time. If the skin is stolen or lost, the selkie cannot return to the ocean.

Tir na nOg   <u>tear</u> na <u>nohg</u>
> Land of Youth. An otherworldly realm beyond the western sea.

túath
> A tribal community in early Christian Ireland, ruled by a king or lord.

Chapter One

My mother knew every tale that was ever told by the firesides of Erin, and more besides. Folks stood hushed around the hearth to hear her tell them after a long day's work, and marveled at the bright tapestries she wove with her words. She related the many adventures of Cú Chulainn the hero, and she told of Fionn mac Cumhaill, who was a great warrior and cunning with it. In some households, such tales were reserved for men alone. But not in ours, for my mother made a magic with her words that drew all under its spell. She told tales that had the household in stitches with laughter, and tales that made strong men grow quiet. But there was one tale she would never tell, and that was her own. My mother was the girl who had saved her brothers from a sorceress's curse, and nearly lost her own life doing it. She was the girl whose six brothers had spent three long years as creatures of the wild, and had been brought back only by her own silence and suffering. There was no need for telling and retelling of this story, for it had found a place in folks' minds. Besides, in every village there would be one or two who had seen the brother who returned, briefly, with the shining wing of a swan in place of his left arm. Even without this evidence, all knew the tale for truth; and they watched my mother pass, a slight figure with her basket of salves and potions, and nodded with deep respect in their eyes.

If I asked my father to tell a tale, he would laugh and shrug and say he had no skill with words, and besides he knew but one tale, or maybe two, and he had told them both already. Then he would glance at my mother, and she at him, in that way they had that was like talking without words, and then my father would distract me with something else. He taught me to carve with a little knife, and he taught me how to plant trees, and he taught me to fight. My uncle thought that more than a little odd. All right for my brother Sean, but when would Niamh and I need skills with our fists and our feet, with a staff or a small dagger? Why waste time on this when there were so many other things for us to learn?

"No daughter of mine will go beyond these woods unprotected," my father had said to my Uncle Liam. "Men cannot be trusted. I would not make warriors of my girls, but I will at least give them the means to defend themselves. I am surprised that you need ask why. Is your memory so short?"

I did not ask him what he meant. We had all discovered, early on, that it was unwise to get between him and Liam at such times.

I learned fast. I followed my mother around the villages, and was taught how to stitch a wound and fashion a splint and doctor the croup or nettle rash. I watched my father, and discovered how to make an owl and a deer and a hedgehog out of a piece of fine oak. I practiced the arts of combat with Sean, when he could be cajoled into it, and perfected a variety of tricks that worked even when your opponent was bigger and stronger. It often seemed as if everyone at Sevenwaters was bigger than me. My father made me a staff that was just the right size, and he gave me his little dagger for my own. Sean was quite put out for a day or so. But he never harbored grudges. Besides, he was a boy, and had his own weapons. As for my sister, Niamh, you never could tell what she was thinking.

"Remember, little one," my father told me gravely, "this dagger can kill. I hope you need never employ it for such a purpose; but if you must, use it cleanly and boldly. Here at Sevenwaters you have seen little of evil, and I hope you will never have to strike a man in your own defense. But one day you may have need of this, and you must keep it sharp and bright, and practice your skills against such a day."

It seemed to me a shadow came over his face, and his eyes went distant as they did sometimes. I nodded silently and slipped the small, deadly weapon away in its sheath.

These things I learned from my father, whom folk called Iubdan, though his real name was different. If you knew the old tales, you recognized this name as a joke, which he accepted with good humor. For the Iubdan of the tales was a tiny wee man, who got into strife when he fell into a bowl of porridge, though he got his own back later. My father was very tall and strongly built, and had hair the color of autumn leaves in afternoon sun. He was a Briton, but people forgot that. When he got his new name he became part of Sevenwaters, and those who didn't use his name called him the Big Man.

I'd have liked a bit more height myself, but I was little, skinny, dark haired, the sort of girl a man wouldn't look twice at. Not that I cared. I had plenty to occupy me without thinking that far ahead. It was Niamh they followed with their eyes, for she was tall and broad shouldered, made in our father's image, and she had a long fall of bright hair and a body that curved generously in all the right places. Without even knowing it, she walked in a way that drew men's eyes.

"That one's trouble," our kitchen woman Janis would mutter over her pots and pans. As for Niamh herself, she was ever critical.

"Isn't it bad enough being half Briton," she said crossly, "without having to look the part as well? See this?" She tugged at her thick plait, and the red-gold strands unraveled in a shining curtain. "Who would take me for a daughter of Sevenwaters? I could be a Saxon with this head of hair! Why couldn't I be tiny and graceful like Mother?"

I studied her for a moment or two as she began to wield the hairbrush with fierce strokes. For one so displeased with her appearance, she did spend rather a lot of time trying out new hairstyles and changing her gown and ribbons.

"Are you ashamed to be the daughter of a Briton?" I asked her.

She glared at me. "That's so like you, Liadan. Always come straight out with it, don't you? It's all very well for you; you're a small copy of Mother yourself, her little right hand. No wonder Father adores you. For you it's simple."

I let her words wash over me. She could be like this at times, as if there were too many feelings inside her and they had to burst out somewhere. The words themselves meant nothing. I waited.

Niamh used her hairbrush like an instrument of punishment. "Sean, too," she said, glaring at herself in the mirror of polished bronze. "Did you hear what Father called him? He said, he's the son Liam never had. What do you think of that? Sean fits in; he knows exactly where he's going. Heir to Sevenwaters, beloved son with not one but two fathers—he even looks the part. He'll do all the right things—wed Aisling, which will make everyone happy, be a leader of men, maybe even the one who wins the Islands back for us.

His children will follow in his footsteps, and so on, and so on. Brighid save me, it's so tedious! It's so predictable."

"You can't have it both ways," I said. "Either you want to fit in, or you don't. Besides, we are the daughters of Seven-waters, like it or not. I'm sure Eamonn will wed you gladly when it's time, golden hair or no. I've heard no objections from him."

"Eamonn? Huh!" She moved to the center of the room, where a shaft of light struck gold against the oak boards of the floor, and in this spot she began slowly to turn, so that her white gown and her brilliant shining hair moved around her like a cloud. "Don't you long for something different to happen, something so exciting and new it carries you along with it like a great tide, something that lets your life blaze and burn so the whole world can see it? Something that touches you with joy or with terror, that lifts you out of your safe, little path and onto a great, wild road whose ending nobody knows? Don't you ever long for that, Liadan?" She turned and turned, and she wrapped her arms around herself as if this were the only way she could contain what she felt.

I sat on the edge of the bed, watching her quietly. After a while I said, "You should take care. Such words might tempt the Fair Folk to take a hand in your life. It happens. You know Mother's story. She was given such a chance, and she took it; and it was only through her courage, and Father's, that she did not die. To survive their games you must be very strong. For her and for Father the ending was good. But that tale had losers as well. What about her six brothers? Of them, but two remain, or maybe three. What happened damaged them all. And there were others who perished. You would be better to take your life one day at a time. For me, there is enough excitement in helping to deliver a new lamb, or seeing small oaks grow strong in spring rains. In shooting an arrow straight to the mark, or curing a child of the croup. Why ask for more when what we have is so good?"

Niamh unwrapped her arms and ran a hand through her hair, undoing the work of the brush in an instant. She sighed. "You sound so like Father you make me sick sometimes," she said, but the tone was affectionate enough. I knew my sister well. I did not let her upset me often.

"I've never understood how he could do it," she went on. "Give up everything, just like that: his lands, his power, his position, his family. Just give it away. He'll never be master of Sevenwaters, that's Liam's place. His son will inherit, no doubt; but Iubdan, all he'll be is 'the Big Man', quietly growing his trees and tending his flocks, and letting the world pass him by. How could a real man choose to let life go like that? He never even went back to Harrowfield."

I smiled to myself. Was she blind that she did not see the way it was between them, Sorcha and Iubdan? How could she live here day by day, and see them look at one another, and not understand why he had done what he had done? Besides, without his good husbandry, Sevenwaters would be nothing more than a well-guarded fortress. Under his guidance our lands had prospered. Everyone knew we bred the best cattle and grew the finest barley in all of Ulster. It was my father's work that enabled my Uncle Liam to build his alliances and conduct his campaigns. I didn't think there was much point explaining this to my sister. If she didn't know it by now, she never would.

"He loves her," I said. "It's as simple as that. And yet, it's more. She doesn't talk about it, but the Fair Folk had a hand in it all along. And they will again."

Finally, Niamh was paying attention to me. Her beautiful blue eyes narrowed as she faced me. "Now you sound like her," she said accusingly. "About to tell me a story, a learning tale."

"I'm not," I said. "You aren't in the mood for it. I was just going to say, we are different, you and me and Sean. Because of what the Fair Folk did, our parents met and wed.

Because of what happened, the three of us came into being. Perhaps the next part of the tale is ours."

Niamh shivered as she sat down beside me, smoothing her skirts over her knees.

"Because we are neither of Britain nor of Erin, but at the same time both," she said slowly. "You think one of us is the child of the prophecy? The one who will restore the Islands to our people?"

"I've heard it said." It was said a lot, in fact, now that Sean was almost a man, and shaping into as good a fighter and a leader as his Uncle Liam. Besides, the people were ready for some action. The feud over the Islands had simmered since well before my mother's day, for it was long years since the Britons had seized this most secret of places from our people. Folk's bitterness was all the more intense now, since we had come so close to regaining what was rightfully ours. For when Sean and I were children, not six years old, our Uncle Liam and two of his brothers, aided by Seamus Redbeard, had thrown their forces into a bold campaign that went right to the heart of the disputed territory. They had come close, achingly close. They had touched the soil of Little Island and made their secret camp there. They had watched the great birds soar and wheel above the Needle, that stark pinnacle lashed by icy winds and ocean spray. They had launched one fierce sea attack on the British encampment on Greater Island, and at the last they had been driven back. In this battle perished two of my mother's brothers. Cormack was felled by a sword stroke clean to the heart and died in Liam's arms. And Diarmid, seeking to avenge his brother's loss, fought as if possessed and at length was captured by the Britons. Liam's men found his body later, floating in the shallows as they launched their small craft and fled, out-numbered, exhausted, and heartsick. He had died from drowning, but only after the enemy had had their sport with him. They would not let my mother see his body when they brought him home.

These Britons were my father's people. But Iubdan had no part in this war. He had sworn, once, that he would not take arms against his own kind, and he was a man of his word. With Sean, it was different. My Uncle Liam had never married, and my mother said he never would. There had been a girl once that he had loved. But the enchantment fell on him and his brothers. Three years is a long time when you are only sixteen. When at last he came back to the shape of a man, his sweetheart was married and already the mother of a son. She had obeyed her father's wishes, believing Liam was dead so he would not take on a wife. And he needed no son of his own, for he loved his nephew as fiercely as any father could and brought him up, without knowing it, in his own image. Sean and I were the children of a single birth, he just slightly my elder. But at sixteen he was more than a head taller, close to being a man, strong of shoulder, his body lean and hard. Liam had ensured he was expert in the arts of war. As well, Sean learned how to plan a campaign, how to deliver a fair judgment, how to understand the thinking of ally and enemy alike. Liam commented sometimes on his nephew's youthful impatience. But Sean was a leader in the making; nobody doubted that.

As for our father, he smiled and let them get on with it. He recognized the weight of the inheritance Sean must one day carry. But he had not relinquished his son. There was time, as well, for the two of them to walk or ride around the fields and byres and barns of the home farms, for Iubdan to teach his son to care for his people and his land as well as to protect them. They spoke long and often, and held each other's respect. Only I would catch Mother sometimes, looking at Niamh and looking at Sean and looking at me, and I knew what was troubling her. Sooner or later, the Fair Folk would decide it was time: time to meddle in our lives again, time to pick up the half-finished tapestry and weave a few more twisted patterns into it. Which would they choose? Was one of us the child of the prophecy, who would at last make peace between our people and the Britons of Northwoods and win back the islands of mystic caves and sacred trees? Myself, I rather thought not. If you knew the Fair Folk at all, you knew they were devious and subtle. Their games were complex; their choices never obvious. Besides, what about the other part of the prophecy, which people seemed to have conveniently overlooked? Didn't it say something about bearing the mark of the raven? Nobody knew quite what that meant, but it didn't seem to fit any of us. Besides, there must have been more than a few misalliances between wandering Britons and Irish women. We could hardly be the only children who bore the blood of both races. This I told myself; and then I would see my mother's eyes on us, green, fey, watchful, and a shiver of foreboding would run through me. I sensed it was time: time for things to change again.

That spring we had visitors. Here in the heart of the great forest, the old ways were strong despite the communities of men and women that now spread over our land, their Christian crosses stark symbols of a new faith. From time to time, travelers would bring across the sea tales of great ills done to folk who dared keep the old traditions. There were cruel penalties, even death, for those who left an offering, maybe, for the harvest gods or thought to weave a simple spell for good fortune or use a potion to bring back a faithless sweetheart. The druids were all slain or banished over there. The power of the new faith was great. Backed up with a generous purse and with lethal force, how could it fail?

But here at Sevenwaters, here in this corner of Erin, we were a different breed. The holy fathers, when they came, were mostly quiet, scholarly men who debated an issue with open minds and listened as much as they spoke. Among them, a boy could learn to read in Latin and in Irish, and to write a clear hand, and to mix colors and make intricate patterns on parchment or fine vellum. Amongst the sisters, a girl might learn the healing arts or how to chant like an angel. In their houses of contemplation there was a place for the poor and dispossessed. They were, at heart, good people. But none from our household was destined to join their number. When my grandfather went away and Liam became lord of Sevenwaters, with all the responsibilities that entailed, many strands were drawn together to strengthen our household's fabric. Liam rallied the families nearby, built a strong fighting force, became the leader our people had needed so badly. My father made our farms prosperous and our fields plentiful as never before. He planted oaks where once had been barren soil. As well, he put new heart into folk who had drawn very close to despair. My mother was a symbol of what could be won by faith and strength, a living reminder of that other world below the surface. Through her they breathed in daily the truth about who they were and where they came from, the healing message of the spirit realm.

And then, there was her brother Conor. As the tale tells, there were six brothers. Liam I have told of, and the two who were next to him in age, who died in the first battle for the Islands. The youngest, Padriac, was a voyager, returning but seldom. Conor was the fourth brother, and he was a druid. Even as the old faith faded and grew dim elsewhere, we witnessed its light glowing ever stronger in our forest. It was as if each feast day, each marking of the passing season with song and ritual, put back a little more of the unity our people had almost lost. Each time, we drew one step closer to being ready—ready again to reclaim what had been stolen from us by the Britons long generations since. The Islands were the heart of our mystery, the cradle of our belief. Prophecy or no prophecy, the people began to believe that Liam would win them back; or if not him, then Sean, who would be lord of Sevenwaters after him. The day drew closer, and folk were never more aware of it than when the wise ones came out of the forest to mark the turning of the season. So it was at Imbolc, the year Sean and I were sixteen, a year burned deep in my memory. Conor came, and with him a band of men and women, some in white, and some in the plain homespun robes of those still in their training, and they made the ceremony to honor Brighid's festival deep in the woods of Sevenwaters.

They came in the afternoon, quietly as usual. Two very old men and one old woman, walking in plain sandals up the path from the forest. Their hair was knotted into many small braids, woven about with colored thread. There were young folk wearing the homespun, both boys and girls; and there were men of middle years, of whom my Uncle Conor was one. Come late to the learning of the great mysteries, he was now their leader, a pale, grave man of middle height, his long chestnut hair streaked with gray, his eyes deep and serene. He greeted us all with quiet courtesy: my mother, Iubdan, Liam, then the three of us, and our guests, for several households had gathered here for the festivities. Seamus Redbeard, a vigorous old man whose snowy hair belied his name. His new wife, a sweet girl not so much older than myself. Niamh had been shocked to see this match.

"How *can* she?" she'd whispered to me behind her hand. "How can she lie with him? He's old, so old. And fat. And he's got a red nose. Look, she's smiling at him! I'd rather die!"

I glanced at her a little sourly. "You'd best take Eamonn then, and be glad of the offer, if what you want is a beautiful young man," I whispered back. "You're unlikely to do better. Besides, he's wealthy."

"Eamonn? Huh!"

This seemed to be the response whenever I made this suggestion. I wondered, not for the first time, what Niamh really did want. There was no way to see inside that girl's head. Not like Sean and me. Perhaps it was our being twins, or maybe it was something else, but the two of us never had any problem talking without words. It became necessary, even, to set a guard on your own mind at times so that the other could not read it. It was both a useful skill and an inconvenient one.

I looked at Eamonn, where he stood now with his sister, Aisling, greeting Conor and the rest of the robed procession. I could not really see what Niamh's problem was. Eamonn was the right age, just a year or two older than my sister. He was comely enough; a little serious maybe, but that could be remedied. He was well built, with glossy, brown hair and fine, dark eyes. He had good teeth. To lie with him would be—well, I had little knowledge of such things, but I imagined it would not be repulsive. And it would be a match well regarded by both families. Eamonn had come very young to his inheritance, a vast domain surrounded by treacherous marshlands to the west of Seamus Redbeard's land and curving around close by the pass to the north. Eamonn's father, who bore the same name, had been killed in rather mysterious circumstances some years back. My Uncle Liam and my father did not always agree, but they were united in their refusal to discuss this particular topic. Eamonn's mother had died when Aisling was born. So Eamonn had grown up with immense wealth and power and an overabundance of influential advisers: Seamus, who was his grandfather; Liam, who had once been betrothed to his mother; my father, who was somehow tied up in the whole thing. It was perhaps surprising that Eamonn had become very much his own man and despite his youth kept his own control over his estates and his not inconsiderable private army. That explained, maybe, why he was such a solemn young man. I found that I had been scrutinizing him closely as he finished speaking with one of the younger druids and glanced my way. He gave me a half smile, as if in defiance of my assessment, and I looked away, feeling a blush rise to my cheeks. Niamh was silly, I thought. She was unlikely to do any better; and at seventeen, she needed to make up her mind quickly before somebody else did it for her. It would be a very strong partnership and made stronger still by the tie of kinship with Seamus, who owned the lands between. He who controlled all of that could deal a heavy blow to the Britons when the time came.

The druids made their way to the end of the line, finishing their greetings. The sun was low in the sky. In the field behind our home barn, in neat rows, the plows and forks and other implements of our new season's work lay ready. We made our way down paths still slippery from spring rains to take up our places in a great circle around the field, our shadows long in the late afternoon light. I saw Aisling slip away from her brother and reappear slightly later at Sean's side, as if by chance. If she thought her move unnoticed, she thought wrong, for her cloud of auburn hair drew the eye however she might try to tame its exuberance with ribbons. As she reached my brother's side, the rising breeze whisked one long, bright curl across her small face, and Sean reached out to tuck it gently behind her ear. I did not need to watch them further to feel her hand slip into his and my brother's fingers tighten around it possessively. Well, I thought, here's someone who knows how to make up his mind. Perhaps it didn't matter, after all, what Niamh decided, for it seemed the alliance would be made one way or another.

The druids formed a semicircle around the rows of tools, and in the gap stood Conor, whose white robe bore an edging of gold. He had thrown back his hood, revealing the golden torch he wore around his neck, a sign of his leadership within this mystic brotherhood. He was young yet by their standards, but his face was an ancient face; his serene gaze held more than one lifetime's knowledge in its depths. He had made a long journey these eighteen years in the forest.

Now Liam stepped forward, as head of the household, and passed to his brother a silver chalice of our best mead, made from the finest honey, and brewed with water from one particular spring whose exact location was a very well-guarded secret. Conor nodded gravely. Then, he began a slow progress between the plows and sickles, the hay forks and heavy spades, the shears and shovels, and he sprinkled a few drops of the potent brew on each as he passed.

"A fine calf in the belly of the breeding cow. A river of sweet milk from her teats. A warm coat on the backs of the sheep. A bountiful harvest from spring rains."

Conor walked evenly, his white robe shifting and changing around him as if with its own life. He bore the silver chalice in one hand, his staff of birch in the other. There was a hush over all of us. Even the birds seemed to cease their chatter in the trees around. Behind me, a couple of horses leaned over the fence, their solemn, liquid eyes fixed on the man with the quiet voice.

"Brighid's blessing be on our fields this season. Brighid's hand stretch out over our new growth. May she bring forth life; may our seed flourish. Heart of the earth; life of the heart; all is one."

So, he went on, and over each of the homely implements of toil he reached his hand and dropped a little of the precious mead. The light grew golden as the sun sank below the tops of the oaks. Last of all was the eight-ox plow, which the men had made under Iubdan's instruction long years ago. With this, the stoniest of fields had been made soft and fertile. We had wreathed it in garlands of yellow tansy and fragrant heather, and Conor paused before it, raising his staff.

"Let no ill fall on our labors," he said. "Let no blight touch our crops, no malady our flocks. Let the work of this plow, and of our hands, make a good harvest and a prosperous season. We give thanks for the earth that is our mother, for the rain that brings forth her life. We honor the wind that shakes the seed from the great oaks; we reverence the sun that warms the new growth. In all things, we honor you, Brighid, who kindles the fires of spring."

The circle of druids echoed his last sentence, their voices deep and resonant. Then, Conor walked back to his brother and put the cup into his hands, and Liam made a comment about maybe sharing what was left in the flask after supper. The ceremony was almost over.

Conor turned and stepped forward, one, two, three steps. He stretched out his right hand. A tall-young initiate with a head of curls the deepest red you ever saw came quickly forward and took his master's staff. He stood to one side, watching Conor with a stare whose intensity sent a shiver down my spine. Conor raised his hands.

"New life! New light! New fire!" he said, and his voice was not quiet now but powerful and clear, ringing through the forest like some solemn bell. "New fire!"

His hands were above his head, reaching into the sky. There was a shimmering and a strange humming sound, and suddenly above his hands was light, flame, a brightness that dazzled the eyes and shocked the senses. The druid lowered his arms slowly. Still between his cupped hands flared a fire, a fire so real I watched with awe, expecting to see his skin burn and blister under the intense heat. The young initiate walked up to him, an unlit torch in his hands. As we stared transfixed, Conor reached out and touched this torch with his fingers, and it flamed into rich, golden light. And when Conor drew his hands away, they were just the hands of a man, and the mysterious fire was gone from them. The face of the youth was a picture of pride and awe as he bore his precious torch up to the house, where the fires of the hearth would be rekindled. The ceremony was complete. Tomorrow, the work of the new season would begin. I caught fragments of conversation as we made our way back to the house, where feasting would commence at sundown.

". . . was this wise? There were others, surely, who could have been chosen for this task?"

"It was time. He cannot be kept hidden forever."

This was Liam and his brother. Then I saw my mother and my father as they walked up the path together. Her foot slipped in the mud, and she stumbled; he caught her instantly, almost before it happened, he was so quick. His arm went around her shoulders, and she looked up at him. I sensed a shadow over the two of them, and I was suddenly ill at ease. Sean ran past me, grinning, with Aisling not far behind. They were following the tall, young man who bore the torch. My brother did not speak, but in my mind I caught his happiness as he passed me. Just for tonight, he was only sixteen years old, and he was in love, and all was right in his world. And I felt that sudden chill again. What was wrong with me? It was as if I were wishing ill on my family, on a fine spring day when everything was bright and strong. I told myself to stop being foolish, but the shadow was still there on the edge of my thoughts.

You feel it too.

I froze. There was only one person I could speak to this way, without words, and that was Sean. But it was not my brother's inner voice that touched my mind now.

Don't be alarmed, Liadan. I will not intrude on your thoughts. If I have learned anything these long years, it is to discipline this skill. You are unhappy. Uneasy. What happens will not be your doing. You must remember that. Each of us chooses his own path.

Still I walked toward the house, the crowd around me chattering and laughing, young men holding their scythes over a shoulder, young women helping to carry spade or sickle. Here and there hands met and clasped, and one or two stragglers disappeared quietly into the forest about their own business. On the path ahead, my uncle walked slowly, the golden border of his robe catching the last rays of setting sun.

I—I don't know what I feel, Uncle. A darkness—something terribly wrong. And yet, it's as if I were wishing it on

*us by thinking of it. How can I do this when everything is so
good, when they are all so happy?*

It's time. Not by so much as a turning of the head did my
uncle show that he spoke with me thus. *You wonder at my
ability to read you? You should talk to Sorcha, if you can
make her answer. It was she, and Finbar, who excelled in
this once. But it may pain her to recall it.*

You said it's time. Time for what?

If there was a way to sigh without making a sound that
was what Conor communicated to me. *Time for their hands
to stir the pot. Time for their fingers to weave a little more
into the pattern. Time for their voices to take up the song.
You need feel no guilt, Liadan. They use us all, and there is
not much we can do about it. I discovered that the hard way.
And so will you, I fear.*

What do you mean?

*You'll find out soon enough. Why not enjoy yourself and
be young while there is still time?*

And that was it. He shut off his thoughts from me as suddenly and surely as if a trapdoor had slammed closed.
Ahead, I saw him pause, waiting for my mother and Iubdan
to catch up; and the three of them went into the house together. I was left none the wiser for this strange conversation.

My sister was very beautiful that night. The hearth fires
of the house had been rekindled, and there was a bonfire out
of doors, and cider, and dancing. It was quite cool. I had
wrapped a shawl around me, and still I shivered. But Niamh's shoulders were bare above her deep blue gown, and
her golden hair was cunningly woven with silk ribbons and
little early violets. As she danced, her skin glowed in the
firelight and her eyes spoke a challenge. The young men
could scarce keep their eyes off her, as she whirled first
with one and then another. Even the young druids, I
thought, were having difficulty in keeping their feet from
tapping and their gaze suitably sober. Seamus had brought

the musicians. They were good; a piper, a harper, and one who excelled at anything he put his hand to, bodhrán or whistle or flute. There were tables and benches set out in the courtyard, and the older druids sat with the household there, talking and exchanging tales, watching as the young folk enjoyed themselves.

There was one who stood apart, and that was the young druid, him with the dark red hair who had held the torch rekindled with a mystical fire. He alone had not partaken of food and drink. He showed no sign of enjoyment as the household exploded in merriment around him. His foot would not be tapping to an old tune; his voice would not be raised in song. Instead, he stood upright and silent behind the main party, watchful. I thought that only common sense. It was wise to have a few who did not partake of strong ale, a few who would listen for unwanted intruders, who would be alert to sounds of danger. I knew Liam had posted men to watch at strategic points around the house, in addition to his usual sentries and forward guards. An attack on Sevenwaters tonight could wipe out not just the lords of the three most powerful families in the northeast but their spiritual leaders as well. So no chances were taken.

But this young man was no guard; or if he were meant to be, he was a pretty poor one. For his dark eyes were fixed on one thing only and that was my lovely, laughing sister as she danced in the firelight with her curtain of red-gold hair swirling around her. I saw how still he was, and how his eyes devoured her; and then I looked away, telling myself not to be stupid. This was a druid after all; I supposed they must have desires, like any other man, and so his interest was natural enough. Dealing with such things was no doubt part of the discipline they learned. And it was none of my business. Then I looked at my sister, and I saw the glance she sent his way from under her long, beautiful lashes. *Dance with Eamonn, you stupid girl*, I told her, but she had never been able to hear my inner voice.

The music changed from a reel to a slow, graceful lament. It had words, and the crowd had drunk enough by now to sing along with the piper.

"Will you dance with me, Liadan?"

"Oh." Eamonn had startled me, suddenly there beside me in the darkness. The firelight showed his face as gravely composed as ever. If he were enjoying the party, he gave no sign of it. Now that I thought about it, I had not seen him dancing.

"Oh. If you—but perhaps you should ask my sister. She dances far better than I." It came out sounding awkward, almost rude. Both of us looked across the sea of dancing youths and girls to where Niamh stood smiling, running a careless hand through her hair, surrounded by admirers, a tall, golden figure in the flickering light.

"I'm asking you." There was no sign of a smile on Eamonn's lips. I was glad he was not able to read my thoughts as my Uncle Conor could. I had been quick enough to assess him earlier that evening. It made my cheeks burn to think of it. I reminded myself that I was a daughter of Sevenwaters and must observe certain courtesies. I got up and slipped off my shawl, and Eamonn surprised me by taking it from me and folding it neatly before he laid it on a nearby table. Then he took my hand and led me into the circle of dancers.

It was a slow dance, couples meeting and parting, circling back to back, touching hands and letting go, a dance well suited to Brighid's festival, which is, after all, about new life and the stirring of the blood that gives it form. I could see Sean and Aisling moving around one another in perfect step, as if the two of them breathed the one breath. The wonderment in their eyes made my heart stop. I found myself saying silently, *Let them keep this. Let them keep it.* But to whom I said this, I did not know.

"What is it, Liadan?" Eamonn had seen the change in my face as he came toward me, took my right hand in his, turned me under his arm. "What's wrong?"

"Nothing," I lied. "Nothing. I suppose I'm tired, that's all. We were up early, gathering flowers, preparing food for the feast, the usual things."

He gave an approving nod.

"Liadan—" He started to say something but was interrupted by an exuberant couple who threatened to bowl us over as they spun wildly past. Adroitly, my partner whisked me out of harm's way, and for a moment both his arms were around my waist and my face close to his.

"Liadan, I need to speak with you. I wish to tell you something."

The moment was over. The music played on, and he let go as we were drawn back into the circle.

"Well, talk then," I said, rather ungraciously. I could not see Niamh; surely she had not retired already. "What is it you want to say?"

There was a lengthy pause. We reached the top of the line; he put one hand on my waist and I put one on his shoulder, and we executed a few turns as we made our way to the bottom under an arch of outstretched arms. Then suddenly it seemed Eamonn had had enough of dancing. He kept my hand in his and drew me to the edge of the circle.

"Not here," he said. "This is not the time nor the place. Tomorrow. I want to talk with you alone."

"But—"

I felt his hands on my shoulders briefly as he placed the shawl about me. He was very close. Something within me sounded a sort of warning, but still I did not understand.

"In the morning," he said. "You work in your garden early, do you not? I will come to you there. Thank you for the dance, Liadan. You should perhaps let me be the judge of your skills."

I looked up at him, trying to work out what he meant, but his face gave nothing away. Then somebody called his name, and with a brief nod he was gone.

I worked in the garden next morning, for the weather was fine, though cold, and there was always plenty to do between herb beds and stillroom. My mother did not come out to join me, which was unusual. Perhaps, I thought, she was tired after the festivities. I weeded and cleaned and swept, and I made up a coltsfoot tea to take to the village later, and I bundled flowering heather for drying. It was a busy morning. I forgot all about Eamonn until my father came into the stillroom near midday, ducking his head under the lintel, then seating himself on the wide window embrasure, long legs stretched out before him. He, too, had been working and had not yet shed his outdoor boots, which bore substantial traces of newly plowed soil. It would sweep up easily enough.

"Busy day?" he asked, observing the well-ordered bundles of drying herbs, the flasks ready for delivery, the tools of my trade still laid out on the workbench.

"Busy enough," I said, bending to wash my hands in the bucket I kept by the outer door. "I missed Mother today. Was she resting?"

A little frown appeared on his face. "She was up early, talking to Conor, at first. Later with Liam as well. She needs to rest."

I tidied the knives, the mortar and pestle, the scoops and twine away onto their shelves. "She won't," I said. "You know that. It's like this when Conor comes. It's as if there's never enough time for them, always too much to be said, as if they can never make up for the years they lost."

Father nodded, but he didn't say anything. I got out the millet broom and began to sweep.

"I'll go to the village later," I told him. "She need not do that. Perhaps, if you tell her to, she'll try to sleep."

Iubdan's mouth quirked up at one corner in a half smile. "I never tell your mother what to do," he said. "You know that."

I grinned at him. "Well then, I'll tell her. The druids are here for a day or two. She has time enough for talking."

"That reminds me," said Father, lifting his booted feet as I swept the floor beneath them. When he put them down again, a new shower of earth fell onto the flagstones. "I had a message to give you."

"Oh?"

"From Eamonn. He asked me to say he's been called home urgently. He left very early this morning, too early to come and see you with any decency, was how he put it. He said to tell you he would speak with you when he returned. Does that make sense to you?"

"Not a lot," I said, sweeping the last of the debris out the door and down the steps. "He never did tell me what it was all about. Why was he called away? What was so urgent? Has Aisling gone as well?"

"Aisling is still here; she is safer under our protection. It was a matter calling for leadership and quick decisions. He has taken his grandfather and those of his men who could be made ready to ride. I understand there was some new attack on his border positions. By whom, nobody seemed sure. An enemy who came by stealth and killed without scruple, as efficiently as a bird of prey, was the description. The man who brought the tale seemed almost crazed with fear. I suppose we will hear more when Eamonn returns."

We went out into the garden. At this chill time of year, spring was not much more than a thought; the tiniest of fragile crocus shoots emerging from the hard ground, a hint of buds swelling on the branches of the young oak. Early flowering tansy made a note of vibrant yellow against the gray-green of wormwood and lavender. The air smelled cool and clean. Each stone path was swept bare, the herb beds tidy under their straw mulching.

"Sit here awhile with me, Liadan," said my father. "We are not needed yet. It will be hard enough to persuade your mother and her brothers to come inside for some food and drink. I have something to ask you."

"You, too?" I said, as we sat down together on the stone bench. "It sounds as if everyone has something to ask me."

"Mine is a general sort of question. Have you given any thought to marriage? To your future?"

I was not expecting this.

"Not really. I suppose—I suppose I hoped, as the youngest, for a couple more years at home," I said, feeling suddenly cold. "I am in no hurry to leave Sevenwaters. Maybe—maybe I thought I might remain here, you know, tend to my ancient parents in their failing years. Perhaps not seek a husband at all. After all, both Niamh and Sean will make good matches, strong alliances. Need I be wed as well?"

Father looked at me very directly. His eyes were a light, intense blue; he was working out just how much of what I said was serious and how much a joke.

"You know I would gladly keep you here with us, sweetheart," he said slowly. "Saying farewell to you would not be easy for me. But there will be offers. I would not have you narrow your pathway because of us."

I frowned. "Maybe we could leave it for a while. After all, Niamh will wed first. Surely there won't be any offers until after that." My mind drew up the image of my sister, glowing and golden in her blue gown by firelight, tossing her bright hair, surrounded by comely young men. "Niamh should wed first," I added firmly. It seemed to me that this was important, but I could not tell him why.

There was a pause, as if he were waiting for me to make some connection I could not quite grasp.

"Why do you say that? That there will be no offers for you until your sister weds?"

This was becoming difficult, more difficult than it should have been, for my father and I were very close and always spoke directly and honestly to each other.

"What man would offer for me when he could have Niamh?" I asked. There was no sense of envy in my question. It just seemed to me so obvious I found it hard to believe it had not occurred to him.

My father raised his brows. "Perhaps, if Eamonn makes you an offer of marriage, you should ask him that question," he said quite gently. There was a hint of amusement in his tone.

I was stunned. "Eamonn? Offer for me? I don't think so. Is he not intended for Niamh? You're wrong, I'm sure." But in the back of my mind, last night's episode played itself out again: the way he had spoken to me, the way we had danced together, and a little seed of doubt was sown. I shook my head, not wanting to believe it was possible. "It wouldn't be right, Father. Eamonn should wed Niamh. That's what everyone expects. And—Niamh needs somebody like him. A man who will—take a firm hand but be fair as well. Niamh should be the one." Then I thought, with relief, of something else. "Besides," I added, "Eamonn would never ask a girl such a thing without seeking her father's permission first. He was to have spoken with me early this morning. It must have been about something else."

"What if I told you," said Iubdan carefully, "that your young friend had planned a meeting with me as well this morning? He was prevented from keeping this appointment only by the sudden call home to defend his border."

I was silent.

"What sort of man would you choose for yourself, Liadan?" he asked me.

"One who is trustworthy and true to himself," I answered straightaway. "One who speaks his mind without fear. One who can be a friend as well as a husband. I would be contented with that."

"You would wed an ugly, old man with not a scrap of silver to his name if he met your description?" asked my father, amused. "You are an unusual young woman, Daughter."

"To be honest," I said wryly, "if he were also young, handsome, and wealthy, it would not go unappreciated. But such things are less important. If I was lucky enough—if I was fortunate enough to wed for love, as you did . . . but that is unlikely, I know." I thought of my brother and Aisling, dancing in a charmed circle all their own. It was too much to expect the same thing for myself.

"It brings a contentment like no other," said Iubdan softly. "And with it a fear that strikes when you least expect it. When you love thus, you give hostages to fortune. It becomes harder with time to accept what fate brings. We have been lucky so far."

I nodded. I knew what he was talking about. It was a matter we did not speak of openly, not yet.

We got up and walked slowly out through the garden archway and along the path toward the main courtyard. Farther away, in the shelter of a tall hedge of blackthorn, my mother was seated on the low, stone wall, a small, slight figure, her pale features framed by a mass of dark curls. Liam stood on one side, booted foot on the wall, elbow on knee, explaining something with economical gestures. On her other side sat Conor, very still in his white robe, listening intently. We did not disturb them.

"I suppose you will find out when Eamonn returns whether I am right," my father said. "There is no doubt he would be a very suitable match for your sister or for yourself. You should at least give thought to it in the meantime."

I did not answer.

"You must understand that I would never force you into any decision, Liadan, and neither would your mother. When you take a husband, the choice will be yours. We would ask only that you think about it, and prepare yourself, and consider any offers that are made. We know you will choose wisely."

"What about Liam? You know what he would want. There is our estate to consider and the strength of our alliances."

"You are your mother's daughter and mine, not Liam's," said my father. "He will be content enough that Sean has chosen the one woman Liam would most have wanted for him. Your choice will be your own, little one."

I had the strangest feeling at that moment. It was as if a silent voice whispered, *These words will come back to haunt him.* A chill, dark feeling. It was over in a moment, and when I glanced at Father, his face was calm and unperturbed. Whatever it was, it had passed by him unheard.

The druids remained at Sevenwaters for several days. Conor spoke at length with his sister and brother, or sometimes I would see him with my mother alone, the two of them standing or sitting together in total silence. At such times they communicated secretly, with the language of the mind, and there was no telling what passed between them. Thus had she spoken once with Finbar, the brother closest to her heart, him who returned from the years away with the wing of a swan instead of an arm and something not quite right with his mind. She had shared the same bond with him as I did with Sean. I knew my brother's pain and his joy without the need for words. I could reach him, however far he might go, with a message nobody but he would ever hear. And so I understood how it must be for my mother, for Sorcha, having lost that other who was so close that he was like a part of herself. For, the tale went, Finbar could never become a man again, not quite. There was a part of him, when he came back, that was still wild, attuned to the needs and instincts of a creature of the wide sky and the bottomless deep. And so, one night, he had simply walked down to the lake shore and on into the cold embrace of the water. His body had never been found, but there was no doubt, folk said, that he drowned that night. How could such a creature swim, with the right arm of a young man and on the left side a spreading, white-feathered wing?

I understood my mother's grief, the empty place she must carry inside her even after so long, although she never spoke of these things, not even to Iubdan. But I believed she shared it with Conor during those long, silent times. I thought they used their gift to strengthen one another, as if by sharing the pain they could make it a little easier to bear, each for the other.

The whole household would gather together for supper when the long day's work was over, and after supper for singing and drinking and the telling of tales. In our family there was an ability for storytelling that was widely known and respected. Of us all, my mother was the best, her gift with words such that she could, for a time, take you right out of this world and into another. But the rest of us were no mean wordsmiths either. Conor was a wonderful storyteller. Even Liam, on occasion, would contribute some heroic tale containing detailed descriptions of battles and the technicalities of armed and unarmed combat. There was a strong following for these among the men. Iubdan, as I have said, never told a tale, though he listened attentively. At such times folk were reminded that he was a Briton, but he was well respected for his fairness, his generosity, and above all his capacity for hard work; and so they did not hold his ancestry against him.

On the night of Imbolc, however, it was not one of our household who told the tale. My mother was asked for a story, but she excused herself.

"With such a learned company in our midst," she said sweetly, "I must decline for tonight. Conor, we know the talent of your kind for such a task. Perhaps you will favor us with a tale for Brighid's day?"

I thought, looking at her, that she still seemed weary,

with a trace of shadow around the luminous green eyes.
She was always pale, but tonight her skin had a trans-
parency that made me uneasy. She sat on a bench beside
Iubdan, and her small hand was swallowed up by his large
one. His other arm was around her shoulders, and she
leaned against him. The words came to me again, *Let them
keep this,* and I flinched. I told myself sternly to stop this
foolishness. What did I think I was, a seer? More likely just
a girl with a fit of the vapors.

"Thank you," said Conor gravely, but he did not rise to his
feet. Instead, he looked across the hall and gave the smallest
of nods. And so it was the young druid, the one who had
borne the torch the night before to rekindle our hearth fires,
who stepped forward and readied himself to entertain us. He
was, indeed, a well-made young fellow, quite tall and very
straight backed with the discipline of his kind, his curling
hair not the fiery red of my father's and Niamh's but a deeper
shade, the color at the heart of a winter sunset. And his eyes
were dark, the dark of ripe mulberries, and hard to read.
There was a little cleft in his chin, and he had a pair of
wicked dimples when he allowed them to show. Just as well,
I thought, that this is one of the brotherhood. If not, half the
young girls of Sevenwaters would be fighting over him. I
dare say he'd enjoy that.

"What better tale for Imbolc," began the young druid,
"than that of Aengus Óg and the fair Caer Ibormeith? A tale
of love, and mystery, and transformation. By your leave, I
will tell this tale tonight."

I had expected he might be nervous, but his voice was
strong and confident. I supposed it came from years and
years of privation and study. It takes a long time to learn
what a druid must learn, and there are no books to help you.
I saw, out of the corner of my eye, Liam looking at Sorcha, a
small frown on his face and a question in his eyes. She gave
a little nod as if to say, never mind, let him go on. For this
tale was one we did not tell here at Sevenwaters. It cut alto-

gether too close to the bone. I imagined this young man knew little of our history, or he would never have chosen it. Conor, surely, could not have been aware of his intention, or he would tactfully have suggested a different story. But Conor was sitting quietly near his sister, apparently unperturbed.

"Even a son of the Tuatha Dé Danann," began the young man, "can fall sick for love. So it was with Aengus. Young, strong, handsome, a warrior of some repute; one would not have thought him so easily unmanned. But one afternoon, out hunting for deer, he was overtaken suddenly by a deep weariness and stretched himself out to sleep on the grass in the shade spread by a grove of yew trees. He slept straightaway, and in his sleep he dreamed. Oh, how he dreamed. In his dream, there she was: a woman so beautiful she outshone the stars in the sky, a woman to tear your heart in pieces. He saw her walking barefoot by a remote shore, tall and straight, her breasts white as moonlight on snow where they swelled around above the dark folds of her gown, her hair like light on beech leaves in autumn, the bright redgold of burnished copper. He saw the way she moved, the sweet allure of her body; and when he woke, he knew that he must have her or he would surely die."

This had, I thought, far too much of a personal touch. But when I looked round me, as the storyteller drew breath, it seemed only I had noticed the form of his words: I and one other. Sean stood by Aisling near the window, and they seemed to be listening as attentively as I, but I knew their thoughts were on each other, every scrap of awareness fixed on the way his hand lay casually at her waist, the way her fingers gently touched his sleeve. Iubdan was watching the young druid, but his gaze was abstracted; my mother had rested her head against his shoulder, and her eyes were closed. Conor looked serene; Liam remote. The rest of the household listened politely. Only Niamh sat mesmerized on the edge of her seat, a deep blush on her cheeks and her lovely blue eyes alight with fascination. He meant it for her, there was no doubt of it; was I the only other who could see this? It was almost as if he had the power to command our reactions with his words.

"Aengus suffered thus for a year and a day," the youth went on. "Every night in visions she would appear to him, sometimes close to his bedside, her fair body clothed in sheerest white, so close it seemed he could touch her with his hand. He fancied, when she bent over him, he felt the light touch of her long hair against his bare body. But when he reached out, lo! she was gone in an instant. He was eaten up with longing for her so that he fell into a fever, and his father, the Dagda, feared for his life, or at least for his sanity. Who was she? Was the maiden real or some creature summoned up from the depths of Aengus's spirit, never to be possessed in life?

"Aengus was dying; his body was burning up, his heart beat like a battle drum, his eyes were hot with fever. And so the Dagda solicited the help of the king of Munster. They sought to the east, and they sought to the west, and along all the highways and byways of Erin; and at length they learned the maiden's name. It was Caer Íbormeith, Yewberry, and she was the daughter of Eathal, a lord of the Tuatha Dé, who dwelt in an Otherworld place in the province of Connacht.

"When they told Aengus this news, he rose up from his sickbed and went forth to find her. He made the long journey to the place called Mouth of the Dragon, the lake on whose remote shores he had first glimpsed his beloved. He waited there three days and three nights, taking neither food nor drink, and at length she came, walking along the sand barefoot as he had seen her in his vision, her long hair whipped around her by the wind over the lake, like coils of living fire. His desire threatened to overwhelm him, but he managed to approach her politely and introduced himself as steadily as he could.

"The maiden, Caer Ibormeith, wore around her neck a collar of silver, and now he saw that a chain linked her to another maiden, and another, and all along the shore thrice fifty young women walked, each joined to the next by chains of wrought silver. But when Aengus asked Caer to be his, when he pleaded his longing for her, she slipped away as silently as she had appeared, and her maidens with her. And of them all, she was the tallest and the most lovely. She was indeed the woman of his heart."

He paused, but not a glance did he make in Niamh's direction, where she sat like some beautiful statue, her intense blue eyes full of wonderment. I had never seen her sit still so long.

"After this, the Dagda went to Caer's father where he dwelt in Connacht and demanded the truth. How could his son, Aengus, win this woman, for without her he would surely be unable to live? How might so strange a creature be had? Eathal was unwilling to cooperate; eventually, pressure was applied that he could not resist. The fair Caer, said her father, chose to spend every other year as a swan. From Samhain she would resume her birdlike guise; and on the day she changed, Aengus must take her to him, for that was the time she was most vulnerable. But he must be ready, warned Eathal. Winning her would not be without a cost.

"It came to pass as Eathal had said. On Samhain Eve, Aengus traveled back to the Dragon's Mouth, and there on the shore were thrice fifty beautiful swans, each with a collar of beaten silver. Thrice fifty and one, for he knew the swan with the proudest plumage, and the longest, most graceful neck, was his lovely Caer Ibormeith. Aengus went up to her, and fell on his knees before her, and she laid her neck across his shoulder and raised her wide wings. At that moment he felt himself changing. A thrill went through his body, from the tips of his toes to the hair on his head, from his smallest finger to his beating heart; and then he saw his skin change and shimmer and his arms sprout forth snowy plumes, and his vision became clear and far seeing, and he knew he, too, was a swan.

"They flew three times around the lake, singing in their joy, and so sweet was that song that it lulled all for many leagues around into a peaceful sleep. After that, Caer Ibormeith returned home with Aengus, and whether they went in the form of man and woman, or of two swans, the stories do not make plain. But they do say, if on Samhain Eve you travel close to Loch Béal Dragan and stand very still on the shore at dusk, you will hear the sound of their voices calling out in the darkness over the lake. Once you have heard that song, you will never forget it. Not in all your living days."

The silence that followed was a sign of respect accorded only to the best storytellers. He had indeed told his tale with skill; almost as well as one of our own family might have done. I did not look at Niamh; I hoped her red cheeks would not draw undue attention. At length it was my mother who spoke.

"Come forward, young man," she said softly, and she stood up, but her hand was still in my father's. The young druid stepped forward, somewhat paler in the face than before. Perhaps, for all his seeming confidence, this had been an ordeal for him. He was young enough, scarce twenty, I'd have thought.

"You tell your tale with spirit and imagination. Thank you for entertaining us so well tonight." She smiled at him kindly, but I noticed the grip she kept on Iubdan's fingers behind her back, as if to steady herself.

The young man bowed his head briefly. "Thank you, my lady. Praise such as this, coming from a storyteller of your reputation, I value highly. I owe my skills to the best of teachers." He glanced at Conor.

"What is your name, son?" This was Liam, from across the room where he sat among his men. The boy turned.

"Ciarán, my lord."

Liam nodded. "You are welcome in my house, Ciarán, whenever my brother chooses to bring you here. We value our tales and our music, which once were all but lost from these halls. Welcome, indeed, all of the brotherhood and sisterhood who grace our fireside on Brighid's night. Now, who will play the harp or flute or sing us a fine song of battles won and lost?"

My uncle was, I thought, deliberately moving them onto safer territory, like the master tactician he was. The young man, Ciarán, melted back into the group of gray-robed figures seated quietly together in a corner; and with the passing around of mead jugs and the striking up of pipes and flute, the evening went on in perfect harmony.

After a while, I told myself I was being foolish. An overactive imagination, that was all it was. It was natural for Niamh to flirt; she did it without thinking. There was no real intention in it. There she was now, laughing and joking with a couple of Liam's young warriors. As for the tale, it was not uncommon to base a description of a hero, or a lady, on someone you knew. A boy brought up in the sacred groves, far from the halls of lord and chieftain, might have precious little to go on when required to speak of a peerless beauty. Not surprising, then, that he fixed on the lovely daughter of the house as his model. Harmless. I was stupid. The druids would go back to their forest, and Eamonn would return, and he would marry Niamh, and all would be as it should be. As it must be. I'd almost convinced myself, as it drew onto midnight and we made ready to retire to bed. Almost. As I reached the foot of the stairs, candle in hand, I happened to glance across the room, and met the steady gaze of my Uncle Conor. He was standing still amid a bustle of people who talked, and laughed, and lit candles from the lamp there, so still he could have been made of stone, but for his eyes.

Remember, Liadan. It unfolds as it must. Follow your path with courage. That is all any of us can do.

But—but—

He had moved away already, and I could no longer touch his thoughts. But I saw Sean turn his head sharply toward me, feeling my confusion without understanding it. It was too much. Nameless feelings of ill; sudden bouts of shivering; cryptic warnings of the mind. I wanted my quiet room, a drink of water, and a good night's sleep. Simple, safe things. I gripped my candleholder, picked up my skirts, and went upstairs to bed.

Chapter Two

It's quite tricky making a tincture of celandine. The method is simple enough; it's getting the quantities just right that's the problem. My mother showed me how to do it both ways, with fresh leaves and dry, her small, capable hands grinding the dried leaves with mortar and pestle while I shredded the newly gathered ones, placing them in a shallow bowl, covering them barely with a little of the precious brew that was the same Conor had used to bring down the blessing of Brighid on our fields this growing season. I followed her instructions, glad I was not one of those who suffered a painful swelling of the skin when working with this particular herb. My mother's hands were smooth and pale, for all her daily labors in the stillroom, and delicately made. The only adornment she wore was the ring her husband had crafted for her many long years ago. Today, she was clad in an ancient gown that had once been blue, and her long hair was tied back with a plain strip of linen. This gown, this ring, these hands each had their own tale; and my mind was on them as I prepared my own bowl of steeping herbs.

"Good," said Mother, watching me. "I want you to learn this well and be able to apply it with other materials as aptly. This tincture will ease most maladies of the stomach, but it is strong. Use it on your patient but once, or you may do more harm than good. Now lay the muslin cloth over your bowl and put it away carefully. That's it. One and twenty nights let it rest, and then strain it and store it in the dark, corked tight. Such a tincture will keep well for many moons. This will see you through the winter."

"Why don't you sit down for a while, Mother?" The pot was boiling on the small fire; I took down two earthenware cups, opened jars of dried leaves.

"You're spoiling me, Liadan," she said, smiling, but she did sit down, a slight figure in her old, working dress. The sun streamed in the window behind her, showing me how pale she was. In the strong light, you could see the traces of faded embroidery at the neckline and hem of her gown. Ivy leaves, little flowers, here and there a tiny, winged insect. I poured hot water carefully into each cup.

"Is this a new mixture?"

"It is," I said, beginning to clean and tidy away the knives and bowls and implements we had used. "See if you can tell me what's in it." The smell of the herbal infusion was spreading through the cool, dry air of the stillroom.

Mother sniffed delicately. "There's all-heal—the dried flowers, that must be; there's figwort in it, maybe a touch of Saint-John's-wort as well, and—goldenwood?"

I found a jar of our best honey and spooned a little into each cup. "You certainly haven't lost your touch," I said. "You needn't worry. I know how to gather that herb and how to use it."

"A powerful combination, Daughter."

I glanced at her, and she looked straight back.

"You know, don't you?" she said softly.

I nodded, unable to speak. I placed a cup of the healing tea on the stone sill beside her and my own near me where I worked.

"Your choice of herbs is very apt. But it is too late for such cures to do more than provide a brief respite. You know this too." She took a sip of the tea, screwed up her face, and gave a little smile. "It's a bitter brew."

"Bitter indeed," I said, sipping my own tea, which was plain peppermint. I managed to keep my voice under control, just.

"I can see we have taught you well, Liadan," said my mother, regarding me closely. "You have my skill with healing and your father's gift for love. He gathers all around him under his protective shade like a great forest tree. I see the same strength in you, Daughter."

This time, I did not risk speaking.

"It will be hard for him," she went on, "very hard. He is not one of us, not truly, though we forget it sometimes. He does not understand that this is not a true parting but simply a moving on, a changing."

"The wheel turns and returns," I said.

Mother smiled again. She had put the tea down almost untouched. "There's a bit of Conor in you as well," she said. "Sit down awhile, Liadan. I have something to tell you."

"You too?" I managed a watery grin.

"Yes, your father told me about Eamonn."

"And what did you think?"

A little frown creased her brow. "I don't know," she said slowly. "I can't advise you. But—but I would say, don't be in too much of a hurry. You'll be needed here for a while."

I didn't ask her why. "Have you told Father?" I asked finally.

Mother gave a sigh. "No. He will not ask me, since he knows I will answer with the truth. I don't need to put it into words. Not for Red. His knowledge is there in the touch of his hand, in his hastening home from plowing, in the way he sits by the bed, thinking me asleep, and holds my hand, looking into the darkness. He knows."

I shivered. "What was it you were going to tell me?"

"Something I have never shared with anyone. But I think now is the time to pass it on. You've been troubled lately; I've seen it in your eyes. Not just—not just this, but something more."

I held my cup between my palms, warming them. "I get—sometimes I get the strangest feeling. As if suddenly everything goes cold, and—and there's a voice . . ."

"Go on."

"I see—I feel as if something terrible is coming. I look at someone and sense a—a sort of doom over them. Conor knows. He told me not to feel guilty. I didn't find that particularly helpful."

Mother nodded. "My brother was about your age when he first felt it. Finbar, I mean. Conor remembers that. It is a painful skill, one few would wish for themselves."

"What is it?" I asked, shivering. "Is it the Sight? Then why don't I go into convulsions and scream and then go limp like Biddy O'Neill down at the Crossing? She's got the Sight. She foretold the great floods two winters ago and the death of that man whose cart went over the edge at Fergal's Bluff. This is—different."

"Different but the same. The way it takes you depends on your own strength and your own gifts. And what you see can also mislead you. Finbar often saw true, and he felt the guilt of not being able to prevent the things from happening. But what his visions meant was by no means easy to interpret. It's a cruel gift, Liadan. With it comes another, which you have not yet had cause to develop."

"What's that?" I wasn't sure I wanted to know. Wasn't one such gift, if gift it could be called, more than enough?

"I can't explain it, not fully. He used it on me once. He and I—he and I shared the same bond you have with Sean, a closeness that lets you speak mind to mind, that tunes you to the other's inmost self. Finbar had greater skill than I; those last days he became adept at keeping me out. There were times when I think he dreaded to let down his guard; he had a wound deep to the spirit, and he would not share it, not even with me. But he had the other skill as well, the ability to use the power of his mind for healing. When I was—when I was hurt and thought the world would never be right again, he—he touched me with his mind; he blocked out the bad things; he held my thoughts with his own until the night was over. Later, he used this same skill on my father, whose mind was deeply damaged by the work of the Sorceress, the Lady Oonagh. She kept Father dancing to her will for three long years while my brothers were under the enchantment. And Lord Colum was not a weak man; he wrestled with his own guilt and shame, and yet he could not deny her. When we returned home at last, he scarcely knew us. Bringing him back to himself took many patient days and nights. There is a heavy price for the use of this healing power. Afterward Finbar was—drained, scarce himself. He was like a man who has undergone the fiercest ordeals of body and spirit. Only the strongest may withstand this."

I looked at her with a question in my eyes.

"You are strong, Liadan. I cannot tell you if and when you may be called to use this gift. Perhaps never. It's best you know, at least. He would be able to tell you more."

"He? You mean—Finbar?" Now we were on fragile ground indeed.

Mother turned to look out of the window. "It grew again so beautifully," she said. "The little oak Red planted for me that will one day be tall and noble, the lilac, the healing herbs. The Sorceress could not destroy us. Together, we were too strong for her." She looked back at me. "The magic is powerful in you, Liadan. And there is one more thing in your favor."

"What's that?" I asked. Her words were both fascinating and terrifying.

"He showed me once; Finbar. I came close to asking him what the future would hold for me. He showed me a moment of time. There was Niamh, dancing along a forest path with her hair like golden fire, a child with a gift for happiness. And Sean, running, running to catch up with her. I saw my children and Red's. And—and there was another child. A child who was—shut out. On the edge, so that I could never quite see. But that child was not you, Daughter. Of that I am certain. Had it been you, I would have known the moment you were born and laid in my arms."

"But—but why wasn't I there? Sean and I are of an age. Why would I not be in your vision, too?"

"I saw the same vision earlier," said my mother slowly. "When I—but both times, you were not there. Only that other child, closed off from the picture. I believe you are somehow outside the pattern, Liadan. If this is so, it could give you great power, dangerous power. It could allow you to—change things. In these visions, it was not foretold that Sean's birth would bring forth a second child. That sets you apart. I have believed, for a long time, that the Fair Folk guide our steps. That they work their great plans through us. But you are not in their scheme. Perhaps you hold some sort of key."

It was too much to take in. Still, I could not but believe her, for my mother always told the truth, no more and no less.

"Then what about the third child in the vision?" I asked. "The child on the margin, in the shadows?"

"I cannot tell who that was. Only—it was a child who had given up all hope. That is a terrible thing. Why I was shown this, there is no telling. In time, perhaps you will find out."

I shivered again. "I'm not sure that I want to."

Mother smiled and got up. "These things have a habit of finding you, whether you like it or not," she said. "Conor was right. There's no point in feeling guilty or worrying about what may come. Put one foot before the other and follow your path. That's all we can do."

"Hmm." I glanced at her. It sounded as if my own particular path might be rather more complicated than I would have wished. I didn't ask for much. The security and peace of Sevenwaters, the chance to use my craft well and be warmed by the love of my family. I wasn't sure if I had it in me to do more than that. I could not see myself as one who might influence the course of destiny. How Sean would laugh at this notion, if I told him.

The season wore on, and Eamonn did not come back. The druids left us again, walking silent footed into the forest at dusk. Niamh became unusually quiet and took to sitting up on the roof slates, gazing out over the trees and humming softly to herself. Often, when I looked for her to help with a piece of sewing or an errand to the settlement, she was nowhere to be found. In the evenings she never wanted to talk anymore but lay on her bed smiling secretly, until her eyelids dropped over her beautiful eyes and she slept like a child. I slept less easily myself. We heard conflicting reports from the north. Eamonn was fighting on two fronts. He had advanced into his neighbor's territory. He had retreated to his inner wall. The raiders were Norsemen, come back to harry a shore we had long thought safe. They had settlements far south, at the mouth of a great river, and they sought to expand their holding up along the coast and even into the heart of our own lands. They were not Norsemen at all but Britons. They were neither, but some more foreign breed; men who wore their identity on their skin in a secret, coded pattern. Men with faces like strange birds and great fierce cats and stag and boar; men who attacked in silence and killed without mercy. One had a face as black as the night sky. Not even men, perhaps, but Otherworld warriors. Their weapons were as odd as their appearance; cunning pipes through which a dart with poison tip might be launched into the air; tiny metal balls studded with spikes that traveled fast and bit hard, clever use of a length of fine cord, no sword or spear, no honest weapons.

We did not know which of these stories to believe, though Sean and Liam favored the theory about Norsemen as the most likely. After all, such invaders were best placed for a quick strike and retreat, for at sea they were as yet un-matched, employing both oar and sail to move faster than the wind over the water. Maybe their ornate helmets had given rise to the strange tales. And yet, said Liam, the Norsemen fought unsubtly, with broadsword, mace, and axe. Nor were they known for their prowess in wooded ter-rain, preferring to keep their hold on the coastal margins rather than venture inland. The theory did not fit quite as neatly as one might have wished.

Eventually around the time when day and night were of equal length and Father was busy with planting, Eamonn sent for help, and Liam despatched a force of thirty well-armed men off to the north. Sean would have liked to go and so, I think, would my uncle himself. But as it was, something stayed them both. There was Aisling, still dwelling in our house where she would be out of harm's way, and anxious for her brother's safety. That was enough to keep Sean at home for now. And Liam said it was too risky, with the threat not fully understood, for either of them to be in the front line along with both Eamonn and his grandfather. They would wait until they got a report from Eamonn himself or from Seamus. That would be fact and not fancy. Then would be time to decide whether to take further action.

I noticed, though, that they spoke long and seriously in the evenings and studied their maps. Iubdan, too. My father might have sworn not to take up arms, not if the enemy might be his own kind, but Liam was enough of a strategist to recognize and make use of the skill his sister's husband had with charts and with the planning of offense and defense. I heard him remark that it was a pity Padriac had never come back the last time he'd sailed off in search of new lands and fresh adventures. Now *there* was a man who knew how to build a boat and handle it better than any Norseman. There was a man who could think up ten different solutions to any problem. But it was three years now since Liam had last laid eyes on his youngest brother. Nobody held out much hope of a safe return after so long. I remembered this uncle quite well. Who could forget him? He'd be home awhile, full of wonderful tales, and then off again on some new quest. He was tanned brown as a nut, with his hair plaited down his back; and he wore three rings in the one ear; and he had a strange, many-colored bird that sat on his shoulder and asked you politely if you wanted a roll in the hay, dear? I knew my mother no more believed him dead than she did Finbar. I wondered if she knew. I wondered if I would know if Sean went away to battle and perished on the point of some stranger's sword. Would I feel it in my own heart, that moment when the blood slows in the veins and the breath stops and a film covers the eyes as they gaze sightless into the wide expanse of the sky?

It was never my intention to spy on Niamh. What my sister did with her spare time was her own affair. I was concerned, that was all. She was so unlike herself, the way she had retreated into silence and spent so much time alone. Even Aisling commented on it, kindly.

"Niamh seems very quiet," she remarked one afternoon as the two of us went up to the fields behind the house to pick wild endive for brewing. In some households it was thought inappropriate for the lord's daughters to touch such menial work, and it would be left to those who served the family. It had never been so at Sevenwaters, not in my memory at least. Here, everyone worked. True, Janis and her women handled the heavier tasks, hefting the huge, iron stew pot, cleaning floors, and killing chickens. But both Niamh and I had our daily routine, and our seasonal tasks, and knew how to perform them capably. In this we followed our parents' example, for Sorcha would spend her whole day between stillroom and village, tending to the sick; and my father, who had once been lord of Harrowfield, was not reluctant to set his own hand to the plow if the occasion demanded it. Niamh and I would make good wives, well able to order the domestic side of our husbands' households. After all, how can you be a good mistress if you have no understanding of the work your folk must undertake? Just how Niamh did manage to acquire her skills I am not sure, since she never stayed long at one task. But she was a clever girl, and if she forgot something it did not take her long to charm Janis or me or someone else into helping her.

However, she was not here for the endive. Aisling picked carefully, stopping now and then to push her unruly bright curls back into the binding they sought to escape. Now the days were warmer, she was getting a light dusting of freckles on her nose.

"Be sure you leave enough to make seed," I cautioned.

"Yes, Mother," chuckled Aisling, as she added a few more of the golden blooms to her willow basket. She was always willing to help with such tasks. Maybe she thought she was preparing herself to be the right sort of wife for Sean. I could have told her that side of it wouldn't matter a bit, not to him. My brother's mind was made up already.

"But seriously, Liadan, do you think Niamh is all right? I

wondered if—well, I wondered if it was to do with Eamonn."

"Eamonn?" I echoed, rather stupidly.

"Well," said Aisling thoughtfully, "he has been away awhile now, and none of us knows what's been happening. I'm not sure how things are between the two of them, but I did think she might be worried. I know I am."

I gave her a reassuring hug. "I'm sure you need not be. If anyone knows how to look after himself, it's Eamonn. Any day now we'll see your brother riding up to the door as large as life, and no doubt victorious with it." And I'll bet a silver piece to an old bobbin, I said to myself, that whatever is bothering my sister, it's not him. I doubt if she's given him a moment's thought since he went away. He's probably been in my thoughts more than he has hers.

We finished our picking, and we brewed the spring wine with honey and jasmine to counter the bitterness of the endive, and we put it away to work in darkness; and still there was no sign of Niamh. Aisling and I went upstairs and washed our hands and faces, and combed and braided each other's hair, and took off our coarse working aprons. It was nearly time for supper, and outside a cool dusk was brushing across the sky, turning it to violet and faded gray. Then at last I saw her from my narrow window, running across the field from the margin of the forest, with a quick look to the right and to the left to see whose curious eyes might be watching her. She disappeared from view. Not long after, there she was at the door, gasping for breath, skirts still held up in one hand, her cheeks flushed scarlet. I looked at her, and Aisling looked at her, and neither of us said a word.

"Good, I'm not late." She went straight across to the oaken chest, lifted the lid, and rummaged for a clean gown. Finding what she wanted, she proceeded to unfasten the one she wore and strip it off, followed by her shift, with never a by-your-leave. Aisling moved tactfully to gaze out the window; I brought my sister the bowl of water and a hairbrush as she wriggled into fresh smallclothes and dragged the gown over her head. She turned her back, and I began to fasten the many small hooks for her. She was still breathing hard, which made my task no easier.

"She's decent again, Aisling," I said wryly. "Perhaps you could take a hand with the hairbrush. It must be nearly supper time." Aisling was clever with her fingers and had a better chance of doing something acceptable with my sister's wildly disheveled locks in the little time we had left. She began to wield the brush with calm, even strokes.

"Where on earth have you been, Niamh?" she asked in amazement. "There's straw in your hair, and leaves, and what are these little blue flowers?" She brushed away, her face as sweetly innocent as ever.

"We missed you this afternoon," I said levelly, still working on the gown. "We made the spring wine without you."

"Is there some criticism intended in that?" asked Niamh, twisting this way and that to settle her skirts and wincing as the brush hit a tangle.

"It was only a statement, not a question," I said. "I doubt if your absence was noted by anyone but Aisling and me—this time. And we did fine without you, so you need not feel guilty on that score."

She gave me a very straight look, but she wasn't saying anything, not with Aisling there. Aisling saw only the good in people and had no concept of secrecy or subterfuge. She was as guileless as a sheep, though perhaps the comparison was a little unfair. Simple as she was, the girl was not stupid.

I felt that uneasiness again that night, as we sat at supper, the whole family together. Our meal was a plain one. In part because my mother never touched meat, we ate quite simply, relying mainly on the grain and vegetables of our home farms. Janis had a wide repertoire of tasty soups and good honest breads, and we did well enough. The men would partake of a roasted fowl or two, or a sheep would be slaughtered from time to time, for they worked hard, whether it be in the field of arms or the labor of farm and stable, and they were not always satisfied with a meal of turnips and beans and rye bread. That night, I was pleased to see that Mother was managing a little soup, a scrap or two of bannock. She had grown so thin, the north wind might snatch her away if it took a mind to; and it had never been easy to persuade her to eat. As I watched her, I felt Iubdan's eyes on me, and I glanced at him and quickly away again, for I could not bear his expression. That look said, this is a long good-bye, yet not time enough. I have no aptitude for this. I cannot learn this. I would hold on, and hold on, until my hands clutch at emptiness.

Niamh sat neat as a cat, drinking her soup, eyes downcast. There was not a hair out of place. The telltale blush was gone, her skin smooth gold in the light of the oil lamps. Opposite her sat Sean, with Aisling beside him, and they whispered together, holding hands under the table. After supper there were no tales, not that night. Instead, the family retired under Liam's directions to a small, quiet chamber where some privacy might be had, and left the men and women of the household to their songs and ale by the kitchen fires.

"You've had some news," my father said, as soon as we had seated ourselves. I poured wine from the flask on the table, serving first my mother, then my uncle, my father, Sean, and lastly the other two girls.

"Thank you, Liadan." Liam gave me an approving nod. "News indeed, which I have kept until now, since it should be Aisling who hears it first. Good news, child," he added hastily, as Aisling started up in fright, no doubt fearing the worst. "Your brother is well and should be here to collect you before Beltaine. The threat is over for now."

"What of the unknown enemy?" asked Sean eagerly. "What news of the battle?"

Liam frowned. "Very sketchy. There were some losses.

The man who rode here with the message knew little, having got it from another. I know that Eamonn has secured his borders again, but exactly how, and against whom, still seems to be shrouded in mystery. It must wait for his return. I, too, am keen for further knowledge of this. It could influence our entire plan of action concerning the Britons. It would be folly to expect victory in a sea battle against Norsemen."

"True," said Sean. "I would not think of such a venture unless I had the skills of their own kind on my side. But the Norsemen have no interest in our Islands; if they needed the use of safe anchorage there, they'd have taken them from the Britons long ago. The Islands are too barren for crops, too remote for settlements, a territory long forsaken by all but the Old Ones. The Britons hold them only as a stepping stone to our own lands."

"And, I think, as a goad to yourselves," added Iubdan quietly. "I heard it said, once, that this was the way to provoke a response from a man of Erin. Start a fight by stealing what is closest to his heart: his horse maybe, or his woman. Start a war by taking away what is closest to his spirit: his heritage, his mysteries. Perhaps they have no more reason for it than that."

"Certainly, their efforts to establish a land base on this coast have not been impressive," said Liam. "Like ours, their skills are less apt for warfare by sea. And yet, they have held onto the Islands these three generations and more. Aided by an ally with a strong fleet, and the Norseman's ability to use it, who knows what they might do."

"That, surely, is an unlikely partnership." Sean scratched his head thoughtfully. "The Britons of the western seaboard have no reason to trust the Norsemen. They have suffered losses more severe than our own through Viking raids. For scores of years they have witnessed the savagery of these invaders. It would indeed be an unholy alliance."

"If our old foe Richard of Northwoods is the yardstick,"

scowled Liam, "I would believe the Britons capable of anything."

"We should wait," put in my mother tactfully. "Eamonn will tell us more when he returns. I'm glad to see you smiling again, my dear," she added, looking at Aisling.

"Your concern for your brother does you credit," said Liam. "The boy's a leader, there's no doubting that. I trust his losses have not been too great. And now there is another piece of news. One that will interest you, Niamh."

"Mm . . . ? What?" She had been far away, deep in thought.

"A letter," said my uncle gravely, "from a man I have never met, but of whom I have heard much. You will know of him, Iubdan. His name is Fionn of the clan Uí Néill, the branch that has established itself in the northwest. They are connected, quite closely, with the high king of Tara. But there is no love lost between the two branches of that family. Fionn is the elder son of the clan chieftain in Tirconnell, a man of great influence and considerable wealth."

"I've heard talk of him, yes," said Father. "He's well regarded. It's not altogether comfortable to be situated neatly, as we are, between the two seats of Uí Néill. Hungry for power, all of them."

"That fact makes this all the more interesting," my uncle said. "This Fionn and his father seek a closer alliance with Sevenwaters. He makes overtures, quite directly, to such an end."

"Is this your roundabout method of telling us he wants to wed one of the daughters of this household?" My mother had a way of bringing her brother sharply to the point when he was being a little too formal. "Has he made an offer for one of our girls?"

"Indeed. The letter says he has heard there is a daughter of exceptional beauty and excellent skills in the household of Sevenwaters, that he seeks a wife, and that his father would view such an alliance as being to our mutual benefit.

He makes a veiled reference to our feud with the Britons of Northwoods, pointing out the manpower at his own disposal, located conveniently close to us. He mentions also the strategic position of Sevenwaters in relation to his kinsfolk farther south, should he face a threat from that quarter. For a short letter, it contains a great deal."

"What manner of man is this Fionn?" put in Aisling rather boldly. "Is he young or old? Ill-favored or well made?"

"He'd be of middle years," said Liam. "Thirty, perhaps. A warrior. I know nothing of his looks."

"Thirty!" Aisling was clearly shocked at the thought one of us might wed so ancient a man.

Sean grinned. "A daughter of exceptional beauty," he murmured. "That'd be Niamh." He glanced at me, brows raised, and I made a face at him.

"It would be Niamh for whom the offer was intended," agreed Liam, missing the point of our interchange entirely. "What do you say, Niece?"

"I . . ." Niamh appeared quite incapable of speech, which was a very unusual state of affairs. She was suddenly extremely pale. "I . . ." And yet, it can hardly have been such a shock. At seventeen, indeed, it was surprising that this was the first formal offer we had received for her.

"This is too much for a young girl to take in at once, Liam," said my mother quickly. "Niamh needs time to consider it, and so do we. I might, perhaps, read this letter to her in private, if you have no objection."

"None whatever," said Liam.

"We'll want to discuss it." My father had been keeping quiet up to this point, but his tone said clearly that nobody else was going to make his decisions for him. "Does this Fionn intend to favor us with a visit in person, or must we assess his qualities solely from his penmanship?" It was at moments such as this that one remembered who my father was and had once been.

"He wishes to hear first if we will consider the matter. If the answer is favorable, he will travel here before midsummer to present himself and would hope to be wed without delay, if we are in agreement."

"There's no need for haste," said Iubdan quietly. "Such matters are weighty and should be given due consideration. What seems the best choice at first may not prove its worth in time."

"All the same," Liam said, "your daughter is in her eighteenth year. She could have been married these two or three summers past. Might I remind you that at her age Sorcha was wed and the mother of three children? And an offer from a chieftain of such standing comes but seldom."

Niamh stood up abruptly, and now I could see that she had indeed been listening and that she was quivering from head to toe.

"You can stop discussing me as if I were some—some prize breeding cow you want to sell off to advantage," she said in a shaking voice. "I won't marry this Uí Néill. I can't. That's—that's just the way it is. It just can't happen. Why don't you ask him if he'll take Liadan instead? It's the best offer she's likely to get. And now, if you'll excuse me—" She blundered to the door, and I could see the tears starting to flow as she stumbled out and away along the hall, leaving the family in stunned silence.

She wouldn't talk to me. She wouldn't talk to Mother. She wouldn't even talk to Iubdan, who was the best listener you could hope for. Liam she avoided altogether. Things began to get quite strained as the days passed and Fionn's letter remained unanswered. There was no sign of a compromise, and my uncle became edgy. Everyone recognized that Niamh's reaction went beyond what might be expected (which was shocked but flattered surprise, followed by a show of maidenly reluctance, and eventually blushing acceptance). What they could not understand was why. My sister was, as Liam had pointed out, quite old to be still unwed, and her such a beauty. Why hadn't she jumped at such an offer? The Uí Néill! And a future chieftain at that! The gossip was, it was Eamonn she really wanted, and she was holding out until he came back. I could have told them differently, but I held my tongue. I had an idea what was in her head. I had a suspicion about where she went those days she made herself vanish from sunrise to dusk. But my sister's thoughts were impenetrable; I could only guess at the truth, and I hoped fervently that my misgivings were unfounded.

I tried to talk to her, but got nowhere. At first I was kind and tactful, for she cried a lot, lying on her bed staring up at the ceiling or standing by the window with her tear-stained face bathed in moonlight, looking out over the forest. When kindness had no effect, I became more direct.

"I don't think you would make a very good druid, Niamh," I told her one night as we sat alone in our room, a small candle burning on the chest between our narrow beds.

"What?" I had certainly got her attention with that. "What did you say?"

"You heard me. There are no warm blankets, no accommodating servants, no silken gowns in the nemetons. There is a lifetime of discipline and learning and self-deprivation. It is a life of the spirit, not the flesh."

"Hold your tongue!" Her furious response told me I had come close to the truth. "What would you know? What would you know about anything? My plain little sister, wrapped up in her herbs and potions and her cozy, domestic round! What man's likely to want you, save a farmer with big hands and mud on his boots?" She flung herself down on the bed, her face in her hands, and I suspected she was crying.

I took a deep breath and let it carefully out again. "Mother chose a farmer with big hands and mud on his boots," I said quietly. "There were more than a few women at Sevenwaters who thought him quite a catch when he was a young man. So they say."

She did not move, did not make a sound. I sensed the deep misery that had given rise to her cruel words.

"You can talk to me, Niamh," I said. "I'll do my best to understand. You know it can't go on like this. Everyone's upset. I've never seen the household so divided. Why don't you tell me? See if I can help?"

She lifted her head to look at me. I was shocked at her pallor and the deep shadows under her eyes.

"Oh, it's all my fault now," she said, in a strangled voice. "Upset everyone, have I? Who was it decided to marry me off so they could win some stupid battle? That wasn't my idea, I can tell you!"

"Sometimes you can't have what you want," I said levelly. "You might just have to accept that, hard as it might seem right now. This Fionn might not be so bad. You could at least meet the man."

"That's good, coming from you! You wouldn't know a real man if you saw one. Didn't you suggest Eamonn as a likely choice for me? *Eamonn?*"

"It did seem—possible."

There was a long silence. I kept still, seated cross-legged on my bed in my unadorned linen nightrobe. I supposed what she had said about me was true; and I wondered again if my father had been wrong about Eamonn. I tried to see myself as a man might, but it was pretty difficult: too short, too thin, too pale, too quiet. You could say all these things about me. I was, however, not discontented with the face and body I had inherited from my mother. I was happy with what Niamh disparagingly called my small, domestic round. I had no wish for adventures. A farmer would suit me just fine.

"What are you smiling at?" My sister glared across the room at me. The candle made her shadow huge and menacing on the wall behind her as she sat up, dashing the tears from her eyes. Swollen with weeping as it was, her face was still dazzling in its beauty.

"Nothing much."

"How can you smile, Liadan? You don't care at all, do you? How can you imagine I would ever tell you anything? Once you know, Sean knows, and then they all know."

"That's not fair. Some things I keep from Sean, and him from me."

"Oh yes?"

I did not reply, and Niamh lay down again, her face to the wall. When she spoke, it was in a different tone of voice, wobbly and tearful.

"Liadan?"

"Mmm?"

"I'm sorry."

"For what?"

"Sorry I said that. Sorry I said you were plain. I didn't mean it."

I sighed. "It's all right." She had a habit of coming out with hurtful words when she was upset and taking it all back later. Niamh was like an autumn day, all surprises, rain and shine, shadow and brightness. Even when her words were cruel, it was hard to be angry with her for she meant no harm by them. "I'm not looking for a husband anyway," I told her, "so it hardly matters."

She gave a sniff and drew the blanket over her head, and that was as far as we got.

The season drew on toward Beltaine, and the work of the farm continued, and Niamh retreated deeper into herself. There were heated words exchanged behind closed doors. The household was quite unlike its usual self. When at length Eamonn did return, he received the warmest of welcomes, for I think we were all glad of anything to ease the building tension among us. The tale he had to tell was indeed as strange as the rumors had suggested.

We heard it the night of his arrival as we sat in the hall after supper. Despite the season, it was cold, and Aisling and I had helped Janis prepare mulled wine. Ours was a safe household, where all were trusted; and so Eamonn told his story openly, for he knew the depth of interest in what had befallen himself and Seamus and their fighting force. Of the thirty from Liam's garrison, but twenty-seven had returned. Eamonn's own losses had been far greater, as had Seamus Redbeard's. There were women weeping in three households. Nonetheless, Eamonn had returned victorious, though not quite in the way he would have wished. I watched him tell his tale, using a gesture here and there to illustrate a point, a strand of brown hair falling across his brow from time to time, to be pushed back with an automatic sweep of the hand. I thought his face bore more lines than it once had; he carried a heavy responsibility for a man so young. It was no wonder some thought him humorless.

"You know already," he said, "that we lost more good men than we could well afford on this venture. I can assure you that their lives were not lightly thrown away. We deal here with an enemy of quite a different nature from those known to us: the Britons, the Norsemen, the hostile chieftains of our own land. Of the one and twenty warriors that perished in my service, not two were slain by the same method."

There was a murmur around the room.

"You'll have heard the tales," Eamonn went on. "It may be they spread the tales themselves to increase the fear. But these rumors are founded in fact, as we discovered for ourselves when at last we encountered this enemy." He went on to tell of a northern neighbor with whom a long-running dispute had flared into action, of cattle raided, of retaliatory strikes.

"He knew the strength of my forces. He would never, in the past, have done more than attempt to herd away a few head or light a small fire somewhat too close to one of my watchtowers. He knew he could not match me in battle and that any action he took would bring about swift and deadly retaliation. But he covets a parcel of land I hold, bordering his own most fertile area, and has long schemed to acquire it. He tried once to buy the disputed territory from me, and I turned him down. Well, he found another use for his silver pieces."

Eamonn took a mouthful of his wine, wiped his hand across his mouth. His expression was somber.

"We began to hear of lightning raids by an unseen enemy. There was no damage to the guard towers, no sacking of villages or burning of barns. Just killing. Highly efficient. Imaginative in its method. First an isolated post, where two lay dead. Then a bolder ambush. A troop of my guards patrolling the western margin of the marshlands taken, all of them. A nightmare scene. I will spare the ladies the details." He glanced quickly in my direction and away again. "Not cruel, exactly. There was no torture. Just . . . extremely efficient and—and different. There was no way to tell what we were dealing with. No way to prepare. And my cottagers, my farmers, were in a state of sheer terror. They thought these silent killers some Otherworld phenomenon, creatures that could appear and disappear in a flash, some hybrid of man and beast, devoid of any sense of right or wrong." He fell silent, and I believed his eyes saw an image he wished he could erase from his mind.

"You would think," he went on finally, "that on our own territory, backed up by Seamus's men, we would have no difficulty in expelling any invader. My men are disciplined. Experienced. They know those marshes like the back of their hands; they know every forest path, every place of refuge, every potential trap. We divided ourselves into three groups and sought to isolate the enemy in one particular area where we believed his force was concentrated. There was success at first. We captured many of my northern neighbor's men and thought the threat all but over. It was strange, though; our prisoners seemed nervous, always looking over their shoulders. I suppose I knew, even before that point, that the attacks were not made by a single enemy. My neighbor's silver had bought him a force he could never have mustered himself, a force such as none of us here has at his disposal."

"Who were they?" asked Sean, who was hanging on every word. I sensed his excitement; this was a challenge he would have relished for himself.

"I saw them only once," said Eamonn slowly. "We rode through the most treacherous area of the marshland, returning to our main camp with the bodies of our slain. It is not possible to mount an attack in such a place. I had not thought it possible. One false move and the ground will shiver and shake and swallow, and all you will hear is the little ripple of the water as it takes a man under. It is quite safe, if you know the path.

"There were ten of us," he went on, "riding single, for the track is narrow. We bore the bodies of our dead across our saddlebows. It was late afternoon, but the mists in that place make day seem like dusk and dusk like night. The horses knew the way and needed no guidance. We kept silence, not allowing our vigilance to lapse even in that forsaken place. I have good ears and sharp eyes. My men were handpicked. But I missed it. We all missed it. The smallest pipe of a marsh bird; the croak of a frog. Some little noise, some signal, and they were upon us. Coming from nowhere, but rising each at precisely the same instant, one to each of us, taking his man from the horse, despatching him neatly and silently, one with a knife, one with the cord, one with the clever thumb to the neck. As for me, my punishment had been selected especially. I could not see the man who held me from behind, though I used all the strength I had trying to break his grip. I felt my own death at my back. But it was not to be. Instead, I was pinned there, watching, listening, as my men died before and behind me, one after the other, and their horses crashed in panic off the path and were swallowed by the trembling waters of the marsh. My own mount stood steadfast, and they left him alone. I was to be allowed to return home. I was to witness, helpless, the slaughter of my own men and then to be set free."

"But why?" breathed Sean.

"I am not sure I understand that even now," said Eamonn bleakly. "The man who held me had a grip around me, and his knife against my throat, and enough skill in his hands to stop me from struggling long. In this kind of combat he possessed an ability such as I could hardly imagine. I could not hope to break free. My heart was sick as I waited for the last of my men to die. And—and I almost thought the rumors true, as the shifting mist showed me a glimpse, here and there, of those who took their lives with cool detachment."

"Were they indeed half man, half beast?" asked Aisling hesitantly, afraid, no doubt, of sounding foolish. But nobody was laughing.

"They were men," Eamonn said, in a tone that suggested there might be some doubt. "But they wore helmets, or masks, that belied the fact. You might think you saw an eagle or a stag; some, indeed, had markings on the skin, perhaps above the brow or on the chin, to suggest the plumage or the features of a wild creature. Some had helms adorned with feathers, some cloaks of wolf pelt. Their eyes . . . their eyes were so calm, as calm as death. Like—like beings with no human feelings."

"What about the man who held you?" asked Liam. "What manner of man was he?"

"Evasive. He made sure I did not see his face. But I heard his voice and will not forget it; and as he released me at last,

I saw his arm revealed when he drew his knife away from my neck. An arm patterned from shoulder to fingertips with a delicate web of feather and spiral and interlocking links, an intricate and permanent design etched deep into the skin. By that I will know this killer again when I avenge the murders of my good men."

"What did he say to you?" I was unable to keep silent, for it was a fascinating tale, though terrible.

"His voice was—very even, very calm. In that place of death, he spoke as if discussing a business transaction. It was only for an instant. He released his grip; and as I drew breath and turned to pursue him, he vanished into the encircling mist, and he said, *Learn from this, Eamonn. Learn well. I am not done with you yet.* And I was alone. Alone save for my trembling horse and the broken bodies of my men."

"You still believe these are not—are not some creatures of the Otherworld?" asked my mother. There was an unsteadiness in her voice that worried me.

"They are men." Eamonn's tone was controlled, but I could hear the anger in it, "men of awesome skills in the field, skills that would be the envy of any warrior. For all the strength of our forces, we neither killed nor captured a single one of them. But they are no immortals, this I discovered when I heard from their leader again."

"Did not you say you had never seen this man?" asked Liam.

"Seen, no. He sent me a message. It was some time later, and we had encountered no more of them. Your reinforcements had arrived, and together we'd flushed out the rest of my neighbor's meager force and sent them packing. Our dead were honored and laid to rest. Their widows were provided for. The raids ceased. The threat appeared to be over, though folk still shuddered with dread at the memory of what had happened. They had given this murderer a name. They dubbed him "the Painted Man." I thought his band gone from my territory. Then the message was brought to me."

"What message?"

"No simple words of challenge; nothing so honest for this miscreant. The message was . . . perhaps I should not relate this here. It is not fit for ladies' ears."

"You'd better tell us," I said bluntly. "We're going to hear it regardless, one way or another."

He looked at me again. "You're right of course, Liadan. But it is—it is not pleasant. None of this story is. I was brought . . . I was brought a leather pouch, which had been left where my men could not fail to find it. Inside this pouch was a hand, a neatly severed hand."

There was total silence.

"By the rings it wore, we knew this was removed, with some skill, from one of our own. I interpret the gesture as a challenge. He tells me he is strong; I know already that he is arrogant. His services, and those of the men he leads, are now for sale in these parts. Of that we must take heed in planning any venture."

We sat stunned for a while. At last my father said, "You think this fellow would have the gall to offer any of us his services after what he has done? To ask for payment?"

"He knows the value of what he has," said Liam dryly. "And he's right. There's many a chieftain whose scruples would not stop him from accepting such an offer had he the resources to finance it. I imagine they would not come cheap."

"One could hardly consider it seriously," said my mother. "Who could ever trust such a man? It appears he would change his allegiance in an instant."

"A mercenary has no allegiance," said Eamonn. "He belongs to the man with the fattest purse."

"Nonetheless," Sean spoke slowly, as if working something out, "I would like to know if their skills by water equal those they showed in ambush. Such a force, used in conjunction with a well-disciplined, larger troop of warriors, would give one a great advantage. Do you know how many men he has?"

"You would not seriously consider employing a rabble such as this?" asked Liam, shocked.

"Rabble? From Eamonn's account, this is no unruly band of oafs. They seem to strike with the utmost control and plan their raids with a keen intelligence." Sean was still thinking hard.

"They may work cleverly, but they are worse than fianna, for they carry out their missions without pride, without commitment save to the deed itself and the payment," said Eamonn. "This man has misread me badly. When he dies, it will be at my hands. He will pay in blood if he sets foot on my territory or touches what is mine. I have sworn it. And I will make sure my intention reaches his own ears. His life is forfeit should he cross my path again."

At this point Sean wisely held his tongue, though I could sense the suppressed excitement in him. Eamonn took another goblet of wine and was soon surrounded by eager questioners. I thought this was probably the last thing he wanted at that moment when his tale had brought the memory of his losses back starkly into his mind. But I was not his keeper.

I suppose that night was the first time I had seen Eamonn come close to conceding he was not in control of a situation. If he had any outstanding quality, it was authority, and next to that was his commitment to what he believed in. It was no wonder, therefore, that the precision and audacity of the Painted Man's attack, and the arrogance of its sequel, had disturbed him deeply. He was due to escort his sister home the next day, for there were many matters to attend to.

I was surprised, therefore, when he came into my garden soon after I had begun my morning's work, as if our previous appointment had merely been slightly postponed.

"Good morning, Liadan," he said politely.

"Good morning," I replied, and I went on cutting the spent blooms from my ancient briar rose. Prune them back now, and they would provide many more flowers as the summer advanced. The hips, later, could be used for a powerful cordial with a multitude of applications, as well as a tasty jelly.

"You're busy. I don't wish to interrupt your work. But we leave soon, and I would like to speak with you first."

I ventured a glance at him. He did indeed look rather pale and extremely serious. This campaign had aged him beyond his years.

"You will, I suppose, have some notion of what it is I wish to discuss with you."

"Well, yes," I said, realizing there was no choice but to stop pretending to work and hear him out. It would have been helpful if I had any idea of how I was going to reply. "Would you like to sit here awhile?" We moved to the stone bench, and I sat down, basket on my knees and pruning knife still in my hand; but Eamonn would not sit. Instead, he paced, with hands clenched. How can he be nervous about this, I thought, after all he has endured? But nervous he was; there was not a doubt about it.

"You heard my tale last night," he said. "These losses have made me think long and hard about many things: death, revenge, blood, dark matters. I did not believe I had it in me to hate so; it's not a comfortable feeling."

"This man has done you a wrong, that is certain," I said slowly. "But perhaps you should set it behind you and move on. Hatred can eat you up if you let it. It can become your whole life."

"I would not see that happen," he said, turning to face me. "My father made bitter enemies of those who should have been his allies; thus he brought about his own destruction. I would not wish to be consumed by this. But I cannot put it by. I was hoping that . . . perhaps I should start this again."

I looked up at him.

"I need to wed," he said bluntly. "After this, it seems even more important. It is—it is a balance to those dark things. I am weary of coming home to a cold hearth and echoing halls. I want a child to secure the future of my name. My estate is significant, as you know, my holdings secure, save for this upstart and his band of cutthroats, and I will deal with them soon enough. I have a great deal to offer. I have—I have admired you for a long time, since you were too young even to contemplate such an alliance. Your industry, your application to a task, your kindness, your loyalty to your family. We would be well suited. And it is not so very far to travel; you could see them often." He shocked me by moving closer and dropping to his knees beside me. "Will you be my wife, Liadan?"

As proposals go, it had been—businesslike. I supposed he had said all the correct things. But I found it somehow lacking. Perhaps I had listened too much to the old tales.

"I'm going to ask you a question," I said calmly. "When you answer, remember that I am not the sort of woman who seeks flattery or false compliments. I expect the truth from you always."

"You will get the truth."

"Tell me," I said, "why have you not offered for my sister, Niamh, instead of me? That was what everyone expected."

Eamonn took my hand in his and touched it to his lips. "Your sister is indeed very beautiful," he said, with a trace of a smile. "A man might well dream of such a woman. But it would be your face he wanted to see on his pillow when he woke."

I felt myself blushing crimson and was quite lost for words.

"I'm sorry. I have offended you," he said hastily, but he held onto my hand.

"Oh no . . . not at all," I managed. "I'm just—surprised."

"I have spoken to your father," he said. "He has no objection to our marriage. But he told me the decision is yours. He allows you a great deal of freedom."

"You disapprove of that?"

"That depends on your answer."

I took a deep breath, hoping for some inspiration. "If this were one of the old tales," I said slowly, "I would ask you to complete three tasks or kill three monsters for me. But there is no need to test you in such a way. I recognize that this would be a highly—suitable match."

Eamonn had put my hand down and was studying the ground at my feet where he still knelt.

"I hear unspoken words here," he said, frowning, "a reservation. You had better tell me."

"It's too soon," I said bluntly. "I am not able to answer, not now."

"Why not? You are sixteen years old, a woman. I am sure of my own mind. You know what I can offer you. Why cannot you answer?"

I took a deep breath. "You know my mother is very ill, so ill that she will not recover."

Eamonn glanced at me sharply, and then he moved to sit beside me on the bench. The tension between us eased just a little.

"I have seen how pale she looks and wondered," he said gently. "I did not know it was so serious. I'm sorry, Liadan."

"We don't speak of it," I said. "Not many are aware that we count each season, each cycle of the moon, each day that passes. It is for this reason that I can make no commitment to you or to any other."

"There is another?" His voice was suddenly fierce.

"No, Eamonn," I said hastily, "you need have no concern

on that score. I'm aware of how fortunate I am to receive even one offer such as yours."

"You underestimate yourself, as always."

A silence fell again. Eamonn stared at his hands, frowning.

"How long must I wait for your answer?" he asked eventually.

It was hard to reply, for to do so was to set a measure on Sorcha's days.

"For my mother's sake, I will make no decision before Beltaine, next year," I said. "That is long enough, I think. I will give you an answer then."

"It's too long," he said. "How can a man wait so long?"

"I must be here, Eamonn. They will need me more and more. Besides, I do not know my own heart. I'm sorry if that hurts you, but I will return your honesty with the plain truth."

"A whole year," he said. "You expect a great deal of me."

"It is a long time. But I do not mean to bind you to me for the passing of these four seasons. You are under no obligation toward me. If you meet another during this time, if you change your mind, you are quite free to pledge yourself, to marry, to do whatever you wish."

"There is no chance of that," he said, with absolute finality. "None whatever."

At that moment I felt a shadow pass over me, and all at once I was cold. Whether it was the intensity of his voice or the look in his eyes or something quite different, for an instant the peaceful, sunny garden grew dark. Something about my expression must have changed.

"What is it?" he asked anxiously. "What's the matter?"

I shook my head. "Nothing," I told him. "Don't be concerned. It's nothing."

"It's nearly time for me to go," he said, getting up. "They'll be expecting me. I would be happier if we had at least some—understanding. A betrothal, perhaps, with the marriage delayed until—until you are ready. Or—or might not the Lady Sorcha wish to see you happily settled before . . . might she not wish to be there at your wedding feast?"

"It's not that simple, Eamonn." All at once I was terribly tired. "I can agree to no betrothal. I want no commitment. I have told you when I will answer, and that will not change. A year may not seem so long."

"It seems forever. A great deal can change in a year."

"Off you go," I said. "Aisling will be waiting. Go home, sort out your household, put your people to rights. I will still be here next Beltaine Eve. Go home, Eamonn."

I thought he would leave with no more said, he was silent so long, arms folded, head bowed in thought. Then he said, "It will be home when I see you waiting there in the doorway with my child in your arms. Not till then." And he strode away through the arch in the wall with never a backward glance.

Chapter Three

My mind did not dwell long on this, for events soon overtook our household with a swiftness that came close to overwhelming us. We were already unhappy, divided among ourselves by Niamh's unwillingness to so much as consider her suitor's offer and her total silence as to the reasons why. By Liam's anger; by my father's frustration at his inability to make peace between them. My mother was distressed at seeing her menfolk at odds thus. Sean was missing Aisling and snapped with irritation at the slightest thing. In desperation, one warm afternoon close to midsummer, I went out into the forest alone. There was a place we used to visit often in our childhood, a deep, secluded pool fringed by ferns and bracken, filled by a splashing waterfall and protected by the gentle shade of weeping willows. The three of us had swum and played there many a time on hot summer days, filling the air with our shrieks and splashing and laughter. We were too old for that now, of course. Men and women, as Eamonn had reminded me. Too old for fun. But I did remember the sweet herbs that grew lush and wild near that place—parsley, chervil, and abundant cresses—and I thought to make a little pie with eggs and soft cheese, that might tempt my mother's failing appetite. So I took a basket and tied back my hair and set off alone into the forest, glad of some respite from the emotionally charged atmosphere of the house.

It was a warm day, and the herbs were plentiful. I picked steadily, humming under my breath, and soon enough my basket was full. I sat down to rest with my back against a willow. The woods were alive with little sounds: the rustle of squirrels in the undergrowth, the song of a thrush overhead, and stranger voices, too, subtle whispers in the air, whose words I could not comprehend. If there was a message in it, it could scarcely be for me. I sat very still and thought perhaps I could see them: faint, ethereal shapes passing between the branches, a scrap of floating veil, a wing transparent and fragile as a dragonfly's, hair that was shining filaments of gold and silver. Perhaps a slender hand, beckoning. And bell-like laughter. I blinked and looked again. The sun must have been making me foolish for now there was nothing. I must return to the house and make my pie and hope my family might become friends again.

There was someone there. Down between the rowans, a flash of deep blue, gone again as quickly as it had appeared. Had I heard footsteps on the soft path? I got up, basket over my arm, and followed quietly. The track led down the hillside toward the sheltered pool, curving under the trees and between thick clumps of bushes. I did not call out. There was no telling if what I had seen was merely a trick of the light on the dark foliage or something more. And I had learned to move through the woods in silence. It was an essential skill for self-preservation, Father said. There it was again, just ahead of me behind the rowans, a hint of blue like a fold of cloth, and a flash of white, a long, delicate hand. This time the gesture was unmistakable. This way, it motioned. Come this way. I went on softly down the path.

Niamh would never believe, later, that I had not come there on purpose to find out her secret. I moved down quietly under the willows until the calm surface of the pool came into view. I halted, frozen with shock. She had not seen me. Nor had he. They had eyes only for each other, as they stood there waist deep, their bodies mirrored in the water under the tree canopy, their skin dappled with the sunlight through summer leaves. Her white arms were wrapped closely around his neck; his auburn head was bent to kiss her bare shoulder, and her back arched with a primitive grace as she responded to the touch of his lips. The long, bright curtain of her hair fell about her, echoing the gold of the sunlight and not quite concealing the fact that she was naked.

Feelings warred within me. Shock, fright, a fervent wish that I had gone elsewhere for my small harvest. The knowledge that I should stop looking immediately. The complete inability to tear my eyes away. For what I saw, though deeply wrong, was also beautiful beyond my imaginings. The play of light on water, of shadow on pearly skin, the twining of their two bodies, the way they were so utterly lost in each other—to see this was as wondrous as it was deeply unsettling. If this was what I was supposed to feel for Eamonn, then I had done well to make him wait. There came a point, as the young druid's hands moved down my sister's body, and he lifted her, pulling her urgently toward him, when I knew I could watch no longer, and I retreated silently back under the willows and walked blindly in the direction of home, my mind in a turmoil. Of the strange guide who had beckoned me to find them, there was now no sign at all.

Bad luck. Bad timing. Or perhaps it was meant that the

first person I should meet was my brother, that this should happen halfway across the home pastures while my mind was filled with the image of those two young bodies wrapped so closely together, as if they were but a single creature. Perhaps the Fair Folk had had a hand in it, or maybe, as Niamh said later, it was all my fault for spying. I have spoken of how it was between my brother and me. When we were younger, we would often share our thoughts and secrets direct, mind to mind, with no need at all for speech. All twins are close, but the bond between us went far deeper; in an instant we could summon one another, almost as if we had shared some part of our spirit before ever the two of us saw the outside world. But lately we had, in unspoken agreement, chosen to shut off that link. The secrets of a young man who courts his first sweetheart are too delicate to share with a sister. As for me, I had no wish to tell him of my fears for Niamh or my misgivings about the future. But now I could not prevent this. For it is the way of things for those who are as close as Sean and I that when one feels sharp distress, or pain, or an intense joy, it spills over so strongly that the other must share it. I had no way to keep him out at such times, no controls with which to set a shield on my mind. I could not block out the small, crystal-clear image of my sister and her druid, mirrored in still water, locked in each other's arms. And what I saw and felt, my brother saw also.

"What is this?" Sean exclaimed in horror. "Is this today? Is it now?"

I nodded miserably.

"By the Dagda, I will kill this fellow with my own hands! How dare he defile my sister thus?"

It seemed to me he would rush into the woods that instant, bent on punishment.

"Stop. Stop it, Sean. Anger will achieve nothing here. This may not be so bad."

He took hold of my shoulders as we stood there in the middle of the field and made me look him straight in the eye. I saw on his face the reflection of what I read in his mind— shock, fury, outrage.

"I cannot believe this," he muttered. "How could Niamh be a willing partner in something so utterly foolish? Doesn't she know she's put the whole alliance at risk? Merciful gods, how could we have been so blind? Blind, all of us! Come, Liadan, we must return to the house and tell them."

"No! Don't tell, not yet. At least let me speak to Niamh first. I see—I see ill from this, a more terrible ill than you can imagine. Sean, stop."

"It's too late. Much too late." Sean's decision was made and he was not listening to me. He turned for the house, gesturing for me to follow him. "They must be told, and now. We may still salvage something from this mess if it is kept quiet. Why didn't you tell me? How long have you known of this?"

As we walked up to the house, a grim-faced Sean striding ahead and I reluctantly following in his wake, it seemed to me we brought a shadow with us, the deepest of shadows. "I did not know. Not until now. I guessed, but not that it had come so far. Sean, must you tell them?"

"There's no choice. She's to wed the Uí Néill. Our whole venture depends on that link. I dare not contemplate what this will do to Mother. How could Niamh have done such a thing? It's beyond all reason."

Father was out working on one of his plantations. Mother was resting. But Liam was there, and so it was he who got the news first. I was prepared for outraged disapproval, for anger. I was completely taken aback by the way my uncle's face changed as Sean told him what I had seen. The look in his eyes was more than shock. I saw revulsion, and was it fear? Surely not. Liam, afraid?

When my uncle spoke at last, it was clear he was exercising the greatest control to keep his voice calm. Nonetheless, it shook as he spoke.

"Sean, Liadan, I must ask you for your help. This matter must go no further than the family. That's of the utmost importance. Sean, I want you to fetch Conor here. Go yourself, and go alone. Tell him it's urgent, but don't speak of the reason to anyone else. You'd better leave now. And keep your anger in check for everyone's sake. Liadan, I am reluctant to involve you, for such matters are not fit for a young woman's eyes or ears. But you are family, and you are part of this now, like it or not. Thank the gods Eamonn and his sister are no longer at Sevenwaters. Now I want you to go down and wait for Niamh; keep watch by your garden entry until you see her on her way home. Then bring her straight to me in the private chamber. Again, I cannot stress too strongly, no talk. Not to anyone. I will send for your father and break this news to him myself."

"What about Mother?" I had to ask.

"She must be told," he said soberly. "But not yet. Let her have a little more peace before she must know."

So I waited for Niamh; and as I waited, I watched Sean ride away under the trees in the direction of the place the druids had their dwelling, deep in the heart of the forest. The dust flew under his horse's feet.

I waited a long time, until it was nearly dusk. I was cold, and my head was aching, and there was a strange sort of fear in me that seemed quite out of proportion to the problem. I had been over and over it in my mind. Perhaps she really loved him and he her. It had certainly looked that way. Maybe he was the son of a good family, and maybe it didn't really matter whether he remained a druid or not, and—then I remembered the look on Liam's face, and I knew that my thoughts were utterly futile. There was far more here than I could rightly understand.

It was very hard to tell Niamh. She was radiant with happiness, her skin glowing, her eyes bright as stars. She wore a wreath of wildflowers on her shining hair, and her feet were bare beneath the hem of her white gown.

"Liadan! What on earth are you doing out here? It's nearly dark."

"They know," I said straight out, and watched her face change as the light went out of her eyes, quenched as quickly as a doused candle. "I—I was picking herbs, and I saw you, and—"

"You told! You told Sean! Liadan, how could you do such a thing?" She gripped my arms, digging her fingers in until I gasped with pain. "You've ruined everything! Everything! I hate you!"

"Niamh. Stop it. I said nothing, I swear. But you know how it is with me and Sean. I could not keep it from him," I said miserably.

"Spy! Snoop! You use your stupid mind-talk, whatever it is, as an excuse. You're just jealous because you can't get your own man! Well, I don't care. I love Ciarán, and he loves me, and nobody's going to stop us being together! You hear me? Nobody!"

"Liam told me to wait for you and bring you straight to see him," I managed, and now I found I had to make an effort not to cry. I swallowed my tears. They would help nobody. "He said we must keep this quiet, keep it in the family."

"Oh, yes, the family honor. Wonderful. Can't ruin the chance of an alliance with the Uí Néill, can we? Never mind, Sister. Now that I've shamed the all-important family, maybe it's you who will wed the illustrious Fionn, chieftain of Tirconnell. It could be the making of you."

Liam's reaction had been deeply unsettling, and a fear had gripped me, a fear whose cause I did not understand. I had tried to be calm, to be strong for my sister. But Niamh's words hurt me, and I found I could not hold back my anger.

"Brighid save us!" I snapped. "When will you learn that

there are more folk in the world than just yourself? You're in real trouble, Niamh. Seems to me you're overeager to hurt those who would help you. Now come on. Let's get this over with."

I walked to the stillroom door. From here, it was possible to go up the back stairs to the chamber where Liam waited and with luck be unobserved. Niamh had fallen silent. I turned, hoping I would not have to drag her after me forcibly. "Are you coming?"

There was a sound of hoofbeats beyond the garden wall, galloping up to the main entrance. Boots crunched on gravel as men dismounted. There had been no way for Sean to return unobserved from his errand.

"Liadan." My sister spoke in a very small voice.

"What?"

"Promise me. Promise me you'll stay in there with me. Promise you'll speak up for me."

I walked straight back and put my arms around her. She was shivering in her light gown, and a tear glinted in one long-lashed, blue eye. "Of course I'll stay, Niamh. Now come on. They'll be waiting for us."

By the time we reached the upstairs room, they were all there. All but Mother. Liam, Conor, Sean, and my father, standing, the four of them, their faces made grimmer by the half-light, for only one small lamp burned on the table and outside it was dark. The air was thick with tension. I could tell they had been talking and had fallen silent as we came in. If there was anything that really frightened me as I stood there beside my sister, it was Conor's face. The expression he wore mirrored that I had seen on his brother's features not long before. Not quite fear perhaps. More like the memory of fear.

"Shut the door, Liadan." I did as Liam told me, and returned to my sister's side where she stood, head held high, like some tragic princess in an old story. Her hair was a glowing gold in the lamplight. Her eyes shone with unshed tears.

"She's your daughter," my uncle said bluntly. "Perhaps you'd better speak first."

Father stood at the back of the room, his face in shadow. "You know what this is about, Niamh." His voice was level enough.

Niamh said nothing, but I saw her straighten her back, lift her head a little higher.

"I have always expected my children to speak the truth, and I want the truth from you now. We had hoped for a good marriage for you. Perhaps I have allowed you more freedom than some thought wise, freedom to make your own choices. In return, I expected—honesty at least, common sense, some exercise of judgment."

Still she said nothing.

"You had better tell us, and tell us truly. Have you given yourself to this young man? Has he lain with you?"

I felt the tremor that ran through my sister's body and knew it for anger, not fear.

"What if I have?" she snapped.

There was a little silence, and then Liam said grimly, "Answer your father's question."

Niamh's eyes were bright with defiance as she glared back at him.

"What's it to you?" she demanded, voice going up a notch, and she gripped my hand so tight I thought she would break it. "I'm not your daughter and I never have been. I care nothing for your family honor and your stupid alliances. Ciarán is a good man, and he loves me, and that's all that matters. The rest of it is none of your business, and I won't sully it by laying it bare before a roomful of men! Where's my mother? Why isn't she here?"

Oh, Niamh. I wrenched my hand from hers and turned away. There was a weight like a cold stone in my heart.

It was Sean who stepped forward, and I had never seen such anger in his eyes or felt in my spirit such an outpouring of rage and grief as I caught from him at that moment. There was no way I could stop him; no way in the world.

"How dare you!" he said, in a voice cold with fury, and he lifted his hand and struck Niamh across her lovely, tear-stained cheek. A red mark appeared instantly on the golden skin. "How dare you ask that? How dare you expect her to endure this? Have you any idea what your selfish folly will do to her? Don't you know our mother is dying?"

And, incredibly, it was clear that she had not known. All this time, as Sean, and I, and Iubdan, and her brothers had watched Sorcha fail just a little each day, had felt our hearts grow cold as she took one step away from us with each waning of the moon, Niamh, blithe in her own world, had seen nothing at all. She turned as white as parchment, save for the mark on her cheek, and she pressed her lips tightly together.

"Enough, Sean." Iubdan looked like an old man as he stepped out of the shadows, and the light showed the lines and furrows of grief on his face. He moved to take my brother by the arm and steer him back, away from Niamh who stood frozen in the center of the room. "Enough, Son. A man of Sevenwaters does not raise his hand in anger against a woman. Sit down. Let us all sit down." He was a strong man, my father. So strong, at times, he put the rest of us to shame. "Perhaps you should leave us, Liadan. We can at least spare you this."

"No!" Niamh's voice was shrill with panic. "No! I want her here. I want my sister here!"

Father glanced at me, raised his brows.

"I'll stay," I said, and my voice came out sounding like a stranger's. "I promised." I glanced at Conor where he sat, ashen faced, his mouth set in a line. He had told me not to feel guilt for what must unfold. But he could not have foreseen this. I scowled at him. *You didn't tell me it would be like this!*

I did not know. This, I would have done much to prevent. Still, it unfolds as it must.

"Now," said Father wearily, when we were all seated, Niamh and I on a bench together, for she had grasped my hand again and this time she was not letting go. "We will get no more out of you tonight; I can see that. I understand also what the answer to my question is, although you did not give it. But it is clear to me you do not comprehend the import of what you have done. Were this merely a youthful escapade, a giving-in to the madness of Imbolc, a surrendering to the urges of the body, it might be more readily accepted, if not excused. Such an error is common enough and can be overlooked if it occurs but once."

"But—" Niamh began.

"Keep silent, girl." Her mouth snapped shut as Liam spoke, but her eyes were angry. "Your father speaks wisely. You should hear what Conor has to say. He must bear some responsibility for this himself; it is in part his own error of judgment that has brought this ill on us. What have you to tell us, Brother?"

I had never heard my uncle utter a word of criticism against his brothers or sister, not in all the years since my childhood. There was some old hurt here that I could guess at only dimly.

"Indeed," said Conor very quietly, looking direct at Niamh with his serene, gray eyes, those eyes that saw so much and held it all in their depths. "It was I who decided to bring him here; it was I who believed it was time for him to step forth and be seen. Despite the heartbreak he has caused, despite who he is, Ciarán is a fine young man and, until now, a credit to the brotherhood. He is very able. Very apt."

"Some credit," Sean growled. "Give him one chance to show himself in public and the first thing he does is seduce the daughter of the house. Very apt indeed."

"That's enough, Sean." Iubdan was keeping his tone steady at some cost. "Your youth makes you speak rashly. This is as much Niamh's doing as the young man's. He has had a sheltered upbringing and perhaps did not fully understand the significance of his actions."

"Ciarán has been with the brotherhood many years, though he is still but one and twenty." Conor still looked straight at Niamh, and in the lamplight his long, ascetic face was as pale as his robe. "He has, as I said, been an exemplary student. Until now. Apt to learn. Willing. Disciplined. Skilled with words, and with other talents he has barely begun to recognize in himself. Niamh, this young man is not for you."

"He told me," said Niamh, her voice cracking. "He told me. He loves me. I love him. There's nothing as important as that. Nothing!" Her words were defiant, but underneath it she was scared. Scared of what Conor had not said.

"There can be no union between you and this young man." Liam spoke heavily, as if some untold grief weighed on him. "You will be suitably married as soon as possible, and you will leave Sevenwaters. None must know of this."

"What!" Niamh flushed scarlet with outrage. "Wed another man after—you can't say that! You can't! Tell them, Liadan! I will wed no man but Ciarán! What if he is a druid, that need not matter; he can still take a wife, he told me—

"Niamh."

At the sound of Father's voice, her torrent of words came to an abrupt, hiccupping stop.

"You will not wed this man. It is not possible. Perhaps this seems unfair to you. Perhaps it seems to you that we make our decision too quickly, without considering all arguments. It is not so. We cannot explain our reasons to you in full, for, believe me, that would only add to your pain. But Liam is right, Daughter. This is a match that can never be. And now that you have given in to your desires, you

must take a husband as soon as it can be arranged, lest—
you must be wed, lest a worse evil befall this house."

He sounded weary beyond belief, and I found his words
strange. What my sister had done was foolish and unthinking perhaps, but it hardly seemed to merit such harsh treatment. And my father was ever the most balanced of men,
his decisions based on a careful weighing of all relevant
matters.

"May I speak?" I ventured with some hesitation.

The response was not encouraging. Sean glared; Liam
frowned. Father did not look at me. Niamh stood frozen,
save for the tears rolling down her cheeks.

"What is it, Liadan?" asked Conor. He had a tight guard
on his thoughts; I had no idea at all what was in his mind,
but I sensed a deep hurt. More secrets.

"I'm not excusing Niamh or the young druid," I said quietly. "But do you not judge too harshly? Ciarán seems a
man of favorable aspect, of good manners, clever and honest. He treated my mother with great respect. Would not
such a match deserve at least some consideration? Yet you
dismiss it outright."

"It cannot be." I knew from Liam's tone that the judgment was final. Further argument was pointless. "As your
father says, it is agreed between us that we can only do
what we must to salvage the situation. It is a very grave
matter; one whose full implications we cannot make known
to you. This must go no further than these four walls. It is
imperative that it be kept secret."

It seemed to me a darkness had come awake and was
present among us in this room. It was there in the red mark
that marred my sister's cheek. It was there in Liam's criticism of his wise brother. It was there in the lines and
grooves etched stark on my father's face. It was in Niamh's
eyes as she turned on me in fury.

"This is your fault!" she sobbed. "If you'd kept out of it,

if you hadn't followed me, snooping after me, none of them would have known. We would have gone away; we could have been together—"

"Hold your tongue, Niamh," said Iubdan, in a voice I had never heard him use before. She hiccupped to a stop, shoulders heaving.

"I want to see Mother," she said in a small voice.

"Not tonight," said Father, now very quiet. "I have told her of this while we awaited Conor's arrival, and she is much distressed. She has agreed to take a sleeping draft and is resting now. She asked for you, Liadan. I told her you would look in before you retired for the night." He sounded terribly tired.

"I want to see her," Niamh said again, like a small child denied a treat.

"You have forfeited the right to make your own choices." My father's words hung in a cruel silence.

I never thought I would hear him say such a thing. He spoke out of the depths of his hurt, and my heart bled for him. Niamh stood mute and still.

"We'll speak further of this later," Father went on. "For now, you'll go to your room, and you'll stay there until we decide what's to be done. That decision must be made quickly, and you'll abide by it, Niamh. Go now. No more tonight. And no talk of this, not to anyone, you understand? Liam is right; this must be kept contained here or more harm will be done."

"What of the boy?" asked Liam.

"I will speak to him tonight," Conor replied, and he too sounded weary to exhaustion. "It will be a measure of his worth how he deals with this."

I sat by Mother until she fell into a fitful sleep. We did not speak of what had happened, but I could see she had been weeping. Then I went to my room, where Niamh sat bolt upright on her bed, staring at the wall. There was no point in trying to talk to her. I lay down and closed my eyes, but rest was impossible. I felt sick and helpless, and for all Conor's wise words, I could not escape a sense that I had somehow betrayed my sister. There was indeed a darkness over our household, as if the shade of a past evil had come to life once more. I did not understand what it was, but I felt its grip on my heart and saw its touch in my sister's pallid, tear-stained face.

"Liadan!"

My eyes came open at Niamh's urgent whisper. She was by the window.

"He's here! Ciarán. He's come for me!"

"What?"

"Look down. Look down to the trees."

It was dark and I could see little, but I heard the muffled hoofbeats as a lone rider came up very fast, too fast, from the margin of the forest. The horse's feet crunched on gravel and then were silent. There was a hammering on the outer door and the flare of a lamp.

"He's here," said my sister again, her voice alive with hope.

"So much for Liam's plan to keep this quiet," I said dryly.

"I must go. I must go down to him—"

"Weren't you listening to anything they said?" I asked her. "You can't go down. You can't see him. This is forbidden. And didn't Father say something about staying in your room?"

"But I must see him! Liadan, you have to help me!" She turned those large, beseeching eyes on me, as so many times before.

"I won't do it, Niamh. Anyway, you're wrong. Your young man is not here to fetch you away in secret. A lover does not do so by knocking down her father's door. He is here because he has heard the news and does not understand. He is here because he is hurt and angry and wants answers."

Downstairs, the nocturnal visitor had been admitted and the door closed after him. It was silent again.

"I have to know," hissed Niamh, grabbing me by the arms right where she had bruised me before. "You go, Liadan. Go down and listen. Find out what's happening; tell me what they're saying. I must know."

"Niamh—"

"Please. Please, Liadan. You're my sister. I'm not breaking any rules. I'll stay here; I promise. Please."

For all her faults, I loved my sister and had never found it easy to refuse her. Besides, I had to admit that I, too, wanted to know what was being said behind closed doors. I was not comfortable living in a house of secrets. But I had seen the look on Liam's face and heard the anger in my father's voice. I had no wish to be discovered where I had no business to be.

"Please, Liadan. You have to help me. You have to."

She went on in this vein for some time, weeping and pleading, her voice growing hoarse with tears. In the end she wore me down.

I threw a shawl over my night robe, and went soft-footed along the hallway until I saw a line of faint light under the door of that room where we had spoken before. There was nobody about. It seemed Liam had been quick to avoid a public scene.

From inside came the sound of voices, but I could not hear the words. It sounded as if there were four of them there. Liam, curtly decisive; the more measured tones of Conor. My father's voice was deeper and softer. Sean, it seemed, had been excluded. Perhaps they considered him too young and rash for such a council. I stood shivering at the top of the stairs. Now Ciarán's voice; the words indistinct, the tone harsh with grief and outrage. I sensed movement within the chamber and sought to retreat. But I was not quick enough. The door slammed open and the young druid strode out, face chalk white, eyes blazing. As the door swung to, I heard Liam saying, "No. Leave him be."

Ciarán halted in his tracks, staring at me as I stood motionless there in my old night robe and woolen shawl. I thought he hardly saw what was in front of him; his eyes were full of ghosts. But he knew who I was.

"Here," he said, reaching into the pouch he had at his belt. "Tell her I'm going away. Tell her—give her this." He dropped something small into my hand, and then he was gone without a sound, down the stairs and away into the darkness.

When I was safely back in my room, I gave Niamh the smooth white pebble with a neat hole through it, and I told her what he had said, and I held her in my arms while she wept and wept as if she would never stop. And deep in my spirit, I heard the sound of hoofbeats as Ciarán rode away, farther and farther, as many miles from Sevenwaters as his horse would carry him by sunrise.

Before midsummer my sister wed Fionn, chieftain's son of the Uí Néill, and that same day he took her away with him to Tirconnell. I rode with them as far as the village of Littlefolds. At least, that was the plan. Silent, frozen, impenetrable as she was in her grief, Niamh had made a single request, and that was for my company to see her on her way.

"Are you sure this is all right?" I had asked Mother.

"We'll manage," she smiled, but there was a sorrow in her eyes these days. "You must live your life, Daughter. We'll do well enough without you for a while."

I thought to ask her what it might mean, that an Otherworld guide had led me to discover my sister's secret and set her on a path out of Sevenwaters and away from the forest. For I had no doubt that the Fair Folk had had a hand in that, but I could not guess their motive. My mother might know, for she had more than once seen these powerful beings face-to-face and been guided by their wishes. But I did not ask. Mother had enough to bear. Besides, it was too late. Too late for Niamh and too late for Ciarán, who was gone away, nobody knew where.

Father was not quite so ready to see me ride off, but he recognized how it was with Niamh, and reluctantly he agreed. "Don't be gone too long, sweetheart," he said, "five or six nights at most. And go nowhere unguarded. Liam will provide armed men to see you home safely."

Before her wedding, I fashioned a fine, strong cord for my sister to wear about her neck. As I wove it I told myself the tale of Aengus Óg and the fair Caer Ibormeith, and I felt the weight of unshed tears heavy behind my eyes. Into this cord I wove one gold thread from my Uncle Conor's robe. There were fibers there of heather and lavender, celandine and juniper; I sought to protect her as well as I could. There were plain linen strands from my own working attire, and a thread of blue from my mother's ancient, most beloved gown. Sean's riding cloak provided dark wool, and the leather strips that bound the ends of it were snipped from an old pair of Iubdan's working boots, a farmer's muddy boots. I fashioned all together into a cord that was fine and smooth and crafted so that it would take more than mortal strength to break it. I didn't say anything when I slipped it into Niamh's hand and neither did she. But she knew what it was for. She took the small white stone from her pocket, and threaded the cord through the little hole in it, and put it around her neck; and I lifted aside the weight of her beautiful fiery hair and tied the leather strips tightly together. When she slipped the stone under her gown, it could not be seen at all.

Since that night, when she had learned that it is men who make decisions and women who must follow them, my sister had not once mentioned Ciarán. Indeed, she had not spoken much at all. Those had been her last tears, her last signs of weakness. I saw the bitter resentment in her eyes as she told Liam she would wed Fionn as he wished. I saw the pain on her face as she made ready her gowns and shoes and veils, as she watched the women sew her wedding dress, as she gazed out the window at the soft, summer woods of Sevenwaters. She would barely speak, even to Mother. Father tried to talk to her, but she tightened her lips and would not hear his quiet words, as he attempted to explain to her that this was indeed best for her, that she would discover in time that the right choice had been made. After that, Father took to staying out late in the fields so he need not speak to any of us. Sean busied himself with the men in the practice yard and gave both his sisters a wide berth.

As for me, I loved Niamh and wanted to help her. But she would not let me in. Only once, the night before her wedding, as we lay sleepless, sharing our bedchamber for the last time, she said very softly, "Liadan?"

"What is it, Niamh?"

"He said he loved me, but he went away. He lied to me, Liadan. If he had truly loved me, he would never have left me, he would not have given up so easily."

"I shouldn't think it was easy at all," I said; remembering the look on the young druid's face in the shadow of the hallway and the harsh note of pain in his voice.

"He said he would love me forever." My sister's voice was tight and cold. "All men are liars. I told him I would be his alone. He did not deserve such a promise. I hope he suffers when he learns that I have wed another and gone far from the forest. Perhaps he will know then how betrayal feels."

"Oh, Niamh," I said, "he does love you; I am sure of it.

No doubt he had his reasons for going away. There is more to this than we know; secrets not yet told. You should not hate Ciarán for what he has done."

But she had turned her face to the wall, and I could not tell if she heard me or not.

Fionn was a man of middle years, as my uncle had said, well mannered, decisive, and accompanied by the retinue one would expect for a man of his standing. His eyes followed my sister, and he made no attempt to conceal the desire in them. But his mouth was cold. I did not like him. What the rest of my family thought was anyone's guess, for we made a convincing pretense of joyful celebration, and the wedding day was not lacking in music and flowers and feasting. The Uí Néills were a Christian household, and it was a Christian priest who spoke the words and heard the couple's vows. Aisling was there and with her Eamonn. I was relieved there was no opportunity to speak with him alone. He would have read the unhappiness in my eyes and demanded to know the cause. Conor was not there, nor any others of his kind. Underneath the jollity there was a freezing wrongness about the whole thing, and there was absolutely nothing I could do about it. Then we rode away to the northwest, Niamh and her husband, and the men of Tirconnell, and the six men at arms from our own household, with me in the middle, feeling just a little ridiculous.

The village of Littlefolds lies tucked under a hill, in a fold of the land amid thickly wooded, undulating country. It is to the west of Eamonn's estates and northwest of his border with Seamus Redbeard. Our journey had taken us, thus far, through familiar and friendly territory. Now it was time to bid my sister farewell and turn for home. It was the third day. We had made camp on the way and had been well provided for. Niamh and I and the maidservant who accompanied her had shared a canopied tent, while the men fended for themselves. I supposed Fionn would wait until they reached Tirconnell to consummate the marriage. For my sister's sake, I hoped he would wait.

We said our farewells. There was no time, no privacy. Fionn was eager to be away. I hugged Niamh and looked into her eyes, and they were empty, like the eyes of a lovely image carved in pale stone.

"I'll come and see you," I whispered. "Just as soon as I can. Be strong, Niamh. I'll hold you in my heart."

"Good-bye, Liadan," she said in a tight little voice, and she turned so that Fionn could help her onto her horse, and they rode away without a word more. I did not weep. My tears would help nobody.

With the men of Tirconnell departed, the atmosphere thawed a little. My six men at arms had done exactly the job Liam had given them, surrounding me, grim faced, on the road so that I was protected from any possible attack; maintaining a watchful, well-armed guard at all other times. Now, as they readied horses and baggage for the return to Sevenwaters, one cracked a joke, and the others laughed, and one asked me quite gently if everything was all right and whether it would suit me to leave by midmorning. Was I tired? Could I ride maybe half a day before we stopped to rest? I said yes, for I wanted nothing more than to be back home and to start mending the hurt of this last painful time. So I sat on a flat-topped stone and watched them as they made their orderly preparations. The sky was heavy with clouds; it would rain before sunset.

"My lady!" It was one of the villagers, a young woman with a worn, lined face, her hair caught back in an old, green kerchief. "My lady!" She was running toward me, breathless in her haste. Liam's men were good. Before she was anywhere near, there were two of them right beside me, hands on sword hilts. I stood up.

"What is it? What's the matter?"

"Oh, my lady," she gasped, holding her side, "I'm so

glad you haven't gone yet. I'm still in time. It's my boy, Dan. I heard—they say you're the daughter of a great healer. My lady, Danny's got a fever on him that won't go down. He shakes and trembles and talks nonsense, and I'm afraid for him, I am so. Won't you come and cast your eye over him, just quickly before you go?"

I was already hunting around for my small pack, for I never traveled without a healer's basic supplies.

"This is not a good idea, my lady." The leader of the men at arms was frowning. "We should leave directly to reach a safe place of shelter by dusk. Liam said, straight there and straight back."

"Have you no healers of your own?" another of the men asked.

"None such as the lady here," the woman said, with a thread of hope in her voice. "They say she has magic in her hands."

"I don't like it," the leader said.

"Please, my lady. He's my only boy, and I'm out of my mind with worry, for I don't rightly know what to do for him."

"I won't be long," I told them firmly, picking up the pack and starting back toward the village. The men glanced at one another.

"You two go with the Lady Liadan," the leader barked. "One at each door, and let nobody in or out, save this woman and the lady herself. Eyes and ears open, weapons drawn. You, stand guard where you can see the path by the cottage. You, down the bottom of the track. Fergus and I will guard the horses. Keep it quick, my lady, if you please. You can't be too careful these days. Lot of rabble around."

It was dark in the cottage, which was no more than a windowless hut of mud and wattle roofed with ragged thatch. A shielded candle burned by the boy's pallet. The guards did as they were told. The one at the back door I could not see; the other stood just outside the front, where he could keep a

watch both on me and on the entrance. I felt the boy's forehead, touched my finger to his wrist where the blood pulsed.

"He is not so very sick that an herbal tea, administered
correctly, may not help," I said. "Here, make this up, one
handful in a large cup of hot water. Let it infuse till the color
is a deep gold; then strain it well and let it cool until you can
put a finger in comfortably. Give the boy a cupful twice a
day. Don't try to make him eat; he will take food soon
enough when he's ready. This summer fever is quite common; I am surprised you—"

I saw the boy's eyes change as he looked over my shoulder and beyond me, and I saw the woman back away
silently, a mute apology on her worn face. I tried to rise and
turn around, but as I stood up a large hand was clapped over
my mouth and a muscular arm seized me around the chest,
and it became clear to me that I had been neatly trapped.
Iubdan's training had made sure I would not be without resources in such a situation. I sank my teeth into my captor's
hand so that his grasp loosened for an instant, just long
enough for me to raise my foot sharply to catch him between his legs. If I expected him to let me go, I was wrong.
He sucked in his breath; that was all. I tasted his blood. I
had marked him. But he remained silent. There was no
cursing, only a tightening of his grip. Where were my
guards? How had he got in? Now even the woman was
nowhere to be seen. The man began to move, trying to drag
me to the back door. I made my whole body limp; he would
have to carry me to get me out of there. I felt the pressure
ease from my mouth, just a little, as he shifted his hold. I
drew a deep breath, ready to yell for help. An instant later,
there was a sickening blow on the back of my head and
everything went dark.

My head was on fire. My mouth was as dry as chaff in a
summer wind. There was scarce a part of my body that did

not ache, for it seemed I had been dropped to the ground and left where I fell, one arm under me, my body sprawled face down on the hard earth. I was not tied up. Perhaps when I worked out what was happening, there would be some chance of escape. They had taken the little knife from my belt. That was no surprise. I lay still, eyes closed. I could hear birds calling, many birds, and a breeze in leaves, and water running over stones. Well out of doors then, somewhere in that vast, wooded area beyond the village. It was no longer full day; when I opened my eyes just a crack, I judged it was approaching dusk. How long, I wondered, before someone raised an alarm? How long before somebody came out to find me? It had been an efficient blow, calculated to put me out of action and keep me silent for long enough, without any permanent damage. In a way that was a good sign. The question was, long enough for what?

"They'll be back by sunset."

"So?"

"So who's going to tell the chief then? Who's going to explain this? Not me, that's for sure."

"Pity we can't keep it quiet. Get him called away on some mission, as far away as possible. She showing any sign of coming round?"

"Not a twitch. Sure you haven't killed her, Dog?"

"Who, me? Kill a little woman like her? With my tender heart?"

Then there was an awful groaning sound, like a man in deathly agony. This shocked me so much I forgot to pretend and sat up quickly. A mistake. The pain in my head was so bad that a wave of nausea hit me, and for a moment all I could see was whirling stars. I held my hands against my temples, eyes shut, until the throbbing began to subside. The terrible groaning went on.

"Here," said a voice. I opened my eyes cautiously. A man was crouched next to me, in his hand a cup. The cup was plain, dark metal. The hand that held it was even darker. I looked into the man's face, and he grinned, showing gleaming white teeth, of which one or two were missing. His face was as black as night. I stared, forgetting all my manners.

"You'll be thirsty," he said. "Here."

I took the cup of water and drained it. Things came into focus slowly. We were on a flat patch of ground by a little stream where the bushes and trees grew less densely. There were great moss-covered rocks and thick ferns on the bank. It had been raining, but we were protected by overhanging willows. There were two other men there, both now standing, hands on hips, looking down at me. All three of them were extraordinary, the stuff of fanciful tales. One had half of his skull shaved clean and the other half left alone, so the hair there was long and knotted, dark save for a streak of white at the temple. Around his neck he wore a strip of leather threaded through three great claws, perhaps a wolf's, though this would have been a bigger wolf than most men would see in their lives or wish to see. This man had a face pockmarked with small scars, and feral yellow eyes. His chin was etched with a neat pattern, the ink marked into the skin in crosshatched lozenges from lip to jawline. The second man bore markings around his wrists, as of twined serpents, and over his tunic he wore a strange garment that appeared to be fashioned of snakeskin. Again, the flesh of the face was etched and colored, this time on the brow, a design of cunningly interlocked scales and a forked, venomous tongue drawn down the ridge of the nose. He was younger, perhaps not yet five and twenty; but like the others, a hard-looking man, a man only a fool would meddle with. The dark one was more simply dressed, and if there were patterns on his inky skin, I could not see them. His only adornment was in his tightly curling hair, which he wore in many braids to the shoulders. Behind the left ear, a single feather made a lighter patch against the black. He saw me looking.

"Gull," he said. "Keeps me in mind of the sea." He nodded at the others in turn. "Dog. Snake. We have no other names here."

"Very well," I said politely, pleased that my voice was coming out reasonably steady. It seemed important not to let them know how frightened I was. "Then I need not give mine. Which of you was it gave me this headache?"

Two of them looked at the one with the wolf's claws and half-shaven head. Dog. He was a very big man.

"Didn't expect you to fight," he said gruffly. "Got a job for you. Couldn't risk you screaming. Women do scream."

The moaning started again. It was coming from the rocks behind us.

"Someone's hurt," I said, getting up carefully.

"That's it," said the black one, Gull. "You're the healing woman, aren't you? The one they said might pass through the village?"

"I have some skills," I said cautiously, for I did not want to give too much away. If they were who I thought they were, then it would be wise to be very, very careful. "What's the matter with this man? Can I look at him?"

"That's what you're here for," said Dog. "Better make it quick. Chief's due back and we need a good answer for him, or this man won't see another sunrise." The language they used was quite odd, a jumbled mixture of Irish and the tongue of the Britons, word and phrase chosen, it seemed, from whichever happened to suit them. Their speech was fluent but accented; Snake, perhaps, was a man of Ulster, but I doubted the others had owned either of these tongues from birth. It was just as well I had a parent of each extraction; I could follow well enough, if I concentrated, though here or there they slipped in a word the meaning of which was quite unknown to me, as if still another language lent its own touch to this peculiar speech.

I had seen and tended to many injuries, some of them severe. A festering knife wound; a nasty accident with a pitchfork. But I had never seen anything like this. The man lay in a sheltered area in a sort of half-cave, safe from rain and wind and the sun's heat. There had been some attempt to make him comfortable on a makeshift pallet, and there was a rough stool by it, and water and a quantity of stained linen. On the ground were a flask and another of the dark, metal cups. The man was gasping now, turning his head from side to side in pain, and his skin was pallid and beaded with sweat. His right arm was bandaged from shoulder to fingertips, and the whole length of it was red with blood. You could see, without unwrapping the stained cloth, that the limb was more than broken. The flesh of bare chest and shoulder was streaked with a dull, angry crimson.

"What have you given him for the pain?" I asked crisply, rolling up my sleeves.

"He can't keep anything down," Dog said. "There's strong wine in the flask; we tried that, but he can't swallow it, or if he does, he'll be retching it back before you can count to five."

"We doctor ourselves here and do well enough," said Gull. "But this—this we can't deal with. Can you help him?"

I was unwrapping the bloody dressings, trying not to screw up my face at the smell.

"When did this happen?" I asked.

"Two days since." Snake was there too now, one eye on me and my patient and the other keeping a lookout. For the chief, I presumed. "He's careful, mostly. Lost his grip, this time, trying to shift a load off the cart by himself. Caught a weight of scrap iron, crushed his arm to nothing. Would've been a goner if Dog here hadn't pulled him away in time."

"Not fast enough," said Dog, scratching the bald side of his head.

I finished unrolling the stained and stinking linen as the injured man bit his lip, feverish eyes fixed on my face. He was conscious, but I thought not really aware of what was before him or of the words that were spoken. I turned away from the pathetic, shattered remnant of his limb.

"This man has little chance," I said quietly. "Ill humors are already spreading through his body from his injury. The arm cannot be saved. He has days of agony ahead of him. I can help with that. But it is unlikely I can save his life. It might, indeed, have been better if he had died then, straight away. You've done your best; I can see that. But this may be beyond the skill of any healer."

They were all silent. Outside it was growing darker.

"I can at least make him more comfortable," I said finally. "I hope you had the sense to bring my things." My heart sank at the prospect of dealing with such an injury out here with no tools, no ready supply of the strong herbal mixtures I would need.

"Here," said Dog, and there it was, my small bag, neatly packed and strapped. He dropped it at my feet.

"What happened to my guards?" I asked, as I crouched to undo the bindings and find what I needed.

"Best you don't know," said Snake from where he still kept lookout. "Less you know the better, if you want to get home."

I rose to my feet. The three of them were all watching me closely. It would have been intimidating had I not been so intent on my task.

"We'd hoped you'd be able to do more," said Gull bluntly. "Save his life, if not the arm. This man's a good smith. Strong. Steady."

"I'm no miracle worker. I've told you what I think. I can promise no more than to make his last days easier. Now, can you fetch me some hot water, and is there any clean linen? Get this out of here, and burn it, for it's beyond washing. I'll need some sort of jug, if you have one, and a bucket or bowl."

"Not now," said Snake sharply. "Chief's coming."

"Curse it." Dog and Snake were gone in a flash. Gull hovered in the entrance.

"I take it this chief's not going to throw out the welcome mat for me?" I asked, trying not to show my fear. "You've broken some rule in bringing me here?"

"More than a few," Gull said. "My doing. Best thing you can do is keep your mouth shut. Chief can't abide women. Let me do the talking." Then he, too, was gone. I heard the sound of voices farther away. My patient let out his breath and sucked it in suddenly, and his body began to tremble all over.

"It's all right. It's all right," I said, silently cursing the isolation and the lack of ready materials and reliable assistance. A pox on them. Asking me to do good here was like—was like expecting a man to plow a field with his bare hands. How could they do this to me? How could they do it to one of their own?

". . . help . . . help me . . ." The injured man was looking right at me now, and there was some sort of recognition in the too-bright eyes. His features were so drained and white, it was hard to tell what manner of man he had been, of what years or origin. He was tall and strongly built, in keeping with his trade. The left arm was well muscled, the heaving chest sturdy as a barrel. It only made the pathetic bundle of flesh and bone on his right side more pitiful. He would take a long time to die.

". . . lady . . . help . . ."

The voices outside came close, and now I could make out the words.

"I'm not sure I heard right. Much against my better judgment, I give you two days to prove to me that you know better than I. Now the time's up. There's no improvement in his condition. All you have done is put off the inevitable. And you bring a woman here. Some girl you abduct off the road. She could be anyone. I've misjudged you, Gull. It seems you value your place in my team less highly than I thought."

"Chief."

"Am I wrong? Is he improved? Has this female effected some miracle cure?"

"No, Chief, but—"

"Where's your sense, Gull? And you? What's got hold of you? You know the way this should have ended when first he came by the injury. I should not have let you stand in the way. If you have not the stomach for such decisions, there can be no place for you here."

They were close to the rocks now, almost in sight. I held my patient's hand and made myself breathe slowly and steadily.

"Chief, this is not just any man. This is Evan we're talking about."

"So?"

"A friend, Chief. A good friend and a good man."

"Besides," put in Dog, "who'll mend our weapons with him gone? Best smith this side of Gaul, Evan is. You can't just . . ." his voice died away as if something had just occurred to him. There was a pause.

"A one-armed smith is of limited use." The tone was cool, dispassionate. "Have you given thought to what the man himself would want?"

At that moment they stepped around the rocks and under the overhang to where I sat by the injured man. I stood up as tall as I could, trying hard to look calm and confident. It scarcely mattered. The chief's eyes swept over me dismissively and settled on the man who lay by my side. I might not have been there for all the notice he took of me. I watched him as he came close and touched the smith's brow with his hand, a hand patterned from the wrist of his shirt to the fingertips with feathers and spirals and interlocking links, as complex and fascinating as some ancient puzzle. I glanced up, and for a moment he looked straight back at me across the pallet. I gaped. This was a face such as I had never seen before, even in the most fanciful of dreams, a face that was, in its way, a work of art. For it was light and dark, night and day, this world and the Otherworld. On the left side, the face of a youngish man, the skin weathered but fair, the eye gray and clear, the mouth well formed if unyielding in character. On all the right side, extending from an undrawn mark down the exact center, an etching of line and curve and feathery pattern, like the mask of some fierce bird of prey. An eagle? A goshawk? No, it was, I thought, a raven, even as far as the circles about the eye and the suggestion of predatory beak around the nostril. The mark of the raven. If I had not been so frightened, I might have laughed at the irony of it. The pattern extended down his neck and under the border of his leather jerkin and the linen shirt he wore beneath it. His head was completely shaven, and the skull, too, was colored the same, half-man, half-wild creature; some great artist of the inks and needle had wrought this over many days, and I imagined the pain must have been considerable. What manner of man needed such decoration to find his identity? I was staring. He was probably used to that. With difficulty, I tore my gaze away to where Gull and Dog and Snake were standing mute amongst a group of other men. Their garb was motley, in tune with Eamonn's description: a shaggy pelt here, feathers there, chain links, leather patches, straps and buckles, silver collars and armlets, and a not inconsiderable display of well-muscled flesh in various shades. It occurred to me, somewhat belatedly, that this was perhaps not the best of places for a young woman on her own. I could almost hear my father's voice. *Haven't you been listening to a thing I've told you, Liadan?*

The leader had drawn a knife from his belt. It was a sharp, lethal sort of knife.

"Let us end this farce," he said. "You should not have delayed me in doing so before. This man has no further use. He can no longer contribute, here or elsewhere. All you have done is prolong his suffering needlessly." He moved subtly, so the injured man could not see his hands, and he shifted his grip on the knife. The others stood silent. Nobody moved. Nobody said a word. He raised the knife.

"No!" I put out a hand across the pallet, shielding the wounded man's neck. "You can't do this! You can't just—finish him off as if he were some snared rabbit or a sheep to be slaughtered for the pot. This is a man here. One of your own."

The chief raised his brows just a fraction. The thin line of his mouth did not change. The eyes were cool.

"Would you not administer such a stroke if it were your dog or your hawk or your mare that suffered thus with deadly injury? You would not wish such agony to be extended without reason? But no, I suppose there was always some man to do your dirty work for you. What could a woman know of such things? Remove your hand."

"I will not," I responded, my anger rising. "You say this man has no further use, as if he were—merely some tool, some weapon in your armory. You say he cannot contribute. For your purposes, maybe that is true. But he still lives. He can love a woman and father a child. He can laugh and sing and tell tales. He can enjoy the fruits of the fields and a tankard of good ale at night. He can watch his son become a smith such as he was. This man can have a life. There is a future, after—" I looked around me at the circle of grim-faced men—"after this."

"Where did you learn of life?" the raven man asked me in the bleakest of tones. "In some fairy tale? We live by the code. We have no names, no past, no future. We have tasks to perform, and at those we are the best. There is no life for this man, nor for any of us, outside that. There can be none. Step away from the bed." It was growing quite dark, and one of the men had lit a small lantern. Crazy shadows fell across the creviced rock walls, and the leader's face held a menace that was as real as the weapon in his hand. You could see how it might strike terror into an enemy, for in the trickery of the uneven light he did indeed seem half raven, his eye piercing bright and dangerous amid the whorls and spirals of the finely drawn pattern.

"Step away," he said again.

"I will not," I said. And he raised his left hand as if to strike me across the face. With a great effort of will, I managed not to flinch away. I held his gaze and hoped he could not see how I was shaking with fear. The man stared back at me, bleak-eyed, and then he slowly lowered his hand.

"Chief," ventured Gull, the only one bold enough to speak out.

"Hold your tongue! You're going soft, Gull. First you beg two days' grace for a man you know has no hope of survival, who wouldn't want to live even if he could. Then you bring some fool of a girl here. Where did you find her? She's got a tongue on her, that's beyond dispute. Can we get on with this? There's work to be done." Perhaps he thought he had intimidated me into silence.

"He does have a chance," I said, much relieved that he had decided not to hit me, for my head ached already from its earlier knock, "a slender one, but a real one nonetheless. He must lose the arm, that I cannot save. But I may save his life. I do not believe he would want to die. He asked me to help him. At least let me try."

"Why?"

"Why not?"

"Because—curse it, woman, I've neither time nor inclination to debate issues with you. I don't know where you came from or where you're going, and I have no wish to be enlightened on either score; but here you are no more than a nuisance and an inconvenience. This is no place for a woman."

"Believe me, I am not here by choice. But now that your men have brought me so far, at least give me a trial. I will show you what I can do. Seven days, eight—long enough to tend to the man properly and give him a fighting chance. That's all I'm asking." I saw Gull's face, a picture of surprise. I had, after all, completely contradicted my earlier words. Perhaps I was a fool. Dog had hope written on his plain features; the others looked at the rock wall, the ground, their hands, anywhere but at their leader. Someone at the back gave a tiny little whistle, as if to say, *Now she's done it*.

The raven man stood very still for a moment, looking at me through narrowed eyes, and then he slipped the wicked knife casually back into its sheath.

"Seven days," he said. "You think that's enough?"

I could hear the labored breathing of the smith, and the cynical tone of the questioner's voice.

"The arm must come off," I said. "Tonight, straightaway. I'll need help with that. I can tell you how to do it, but I don't have the strength for the cutting. After that, I'll tend to him. Ten days would be better."

"Six days," he said levelly. "In six days we move. It can be no later; we are required elsewhere and must allow time for travel. If Evan is not fit to accompany us, he'll be left behind."

"You ask the impossible," I whispered, "and you know it."

"You wanted a trial. This is your trial. Now if you'll excuse us, we have work to do. You, Gull, and you," nodding at Dog, "since your folly brought her here, you can help her with the job. Fetch what she wants. Do her bidding. And the rest of you—" He glanced around the circle of men, and they fell silent. "The woman is out of bounds. I should not need to tell you that. Lay a hand on her, and you'll have extreme difficulty in picking up your weapon the next day. She'll remain here with a guard outside at all times. If I hear so much as a breath of any breach, you'll be painfully aware of it."

Chapter Four

I kept a brave face, but under it I was petrified with fear. I, the girl who wanted nothing more than to stay at home and tend her herb patch; I, the girl who loved above all to exchange tales with her family of an evening after supper, instructing fierce strangers on how to hack off a dying man's limb and cauterize the wound with hot iron. I, the daughter of Sevenwaters, alone in the lair of the Painted Man and his band of feral killers; for it had become blindingly clear to me that these must be the very outlaws Eamonn had told of. I, Liadan, making bargains with a man who—what was it Eamonn had said? That he carried out his missions without pride or commitment? I wasn't sure, now, that this description was accurate. I thought both qualities were present, though not perhaps in the way Eamonn would have defined them. The man was singularly unpleasant, there was no doubting that. But why had he agreed to what I proposed if he thought me so misguided?

I pondered this as I told Dog to make ready a brazier just

outside and to keep the heat up, and to get a broad dagger ready, red hot, if he could. Gull fetched the other things that were needed. In particular, a small bowl of warm water and a very sharp knife with a toothed edge. Snake brought more lanterns and stood them around the rock shelter. Meanwhile I sat by the smith, Evan, and tried to talk to him. He slipped in and out of awareness, one moment speaking nonsense in his fever, then suddenly back with us, staring up at me in a blend of hope and terror. I tried to tell him, during these brief, lucid moments, what would happen.

". . . your arm is beyond saving . . . To save your life, we must cut off your arm. . . . I will put you to sleep as well as I can, but you'll probably still feel it. It will be very bad for a while. . . . Try to keep still. Trust me. I know what I'm doing . . ." There was no telling if he understood me or believed me. I wasn't sure if I believed myself. Outside there were sounds of quiet, orderly activity: horses being attended to, buckets clanking, weapons being sharpened. Not much talk.

"We're ready," said Gull.

I had taken a small sponge from the deepest corner of my pack, and this had been soaking in the little bowl for a time, not too long. Gull sniffed.

"That takes me back a long way. Reminds me of my mother's potions. Pretty strong stuff. Mulberry, henbane, juice of hops, mandrake? Now where would a good little lass like you learn how to make up a draft like that? As soon kill a man as cure him, that would."

"That's why we need the vinegar," I told him, eyeing him curiously. Did a man with no past have a mother? "The herbs are dried into the sponge. Very useful when you're on the road. You know a bit about these things then?"

"Most of it I've long forgotten. It's women's work."

"It could be useful to learn it again. For men who take such risks, it seems you have few resources to deal with your injuries."

"It doesn't happen much," said Dog. "We're the best.

Mostly, we come out untouched. This, this was an accident, pure and simple."

"His own fault," agreed Gull. "Besides, you heard the chief. We've got our way of dealing with it. No passengers in this team."

I shivered. "You've done this yourselves? Slit a man's throat sooner than try to save him?"

Dog narrowed his yellow eyes at me. "Different world. Couldn't expect you to understand. No place in the team if you're hurt so bad you can't do your work. No place to go outside the team. Chief's right. Ask any of us. All of us. Put us in Evan's place, and we'd be begging for the knife."

I thought about this as I coaxed the smith to swallow a few drops squeezed from the little sponge.

"That doesn't make sense," I said. "Maybe it's part of the code, whatever that is. But then, why did you try to save this man's life against your chief's orders? Why not just finish it, as he would have done?"

They seemed reluctant to answer. I pressed the sponge in my hand, and a little more of the highly toxic mixture dribbled into Evan's mouth. His eyelids closed. At last Gull spoke in an undertone.

"Different, you see. Evan's a smith, not a fighter. Got a trade. Got a chance of a life outside, once he saves enough to take himself away. Right away, it'd have to be; Armorica, Gaul, across the sea. He's got a woman waiting for him in Britain; he can up and go as soon as he has the silver for bribes to secure safe passage. There's a price on his head, like all of us. Still, he's got that hope."

"Couldn't tell the chief that," said Snake in a murmur. "It was hard enough work, begging a couple of days for him. Hope you can do miracles, healer girl. You'll need one."

"My name's Liadan," I said, without thinking. "You can call me that; it'll be easier for all of us. Now we'd better get started. Who's doing the cutting?"

Gull looked at Dog, and Snake looked at Dog, and Dog eyed the lethal, toothed knife.

"Looks like it'll have to be me," he said.

"Size and strength aren't all of it," I cautioned. "You'll need very good control as well. The cut must be neat and quick. And he'll scream. This potion may be strong, but it's not as strong as that."

"I'll do it."

Nobody had heard the chief coming. It seemed that, good as his men were, he was better. I hoped he had not been listening for long. His cold, gray eyes swept once around the area, and then he stalked over and helped himself to the knife. Dog wore an expression of acute relief.

"You don't escape so lightly," I told him. "You seem to be the biggest, so you'd better hold onto his shoulders. Keep your hands well away from where the—from where this man is cutting. You two, take his legs. He may look unconscious, but he'll feel the pain of this and its aftermath. When I tell you, you must use all your weight to hold him."

They moved into position, well drilled in obeying orders.

"Have you ever done this before?" I asked the man with the knife.

"Precisely this, no. You are about to instruct me, no doubt."

I made a quick decision not to lose my temper however arrogant his manner.

"I'll take you through it step-by-step. When we start, you must do as I tell you straightaway. It will be much easier if you give me a name to use. I will not call you Chief."

"Use what you will," he said, brows raised. "We have no names here, save those you have heard."

"There are tales about a man named Bran," I said. "That name means raven. I will use that. Is the dagger heated? You must fetch it quickly when I tell you, Dog."

"It's ready."

"Very well. Now, Bran, you see this point near the shoulder, where the bone is still whole?"

The man whom I had named after a legendary voyager gave a nod, his face tightlipped with disapproval.

"You must cut here to finish cleanly. Don't let your knife slip down to this point, for the wound has no hope of healing if we leave fragments within. Concentrate on your job. Let the others hold him. I will cut back the flesh first with my small knife. . . . Where is my small knife?"

Gull reached down and extracted it from where he had stuck it in his boot.

"Thank you. I'll start now."

I wondered, later, how I could possibly have stayed in control. How I managed to sound calm and capable when my heart was racing at three times its usual pace, and my body was breaking out in a cold sweat, and I was filled with fear. Fear of failure. Fear of the consequences of failure, not just for the hapless Evan, but for myself as well. Nobody had spelled out exactly what would happen if I got this wrong, but I could imagine.

The first part was not so bad. Cut neatly through the layers, peel back the skin, as far as the place where somebody had tied a narrow, extremely tight strip of linen around the arm, just below the shoulder. My hands were soon red to the wrists. So far, so good. The smith twitched and trembled, but did not wake.

"All right," I said. "Now you cut, Bran. Straight across here. Dog, hold tight. Keep him still. This must be quick."

Perhaps the best assistant, at such times, is a man who has no understanding of human feelings, a man who can cut living bone as neatly and decisively as he would a plank of wood, a man whose face shows nothing as his victim jerks and thrashes suddenly, straining against the well-muscled arms that hold him, and lets out a shuddering moan straight from the depths of the gut.

"Sweet Christ," breathed Snake, leaning his weight across

the smith's legs to keep him down. The horrible sawing noise went steadily on. The cut was as straight as a sword edge. By my side, Dog had his massive forearms planted one on the patient's left arm, one across the upper chest.

"Careful, Dog," I said. "He still needs to breathe."

"I think he's coming to." Gull's hands pressed heavily down on Evan's right side. "Having trouble holding him still. Can't you give him some more of the . . . ?"

"No," I said. "He's had as much as he can safely take. We're nearly done." There was a truly horrible sound as the last shard of bone was severed, and the mangled remains of the limb fell to the ground. Across the pallet from me, Bran looked up. There was blood on him to the elbows, and his shirt front was spattered with crimson. I detected no change at all in his expression. His brows rose in silent question.

"Fetch the dagger from the fire." Díancécht help me; I must do this part myself. I knew what would happen and steeled my will. Bran walked outside and returned with the weapon in his hand, hilt wrapped in a cloth, blade glowing as bright as a sword half forged. His eyes asked another question.

"No," I said. "Give it to me. This part is my work. Untie the last binding there. There'll be blood. Then come around and help Dog hold him down. He'll scream. Hold on tight. Keep him still."

The binding came off, and there was a flow of blood, but less than I expected. That was not a good sign, for it might signify the flesh was already dying. Without a word I moved to the other side, and Bran took my place, ready to hold the smith as soon as he moved.

"Now," I said, and touched the red-hot iron to the open wound. There was an unpleasant sizzling sound, and a sickening smell of roast meat. The smith screamed. It was a hideous banshee scream such as you might hear again and again in your dreams for years after. His whole body convulsed in agony, chest heaving, limbs thrashing, head and shoulders kept still only by the efforts of both Dog and Bran, who forced him down, muscles bulging. Big, ugly Dog was as white as a wraith.

"Sweet Jesus," muttered Snake.

"Sorry, not finished," I said, blinking back tears, and I touched the dagger to the wound again, moving it firmly so the whole area would be sealed. Forced myself to keep it there long enough, as another shuddering scream filled the air of the small shelter. Took the hot iron away, finally, and stood there as the smith's voice died down to a wheezing, gasping whimper. The four men relaxed their grip and straightened up slowly. I didn't seem to be able to move. After a bit, Gull took the dagger from my hands and went outside with it, and Dog began quietly picking things up off the ground and dropping them into a bucket, and Snake took the little cup of vinegar and, at a nod from me, began to sponge it, a few drops at a time, between Evan's swollen lips.

"I'm not going to ask where you learned that," Bran commented. "Are you happy you put him through this? Still convinced you're right?"

I looked up at him. His severe features with their strange half pattern blurred before my eyes, the feathered markings moving and twisting in the lamplight. I was aware, suddenly, of how weary I was.

"I stand by my decision," I said faintly. "The time you have set me is too short. But I know I'm right."

"You may not be so sure after six days in this camp," he said ominously. "When you've seen a little more of the real world, you will learn that everyone is expendable. There are no exceptions, be it skillful smith or hardened warrior or little healer girl. You suffer and die and are soon forgotten. Life goes on regardless."

I swallowed. The rock walls were moving around me.

"There will be people looking for me," I whispered. "My uncle, my brother, my . . . They will be searching for me by now, and they have resources."

"They will not find you." His tone allowed for no doubt.

"What about the escort that traveled with me?" I was clutching at straws now, for I suspected they were all dead. "They cannot be far away. Someone must have seen what happened—someone will follow—"

My voice trailed away, and I put out a hand for balance as my vision filled with spinning stars.

"Sorry," I mumbled foolishly, as if excusing myself from polite company. Suddenly there was a very firm grip on my arm, and I was propelled to the wooden stool and pushed unceremoniously onto it.

"Snake, leave that for now. He's still breathing; he'll keep. Fetch the girl clean clothes, if you can find anything small enough. A blanket, water for washing. Go down to the fire, get yourself food, and bring some for her when you come back. She's little enough use at her best; she'll be none at all if we let her starve." He turned back to me. "First rule of combat: Only the most battle tested can function well on little food and less sleep. That comes only with long practice. You want to do your job properly, then prepare for it properly."

I was far too tired to argue.

"You'll get two guards tonight. One for outside, one to watch the smith while you sleep. Don't let it make you complacent. You chose this task yourself, and you're on your own after tonight."

At last he was leaving. I closed my eyes, swaying with exhaustion where I sat. The smith lay quiet, for now.

"Oh, and one more thing."

My eyes snapped open.

"This will have earned you a certain—respect—among the men. Make sure you don't let it develop into anything more. Any of them who breaks the code will face the severest penalty. You'll have enough on your conscience without that as well."

"What would a man like you know about conscience?" I muttered, as he turned on his heel and walked away. If he heard me, he gave no sign of it.

It was a strange time. There are tales of men and women taken by the Fair Folk of a moonlight night in the woods, who journey into the Otherworld and experience a life so different that, on return, they scarcely know what is real and what a dream. The Painted Man and his motley bunch of followers were about as far from the visionary beings of the Otherworld as was imaginable, but still I felt removed utterly from my normal life; and although it may be hard to believe, while I dwelt there in the hidden encampment I did not spend much time thinking of my home or my parents or even of how Niamh was faring, all alone and sharing a stranger's bed. There were moments when I grew chill with fear, remembering Eamonn's tale. I recognized that my situation was perilous indeed. The guards Liam had sent with me had almost certainly been dispatched with ruthless efficiency. That was the way these men went about things. As for the code, it might protect me and it might not. In the end, my survival probably depended on whether the smith lived or died. But my father had told me once that fear is no winner of battles. I rolled up my sleeves and told myself I had no time for fits of the vapors. A man's life was in the balance. Besides, I had something to prove and was determined to do it.

That first night and day they guarded me so closely it was like having a large, well-armed shadow always a step behind. I even had to remind them that women do have some bodily needs best attended to in private. We then developed a compromise whereby I could at least be out of sight briefly, provided I did not take too long and came straight back to where Dog, or Gull, or Snake would be waiting, weapon in hand. Nobody needed to point out to me the utter futility of any attempt to escape. They brought me food and water; they brought me a bucket so I could wash myself. Clad in someone's old undershirt, which came down well below my knees, and a roomy sort of tunic with useful pockets here and there, I braided my hair severely down my back, out of the way, and got on with what had to be done. Carefully measured drafts for the pain; mixtures to be burned on the brazier, encouraging the ill humors to leave the body; dressings for the ugly burn, compresses for the brow. Much of the time I would simply sit by the pallet, holding Evan's hand in mine, talking quietly or singing little songs as to a feverish child.

On the second night I was allowed out as far as the cooking fire. Dog walked by me through the encampment, where many small, temporary shelters were dotted between the trees and bushes, until we came to a cleared area where a hot, smokeless fire burned neatly between stones. Around it a number of men sat, stood, or leaned, scooping up their food from the small vessels most travelers carry somewhere in their packs. There was a smell of stewed rabbit. I was hungry enough not to be too particular and accepted a bowl shoved into my hands. It was quiet, save for the buzz of night crickets and the faint murmur of a bird as it fell asleep in the branches above.

"Here," said Dog. He handed me a small spoon crafted of bone. It was none too clean. There were many eyes turned on me in the half darkness.

"Thank you," I said, realizing I had been accorded a rare privilege. The others used their fingers to eat or maybe a hunk of hard bread. There was no laughter and little talk. Perhaps my presence stifled their conversation. Even when ale was poured and cups passed there was scarcely a sound. I finished my food; declined a second helping. Somebody offered me a cup of ale, and I took it.

"Did a good job," someone said curtly.

"Nice piece of work," agreed another. "Not easy. Seen it botched before. Man can bleed to death quicker than a— that's to say, it's a job that has to be done right."

"Thank you," I said gravely. I looked up at the circle of faces from where I sat on the bank near the fire. All of them kept a margin of three, four paces away from me. I wondered if this, too, were part of the code. They were a strangely assorted group, their bizarre polyglot speech indicating a multitude of origins and a long time spent together. Of them all, I thought, perhaps but two or three had had their birthplace here in Erin. "I had help," I added. "I could not have performed such a task alone."

One very tall man was studying me closely, a frown creasing his features. "Still," he said after a while, "wouldn't have been done at all, but for you. Right?"

I glanced around quickly, not wishing to get anyone into trouble. "Maybe," I said, offhand.

"Got a chance now, hasn't he?" the very tall man asked, leaning forward, long, skinny arms folded on bony knees. There was an expectant pause.

"A chance, yes," I said carefully, "no more. I'll do my best for him."

There were a few nods. Then somebody made a subtle little sound, halfway between a hiss and a whistle, and suddenly they were all looking anywhere but at me.

"Here, Chief." A bowl was passed, a full cup.

"It's very quiet here," I observed after a little while. "Do you not sing songs or tell tales of an evening after supper?"

Somebody gave a snort, instantly suppressed.

"Tales?" Dog was perplexed, scratching the bald side of his head. "We don't know any tales."

"You mean, like giants and monsters and mermaids?" asked the very tall, lanky fellow. I thought I detected a little spark of something in his eye.

"Those and others," I said encouragingly. "There are also

tales of heroes, and of great battles, and of voyages to distant and amazing lands. Many tales."

"You know some of these tales?" asked the tall man.

"Shut your mouth, Spider," someone hissed under his breath.

"Enough to tell a new one each night of the year and have some left over," I said. "Would you like me to tell you one?"

There was a long pause, during which the men exchanged glances and shuffled their feet.

"You're here to do a job, not provide free entertainment." There was no need for me to look up to know who spoke. "These men are not children." Interesting, when this man addressed me, he used plain Irish, fluent and almost unaccented.

"Is telling a tale against the code?" I asked quietly.

"What about this Bran character?" Gull put in with no little courage. "I'll wager there's a tale or two about him. I'd like to hear one of those."

"That is a very grand tale to be told over many nights," I said. "I will not be here long enough to finish it. But there are plenty of others."

"Go on, Chief," said Gull. "It's harmless enough."

"Why don't I start," I said, "and if you feel my words are a danger, you can stop me when you choose. That seems fair."

"Does it?"

Well, he hadn't said no, and there was an air of hushed expectancy among the strange band gathered around the fire. So I started anyway.

"For a band of fighters such as yourselves," I said, "what could be apter than a tale of the greatest of all warriors, Cú Chulainn, champion of Ulster? His story, too, is a long one made up of many tales. But I will tell of the way he learned his skill and honed it so that no man could master him on the field, be he the greatest battle hero of his tribe. This Cú Chulainn, you understand, was no ordinary man. There were rumors, and maybe there was some truth behind them, rumors that he was a child of Lugh, the sun god, by a mortal woman. Nobody seemed quite sure, but one thing was for certain: when Cú Chulainn was about to fight, a change would come over him. They called it riastradh, the battle frenzy. His whole body would shake and grow hot, his face red as fire, his heart beating like a great drum in his breast, his hair standing on end and glowing with sparks. It was as if his father, the sun god, did indeed inspire him at such times, for to his enemies it appeared a fierce and terrible light played around him as he approached them, sword in hand. And after the battle was won, they say it took three barrels of icy river water to cool him down. When they plunged him into the first, it burst its bands and split apart. The water in the second boiled over. The third steamed and steamed until the heat was out of him, and Cú Chulainn was himself again.

"Now, this great warrior had exceptional skills, even as a boy. He could leap like a salmon and swim like an otter. He could run swifter than the deer and see in the dark as a cat does. But there came a time when he sought to improve his art, with the aim of winning a lovely lady called Emer. When he asked her father for Emer's hand, the old man suggested he was not yet proved as a warrior and should seek further tuition from the best. As for the lady, she'd have taken him then and there, for who could resist such a fine specimen of manhood? But she was a good girl and followed her father's bidding. So Cú Chulainn asked and he asked, and at length he learned that the best teacher of the arts of war was a woman, Scáthach, a strange creature who lived on a tiny island off the coast of Alba."

"A woman?" someone echoed scornfully. "How could that be?"

"Ah, well, this was no ordinary woman, as our hero soon found out for himself. When he came to the wild shore of Alba and looked across the raging waters to the island where she lived with her warrior women, he saw that there could be a difficulty before he even set foot there. For the only way across was by means of a high, narrow bridge, just wide enough for one man to walk on. And the instant he set his foot upon its span, the bridge began to shake and flex and bounce up and down, all along its considerable length, so that anyone foolish enough to venture farther along it would straightaway be tossed down onto the knife-sharp rocks or into the boiling surf."

"Why didn't he use a boat?" asked Spider, with a perplexed frown.

"Didn't you hear what Liadan said?" Gull responded with derision. "Raging waters? Boiling surf? No boat could have crossed that sea, I'll wager."

"Indeed not," I said, smiling at him. "Many had tried, and all of them had perished, swallowed up by the sea or by the huge, long-toothed creatures that dwelt therein. Well, what was Cú Chulainn to do? He was not the sort of man to give up, and he wanted Emer with a longing that filled every corner of his body. He measured the distance across the bridge with his keen eye, and then he drew in his breath and let it out, and drew it in again, and the riastradh came on him until his heart threatened to burst out of his chest, and every vein in his skin swelled and stood out like a hempen cord stretched tight. Then Cú Chulainn gathered himself and made a mighty leap, as of a salmon breaching a great waterfall, and he landed lightly in the very center of the shaking bridge, neatly on the ball of his left foot. The bridge bounced and buckled, trying to throw him off, but he was too quick, leaping again, such a leap that when his foot touched ground he was on the shore of Scáthach's island.

"Up on the ramparts of Scáthach's dwelling, which was a

fortified tower of solid granite, the warrior woman stood with her daughter, watching.

" 'Looks a likely fellow,' she muttered. 'Knows a few tricks already. I could teach him well.'

" 'Wouldn't mind teaching him a few tricks myself,' said the daughter, who had something quite different in mind."

There was a ripple of laughter. Unused to stories these men might be, but it seemed they knew how to enjoy one. As for me, I was warming to my task and wondered, fleetingly, what Niamh would say if she could see me now. I took up the tale again.

" 'Well then,' said the mother, 'if you want him, take him. Three days, you can have, to teach him the arts of love. Then he's mine.'

"So it was Scáthach's daughter who went down to welcome the hero, and very welcome indeed did she make him, so that after three days there was little he did not know of the needs of a woman and how to please her. Lucky Emer. Then it was the mother's turn, and when his lessons began, Cú Chulainn soon realized Scáthach was indeed the best of teachers. She taught him for a year and a day, and it was from her he learned his battle leap, with which he could fly high above a spear flung through the air by his adversary He learned to shave a man with quick strokes of the sword, a skill with little practical use, maybe, but sure to drive terror into an enemy."

Dog ran a hand nervously over the bald side of his scalp.

"Cú Chulainn could cut away the ground under the enemy's feet, his sword moving so quickly you could scarce see it. He could jump lightly onto his adversary's shield. He learned to maneuvre a chariot with knives on its wheels so that his opponents would not know what hit them until they lay dying on the field of battle. He learned, as well, the art of juggling, which he could do as cleverly with sharp knives or flaming torches as he could with the leather juggling balls. While he was on that island, Cú Chulainn lay with a warrior woman, Aoife, and she bore him a son, Conlai, and that began another tale, a tale of great sadness. But Cú Chulainn himself returned home, after a year and a day, and again sought the hand of the lovely Emer."

"And?" asked Gull impatiently when I paused. It was late. The fire had died to a glow, and a network of stars had spread across the dark sky. The moon was waning.

"Well, Emer's father, Fogall, had never expected the young man to return. He had been hoping Scáthach would finish him off, if the bridge and the sea didn't. So Cú Chulainn met with armed resistance. But he had not studied with the best in the world for nothing. With his small band of warriors, each of them carefully picked, he routed Fogall's forces with little effort. Fogall himself he pursued to the very edge of the cliffs and fought there man-to-man. Soon enough Fogall, completely outclassed, fell to his death on the stones far below. Then Cú Chulainn took the fair Emer as his bride, and much joy they had in each other."

"I'll bet he taught her a thing or two," said somebody in an undertone.

"Enough." Bran stepped around from behind me, his voice commanding instant silence among the men. "The tale is ended. Those men on relief watch, be off with you. The rest, to your beds. Don't expect a repeat performance."

They went with never a word. I wondered how it would feel to be so in fear of a man that you never questioned his orders. There could be little satisfaction in such an existence.

"You, back to work."

It took a moment or two before I realized Bran was speaking to me.

"What am I supposed to say to that? Yes, Chief?" I got up. Dog was close behind me, a constant shadow.

"What about keeping your mouth shut and doing as you're told? That would be easier for all of us."

I shot him a glance of dislike. "I am not answerable to you," I said. "I'll do the job I'm here to do. That's all. I will not be ordered about like one of your men. If they choose to follow you like terrified slaves, that's their business. But I cannot work if I must go in fear and be always restricted. And you said yourself, be properly prepared so you can do your job effectively. Something like that."

He did not answer for a while. Something I had said had clearly touched a nerve, although that strange face, summer and winter, scarcely moved a muscle.

"It will help, too, if you use my name," I added severely. "My name is Liadan."

"These tales," said Bran absently, as if his mind were on something else entirely. "They are dangerous. They make men dream of what they cannot have, of what they can never be. They make men question who they are and what they may aspire to. For my men, there can be no such tales."

For a moment, I could not speak.

"Oh, come on, Chief," protested Dog unwisely. "What about Cú Chulainn and his son, Conlai? A tale of great sadness, that's what she said. What about mermaids and monsters and giants?"

"You talk like an infant," Bran's tone was dismissive. "This is a troop of hardened men with no time for such trivial nonsense."

"Perhaps you should make time," I said, determined to get my point across. "If what you want is to achieve a victory, what better to inspire your men than a heroic tale, some tale of a battle against great odds, won by skill and courage? If your men are weary or downhearted, what more fit to cheer them than a foolish tale—say, the story of the wee man Iubdan and the plate of porridge, or the farmer who got three wishes and squandered them all? What better to give them hope than a tale of love?"

"You take a risk, talking of love. Are you so innocent, or so stupid, that you cannot imagine what effect such words will have in this company of men? Or perhaps that's what you want. You could take your pick. A new one every night. Two, maybe."

I felt myself grow pale.

"You show the man you are when you insult me thus," I said very quietly.

"And what sort of a man is that?"

"A man with no sense of right or wrong. A man who cannot laugh and who rules by fear. A—a man with no respect for women. There are those who would seek a terrible vengeance if they heard you speak to me thus."

There was a moment's silence.

"And on what do you base this judgment?" he asked eventually. "You have spent but the briefest time in my company. Already you believe me some kind of monster. You are indeed quick to assess a man's character."

"As are you to judge a woman," I said straightaway.

"I need not know you, to recognize what you are," he said bleakly. "Your kind are all the same. Catch a man in your net, draw him in, deprive him of his will and his judgment. It happens so subtly he is lost before ever he recognizes the danger. Then others are dragged in after him, and the pattern of darkness stretches wider and wider so that even the innocent have no escape." He stopped abruptly, clearly regretting his words.

"You," he said to Dog, who had been listening openmouthed. "Take her back to her charge, then go to your bed. Gull will stand guard tonight."

"I could do it, Chief. I'm good for another watch—"

"Gull will stand guard."

"Yes, Chief."

That was the second day. The smith, Evan, held his ground, though I was not happy with the way his body trembled and shivered, or the heat of his brow that could not be relieved,

however much I sponged him with cool water in which I
had steeped wild endive and five leaf. A certain competition
developed among my three assistants. All were eager to
help with nursing duties and, though they lacked skill, I
welcomed their strength in lifting and turning the patient.

Bran's men seemed always busy, rehearsing combat,
tending to horses or harness, cleaning and sharpening
weapons. Eamonn had been wrong on one count. They used
the conventional armory of sword, spear, bow, and dagger,
as well as a wide range of other devices whose names and
functions I had no wish to learn. The camp was self-
contained and highly organized. I was amazed, on the third
morning, to find my gown and shift neatly folded on the
rocks outside my shelter, washed and dried and almost as
good as new. There was evidently at least one capable cook
there, and no shortage of efficient hunters to provide a supply of fresh meat for the pot. Where the carrots and turnips
came from, I did not ask.

Time was short. Six days until they moved on. The smith
was in pain and needed the soporific herbs to control it.
Still, if he were to be ready to go on without me, he must
know the truth. There were times when he looked down at
what lay where his strong arm had once joined his powerful
shoulder. But his fevered eyes showed no real recognition,
as I spoke to him of what had happened and how things
would be.

I walked through the camp on the third day with Snake
close by me. My borrowed clothes were in need of washing,
for they were now, in their turn, stained with my patient's
blood, and here and there with drafts Evan kept in his stomach no longer than the count of ten before he retched them
up again.

When we reached the bank of the stream, we found the
tall man, Spider, and another whom they called Otter
wrestling on the grass. Otter was winning, for in such a
sport, height gives little advantage if your opponent is swift

and clever. There was a big splash, and there was Spider sprawled in the water, looking very put out. Otter wiped his hands on his leather trousers. The upper part of his body was naked, and he bore a complex pattern on the chest of many links forming a twisting circle.

"Morning, Snake. Morning, lady. Here, you oaf. Get up. Need to put in a bit more practice, you do." Otter reached out an arm and hauled the embarrassed Spider out of the water.

"Fools," commented Snake mildly. "Don't let the chief catch you mucking about."

I unrolled my bundle and began to rub the stained cloth on the smooth stones in the shallows.

"Better go back up to camp, or wherever you're meant to be," Snake went on. "Chief wouldn't be happy to see you talking to the lady here."

"All right for you," mumbled Spider, clearly put out to be seen thus, dripping wet and defeated. "How did you score permanent guard duty then?"

"None of your business."

"Why are you all so frightened of him?" I asked, pausing in my labors to look up at the three of them. It was a pity there was no soapwort growing nearby. I must ask how they had gotten my gown so clean.

"Frightened?" Spider was perplexed.

Snake frowned. "You've got it wrong," he said. "Chief's a man to respect, not to fear."

"What?" I sat back on my heels, amazed. "When all of you fall silent at his least word? When he threatens the direst punishment if you transgress some code which no doubt he himself invented? When you are somehow bound to him in a brotherhood from which it seems you can never escape? What is that but a rule of fear?"

"Ssh," said Snake, alarmed. "Keep your voice down."

"See?" I challenged, but more quietly. "You dare not even speak of these things openly lest he should hear and punish you."

"That's true enough," said Spider, settling his long, ungainly form on the rocks near me, but still that careful three or four paces away. "He knows how to set rules and enforce them. But it's fair. The code's there to protect us. From each other. From ourselves. Everyone understands that. If we break it, that's our choice, and we take the consequences."

"But what holds you here if not fear of him?" I asked, perplexed. "What sort of a life is it, killing for money, never able to go out into the real world, never able to—to love, to see your children thrive, to watch a tree you planted grow to shade your cottage, or fight in a battle where right is on your side? It is no life."

"Don't suppose you could understand," said Snake diffidently.

"Try me," I said.

"Without the chief," it was Otter who spoke, "we'd be nothing. Nothing. Dead, imprisoned, or worse. Scum of the earth, every one of us. You can't say this is no life. He's given us a life."

"Otter's right," said Snake. "Ask Dog. Ask him his story; get him to show you the scars on his hands."

"We're the men nobody had a use for," said Spider. "The chief made us useful; gave us a place and a purpose."

"What about Gull?" Snake went on. "Comes from foreign parts, Gull does, some place far off, hot as hellfire and all over sand. Land of black people, like himself. Anyway, somebody had really put him through it. Saw his people hacked to death right before his eyes. Wife, children, old folks. All he wanted was to die. Chief got him out, talked him around. Tough job. Now Gull's the best we've got, barring the chief himself."

I had completely forgotten my washing, and it was in danger of floating away. Snake reached past me to grab it, put it into my hands, moved back three, four paces.

"Every man here has a story," said Otter, "but we try to forget. No past, no future, just today. Easier. We've all been cast out. Not one of us can go back, except perhaps the smith. This is our existence, here in these woods, or out there on a job, knowing we can be the best at what we do. It's our identity: the band of the Painted Man. He commands a good price and shares what he gets. Me, I'd sooner be here working for him than in the uniform of some jumped-up lordling's private army."

"Who'd have you?" chuckled Snake. "Too full of funny tricks, you are. You'd be in trouble before you had the chance to hear your first order."

"I'll take his orders any day," replied Otter seriously. "The chief saved my life. But life's cheap enough. I owe him something far more valuable, my self-respect."

"But . . ." I was totally confused. I began to wring the garments out. "But . . . I don't understand. Can't you see that what you do is—monstrous? Evil? Killing without scruple, for money? How can you call that a trade, as if it were no different from—from breeding pigs or building boats?"

"You grow pigs to eat 'em," put in Otter. "Not much difference really."

"Oh!" It was like arguing with a stone wall. "We're talking of men here, not of animals bred for the pot. Doesn't it bother you to have no livelihood but killing? Killing where and how your chief determines, wherever he can command the best price? One day you may take your instructions from a Briton, the next a lord from Connacht or a Pictish chief. There's no meaning to it."

"Couldn't take one side or another," said Spider, apparently surprised. "Not on a permanent basis, you understand. All sorts, we are. Saxon, Pict, Southerner, and some like Gull from places you can't even say the name of. Mixed bag, that's us."

"But that doesn't mean you—oh!" I gave up in frustration.

"What about Cú Chulainn?" asked Snake. This was unexpected. "He killed his lady-friend's father. I wonder what she thought of that? His men killed her father's army. What for? So he could have a woman, satisfy his lust. So he could show he was the strongest. How different is that from killing for payment? Not so different, I'd say."

For now, I had run out of answers. Besides, it was time to go back. Dog could not be left in charge of the smith for too long, given his limited nursing skills.

But when we came close to the shelter, the quiet voice I heard was not Dog's. I motioned Snake to silence.

". . . a man, his name you need not know . . . from the coast of Wessex across to Gaul . . . can arrange for you to travel on to . . . no, don't mention that, it will be taken care of . . ."

"Chief." Evan's reply was weak, but he sounded as if he understood. So he was awake, and his mind was clear again, for now. Snake had retreated farther down the bank and busied himself with something or other. I waited, remaining just out of sight, my curiosity getting the better of me.

"What held you back," Evan asked, "when you saw what was left of me? What stopped you?"

There was a brief pause.

"I won't lie to you, Evan," Bran said quietly. "I would have done it. And I am not persuaded, thus far, that this is right."

Again a silence. The smith was growing tired.

"Bossy little wench, isn't she?" he said eventually, summoning a ghost of a chuckle. "Likes to take charge. Talked me through it. Couldn't tell if I was waking or sleeping half the time, but I heard her all right. Told me straight, she did. Arm's off, she said. Not the end of the world, she said. Told me what I could do without it. Put a few ideas into my head, stuff I'd never have dreamed of. Ask me yesterday, I'd have cursed you for not finishing it then and there. Now I'm not so sure."

"You'd better rest," Bran said, "or I'll be accused of subverting her plans, I've no doubt."

"Got a mind of her own, that one. Just your type, Chief. Easy on the eye, too."

It was a little while before Bran answered this. When he did, the warmth had left his voice. "You know me better than that, Smith."

"Uh-huh."

He was coming out. Suddenly, I was busy spreading out the wet garments to dry on the hawthorn bushes nearby. He halted in the entrance.

"Where's Dog?" I asked, without turning.

"Not far. I will remain until he returns."

"You don't need to," I said. "Snake is still here. One guard is plenty. I can be trusted not to desert my charge. I would not have agreed to this task if I had intended to turn and run at the earliest opportunity."

I looked up at him. He was regarding me gravely, and I thought, not for the first time, about his strange two-in-one features. The intricately detailed pattern on the right side gave his eye a look of menace, his nostril an arrogant flare, his mouth a severe, reined-in tightness. And yet, if you took the other side in isolation, the skin was fair, the nose neat and straight, the eye a steady, clear gray like lake water on a winter morning. Only the mouth was the same, hard and ungiving. He was like two men in one body. I was staring again. I made myself look away.

"Trust?" he said. "That word is meaningless."

"Suit yourself," I said, and made to go back inside the shelter.

"Not yet," said Bran. "You heard, I suppose? Heard the smith talking?"

"Some of it. I am pleased to hear him lucid. He seems to be improving."

"Mmm." He did not sound convinced. "Thanks to you, he sees some hope of a future. You have painted this for him with your words, I imagine, as you did last night for my men. A rosy new beginning, full of love, life, and sunlight. You do this, and yet you dare to judge us."

"What do you mean?" I asked quietly. "I told him only the truth. I did not hide the facts nor falsify the extent of his injury and how it would limit him. As I told you before, his life need not be over. There are many things he can do."

"False hopes," Bran said bleakly, frowning as he kicked the earth with the toe of his boot. "It is no life for an active man. In your soft way you are more cruel than the assassin who takes his victim quickly and efficiently. That prey does not suffer long. Yours may spend a lifetime learning that things can never be the same again."

"I have not told him it will be the same. Good, but different, I said. And I have spoken of the need to be strong, strong in mind and will rather than body. The need to fight against despair. You judge me unfairly. I have been honest with him."

"You can hardly speak of judgment," Bran said. "You think me some kind of monster, that is clear."

I regarded him levelly. "No man is a monster," I said. "Men do monstrous things, that is certain. And I have not judged quickly, as you do. I knew of you before I was rudely snatched and brought here against my will. As you are doubless aware, your reputation goes before you."

"What did you hear and from whom?"

I was already regretting my words. "This and that, around the household," I said cautiously. "Rumors of killings, seemingly at random, carried out in a way that was both effective and—and eccentric. Tales of a band of mercenaries for hire who would do anything if you paid them well enough and who did not let paltry considerations such as loyalty, honor, or justice stand in the way of their work. Men with the appearance of wild beasts or of creatures from the Otherworld led by a shadowy chief they called the Painted Man. You'll hear these tales in many parts."

"And what household was this in which such rumors came to your ears?"

I did not reply.

"Answer my question," he said, still softly. "It's time you told me who you are and where you come from. My men were strangely vague in their account of how they found you and who accompanied you on the road. I still await an adequate explanation from them."

I remained silent, my eyes steady as I looked back at him.

"Answer me, curse you!"

"Are you going to hit me this time?" I inquired, not raising my voice.

"Don't tempt me. What is your name?"

"I thought we had no names here."

"You do not belong here and cannot," Bran snapped. "I can extract this information from you if I must. It will be easier for both of us if you simply tell me. I am amazed you do not realize the danger of your current situation. Perhaps you are a little slow in the wits."

"Very well," I said, "fair trade. I'll tell you my name and where I come from if you tell me yours—the real one, I mean—and where you were born. Your origins were in Britain, I would guess, though you speak our tongue with fluency. But no mother gives her son the name Chief."

There was a brief silence. Then he said, "You tread on perilous ground."

"Let me remind you," I replied, my heart thumping, "I am not here of my own will. There will be those of my household out searching, and they are both well armed and skillful. You think I would jeopardize their efforts to find me by telling you who they are and whence they come? Slow in the wits I may be, but not that slow. I have told you my name is Liadan, and that must be enough for you until you give me yours."

"I cannot imagine why anyone would take the trouble of

searching for you," he said in frustration. "Does not your habit of biting back, like a meddlesome terrier, make your folk soon weary of your company?"

"Indeed no," I told him sweetly. "At home I am known as a quiet, dutiful girl, well mannered, industrious, obedient. I think you must bring out the worst in me."

"Mmm," he said. "Quiet, dutiful, I doubt it. It requires too great a leap of the imagination. More likely, true to your kind, you lie when it suits you. To such a teller of tales, that should come easily."

"You insult me," I said, keeping my voice calm with increasing difficulty. "I would have preferred a blow to the cheek. Tales are not lies, nor are they truths, but something in between. They can be as true or as false as the listener chooses to make them, or the teller wants him to believe. It is a sign of the tight circle you draw around yourself, to keep others out, that you cannot understand this. I do not lie easily, nor would I do so for so superficial a reason."

He glared at me, gray eyes icy. At least I had sparked some sort of reaction.

"By God, woman, you work an issue threadbare with your twisted logic!" he said impatiently. "Enough of this. We've work to do."

"Indeed," I said quietly, and I turned and went in to my patient and did not look back.

Evan was holding on, talking sense, and sleeping more naturally. I made sure nobody saw how greatly this surprised me. Gull was on watch that evening, and I asked him how the sick man was to be moved in safety when the time came, but he was evasive in his answers. Then I sent him outside for a while so that I could wash and ready myself for the evening meal. The smith was nearly asleep, eyes narrowed to slits, breath calm enough after the painful changing of his dressing. He had taken a little broth.

"This is rather awkward," I told him. "Shut your eyes, and turn your head away, and don't move till I tell you."

"Still as the grave," he whispered with a certain irony and closed his eyes.

I stripped off quickly, shivering as I sponged my body with water from the bucket and used the sliver of coarse soap Dog had found for me. As I rinsed myself off again I felt the goosebumps rise, summer or no. I turned to grab the coarse towel, with the aim of dressing as swiftly as I could and found myself looking straight into Evan's deep-set, brown eyes as he lay prone on his pallet, staring for all he was worth and grinning from ear to ear.

"Shame on you!" I exclaimed, as a blush crept across my naked body. There was nothing for it but to dry off sketchily and struggle as fast as I could into my smallclothes, shift, and gown, glad that I could reach the back fastenings without assistance. "A grown man like you, acting like a—an ill-bred youth who spies on the girls. Didn't I tell you—"

"No offense, lass," said Evan, the grin relaxing to a smile that gave his blunt features a surprising sweetness. "Quite beyond me not to look. And a pleasing eyeful it was, may I say."

"No, you may not say," I snapped, but I had forgiven him already. "Don't do it again, you understand? It's bad enough being the only woman here, without . . ."

He was suddenly serious.

"These men would never harm you, lass," he said gently. "They're not barbarians who rape and spoil for the thrill of it. If they want a woman, they've no need to force one. Plenty of willing takers, and not all put a price on it, believe me. Besides, they know they can't touch you."

"Because of what he said? The chief?"

"Well, yes, he did tell them hands off, so I'm informed. But he could have saved his breath. Anyone with eyes in his head can see that you're a woman for the marriage bed, not a quickie by the road, if you'll pardon me. Got a man back home, have you?"

"Not exactly," I said, unsure of the best answer to this.

"What's that mean? Either you have or you haven't. Husband? Sweetheart?"

"I have a—suitor, I suppose you'd call him. But I have not agreed to marry. Not yet."

Evan gave a long sigh as I tucked the blanket firmly around him, and smoothed the makeshift bolster.

"Poor lad," he said sleepily. "Don't make him wait too long."

"Next time I tell you to close your eyes, keep them closed," I said severely.

He mumbled something and settled to rest, still with the hint of a grin on his face.

That night I told stories to make them laugh. Funny stories. Silly stories. Iubdan and the plate of porridge. He got his own back on the big folk, make no doubt of it. The tale of the man who got three wishes from the Fair Folk so that he could have had health, wealth, and happiness. Poor fool, all he ended up with was a sausage. By the end of it, the men were roaring with laughter and begging for another one. All but the chief, of course. I ignored him as best I could.

"One more," I said. "Only one. And now it is time to grow sober again and ponder on the frailty of all creatures. I told you last night of one of our great heroes, Cú Chulainn of Ulster. You will recall how he lay with the warrior woman Aoife, and how she bore him a son long after he was gone from those shores. Not that he left her entirely without token. He gave her a little gold ring for her smallest finger before he went off to wed his sweetheart Emer."

"Big of him," somebody commented dryly.

"Aoife was used to it. She was her own woman, and strong, and she'd little time for the selfish ways of men. She bore her child one day, and the next she was back out of doors swinging her battleaxe around her head. She named the boy Conlai, and as you can imagine, he grew up expert in all the arts of combat so that there were few could match him in the field. When he was twelve years old, his mother, the warrior woman, gave him the little gold ring to wear on a chain around his neck, and she told him his father's name."

"Not a good idea?" hazarded Snake.

"That depends. A boy needs to know who his father is. And who is to say this tale would not have had the same ending had Aoife kept this knowledge from the boy? It was Cú Chulainn's blood that ran in his veins, whether he bore the name or not. He was a youth destined to be a warrior, to take risks, full of his father's impetuous courage.

"She held him back as long as she could, but there came a day when Conlai was fourteen years old, and thought himself a man, and he set forth to find his father and show him the fine son he had made. Aoife had misgivings and sought to protect the boy. He'd need to be careful, she reasoned, not to let on he was the offspring of the greatest hero Ulster had ever known. At least, not until he came to his father's hall. He'd be safe there; but on the way, he might well meet those whose sons or brothers or fathers had fallen foul of Cú Chulainn, and who was to say they might not take their vengeance on the father by killing the son? So she said to Conlai, tell no single warrior your name. Promise me. And he promised, for she was his mother. So, unwittingly, did she seal his doom, who sought only to keep him safe."

There was utter silence, save for a little breeze stirring the shadowy trees above us. It was dark of the moon.

"Across the sea from Alba, across the land of Erin came Conlai, all the way to Ulster, and at last to the home of his father, the great hero Cú Chulainn. He was a tall, strong boy, and in his helm and battle raiment none could tell him from a seasoned warrior. He rode up to the gates and raised his sword in challenge; and out came Conall, foster brother of Cú Chulainn, in answer.

"'What name have you, bold upstart?' shouted Conall.

'Tell me so that I may know whose son lies vanquished at my feet when this duel is over!'

"But Conlai answered not a word, for he kept his promise to his mother. A short, sharp fight ensued, watched with interest by Cú Chulainn and his warriors from the ramparts high above. And it was not the challenger who lay defeated at the end of it."

Then I told how the lad vanquished each man who went forth with sword or staff or dagger, until Cú Chulainn himself determined to meet the challenge, for he liked the set of the young man's shoulders, and the neatness of his footwork, seeing something of himself in it, no doubt.

" 'I will go down and take on this fellow myself,' he said. 'He seems a worthy opponent, if somewhat arrogant. We shall see what he makes of Cú Chulainn's battle craft. If he can withstand me until the sun sinks beyond those elms there, I will welcome him to my house and to my band of warriors, should he be so inclined.'

"Down he went and out before the gates, and he told the lad who he was and what he intended. *Father,* whispered Conlai to himself, but he said not a word for he had promised his mother, and he would not break his oath. Cú Chulainn was offended that the challenger had not the courtesy to give his name, and so he started the encounter already angered, which is never good."

There was a murmur of agreement from the men. I was watching Bran; I could not avoid it, for he sat quite near me, face lit by the fire into which he gazed, his expression very odd indeed. There was something about this story that had caught his attention where the others had not; and had I not known the kind of man he was, I would have said I saw something akin to fear in his expression. Must be a trick of the light, I told myself, and went on.

"Well, that was a combat such as you see but rarely: the hardened, experienced swordsman against the quick, impetuous youth. They fought with sword and dagger, circling, to and fro, around and about, ducking and weaving; leaping and twisting so that at times it was hard to see which of them was which. One of the men watching from above commented that in stature, the two men were as like as peas in a pod. The sun sank lower and lower and touched the tip of the tallest elm. Cú Chulainn thought of calling it a day, for he was, in truth, merely playing with the upstart challenger. His own skills were far superior, and he had always planned to test the other only until the allotted time was up, and then to offer him the hand of friendship.

"But Conlai, desperate to prove himself, gave a nifty little flick of the sword and lo! there in his hand lay a fiery lock of Cú Chulainn's hair, neatly cut from his scalp. For a moment, just a moment, battle fury overcame Cú Chulainn, and before he knew what he did, he gave a great roar and plunged his sword deep into his opponent's vitals."

There was a murmur around me; some in my audience had seen this coming, but all felt the sudden weight of such a horror.

"As soon as he had done this, Cú Chulainn came to himself. He wrenched the sword out, and Conlai's lifeblood began to spill crimson on the ground. Cú Chulainn's men came down and took off the stranger's helmet, and there he was, just a boy, a youngster whose eyes already darkened with the shadow of death, whose face paled and paled as the sun sank behind the elms. Then Cú Chulainn loosened the boy's garments, trying to make his end more comfortable. And he saw the little ring hanging on its chain around Conlai's neck, the ring he had given Aoife nearly fifteen years before."

Bran had a hand over his brow, concealing his eyes. Still he stared into the flames. What had I said?

"He killed his own son," somebody whispered.

"His boy," said someone. "His own boy."

"It was too late," I said soberly, "too late to make amends. Too late to say farewell, for at the moment Cú Chulainn recognized what he had done, the last breath of life left his son, and Conlai's spirit fled from his body."

"That's terrible," said Dog, in shocked tones.

"It is a sad story," I agreed, wondering if even one of them might relate the tale in any way to their own activities. "They say Cú Chulainn carried the boy inside in his own arms and later buried him with full ceremony. Of how he felt, and what he said, the tale does not tell."

"A man could not do such a deed and put it behind him," said Gull very quietly. "It would be with him always, whether he wished it or no."

"What about his mother?" asked Dog. "What did she have to say about it?"

"She was a woman," I said dryly. "The tale does not concern itself further with her. I suppose she bore her loss and went on, as women do."

"In a way it was her fault," somebody offered. "If he'd been able to give his name, they'd have welcomed him instead of fighting."

"It was a man's hand that drove the sword through his body. It was a man's pride that made Cú Chulainn strike. You cannot blame the mother. She sought but to protect her son, for she knew what men are."

My words were greeted with silence. At least the tale had made them think. After the earlier jollity, the mood was somber indeed.

"You believe I judge you too harshly?" I asked, getting up.

"None of us has ever killed his own son," said Spider, outraged.

"You have killed another man's son," I said quietly. "Every man that falls to your knife, or your hands, or your little loop of cord is some woman's sweetheart, some woman's son. Every one."

No one said anything. I thought I had offended them. After a while somebody went around refilling cups with ale, and somebody threw more wood on the fire, but nobody was talking. I was waiting for Bran to speak, maybe to tell me I should shut my mouth and stop upsetting his fine band of warriors. Instead, he got up, turned on his heel, and went off with never a word. I stared after him, but he had disappeared like a shadow under the trees. The night was very dark. Slowly, the men began to talk again among themselves in low voices.

"Sit down awhile, Liadan," said Gull kindly. "Have another cup of ale."

I sat down slowly. "What's wrong with him?" I whispered, looking beyond the circle. "What did I say?"

"Best left alone," mumbled Dog, who had overheard. "He'll be standing guard tonight."

"What?"

"Dark of the moon," said Gull. "Always takes the watch, those nights. Told us both to get our rest. He'll have gone up to relieve Snake now. Stands to reason. If he's going to be awake anyhow, he may as well do it."

"Why doesn't he sleep? You're not going to tell me he turns into some sort of monster with the quenching of the moon, I hope—half man, half wolf maybe?"

Gull chuckled. "Not him. Just doesn't sleep. Can't tell you why. Been like that as long as I've known him. Six, seven years. Keeps himself awake until the dawn comes."

"Is he afraid to sleep?"

"Him? Afraid?" It seemed the very idea was laughable.

Gull walked back up to the shelter with me and left me there. Bran was inside, his hand on the smith's brow, speaking quietly. There was one lantern lit, and it spread a golden glow over the rock walls and the man lying on the pallet there. It touched Bran's patterned features with light and shadow, softening the grim set of the mouth.

"He's awake," he said, as I came in. "Is there anything you require help with before I go outside?"

"I'll manage," I said. Snake, on my instructions, had prepared a bowl of water with some of the dwindling stock of healing herbs, and I placed this on the stool by the bed.

"You're a good lass," Evan said weakly. "Told you that before, but I will again."

"Flattery will get you nowhere," I said, unbuttoning his sweat-soaked shirt.

"Don't know about that." He managed a crooked grin. "Not every day I find a fine woman like yourself undressing me. Almost worth losing an arm for, that is."

"Get away with you!" I said, wiping the damp cloth over his body. He had lost flesh alarmingly; I could feel the ribs stark under the skin and see the deep hollows at the base of the neck. "You're too skinny for my tastes, anyway," I told him. "Have to fatten you up, I will. You know what that means. More broth, before I let you sleep."

His eyes were as trusting as those of a faithful hound as I sponged his brow.

"Bran, Snake will have left the pot of broth to cool by the little brazier. Could you fetch me some in a cup?"

"Broth," said Evan in disgust. "Broth! Can't you give a man a proper meal?"

But in the event, it was hard enough for him to swallow even the mouthful or two he took. And I did have to ask Bran to help me, his arm lifting the smith's head as I spooned the mixture little by little between his lips. Evan gagged, despite his best efforts.

"Breathe slowly, as I told you," I said quietly. "You must try to keep this down. One more spoonful."

He was soon exhausted. And he had swallowed so little. Beads of sweat were already breaking out on his brow. I would need to burn some aromatic herbs for there was no way I could get enough of a sleeping draft into him to give any relief. He never spoke of the pain, save in jest, but I knew it was extreme.

"Could you move the little brazier farther in?"

Bran said nothing, but carried out my orders. He watched

me in silence as I got what I needed from my pack and sprinkled the mixture onto the still-glowing coals. There was not much left. But then, three days was not long. I did not allow myself to think beyond that point. The pungent smell rose into the night air: juniper, pine, hemp leaves. If only I could have gotten some tea into the man, for a mere half cup of lavender and birch-leaf infusion can give good relief from pain and bring healing sleep. But I had not the ingredients to make such a brew, nor would Evan have had the energy to swallow it. Besides, it was past midsummer. Birch leaves are only good for this purpose used fresh and plucked in spring. I wished my mother was there. She would have known what to do. The smith grew quiet, eyes closed to slits, but his breathing was labored. I wrung out the cloth and began to tidy up.

"What if Conlai had never learned his father's name?" said Bran suddenly from the entrance. "What if he had grown up, say, in the family of a farmer, or with holy brothers in a house of prayer? What then?"

I was so surprised, I said nothing at all, my hands still working automatically as I emptied the bowl and wiped it out and unrolled my blanket on the hard earth.

"You said it was his father's blood flowed in his veins, his father's will to be a warrior that ran deep in him. But his mother trained him in the warlike arts, set him on that path, before ever he knew what Cú Chulainn was. Do you say that whatever his upbringing, this boy was destined to be another in his father's mold? Almost that the manner of his death was set out the moment he was born?"

"Oh no!" His words shocked me. "To say that is to say we have no choice at all in how our path unfolds. I do not say that. Only that we are made by our mothers and our fathers, and we bear something of them in our deepest selves, no matter what. If Conlai had grown up as a holy brother, it may have been much longer before his father's courage and his wild, warlike spirit awoke in him. But he would have found it in himself, one way or another. That was the man he was, and nothing could change it."

Bran leaned against the rock wall, his figure in shadow.

"What if . . . ," he said, "the—the essence, the spark, whatever it is, the little part of his father that he bore within him—that could be lost, destroyed, before he knew it was there. It could be . . . it could be taken from him."

I felt a strange sort of chill, and the little hairs rose on my neck. It was like a darkness stretching out over me, over the two of us. Images passed before my eyes so rapidly I could scarcely make them out before they were gone.

. . . dark, so dark. The door shuts. I cannot breathe. Keep quiet, choke back your tears, not a sound. Pain, cramp like fire. I have to move. I dare not move; they will hear me . . . Where are you? Where are you . . . where did you go?

I wrenched myself back to the real world, shaking. My heart was hammering.

"What is it?" Bran stepped out of the shadows, eyes fixed intently on my face. "What's wrong?"

"Nothing," I whispered. "Nothing." And I turned away, for I did not want to look into his eyes. Whatever the dark vision was, it was from him it had come. Beneath his surface there were deep, uncharted waters, realms strange and perilous.

"You'll be needing your sleep," he said, and when at length I turned around, he was gone. The brazier burned low. I made the lamp dim, but did not quench it, lest the smith should wake and need me. Then I lay down to rest.

Chapter Five

Something woke me. I sat up abruptly, heart thumping. The fire in the brazier had gone out; the lantern burned low, casting a circle of faint light. Outside, it was completely dark. Everything was still. I got up and went over to the pallet, lantern in hand. Evan was sleeping. I tucked the covers over him and turned to go back to bed. For a summer night, it was quite chill.

Then I heard it. A sound like a stifled gasp, the merest indrawn breath. Could such a little thing have woken me so instantly? I went out, hesitant in my bare feet and the borrowed undershirt I wore for sleeping, shivering slightly and not just from cold. It was a deep, deep darkness, intense in its presence. Even the night birds were silent before it. With my small, dim lantern, I felt as if I were the only creature stirring in this black, impenetrable world.

I took a step forward, and another, and saw that Bran sat against the rocks at the entrance to the shelter, staring straight ahead of him into the darkness. Perhaps he, too, had heard something. I opened my mouth to ask him, and he shot out a hand and grabbed me violently by the arm, without looking at me, without saying a word. I bit back a scream of fright and struggled to keep the lantern from falling. The clutching hand gripped so tightly I thought my arm would break. Still he said nothing, but I heard it again in my mind, a voice like a terrified child's, the voice of a boy who has wept so long he has no more tears in him. *Don't go. Don't go away.* And in the light from the lantern, which wobbled dangerously now in my free hand, I could tell that Bran did not really see me. He held me fast, but his eyes stared ahead, unfocused, blind in this night of no moon.

I felt the pain of his grip all the way up my arm. It no longer seemed to matter. I remembered that I was, after all, a healer. I lowered myself cautiously to the ground beside him. His breathing was fast and uneven; he was shivering. This seemed some kind of waking nightmare.

"All right," I said quietly, not wishing to startle him and make things worse. I set the lantern down. "I'm here. It's all right now." I knew full well it was not me he wanted. That child I heard cried out for something that was long gone, but I was here. I wondered how many such nights he had endured, nights when he would not sleep lest these dark visions should engulf him.

I tried to loosen his fingers where they bit into my flesh, but the grip could not be slackened. Indeed, when I touched that hand it tightened still further, like that of a drowning man who, in panic, comes close to taking his rescuer down with him. Tears of pain came to my eyes.

"Bran," I said softly, "you're hurting me. It's all right now; you can let go now."

But he made no reply, simply gripped all the harder, so that despite myself I whimpered with the pain. I would not wake him from the trance that held him fast. Such intervention is unwise, for these visitations have a purpose and must be allowed to run their course. Still, he need not face them alone, though it seemed that was exactly what he had intended to do.

So I sat there and made my breathing slow and calm, and told myself what I had told others many a time: Breathe, Liadan, the pain will pass. The night was very quiet; the darkness like a living thing, creeping in around the two of us. I felt how tight strung his body was; I sensed his terror, and how he fought to conquer it. I could not hope to touch his mind, nor did I wish to see more of the dark images it held. But I could still speak, and it seemed to me words were the only tool I had for keeping out the dark.

"Dawn will come," I told him quietly. "The night can be very dark, but I'll stay by you until the sun rises. These shadows cannot touch you while I am here. Soon we'll see the first hint of gray in the sky, the color of a pigeon's coat, then the smallest touch of the sun's finger, and one bird will be bold enough to wake first and sing of tall trees and open skies and freedom. Then all will brighten and color will wash across the earth, and it will be a new day. I will stay with you until then."

Gradually, the grip of his fingers relaxed a little, and the pain in my arm became easier to bear. I was very cold, but there was no way I was going to move any closer to him. That would most certainly be against the code. He was going to find this extremely awkward in the morning. Time passed and I talked on and on, of harmless, safe things, images of light and warmth. I made with my words a bright web of protection to keep away the shadows. At length it grew so cold I admitted defeat and edged in to sit close beside him, leaning against his shoulder and laying my other hand over his fingers where they still clutched me. Inside the shelter, Evan had not stirred.

We were there a long time, I talking steadily, Bran quiet save for a shuddering, indrawn breath here and there, a muttered word. I wondered greatly. I could scarcely believe that somewhere inside this stern outlaw there was a small child afraid of being alone in the dark. I wanted badly to understand, but I would never be able to ask him.

At the moment I had described, when the sky showed the first, faintest traces of gray, he came back to himself abruptly. The shivering stopped, and he went extremely still, and his breathing was deliberately slowed. There was a short time in which he must have become aware that he was not alone. He must have felt the touch of my hand on his, the weight of my head on his shoulder, the warmth of my body against his own. The lantern stood before us on the ground, still dimly glowing in the dark before dawn. Neither of us said anything for a while. Neither of us moved. It was Bran who spoke first.

"I don't know what you think you're doing," he said, "or what you hope to achieve by this. I suggest you get up quietly and go back inside to your job and in future behave less like a cheap roadside slut and more like the healer you're supposed to be."

My teeth were chattering with cold. I couldn't decide whether to laugh or cry. It would have been very satisfying to slap his face, but I couldn't even do that.

"If you would let go of my arm," I said, as politely as I could, and I could not stop my voice from shaking just a little, "I would be happy to oblige. It is rather cold out here."

He looked down at his hand as if he had never seen it before. Then, very slowly, he uncurled his fingers, releasing the vicelike grip he had maintained on me the whole night. My throat was parched with talking, my hand was numb, and a deep ache was spreading through my arm. Did he remember nothing? He turned his head, looking at me in the faint light of earliest daybreak as I sat there barefoot in my old shirt, moving and flexing my hand to bring it back to life. By Díancécht, it hurt. I got stiffly to my feet, for I did not wish to be in his presence one instant longer than I must.

"No, wait," he said. And as the first bird sent its liquid call through the crisp, morning air, he rose and took off his coat and placed it around my shoulders. For a moment I lifted my face and looked straight into his eyes, and what I felt just then terrified me more than any of the demons I'd glimpsed lurking there. I turned without a sound and fled inside, and was just in time for the smith's first waking. It was another day; the fourth day.

A busy morning. Dog helped me to lift the smith and wash his body again, strip off the sweat-soaked garments and replace them with fresh. Both of them remarked that I was yawning a lot. I did not respond. My arm hurt. My head was full of confusion. I tried to imagine how it would be when I finally went home. If I went home. The girl who returned to Sevenwaters, I thought, would be a different one from the girl who'd ridden out not so very long ago. What would Father and Mother and Sean say when they saw me? What would Eamonn say? I tried to picture Eamonn, striding around the garden nervously as he attempted to tell me what he felt. His face would not come clear into my thoughts. It was as if I had forgotten how he looked. My hand shook; water slopped over the sides of the bowl I was holding.

"Hey! Whoa!" Dog reached out quickly to grab it, his big hand bumping my arm as he did so. I let out a gasp of pain. Evan looked at me from where he lay, and Dog looked at me as he put the bowl carefully down.

"What is it, lass?" Evan's voice was weak, but his eyes were shrewdly assessing.

"Nothing. I have a strain or something; it will pass."

"Some strain," commented Dog, taking my sleeve delicately between his large fingers and rolling it up a little to show the deep, purple bruises flowering across the pale skin of my arm.

"Who did this to you, Liadan?" Just as well the smith was too weak to get up.

"It's nothing," I said again. "Forget it."

They exchanged a glance, faces identically grim.

"Please," I added. "It was an accident. Done with no intent to hurt."

"A man should take care to avoid such—accidents," growled Evan. "A man should keep his hands to himself."

"Should know better," agreed Dog, scowling. "Little dainty thing like you; puff of wind would blow you away. Easily hurt. Should have known better."

"I'll be fine, really," I said. "Let's forget this, shall we, and get on with things? Broth perhaps, and maybe a sop or two of bread?"

Evan rolled his eyes. "Have mercy! She'll kill me with her endless flow of broth."

He ate a little, and slept again, and I chatted with Dog and played a makeshift game of ringstones on the ground. It was not easy. We found the flattest stones we could, but they could not be made to balance properly, and we ended up near hysterical with laughter, both of us woeful losers. At length I scooped the stones into a little heap, my hands brushing away the neatly drawn circle and its network of intersecting lines. When I looked up, Dog was staring at me, serious again.

"Got a man at home, I hear," he said.

"Not exactly," I replied cautiously, "an offer. That's as far as it goes."

"You might think about another." His tone was carefully offhand. "Offer, I mean. Got a lot saved. Been with the chief three, four years, now. Got enough put away to buy a good piece of land, few cattle, build a place, somewhere far enough away. Islands up north maybe. Or a boat, sail off and start again. Never met a woman like you before. I'd look after you. May not be much to look at, but I'm strong. I can work. You'd be safe with me. What do you think?" He fingered one of the long claws hung around his neck, his yellow eyes hesitant as he watched my face.

I gaped at him, astounded. I imagined going back to Sevenwaters with Dog in tow. I imagined my father's expression as he took in the half-shaven head, the patterned chin, the feral eyes and pockmarked face, the wolfskin cloak and barbaric necklace.

"You're laughing at me," said Dog, his blunt features crestfallen. "Knew the answer would be no, of course. Just thought I'd ask."

"I'm sorry," I said gently, curling my hand around his. "I am not laughing, I promise. I do not want to offend you. I appreciate your offer, I really do, for I can see you're a fine man. But I will not choose a husband yet, not till the season comes back to summer again. Not you, nor any other." Under my fingers the palm of his hand was ridged and hard. I turned the hand over, looking at the terrible callused scars that slashed across it.

"Where did you get these?" Someone had said, ask Dog his story. I could hazard a guess at part of it.

"Viking ship," he said. "I'm from Alba, same as your warrior woman, Scáthach. Me and my brother had a herring boat, and we made a tidy living. Norsemen raided the village. Took the two of us for the oars, seeing the strength in us, you understand. That was a time, that was." His eyes clouded, and he ran a hand over his scalp. "Long time we were rowing for them. Too long. Mostly they used their own crew, but these were short of men, and they'd six pair of rowers in chains, kept there permanent like. Me and Dougal, we were always in trouble. But they kept us alive; strongest men they had, we were. Dougal took it too far one day and caught the end of a whip across the face. He died. Maybe it was best. He'd seen his wife and daughters taken. Filled with hate. Me, I just kept on. Too strong for my own good."

"So how did you escape?"

"Ah, that's a tale. Chief got me out. Thought he was mad at the time. We were in some eastern port, hot as a furnace, air you could cut with a knife. Shackled in our places, that was the usual thing, while the crew went ashore. You'd die of heat and thirst as easy as you'd draw breath. There we are, one night, sleeping as best we can, bum on the bench, head anywhere you can find for it, not the most comfortable bed you ever had. Place stank of piss and sweat, begging your pardon. Then there's a little jingle of keys, and here's this black man walking along between the benches, cool as you like, and he says to us, who wants to make an agreement with us? We're all staring at him, waiting for the Norsemen to come back and finish him off; but nothing happens except the ship begins to creak and groan like it's putting out from port. But nobody's rowing. We say nothing. Some of the men can't understand anyway; speak half a dozen tongues, they do. Then the black man (which was Gull, you understand, feather in his hair and all) says, the chief's up yonder and getting ready to cast off. You won't see your Norsemen anymore. You've got a choice. Row this tub to Gaul, and when we touch shore there's a little bag of silver in it and freedom. You'll row without shackles if you don't make trouble. What about it?"

"So I speak up. 'What's the other choice,' I ask him? And this other man steps up behind him, it's the chief, but his face was a bit plainer then. He's young, not much more than a lad, and I'm thinking, what's this whippersnapper think he's up to? Then the chief says, 'Depends how well you think you'll do, chained up here. The Norsemen won't be coming back. How long before somebody notices a dead Viking or two feeding the fish under the jetty? Maybe not long. Maybe a while. It's a busy port, and nobody gives a toss what happens to you. That's the choice,' he said. Showed it in signs, with his hands, so all the men could understand. 'Row well for me,' he says, 'and you'll be free men before the next full moon.' And I'm thinking, this fellow's crazy. What about attackers on the way? What about the Norsemen avenging their own? Besides, there's two of them and twelve of us, my brother's place having been taken by a long-faced Ulsterman. What's to stop us dumping them overboard the moment the chains come off? We all say yes, of course. Nothing like a sniff of freedom to make up your mind for you.

"He kept his word. We had a few adventures on the way to Gaul, but we got there, and he gave me the choice to stay with him or move on. Been with him ever since."

"How old is—how old is the chief now? You said you'd been with him three or four years; but you said he was just a lad when you first met him. How can that be?"

Dog was counting on his fingers.

"That'd be right," he said eventually. "Two and twenty, three and twenty. He'd be around that. Not so much older than you, lass."

"But—" I was quite taken aback. "He seems a great deal older than that. I mean—how can such a young man be what he is? It's as if he has already lived as much as another man does in a lifetime. He's very young to be such a leader. He's overyoung to be so—so bitter."

"That man's been old since he was a child," Dog said soberly.

Around midday there was an unusual stirring in the encampment, the sound of harness jingling, the bustle of orderly but hurried activity. I couldn't see much, but what I did glimpse sent a chill right through me. Shelters were being dismantled, saddlebags packed. The signs of occupation were being quietly erased. They were leaving. They were leaving, and nobody had told me. He had promised me six days. Even that would have been barely enough.

"You'd better go down and find out what's happening," I told Dog, keeping my tone calm as fear and fury began to rise in me. I went back inside and busied myself, with an ear out for his return. I felt Evan's eyes on me, anxious, but he did not ask. It grew later, and Dog did not come back. I was kneeling on the ground, washing dishes in the bucket and trying to focus my mind on the autumn planting of my garden at Sevenwaters, when a familiar voice spoke behind me.

"There's been a change of plan."

I got up slowly, hands dripping, sleeves rolled to the elbow. "So I see. I see also how easily you break your word. The man cannot travel. I told you that before. Nothing has changed here."

Bran glanced across at the smith, who was awake and listening. "He must travel or be left," he said grimly. "There is no choice. It's imperative that we move on today."

"We had an agreement. Six days, you said. I suppose you never had any intention of keeping your word."

"You judge overquickly, as always. I am responsible for these men. I will not order them to sit here and be trapped when I can move them out in secret before others reach this place. I will not keep them back when there is an urgent need for their services elsewhere. To sacrifice the entire troop for one man's life would be an act of sheer folly."

I was silent for a time, thinking about this. "The smith cannot travel," I said at last. "You see how weak he still is. He can barely sit alone. How can you transport him with safety? Who will look after him?"

"That is no longer your concern." He glanced over his shoulder. "Pack up these things," he ordered Dog, who had appeared behind him, anxiously hovering.

"Just a moment," I said. "I have stayed here and nursed this man because we had an agreement, a fair trade. You've broken your side of it. But I am responsible for him, as you are for the others. This is my job. I will not see my work thrown away on—on some whim of yours."

Bran hardly seemed to be listening. Instead, he was staring at my arm, where the rolled-up fabric revealed the florid bruises his fingers had made. Angrily I pulled the sleeve of my dress back down to cover the marks. Dog was beginning to pack up, his face expressionless.

"Sit down," Bran commanded. I stared back at him. "Sit down," he said more quietly, folding his arms and leaning a shoulder against the rock wall. I sat. "It is no whim," he said. "I do not act on impulse; I cannot afford such a luxury. I had no intention of breaking my word, else why would I give it? Events have overtaken us, that is all. You understand, I and my men are far from welcome in many parts of this land and beyond its shores. We have made numerous enemies. So we move by stealth and frequently. Because of the smith's injury, and your presence among us, we have already stayed here far longer than was intended and taken great risk in doing so. Now I have a report of a considerable force of armed men on the road and limited time to move in safety. To remain here is to court death. For myself, I would face that with equanimity. But I will not risk my men for such a trivial reason. Besides, our next mission lies north, and those for whom we undertake it have asked us to put forward our departure for those parts. I have made the decision, and it will be carried out quickly. By sunset, no sign of us will be left in this place."

There was a brief silence.

"Trivial," I said, staring up at him. "You consider Evan's life, and my safety, to be trivial."

"As a woman," Bran replied carefully, "you would not be able to understand. In the scheme of things, one life, or two, matters little. I will not put my men at unnecessary risk for you or for him. Nor will I jeopardize their next mission. Already I waste time listening to your circular arguments. Were it not for you, we would be safe on our way by now. I should never have—"

"Chief." The smith was trying to sit up. His face was pale and beaded with sweat.

"What is it?"

"I can ride. Still strong. Got it in me. Strap me up behind Dog here, I'll last as far as I must. But, Chief, what about the lass?"

A heavy silence. Dog ceased his packing and straightened up, glaring at his leader ferociously. "Well?" he growled.

Bran was still looking at me. "Can you understand what I am telling you?" he asked with exaggerated patience. "This is a decision made carefully, weighing all the options. I do not act on a whim."

I gave a shrug. "I understand that a man such as yourself sees his warriors as units with a value, like playing pieces in some lethal game, to be disposed to best advantage, to be protected for their worth to the player. I know that it is women who wait until the game is over to pick up the broken pieces and try to salvage something from them."

"Oh, no." His voice was cold. "That is a half-truth such as I would expect from your kind. It is women who inflict the deepest damage, who guide their men onto a path of destruction. My life has been shaped by this. Don't preach to me about the healing powers of a woman. You know nothing. You understand nothing." His hands were clenched tight, though he kept his arms casually folded.

"Evan asked you a question," I said very cautiously. "What's supposed to happen to me? Can I go home now?"

The chilly, measuring eyes stared straight into mine. "It's clear you know little of the real world," he remarked. "You still don't understand, do you? Perhaps that explains your lack of fear. Tell her, Dog."

"Chief—"

"Tell her."

"It's like this," Dog mumbled. "What the chief's saying is, he's got a problem. Can't take you, not safe; would slow us down, too much of a distraction for the men, and so on. Can't leave you behind either. There's no such thing as visitors in the Painted Man's camp. If a man comes in on business, he's blindfolded. You've seen and heard too much. That's the problem."

"But—" My heart started to thump. They couldn't mean—surely they didn't mean . . . Great Dana help me; the chief was right. I really was stupid. "You're telling me," I whispered, "that it's the solution you would have used for Evan here but for my intervention. The solution of the sharp little knife, the clean cut and quick, neat disposal? Is this what you plan for me?"

"Over my dead body," growled the smith.

"Believe me, I considered that, too," said Bran smoothly. "You're both a damned nuisance, and I bitterly regret ever agreeing to give this a trial. But you," nodding at Evan, "you've earned your chance by surviving this long. You'll come with us. As for you," looking at me, "my men have placed me in a very awkward situation. They've asked me if you can remain with us for now. Indeed, it was made quite plain to me that a refusal on my part could lead to some kind of mutiny. Such is the influence of a few outlandish tales, told by one who knows well the feminine art of persuasion, who uses her face and her body and her honeyed words to make a man do what he should not."

"That's quite ridiculous!" I exclaimed crossly, fear replaced by outrage. "How dare you criticize me? I have no base motives such as you insinuate! I have sought only to help in everything I have done here. Everything. I am no—no seductress. Look at me; how can you even think . . . ? Besides, you broke your promise. You yourself are on shaky ground."

"Oh, no," said Bran softly. "I'm keeping my side of the bargain as best I can. You'll stay and tend your patient, if he survives the journey. My men allow me no other alternative here. And, whatever you may choose to believe, I do respect their wishes if I can. A good leader must be prepared to do so. You must understand, though, that there will be a decision to face later. The longer you stay with us, the more you see, the more impossible it becomes to let you go back. Is that what you want?"

"When was what I want ever a factor in this?" I demanded, angry tears threatening to spill. I blinked them back. I had not realized, until now, how much I longed to see my mother again. What did Bran mean, that I would never be allowed to go home? I pictured Sorcha's fragile form and shadowed eyes, my father's steadfast, watchful presence. I thought of Sean and of Aisling, and of long, peaceful days spent in the deep quiet of the forest or busy about the domestic tasks I loved: baking, sewing, drying herbs. I glanced around me. This grim encampment was no home; this secret, perilous existence was no life. For the first time the weight of what this might have done to my family hit me, and a single tear did escape to trickle down my cheek.

"You will achieve nothing that way," said Bran. "A woman's tears are turned on as readily as the flow from a pump. I am immune to this."

But others, it seemed, were not. I felt Dog's big hand on my shoulder, and Evan said, "Don't weep, lass. When it's over, you'll be home again in no time, and your man there waiting for you."

Bran was looking at Dog. "Take your hand off her," he said, in a terrible, soft voice. Dog snatched it away as if touched by a lash.

"We're wasting time," I said, dashing the tears from my eyes. "Show me how you will transport this man. I may be able to advise you. I hope you don't expect me to ride blindfold. You're likely to need me on the way."

"You can ride then?"

"Indeed, I was doing so quite capably before your men snatched me off the road. You will find I am not entirely without resources."

He did not respond to this, merely indicated with a jerk

of the head that I was to follow him outdoors. I was
tempted, not for the first time, to say something I might regret. But I swallowed my rage and tagged along in his wake
as he strode off across the encampment. Nothing mattered,
really, except keeping Evan alive. I was a healer, and I had a
job to do. Later, perhaps, there would be time for questions.

This journey was the stuff of nightmares. I kept my mouth
shut and my eyes open. I was aware that we traveled somewhat east of due north, but I could not have judged the distance with any accuracy. The pace was unrelenting, as fast
as we could maintain in near silence, going by wooded and
concealed ways, making use of streambeds and marshlands
to hide our tracks. There was always a man out ahead and
one behind. It grew darker, and still we rode on. My back
hurt and my mouth was parched, but I held my tongue and
willed myself to keep going. My own discomfort was nothing to Evan's, strapped as he was to Dog's broad back,
bounced helplessly by the horse's rapid pace on uneven
ground, his wound protected only by a wadding of linen
hastily applied before our unceremonious departure. I had
hoped we would stop on the way so I could help him. It appeared this was not to be. I could not ask. The men kept silence, communicating only by subtle signals, and with good
reason. Once, as we traversed a heavily treed ridge above an
open stretch of land, we glimpsed other horsemen below us,
riding in an orderly, well-armed group parallel to our own
path, but in the opposite direction. Bran halted us with a
single small movement of the hand, and we sat in silence
until the riders were well past. They were men in deep
green tunics with the sign of a black tower on them, worn
over field armor: Eamonn's colors. Whether they were
looking for me, or on some other errand, there was no
knowing. I remembered what Eamonn had said about the

Painted Man and his arrogant challenge and knew I trod a perilous path.

At last, when I had grown so weary I was in danger of falling from the saddle, and Evan was slumped gray-faced and motionless in his bindings, we halted. We were under tall trees, at the entrance to some sort of structure, and it seemed we had reached our destination, for lanterns were lit and quiet instructions given. Dog had dismounted, and they were lying Evan's limp form on a blanket. I wanted to get down, they needed me, but my cramped limbs would not obey me. The horse stood patiently.

"Here." I felt firm hands on my waist and was lifted to the ground as easily as if I had been a small child. He let go immediately, and my legs buckled under me. I grabbed at the horse's harness for support, gasping at the pain.

"You weep for others, but not for yourself," said Bran. "Why is that, I wonder? Someone has taught you self-discipline."

I took a deep breath and another. "Not much point, is there?" I whispered, dry mouthed. "Could you show me where they're taking the smith? I'll be needed."

"Can you walk?"

I tried a step, still grasping the harness in one hand. The horse shuffled sideways.

"Not very convincing," said Bran. "Second rule of combat. Don't bluff if you can't go through with it. Your enemy sees your weakness a mile off. If you haven't the strength to fight, admit it and retreat. Regroup, or use your wits instead. If you must, accept help. Here."

He put out a hand, and I found myself supported and steered in the direction of a low doorway, whose lintel and supports were massive stone slabs, and an old passage that appeared to go straight into a grassy hill. The night was growing stranger by the instant. An owl hooted, and I looked up. Above us, through the web of branches, a fledgling moon hung delicate in the black sky. I could feel the weight of Bran's gaze on me as he helped me along, but I said not a word. We reached the entry through which the others had disappeared and something halted me abruptly.

"I don't think we should be here," I said, as a cold chill settled about me, and a dark mist seemed to envelop the two of us standing there outside the door. "This place is—this is very old, it is a place of the Old Ones. We should not be here."

Bran was frowning. "This mound has sheltered us well many times before," he said, resting a hand casually on the ancient lintel, where tiny inscrutable faces gazed at us between the whorled and spiraled patterns carved deep in the stone. If anyone's hand belonged there, it was his. "Whoever once used the place is long gone; now it is ideal for us, secret, secure, easy to guard, with concealed exits for a quick departure. It is quite safe."

But I was filled with dread, a freezing sense of foreboding that I could ill explain, least of all to him. "There's death here," I said. "I see it. I feel it."

"What do you mean?"

Then I looked up at him and for a moment, instead of the face of a hard, vital young man, half patterned, half plain, I saw a hideous mask, ashen hued, the mouth stretched in a ghastly rictus of death, the clear, gray eyes now staring and lifeless. Somewhere I heard a child screaming. *You let me go . . . you let go . . .* A small hand stretching out, clutching in desperation, but I couldn't reach, they were taking me away, I couldn't reach him. . . .

"What is it? What do you see?" His hands were on my shoulders; the strength of his grip wrenched me back into the present.

"I . . . I . . ."

"Tell me. What did you see?"

I fought to make my breathing steady. There was work to do, I must not let this overwhelm me.

"N-Nothing. It's nothing."

"You don't lie well. Tell me. What is it that troubles you so greatly? You look at me, and you see—something that terrifies you. Tell me."

"Death," I whispered. "Terror. Hurt. Sadness and loss. I cannot tell if it is the past or the future I see, or both."

"Whose past? Whose future?"

"Yours. Mine. This shadow encompasses the two of us. I share your nightmare. I see a path that is shattered and broken. I see a way leading into darkness."

We stood there in silence, with the night behind us and the open door in front.

"This is our only shelter here," he said after a while. "There is no choice but to go in."

I nodded. "I'm sorry," I said.

"Do not be sorry," said Bran. "This visits you unbidden, I see that. You will be safe enough with us. But that's not what frightens you, is it?"

"Safe," I echoed. "I am not concerned for my own safety."

"Whose then? You cannot mean mine? Why should you trouble yourself over that?"

I could not reply.

"You see my death? This concerns you? It should not. I do not fear it. There are times when I would welcome it."

"You should fear it," I said very softly. "To die before you know your true self, that is a terrible thing."

I had never felt the burden of my strange gift more strongly than on that night, and as we passed through the doorway into the subterranean chamber I made a sign in the air before me, one I had seen Conor use, and I sent a silent call to whatever ancient spirits inhabited the chill realm below. *We honor this space, and the shades therein. We mean no harm. We mean no disrespect in using this place for shelter.* And I heard, deep inside me, my mother's voice. *You are outside the pattern, Liadan. It could give you great power. It could allow you to change things.*

We went in through a short passageway and into the central chamber, around which the huge structure of balanced stones and wooden supports had been built. It had been empty. Now there were bedrolls and packs stacked neatly around the walls. The place was full of orderly, quiet activity as Bran's men readied themselves for the next departure. Rations of hard bread, dried meat, water and ale were distributed, unusual weapons given a last check, a map was consulted, quiet words exchanged. They were well-seasoned men; while I was exhausted to the point of dropping in my tracks, they seemed none the worse for wear after the long ride. Then I heard the smith groaning as he returned to consciousness, and I was suddenly too busy to think of anything but my task.

It was a long time before Evan slept fitfully, dosed with the strongest infusion I could safely give him. I sat cross-legged on the earthen floor by him, keeping a close watch, sponging his pallid, sweaty face from time to time with cool water. The flesh around shoulder and chest was an angry red. Some of the men lay resting, others had been dispatched to stand guard at entry or exit. There was a strong smell of horse, for they had brought the creatures in; they stood loosely tethered at the far end of the chamber. Otter passed among them, a bucket of water in his hands.

Dog sat close to me. His small eyes were very serious and his mouth unusually grim. Across the dimly lit chamber, Gull and Snake stood with their leader, apparently arguing a point. Gull's dark hands moved in quick, expressive gestures, but the meaning was not clear, and they all kept their voices down. Snake glanced in my direction and then said something else to Bran, frowning. Bran's features were stern, as always. I saw him shrug as if to say, if you don't like it, that's your problem.

"We'll be off early in the morning," said Dog quietly. "Might not see you again for a while. You'll stay here, of course. Do you think he's going to make it?"

For a moment we listened to the rasping, rattling sound of Evan's breath.

"I'll do my best to keep him alive. But I must tell you straight. It isn't looking good."

Dog sighed heavily. "My fault. Look at the mess I've got you into. And for nothing."

"Ssh," I said, patting his large hand. "We're all responsible. But him most of all." I glanced across the chamber.

"You can't blame the chief," said Dog under his breath. "He didn't want to leave. Got a message someone was onto us. When that happens you get out quick, no matter what We'd have been finished, all of us, if we hadn't moved on."

"I might have been safe," I said dryly. "Perhaps those who pursued you were looking for me."

"Maybe. Maybe not. We could hardly have left you, not knowing."

My small lantern was now the only one burning in the dark, subterranean space. Under the arch of the roof, where stone lapped carefully shaped stone in a miracle of balance, a network of shadowy webs housed countless small creatures. The floor was smooth, hard earth. At one end of the chamber lay a single monumental slab of dark stone, its surface glossy as if polished from long use. What its purpose was, one could only guess. Above this, at a slight angle, there was a single narrow opening in the roof, cut right through the overlying turf. There would be one day of the year when the sun struck down through this opening straight onto the stone below; one day when the old powers of the place might waken. They were not fled, not yet. I could feel them in the still air around me, in the rough-hewn walls, where here and there a small, subtle sign was carved. I thought suddenly of the young druid, Ciarán, striding out of Sevenwaters in his hurt and fury. Maybe it was better not to feel too much. Not to want too much. No past, no future. Only today. Much safer. As long as the past didn't come back uninvited.

"You're weary," Dog said. "Still, we'll be gone tomorrow. Was going to ask—no, maybe better not."

"What? You can ask."

"You're tired. Long ride for you. We'd dearly like another tale, one last tale before we—too much to ask. Forget I said it."

"It's all right." I smiled, stifling a yawn. "I can sleep tomorrow, I expect. One more tale I can surely manage."

Strangely, although we had been speaking quietly, all of them seemed to know. I was soon surrounded by silent men, leaning against the wall or squatting on their haunches. Some sat cross-legged, sharpening knives or spearheads in the lantern light. Spider reached a long arm over and put a tankard of ale in my hands. Behind the others, Bran and Gull stood together. In the darkness Gull was near invisible, save when his grin revealed a flash of gleaming teeth. Bran watched me with folded arms, expressionless. No sign of weariness there. And he'd been longer without proper sleep than any of us, as I had good cause to know.

"I had thought," I began, "that on the eve of your mission, I should inspire you with another heroic tale, perhaps of sacrifice and courage on the field of battle. But I have not the heart for this. For all I know, the men you go out to attack may be my own kind. Besides, I have heard you are the best at what you do. I expect you need no encouragement to excel. So I will seek instead to divert you, and I will tell you a tale of love. It tells how a woman kept faith against all odds."

I took a mouthful of the ale. It tasted very good, but I set the cup down. If I had any more I would risk falling asleep right here where I sat. I looked up around the circle of grim, hard-bitten faces. How many of them would I see again? How many of them would still be alive this time tomorrow?

"She was an ordinary girl, a farmer's daughter, and her name was Janet. But her sweetheart called her Jenny; it was his special name for her that nobody else used. When he called her that, she felt she was the most beautiful woman in the world. Her Tom certainly thought so. Tom was her sweetheart, and he was a smith, like Evan here, a strong young man, broad shouldered and skillful at his trade. He was not too tall and not too short. He had curling, brown hair and a merry face. But the thing Jenny liked best about him was his deep, gray eyes; trustworthy eyes, she called them. She knew that whatever happened, Tom would never let her down.

"Jenny was a quiet girl. A good girl. Obedient to her father, helpful to her mother, skilled at all the things a good wife should know. She could sew and make preserves and brew ale. She could pluck a chicken and spin wool and tend to a sick lamb. Tom was proud of her, and he was hard put to it to wait until their wedding day, which was set for midsummer. He loved her yellow hair down to her waist, which she took out of its braid sometimes, so he could see it ripple like a field of wheat in sunlight. He loved the way she was just the right height for his arm to go neatly around her shoulders as they walked along. She made his heart beat quicker and his body stir, and he sang at his forge as he hammered the hot iron into pitchfork or plow share and smiled to himself, waiting till Midsummer Day.

"Quiet and sweet as Jenny was, there was one thing that made her lose her temper and that was the other girls looking sidelong at her Tom or trying to flirt with him as he passed them on the pathways. 'Keep your eyes to yourself,' she'd say, furious, 'or you'll be sorry. He's mine.' Tom used to laugh at her, and say she was like a little fierce terrier protecting a bone. Didn't she know he'd never dream of looking at another? Wasn't she the woman of his heart?

"Ah, but they reckoned without the folk under the hill. Meddlesome they are and love nothing better than to snatch away a likely lad or lass on a whim and use the poor mortal for their own pleasure. Some they keep for a year and a day, and some forever. Some they spit out again when they've had their fill, and these poor lost ones are never quite the same again. One night Tom had been working late down at the forge, and he took a short cut through the woods to the farm where his Jenny lived, thinking to steal a kiss or two before he went home. Foolish Tom. What did he do but put a foot in a mushroom circle, and quick as a heartbeat there were the fairy folk all dressed in their finest, and at their head the fairy queen on her white horse. One look into her eyes and he was lost. The queen took him up behind her and off they galloped, far, far away, beyond the reach of mortal being. Jenny waited and waited that night, with a candle burning in the window. But her Tom never came."

I had wondered if they might find this story too childish or whimsical; not a fit tale for grown men. But there was the utter silence of rapt attention. I took another sip of ale.

"Go on," said Snake. "I thought you said he was trustworthy. Sounds pretty stupid to me. Should've gone by the road and carried a lantern."

"Once the fairy folk decide they want you, you can't do much about it," I replied. "Well, Jenny was no fool. Next morning, early, she went down through the woods toward the forge, and she saw the grass all trampled with hoofmarks and the mushroom circle, what was left of it; and she saw the red scarf Tom had been wearing, the scarf she had spun and dyed and knitted for him with her own hands. She knew who'd taken him all right, and she was determined to get him back. So off she went to the oldest woman of the village, a crone so old she'd bare gums instead of teeth, and gnarled, curling fingernails, and as many wrinkles on her as the last of winter's dried apples. Jenny sat down with this ancient one and fed her a little bowl of gruel she'd made specially, and then she asked her what to do.

"The old woman was reluctant to speak. Such things are best kept quiet. But she'd had many little kindnesses from Jenny, treats and help around the house, and so she told her. On the next full moon, she said, the fairy folk would ride out along the wide, white path that led through the heart of the woods and on to the crossroads on the moor. Jenny must wait at the crossroads, silent, until midnight. When they came by, she must grab hold of her Tom by his hand, and she must hold on till dawn. Then the spell would be broken, and he would be hers again. 'That sounds easy,' said Jenny. 'I can do that.' The old one cackled with laughter. 'Easy!' she choked. 'That's a good one! This will be the hardest thing you ever did, chicken. You'll need to want him bad to keep hold. Be prepared for a few surprises. Sure you can do it?' And Jenny said fiercely, 'He's mine. Of course I can do it.'"

Snake reached over with a pitcher and refilled my cup. The forked tongue inscribed on his nose seemed to flicker in the lamplight, as if preparing to strike.

"Well, Jenny did as she'd been bidden. At midnight on the full moon, she waited alone at the crossroads in her homespun gown and sensible boots, with a dark, hooded cloak concealing her bright hair. Like a little shadow in the moonlight she waited. Around her neck she had wrapped the red scarf that had been his. And they came; a long glittering cavalcade of riders, the horses all white, the gowns and tunics beaded and jeweled, the hair dressed long and wild with sparkling gems and strange leaves braided into its silvery flow. The fairy queen rode in the middle, tall, regal, her skin pale as milk, her hair a glorious glossy auburn, her dress cut low to show the elegant curves of her figure. Behind her rode Tom the smith, his gray eyes distant, his once merry face an expressionless mask. He wore a strange tunic and leggings of silver and boots of softest kidskin. Jenny was filled with fury, but she stood still and silent until the queen reached the very center of the crossroads, until her Tom was just before her within easy reach. Then, quick as a flash, she darted out and seized his hand, and she pulled as hard as she could, and he tumbled down from his horse and sprawled at her feet on the white path.

"There was a hiss of outrage from the fairy folk, and in a trice they had circled their horses around her and poor Tom, and there was no getting away. The fairy queen's voice was terrible to hear, both sweet and deadly in its fury. 'You!' she spat. 'What are you playing at? Who put you up to this? This man is mine! Take your filthy mortal hands off him! No woman challenges me!' But Jenny held on, while Tom sat at her feet in a daze, and she stared at the beautiful creature on the white horse and spoke defiance with her eyes. Then the fairy laughed a dreadful laugh, and she said, 'We shall at least have some sport from this. Let us see how long you can hold on, farm girl! You think yourself strong? How little mortals comprehend.'

"At first Jenny hardly knew what she meant, for Tom's hand was limp and passive in hers. Then all at once the fingers changed to razor-sharp claws and the flesh to rough hair; and instead of a man, she held the leg of a great, slavering wolf that opened its jaws and bared its long, sharp teeth at her. Jenny flinched in terror, with the creature's rancid breath on her face and its strong body thrashing and straining against the grip of her hands. But she wound her fingers into the wolf's long hair and she held on and held on as the creature dragged her across the path. She felt the white gravel tearing at her gown and at her skin. There was a murmur from the circle of watchers; and a single word was spoken in a strange tongue. Then the rough hair changed to a smooth, slippery surface that made her almost let go, it was so hard to grip. There was a swelling and coiling, and now, instead of a great wolf, she held a massive, sleek serpent with scales the color of jewels from deep in the earth, a monster that writhed and swirled and sought to wrap her tight in the coils of its immense body. To keep hold, Jenny was obliged to embrace this creature within the circle of her arms, and lock her hands together, pressing her face against the cold scales of its body, willing herself not to faint with terror as the small, evil head darted down toward her again and again, the forked tongue flicking close to her eyes. 'This is Tom,' she told herself, her heart thudding like a drum. 'This is my sweetheart. I will hold on. I will. He is mine.'

"Another word fell into the moonlight silence. The snake became a huge spider, a hairy, bristling creature with many-faceted eyes and thick legs that curled around the hapless girl. Its venomous fangs probed toward her where she clutched its leg, the spines of its body piercing her flesh until she put her teeth through her lip to keep from screaming. After the spider came a boar with yellow tusks and tiny, mindless eyes; and after the boar a strange creature whose name she did not know, with long, snapping jaws and a gnarled, knobbled skin. Still Jenny held on, though her poor hands were bleeding and would scarce obey her will, so cramped were they. Once she looked up, and she thought she could see the smallest lightening of the night sky. The folk around her were very quiet. Then the fairy queen laughed again. 'Not bad, not bad at all! You've given us some fine sport. Now we must be off. I'll have my boy back, if you'll be so good as to release him.' She gave an imperious sweep of the hand, and Jenny felt her shoulders pierced as with a hundred sharp knives, and she almost let go. There was a flapping of great, dark wings, and in her hands was the foot of a gigantic bird, its beak as large as a horse's head, its claws flexing as it sought to break her grip. The other foot had closed about her arm and shoulder, and the monstrous creature jumped and flapped and squawked, and stabbed with its deadly beak to the right and to the left, trying to dislodge her. There was a tinkling of fairy laughter. 'This is my man,' Jenny whispered to herself. 'I love him. She shall not have him. I will not let go.' And fight as the great bird might, it could not break free of her hold. Then all at once there was a rustling and a sighing, and the delicate clatter of many hooves; and as the first light of dawn turned the edges of the world to silver, the fairy folk

were gone like wisps of mist, and there in her arms was her
sweetheart, limp as if dead, his shining clothes turning to
plain gray as the sky lightened. 'Tom,' she whispered,
'Tom.' She hadn't the strength to say more. After a while
she felt him move and slip his arms around her waist, and
he laid his head on her breast, and he murmured, 'Where
are we? What happened?' Then Jenny took off the red scarf
and wound it around her sweetheart's neck, and she helped
him to his feet with her bleeding, damaged hands. They put
an arm around each other; and as the sun rose on a perfect
day, they walked slowly homeward. And, though the tale
does not tell it, I should think they had a good life together,
for they were two halves of the one whole."

Around me, there was a collective release of breath. Nobody said anything. After a little the men moved away and
settled to rest as well as they could on the hard ground.
There would be no privacy here. I dimmed the lantern as
low as it would go, and made ready to sleep, fully clothed
as I was. I might at least take off my boots. But when I bent
to unlace them, I found I was so tired my fingers would not
obey me, so tired I was on the verge of weeping over everything and nothing. A curse on them all. It would have been
so much easier to hate them, as Eamonn did.

"Here." Dog was kneeling by me, his big hands delicate
as they unfastened the laces and drew the boots off my feet.
"Such little feet you've got."

I nodded thanks, aware of eyes fixed on us from across
the chamber. It was almost dark. I heard a tiny, snipping
noise and then something smooth and sharp was slipped
into my hand, and Dog's large, lumbering form retreated
back into the shadows. As I lay down and felt deep weariness overwhelm me, I slipped the wolf claw into my pocket.
These were hired killers. Why should it matter to me what
became of them? Why couldn't life be simple, the way it
was in the tales? Why couldn't . . . I dropped into a deep,
dreamless sleep.

* * *

I blinked, once, twice. Light was streaming in through the entranceway. It was morning. I sat up. The chamber was empty, the floor bare, all sign of human habitation gone. All but my blanket and my small pack and the tools of my trade, and the smith lying asleep near me, his breath difficult.

I looked around again. Nothing. They were gone, all of them. They had left me to deal with this alone. Don't panic, Liadan, I said to myself as my heart began to thump. There would be limited time before Evan awoke and needed me. So, find a source of water. See if it was possible to make a fire. Beyond that, there could be no planning.

There was a small bowl and a bucket by my pack. With these in hand, I made my way out through the narrow entry, screwing up my eyes as I emerged into a glorious summer morning.

"There's a stream at the northern end of the mound, and a pool where you can wash."

He had his back to me, and a bow over the shoulder. Nonetheless, the shaven head and bizarre, decorated skin made his identity instantly plain. My shock and resentment were almost as strong as my relief, and I spoke incautiously.

"You! You are the last man I expected to find here."

"You'd have preferred another?" he queried, as he turned toward me. "One who would flatter you and speak sweet words?"

"Don't talk rubbish!" I was determined not to let slip that I had believed myself alone. I would show him no sign of fear. "I prefer none of you. Why are you not with your men? They look to you for leadership: the chief, almost godlike. I cannot understand how you could send them on this mission and remain behind. Any of them could have been left here to guard me."

He narrowed his eyes at me. The morning sun threw the light and dark of his patterned features into harsh relief.

"There's not a single one of them I would trust for this job," Bran said. "I saw the way they watched you."

"I don't believe you." This was nonsense.

"Besides," he added casually, stowing away the bow in a crevice between the rocks, "it's good training. They must learn to deal with the unexpected, to assume command instantly if they must, and not to question. They must learn to be always ready. There are other leaders among them. They will accept this challenge."

"How—how long will they be gone?"

"Long enough."

Since I could think of no more to say to him, I went off to find the stream, to wash my face and hands and fetch water for my patient. There was a still pool between the rocks, and as I dipped the bucket I half imagined I saw my sister there, waist deep, locked in her lover's arms, her fiery hair flowing about her white body. Poor lovely Niamh. I had scarce given her a moment's thought since I bade her farewell. She would be settling in at Tirconnell by now, learning to cope with her new life among strangers. I shivered. I could not imagine living away from Sevenwaters, away from all that was so much a part of me. Maybe, if you cared enough about someone, you could do it and not feel your spirit torn in two. But the forest keeps her hold on all those who are born there, and they cannot travel far without the yearning in them to return. In my heart I feared for my sister. As for Ciarán, there was no telling what path he had taken.

The day unfolded. Evan was in pain, sweating, retching, and babbling nonsense. Bran would appear and disappear, saying little, helping me lift and turn the smith, heating water, doing whatever I asked. I was forced to admit, grudgingly, that he was quite useful. Once, when Evan lay quiet, he called me outside, made me sit down, and gave me a platter of stew and dry bread and a cup of ale.

"Don't look so surprised," he said, settling on the ground opposite me and starting on his own meal. "You must eat. And there is nobody else to provide for you."

I said nothing.

"Or maybe you believe you could have managed this task alone? Is that it? The little healer girl, worker of miracles. You did not imagine we would leave you here on your own, did you?"

I did not look at him, concentrating instead on the stew, which was remarkably good. The bow must be for hunting.

"You did believe it," he said incredulously, "that we had gone on and left you out here alone with a dying man. You must think us little better than savages."

"Isn't that what you want?" I challenged, looking direct at him now and glimpsing for an instant a rather different expression in his gray eyes before he turned them away. "The Painted Man, a creature who inspires terror and awe? A man who can, and will, do almost anything if you pay him well enough? A man without conscience? Why should such a man have second thoughts about leaving a woman on her own, especially when he seems to despise the female sex so utterly?"

He opened his mouth, thought better of what he was about to say, and closed it again.

"Why do you hate us so much? What woman let you down so badly that you must take it out on the whole of our kind for the rest of your life? You bear such resentment. It eats you from the inside like a canker. You would be a fool to let this destroy you. That would be a terrible waste. What happened to make you so bitter?"

"None of your business."

"I'm making it my business," I said firmly. "It was your choice to stay here, and you will listen. You heard my tale of the farmer's daughter, Jenny. Maybe it was true, and maybe it wasn't. But there are many fine, strong women such as her in the world, as well as those less admirable. We are human like you, and each of us different. You see the world through the shadow of your own hurt, and you judge unfairly."

"Not so." His features had a pinched look, and the eyes were distant. I began to regret speaking so boldly. "It was a woman's guile and her power over a man that robbed me of both family and birthright. It was a woman's selfishness and a man's weakness for her that set me on this path, that made me the creature you so despise. Women are spoilers. A man should beware not to get too close and be caught in the net."

"But I am a woman," I said, after a while. "I do not—entrap, seduce, or commit acts of evil. I speak my mind, but there's nothing wrong with that. I refuse to be categorized as a—what was the word? A spoiler? My mother has been my example. She is fragile, but strong. She knows nothing but giving. My sister is beautiful and completely without guile."

"You're crying."

"I am not!" I scrubbed an angry hand across my cheek. "All I'm saying is, you must have encountered very few women to cling to this narrow view."

"For you, perhaps, I might make an exception," he said grudgingly. "You are not so easily classified."

"You think me more akin to a man?"

"Hah!" I could not tell if this sound indicated amusement or scorn. "Hardly. But you show some qualities I did not expect. A pity you cannot wield a staff or draw a bow; we might have recruited you to the troop."

It was my turn to laugh. "I think not. But as a matter of fact, I can. Wield a staff and draw a bow, that is."

He gazed at me. "Now that I cannot believe."

"I'll show you."

Iubdan had taught me well. This bow was rather longer and heavier than I was used to, and I could not draw it fully. But it would do. Bran watched me in silence, brows raised in derision as I adjusted the string.

"What would you have me strike with this arrow?"

"I suppose you could try for the large knothole on that elm trunk."

"A child could find that mark," I said with some scorn. "You insult me. What target would you choose for a young man who wished to join your band of warriors?"

"He would not have got this far without proving himself. But if you insist, I suggest the apple tree that grows down there between the rocks. Here, let me show you."

He took the bow from me, and drew it fully, eyes narrowed against the light. It was quick. A twang as he released the string, and I saw a small green apple fall to the ground, split by the arrow's point.

"Your turn," he said dryly.

This was a game Sean and I had practiced over and over. I drew the bow as far as I could, said a word under my breath, and released the string.

"Beginner's luck," said Bran as another apple fell. "A fluke. You couldn't do it twice."

"I could," I said, "but I really don't care if you believe me or not. Now, we have work to do. If I told you what I needed, could you find some herbs for me? My supply is nearly gone, and Evan will be in increasing pain."

"Tell me what you want."

It was just as well I had slept so soundly that night, for there was to be little sleep in the days to come. The smith grew steadily sicker, his features becoming hectically flushed, the flesh around his wound now mottled and bluish. Bran had brought back what I had asked for, and I had made up a tea, which I fed Evan drop by drop until he grew quieter.

"Where are you, Biddy?" he muttered, still moving his

head restlessly from side to side. "Biddy? Woman? I can't see you."

"Hush," I said, sponging his burning face. "I'm here. Sleep now."

But he took a long time to sleep and, despite the herbs, did not rest long before the pain woke him anew. Bran was outside, and I did not call him. What was the point? There was nothing he could do. I sat by Evan's side, the two of us in the small pool of lantern light, and held his hand. I told him not to talk, but there was no stopping him.

"Still here. Thought you'd have gone home by now."

"Yes, I'm still here, as you see. You don't get rid of me so easily."

"Thought it was Biddy for a bit. Silly. She'd make three of you; fine big girl she is, my Biddy."

"She's waiting for you; make no doubt of it," I said.

"You think she'll still want me? You think she wouldn't mind the . . . you know?"

I gave his hand a little squeeze. "A strong, strapping fellow like you? Of course she'll want you. You'll have them lining up, man."

"Don't like to complain; know you're doing your best. But God, it hurts . . ."

"Here, see if you can swallow more of this."

"Need some help?" Bran had come in silently, with a small flask in his hand. "Gull left me this. It is a drink from his own country, very potent. Saved for special occasions."

"I doubt if he could keep it down. A few drops, maybe. Here, put a little in this tea; you are right; it is time for strong measures. Can you lift his head and shoulders for me? Thank you."

The flask was silver, lined with fine yew wood, and its surface was chased with an elaborate spiral pattern. The stopper was of amber glass, fashioned in the shape of a little cat.

"Not too much. We want it to stay in his stomach long enough."

Little by little, sip by sip, I fed Evan the potent brew, while Bran sat behind, supporting him.

"Trust you, Chief," said the smith weakly. "Wait till I'm down, then try to poison me. Better leave it to the lass here."

"Indeed, what am I here for but to do her bidding?"

"That'll be the day, Chief . . ."

"Hush," I said. "Too much talk. Drink this, and keep quiet."

"You hear that?" said Bran. "She likes to give orders. No wonder the others couldn't wait to get away."

Evan's eyes closed. "Told you she was just your type, Chief," he said faintly. Bran refrained from comment.

"Sleep," I said, putting down the cup of herbal tea. It was half empty. He had managed more than I expected. "Rest. Think of your Biddy. Maybe she can hear you, across the water as she is. It happens that way sometimes. Tell her you're coming for her soon. She won't have to wait long."

After a while Bran lowered Evan gently to the ground, his head supported on a roll of blankets so he could breathe more easily.

"Here," he said, and he was offering me the silver flask.

"Maybe not." But I took it from him, thinking its intricate pattern seemed to flow across his hand and up his arm under the sleeve of his plain, gray shirt, rolled to the elbow. "I must be able to wake when he does."

"You have to sleep sometime."

"So do you."

"Don't concern yourself with me. Drink a mouthful, at least. It will help you rest."

I put the flask to my lips and swallowed. It was as strong as fire. I gasped and felt a warm glow spread through me. "You, too," I said, passing it back.

He took a drink, then stoppered the flask and stood up.

"Call me when he wakes." For the first time there was a sort of diffidence in his tone. "You don't have to do this alone, you know."

Brighid help me. I was suddenly overtaken by the most profound sadness. Arrogance, scorn, indifference I could deal with. Quiet competence was just fine. Arguing with him was almost enjoyable. It was the unexpected words of kindness that threatened to shatter me in pieces. I must indeed be weary. I fell asleep with a vision of Sevenwaters before my eyes: dark, shadowy trees, dappled sunlight, the clear waters of the lake. Tiny and perfect and oh, so far away.

Chapter Six

We fell into a routine. We became used to each other. While I slept, Bran kept guard and tended to the smith. When Bran slept, which was seldom, he made me stay inside; and I did as I was told. Day followed day, and we watched the fever strip the flesh from Evan's bones and slowly drain the life from his eyes. It would have been easy for Bran to remind me that I had insisted on keeping this man alive long enough to suffer a lingering and painful death. It would have been easy for me to blame Bran for moving the smith before he was fit to travel. But we did not speak of these things. We did not speak much at all. It hardly seemed necessary. He knew when I needed him and was there. I began to recognize the times when he needed to be alone, and I would retreat silently indoors or up to the pool to sit on the rocks and will my mind to quiet. There were carven stones there, ancient, monumental slabs encrusted with creeping lichens and shawled by soft ferns. That they were somehow guardians of the old truths that had their center here, I was in no doubt whatever, and I nodded to them with respect as I passed.

Our talk became different, as if there were no need any longer to play a game of strategy with our words. Evan held on, and I allowed myself a slim hope that all was not lost. There was a brief respite one night, time for the two of us to sit outside, under the waxing moon and the arch of a thousand stars, eating rabbit baked in the coals with wild garlic, while the only sounds around us were the tiny rustling of night creatures in the undergrowth and the solitary hoot of a hunting owl. It was a companionable silence. I realized I had come to trust this man, something I would never have believed possible.

"Give me your honest opinion," he said, when we had finished eating. "Has he any real chance?"

"He'll survive until morning. I'm trying not to look too far ahead."

"You learn quickly."

"Some things. It's another world out here. The old conventions don't seem to work anymore."

"Tell me. You seem to know a great deal about herbs and potions. What you used when you put him to sleep, when we took off his arm; it was powerful. Have you any left?"

I could not see his face clearly in the shadows, but the eyes were watchful, intent.

"Some. Gull commented on it. He took one sniff and named almost every ingredient. That surprised me."

"His mother was an herbalist, famous in her own country. There were those who called her a witch. That led in time to persecution and death. Gull has been tried almost beyond endurance."

I could not resist asking, "I thought these men had no past?"

"They learn to put it behind them. To do the kind of work we do, a man must travel light. He must carry neither memories nor hopes. To be what we are, you must think only of today's task."

"I knew Gull's story."

"He told you?"

"The others told me. Each has his tale. Not buried so very deep. Each has his hope. No man can be truly without it."

"No?"

I decided it would be wise to pursue this no further.

"Haven't you ever been tempted," he asked quietly, "when your patient is in pain and you know he cannot survive? It would be easy, wouldn't it, to make the draft just a little stronger? So instead of suffering further, he simply sank into sleep and never woke?"

I had been thinking the very same thoughts.

"One must be careful," I said. "Meddling in such matters can be dangerous, and not just for the victim. We each have our time to move on. The goddess wills it. I would act thus only if I believed she moved my hand."

"You follow the old faith?"

I nodded, reluctant to be drawn into talk of my family.

"Would you do it?" he asked me, "if he keeps getting worse?"

"Then I would be no different from you with your little knife, your convenient solution. I heal, I do not kill."

"You would, I think, if you had to."

"I would not wish to offend the goddess, nor would I take such a step unless I was sure that was what Evan wanted. I suppose I cannot say what I would do unless I was faced with the choice."

"You may get the chance to find out."

I did not reply.

"Did you believe," he went on after a while, "that I would have done it? Used this convenient solution for yourself because you were in my way?"

"At the time, yes. I believed it was possible And—what I had heard of you seemed to support it."

"I would never have done such a thing."

"I know that now."

"Don't get me wrong. I am not soft. Conscience does not trouble me. I make decisions quickly and I do not allow myself to regret them. But I am no arbitrary destroyer of the innocent."

"Then why did you—" It was too late to bite my words back.

"Why did I what?" The tone had suddenly become dangerous. He had trapped me with his kindness.

"Nothing."

"Tell me. What tale was it you heard of me?"

"I—" It was plain that silence was not going to be an option, and he would know if I lied. "I was told of a time, not so very long ago, when a party of men, on their own land, were ambushed and slain while bearing the bodies of their dead for burial. I heard that their leader was held and forced to watch his friends die, one by one—for nothing, for nothing more than a demonstration of skill. The description he—the tale was told in a way that made it clear you were responsible."

"Uh-huh. Who told this tale? Where did you hear it?"

"Who was your father? Where were you born? Fair trade, remember?"

"You know I will not tell you."

"One day you will." There was the sudden cold again, as if a wraith had passed by and touched me with its breath. I did not know why I had said these words, but I knew they were the truth.

"Did you feel that?" asked Bran, in a strange voice.

I stared at him. "Feel what?"

"A—a chill, a sudden draft. Maybe the weather is breaking."

"Maybe." This was getting ridiculous. Not only was I sharing his nightmares, but he was feeling it when the Sight touched me. It was most certainly time I went home.

"His name is Eamonn," he said slowly. "Eamonn of the

Marshes, they call him. His father had a bad reputation, and the son has done nothing to improve on that. My men picked you up in Littlefolds, didn't they? Right on the border of this Eamonn's land? What is he to you? Cousin? Brother? Sweetheart?"

"None of these," I stammered, my heart pounding. I must not tell him who I was, must not leave my family vulnerable. "He is known to me. I heard him tell the tale, that's all."

"Where?"

"None of your business."

"You would do well not to ally yourself with that man. His kind is the most dangerous. You do not cross such a man and come out unscathed."

"You speak of yourself, surely, not of Eamonn."

"You spring quickly enough to his defense. Is he not the one who waits anxiously for your return, as my men so touchingly related?"

"Your men have overactive imaginations, born of too little entertainment. There is no sweetheart waiting for me at home. Only my family. That's the way I choose it."

"That sounds implausible."

"It's the truth."

We sat quiet for a while. He refilled my cup and his own. I was starting to feel drowsy.

"It was not arbitrary." Bran spoke into the space between us. "The killing. It was no massacre of the innocent. We are men. We do men's work. You might ask this Eamonn of yours how many he has slain in like fashion. We were well paid to do as we did by an old and powerful enemy of his. His father wronged many in his time; the son continues to pay the price. I did add a little touch of my own; I heard he was unimpressed."

"To me it sounded like an act of mindless slaughter. And the aftermath, the arrogant gesture of a man who believes himself untouchable."

This was greeted with a frosty silence. I began to regret

my words, true as they were. When he spoke again his tone had changed. Now it was constrained, almost awkward.

"I hope you will take heed. You should not trust this man Eamonn. Take him as your husband, your lover, and he'll suck you dry. Don't throw yourself away on him. I know his kind. Such a man will give you the fair words you want; he will lull you into believing in him. Such a man knows only how to take."

I gaped at him. "I cannot believe this! You, giving me advice on how to live my life? Besides, did I ever say I wanted fair words?"

"All women want to be flattered," he said dismissively.

"Not true. All I have ever wanted is honesty. Words of affection, words of—of love, such sweet words are meaningless if spoken merely to gain an end. I would know, if a man lied to me on such a matter."

"You have much experience in these things, I suppose." There was no way to tell if he were serious or not, save that I believed him incapable of humor.

"I would know. In my heart, I would know."

A day arrived when Evan could no longer keep anything at all in his stomach. His throat was cruelly swollen, his fever replaced by a hollow-cheeked lethargy that spelled the end for him. Without my herbal infusions his pain must have been acute; but he had already moved one foot onto the final path, and being a strong man, he suffered without complaint. There was no easy sleep, made deeper by expert assistance, from which to drift peacefully on into the next world. Not for him. He knew it was time and faced it open-eyed.

The day wore on slowly to afternoon, and it seemed to me the cool, dry air inside the old enclosure was full of subtle whisperings and rustlings, as if some ancient forces beckoned the smith away.

"Tell me straight," Evan said. "It's the end for me, isn't it?"

I was sitting on the ground by him, holding his hand. "The goddess calls you. It may be your time to move on. You bear it bravely."

"Been good. Been a good lass. Did your best."

"I tried. I'm sorry it wasn't enough."

"Oh, no. No, don't weep for me, lass . . ." His breath rattled. "Dry those tears. You've got time ahead of you. Don't waste your sorrow on a plain man like me."

That only made the tears flow faster, not just for the loss of a good man, but for my mother who was on the same path, and for poor Niamh who had been denied her heart's desire, and for the world that made it necessary for men to waste their best years living a life of flight and concealment and killing. I wept because I did not know how to put it right. Evan was quiet for a long time. Later he began to talk of his woman, Biddy. Couple of boys, she had, another man's children. Fine lads, the pair of 'em. Their father had been a nasty piece of work, used to beat her black and blue. Hard life, she'd had. Well, the fellow had died. Best not to tell exactly how. And she was his now, waiting for him to give all this up and come back to her. They'd move on someplace, him and Biddy and the lads, set up a little forge in a village, perhaps in foreign parts. There was always work for a skilled man, and Biddy, she'd turn her hand to anything. He'd teach the lads the trade, give 'em a future. Once or twice he spoke as if it were Biddy there holding his hand, and I nodded and smiled back at him.

There was a chance, later, to ask him that question, and I took it.

"Evan, I must speak to you plain, while you can understand me."

"What is it, lass?"

"There isn't a lot of time left. We both know that. You're in pain, and it will get worse. I was—I was going to offer

you a very strong sleeping draft, one that would see you
through to the end. But you wouldn't be able to take it, not
now. If you want—if you want to shorten this, I could ask
Bran . . . I could ask the chief to . . . to. . . ." I found, after
all, that these words were beyond me.

". . . know what I want. Call the chief in, tell you
both . . . save the breath."

So I had to go outside and fetch Bran, after scrubbing my
face with my hand in an attempt to erase the tears. He was
not far away, leaning his back against the stone wall of the
ancient barrow, staring far off into the distance, apparently
deep in thought. His mouth was set in a grim line.

"Could—could you come inside, please?"

He started as if I had struck him, then followed me without a word.

"Got a couple of things to ask. Sit down, Chief. Not
much breath left. Got to talk quiet."

"I'm here. We're both here."

"Know what she asked me?" There was a tiny, rattling
ghost of a chuckle.

"I can't imagine."

"Said would I like you to finish me off? Seeing as she
can't do it herself. Would you believe that? What a girl."

They were both looking at me, their expressions identi-
cal. Sweet Brighid, why couldn't I stop these tears from
flowing?

"Don't want that. Glad of the offer though. Never easy.
Want—want to be outside. Under the stars. Little fire. Smell
of pine cones burning, feel the night breeze on my face.
Drop of strong drink, maybe, to keep the chill out. Tell a
story. A good long one. That's what I want."

"I should think we can manage that." But it was at me
Bran was looking, and there was that expression again, less
fleeting this time. The gray eyes clear and true, the eyes of a
trustworthy man. The mouth softened by concern and by

something else. I sensed this unmasked Bran was infinitely more dangerous to me than the Painted Man could ever be.

"One more thing," whispered Evan. "Chief, about my woman. Gull knows where my stuff's hidden. Need to look after her and the lads. Been saving. Should be plenty. Gull knows where she is."

Bran nodded soberly. "Have no concerns on that score. I will make sure they are protected, and provided for. There are plans in place."

A faint grin lightened the smith's gaunt, gray features, and he was looking at me. "Good man, the chief," he murmured.

"I know," I said.

Bran carried the smith outside with little apparent effort, despite Evan's far greater height and weight. I fetched blankets, water, cloths. It was dusk at last, after an endless day. There was time to settle Evan, propped half sitting against the rocks, his body wrapped as warmly as possible. We chose a spot where he was well sheltered but still able to feel the movement in the night air. There was a scent of rain; I hoped it would not come down before morning. Bran made a small fire, bordered by flat stones from the stream, and then he disappeared. Evan was silent now. The short move had taken most of his remaining strength.

I wondered what sort of tale was right for a dying man's last night in this world. A long one, he'd said, long enough. I sat with my hands around my knees, staring into the flames of the small fire. A tale with hope in it. A tale I could get through without weeping. Bran came back as silently as he had left, holding something in the front of his shirt. He spilled the load on the ground. Pine cones. I collected one or two and tossed them on the fire, with a silent word to the goddess. It was a smell that held the promise of high mountains, of snow, and great birds circling in a pale sky.

"Chief." The voice was thready.

"I'm here." Bran settled on the smith's other side. This placed him somewhat closer to me than the three or four paces demanded by the code.

"The lass. Give me your promise. She's to go safe home when this is finished. Promise, Chief."

Bran did not reply. He was staring into the fire.

"I mean it, lad." Faint as it was, the smith's voice demanded an answer.

"I wonder what value can be placed on the promise of a man such as myself. But I will give you my word, Smith."

"Good. Tell the tale now, lass."

So while he sat there quietly, I began. I wove into this story as much wonder and magic and enchantment as I could. But I did not forget the ordinary things, the things that are wonderful in themselves, without being in any way unusual. The hero of this tale fell in love and married and held his firstborn son. He knew the friendship and loyalty of comrades in arms. He journeyed through far-off lands and mysterious seas, and he experienced the joy of homecoming. Mostly I looked at the flames as I talked, but sometimes I watched Evan's blunt, honest features and his wide-open eyes gazing up at the stars. Once or twice Bran took out the silver flask and put a little of its contents on his fingertip then touched it to the smith's lips. But after a while, he stoppered the flask and returned it to his pocket; and then he just sat there listening. The tale went on. Some of the adventures I borrowed, and some I made up as I went along. The waxing moon rose and spread a faint light over us, and still I talked steadily on. The breeze came up, with a scent of the sea in it, and the night became chill. Bran got up and fetched his coat.

"Here," he said diffidently, and dropped it neatly around my shoulders. Another time, he brought me a cup of water. It was a long, long tale. I could have done with Sean or Niamh or Conor to help me with it, but there was nobody. Careful, I must not begin to weep again. The stars were like bright jewels on a cloak of deepest velvet. But you could never sew a cloak so wondrously lovely.

"There came a time," I said at last, "when the goddess called Eoghan back to her. For it was the appointed day for him to move on, to let his spirit free from this life and send it forth into the next. When she calls you, there is no refusing. Still, Eoghan thought of his wife and his son who was still half grown, and he sat by the carven stones where he had heard this call and asked himself how could he leave them? How would they manage without him? Who would chop the wood for his wife? Who would teach his son to hunt? Then the goddess sent her wisdom deep into his heart, and he understood. Your wife will grieve for you, but her love will keep her strong. She will sew her love into every stitch of the gowns she makes (for his wife was a seamstress). Your son will learn his father's true self as he practices the craft you taught him. In time, he too will be a man, and he will love and be happy and take forward in his life the questing heart, the eager will he learned at your knee, when you told of your adventures. In time, your spirit will be with them again, perhaps in a great, spreading tree that shades the place where your grandchildren play. Maybe in a wide-winged eagle soaring aloft, watching as your dear one spreads her linen on the hawthorns to dry and looks suddenly to the sky, shading her eyes against the sunlight. You will be there, and they will know. I am not cruel. I take, and I give."

My fingers moved to Evan's wrist, feeling for the spot where the blood pulsed under the skin.

"He still breathes," said Bran softly. "But barely. I don't know if he can hear you."

A long tale, Evan had said; that meant I had to keep going. Not much longer. My whole body felt stiff and wretched; I was so tired I suspected I was talking nonsense.

"That same day Eoghan's son had been out checking on the sheep, and he chanced to come home by the carven stones, for he liked to trace the strange shapes on them with his finger. A long spiral, a chain of many curious links, a grinning wolfhound, a small cryptic face. But when he came to the place, there was his father, lying at peace on the earth with his eyes open to the sky. The boy was not yet twelve years old, but he was his father's son. So he crossed Eoghan's hands on his breast, and closed the sightless eyes, and he ran to the village and fetched two men and a board. Only then did he go in quietly and break the news to his mother. And it was as the goddess had spoken. They grieved, but they went on and built their lives. Eoghan's love had made them strong. It had wrapped them like a shining cloak to keep their hearts warm and their minds clear, and his passing only made it stronger. It remained also in the spirits of his true friends, who honored his memory in their brave deeds and their bold journeys of discovery. Eoghan had moved on, through the Otherworld realms to his next life. But what he had done, and who he had been, that remained bright and true for many a year after his passing. Such is the legacy of a good man."

There was a rattling, rasping sound as Evan drew in a breath, and a spasm went through his body. Bran put an arm beneath his shoulders, lifting him slightly.

"Turn him this way," I said. "Face the west." It was time. My tale had lasted just long enough. I stood up, looking into the star-washed sky.

"Manannán mac Lir, son of the sea!" I called with the last strength of my voice. "Take this man on his journey! He has worked long and hard and is ready to depart. Let him set sail now on his voyage, with favorable winds and fair seas." I raised my arms, stretching them out toward the west. A cloud moved across the moon, and the leaves stirred around us. I thought, as the gust of wind passed across the opening on top of the barrow, there was a faint, deep vibration, almost too low to hear, like the note of some giant instrument, like the ancient voice of the earth itself. My hands made a sign of protection in the darkness. *Dana watch over us. The goddess guide our steps.*

Beside me, Bran was lowering the smith back to the blanket. I had no need to ask, it was over. Today was over. I would not think about tomorrow. My back ached, and my head was stuffy with unshed tears; and I was so weary I did not think I could move from where I stood, still gazing westward but seeing nothing. What I needed was impossible. At home there would have been someone near to put loving arms around me, to say, all right, Liadan, it's finished now. You've done well. Cry if you want to. Here there was nobody, only him. And that was unthinkable.

I forced myself to move. Evan lay tranquil, arms by his sides, his eyes closed. Perhaps the spirit was not quite fled, but it would be gone by dawn. I knelt by him and bent to brush my lips against his, to touch his cheek and marvel at the deep expression of peace that now spread across his exhausted face.

"Farewell," I whispered. "You died bravely, as you lived. Rest now."

When I got to my feet again, my legs felt like jelly and the stars were wheeling across the sky. Bran moved swiftly to grab my arms before I fell.

"You must rest. Go back inside. Take the lantern. I'll watch over him. Time enough in the morning for what needs to be done."

I shook my head. "No. I'm not going in there. Not by myself." My voice sounded odd, distant.

"Lie down here." A firm hand guided me to the far side of the fire. Then I was lying on a blanket and the coat settled over me.

"I don't—you must wake me when—"

"Ssh. Get some sleep. I'll wake you in time."

Too tired to weep, too tired to think, I did as I was told and slept.

* * *

I did not want to cry anymore. Instead I felt hollow, empty, as if all the meaning had been sucked out of me and I was drifting, light as a skeleton leaf, at the mercy of the four winds. I was drained of tears. My brief sleep had been visited by dreams of strange intensity, which I could not have recounted clearly. I remembered standing on the edge of a cliff so high that all you could see below was a swirling mist, and a voice saying to me, *Jump. You know you can change things. Do it; jump.* I was relieved to wake, soon after dawn, and occupy myself with washing the smith's body with clean water in which I had floated a few leaves of the creeping pennyroyal that grew abundantly by the stream. The scent was fresh and sweet. I worked quickly but with respect. Soon the body would begin to stiffen. We should move him before then. Bran was down the hill, busy with a shovel. I did not ask him where he had found it or what he was doing. I was discovering, now that my task was almost over and I had time to look around me, that things outside were not quite as I had imagined. For a horse had startled me by stepping quietly out from between the bushes and whickering gently at me as I knelt there. She was a stocky, long-maned creature, her coat a delicate gray. She wore a rudimentary bridle, but was untethered. I assumed she was Bran's and well disciplined not to wander. It might, therefore, be possible to leave here.

The sun rose, but there was a sharp breeze and an increasing heaviness of clouds. I could smell the sea. I thought it would rain before nightfall. Maybe I would be gone by then. I finished the job and tidied up, and then I called Bran.

"We should do it now." It would have been better to wait, to be quite sure. Three days after the last breath, it could take, for the spirit to depart. Another man might have lain in peace in some dim chamber, with candles around him, while friends and kinsfolk made their farewells. But this man must be buried now while we still could do it; and his grave would be unmarked. The Painted Man would leave no tracks behind him.

We laid Evan down with his head to the north. The grave had been efficiently prepared, the pile of soil ready to be replaced, the length and depth perfectly calculated. I glanced at my companion. His features were quite calm, if rather pale. I supposed this meant little to him. He was good at it because he had done it so many times before. What was the loss of one more man when your life was one long dice with death?

The sun touched Evan's worn features with gold. Around us the bushes stirred and rustled.

"If you don't object, I would like to do this properly. If you don't mind."

Bran nodded, tight-lipped. I circled around the grave, walking slowly, then stopping to face the east, feeling the touch of the breeze on my skin.

"Beings of air, we honor your presence. This man's spirit flies forth from his body and journeys through your realm on his way to the Otherworld. Bear him aloft with your wings; shelter him and speed him on his flight, straight and true as an arrow."

I moved to the other side, to face the west. Dappled shadow spread across the ground. A solitary drop of rain fell, making a dark circle on the earth.

"Creatures of the deep, Manannán's folk, you who abide in the dark, mysterious waters, be with us now. Bear this man on his journey like a strong, sound vessel of oak, which breasts the waves with pride and strength. For such a one he was in life."

Now I moved again, to look northward, back up the hill toward the huge, turf-covered barrow.

"You who dwell in the earth, whose secret songs vibrate deep in her memory, you who are close to the beating heart of our great mother, hear me now. Take the broken shell of a good man and use it well. In death, may he nourish life. May he be part of the old and the new that twine together in this place of deep mystery."

Almost done. I walked to the head of the grave, so I was standing next to Bran, facing the south.

"Last I call upon you, bright salamanders, spirits of fire! Arise and shine forth, and take back one of your own. For this man was a great smith, the best this side of Gaul and beyond, so they said. His trade was with fire and he used it skillfully, respecting its power. With heat he forged weapon and tool, he labored and sweated and bent the iron to his will. Spark to spark, flame to flame, let his spirit soar to the sky as the heat rises from a great conflagration."

Up the hill, our own little fire still burned. You could smell it now, the smoke borne by gusting, contrary breezes. You could catch the scent of the powder I had strewn on the coals, a very small amount, but pungent and pure. The roots of wolfbane and chervil, ground fine as dust, stored in the depths of my bag for just such a use. I had never had to do this before, and I hoped fervently I would never have the need again.

We stood silent for a moment, and then I scooped up a handful of soil and dropped it into the grave. I found, after all, that I did have more tears to shed, but I held them back and made myself wait there while Bran used the shovel to finish the job. It was quick and neat. Level the soil. Spread the leaf litter on top, a fallen branch or two. It was as if nobody had been there, no creature save a scampering squirrel or foraging woodmouse. The body would go back to clay. The spirit was flown. I had done what I could to speed its journey.

Now it was over, and I could no longer avoid asking the question. I could no longer go on living today and pretending tomorrow did not matter. I would have to talk to him. I would have to ask him what came next for the two of us?

But neither of us was talking. We returned to the fire, and I tidied up my things, and he prepared some sort of meal, I cannot remember what it was; and we sat there and ate it in complete silence. Then he took the silver flask out of his pocket, uncorked it, and drank. He passed it to me, and I took a mouthful. It was strong stuff. I felt slightly better. The fire was down to coals, but the sharp scent of wolfbane still lingered. I passed the flask back. We did not look at one another. Neither of us spoke. Maybe each of us was waiting for the other to begin. Time passed; the sun moved across to the west, and the clouds built. The air was heavy with moisture. Home, I thought vaguely. I must go home. I have to ask him. But I did not ask. There was a sadness on me, a feeling of being cut adrift, of being set suddenly on an unknown path in an unmapped land. So instead of thinking it through, I sat there quietly, accepting the flask when it was offered, handing it back so he could share. And after a while it was empty, and still we had said nothing at all. My head was hazy; my thoughts drifted. How could you live without human touch? Wasn't that the first thing you knew when you came into the world and they laid you on your mother's belly? Her hand would come across and stroke your back, and cup your head, and she would smile through tears of exhaustion and wonderment. That touch of love would be the very first thing for you. Later she would hold you in her arms and sing to you. Something simple, something very old, like—how did it go? There was a lullaby, a tiny fragment of song in a language so old that nobody remembered what the words meant. I hummed it softly under my breath. My mother had sung this song to me and Sean so often it was lodged deep inside us. Here in this place of ancient spirits, the song felt right. As I sang, the rising wind passed over the great mound with its hidden opening, and I heard that faint, deep tone again, coming and going as if it were part of my song, as if my words came from the depths of the earth itself. *Jump,* said the voice. *Jump now.* A tear rolled down my cheek, or was it a drop of rain? If I was weeping, I did not understand why. The song ended, but the deep voice of the wind cried on and the clouds gathered. I glanced at Bran, ready to suggest a move in search of shelter. The strange, gray-horse had already retreated under the trees.

Bran was asleep. Not surprising, for he had not had the benefit of the brief rest I had enjoyed before dawn. He was an incongruous sight, the fiercely marked skin, the studded leather belt, and the weapon at his side at odds with his posture, knees drawn up, head resting on one arm, the other fist against his mouth. Sleeping thus, he seemed as vulnerable as a small child. There were deep shadows under his eyes. Even such a man as he could not go without sleep for so long and not be marked by it. I got up quietly and fetched the coat, and I laid it carefully over him. I did not want to risk waking him, for I knew he would not appreciate being seen like this, with all his safeguards down. The best thing would be to leave him alone. The best thing, in fact, would be to take the horse and a sharp knife and leave him altogether. Go home. Head south and make for Sevenwaters. I could reach the road before dusk if I rode quickly.

But I did not go. At least, I went only far enough to give him his privacy. I wrapped a blanket around myself, against the likelihood of rain, and I took the lantern for later, and I went up to the other end of the mound, by the pool, and settled myself on the smooth rocks as the sky darkened and changed to the violet of early dusk. Still the clouds passed overhead, metal-dark, edged with rose. In the distance thunder rolled. Coward, I said to myself. Why didn't you go while you could? You want to go home, don't you? Then why not grab the opportunity? Fool. But under these words, there was a strange sort of calm, the feeling that comes when you step into the unknown, when everything has changed and you are waiting to make sense of it.

I sat there a long time. It grew dark, save for the small

circle of lantern light mirrored in the black water. A few fat drops of rain splashed on the rocks. Time to move inside, I thought. But I could not do it. Something held me, something called me to stay where I was, among the strange, carved stones that lifted their heads above the ferns and bracken, here where the voice of the earth called to me on the wind. Perhaps I would wait here all night. Perhaps I would stay here in the dark, and in the morning there would be one more curious, patterned stone, and Liadan would be gone. . . .

It was cold. The storm was close. At home, my mother would be resting, and Father would be sitting by the bed, maybe working on his farm records by candlelight, dipping his quill carefully in the ink pot, glancing at Sorcha as she lay there like a little shadow, her hands small and fragile, whiter than the linen coverlet. My father would not weep, not so that you could see. He buried his pain deep inside him. Only those closest to him knew how it shredded his heart. I stood up, wrapping my arms around myself. Home. I had to go home. They needed me. I needed them. There was nothing for me here; I was stupid even to think that— that—

"Liadan." Bran's voice was quite soft. I turned around slowly. He was very close, not two paces away. It was the first time I had heard him use my name. "I thought you were gone," he said.

I shook my head, sniffing.

"You're crying," he said. "You did your best. Nobody can do more than that."

"I—I should not have . . . I . . ."

"It was a good death. You made it so. Now you can— now you can go home."

I stood there looking at him, unable to speak.

He took a deep breath. "I wish—I wish I could dry these tears," he said awkwardly. "I wish I could make this better for you. But I don't know how."

I cannot say what it was that made me take that one step forward. Maybe it was the hesitation in his voice. I knew what it cost him to let himself speak thus. Maybe it was the memory of how he had looked as he slept. I just knew, overwhelmingly, that if I did not touch him I would shatter in pieces. *Jump,* cried the wind. *Jump over.* I shut my eyes and moved toward him, and my arms went around his waist, and I rested my head against his chest and let my tears flow. *There,* said the voice deep inside me. *See how easy it was?* Bran went very still; and then his arms came around me quite cautiously, as if he had never done this before and was not at all sure how one went about it. We stood there awhile, and the feeling was good, so good, like a homecoming after long troubles. Until I felt this touch, I did not know how much I had longed for it. Until I held him, I did not realize he was just the right height to put his arms comfortably around my shoulders, for me to rest my brow in the hollow of his neck, where the blood pulsed under the skin—a perfect fit.

I could not say at what point this embrace, which began as one of simple comfort, turned into something quite different. I could not say what came first, his lips moving to touch my eyelid, my temple, the tip of my nose, the corner of my mouth; my hands twining up around his neck, my fingers slipping inside his shirt to move against the smooth skin. Both of us recognized the moment of danger. Once his lips brushed across mine, it was not possible to keep our mouths apart; and this kiss was no chaste symbol of friendship, but a desperate, hungry meeting of lips and teeth and tongues that left us shaking and breathless.

"We can't do this," muttered Bran, as his hand moved over the swell of my breast through the old shirt.

"Indeed not," I whispered as my fingers traced the spirals and swirls that covered the right side of his smoothly shaven head. "We should . . . we should forget this ever happened . . . and . . ."

"Ssh," he breathed against my cheek, and his hands moved farther down my body, and the moment of drawing back was lost forever. Need flared between us as violent and sudden and unstoppable as a great wildfire that consumes all in its path, a fierce coming together that was both joyous and terrifying in its power. It began to rain heavily, and the rocks where we lay locked in each other's arms ran with water, and we were soaked through; but we barely noticed it as hand explored soft skin, and lips tasted secret places, and we moved together as if we were indeed two halves of the one whole, made complete again. As I took him inside me, I felt a sharp throb of pain; and I must have made some sound, for he asked, "What is it? What's wrong?" I stopped his words with my fingers. Then pain was forgotten as I felt myself turn to liquid gold under his touch, and I wrapped my arms around his body, held him to me as tightly as I could. I thought I would never let go, never. But I did not say it aloud. This man had never learned tenderness. He had never been taught how to love. As he had said, he knew no fair words. But his hands and his lips and his hard body spoke sweetly enough for him. As he rolled to hold me above him, I looked into his eyes in the light of the guttering lantern and the mixture of astonishment and longing there nearly broke my heart. I stretched out over him, touching my lips to his body, and found from somewhere deep inside me a rhythm, like a strong, slow drumbeat, that moved me against him, the clenching and loosening of muscles, the touching and letting go, the fierce building sweetness—blessed Brighid, when it came it was nothing like I'd imagined. He cried out and pulled me down toward him, and I gasped with the heat that flooded my body. I felt the vibration deep within me, and knew that things could never, never be the same again. They tell of this in tales, the tales of great lovers who are parted, and long for each other, and at length find joy together. But no tale matched up to this. Afterward, we lay still in each other's arms, and neither of us could find a word to say.

Some time later, we got up and went inside, and by the lantern light we took off each other's wet clothes and dried each other, and he told me, rather haltingly, that I was the loveliest thing he had ever seen. For a little while I let myself believe it. He knelt before me, wiping the rain from my body. And he said, "You're bleeding. What is it? I've hurt you."

I concealed my surprise. "That's nothing," I said. "It's quite usual the first time. So I've heard."

He did not reply, simply looked at me; and I thought, this is a different man, quite different from the man who threatened and insulted me. Still it is the same man. He brushed my cheek with his fingers very softly. His words, when they came, were hesitant. "I don't know what to say to you."

"Then don't say anything," I told him. "Just put your arms around me. Just touch me. That's enough."

And I did what I had long wanted to do. I began at the top of his head, where the intricate markings of his body began, and I traced the edge with my fingers, slowly, down the high bridge of his nose, across the center of his severe mouth, down chin and neck and well-muscled chest. Then I touched my lips to his skin, and followed the line downward. This pattern did indeed cover him entirely, on all the right side of his body. It was indeed a work of art; not just the finely detailed drawing, but the man whose identity it had become. He was not too tall, nor too short; he was broad in the shoulder and lean with it, and his body was hardened with the life he led, but still, the skin of the left side was fair and young.

"Stop it, Liadan," he said unevenly. "Don't—don't do that, not unless—"

"Not unless what?"

"Not unless you want me to take you again," he said, lifting me up very gently.

"That would be—quite acceptable," I answered. "Unless you have had enough?"

He let out his breath and put his arms around me, and I felt the rapid beat of his heart against me. "Never," he said fiercely, his lips against my hair. "I could never have enough of you." Then we lay down again together, and this time we were slow and careful and it was different, but just as sweet, as we touched and tasted and learned each other.

We did not sleep much that night. Perhaps each of us knew that time was passing all too quickly; that when dawn broke, tomorrow would be today, and choices would have to be made, and the unthinkable faced. Who would squander such a precious night in sleep? So we touched and whispered and moved together in the darkness. My heart was so full it threatened to spill over, and I thought: This feeling I will keep always, no matter what happens. Even if . . . even when . . . Toward daybreak he did fall asleep, with his head on my breast; and once in his dreams he cried out words I could not distinguish, and moved his arm violently as if pushing something away.

"Hush," I said, my heart thumping. "Hush, Bran. I'm here. You're safe. It's all right." I held him in the circle of my arms as I stared up at the arch of the high roof and watched the slow brightening of the light through the narrow space there. *Let it not be dawn yet,* I pleaded silently. *Please, not yet.* But the rain was gone, and the sun was rising, and the song of woodland birds began to flute through the crisp air. And at last I could pretend no longer that this dark, secret space that held the two of us was real and that other place the dream.

In silence we rose and dressed, and I folded blankets while he went out and tended to the horse and searched for dry wood. What could be said? Who would dare to begin? When the fire was made and water heating over it, we did not sit on opposite sides as we had always done before but close by each other, bodies touching, hands clasped fast.

The light brightened around us. There were no signposts here, no landmarks. We were adrift in this place together.

"You said, a fair trade," Bran managed finally, sounding as if he had to drag the words out. "Question for question, maybe?"

"That depends. Who asks the first question?"

He touched his lips to my cheek, very lightly. "You do, Liadan."

I took a deep breath. "Will you tell me your name now? The real one? Would you trust me with that?"

"I am content with the name you chose for me."

"That's no answer."

"What if I told you the name I was given is forgotten?" His hand grew tense in mine. "That I came to believe my name was wretch, scum, cur, filth, that I heard these names so long I could remember no other? A name is pride; it is a place. A worthless creature has no name but a curse."

I could hardly speak. "Is this why you . . . can you tell me when you . . ." My fingers moved softly against the inside of his wrist, where there was a tiny break in the intricate pattern. A plain space, a neat oval; and in the center, a small design of an insect, a bee I thought it was. Simply done, but perfect in every detail, finely veined wings, delicate legs, fat, neatly striped body. It was the only place on him where such a clear picture was made.

"You understand almost too well," he said grimly. "I bore those curses a long time. When I was nine years old I determined I was a man, and I—broke away from that life. Moved on. From that time I have made my own way. This," and he touched the little insect, "was the beginning. I had heard of a craftsman who did such work for a price. He told me I was too young, too small for what I asked him. But all that I had was this body, these hands. The past was gone; I'd erased it. The future was unimaginable. I needed . . . well, he listened to me and he told me, come back when you are fifteen years old and grown. Then I will do as you ask. But

I insisted, and in the end he said, very well, one little pattern now, the rest when you are a man. I am a man, I said. At least he did not laugh at me. And he made this, very small as you see, but it was a start. The rest came later and over a long time."

"Did you choose this pattern? This—small creature?"

He nodded.

"Why this?"

"You've had four questions," he said, with a trace of a smile. "I—I am not sure. Perhaps I remembered it from somewhere. I cannot tell you."

He got up and busied himself with the fire. There was food: little wild plums, crisp and sour; hard bread that could be chewed if you dipped it in a cup of hot water. Suitable rations for a traveling man.

"My turn," he said. I nodded, expecting that he would ask who I was and where I came from. I would have to tell him. I would have to trust him.

"Why me?" he asked, staring into the distance. "Why me, of all the men you could have chosen, to be the first; why take a—why choose an outcast, a man whose every action you despise? Why throw yourself away on—on gutter scum?"

The silence drew out, as birds busied themselves in the trees around us.

"You must answer," he said severely. "I will know if you lie to me." He was not touching me now but sat slightly apart, arms around his knees, his expression forbidding. How could I answer? Didn't he know? Couldn't he tell the answer from the way I touched him, from the way I looked at him? Who could put such feelings into words?

"I—I did not intend it to happen this way," I said faintly. "But—I had no choice."

"You did this out of pity? You gave yourself, thinking to change me, perhaps, to remake me in a form more acceptable to you? The ultimate act of healing?"

"Stop it!" I exclaimed violently, jumping to my feet. "How can you say that? How can you think that after last night? I have not lied to you, not in my words nor in my actions. I chose you willingly, knowing what you are and what you do. I want no other. I will have no other. Can't you see that? Can't you understand that?"

When I turned back toward him, he had both hands over his face.

"Bran?" I said softly after a while, and I knelt in front of him and lifted his hands away. No wonder he had shielded his eyes, for they were stripped of any armor now and their clear, gray depths held hope and terror in equal parts.

"Do you believe me?" I asked him.

"You've no reason to lie to me. But I did not think . . . I could not believe . . . Stay with me, Liadan." His hands tightened around mine and there was a sudden violence in his tone that made my heart thump.

"That's not the most practical suggestion I've heard you make," I said shakily.

Bran drew a deep breath, and when he spoke again it was with extreme diffidence, his voice under tight control. "This is no life for a woman, I know that. I would not expect that. But I am not without resources. I have a place; I think you would like it. I could provide for you." He would not meet my eyes as he said this.

"I can't," I said bluntly. "I must go home to Sevenwaters. My mother is very sick, she has little time left. They need me. At least until Beltaine, I must remain there. After that, there may be choices."

I knew, the instant I said this, that something had gone terribly wrong. His face changed as abruptly as if a mummer's mask had been slipped over it, and he unclasped his hands from mine quite slowly and carefully. He was again the Painted Man. But his voice was dark with shock and pain.

"What did you say?"

"I . . . I said I must go home now. I am needed. . . . Bran, what is it? What's wrong?" My heart was hammering. His eyes were so cold, remote as a stranger's.

"Home to Sevenwaters. That was what you said, wasn't it?"

"Y-Yes. That is the name of my home. I am a daughter of that household."

His eyes narrowed. "Your father—your father's name is Liam? Lord of Sevenwaters?"

"You know him?"

"Answer the question."

"Liam is my uncle. My father's name is Iubdan. B-But my brother is heir to Sevenwaters. We are all of the same family."

"You'd better tell me straight. This man—Iubdan. Liam's brother? Cousin?"

"What does that matter? Why are you so angry with me? Surely nothing has changed, surely—"

"Don't put your hand on me. Answer the question. This man Iubdan, has he another name?"

"Yes."

"Curse you, Liadan, tell me!"

My whole body was cold. "That is the only name he bears now. The name was chosen for its likeness to the name he had once, before he wed my mother. His name was Hugh."

"A Briton. Hugh of Harrowfield." He spoke this name as if its owner were the lowest form of life imaginable.

"He is my father."

"And your mother is—is—"

"Her name is Sorcha." Through my shock, I was starting to feel the first spark of anger. "Liam's sister. I am proud to be their daughter, Bran. They are good people. Fine people."

"Hah!" That explosion of scorn again. He got abruptly to his feet, striding away to stand staring out toward the trees. When he began to speak again, it was softly; and it was not to me he was talking.

"*. . . this was never for you, bitch's whelp . . . weak, you are, piss-weak, fit to live only in the darkness . . . how could you believe for an instant . . . go back to your box, cur . . .*"

"Bran,"—I spoke as firmly as I could, despite my thudding heart—"what is this? I am still the same woman you held in your arms at daybreak. You must tell me what's wrong."

"She taught you well, didn't she?" he said, with his back to me. "Your mother. How to turn a man from his path and weaken his resolve and twist him to your will? She was expert at that."

I was speechless.

"When you go home, tell her I am not as weak as he was, the estimable Hugh of Harrowfield. I see through your tricks; I know your performance for what it is. That I ever believed—that I was fool enough to trust—that was indeed stupid. I will not make such an error again."

There was no way I could make sense of his words.

"My mother never—if you knew her, you would realize—"

"Oh, no, that won't do," he said, turning back toward me. "That woman and the man she bewitched, they made me this creature you see here: the man without a conscience, the man with no name, who has no talents save for killing, who has no identity but the one graven on his skin. They took from me my family and my birthright; they took my name. Maybe they told you different. But she stole your father away from his rightful place. He abandoned his duty to follow her. Because of that I lost everything. Because of them, I . . . I am indeed worthless, scum of the earth."

"But—"

"The irony of it. You would think someone out there played a game with us. How could it be by chance that the one woman I—that the woman who brought me so close to forgetting—that you should be her daughter. That cannot be random. This is my punishment, my doom for daring to believe there could be a future."

"Bran—"

"Hold your tongue! Don't use that name! Pack your things and go; I don't want you here one instant longer."

A cold stone in the heart. That was how it felt. There wasn't much to pack. When it was done, I went down the hill and stood for a moment by Evan's grave. I could barely tell where the earth had been disturbed. It would not be long before every sign was gone.

"Farewell, friend," I whispered.

Bran had brought the horse out, and now she wore a blanket saddle, neatly strapped in place. He had tied my small bag behind this. A water bottle. His coat, rolled up and fastened with a length of rope. That was a little odd.

"She will carry you safely home," he said. "You need not trouble yourself to return her. Call it—payment for services rendered."

I felt the blood drain from my face. I lifted my hand and struck him hard across the cheek, and watched as a red mark stained the clear skin. He made no attempt to avoid the blow.

"You'd better go," he said coolly. "Make for the east; the road goes through that way, then south to Littlefolds. It's not so very far."

Then his hands came around my waist, and he lifted me into the saddle; but one hand still lay against my thigh as if he could not quite let go.

"Liadan," he said, staring intently at the ground.

"Yes," I whispered.

"Don't wed that man Eamonn. Tell him, if he takes you, he's a dead man." His tone was intense. It was a vow.

"But—"

Then he slapped the horse on the rump, and, obedient beast that she was, she headed off at a sharp canter. And be-

fore I could form the words for good-bye, he was lost from
sight, and it was too late.

There was no point in being angry. This was over. I would
never see the Painted Man again. It was time to go home;
and before it was dark of the moon again, all this would be
fading into memory like some fantastic dream. I whispered
this to the sturdy gray mare as she made her steady way
eastward under the trees, and by lonely brooks and still
tarns, and carefully between the rocks toward the road. I
had no need to direct her steps; she seemed to know her
way.

When the sun was high in the sky, we rested by a stream.
She drank and cropped the grass. I unfastened my pack and
discovered hard cheese and dry bread wrapped in a cloth.
For a man who could not wait to see the last of me, he had
been surprisingly thorough. I supposed he simply followed
the well-practiced pattern of hasty departures, of decisions
taken on the run. That was his life. It dealt him one blow after another, and he took them and moved on. I tried very
hard not to think of him. Home. That was where I must direct my thoughts. Sometime, when I was far enough away, I
must use the power of the mind to send a message to my
brother Sean, so he could ride out to meet me. Not yet, I
thought. Do this too early, and I risked drawing the forces
of Sevenwaters down on Bran and his men. I had felt it
from time to time in the encampment, a tug at the thoughts,
an intrusion in the mind, my brother calling silently, *Liadan! Liadan, where are you?* But I had shut myself off
from him. If anyone were to betray the band of the Painted
Man and destroy their fellowship, it would not be me.

We moved on. I was growing weary. There had been little sleep; and despite myself I heard, over and over, the
words of that morning in my head. *Don't put your hand on
me. I don't want you here one instant longer. Call it pay-*

ment for services rendered. I told myself not to be foolish. What had I expected? That I could change his life forever as he had changed mine?

I set my thoughts ahead, to home and to my return. What could I tell my family? Not where I had been; nothing of the outlaws who had sought my help, and who had, against all odds, become my friends. Certainly, nothing of the man to whom I had so rashly given myself. Had I not repeated my sister's error? It followed, then, that if the truth were known I could expect no better treatment than poor Niamh had been given: a hasty marriage and prompt banishment, away from family and friends, away from the forest. A shiver ran through me. Sevenwaters was my home; its dark loveliness was lodged in my very spirit. But I had changed things; I had lain with the Painted Man; and no matter how cruel his words of rejection, he, too, was now a part of me. I wanted to tell the truth; I wanted to ask my father what dark secret of the past had led to this man's bitter hatred of me and mine. If I did not tell, I would never know why Bran had sent me away. And yet, I could not tell.

There were hoofbeats alongside me, to left and to right. Little, trotting hoofbeats; a prancing, delicate gait. My horse shivered, twitching her ears nervously. I glanced around. There was nobody there. Afternoon shadows trembled in the summer breeze. I thought I heard a faint tinkle of laughter. And still the accompanying footsteps, as of unseen creatures by my side. My heart thumping, I reined in the mare and waited, silent. The sound ceased.

"All right," I said as calmly as I could, trying to remember everything Iubdan had taught me about self-defense. "Where are you? Who are you? Come out and show yourselves!" And I took the little dagger my father had given me from my belt and held it ready, for what I did not know.

There was a short pause.

"You won't be needing that. Not yet." On my right sat a man on a horse. An almost-man on an almost-horse. He had not materialized in an instant; it was more as if he had been there all along, but I had been unable to see him until he wished to be seen. His hair was the same improbable shade as his mount, bright poppy-red, and his garments were many hued, changeable as a sunset. He was extremely tall.

"Keep riding," advised a voice from my other side, and my mare moved forward without guidance. "It's a long way back to the forest." The woman who spoke was black-haired, blue-cloaked, palely beautiful. I had sometimes wondered if I would ever see them as my mother had: the Lady of the Forest and the flame-haired lord who was her consort. I swallowed and found my voice.

"Wh-what is it you want of me?" I said, still staring in wonder at their tall, stately forms and the fragile not-horses that they rode.

"Obedience," said the lord, turning his too-bright eyes on me. Looking at him was like gazing into the heart of a great fire. Stare too long and you would be burned.

"Common sense," said the lady.

"I'm on my way home." I could not imagine how anything I did could interest such grand folk in the slightest. "I have a good horse to take me, and warm clothes, and a weapon I know how to use. In the morning I will send for my brother. Is not that common sense?"

The lord roared with laughter, a sound so full throated the very ground shook with it. I felt the shudder through the little gray horse's body, but she went gamely forward.

"It's not enough." The lady's voice was softer, but very serious. "We want a promise from you, Liadan."

I did not like the sound of that. A promise made to the Fair Folk was a promise that must be kept, if one had any sense whatever. The consequences of breaking such a vow were unthinkable. These folk possessed power beyond imagining. It was in all the tales.

"What promise?"

"The very fate of Sevenwaters, and of the Islands, may be in your own hands," said the bright-haired man.

"The very future of your kind, and of our kind, may depend on you," agreed the lady.

"What can you mean?" Perhaps I sounded a little churlish. It had been a long day.

The lady sighed. "We hoped to see, in the children of Sevenwaters, one who might combine the strength and patience of your father with the rare talents of your mother. One who might at last fulfill our long quest. You have disappointed us. It seems you are a coarser kind, understanding little beyond the lusts of the flesh. Your sister was enticed to lose her way; your own choice was most unwise. You should not have listened to the voices."

"Voices?"

"The voices of the earth, there in the Old Place. You should not have heeded them."

I was trembling, poised between fear and anger. "Forgive me," I said, "but were not they voices of Fair Folk such as yourself?"

She shook her head, brows raised in disbelief at my ignorance. "An older kind. Primitive. We banished them, but still they linger. They will lead you astray, Liadan. Indeed, they have done. You must not heed their blandishments."

I scowled. "I'm capable of making my own choices without need for any—blandishments, as you put it. I don't regret anything I have done. Anyway, what about the prophecy? Won't that come true some day? Although you dismiss me and my sister, there is another child, my brother Sean. A fine young man who never set a foot wrong. Why don't you just ignore me and let me get on with my life?"

"Oh no, I don't think we can do that—not now."

"What do you mean, not now?"

"Prophecies don't simply come about of themselves, you know. They need a little helping along." The lord wore a sly expression as he glanced at me sideways with his glowing eyes. "We hoped for children. I'll tell you one thing. We weren't expecting *you*."

I thought of my mother's words, about how I had come as a surprise to all of them, the unexpected twin. How it gave me the power to change things.

"I have a question," I said.

They waited.

"Why did you lead me to discover my sister and—and her lover, in the woods? They sent her away, and she was bitterly unhappy. Ciarán, too. It made the family blame each other and turned everything to sorrow. Why would you do such a thing?"

There was a silence. He looked at her, and she looked at him.

"The old evil is awake," said the lady eventually, and there was a shadow in her voice. "We must use what strength we have to stop it. What we did was for the best. What your sister wanted could not be. These men and women, they are unimportant with their petty woes and grievances. They serve their purpose, that is all. Only the child is important."

"The old evil?" I asked through gritted teeth. Perhaps she did not realize how angry her words had made me, with their callous disregard for the suffering of my own kind.

"It is returned," she said solemnly, her deep blue eyes intent on my face. "We thought it defeated; we were wrong. Now all of us face the end; we are squeezed tighter and tighter, and without the child, we will not overcome this. You must return home, Liadan, straightaway. This dalliance is over."

"I know that," I said, annoyed to find tears pricking my eyes. "I told you, I'm going now."

The lord cleared his throat. "There are two young men who lust for you: the one you leave, and the one to whom you return. Neither is suitable. You show regrettable taste in your choice of a mate. Still, there is no need for you to wed. Forget them both. Return to the forest and stay there."

I gaped at him. "It would help if you explained a little. What evil? What end?"

"Your kind cannot understand," he said dismissively. "Your scope is very limited. You must learn to disregard the stirrings of the flesh and the achings of the heart. These are paltry things, fleeting as youth. It is the greater good that counts."

"You insult me," I said, "and then expect blind obedience."

"And you waste time when there is none to spare." The lord's voice now held a new edge of menace. "You snap back like a little wild thing caught in a trap. You would do better to recognize your weakness and comply. We can help you. We can protect you. But not if you follow this willful path. That way lie dangers you can scarce dream of." He lifted his hand, sweeping it in a long arc before him, and it seemed to me a shadow passed there; grasses flattened as if cowering before it, trees shivered, bushes rustled, birds gave a sudden outcry, then fell silent.

"We face again a foe who threatened us long since," the lady said. "We thought her defeated, but she found a way to slip under our guard. She has evaded both Fair Folk and human folk, and now she twists her evil hand around the very future of our race."

I stared at her, horrified. "But—but I am an ordinary woman, as you see. How can my choice play any part in such grand and perilous things? Why must I promise to remain at Sevenwaters?"

The lord sighed. "As I said, this is beyond your comprehension. I see no reason for your resistance, save sheer stubbornness. You must do as we bid you."

He seemed to grow larger as I watched, and flickering

light ran up his body, as if he were aflame. His eyes were piercing; he held my gaze relentlessly, and my head throbbed with pain.

The lady spoke softly, but there was a core of iron in her tone. "Do not disobey, Liadan. To do so is to endanger more than you can understand."

"Promise," said the lord, and his hair seemed to rise around his noble head like a crown of glittering fire.

"Promise," echoed the lady, with a sadness in her voice that wrung the very heart.

I squeezed the gray mare's sides with my knees, and she moved forward; and this time they did not ride alongside but remained behind. Their voices followed me, commanding, beseeching: *Promise. Promise.*

"I can't," I said, in a little whisper that came from deep inside me. It was very strange, for up to that point I had intended to do just as they wished: return to Sevenwaters, take up the threads of my old life and do my best to forget all about the Painted Man and his followers. But something had changed. I would not offer unquestioning obedience to folk who dismissed the anguish of those dear to me as too paltry for consideration. Somehow I knew I could not agree to their request. "I must make my own decisions and go my own way," I said. "For now, I will indeed ride home to Sevenwaters and can see no reason why I would not stay there. But the future—that is unknown; who knows what may come to pass? I will make you no promises."

Their voices came again, with an angry power that sent a deep shudder through my body. The mare felt it, too; she trembled under me. *You will do as we command, Liadan. Indeed, you must.* But I did not reply; and the next time I looked behind me, they were gone.

It was late afternoon, almost dusk. I had reached the road and followed it southward as the sun set in a brilliant display of gold and rose. What was the old saying? Red sky at night, shepherd's delight. Red sky in the morning, shep-

herd's warning. I smiled to myself. No doubt where I had
heard that one. My father, holding me up in his arms as he
stood on a hilltop with his young oak trees around him,
showing me how the sun went down in the west, over the
land of Tir na nOg beyond the sea. Every night it went
down, and tonight's sky would tell of tomorrow. Learn to
read the signs, little one, he told me. The Fair Folk had chosen him as the father of a child they wanted born, had chosen him for his strength and patience. Surely, then, Bran
was mistaken. The Big Man, so quiet and deep, with his
reverence for all things that lived and grew, could never
have committed some act of evil that blighted a man's
whole existence.

The mare whinnied softly and came to a sudden halt.
There was a disturbance ahead of us on the road. Men's
voices, hoofbeats, the clash of metal. We retreated in silence under the shelter of the trees, and I dismounted in the
shadows. The sounds came closer. In the fading light I
could distinguish four or five men in dark green and one
dressed in a strange garment of leather and wolfskin, a man
with a half-shaven head who fought like a mad thing, so
that at times you might almost believe he would be a match
for them, outnumbered as he was. A man whose great
height and massive build gave him an advantage, but not
such an advantage that he could not at length be unhorsed
and disarmed and at the mercy of his enemy. There were
shouts of derision and words of defiance. There were growls
and hisses and oaths, and somebody yelled something
about retribution, and there were cries and curses as
weapons found their mark. But at the last, there was near silence, save for the thud of kicks and blows raining down on
the man who lay huddled in the road, with his attackers
around him in a tight circle. There was nothing I could do.
How could I step out and identify myself? How could I seek
to prevent this one-sided act of barbarity without, at the
same time, revealing where I had been? What cause would

a good girl like myself possibly have for defending a thug of an outlaw? Besides, in the bloody melee they might well not notice me before I fell to thrusting sword or swinging axe myself. So I stood completely still, with the horse obediently silent by me, until one of them said, "Enough. Leave him to stew in his own juice." The men in green mounted, took the other man's horse by the bridle and rode away to the south.

I came out cautiously. There was not much light left; I found him as much by the faint, bubbling sound of his breathing as by sight. I knelt down beside him.

"Dog?"

He was lying on his side, face contorted in agony. He had both hands on his stomach, and something lying on the ground by him. Blood, and . . . Díancécht help me, his belly had been slit two ways and spilled his vitals forth, and he strained to hold his very self together.

There were words, gasped out on a desperate, squealing mouthful of air. But I could only make out one.

". . . knife . . ."

And I found that, when it came to the point, there was indeed no choice. My hands shook violently as I out took the little sharp dagger my father had given me.

"Shut your eyes," I whispered shakily. I knelt by his convulsing body in the fading light, and I touched the point of the dagger carefully to the hollow below his ear. Then I shut my eyes and drew the blade across his neck, fast, pressing down with all my strength, while my heart pounded and my throat tightened and my stomach heaved in protest. Warm blood gushed over my hands. The horse shifted uneasily. Dog's body went limp, and his arms fell away from the great slicing wound in his belly, and . . . I got up abruptly and backed away, and for a long time I could only lean against a tree, retching, gasping, emptying my stomach of its contents, eyes and nose streaming, head throbbing with outrage. Logical thought was not possible. Only a blazing resentment, a gut-wrenching revulsion. The Painted Man. Eamonn of the Marshes. It was six of one and half a dozen of the other. Between them, they had made sure there would be no tomorrow for this man. It would be I who bore the scar of this on my spirit, while they shrugged it off and went on with their mindless pursuit of each other.

At last the moon spread a faint silver light over the desolate stretch of road, and I felt the mare nuzzle my shoulder, gentle but insistent.

"All right," I said. "All right, I know." Time to move on. But I could not leave him like this. Could not shift him; too heavy. In the delicate light his face was peaceful, the yellow eyes closed, the pockmarked features at rest. I tried not to look at the gaping wound in his neck.

"Dana, take this man to your heart," I muttered, slipping off the borrowed shirt I wore over my gown. Something glinted in the moonlight. The leather strip was severed neatly; when I lifted the necklace it left blood on my fingers. "Fierce as a great wolf," I said, as my tears began to flow. "Strong as a fearless hound that gives its life for its master. Gentle as the most faithful dog that ever walked by a woman's side. Go to your rest now." I laid the shirt over his face and chest. Then I struggled back onto the mare and we made our way southward until I judged it was far enough. There was a place of shelter in the lee of a stack of straw. I unrolled Bran's coat and put it around me. I lay down, and the horse settled beside me, as if she knew I needed her warmth to keep away the dark. I had never come closer to wishing I would fall asleep and never wake up.

The next morning I rode farther south, and I saw a few farmers in their carts and one or two other travelers; and all looked at me curiously, but nobody spoke. I suppose I did look a bit of a sight, with my hair straggling down my back, and my clothes marked with blood and vomit. Some crazy woman. When I judged I was near enough to Littlefolds, I stopped by the way, and I opened my mind to my brother at last. Showed him just enough, with images carefully chosen, so he could find me. I sat down under a rowan tree and waited. He cannot have been so far away. Before the sun was at its peak, there was a thundering of hooves on the road, and Sean was there, leaping off his horse, hugging me hard, and looking searchingly into my eyes. But they were as carefully guarded as my thoughts. I had reached out to him; but I had told him nothing. After a while I noticed that Eamonn was there, too, and several of his men. Eamonn's face wore a strange expression; eyes burning, face ash white. He did not embrace me; that would not be correct. But his voice shook as he greeted me.

"Liadan! We thought—are you harmed? Are you hurt?"

"I'm fine," I said wearily, as the men in green brought their horses to a halt behind him.

"You don't look fine," said Sean bluntly. "Where were you? Who took you? Where have you been?" My brother knew I was keeping him out, and he used all the tricks he knew with his mind to try to make me open up.

"I'm fine," I said again. "Can we go home now?"

Eamonn was looking at my horse; and he was looking at the big gray coat I wore, a man's coat. He was frowning. Sean was looking at my face and at my bloodstained hands.

"We'll ride as far as Sídhe Dubh," he said soberly. "You can rest there."

"No!" I said a little too vehemently. "No," I added more carefully. "Home. I want to go home now."

The two men exchanged glances.

"It may be better if you ride ahead with your men," Sean said. "Get word to the Big Man. He'll want to meet us. We'll rest by the way, take our time."

Eamonn gave a curt nod and rode off without another word. The men in green followed him. There was just my brother and two men at arms and me.

All the way home Sean questioned me. Where had I been? Who had taken me? Why wouldn't I tell him; didn't I understand there must be vengeance if I had been harmed in any way? Did I forget that he was my brother? But I would not tell. Bran had been right. You could not trust; not even those closest to you.

So I rode back to Sevenwaters on the Painted Man's horse, with his coat to keep me warm, with a necklace of wolf claws in my pocket and blood on my hands. So much for being able to change things. So much for the Fair Folk and ancient voices and visions of death. What was I but one more powerless woman in a world of unthinking men? Nothing had changed. Nothing at all, save deep inside, where nobody could see.

Chapter Seven

The day after I came home, I made a candle. There was nothing so remarkable about this; such crafting was a regular part of the household's work. But I was supposed to be resting. Mother checked my bedchamber, found the floor swept clean and the quilt neat and flat, and sought me out where I worked in the stillroom, my newly washed hair drawn back tightly by a linen band. If she saw my lips swollen and bruised, if she recognized bite marks on my neck, she did not comment on them. Instead, she watched my hands as they marked one side of the beeswax methodically in an intricate design of spiral and whorl and cross-hatching. The other side was plain. I said nothing. When it was done to my satisfaction, I set it in a sturdy holder, and around the base I tied the severed strip of leather with wolf claws strung on it and a little garland I had fashioned. At last my mother spoke.

"This is a powerful charm: dogwood, yarrow, and juniper, apple and lavender. And are those the feathers from a raven's wing? Where will this candle burn, Daughter?"

"In my window."

Mother nodded. She had asked me no real questions.

"Your beacon has been made with herbs of protection and herbs of love. I understand its purpose. Perhaps it is as well your father and brother do not. You close yourself off from Sean. That hurts him."

I glanced at her. Concern was written on her small features, but her eyes, as usual, were deep and calm. Of them all, only she had believed me when I said I was all right. The others saw the fading bruises on my wrist, the bite marks, the stains on my clothing, and leapt to conclusions. Their anger burned bright.

"I have no choice," I said.

"Mmm." Sorcha nodded. "And it is not yourself you are protecting. You have a great capacity to love; you give freely, Daughter. And like your father, you lay yourself open to hurt."

The candle was finished. It would burn for many nights. It would burn steadfast at dark of the moon, lighting the way home.

"I have no choice," I said again, and as I went out I bent to kiss my mother's brow. Her shoulder under my fingers was fragile as a bird's.

There were many questions. Liam had questions. How were you taken? What manner of men were they? Did you know three of my men were slain guarding you? Where did they take you? North? Morrigan curse your stubbornness, Liadan! This could be vitally important! Sean had his own questions, but after a while he stopped asking them. I felt his hurt and his worry as if it were my own, for thus it always was with the two of us. But this time I was unable to help him.

As for my father, with him I needed all my will to remain

silent. He sat quietly in the garden, watching me work, and he said, "For all that time I did not know if you were alive or dead. I have lost one daughter already, and your mother walks in shadow. I would do anything in my power to keep you safe, Liadan. But I will wait until you are ready to tell me, sweetheart."

"You might have a fair wait."

Iubdan nodded. "As long as you are home, and safe," he said quietly.

Eamonn came to visit, and I refused to see him. Maybe that was discourteous of me, but nobody insisted. It was put down to my feeling poorly after my experience and needing to rest. What Eamonn said, I did not know, but the men of the household were rather tight-lipped after his departure. In truth I had recovered remarkably quickly and soon found myself full of energy, eating heartily, and sleeping sound as a child while my candle conjured strange shadows on the walls around me. The one thing I could not come to terms with, for it was a feeling quite new and strange to me, was the ache within me, the longing to be held, the need to touch and be close and at length to rise again to that peak of joy that no words can describe. It is hard to explain. There was no doubt I felt the lusts of the body, the hot urge of a creature for its mate. But that was not all. I had seen the hand of death over Bran, and over myself, at the mouth of the ancient barrow. I sensed our fates were intertwined; we were closer than any mates or lovers or partners. This was a link that would transcend death, an unbreakable bond. This seemed ever clearer to me, a certainty that could not be questioned. It made no difference that he had sent me away. This was and would be. And as for the Fair Folk, if they wanted me to make some sort of commitment, they would need to provide better explanations. Unquestioning compliance with their wishes was not my idea of common sense.

I longed for Niamh to be home. Some things you can talk of only with your sister. I wanted to tell her that I understood now why she had acted as she did, though at the time it had seemed to me blind and selfish. That I knew how it must hurt her, each day without Ciarán, giving herself to another man, each day alone among a sea of strangers, thinking only of him, wondering where he was, if he was safe, dreaming of the touch she would never feel again.

Life went back to its old pattern. The same, and yet not the same. We all missed Niamh, but nobody spoke of that. What was done was done; you could not rewrite the past. As for me, it seemed all of them were just a step farther away from me. They mistrusted my silences, my need to be alone with my thoughts. It was different with Mother. She had her own idea of the truth, and she stopped Liam from questioning me further.

One evening not long past Lugnasad, in the chill of the season's change, a messenger came from Tirconnell with welcome news. There was to be a gathering in the south; the chieftains of many clans were summoned to Tara by the high king, and Fionn would go as his father's representative. There might be no love lost between the two factions of the Uí Néill, but it would be more than folly to spurn such an invitation. Often enough, as the generations passed, the title of Ard Ri, or high king, had gone from one branch of this great family to the other and back again. Liam, too, was to attend. Best news of all, Fionn would bring his wife with him, at least as far as Sevenwaters, so I would see my sister again.

Linen was aired and floors swept; preparations were made in kitchens and stableyard for an influx of visitors. I had intended to make myself useful, helping Janis and her women with salting and brewing. But the strong smell of the ale seemed to turn my stomach, and I had to make a hurried excuse and retreat outside to retch up my breakfast under a rowan bush. I supposed I had eaten too much. I always seemed to be hungry these days. Later, I felt fine, and dismissed my malady as nothing important. But when it happened again the next day, and the next, I stayed away from the kitchens in the mornings, restricting myself to pruning, sweeping, harvesting seed, drying and storing herbs. I worked extremely hard. I was always busy. I allowed myself no time to think.

Dark of the moon came and went, and came again. On these nights I did not sleep. Instead, I would sit by the window where the candle burned, and I would think of that small child who had stretched out his hand to me in the darkness, in the nightmare. *Don't let go.* In my mind I took this child, who was also a man, and I wrapped my arms around him and held him next to my heart until the first touch of dawn brushed the sky. And although I never spoke aloud, I talked to him constantly through the shadows that encircled him. *I'm here. You're safe now, I have you safe. I won't let go.* Dawn always came at last. The sun always rose, and it was a new day. I told him that; and when it was light enough for him to see his way, I blew out the candle, touched the raven feather gently with my fingertips, and went out, yawning, to start the day's work.

It was a year of good harvest. Iubdan could be seen everywhere, his great height and his bright hair marking him out from the other men of the household as he oversaw the gathering of root crops, the culling of cattle, the slaughtering of sheep for salting and drying, the mending of roof and wall to guard cottager and herd beast against winter's eager grasp. Sean was often by his side, a slighter figure, his hair as dark and wild as our mother's. There was no Aisling to divert him, for their own harvest kept her and her brother away from Sevenwaters, and I was glad of it. Liam was preparing for his journey south, sending and receiving many messages, planning, consulting with his captains. Although Sean was privy to these meetings, he would not travel to the high king's gathering. Ever a strategist, Liam was taking his time before he exposed his nephew too openly to that influential and dangerous circle. He thought my brother still too young to play the delicate games of power. In time Sean would be lord of Sevenwaters. He must learn to be always a step ahead of his neighbors, for a neighbor could turn from ally to enemy in an instant. Liam taught these lessons well, biding his time until Sean should lose the rashness of youth and prove himself a true leader of men.

It suited me well that the household was so busy, for harvest and gathering took folk's attention away from me. Niamh and her husband would be here at Meán Fómhair, when night equals day, and we stand on the threshold of darkness. Through that doorway is the keeper of births and deaths. Ancient crone she may be, but with great age comes a wisdom beyond measure. At the turning time, her counsel can be sought by those with the courage to open their minds to her voice. And oh, I needed wisdom, I needed guidance, and soon. But not from the Fair Folk. I knew what they would say, and I was starting to have an inkling of what might lie behind it. I was starting to feel trapped, and I did not like it at all.

I cut off the hem of Bran's coat, so I could wear it out of doors without picking up too much mud. Once I had cleaned the length of fabric I cut it into neat squares, and laid them away in the small oak chest by my bed. I had some other pieces ready. Fragments of an old shirt of my father's softened with wear. A pretty rose-colored wool from one of Niamh's gowns. I had prepared the dye for this myself, a long time ago. She had worn it happily until another became her favorite. There were scraps of a practical homespun, part of my ruined riding dress. Cut from the back because, when I looked at it, that was the only part that was not beyond saving, so stained was the gown with blood and vomit and other unthinkable things. After I cut my small patches, the garment was burned. I shed no tears over it. I tried not to think about it. Instead I worked. The stillroom had perhaps never been so well stocked, the garden seldom so tidy, not a ragged shoot or unwelcome weed in sight. And then it was almost dark of the moon again, and my mother came in one day as I was stringing rosehips for drying, and I realized I had been humming under my breath a little fragment of an old, old lullaby.

"Don't stop," said Sorcha, settling herself on the window seat, a tiny shadow with huge eyes like the smallest and most delicate of white owls. "I like to hear you singing. I know then that you are well, despite everything. An unhappy woman does not sing."

I glanced at her and went back to my rosehips. They hung on my thread like bright drops of lifeblood. Where was he? In what distant land did he risk his life now for some stranger's bag of silver? Under what exotic tree, in what odd company did he lie awake at night, weapon in hand, waiting silent for the dawn?

"Liadan."

I turned toward her.

"Sit down, Liadan. I've brought something for you."

Taken aback, I did as I was told. She shook out the bundle of cloth she was holding.

"You know this gown, of course. It's very old. Too old, now, to be worn anymore." Her hand stroked the faded blue fabric; her thin fingers touched the ancient embroidery, now almost invisible. "I thought you might salvage a section here, and maybe here. You'd have to hem the edges very finely. But you're clever with a needle. There was a day when the sea and the sand touched these skirts, such a day as you see but once in a lifetime . . . and I wore it again on a day of fire and blood. I need keep the gown no longer to remember; both days are imprinted on my heart. Whatever it is you are making for your child, this fabric must be a part of it."

There was a lengthy silence, during which, eventually, I got up, brewed a pan of mint tea and poured it into two cups. I placed one on the stone sill by my mother and could no longer avoid meeting her gaze. She was smiling.

"Were you going to tell me, Daughter, or were you waiting for me to tell you?"

I choked on my tea.

"I—of course I would have told you. It's not you I fear telling, Mother."

She nodded. "I've only one question," she said, "and not the one you might expect. I would ask, was this child conceived in joy?"

I looked her straight in the eyes, and she read the answer on my face.

"Mmm." She nodded again. "I thought no less. Your walk, your little half-smile, your demeanor are not those of a woman injured or frightened. And yet he did not stay by you? How can that be?"

I sat down opposite her on a three-legged stool, letting the cup warm my hands. "He does not know of this child. Clearly, he could not. And he asked me to stay with him. I said no."

There was a pause. She sipped the tea, I think more to please me than out of any real appetite for it. "I thought perhaps," she said cautiously, "I thought perhaps this child was fathered by one of the—by one of those Others, and that this was how you disappeared without trace so that even the best efforts of Liam and Eamonn could find no sign of you. Is this the reason you hug this secret so tight within yourself, Liadan?"

An Otherworld child. I was almost tempted to say yes; it would have been a handy explanation.

"I did not journey beyond the margins, Mother, though I did—I did see the Fair Folk, and they spoke to me. This child's father is a mortal man, and I will not give his name."

"I see," she said slowly. "You saw them. So this, too, is part of the same pattern. Are we to know, in time, who has done this to you? Got you with child and vanished as if he had never been? Your father will expect to call this man to account; both Sean and Liam are likely to go further and speak of vengeance."

I said nothing. There was a breeze coming up outside; shadows of twig and dry leaf moved against the stone walls. There was the bright, slanting sun of an autumn morning, a light that teased, promising a warmth that would never follow.

"Mother." I could not stop my voice from shaking just a little.

"It's all right, Liadan. Tell me, if you can."

"That's part of the problem. I can't tell anyone, not even you. Mother—how can I speak of this to Father? I can't—I won't be married to a stranger as Niamh was. Nor will I bear my child in shame and silence. How can I tell him? How can I tell Sean, and Liam, and—and—"

"And Eamonn?" she asked gently.

I nodded miserably.

"Would your man return for you?" Mother asked, her face still tranquil. "Surely a man deserving of your love could not fail to do so."

"He—he lives a life of great risk," I managed. "There is no place in such a life for a wife and a child. And besides— no, never mind. He is—he is not a man Father would think . . . suitable. That's all I can say."

"Your father and Liam will wish you married," said Sorcha quietly. "You know this. They will not understand that you would rather bear your child alone."

"I've an answer to that," I said. "The Fair Folk gave me strict instructions to stay here at Sevenwaters. Forever, I think they meant. No need to wed, they said, neither Eamonn nor another. At the time I had no idea why they would bid me do so. Now I begin to understand."

Mother nodded, seemingly not at all surprised. "The child," she said softly, "it is the child who must stay in the forest. They intend you to raise the infant here. It's apt, Liadan. With—with what happened to Niamh, we saw the stirring of an evil we thought long gone. Perhaps your child is their weapon against that."

"The old evil? That is what they called it. What evil? What can be so terrible it threatens the Fair Folk themselves?"

Sorcha sighed. "We cannot be sure. Who can say what form such forces may take? You should heed the warnings you were given."

I frowned. "I don't like this. I told them so. I refused to promise. I will not be used as some tool for their purposes. Nor will my son." I had no doubt whatever this child would be a boy. His father, I thought, was surely a man who would breed sons.

"It's not wise to disregard their bidding," Mother said gravely. "We are the smallest of players in their long game. Its span is greater than we can recognize, Liadan. Still, in time their intent may become clearer to us. It concerns me that you will not name this man. How could one who would abandon you without a thought be worthy of such loyalty? Or is it shame that stops your words?"

I flushed scarlet. "No, Mother," I said firmly. "It's true, at first I did my best to deny this to myself. Not out of shame, but because I knew how difficult it would be, I suppose. I pretended I had not noticed the changes in my body, I ignored the passing of the season, the waxing and waning of the moon. But as his child grows inside me, I have been filled with a joy so strong, a power so intense I can think of nothing to which I can liken it. I feel as if—I feel as if I can hear the heart of the earth beating inside me."

Sorcha was quiet for a while.

"Believe me, Daughter," she said eventually, "this child is as precious to me as he is to you. Your words gladden me and frighten me. I will make you a promise, and you must trust me to keep it. I promise you I will still be here, in spring, to deliver your babe with my own hands. I will be here, Liadan."

I burst into tears, and she put her arms around me and hugged me as hard as she could; and I felt again how small and frail she had become. And yet, in that embrace there was a strength that flowed into me and through me; and I knew Bran had been wrong, wrong about Sorcha, wrong about Hugh of Harrowfield, who was my father. There was no evil here. Somewhere, somehow, the story had been twisted and changed, and I longed to put it right. Someday I would put it right.

"Don't weep, Daughter. Not for me."

"I'm sorry." I dashed the tears from my face.

"It's hard to understand your loyalty to this man. He loves you and will not return. He gives you his child and disappears. And yet you do everything to protect him. You guard his safety with an impenetrable wall of silence that shuts out even your brother. And you believe even that may not be enough. For something still gives you sleepless nights."

I did not respond.

"Is it love that binds you to this man?" she asked me.

There was a small, clear image in my mind. Myself seated on the little horse, and Bran standing by me, scowling, staring fiercely at the ground, his hand belying his expression, his patterned fingers lying warm against my thigh, the last touch. *Don't wed that man Eamonn. Tell him, if he takes you, he's a dead man.*

"What is it, Liadan?" There was alarm in Mother's voice. The goddess only knew what my face had shown.

"He and I—we share a bond. Not love, exactly. It goes beyond that. He is mine as surely as sun follows moon across the sky. Mine before ever I knew he existed. Mine until death and beyond. He is in terrible danger. From others and from himself. If I could do more to protect him, I would. But I will not speak of who, and what, he is. I cannot."

Sorcha nodded, her expression somber. "You cannot delay making this known for much longer. You have some difficult days ahead of you. I think you must tell Red this news yourself."

"I—I don't want him to speak to me as he did to Niamh. I don't want him to send me away with no kind word, as if I had become a stranger."

She sighed. "It was hard for them both. He has always seen something of himself in Niamh; he felt responsible, I think, for her weaknesses. He did try to make his peace with her; he wanted so much to explain his decision to her, as best he could, but she refused to listen. She shut herself off from the two of us. Your father regretted bitterly that he could not wait longer and explore other paths for Niamh. Conor bound us to silence, Liadan; we could not give you the full truth and cannot. My brothers believed that doing so would bring ill things down on all of you. They had good reason for this; in time, perhaps all will be made known. It is just because of what happened with Niamh, and the way it troubles him so, that your father is not likely to treat you so harshly. He sees in you and in Sean the strengths of my own family, the people of the forest. He has always trusted your judgment, as he does mine. Be honest with him, and he will do his best to understand."

"I scarcely know where to begin."

She rose, ready to depart. "Tell your father soon. Then I will tell Liam and Sean. You need not give this news over and over."

"Thank you." My throat was dry; I was suddenly terribly tired. "I would—I would rather wait, to make this known. I would like to wait until Niamh comes and tell her first."

There was a little frown on Sorcha's brow. "Your father can read me very well, especially now. I will not tell him; but he will sense it, and so you should not delay too long. We have no secrets from each other. Besides, soon enough it will be plain for all to see."

Neither of us mentioned Eamonn, but I had not forgotten

the roadside, and the men in green, and the friend whose throat I had slit in the darkness. Some things you never forget.

Our guests were expected any day. All was prepared. The evenings grew cold, and folk drank Janis's potent mulled wine; but I drank water, for the wine's strong smell still sickened me. Janis had her eye on me, and so did her kitchen women, but she kept their gossip under tight control. The men had no such insight. Their talk was all of strategies and dealings, and at times it grew heated. There was a simmering disquiet between Sean and Liam, and one night it came to a head.

A fire burned on the hearth in the small room where the family gathered for private talk. My mother was seated on a bench with Iubdan's supporting arm around her. He was quiet, tired perhaps after a long day in the fields. I registered the voices of Sean and Liam without really listening to their words. I was sewing a blanket. It was quite small. A square of gray here, a square of rose there. A border of homespun. A scrap of palest blue-violet, with a tracery of old, old embroidery. Delicate stitches; a trail of leaves, a tiny insect. My needle moved with precision, linking all together. My thoughts were far away. Then Sean spoke again.

"Perhaps you are too old," he said bluntly, jolting me back to the here and now. "Perhaps you cannot see that your caution prevents this matter from resolution."

"Sean." Iubdan spoke mildly enough. "You are not yet master of this house."

"Let him speak," said Liam, tight jawed.

Sean was pacing, arms folded. I sensed the frustration in him without understanding its cause.

"Haven't we tried, over and over, and been beaten back every time? Good men lost, their places taken by more good men, and those in their turn slain? This feud has poisoned our lives for generations. We fall in the cause, and fall again, and still we keep on coming. An outsider would call it senseless."

"An outsider cannot understand what the Islands mean to our family and to our people." My mother spoke softly. "There can be no harmony here, no balance, until they are returned. It's the Fair Folk who demand it of us."

"What about the prophecy?" I asked.

"A pox on the prophecy," snapped Sean. "Have we ever seen any sign of this mysterious individual who's supposed to deliver us? Neither of Erin nor of Britain, but both; sign of the raven, whatever that means. Somebody probably invented it one night after a bit too much ale. No, what's needed is a new approach. We must get away from the idea of a straightforward assault. We must think beyond the notion that we can only overcome by superior manpower or the timeworn strategies of our grandfathers. We must be prepared to take risks, to outwit the Briton at his own game. His position is near impregnable; long years of failure bear that out. To solve the problem we must be prepared to think the unthinkable, touch the untouchable."

"Never." Liam's tone was heavy. "You don't know what you're saying. It's your youth and inexperience that speak. I've heard this argument before, and I find it no more palatable now than I did then. This family has never used dishonorable methods to win a fight, and it shames me that it should be you, my heir, who suggests such a thing. Besides, we're not alone in this venture. What of our allies? What of Seamus Redbeard?"

"He could be persuaded." There was not a shadow of doubt in my brother's voice.

"You'd be hard put to do it."

"He could be persuaded. There is nothing more important than the recapture of the Islands. And we are poised now to do it, for Fionn will surely agree to join our alliance, and—"

"What of Eamonn? His support is essential. He will be of like mind with myself. Eamonn is immovable. There is no inducement in the world that would bring him to consider this."

"I could convince him."

"Eamonn?" Liam gave a bark of humorless laughter. "You don't know your friend as well as I thought. On this, he would never move ground. Never."

I was starting to get a very uncomfortable feeling about this conversation. "What exactly is it Sean is suggesting?" I forced myself to ask, although I dreaded the answer. There was a shadow on the edge of my thoughts, and I did not want it any closer.

"It's like this." Sean came over to my chair and squatted down beside me. His excitement was intense; his energy seemed to crackle through the air. I kept the shield tight around my mind. "You can't win with an onslaught, however strong. That's been proved. Two of our uncles fell in the last attempt, and many brave men along with them; so many it has taken us nigh on a generation to recover. And yet, our forces were strong and disciplined, our allies backed us; between our own positions and the Norse settlements, the Britons had no chance of establishing a base on this shore. So why did we fail? First, because they have the advantage of possession. Their watchtower on Greater Island commands a wide view. There's only one safe approach, and they have that covered. Second, they have an unsurpassed network of informants here. We all know who set that up years ago. Perhaps it's his father's treachery that causes Eamonn's inflexible attitude now. In any case, whatever action we plan, the Britons seem to know it in advance. So what do we learn from this?" His long hands moved to illustrate his point. "We learn it's useless to follow any predictable course. We learn that there are no secrets from our enemy. However strong an alliance we have on this side of the water, he will match and better it. He has the position of advantage. No man among us has the skills and knowledge to devise an alternative approach to Greater Island." He drew breath, his gaze intense. "At present we are particularly well placed. Seamus has a disciplined force and years of experience to draw on. We know Eamonn's capacity. And there are the Uí Néill, for Fionn is family and will be easily convinced to support us in this. He needs the security of our lands, and Eamonn's, as a buffer against any possible attack by his kinsfolk in the south. We can do business with Fionn. So our resources are greater than ever before."

"Sufficient, I suggest, to take back the Islands with no need of trickery," said Liam severely.

"No, Uncle. You believe that no more than I do. Northwoods can summon what forces he needs, and his intelligence can warn him of our plans long before we set sail. We require two things. First, a superior skill at seamanship, one that will surpass any seen before in these parts. Vessels that can go by stealth and land under cover of darkness in places hitherto thought impossible. Men who can infiltrate the Briton's camp unnoticed. A force that will be in the midst of his stronghold before he recognizes it for what it is. An ally with the capacity to detect and destroy the Briton's network of informants."

"And second?" My heart was thumping. I knew what was coming.

"To gain the first, we must do the second. The second is to cast away our scruples. We must engage the services of the Painted Man, whoever he is."

My mother drew her breath in sharply. Iubdan was grave. Liam simply set his jaw a little tighter. No doubt he had heard it all before.

"I've investigated this," Sean went on. "Among that band of men there is one, a strange, black-skinned fellow who has a knowledge of seagoing craft and a skill with them far beyond what we might dream of. There are others among them, Norsemen and Picts, who together could teach us all we need to know. I have heard tales of their exploits such as you would scarce believe were they not backed up by hard evidence. Their leader is a man with much to offer us. He's expert in false intelligence. I'm told he can outwit the most subtle strategist. With this man and his band in our employment, I believe we could not fail."

"He'd never consider it." I spoke without thinking, and my voice was shaking. Four pairs of eyes turned curiously in my direction. "Eamonn," I said quickly, wincing as I jabbed my finger with the needle. "He would never consider working with—with the Painted Man. You remember what he said. 'If that man sets foot on my land again, his life is forfeit.' Something like that. You'd never persuade him."

There was a brief silence.

"I understand Liam's reluctance," Iubdan said calmly. "You might have high hopes of such a venture. I, too, have heard this mercenary spoken of with a mixture of terror and admiration. Perhaps what they say of his skills is true. But you could never trust such a man, for part of his very value lies in his ability to deceive, in his lack of allegiance. The man is a trickster, without conscience or scruples. He has the ability to make your venture. Or to break it. You would not know until the very last moment which way he would jump."

Liam nodded. "He might extract a price from us and simply walk away. Indeed, he might set his price too high."

"For this," Sean was fierce with determination, "surely no price is too high?"

In that moment the shadow came. The room dissolved around me, and I saw instead two men locked in combat, straining one against the other. Behind them were dark pillars carven with fanciful beasts, a small dragon, a wyvern, a gryphon dagger-clawed. The man in green had his hands tight around the other's neck, squeezing, squeezing. The man in green was square jawed, with a wayward lock of brown hair falling into his eyes. It was Eamonn. He seemed to be winning the struggle. Why, then, was he gasping for air, why were his features so ghastly pale? The shadow passed over the two of them, close in their embrace of death. Then I saw the dagger driven deep into the breast of the green tunic, a dagger held tight in a hand whose white knuckles and straining sinews bore a delicate pattern of spiral and whorl and crosshatching. I did not need to look at the half-strangled features of this man to know him. But I did look; and the vision melted and changed, and one man's face became the other's, suffused with hatred, and I could no longer tell the two of them apart. I let out some sort of cry; and the shadow released me back into the firelit room. I must have fallen forward from my seat into a kind of faint, for I was half lying on the floor with Sean's arm around my shoulders. Liam was looking at my mother, and she was looking at him, as if what they saw was all too familiar. My father brought me a cup of water, and I drank. And soon I was well again, outwardly at least. But I would not tell them what I had seen.

"Sean argues his case well enough," my father said sometime later. "It should be given consideration at least. Maybe he is right. Maybe there has been enough blood shed."

"You think the Painted Man will not shed more?" asked Liam, brows raised in disbelief. "His hands reek of it. You heard the tale Eamonn told."

"We have all killed in our time. And there are many tales. I'm not supporting either of you. I'm simply suggesting you don't dismiss Sean's idea out of hand. Put it before our allies, while you have them all assembled here. I would not broach such a topic in the halls of Tara, but here at Seven-waters it is safe. Put it to them before you leave for the high king's assembly. You can judge their mood."

Liam was silent.

"You should ask Conor," said my mother. "He will be

here tomorrow. Ask him whether he believes it wise to disregard the prophecy."

"Conor!" Liam's tone was cold. "Conor's judgment can
no longer be trusted."

"That's harsh," said Iubdan. "All of us had a part in what
happened with Ciarán. You cannot lay all the blame on your
brother."

"I know that, Briton," snapped my uncle. "Your daughter's lack of self-control was also a factor."

My father rose slowly to his feet. He was a good head
taller than Liam. Beside him, Sorcha raised her hand to
shield a delicate yawn.

"It's late," she murmured. "Time to retire, I think. Liadan, you're not well. Come, I'll see you to bed. Red, could
you bring a candle, please?" She got up, moving over to her
scowling brother. "Good night, Liam." She stood on tiptoes
and kissed him on both cheeks. "The goddess give you
sweet dreams and a clear head in the morning. Good night,
Sean." All three men fell silent, the anger gone from their
eyes. Dana only knew how they'd manage when my mother
was gone.

At dawn the next day we stood under a great oak deep in
the forest ready for the ritual of Meán Fómhair. Conor was
there with several others of his kind, but this time no red-
haired apprentice shadowed his still, upright figure in its
gleaming white. We bore in our hands the fruits of this season's good harvest, one perfect example of each. A flawless
apple, a fine leafy cabbage, a handful of silken grain, a
small flask of mead, cider, honey, fresh herbs. My fingers
held an acorn, safe in its glossy protective shell, nestled
firm in its little cup. We stood about the ancient tree, shivering in the chill before dawn. Liam, solemn and pale, and by
him Sean, a younger version of the same man. My father,
who held no particular beliefs, stood very still by the immense trunk with my mother in the circle of his arm. She
was heavily cloaked against the cold. None of us had been

able to persuade her to stay indoors and rest. Kitchen woman and warrior stood there quiet, horse boy and forester side by side, the people of household, farm, and settlement. It was fortunate that Fionn and his company had not yet arrived. He knew, of course, that our family followed the old ways, but it was wise not to make him aware of quite how significant this was in our lives, for it sat uneasily with the strong Christian faith of his own household. If he were to be wooed into the alliance, we must set no foot wrong.

Conor spoke the words as the first cold light of dawn pierced the autumn canopy, and we began to lay our offerings about the gnarled and tangled roots of this oldest inhabitant of the forest, touching the rough bark, giving a nod of reverence here, a whispered greeting there. This time there were no pyrotechnics, no wizard's tricks. My uncle spoke simply, from the heart.

"Our gratitude is too deep for words. We give it what voice we can here under the oaks. To the sun that brought forth life from the earth. To the guardians of the forest, who watch over what is good all through the growing time, who watch over all things from birth to death and beyond. In you is the wisdom of ages. We honor your presence and offer you the finest fruits of this abundant season for we, too, are the dwellers of the forest, we too are Dana's folk, although we are mortal; and we follow the paths you open for us from our first breath to our last and beyond."

Conor seemed weary, as if he must summon up a great effort of will to continue. There was some weight in his thoughts, some great quandary that burdened him. I felt this in my own heart, and yet I could not have said what it was. His face was serene as always, the gray eyes deep and calm in the growing light.

"We honor no less the coming darkness. All things must sleep. All things must dream and become wise. Welcome, Queen and Enchantress, you who open for us the way of secrets. We acknowledge your insights. Your wisdom we both crave and fear. You give birth; you reap death. We welcome your return. We ready ourselves for the time of shadows."

We stood there awhile, heads bowed, as the sun came up and the gray world of early dawn warmed slowly to brown and green and gold. Iubdan still sheltered my mother with his arm, and his eyes were bleak. Conor spoke but the truth; death comes, and there is no halting it. The movement of the wheel is relentless. All changes; all moves on. A Briton might grow to understand that if he lived among our kind long enough, but he would never accept it.

The ritual over, folk made their way back along the forest paths, thoughts of a warm fire and a bowl of porridge doubtless strong in their minds. After a while I found myself walking beside my Uncle Conor, and in a flash, it seemed, the rest were gone and it was just the two of us, keeping pace together in the immense quiet of the forest.

"I'm glad you have a warm cloak and a good pair of boots," observed my uncle. "We have a fair way to go."

I refrained from comment. It did not seem necessary. But after we had walked awhile I said, "My father might be worried."

A small grin flashed across Conor's calm features.

"Iubdan knows you are with me. Of course, he may not find that totally reassuring. I no longer have their trust as I once did. And you do seem to have a capacity to attract— complications."

Our feet were soft on a carpet of damp leaves.

"What if Niamh comes today?" I asked him. "I could miss her. I need to be home when my sister comes."

He nodded gravely. "I understand, Liadan. I understand better than you think. But for you, this is more important. We'll be back before nightfall."

I raised my brows but made no response.

After a while, my uncle said, "Skillful, aren't you? Even I cannot get under your guard. Where did you learn to put such an iron barrier around your mind? And why? What is it you hold there? I've seen such control but once before, when Finbar held out against your mother long ago. That hurt her badly."

"I do what I must."

He glanced at me. "Mmm," was all he said. And we walked on in silence, keeping a brisk pace, as the day brightened and the forest came alive around us. We walked down the avenues of oaks, as golden leaves spiraled around us in a freshening breeze and squirrels busied themselves, preparing for the dark time. We went by the lake's gray waters and up the course of the seventh stream, swelling with autumn rains to a miniature torrent. It was a steep climb over tumbled stones whose surfaces were curiously patterned, as if some strange finger had marked each with a secret language, whose codes existed only in the mind of one long departed. At the top of the rise we rested, and he produced a frugal meal of dried bread and wrinkled fruit. We drank from the stream, and the cold of the water made my head ache. It was a strange sort of morning but companionable enough.

"You don't ask me where we are going," Conor said, as we started off again, up a slope between thickly clustered rowans laden with scarlet berries.

"No, I don't," I responded mildly.

He grinned again, and for a moment I could see the boy he had once been, running wild with his five brothers and one little sister in the vast spaces of the forest. But the serene mask of the archdruid settled over his features almost immediately.

"I said this was important to you. I had hoped to explain a little to you direct, mind to mind. But I see you will let nobody in. You're guarding a powerful secret. I must use words then. There is a spring, and a pool, hidden so well that few know of its existence. I'm taking you there. You need to understand the gifts you have, and what you can do, or you risk running blind with a power you scarcely recognize. I will show you."

"You underestimate me," I said coolly. "I am not a child. I know the dangers of power exercised unwisely, without thought." Bold words, for I understood only vaguely what he meant.

"Maybe," he said. We moved sharply left between drooping branches of willow and suddenly, there it was, a small, still pool between mossy stones, where fresh water welled up from underground. Insignificant in itself; a place you would almost certainly miss if you did not know it was there. "This place does not reveal itself to every traveler," said Conor, making a quick sign in the air before him and halting two paces from the water's margin.

"What now?" I asked him.

"Sit on the stones. Look into the water. I will not be far away. This is a place where secrets are safe, Liadan. These stones hold a thousand years of secrets."

I sat down and fixed my gaze on the unruffled surface of the pool. There was a feeling of deep shelter about this place, a sense of protection. It was as if nothing had changed here for a very long time. Words came to me in silence. *This rock is your mother. She holds you in the palm of her hand.* My uncle had moved back under the willows and out of sight. I tried to clear my mind of thoughts and images, but one at least would not be erased, and I refused to relax the shield I had set up there. If anyone tracked down the Painted Man, it would not be because I had betrayed what I knew. Nobody was to be trusted. Not even an archdruid.

The water moved and shifted. But here in this little glade, closely encircled by tree and rock, there was not a breath of wind. The water rippled. A momentary flash of white showed in the depths and was gone. I forced myself to stay there, not to look up. The air was as still and heavy as if a summer storm were brewing, and yet the day held autumn's chill. The water stirred and bubbled and was still again. Somebody was standing on the other side of the little pool, and it was not my Uncle Conor.

You are very like your mother. Whoever it was, he had got through the barrier around my mind in a flash, with a skill far beyond even Conor's. I had no hope of countering such strength. *The same, but not the same.* I sat there, unable to look up. *You don't need to look. You know who I am.* The water turned opaque, then reflective. And his image was there. It could have been Conor. It could almost have been Conor. The clothes were different, of course. In place of the snowy white robe, this man wore shapeless garments of an indefinable hue between gray and brown. His feet were bare on the stones. Conor's hair was in the small, neat braids of the druids. This man's black curls tangled wild around his shoulders. Conor's eyes were gray, quiet, and calm. This man had a gaze so deep it was unfathomable, and his eyes seemed as colorless as the water in which I saw them reflected. I could not force myself to look up.

You know who I am. He moved slightly, and there was that flash of white again. He wore a voluminous cloak of dark homespun, a worn old garment that hung unevenly to the ground, fastened at one shoulder. He shifted again, and I acknowledged the truth. My eyes had not deceived me. In place of his left arm, this man had the wing of a large bird, powerful and white plumed. He drew the folds of the cloak across again.

Uncle. If it is possible for the voice of the mind to tremble, that was how mine sounded.

Sorcha's daughter. You are so like her. What is your name?

Liadan. But—

Look up now, Liadan.

I half expected that there would be nobody there. He was standing so still you could hardly see him, as if he were a part of the stones themselves and of the mosses and ferns that grew there. A man who was neither young nor old, his features made in the image of my mother's; but in place of her fey, green eyes, his were clear and far seeing, the color of light through still water. His reflection had been true. A man of middle height, lean, straight backed, a man who bore forever the mark of what had happened to them, the six brothers with the one small sister.

What are you? Are you a druid?

It is my brother who is the druid.

What are you then? Are you one of the filidh?

I am the beat of a swan's wing on the breath of the wind. I am the secret at the heart of the standing stone. I am the island in the wild sea. I am the fire in the head of the seer. I am neither of that world nor of this. And yet, I am a man. I have blood on my hands. I have loved and lost. I feel your pain, and I know your strength.

I stared at him, awestruck. *They thought you were dead. Everyone. They said you drowned yourself.*

Some knew the truth. I cannot live in the one world or the other. I walk the margin. That is the doom the Sorceress laid on me.

I hesitated. *My mother—you know she is very sick? She comes near the time of her journey.* My uncle seemed quite calm. *Wouldn't you come to see her before that time comes? Couldn't you do that?*

I need not be there for her to see me. Beneath the tranquil exterior there was a deep sadness. Much had been lost through the work of the Lady Oonagh.

So she knows? She knows where you are?

At first she did not. Now it is different. They all know: my sister, my brothers, those who are left. It is better that others do not know. Conor's initiates visit me from time to time.

It must be—it must be very hard for you. How hard, I could scarcely imagine.

Let me show you. Make your mind quiet, Liadan, quiet and still. Breathe deep. That's it. Wait a little. Now feel what

I do. Feel my thoughts as they fold into yours. As they wrap you safe. Feel my mind as it becomes one with your own. Let what I am become a part of you for a time. See as I see.

I did as he asked me, not fearful, for somehow I understood there was no danger in this place. I breathed the same breath; I felt his mind as it slipped into mine as subtle and mysterious as a shadow, and held me fast. But not as a prisoner, for within the protective cloak of his thoughts, I was still myself, and at the same time I was young Finbar, standing by the lake in the chill of a misty dawn, staring into the face of evil, feeling myself changing, changing, so my mind knew only what a wild creature comprehends: cold, hunger, danger . . . food, sleep . . . the eggs in the nest, the mate with her graceful, arching back and glossy feathers . . . birth, death, loss . . . the cold, the water, the rushing terror of transformation. *That was how it was for us. That is how it is for me.* He released me gently, leaving me shivering and close to tears.

"I don't understand," I whispered. "I don't understand why I was brought here. Why would you choose to reveal yourself thus to me? I am no druid."

Maybe not. Still, you have gifts. Powerful and dangerous gifts akin to my own. The Sight. The healing power of the mind, which you have scarcely tapped as yet. I see you in peril; I see you as a link in the chain, a link on which much depends. You must learn to harness your gifts, or they will become no more than a burden.

"Harness them? My visions come unbidden. I cannot tell if they are true or false, past or future."

This time he spoke aloud, his voice cracked and hesitant as if long unused. "They can be puzzles, cryptic and misleading. Sometimes they are terrifyingly clear. Here in this place of protection, it is easier to keep control. Outside the grove, the shadows move closer. Let me show you. What is it you carry so deep in your heart? What is it you would see, above all else? Look in the water. Make your mind quiet."

I could not help glancing around to see if Conor was watching; there was no sign of him. Then I willed myself to utter stillness. I made my breathing slow and deep, felt time and place change and settle around me. There was a flicker of light, a flash of color in the water, and an image growing steadily clearer. The image rippled and changed. It was dark. Dark save for a small lantern burning under the shelter of strange, fronded trees. There were two men there, one sleeping, rolled in a blanket, braided hair falling back from ebony skin. Perhaps he had tried to stay awake, to be there for his friend during the dark time, but battle weariness had overwhelmed him at last. The other man sat cross-legged, with a long knife in one hand and a stone in the other, and he sharpened the knife with deliberate, even strokes, one and two and three. His eyes seemed to follow the steady movement of the weapon, but he was not seeing it. At times he glanced up as if in hope of some lightening of the sky, and then, resigned, took up his task again. The blade of that knife would have sliced straight through a man, armor and all.

My hand stretched out, despite myself, and I made some small sound. And at that instant, the man in the water looked up, looked straight at me. His expression struck me to the heart. Bitterness, resentment, longing: I could not say which was written most starkly on his features. His eyes widened in shock and slowly, very slowly, he put the knife down. He lifted his hand, reached his patterned fingers out toward me, and I stretched my own hand out just a little farther, just a little more . . .

Do not touch the water's surface.

But I had, and the ripples came up again, and Bran's image was gone. I let my breath out and sat back, with tears in my eyes.

"You'll have need of this, Liadan. You must learn, while you are here. You must learn quickly and practice the skills. Soon enough, this walk and climb will be too much for you, for a while at least."

I gaped, almost forgetting to keep my eyes down. Was nothing secret?

"Secrets are safe here."

"You saw, I suppose. Saw what was shown to me."

"Oh yes. And he saw you, make no doubt of it. But that is nothing new to him. Your image is before his eyes through every battle, through every flight, through every subtle knife stroke, through every long, dark night. You bound him to you with your courage and with your tales. You hold him to you now. You captured a wild creature when you had no place you could keep him. He cannot escape you, however hard he might wish it to be otherwise."

"You are wrong. He said he did not want me. He sent me away. I seek only to keep him safe, to light his way. There is no one else to do it." I was not comfortable with his words. They made me sound like some seductress who possesses a man against his will.

"You speak no more nor less than the truth. You are responsible. You changed his path. Now you shut him out. Would you deny him his child?" Finbar looked very serious, but there was no judgment in his tone. Still I felt a flare of anger at his words.

"What am I supposed to do? I don't even know who he is. And besides, he despises me. He will never come to Sevenwaters. He blames us—he blames my father, and my mother, for what he has become. Are you suggesting I should seek him out?"

"I suggest nothing. I simply show you what is to be seen."

"I—I met the Fair Folk. The Lady of the Forest and a lord with hair like flames. They said—they told me to give this man up. They wanted me to promise to stay in the forest and not to marry. But I would not promise."

"Ah."

"I don't know what to think. There were other voices, too, in that place. Older voices, and they told me—they seemed to tell me my own choices were right. Now I don't know what to do."

"Don't weep, child."

"I'm not—I—" My feelings threatened to overwhelm me. I had longed to see Bran, yet seeing him had awoken an aching sadness within me for what could not be.

"I had a chance to change the course of events, once, long ago," Finbar said, "the chance to save a man's life and liberty at great risk. I took it and am glad that I did, though there is no telling if my choice was right or wrong. Perhaps what happened later was my punishment for believing I might make a difference. For, as you see, I am prevented from taking my part in the world of affairs. I am set outside and belong neither to one realm nor the other, a mere conduit." Behind his look of tranquil resignation, his tone of calm acceptance, I sensed a deep sorrow. "I know what I would wish to see you do. But I will not offer you advice. For now, I see you bear a heavy burden for one so small. Let me at least ease this for a while. Let me show you, for you will need to use this skill yourself in time. Sit quiet. Let the things that trouble you go."

Subtly, images began to creep into my thoughts: a full moon rising above a lake, with a wide pathway of silver spreading across the still water. A lark spiraling up into a morning sky, its song a pure anthem of joy. The feeling of being held in strong arms, warm and comforting. Myself and Sean racing along the lake shore, hearts pounding, hair tangled by the wind as we laughed and shouted with the thrill of being alive and young and free. A hillside planted with young oaks; the slanting sunlight catching their new leaves and turning them to brilliant gold. The sound of a baby's gurgling laughter. More images, all beautiful, all with some special meaning that reminded me of the good things in my life, the things that made me glad to be a part of Sevenwaters and of the family that belonged there. I was full of hope, full of well-being. The vision darkened momentarily, and I looked into a pair of gray eyes that were steady as a rock, trustworthy eyes. I heard a voice, and it was not Finbar's, saying, *You don't have to do this alone, you know.* Then as gently as they had come to me, the images faded, and my mind came back to itself; and I opened my eyes and saw before me the still waters of the pond and the figure of my uncle, gazing calmly at me across its reflective surface.

There were so many questions in my mind, I did not know where to begin.

"You will learn to do this as I do. It takes an effort of will. You must make yourself stronger than the other, strong enough to bend his thoughts with your own."

"You think I will be called upon to do this? When?"

"I know you will be. I cannot tell you when. You will recognize the need. Now, Liadan. What of the child?"

Fear struck me suddenly. "The child is mine," I said, and my tone was fierce. "I will decide his future. It is not for Fair Folk, nor human folk, to set his path for him."

"So you say. The child is yours. And you want the man as well; I saw that in your eyes as you reached for his image. But this man cannot be tamed, Liadan. You will not keep him at Sevenwaters. And the child must stay here, for all our sakes. The child may be the key. Doubtless the Fair Folk told you that as well. Has it occurred to you that perhaps you cannot have both?"

"Surely it need not be so," I said, not liking at all the sound of where he was heading.

"Your man bears the mark of the raven."

"He is a Briton. So I believe. I would swear not one drop of Irish blood flows in his veins. He cannot be the one of the prophecy. It is no more than coincidence."

"You respond instantly." Finbar's expression was grave. "Clearly, this has been in your thoughts. But you are right. His face is patterned in the raven's image, fierce enough to keep away all but the most determined. And yet he does not match the words of the prophecy. Neither of Britain nor of Erin, but at the same time both. This man does not match; but his son will."

I made a gesture of denial.

"Be still, Liadan. I tell you this only to warn you. The son bears the mark of his father in his blood and in his bearing. There is no escaping it. Your son will be the son of the raven. He will carry forward the lineage of both mother and father. A Briton, a woman of Erin who herself is a child of both races. It matches. It is time. Once his parentage is known, that is what everyone will say."

I was chilled to the bone.

"Are you telling me it is better if nobody knows whose child he is?"

"I did not say that. It is a terrible thing for a son never to know his father, for a father never to meet his son. Ask yourself why you chose the tales you did to tell while you were among the fianna. I do not seek to influence you; I know better than that. You will make your own choices, and so will this man with the raven mask who does not know he is a father. Perhaps you will continue to break the pattern. Still, it would be wise to take steps to protect the child. Forces are astir that we thought long gone. There are those who will not want this child to grow to be a man. Here in the forest, he will be safe."

"How do you know so much?"

"I *know* nothing. I tell you only what I have seen."

I frowned. "Everyone keeps saying—you, Mother, Conor, even the lady herself—they keep talking about the old evil. Something returning and having to be fought. What evil? Why doesn't anyone explain?"

He gazed at me with something like pity. "They have not yet told you then?"

"What? Told me what?"

"This, I think, is not for me to reveal to you. Conor bound us to silence. Perhaps you will know in time. Meanwhile, keep your candle burning, child. Your man has gone far away. He is encircled by shadows."

"I am strong," I said. "Strong enough to hold onto him and to my child. I will keep both. I will not give them up." My own words surprised me; they did not seem at all the words of common sense, yet somehow I knew them for truth.

There was a brief silence and then the unexpected sound of quiet laughter.

"How could I doubt you?" said Finbar, with a grin like his brother's, incongruous in the fragile, shadowed face. "You are your mother's daughter."

Then, without a sound, Conor was standing beside me, laying a reassuring hand on my shoulder.

"We should be going," he said, and whether he had heard any of what had passed between me and his brother there was no telling. "No doubt your father is biting his nails." Before us the pool was as flat as glass.

Go home now, Liadan. I will be here when you need me. Practice your art.

I nodded, and we turned and made our way beneath the overhanging trees and began the long walk home. I took my chance when we were nearly in sight of the lake and asked Conor, "Uncle? Do you know what became of the young druid, Ciarán? Did he return to the nemetons?"

There was a very long silence, and then he said quietly, "No, Liadan. He did not return."

"Where did he go?"

Conor sighed. "On a long journey. He chose a path of great peril in order to seek his past. He vowed never to return to the brotherhood. It is a great loss; greater than he knows."

"Uncle—has this something to do with the thing, the evil my mother speaks of, some shadow from the past that has returned?"

Conor's mouth tightened. He made no reply.

"Why won't you tell me?" I asked him, both exasperated and a little frightened. "Why won't anyone tell me?"

"This cannot be told," Conor said gravely, and we fell back into silence.

It was dark by the time we reached the forest's margin and crossed the fields to the house, where lighted lanterns hung outside the main door and folk bustled around the courtyard.

"You're tired," observed Conor, as we came up the gravel walkway. "Even I am a little weary. But there will be no early bed tonight. I would say, from the looks of it, that the Uí Néill and your sister are expected this same day. Will you manage this?"

"I always manage."

"That has not gone unnoticed."

We entered the bright hall. Conor had been right. My sister was expected before supper time, and during our absence other guests had arrived, and the house was full of light and talk and the smell of good food. There was Seamus Redbeard, warming his generous rump in front of the fire, and his young wife giggling shyly as he whispered in her ear. Sean and Aisling hand in hand, radiant with happiness to be together again. My father, frowning at Conor. And Eamonn. Eamonn rising to his feet as we came in, white faced, eyes fixed on me as if he had been waiting for this very moment. I fled upstairs to change. Never had I longed so much to curl up under the covers and go straight to sleep. The fire in my room had been lit, as if Janis knew when I would be home, and a green gown was laid out on the bed. I dragged off my old garments and struggled into the new. My stomach was just a little more rounded. Not so you'd notice, if you weren't looking for it. Soon enough everyone would know. I fastened the gown and splashed my face with water from the bowl left ready for me. I bent to the fire, held a stick in the heart of the flames until it caught. The candle had burned a long way down. Soon, I must fashion another. I lit the wick, and the scent of herbs began to drift in the evening air. Herbs of love, herbs of healing. *Hold on, wherever you are. Hold on.*

Back downstairs, there was no avoiding Eamonn. Before I could involve myself in conversation with Aisling, or with Seamus's young wife, he was beside me, taking my arm to steer me to a bench, bringing me a cup of wine.

"Just water, please."

"You're looking very pale," said Eamonn, as he fetched another goblet. He sat down beside me, and his fingers brushed mine as he put the cup in my hand. "You're not taking care of yourself, Liadan. What's wrong? Why wouldn't you see me?"

I took a deep breath and let it go again without speaking.

"Liadan? What is it?" His voice was kind, the brown eyes concerned.

"I'm sorry, Eamonn. It's better if we don't speak of this. I'm quite tired. I've been for a long walk."

He frowned. "Somebody should be taking better care of you."

I had no answer for this. Amid the laughter and bustle, we were an island of silence.

"I won't accept this," he said suddenly. "You can't do this."

"Do what?" Brighid help me, I was so weary. The touch of his hand on me brought memories alive, stirred something best left asleep.

"Sh-shut me out." Eamonn was scowling, annoyed with himself. The childhood stammer had long been under control. "You owe me better, Liadan. I must speak with you alone before I go."

I drew in my breath. All of a sudden there were tears in my eyes. How could I tell him? How could I do any of it? I spoke without thinking.

"I'm tired, I'm just so tired."

His face changed. He glanced around quickly, making

sure nobody was looking; and then his hand moved very subtly, and he brushed my cheek just once with his fingers, wiping away the single tear that had escaped.

"Oh, Liadan."

The intensity of his expression scared me. It seemed to me there was a fine line between love and hate, between passion and rage. I was saved from responding by the sound of hooves outside, by the movement of folk to the door. But as we got up to follow, Eamonn's hand was on my back, lightly, shielding me from the crowd. Soon I was going to have to tell him. Somehow I would have to find the words.

Clattering hooves. Torches smoking and flaring in the darkness. A starless sky, heavy with clouds. They rode into the yard two and two, no sign of weariness in the straight backs and proud carriage of the Uí Néill's men. One bore his standard, white with a red symbol, a serpent curled around to devour its own tail. Then Fionn himself, broad shouldered, tight-mouthed, and beside him my sister. I had longed so much to see her, Niamh, who had teased and tormented me throughout my childhood, Niamh, who would rage at me one moment and entrust to me her deepest secrets the next; Niamh, laughing and golden, whirling around and around in a shaft of sunlight, in her white dress. *Don't you long for something that makes your life blaze and burn so the whole world can see it? Don't you long for that, Liadan?* I had missed her terribly, and I could not wait to talk to her, long journey or not. So I moved forward and down the steps, next to Liam where he waited to greet his guests; and my sister's horse drew to a halt right in front of me. I looked up at her; and I knew in that moment that, whatever else I might say to her, I could not tell her my secret. For I stood there in my green gown, glowing with the new life I had been granted; and she glanced at me and away, and her face was frozen, her wide, blue eyes hollow and empty, quenched of their passions and hopes and wild dreams. Fionn came around to offer his hand, and she dismounted with elegance. Her fur-lined riding cloak and soft, kid boots were immaculate. Her shining hair was veiled in snowy linen and warmly hooded. She was like some exquisite shell scoured clean of its living inhabitant by a sudden storm, the lovely remnant of a creature gone forever. I took a step forward and put my arms around her, hugging her close as if to deny what I saw, and she flinched away from my touch.

"Liadan." It seemed to take a great effort of will for her to manage even this.

"Oh, Niamh. Oh, Niamh, it's good to see you."

But it was not good, it was not good at all. I looked into my sister's beautiful, blank face and felt my heart turn cold with foreboding.

Chapter Eight

Something was terribly wrong, and I could not find out what it was. Niamh was avoiding me. She was refusing to talk, as if denying to herself that she was home. And yet, so devoid of will was her face, so empty of soul were her eyes, I found it hard to believe her capable of the effort required for such evasion. Even when the men were gathered around the great oaken table deep in strategies, still I could not find Niamh alone. Often I could not find her at all.

"Niamh's not looking well," observed Aisling, with a little frown. "I wonder if she's expecting."

The third night of the visit I asked Liam a favor.

"You see how Niamh is, Uncle. She seems exhausted, defeated. She cannot go on to Tara. Surely Fionn must recognize that. Ask him if she can stay with us while the men travel on."

Liam regarded me sternly. "Tell me, Niece, why should I be doing Niamh any favors?"

"You ask me that? Can't you see what this marriage has done to her? Can't you remember what she was?"

"That's unfair, Liadan. A woman must submit to her father's ruling and later to her husband's. That is only right and natural. Fionn is a respected man, a man of standing. He is of the Uí Néill. Niamh must grow up, adapt, if she's to contribute anything of value to his household. She must put the past behind her." He sounded as if he was trying to convince himself as well as me.

"Uncle, please ask him."

"Very well. I won't deny it is a practical idea. Eamonn has already suggested that you and your sister travel back with Aisling in a day or two. I prefer that arrangement. You would be very safe in his house, company for Aisling while her brother is away, and it breaks the journey home for Niamh. You're right; she doesn't look well."

Sean had presented his plan of action to the allies on the second morning. They were in the smaller private room this time. Carrying linen along the upper hallway, I heard voices raised, not in anger, more a mixture of shock and excitement. I caught a sense of Sean's urgency and his passion to convince them. The midday meal grew cold on the table while they stayed behind closed doors debating the issue; and when they emerged, Fionn and Sean were still in deep conversation, and Eamonn was pale and silent, with a pinched expression about his face. Intense discussion continued as they ate and drank. They were divided. Fionn was open to the idea, Seamus wavering. Liam stood firm; he would do business with no fianna, he would deal with no faceless mercenaries, he would undertake no mission unless he himself had full control. And everyone knew there was no controlling the Painted Man. He was a law unto himself, if law was the right word for one so patently lawless; and trusting him was a bit like putting your head into a dragon's mouth. Sheer folly. Besides, Seamus put in, how would you even start? The outlaw came and went as he pleased; nobody knew where his headquarters were. Slippery as an eel, he was. How would you get a message to him to let him know you were interested? Sean replied that there were ways, but he did not elaborate. Eamonn contributed very little. When the meal was cleared away, he did not return with the others to continue the debate but headed off outside alone.

I forced myself to go after him. There could be no waiting for him to seek me out; I would give him the bad news and that would be that. Better that he know as soon as possible. This was not as my mother and I had planned, but Eamonn had given me no option.

I found him in the stables. He was watching the gray horse that had carried me home, as one of the lads exercised her around the yard. One and two, three and four, she picked up her feet as neatly as a dancer. Her coat was shining, silvery mane and tail glossy with good care.

I came up to Eamonn's side where he stood in the shadows, watching.

"Liadan." There was restraint in his tone.

"You wanted to talk to me," I said. "Well, I'm here."

"I don't know if—this is not the right time. I am—your brother has disappointed me, shocked me with an error of judgment. I'm afraid my thoughts are not fit for sharing."

"I know this is not a good time, Eamonn. But I have something to tell you, and it has to be now, while I have the courage for it."

I had his attention instantly.

"You are—afraid to tell me? You need never be afraid of me, Liadan. You must know I would never harm what is most precious to me."

His words did nothing to make my task any easier. We moved quietly around to a spot behind the stables where you could sit on the steps in the sun. It had been a good place for childhood secrets. Here nobody could see you, except maybe a druid.

"What is it, Liadan? What can be so bad that you fear to tell a friend?" And he imprisoned both my hands in his so that I could not move away. "Tell me, my dear."

Brighid help me. I was shivering from head to toe. "Eamonn, we've known each other a long time. I respect you, and I owe it to you to tell you the truth, as much of it as I can. Before, you—you asked me to be your wife, and I told you I would answer you at Beltaine. But I find I must give you my answer now."

There was a pause.

"I see I have pressed you unduly on this," he said carefully. "If you prefer it, I will wait as long as you wish. Take what time you need to make your decision."

I swallowed. "That's just it. I cannot take time. And I cannot marry you, now or then. I am carrying another man's child."

And then there was a very long silence, during which I stared miserably at the ground and he sat motionless, still holding my hands. Eventually he spoke in a voice that was calm and even, a stranger's voice.

"I don't think I heard you correctly. What did you say?"

"You heard me, Eamonn. Don't make me say it again."

Another silence. He relinquished my hands. I could not look at him.

"Who has done this?"

"I can't tell you, Eamonn. I won't tell you."

He moved then, and I felt his hands on my shoulders, gripping hard.

"Who has done this? Who has taken what is mine?"

"You're hurting me. I have told you what I must, and now you are free of me. I will not tell any more."

"Not tell? What do you mean, not tell? What are they thinking of, your brother, your father? They should be out hunting down the scum who did this to you, making him pay for this—this outrage!"

"Eamonn—"

"The moment I saw you, the moment Sean and I found you, I feared such a wrong had been done. But you would not talk to me, and you seemed calm, almost too calm . . .

and they said no more of it, so I thought . . . but I will avenge this act of barbarism if they will not. I will make him pay. This ch-child should have been mine."

"They didn't know." My voice was shaking. "Sean, Liam, my father, they still don't know. You are only the second person to hear this news, after my mother."

"But why?" He was up and pacing now, opening and closing his hands as if they were eager to do some damage. "Why not tell? Why not allow your menfolk the satisfaction of just vengeance?"

I took a deep breath. "Because," I said very clearly, so that he could not possibly mistake my meaning, "I was a willing partner in this. The child was conceived in love. This, I know, will hurt you more than the thought of some violence committed against me. But it is true." Still I could not force myself to look him in the eyes.

He strode up and down, up and down. At least now I had given him the truth, and his strong sense of propriety would give him no choice but to leave me. He would mutter an apology and be off to Tara to nurse his wounded pride and look for another wife.

"I don't believe you." He came to a halt in front of me and, reaching down, took my hands and pulled me up to stand before him. This time I was obliged to look at him, and I could see from the bewilderment in his eyes that he meant what he said. "I know you too well. You are incapable of such an act; you are the wisest and most prudent of women. I refuse to believe you would give yourself thus, unwed, and promised to another. This cannot be the truth."

He could hardly make this more difficult for me if he deliberately set out to do so. "It is the truth, Eamonn," I said quietly. "I love this man. I'm carrying his child. I cannot put it more plainly. Besides, I made you no promise."

"Has he offered to marry you? To give your child a name?"

I shook my head. If only he would stop. If only he would leave. Each word made the hurt worse.

"This wretch has taken advantage of your innocence, and now you protect him through some misguided sense of loyalty. I will hunt him down, and I will strangle him with my bare hands. Watching him die will give me intense satisfaction."

For a moment that image returned, the squeezing hands, the gasping for life, the knife, the blood. Then it blurred again, and I swayed where I stood.

"Liadan—what is it? Here, sit down. Let me help you. You are not well."

"I want you to go now. Please go." I put my head in my hands so that I did not have to see the look in his eyes.

"You need help—"

"I'll be better in a moment. I really do need to be alone. Please go away, Eamonn." My own weakness made me cruel.

"If that's what you want." His voice was tightly controlled now. He turned to go.

"Wait."

I heard his indrawn breath, but I did not say what he wanted to hear.

"I'll have to ask you a favor. I have yet to make this news known. Please give me time to tell my father and Sean and my uncle before you make any mention of it. And—and, Eamonn, I am sorry I have hurt you."

He did not respond.

"Eamonn?"

"You would have said yes, wouldn't you?" He spoke abruptly, as if the words tumbled out despite his better judgment. "At Beltaine. You would have accepted me, if not for this?"

"Oh, Eamonn. What good is it to either of us for me to answer that question? It's all changed. Everything is changed. Now go, please. There's no point in talking anymore. It's happened; no shedding of blood can alter it."

"I'll need time." This, too, surprised me. "Time to come to terms with this."

"So will others," I said wryly. "There are many I have yet to tell. I must ask you again not to speak of this, until . . ."

"Of course I will not. Always, you have had my deepest respect, and you have it still." He gave a stiff little half bow, turned on his heel, and, finally, was gone.

There was a strange supper, full of glances and gestures and unspoken words. Niamh wore a demure gown in a soft, gold-colored fabric, high necked, long sleeved, and she sat mute by her husband as he debated strategies with Liam. She ate little. My mother was absent, my father abstracted. From time to time I caught him watching Niamh and watching Fionn, and there was a grimness in his face that echoed my own thoughts. For once I was not hungry. I had crossed only my first bridge. As for Eamonn, he had been obliged to put in an appearance, as my father had, because an absence might have caused offense. He drank his wine, and the cup was refilled, and he drank again. A platter of food was set before him and taken away untouched. There were dark thoughts in his eyes.

Next day dawned fair. I was up early, and dressed warmly in an outdoor gown with the gray coat over the top, an inelegant but practical combination. The water in the little bowl was bracingly cold. I went out to find my father. Most of our lambs were born in spring, but some ewes dropped lambs in autumn, and when the season was harsh that could be a problem. Iubdan was up in the top pastures, checking his stock with an ancient shepherd and a couple of young lads who acted as the old man's eyes and hands. There was a very new lamb, upright but tottering, and they were debating whether to take the ewe down to the barn to try to save her or to put her out of her misery then and there.

"Give her a chance at least," I said, coming up behind them. "That young one might be your prize breeding ram in a couple of years. Give her a day or two."

"Dunno. Not rightly." The old man scratched his chin,

which bore a sparse bristling of white hairs. "Wasting your time, maybe."

"Give her a day or two," I said again, as the ewe rolled her guileless eyes at me. Iubdan got up from where he had been squatting beside the stricken animal. "You lads take her down to the barn. You know what to do."

"Aye, we do. Take the skin off the lamb that died, and rub it on this one and try him with the other ewe. Like as not she'll take him as her own." The lad was eager to demonstrate his knowledge.

"Well, get on with it then," said my father, grinning.

"Father, can you spare a little time?"

"Of course, sweetheart. What is it?"

The three of them, young and old, maneuvered the ewe onto a board and set off down the hill toward the barn. The gnarled old shepherd followed the two lads, with the tiny lamb borne precariously in his arms.

"What's troubling you, Daughter? Is it about Niamh?"

"I'm worried about her, yes. But I've other matters to talk about just now. Very serious matters, Father, that can't wait. You'll be—you'll be more than displeased, I'm afraid."

"Come, sit down here, Liadan. This sounds weighty. It takes a lot to displease me; you know that."

We sat side by side on the drystone wall. From here, the lower reaches of the forest spread down to surround the grim fortress walls of Sevenwaters. The keep was softened by the myriad branches of oak and beech, rowan and birch. Leaves were turning, and the crisp air was clear save for the rising plumes of wood smoke from early cooking fires.

"It'll be a fair morning," said Iubdan.

"The ewe," I blurted out, starting in the middle, "you let her have a couple of days. You could have killed her. Why?"

He thought for a moment. "I'd follow the old man's judgment, normally. He's been a shepherd since before I was born. I did it because you bid me. Maybe the ewe will die, and maybe she won't. Why do you ask?"

"When—when I was away, I killed a man. I-I slit his throat with my knife, and he died. I've never done that before."

My father said not a word. He waited for me to go on.

"It was the only thing to do, you understand? He was dying, he had been left to die, he was in terrible agony, I could not do otherwise. You said once you hoped I would never have to use those skills you taught me, with knife and bow and staff. Well, I have used them now, and I do not feel the better for it. And yet, at the time, it was the only choice."

Iubdan nodded. "Was this what you had to tell me?"

"Only part of it." My throat was suddenly constricted. "There was another man whom I tried to heal. Like the ewe. I insisted on keeping him alive, and he suffered; and in the end he died anyway. I made the wrong choice, but at the time I was so sure."

My father nodded again. "You do what you must. Not every choice can be right. And you cannot be sure yours was wrong. Your mother would say, forces outside yourself have a hand in these things. You are an able healer; if anyone could have saved this fellow, it would have been you. There may have been another reason why this man's life was prolonged."

I said nothing.

"You know," said Iubdan conversationally, "if there's anything I've learned from living among the folk of Erin all these years, it's that a story's not likely to have just two of anything in it. It's always three. Three wishes; three dragons. Three men."

I drew a deep breath. "Father, you told me not so long ago that, when it was time for me to wed, I might make my own choice. Do you remember that?"

He waited a moment before he spoke. "This is not what I

expected." The sun was climbing higher; morning light turned his hair to the exact red-gold shade of Niamh's. Autumn red; oak-leaf red. "But yes, of course I remember."

"I . . ." I could not force the words out. "Father, I . . ."

"You have met some man you fancy? Perhaps the ancient, ugly pauper whose trustworthy character we once discussed?" He was smiling, but the blue eyes were questioning, intent on my face.

"I must tell it straight, Father, though it will hurt you, and that grieves me. I am expecting a child. I cannot name the child's father, and I will not marry him or any other. No wrong was done to me, no ill deed. This man is—he is the one I would choose above all others. But I will bear and raise my child alone, for this man will not come to Sevenwaters. I have told Mother and Eamonn. Now I tell you, and I am afraid because—because above all, I do not want to lose your respect. If you lost your faith in me, I might begin to doubt myself. And I cannot afford to do so. I need all my strength for this."

Unlike Eamonn, my father sat still while he absorbed the news. He looked out over the wide reaches of the forest, his expression giving nothing away. He did not ask me to repeat myself. He did not pace up and down. Finally he asked me, "What did your mother say?"

"That she treasured the child as I do. That she would be here to deliver him with her own hands in spring."

"I see," he said, and there was a grimness in his voice, and a set about his jaw, that told me he was working hard to hold back anger. "I think you must tell me. I think you must give me this man's name. Niamh's ill-chosen lover at least had the courage to face me and account for himself. Yours, it seems, simply takes what pleases him and moves onto the next opportunity."

I felt the heat rise to my cheeks. "You cheapen what was between us," I said, alarmed to be arguing with my father, whom I respected more than anyone in the world. "This was no—no casual liaison, no careless coupling—It was—"

"Remind me, how long was it you were away?" Father asked.

"Stop it! This is all wrong! Oh, what is happening to us that all of us hurt each other and cannot listen anymore!"

There was a little silence, and then he spoke again, very softly.

"Very well," he said. "I have seen the result of Niamh's error, how it has changed her, and that makes me more than uneasy. I will hear you out. Perhaps the man's name is not so important, it is his actions I find hard to understand. You said he would not come to Sevenwaters. Why not? What man would not follow such a woman and seek to keep her as his wife? What man would not wish to know his own son? Unless he is already married, or otherwise unworthy of you. But your judgment is seldom faulty, Daughter."

"He—he did ask me to stay with him, and I said no. There's Mother; I needed to come home. Then, later, he . . . when he found out who I was, he was all too eager to be rid of me." Tears were close, suddenly.

"I don't like the sound of this at all. Was a reason given?"

I hadn't planned to tell him. But it came out anyway. "Something a long way back. When you left Harrowfield. Some sort of wrong he said was done. He said—he said you took away his birthright. Something like that. Father, you must tell nobody of this, you understand?"

He was frowning. "That's a long time ago. Of what years is this man of yours?"

"Not so old. Around Eamonn's age, maybe younger."

"And he's a Briton?" There was a question in his tone, but I did not reply, for I was not prepared to admit I did not know the answer. "He could have been little more than an infant when I left Harrowfield," Father went on. "This cannot be right, surely."

"You've never talked about that time. Was there anything—did anything happen that might explain what he said? Was any ill done to a child? There is some past evil that bears heavily on him."

Iubdan shook his head. "There were children there, of course, in the household, in the villages, on the farms. But I left my estate in good hands. I made sure all was safe and ordered before I came here. My people were well protected, their future as secure as any can be in these troubled times. Perhaps if I could speak with him . . ."

"No," I said. "That's not possible."

"Are you ashamed of him? Or of me?"

"Oh, no, Father. Don't even think that. He cannot come here. He lives a life of—of danger and flight. There is no room in such a life for me or for his child. Best if I just get on with this by myself."

"But you would not marry Eamonn."

"If I cannot have this man, I will have no other."

"Did you tell Niamh?"

"How could I tell her? You've seen how it is with her. She's hardly spoken to me since she came home."

We got up and began to walk slowly down the hill toward the barn. We were silent for a while and then he said, "Since Niamh's return, I seem unable to reach her, Liadan. She will not see her mother, who longs so much to salve the wounds that were inflicted when Niamh was denied her lover. It is as if another woman has returned in our daughter's place, as if something has turned that shining girl into the merest shadow of herself. I have lost one daughter, and your mother walks a dark pathway. I don't wish to lose you as well."

I slipped my arm around his. "I always intended to stay here. You know that."

"Yes. My little daughter, so skilled in all the domestic arts, always happiest with her own people around her. You are the heart of the household, Liadan. But are you sure this is still all you want?"

I did not reply. My father and I did not lie to each other.

"What if this man turned up on your doorstep tomorrow and asked you to go with him? How would you answer him?"

If he turned up on my doorstep tomorrow while Eamonn is still here, he'd be lucky to get away with his neck intact. "I don't know. I don't know what I would do."

We had come out beneath the tree line and could see the whitewashed walls of the barn before us.

"I have a proposal for you, which we'll follow if your mother agrees." Father might have been outlining a plan for building a wall or setting out an orchard. But his eyes were less than tranquil. "When Aisling goes home, you will accompany her to Sídhe Dubh and stay there while Eamonn is at Tara. Take Niamh with you and make it your task to find out what is amiss with her. I sense a wrong there greater than we know of, something deep and wounding. I have done my best to reach her, but she sees me as her enemy and will not talk to me. It is hard enough for your mother to bear her own weakness and pain without the daily hurt of seeing her daughter thus and being shut out from helping. Your mother said if Niamh will talk to anyone, it will be to you. I'm asking you to do this for me. Just until Fionn returns for her, and then you must come home. You will not wish to linger at Eamonn's house once he comes back. You say you have told him this news already. That must have been hard for both of you. Eamonn is a proud man; he does not suffer losses easily."

"It was horrible."

My father slipped an arm around my shoulders. "Well, then, what do you say?"

"If this is what you wish, I will go." My heart sank at the prospect. I was not sure I wanted to know what was behind Niamh's beautiful, blank eyes. I knew I did not want to visit Eamonn's home, even in his absence.

"You will do this for me and for your mother. In return, I will provide protection for you and for my grandchild. I will make sure Liam knows of this before he leaves for Tara. I will tell Sean and Conor."

"Mother said she would—"

"I will do it. And I will do it in such a way that no questions are asked and no demands made of you. You are my daughter. You and your infant will be safe here at Sevenwaters for as long as you choose to stay."

"Oh, Father." I put my arms around him and hugged him.

"I will not see you fall into despair, as Niamh has. I, too, broke the rules to have what I wanted, Liadan. I have never forgotten what I left behind when I came here. But I have never believed, not for a single moment, that what I chose to do was wrong. You are your mother's daughter. I do not have it in me to believe your choices can be faulty. Surely good must come of this in the end. There, sweetheart, weep if you will. Later you must find Aisling and plan your visit. Perhaps you should travel by cart; it may not be wise for you to ride."

"Cart!" He had jolted me out of my tears. "I'm not an invalid. I will be safe enough on the little mare. We'll go gently."

He was true to his word. Just how he achieved it I do not know, but by the eve of the men's departure for Tara, my news was known to Liam and to Sean and also to Conor, but perhaps he had known already. I was aware, constantly, of how different this was from Niamh's experience. For my sister there had been the cold disapproval, the harsh censure, the shutting out, the hasty, forced marriage. For me there was simply acceptance, as if my fatherless child were already part of the family at Sevenwaters. My transgression broke more rules than Niamh's. I still could not understand why the family had considered Ciarán an unsuitable match for her, why their reasons had been kept secret. There had been no child on the way. Yet Niamh had received none of the love and warmth that surrounded me. There was a terrible injustice about it. I was aware of my sister as she moved stiffly about the house, closed off behind her invisible barrier, eyes expressionless, arms wrapped around herself or hands clutched tightly together as if she could not afford to let down her guard for one instant, as if she believed us all to be her enemies.

Despite the unfairness of it, I was deeply grateful to my father for easing my path so miraculously. News travels fast. I went downstairs before supper, and there was Janis herself, making sure there were enough goblets and platters and knives for the household and the guests. Janis was ageless. She had been my mother's wet nurse; she must be quite old in years, but her dark eyes still gleamed with keen interest in whatever was new, and her hair, scraped back into a severely plaited bundle at the nape of the neck, was as black and shining as a crow's wing. Her family were traveling folk, but Janis had settled at Sevenwaters long ago; it was with us she belonged.

"Well, lass," she said with a grin, "no need to keep the secret any longer, I hear."

"My father told you?"

"He put the news about in his own way. Not that I didn't know. A woman does know. I'm just glad you're well. You'll carry safely for all you're a little thing."

I managed a smile.

"I'll help you when it's your time," Janis went on quietly. "She might not have the strength for it by then. She'll tell me what to do. I'll be the hands. There now, no tears, lass. This news has brought a smile to your mother's face. That makes him happy, the Big Man. You've no need for shame."

"It's not that," I said, blinking hard. "I feel no shame. It's my mother, and Niamh, and—and everything. It's all changing; it's changing too fast. I don't know if I can keep up."

"Here, lassie." She put her arms around me and gave me

a firm hug. "Change will follow you. You're one of those who invite it. But you're a strong girl. You'll always know what's right for you and your babe—and your man."

"I hope so," I said soberly.

Looking around the hall that night, it occurred to me that this might be the last occasion for some time that we were all together. Liam sat in his carven chair, his stern image somewhat softened by the young wolfhounds that played a game of pursuit around his booted legs. My brother stood next to him, the resemblance as always striking. Sean had the same long face and hard jaw, the features of a leader in the making. Conor's was the same face again, but subtly different, for it was ever filled with an inner light, an ancient serenity. Niamh was seated silent beside her husband. Her back was held straight, her head high, and she did not look at anyone. Her hair was veiled, her dress demure in the extreme. So quickly, it seemed, was her light quenched, which had shone so strongly as she danced and dazzled at the feast of Imbolc. Fionn ignored her. On my sister's other side was Aisling, keeping up a one-sided conversation with no difficulty at all. And Eamonn was there, seated in the shadows, tankard of ale between his palms. I tried to avoid catching his eye.

My mother was tired, I could see it, and distressed to see her elder daughter so changed. I saw her glancing in Niamh's direction and looking away, and I saw the little frown that never left her brow. But she smiled and chatted with Seamus Redbeard and did her best to make things seem as they should be. Father watched over her, saying little. When we had finished our meal, my mother turned to Conor.

"We need a fine tale tonight, Conor," she said, smiling. "Something inspiring to send Liam and his allies on their way to Tara strengthened. There will be many departures, for Sean escorts the girls west in a day or two, and we shall be very quiet here for a time. Choose your tale well."

"I will do so." Conor rose to his feet. He was not a very

tall man, but there was a presence about him that made him imposing, almost regal in his white robe. The golden torc around his neck gleamed in the torchlight, and above it his features were pale and calm. He stood quiet for a little, as if summoning the right story for this particular night.

"At this time of parting, of new ventures, it is apt to tell a tale of those things that have been, and are, and will be," Conor began. "Let each of you listen and make of this tale what your heart and spirit will, for each brings to the thread of words his own bright vision, his own dark memory. Whatever your faith, whatever your belief, let my tale speak to you; forget this world for a while and allow your mind to go back through the years, back to another time when this land was untrodden by our kind, when the Tuatha Dé Danann, the Fair Folk, first set foot on the shores of Erin and discovered unexpected opposition from those who were here before them."

"Fine tale, fine tale," rumbled Seamus Redbeard, setting his cup heavily down on the table.

"The Tuatha Dé were folk of great influence, gods and goddesses all," said Conor. "Among them were powerful healers; warriors with an awesome capacity for regeneration; practitioners of magic who could drain a lake dry, or change a man into a salmon or turn a soul off his chosen path with a flick of the fingers. They were both strong and willful. And yet they did not take Erin without a good fight.

"For they were not the first on these shores. There were others here before them. The Fomhóire were plain folk, folk with both feet on the ground. Some tales say they were ugly and deformed; some that they were demonic. Thus speak those whose understanding is limited to the surface of things. The Fomhóire were no gods. But they had their own crafts and their own kind of power. Theirs was an ancient magic, the magic of the belly of the earth, of the bottomless caves, of the secret wells and the mysterious depths of lake and river. Theirs were the standing stones we have employed for our own rituals, the solemn markers of the paths of sun, moon, and stars. Theirs were the great barrows and passage tombs. They were older than time. They did not simply live in the land of Erin. They *were* the land.

"Then the Fair Folk came, and others after them, and many were the grueling battles and subtle acts of treachery and feigned overtures of friendship that occurred before at last there was a kind of peace, a delicate truce, a dividing of the land that was so inequitable that the Fomhóire would simply have laughed at it, had not they been so weakened that they dared not risk further losses. So they agreed to the peace, and they retreated to the few places grudgingly allowed them. The Tuatha Dé possessed the land, or thought they did, and they ruled here until the coming of our own kind drove them in their turn into secret places, Otherworld places, under the surface, in the deep forests, in the lonely caverns beneath the hills, or back to the depths of the ocean across which they had first journeyed to Erin. So both races of magical beings seemed lost to this world.

"Time brings change. One people follows another and holds sway for a span, and then a new conqueror comes to take their place. Even for our people, even within the span of our fathers' fathers' lives, we have seen this. Our own faith was stretched very thin for a time. Even here, in the great forest of Sevenwaters, its sacred lore was all but forgotten. For once that lore exists only as a memory in the mind of one very old man, it is as frail and tenuous as the gossamer wing of a butterfly, as a single thread of a cobweb. We nearly let it slip through our fingers. We came so close."

Conor bowed his head. There was a hush in the room.

"You have brought it to life again, Conor," my mother said softly. "You and your kind are a shining example to us. In these times of trouble you have preserved the old ways and fanned the spark into a flame."

I glanced at Fionn; he was a Christian, after all. Perhaps

this had not been the wisest tale to choose. But Fionn did not seem to be perturbed. Indeed, I wondered if he had even been listening. He had his fingers lightly around Niamh's wrist, and his thumb was moving against her skin. He was looking at her sideways, with something like amusement in his expression and a little smile on his lips. Niamh sat rigidly upright, her blue eyes wide and blind like those of a trapped creature staring into the light of a flaring torch.

"We forget sometimes," Conor resumed the tale, "that both these races, the Fair Folk and the Fomhóire, dwelt here a very long time, long enough to set their mark on every corner of Erin. Every stream, every well, every hidden cave has its own tale. Every hollow hill, every desolate rock in the sea has its magical dweller, its story and its secret. And there are the smaller, less powerful folk who have their own place in the web of life. The sylphs of the upper canopy, the strange, fishlike dwellers in the water, the selkies of the wide ocean, the small folk of toadstool and tree stump. They are a part of the land as great oak and field grass are, as gleaming salmon and bounding deer are. It is all one and the same, interlinked and interwoven; and if a part of it fails, if a part of it is neglected, all becomes vulnerable. It is like an arched doorway, in which each stone supports the others. Remove one and the whole structure collapses.

"I have told you how our faith weakened, and was driven into hiding. But this is not a story of the Christian way and how it grows in strength and influence throughout our land. It is a tale of custodianship and of trust. It is a tale you ignore at your peril when you go forth as an ally of Sevenwaters."

There was a pause.

"Very cryptic," murmured Liam, reaching down to scratch one of the dogs behind the ear. "I sense the tale is not yet begun, Brother."

"You know me well," Conor responded with a half smile.

"I know druids," said his brother dryly.

Conor was standing just where Ciarán had stood to tell the tale of Aengus Óg and the fair Caer Ibormeith, whom he created in my sister's image, with her long, copper hair and her milk white skin. I glanced at my sister, wondering if she was thinking the same, and I saw her husband's fingers where they played against the palm of her hand, stroking, teasing, pinching so that she flinched in sudden pain.

"Come and sit by me awhile, Niamh." My voice rang out clearly in the silence while Conor pondered the next part of his tale. "We have seen nothing of you. I'm sure Fionn can spare you for a little."

Fionn's lip curled in a show of surprise. "You are bold, young sister," he said, arching his dark brows. "I ride to Tara in the morning; I will be without my lovely wife for the best part of a moon, maybe longer, since she has been prevailed upon to desert me. Would you deprive me still further? She is such a . . . comfort to me."

"Come, Niamh," I said, suppressing a shudder as I looked him straight in the eye and held out a hand toward my sister. Everyone was watching now, but nobody said a word.

"I . . . I would . . . ," said Niamh faintly, but her husband still held her wrist imprisoned. So I got up and walked across and I slipped my hand through her other arm.

"Please," I said sweetly, smiling at my sister's husband in what I hoped was a placatory manner, though I suspect the message of my eyes was somewhat different.

"Oh, well, there's always later," he said, and his fingers uncurled from her wrist.

This is the Uí Néill, Liadan. Sean was frowning at me. The voice of his mind was stern. *Don't meddle.*

She is my sister. And yours. How could he forget that? But it seemed they had all forgotten when they sent her away.

Niamh sat down by me as Conor resumed the tale. I felt her draw a deep, shuddering breath and let it out all at once.

I kept her hand in mine, but loosely, for it seemed to me I had to move slowly, as carefully as if I walked on eggshells, if I were to win back her trust.

"This is a tale of the first man to settle at Sevenwaters," said Conor gravely. "His name was Fergus, and it is from him that our folk are all descended. Fergus came from the south, from Laigin, and he was a third son with little chance of claiming his father's lands. He was one of the fianna, those wild youths who ride out to sell their swords to the best bidder. Well, one fine summer morning Fergus was separated from his friends right on the edge of a great wood; and try as he might, he could not find their trail. And after a while, lured by the beauty of the arching trees, the dappled pathways and slanting light, he rode on into the old forest, thinking, I will go where this path takes me and see what adventure comes my way.

"He rode and he rode, deeper and deeper into the heart of the forest, and the farther Fergus traveled the more that place took hold of his spirit and the more he marveled at its beauty and its strangeness. He felt no fear, even though by now he had completely lost his way. Instead, he was compelled to go ever forward, high on hills crowned with great oak, ash, and pine, down into hidden valleys thick with rowan and hazel, along streams fringed with willow and elder, until at last he reached the shore of a magnificent lake, glittering gold in the light of late afternoon. He did not know if this journey had taken a single day or two or three. He was not weary; instead, he felt refreshed, reborn, for something had awoken in his spirit that he had never known was there until now.

"Fergus stopped by the lake and dismounted from his horse. He bent to cup his hands in the clear water and take a welcome drink. The water was good. It sharpened his mind and emboldened his heart.

" 'What is it you want most in the world, Fergus?'

"Fergus whirled around in shock. There behind him

stood a man and a woman, so close he could not understand how he had not seen them before. Both were very tall, taller far than mortal kind. The man had hair the color of flame that curled and flickered around his brow as if it were indeed living fire. The woman was very fair, with long dark tresses and deep blue eyes that matched her flowing cloak. Fergus recognized that they must be folk of the Tuatha Dé Danann, and that he must answer the question. Strange, though; his answer came out quite different from what it might have been a few days before.

" 'I want to stay here and make my home,' he said. 'I want to be part of this place. I want my children to grow up under these trees and taste the fresh water of the lake. Then they will be clear-sighted and rich in spirit.' So short a time had it taken for this place to set its imprint on his soul.

" 'You know who we are?' asked the lady.

" 'I—I've an idea, yes,' said Fergus, suddenly abashed, for he had never encountered fairy folk before. 'I don't intend to be presumptuous, my lady. I expect this is your land. I can hardly claim it as my own. But you did ask.'

"The flame-haired man laughed. 'It's yours, son. That's why you were brought here.'

" 'Mine?' Fergus's jaw dropped in shock. 'The forest, the lake—mine?' It was a dream, surely.

" 'Yours to keep as guardian, if you fancy the job. As custodian. Make your home here by the lake of Sevenwaters. The forest is old. It is one of the last safe dwelling places for our people and for—the others. The forest will guard you and yours, and you will enjoy great power and prosperity if you remain true. But you must play your part as well. The old ways dwindle, and the secret places are safe no more; they are laid open, despoiled. You and your heirs will be the people of Sevenwaters, and your influence in the mortal world must be used to keep the forest and its dwellers safe—all of its dwellers. There are few such places of refuge left in the land of Erin, and they grow fewer with each turn of the wheel. It is not our way to seek help from your kind, but the world changes, and we need you and yours, Fergus. Will you be this guardian? Have you the strength for it?'

"What could he answer but yes? So Fergus built his keep of strong stone, and in time he gathered around him some of his old friends from the wild fianna, and some of the farm folk from these parts, and he cleared a few trees, just enough to make room for his grazing land and his small settlements. And he took a wife. Not the daughter of a farmer nor the sister of one of his friends, as you might expect. No, his wife was of another kind entirely. He found her one day when he was out scouting on the hills above the lake, seeking a good place for a watchtower. He came up a rise between rowans, and there she was, sitting high on the rocks in a ragged dress the color of willow leaves, combing her dark hair and gazing out over the trees toward the lake; and he took one look into her strange, clear eyes and was lost. She never said where she came from, or what she was. She was a wee, small thing, a slip of a girl; she was never one of the Tuatha Dé. Fergus remembered, sometimes, how the mysterious lady had spoken of *the others,* but he never asked.

"Her name was Eithne, and she was a good wife to him, and bore him three bold sons and three brave daughters. His first son he taught the arts of war, and the second the arts of good husbandry, so that together they might preserve the forest and lake of Sevenwaters and keep it safe. The third son was claimed, on his seventh birthday, by a very old man with braids in his hair who came limping out of the forest, leaning on a staff of oak. This son became a druid, and that was how the old ways were rekindled among the people of Sevenwaters."

"What about the daughters?" I could not resist interrupting, although it was not good manners to stop the flow of a druid's tale.

"Ah, the daughters," said Conor, smiling. "All three had their mother's small stature, and her dark hair and her strange eyes, and many a suitor was there for them when they became women. Fergus was a good strategist. The first he wed to the holder of the túath to the west of the forest. The second he wed to the son of another neighbor, who dwelt in the heart of the marshlands bordering the pass to the north. The third daughter stayed home and became skilled in herb lore and healing, and folk called her the heart of Sevenwaters."

"What about the Islands?" Sean asked, eager for the tale to unfold further.

"Ah, yes." Conor grew solemn. "The Islands. That is the next part of this tale. But maybe my audience grows weary. It is a long story, perhaps best told over two nights." He glanced around him, brows raised in question.

"Tell the rest, Conor," my mother said softly.

"As I said, Fergus never asked his wife, Eithne, what she was or where she came from. He never knew if she was an ordinary mortal or something else. She grew older just as a mortal does. But they do say that if one of the Otherworld folk makes the choice to wed one of our kind, she loses her immortality. If this is true, Eithne must have loved her man deeply indeed, and that perhaps is the root of the way the folk of Sevenwaters love to this day. Eithne gave her husband good cause to believe that she might indeed be one of the Old Ones. They say the Fomhóire are folk of the sea, that it was from the depths of the ocean that they emerged, long ago, to dwell in the land of Erin. Eithne's secret was a sea secret. She told Fergus of three islands, three rocks in the great water that separates our land from Alba and Britain. Secret islands they were, very small, very hard to find, save by those who knew. Knew what? asked Fergus. Knew how to find them, said Eithne. The Islands were the heart. The heart of everything, the center of the wheel. Fergus must go there, and then he would understand. When all else failed, when all was lost, the Islands would be the Last Place. Even more than the lake, even more than the forest, the Islands must be kept safe.

"What Eithne said turned Fergus cold, and he did not ask her to explain. But he had his men build a sturdy boat, a big curragh with a bit of a sail, and he followed the map Eithne had shown him how to make, and set out from the eastern shore toward the Isle of Man. That was before the worst of the raids; still, it was not the safest stretch of water for a boat manned by a bunch of woodsmen and farmers. Eithne did not come with her husband. She was carrying a child and besides, she said, sea travel made her sick. So Fergus and his men traveled east and a little south, and as they neared the coast of Man a mist came down, so thick you couldn't see your finger in front of you. They took down the sail and stilled the oars, but the boat moved on, pulled by an invisible current, while the crew sat shivering in fright, their minds full of long-toothed sea monsters and knife-edged rocks. And after a long time, the keel of the boat scraped onto a shelly beach, and the mist lifted as suddenly as it had come down. They were on the shore of a small, rocky island, not more than a speck in the sea, a desolate place surely inhabited only by seals and wild birds. The men were dismayed. Fergus reassured them, although truth to tell he himself was less than happy with their situation. There was a strange hush about the place, a feeling that something large was watching their every move. He bade the men haul up the curragh and make camp under the shelter of overhanging rocks, while he climbed higher to see how the land lay.

"Scrambling up the rocks, he observed with surprise that a remarkable variety of life existed in this forlorn place: low, creeping plants, wind-bent bushes, crabs and shellfish and little scuttling things. And many, many birds passing and wheeling overhead. Fergus stood at the topmost point of the small island and looked north. There was the Isle of

Man in the distance, but still too close for comfort. To the east, much nearer, lay another rocky island, larger than the one where they had landed, an island with bays and level ground covered with rough grass rising to cliffs in the south, a place where some sort of presence might be established if there were fresh water to be found. And to the west—there was the third island. Fergus knew instantly that this was the island Eithne had meant. It stood in the sea like a great stone pillar, steep, sheer, its base a mass of sharp, tumbled rocks over which the sea boiled and seethed. Incredibly, a set of rough steps had been hewn into the rock all the way to the top. There was a sort of ledge there and trees. Trees! Fergus could scarce believe it, but a grove of what seemed to be rowans crowned this stark pinnacle, and above them birds circled.

"Fergus thought for a while, and then he went back down to the men, and helped them to make a fire, and promised them they'd be going home in the morning. The men were relieved. This trip had been altogether too strange. Then Fergus said, but first I want you to take me over there. Where? asked his men. There, said Fergus, pointing. You could see no more than the top of the third island from where they stood on the shore, and so the men agreed. It was the next morning, when they were in the boat and rowing across, that they caught sight of the rocks and the frothing surf around them, and felt cold terror grip their vitals. Row on, said Fergus grimly, and they did, despite themselves. Then the current took them, and they shipped their oars, and the boat was sucked forward, closer and closer to the rocks, until the men began to scream and call on Manannán mac Lir to save them. And at the instant when they were about to be dashed to pieces, the boat was all of a sudden drawn between the rocks and into a sort of cavern where the water swirled, and at the side of the cavern was a shelf, and an opening, and steps cut in the rock, going up.

"Before anyone could speak, Fergus was out of the boat

and onto the shelf, and he was tying up the craft to an iron spike driven into a crack between the wet rocks. I won't be long, he said, as he set off up the steps. The men sat in the boat, very quiet indeed. It was dark in the cave, and the water moved strangely against the keel, as if there were creatures there just below the surface. The sea rushed in one opening and out another, where there was barely enough clearance even with the mast down. They tried not to think about tides. Nobody asked who would take charge if Fergus never came back.

"They waited a long time—at least, it seemed long, what with the churning waters and the shifting shadows and their imaginations playing nasty tricks. Eventually Fergus returned with a strange look on his face, as if what he had seen was beyond his wildest dreams, something that could never be put into words. He stepped into the curragh and untied the rope, and the men ducked as the current swept them out through the low opening and shot them forward, clear of the white water and the rocks, spewing their craft out into the open sea. Then they put up mast and sail, and took up the oars as well, and made haste homeward. And never a thing did they ask Fergus until they made safe landfall on the shores of Erin once more.

"He didn't tell what he'd seen. Maybe to Eithne, but not to the rest of his household. It was secret, he told them. But what Eithne had told him was true: the Islands were the Last Place, and the tallest one, which he named the Needle, was most precious of all. Here were the caves of truth, guarded by sacred rowan trees that grew where no ordinary tree could survive. The Islands must be protected from the outside world. If they were disturbed, if they were taken, the balance would shift; and then, however careful the husbandry of the forest, however secure the lands of Sevenwaters, things would begin to go wrong. When Fergus told people this, they believed him, for there was a light in his eyes, an awe in his expression that told them he had indeed seen something wondrous beyond telling.

"From that time on, a guard was put on the Islands, a camp established on Greater Island, a watch set on the seas south of Man, so neither Norseman nor Briton nor curious fisherman would dare come close. Fergus had to learn fast. The folk of Sevenwaters were not a seafaring breed, and they lost more than a few good men over the years, for the Islands are far out to sea, as near the coast of Britain as they are to Erin. But the will was strong. There came a time when the druids of the forest ventured across the sea to the Needle and performed the ritual of Samhain on the pinnacle beneath the sacred rowans. Ah yes," breathed Conor, his eyes seeing it, his expression full of wonder.

"For generations the family at Sevenwaters kept their promise and looked after the forest and its folk, and watched over the Islands, and the forest in turn gave them its bounty and ensured their enemies stayed away. In each generation there would be a druid, and there would be one or two who led the household and kept folk fed and stock healthy and ensured the people could defend themselves. In each generation there would be a healer. Outside the forest, the Christian faith spread across the land, sometimes enforced with violence, but more often subtly and quietly. Outside the forest, the Norsemen came and other raiders, and nothing was safe, not tranquil village nor king's fortress nor cloistered house of prayer. People no longer believed in the Tuatha Dé nor in the manifestations of the Otherworld, for in their fear folk saw only the barbarian with his axe dripping the blood of their dear ones. But Sevenwaters was safe, and so were the lands that bordered it, allies by marriage and long association, united against every foe. Inevitably there came a time when the family grew complacent. There was a generation that gave no child to the wise ones. Daughters wed farther away and died early. A leader was distracted, and his farmers fell into bad habits. Once things started to slide, they got rapidly worse.

"As they lost their grip, their enemies scented blood. In particular, the Briton, Northwoods of Cumbria, had a wish to extend his control beyond the sea; and at a black time for Sevenwaters, he came with a fleet of ships, manned by seasoned warriors, and took control of the Islands. The watch had been relaxed; the garrison allowed to run down. It was all too easy for Northwoods. Then there were British craft moored at Greater Island, and British boots trampled the soil of the sacred places, and British voices echoed in the caves of truth. They butchered the ancient rowans to fuel their fires. And it was as Eithne had said. From that moment on, things started to go wrong for Sevenwaters. Sons fell in battle with the Britons. Daughters died in childbirth. Trees were felled in error, and there were fires and floods. Allies turned their backs. Crops failed and the sheep got the murrain. So it went on, and the family struggled to keep control. They mounted attack after attack, but Northwoods held on and his descendants after him.

"It was later, much later, in the time of my father's grandfather, whose name was Cormack. That name was also my brother's, another who gave his life for the cause, and in the telling of this tale I honor him." Conor's tone remained calm, but there was a shadow over his features as he said this. Cormack had been his twin. I could imagine how such a loss must feel. "The Cormack of this tale was a good, strong man, another such as his ancestor Fergus. He struggled and worked, and saw himself going backward, and one day he ventured deep into the forest and sought help from the oldest of the druids, a man so ancient his face was all wrinkles and his eyes filmy and blind. Cormack asked him, 'How can I save my people? How can the forest be preserved and the dwellers of the forest? I will not give up my task; I am the custodian of these lands and all that live here. I am the lord of Sevenwaters. There must be a way.'

"The old druid looked into the fire and was silent so long Cormack began to wonder if he was deaf as well. The smoke rose and curled and the fire glowed with strange colors, green and gold and purple. 'There is a way,' said the old man, and his voice was deep and strong. 'Not for you, but for your children's children, or for their children's children. The balance must be restored, or all will be lost.'

"'How?' asked Cormack eagerly.

"'Many will fall,' the druid went on. 'Many will die for the cause. That is nothing new. The evil ones will gain in strength. Sevenwaters will come within a hair's breadth of losing everything, family and forest, heart and spirit. But it can be put right.'

"'When?'

"'Not in your time. There will come one who is neither of Britain nor of Erin, and at the same time is both. This child will bear the mark of the raven, and it is through that intervention that the Islands will be saved and the balance restored.'

"'What can I do?'

"'Hold on. Hold on, until it is time. That is all you can do.'"

Conor fell silent. It was a strange way to end a tale, but it was unmistakably the end. There was not a sound in the hall. My mother took up a flask of parsnip wine and poured some into a goblet.

"Liadan? Pass this to your Uncle Conor. He has worked hard for us tonight."

I let go Niamh's hand, which was limp and cold in mine, and carried the wine to my uncle.

"Thank you," he said with a nod. "Now tell me, Liadan, what does this tale mean to you? If you were to take one truth from it, what would that be?"

I looked him in the eye. "That even one of the fianna, a mercenary with no allegiance, can be a good and trustworthy man, given a chance," I said. "We should not be too quick to judge on appearances, for we are all descended from just such a man."

Conor chuckled. "Indeed. What about you, Sean? What truth did my tale speak to you?"

Sean was scowling. "No doubt it's meant to tell me I cannot ignore the prophecy," he said.

"Ah." Conor sat down, his cup between his long hands. "A tale is not *meant* to tell anything. It tells what the listener chooses to hear."

"It speaks to me," said my mother. "It tells me now is the time. Now or very soon. I feel it."

"You are right." Liam had one pup sleeping on his knee, the other sprawled across his feet. It was a measure of his stature that he still managed to look dignified. "Conor chose his tale well for this night. When we are in Tara we must not lose sight of our own goal. We will be prevailed upon, I expect, to lend our support to other ventures. We must not forget what our first true quest must be."

"And indeed, if Sorcha is right, we should consider all options to achieve it quickly." I had thought Seamus Redbeard asleep, but he'd been listening, slumped comfortably back in his chair.

"I find it hard," said Fionn with a half smile, "to accept the way you view fantasy as truth. It's a somewhat different way of looking at the world. Be that as it may, there are practical reasons for your venture. The Islands have long provided Northwoods with safe harbor. Take that from him and you weaken his influence greatly. As for your own lands, you have them secure again now; and Liam is held in high regard throughout Ulster and beyond. A man would be foolish to want Sevenwaters as anything other than an ally."

"Still," said my father quietly, "as the tale tells, generations of good men have died for the cause, and not just the people of Erin. There have been widows and fatherless children on both sides of the water. It may be worth looking at the words of the prophecy more closely if we would not lose more than we must. It says nothing of a battle."

Fionn raised his brows. "You yourself are close kin to Northwoods, are you not? That creates an interesting complication. It is inevitable that you would view the situation somewhat differently."

"The man who bears that name is kin to me, yes," my father said. "A distant cousin. He made a successful claim for the estate when my Uncle Richard died. I make no secret of my link with that family. And since you married my daughter, you, too, can now claim a tie of kinship."

Conor got to his feet, yawning. "It grows late," he said.

"Indeed," said Liam, rising and dislodging the pups unceremoniously to the floor. "Time for bed. We have an early start tomorrow, and not all of us are young."

"Come, Niamh." Fionn held out a hand toward my sister, but his eyes were on me, challenging. She went to him without a word, and he put his arm around her waist, and they were away up the stairs. I turned to fetch my candle, but Eamonn was there before me, lighting it from the torch nearby, putting it in my hand.

"I won't see you for a while," he said. The flickering candlelight made strange patterns on his face. He was very pale.

"I wish you well on your journey to Tara," I managed, wondering why he should take the trouble to talk to me at all now that I had told him. "And—I'm sorry."

"You sh-should not concern yourself with me. Be safe until I return, Liadan." His fingers brushed mine where they held the candle, and then he was gone.

Chapter Nine

Eamonn's home had a real name, the one they put on the maps. It meant the dark fortress. But everybody called it Sídhe Dubh, as if it were a fairy fort and not the home of a chieftain of Ulster, at least not the human kind. The story went that once, long ago, the mysterious hill that rose, mist enshrouded, from the encircling marshlands had indeed been an Otherworld residence, peopled by the Fair Folk or, more likely, the older folk who came before them. Bogles, perhaps, or clurichauns. They were all gone now, fled with the coming of Eamonn's ancestors to set their stamp on this unlikely domain. But the strangeness lingered.

There were small peat bogs on our own estate and on Seamus Redbeard's holdings, providing good turf for hearth fires. On Eamonn's land it was different. Here the marshes were immense, daunting, wreathed in eerie mists, dotted here and there with clumps of oddly misshapen trees, whose roots clung close to the tiny islands amid an ocean of black, sucking ooze. In some places there were stretches of open water, but it was water such as you would see nowhere else, dark even when the sun shone and coated with an oily sheen. In such an inhospitable landscape there were few places where dwellings might be safely built. Isolated stretches of higher ground held small settlements, with barn or storehouse in the middle, and the folk living around them on crannogs built out over the bog. These little islands, constructed from stones and brushwood with rough, wooden palisades to keep out intruders, were linked to dry land by precarious walkways. In warm weather, clouds of insects gathered and the air was filled with a sweet, decaying smell. Still, folk stayed on there as their fathers and their fathers' fathers had done before them. Eamonn was a strong leader, and his people were loyal. Besides, they knew no other life.

To the north, Eamonn had grazing lands and grain fields and other projects of different kinds. Still, he chose to make his home, as his forebears had done, right in the very center of the marshlands. There was a single approach, across a causeway wide enough to take three riders abreast or a heavy cart drawn by oxen. In its way, Sídhe Dubh was even safer than Sevenwaters, for this entry could be easily guarded, and no human invader would be foolish enough to attempt an onslaught through the marshes. For this was no mere peat bog; it was a landscape of tricks and treachery. A man might step out to cut turves, and load his barrow and be away home before sunset. Or he might step but one pace to the right, or to the left, and be sucked under before he had time to call on the Dagda to deliver him. As Eamonn himself had said, it was quite safe if you knew the way.

Since the Painted Man had surprised Eamonn's warriors, the defenses had clearly been strengthened. This was not my first visit here, but I did not remember the seven sentry posts between the borders of Eamonn's land and the start of the causeway. I did not recall the chained and bolted gates that closed the entry and required three keys to be opened. It was just as well we were traveling with Aisling, who was the lady of this grim house, or even Sean and Niamh and I might have been turned away.

Sídhe Dubh was a ring fort little changed since it was built. It first appeared as a low, rocky hill, shield shaped, rising from the gloom of the mist-cloaked landscape. Riding across the causeway, trying not to take too much notice of the strange creakings, ploppings, and gurglings arising from the inky water on either side, a traveler would realize that the hill was crowned with a strong, impenetrable fortress wall of dark stone, concealing all within. Then it became evident that the rocks on the hill were carefully placed, a wall of sharp points laid with great skill and cunning almost all the way around. A horse could never ride up this hill. A man who tried to climb it would be picked off by many arrows before he advanced an arm's length across the jagged circle of stones. The only entrance through this toothed barrier was a heavy iron-barred door that seemed to open into the hill itself, and was guarded by two very large men with axes and two huge black dogs on short, tight chains. As we rode closer, the dogs began slavering and growling and showing their teeth. Aisling slipped down from her horse and walked casually over, reaching out a slender white hand to pat one on its round, brutish head. The great creature panted with delight, and the other one whined.

"You've done well," she said to the guards. "Now open up and let us in. My brother's orders are to make our guests welcome until he returns. And maintain your vigilance. He wants them safe. He asks, have there been any further sightings of the fianna? The Painted Man and his band?"

"No, my lady. Not a skerrick. They say the fellow's gone over the water, doing a job for some king in foreign parts. That's what they're saying."

"Nonetheless, maintain the guard. My brother would not forgive me if any ill came to our guests."

I thought about Aisling as we were admitted to the long, dim, covered way that dipped down and then rose, spiraling up around the contour of the hill. She was so sweet and compliant at Sevenwaters, yet here she was quite different. In her brother's absence, she assumed instant control, and they all obeyed her, little slip of a thing that she was. By the light of the torches flaring in brackets on the stone walls, I saw Sean grinning as she gave orders. As for Niamh, she hadn't said a word since we left Sevenwaters. She had bid our parents a stiff good-bye, and I had seen how my mother held back her tears and how my father was hard put to remain calm before the assembled household. I had seen again how secrets were splitting our family apart, how we began to hurt one another, and I was thinking hard about Conor's tale and what it meant. I was trying not to think about what Finbar had told me. *Perhaps you cannot have both.*

The underground way led ever upward with dark passageways branching off to right and left, full of shadowy corners and unexpected tricks of the torchlight. I was pleased to emerge into the upper courtyard, where we dismounted at the entry to the main building. The high, circular stone wall that blocked our view of the surrounding countryside was topped with a concealed walkway punctuated by guard posts, and many men in green were deployed there, watching, ready. Within the fortress wall was a whole settlement: forge, stables, storehouses, mill, and brewery. It was an entire community, going about its business in orderly fashion as if living thus enclosed were not at all out of the ordinary. I allowed my mind to dwell briefly on the thought that, if certain events had not prevented me from accepting Eamonn's offer of marriage, I might myself have been mistress here in a year or so. I would have needed a powerful incentive to be prepared to live thus, unable to look out over trees and water, prevented from wandering the forest paths in search of berries or climbing the hill under the young

oaks. I would have had to want him very much to agree to
that. But then, Niamh had not wanted Fionn. She had not
wanted to go away from the forest and live in Tirconnell,
but she had gone. My sister had not been given the luxury
of a choice.

We settled in. Niamh overcame her lethargy for long
enough to protest about sharing a bedchamber with me, although she had in fact done so for sixteen years without so
much as a murmur of complaint. Aisling was not swayed;
everything was organized, she said, and there was no suitable chamber available, except her own of course, which
Niamh was welcome to share. Niamh looked at me, waiting
for me to suggest I would gladly share with Aisling and allow her to be alone. I said nothing. So Niamh fell silent
again, frowning and twisting her fingers together.

"Maybe an Uí Néill is too grand for the likes of me," I
said, trying to smile without much success as we went up
the stairs to our quarters. The room was spacious though
dark, its single, narrow window slit looking down into the
courtyard. There were two plain bed frames made up with
snowy linen and dark, woollen blankets. There was a table
with a jug of water and a bowl and soft cloths. Everything
was immaculately tidy and scrupulously clean. I had noticed green-clad guards at the foot of the stairs and in the
upper hallway.

"You might like to wash and then rest until supper time,"
suggested Aisling, who was hovering behind us. "I told
them to leave warm water for you. I'm sorry about the
guards. Eamonn insisted."

I thanked her, and she was away again. Sean was still
down in the courtyard, deep in discussion with one of our
own men. He would not be staying long, for in Liam's absence he was responsible for Sevenwaters and must return
home to fulfill his duties there. My father could have handled it quite capably; but although folk liked and trusted the

Big Man, they did not entirely forget that he was a Briton, and so he could never step into Liam's shoes even if he had a mind to. In a way that was a waste, for if ever a man was cut out to be a leader, it was Hugh of Harrowfield. Still, he had chosen his own path.

Once the door was closed, I stripped off my outer garments and removed my boots. I poured a little water into the bowl and splashed face, arms, and hands, glad to remove some of the dust and sweat of the journey. I rummaged through my bags for comb and mirror.

"Your turn," I said, as I sat down on the bed and began to tackle my wind-tangled curls. But my sister had done no more than take off her riding boots. She lay down on her bed fully dressed and closed her eyes.

"You should at least wash your face," I said, "and let me comb out your hair for you. And you'll sleep more comfortably if you take that gown off. Niamh?"

"Sleep?" she said flatly, not opening her eyes. "Who said anything about sleep?"

My hair was a disaster. I'd be lucky to get all the knots out by suppertime. I tugged the bone comb through, strand by strand, starting with the ends and working painfully back to the roots. There was indeed something to be said for shaven heads, it one must live out of doors. Niamh lay on her back unmoving, breathing slowly, but she was not asleep. Her knuckles were tight, her body tense.

"Why don't you tell me?" I said quietly. "I'm your sister, Niamh. I can see something's wrong, something worse than just—than just being married and going away. It could help to talk about it."

All she did was move a little farther away from me. I went on combing my hair. Sounds drifted in from the courtyard, the movement of horses, men calling, an axe falling on wood, crack, crack. A terrible suspicion was forming in my mind, one I could scarce give credence to. I could not ask her. I closed my eyes, sitting there, and imagined I was my sister, lying quiet in the dim, stone room. I felt the softness of the blanket beneath me, the weariness of my body from riding, the heavy bundle of bright hair around my head under the concealing veil. I let myself drift in the quietness of the room. I became my sister. *I felt how alone I was, now that I was no longer part of Sevenwaters, now that my mother and father and my uncles, and even my sister and brother, had thrown me away like a piece of rubbish. I was worthless. Why else had Ciarán, who said he would love me forever, gone away and left me? What Fionn said was right—I was a complete disappointment, with no skills as a wife and no aptitude as a lover. Unaccommodating with guests, he said. Incompetent around the house. Unimaginative in bed, despite all his efforts to teach me. Altogether a failure. Just as well I was who I was, or there would have been no point to it at all. At least, my husband said, there was the alliance. I felt the aches and pains all over me, the hurt that made it so hard to ride, the damage I must be careful not to show or it would get worse, all of it. I must not let them see how I had failed, even at this. If I let nothing show, then somehow it made the bad things less real. If I let nothing out, then I might hold myself together just a little longer.*

I wrenched myself back, feeling sweat break out all over my body. My heart was racing. Niamh lay there unmoving. She was quite unaware that I had seen into her thoughts. I was shaking with outrage. A pox on my Uncle Finbar! I would rather never have known I could do this; I would gladly give this gift back to whoever had bestowed it upon me and be endowed with a practical skill instead, such as the ability to catch fish or to add up numbers in my head. Not this, not the art of reading people's inner thoughts, not the understanding of their secret pain. Nobody should be given such a perilous gift.

After a while I admitted I was being unfair to my uncle. He had been wise to warn me. Besides, this was not the first time. What about that night when Bran had shivered and gripped my arm so tight he came close to breaking it, and I had heard a child cry out not to be left on his own? I had shared his pain as well and tried to help him. Even after his rejection of me, still I lit my candle, still I kept my vigil in times of darkness and carried his image in my thoughts. If I had the gift to see those wounds inside, hidden deep, then with it I must have the capacity to heal. The two went together; that much both Mother and Finbar had told me. I would give much never to know the rest of what Niamh had in her head behind that empty, closed expression; my imagination conjured up images that made me shudder. But I must know if I were to help her.

Tread slowly. Tread light as a wren that makes barely a rustle in the leaves of the hazel thicket. Tread softly, I told myself, or she will shatter in pieces, and it will be too late. There was time; a moon, maybe, until Fionn returned with Eamonn, and Niamh must leave us again. That was long enough for—for what? I could not imagine, but something. I would find out the truth first, and then I would make a plan. But not so fast that I tipped my sister over the edge. So when she excused herself straight after supper and fled back upstairs, I gave her some time to be alone. There was only so much a person could take when stretched as thin as she was. The weight of it hung heavily on me, and my thoughts were far away when Sean spoke to me. Aisling had gone out to the kitchens, and my brother and I sat alone over our ale at some distance from the men and women of the household.

"I'm leaving in the morning, Liadan," Sean said quietly. "Liadan?"

"Sorry. I wasn't listening."

"Mmm. They say women get like that when they're

breeding. Fuzzy in the head. Not quite all there." It was the first time he had mentioned the subject, and his tone was light, though his eyes were questioning.

"You'll be an uncle," I told him severely. "Uncle Sean. Sounds old, doesn't it?"

He grinned, then was suddenly serious. "I'm not happy about the whole thing. I think I deserve the truth. But I'm under orders not to question you, and I won't. Liadan, I'm riding north tomorrow. I'm not going home, not yet. I'm telling you because I know you'll keep it to yourself. And somebody needs to know where I've gone just in case I don't come back."

"North?" I asked flatly. "Where north?"

"I'm going to present a man with a proposition and hear what he has to say. I should think you can fill in the rest of the story."

"Uh-huh," I said, feeling myself turn cold. "That's not a very good idea, Sean. It's a big risk to take when the answer must be no."

Sean's eyes were fixed very directly on mine. "You seem quite sure about the answer. How can you know such a thing?"

"You're in danger if you go," I said bluntly.

Sean scratched his head. "A warrior is always in danger."

"Send someone else if you are determined to contact this man. It is foolhardy to go yourself and alone."

"From what I've heard, this may be the only way to find him. To walk straight into the dragon's lair, so to speak."

I shivered. "Your journey will be wasted. He will say no. You'll find out that I am right."

"A mercenary only says no when the price is not high enough, Liadan. I know how to bargain. I want the Islands back. This man can win them for me."

I shook my head. "This is no mere transaction, no simple purchase of services. It is quite different. There is death and loss in this, Sean. I've seen it."

"Maybe. Maybe not. At least let me put my theory to the test. And, Liadan, this is secret, that goes without saying. Even Aisling believes I'm traveling home. Keep it so, unless . . . you know."

"Sean—" I hesitated, not sure how much I might say.

"What?" Sean frowned.

"I will keep this to myself of course. And I must ask—I must ask that if you find the man you seek, you will speak to him only of your proposition and not of . . . other things."

Now he was really scowling, his eyes fierce.

Please, Sean. I am your sister. Please. And do not—jump to conclusions.

He looked as if he'd like to pick me up and shake the truth out of me. But Aisling was returning and he gave a reluctant nod. *I can't help jumping to conclusions, but I think they cannot be correct. They are altogether too outrageous.*

The next day Sean was gone, and I said nothing, but I feared for him, knowing he sought out the Painted Man and his band to buy their services. After Bran's repudiation of all I held dear, my mother and father, my very name, I could not believe he would give Sean a hearing. More likely my brother would walk into some sort of trap. Likelier still, he would simply never be able to find them. Wherever he went, they would always be one step ahead. Besides, hadn't the men in green said Bran was far away over the sea? My vision had shown him in some distant place under strange trees. Probably they were all gone, Gull, Snake, Spider, all the motley band of warriors. If so, that was good. That meant, at least, that my brother would come home safe, if disappointed.

Meanwhile there was Niamh. I did not know how to tell her what I had seen in her thoughts, but as it happened there was no need, for the truth came out in a few days, despite her efforts to conceal it. It was not long before dusk, and I was restless, finding the closed environment of Sídhe Dubh oppressive, longing already for open air and trees and water. I had left Niamh to her own devices and gone up to the heavily guarded walkway around the circular fortress wall, high above marshes and settlements, high enough so that if you looked eastward you could glimpse the edge of the forest of Sevenwaters, a gray-blue shadow in the distance. Slowly I made my way right around, pausing here and there to look out through the narrow gaps in the stonework, mere slits formed so that an arrow might be shot without the archer being exposed to a returning shaft. I was not tall enough to see over the parapet; it was designed to protect a man standing, and I am small, even for a woman. The guard posts, set high with steps leading up, and themselves well fortified, gave a vista all around. I charmed my way into the northern one and was allowed to step up and look. The man in charge rumbled about Lord Eamonn and what the rules were, and I smiled sweetly and said how brave they all must be, and what a risky job they did, and how I was sure Eamonn wouldn't mind them showing me the view just this once. But if they were worried, well, I wouldn't tell him if they didn't either. The three guards grinned and set about educating me on what was what.

"Look up northward, my lady. It's not so very far to those hills, dry land, that is, with some cover. But you can't go straight across, too treacherous. Sucking bog, you see. Nightmare stuff."

"Means you have to go all the way around," said the second man. "Back the way you came in, east to the cross-roads, then north again and double back. Adds half a day, moving on foot, till you get to the pass. Of course, there is a way straight across, a quick way."

The first man gave a mirthless chuckle. "It's quick all right. Quick to drag you under if you set a foot wrong. Wouldn't catch me trying that way. Not if my life depended on it."

The third guard was somewhat younger, not much more than a lad, and he spoke diffidently. "Go out there at night, and you'll hear the call of the banshee across the boglands—fair curdles your innards—foretelling another death. Another soul the dark one set her cold hand on."

"But there is a quick way across?" I asked, staring out over what appeared to be a continuous stretch of marshland all the way to the distant line of low hills in the north.

"Uh-huh. Quick and secret. Lord Eamonn uses it, and some of the men. There're only a handful know it. Step by step, single file, have to remember every part of it, two to the left, one to the right, and so on. Or you're gone."

"Was this the sort of place where that mercenary, you know the one, they call him the Painted Man . . . ?"

"Where he set upon our men and slaughtered them like quarry in a hunt? Not this place, my lady, but another much like it. How he learned the way, the Morrigan only knows. A curse on the murdering scum."

"We got one of them, at least," said the first man. "Got one of the butchers later on. Spilled his guts for him."

"Me, I won't be satisfied until they're all dead and buried," said the other. "Only burial's too good for them. Especially the one they call the chief. Black-hearted, that man is, evil through and through. Tell you something; he'd be a fool to set so much as his little toe on my lord's land again. Death sentence, that'd be."

"Excuse me." I slipped between them out of the guard post and down the steps to the walkway.

"Sorry, my lady. Hope we didn't upset you. Men do talk plain, you understand."

"No, no, it's all right. Thank you for explaining."

"Take care walking back, my lady. Stones are a bit uneven here and there. No place for a woman, this."

When I got back to the bedchamber, the door was closed. I gave it a push, but something was blocking it. I pushed harder, and the door opened halfway, dislodging a small chest that had been set behind to keep it shut. A large pan had been carried to the room, and water for bathing. Niamh heard me and grabbed for a cloth to cover herself, but it was too late for her to hide. I had seen. I stepped inside very quietly and closed the door behind me. I stood there staring at the bruises that covered every part of my sister's body. I saw how her once buxom, fair-skinned form had shrunk and faded, so that her ribs stuck out and her hip bones jutted beside her sunken stomach as if she were starving. I saw how the long, shimmering hair that had once cascaded down to clothe the curves of her womanhood was now hacked off crudely at the level of her chin, the ends ragged as if severed with an angry sawing of the knife. It was the first time I had seen her without her veil since she had come back from Tirconnell.

Without a word, I walked over and, taking the cloth from her shaking hands, placed it around her shoulders, shielding her poor, damaged body from the light. I took her hand and helped her from the bath, and sat her down on the bed as she began to weep, at first softly and then with great hiccuping sobs like a child. I did not try to hug her, she was not ready for that, not yet.

I found fresh smallclothes and a plain gown and got her into them. She was still weeping when we were finished, and I found my comb and began to draw it carefully through the tattered remnants of my sister's lovely hair.

After a while, the sobs subsided and her words became more coherent, and what she said was: "Don't tell! Promise me, Liadan. You mustn't tell any of the family, not even Father or Mother. Not Sean. Especially not the uncles." She gripped me by the wrist, quite hard, so that I almost dropped the comb. "Promise, Liadan!"

I looked directly into her big, blue eyes, which brimmed with tears. Her face was ashen; her expression full of fear.

"Did your husband do this, Niamh?" I asked quietly.

"Why would you think that?" she snapped immediately.

"Someone has done it. If not Fionn himself, then who? For surely your husband could protect you from such abuse."

Niamh drew a shuddering breath. "It's my fault," she whispered. "I've got everything wrong, everything. It's a punishment."

I stared at her.

"But, Niamh—what cause could Fionn have to do such a thing? Why hurt you so terribly? Why cut off your hair, your beautiful hair? The man must be mad."

Niamh gave a shrug. She had become so thin, her shoulders were as bony and frail as our mother's under the soft blue wool of her gown. "I deserved it. I made one mistake after another. I'm so—so clumsy and stupid. I am a disappointment to him, a failure. No wonder Ciarán—" Her voice cracked. "No wonder Ciarán went away and didn't come back for me. I was never any good."

This was such utter nonsense I was tempted to speak to her sharply, as I would once have done, to tell her to stop being silly and to count her blessings. But this time she really believed her own words; there were bruises and scars, not just on the tender flesh of the body, but deep in the spirit, and no quick words would heal those wounds.

"Why did he cut your hair?" I asked again.

She put her hand up to run it through the crudely shorn locks, as if she herself could not quite believe that weight of silken gold was gone.

"He didn't," she said. "I cut it."

I stared at her. "But why?" I asked, incredulous. Niamh had always looked after her hair, knowing without vanity that it was one of her chief beauties; and while she had sometimes railed at being made in the mold of her father, so clearly a Briton, she nonetheless liked the way her long tresses shone bright in the sun and flew out around her as she danced and caught the men's eyes. She had washed them in chamomile and tied them with flowers and silk ribbons.

"I don't think I can tell you," my sister said, in a very small voice.

"I want to help you," I told her. I was mindful of what I had been shown before, when her thoughts were revealed to me. Still, far better that she told me herself, willingly. Already, once, she had believed me a spy. "But I can't help if you won't tell me what this is all about. Did your husband find out about Ciarán? Was that it? Was he angry that you had already lain with a man before your wedding night?"

She shook her head miserably.

"What, then? Niamh, a man cannot beat his wife thus and be left unpunished. Under the law you could seek to divorce him on such grounds. Liam would pursue this for you. Father would be outraged. We must tell them."

"No! They must not know!" She was shaking.

"This is crazy, Niamh. You must let your family help you."

"Why would they help me? They hate me. Even Father. You heard what he said to me. Sean hit me. They sent me away."

After that, we sat there silent for a while. I waited. She twisted her thin fingers together, and picked at the fabric of her gown, and gnawed at her lips. When she did speak at last, her tone was flat and final.

"I'll tell you. But first you must promise not to tell Father or Liam or any of the family. Not Eamonn or Aisling either. They are almost family. Promise, Liadan."

"How can I promise such a thing?"

"You must. Because it's all been wrong, all of it, and if you tell, it will wreck the alliance; and then I will have failed at that as well and disappointed them all again, and they will all despise me even more than they do now, and there will be no point at all in going on, no point. I might as well take the knife to my wrists and finish it, and I will if you tell, I will, Liadan. Promise me. Swear it!"

She meant it. As her words spilled out, there was a terror in her eyes that was real and chilling.

"I promise," I whispered, realizing this vow left me all alone, cut off from any help I might have sought. "Tell me, Niamh. What has gone wrong?"

"I thought," she said, drawing an uneven breath, "I thought it would be all right in the end. Up to the last moment, somehow I still believed Ciarán would come back for me. It seemed impossible that he would not, that he would let me be wed and sent away, and not attempt to intervene. I was so sure. So sure he loved me as I loved him. But he didn't come. He never came back. So I thought—I thought—"

"Take your time," I said gently.

"Father was so angry with me," she said, in a thread of a voice. "Father, who never raises his voice to anyone. When I was little he was always there, you know, to pick me up when I fell, to keep us all safe and happy. When I was upset, I always went to him for a hug or a kind word. When things went wrong, he always made them better. Not this time. He was so cold, Liadan. He never even listened to me or to Ciarán. He just said no, without any reason for it. He sent me away forever, as if he never wanted to see me again. How could he do that?"

"That's not quite fair," I said quietly. "He is very worried about you now, and so is Mother. If he seems angry, perhaps it is because he wants to protect her from these things. And you're wrong about not listening. They did listen to Ciarán at least. Conor said it was Ciarán's own choice to leave the forest. He said it was a—a journey to find his past."

Niamh sniffed. "What use is the past if you throw away the future?" she said bleakly.

"So you were hurt by what Father did, and then you went to Tirconnell. What next?"

"I—I just couldn't do it. I meant to get it right; I thought, too bad for Ciarán, if he didn't love me enough to come back for me; then I'll marry another man, and make a new life, and show him I don't care, show him I can manage without him. But I couldn't, Liadan."

I waited. And she told me, told me so clearly it was as if I could see them, Niamh and her husband, there in a bed-chamber together. There had been many such scenes since she wed, since she found she could not pretend.

Fionn was naked, and he was watching my sister as she brushed out her long hair, stroke by careful stroke. I could feel her fear, feel the thudding of her heart, the chill that prickled her flesh. She wore a sleeveless nightrobe of fine lawn, and the bruises on her body, new ones, old ones, were clearly visible. Fionn stared at her, and he had his hand between his legs, fondling himself, and he said, "Make haste then! A man can't wait forever."

"I—" said Niamh, looking like some trapped animal, "I-I don't really want . . . I don't feel like—"

"Mmm." Fionn strode over to her, making no secret of the desire that hardened his body. He stood close behind her and took the fall of her red-gold hair in his hands. "Have to do something about that, won't we? A wife needs to feel like it, Niamh, at least some of the time. Be different if you were breeding, that might give you some excuse. But it seems you can't even do that for me. It's enough to make a man look elsewhere. And it's not as if there isn't plenty on offer. There's many a likely lass in this household has felt the length of me inside her before ever you came here, and been grateful for it. But you—" He pulled her hair tight so that her head was jerked back and she gasped with pain and fright. "You just don't seem to care, do you? You just don't seem to warm to me." He tugged again, and she bit back a scream. Then he let go all of a sudden, and his hands were on her, pulling up the nightrobe roughly, pressing her body toward him, and he thrust into her from behind without further ado, and this time she could not hold back her cry of pain and outrage.

"Bad girl," Fionn said, taking his pleasure with grim efficiency. "What's a wife for but to satisfy her husband? Though you could hardly call this satisfaction. A bit like doing it to a corpse. A mere—outlet—for the—urges of the—body—aahhh," he said, withdrawing from her with a shudder, reaching for a cloth to dry himself. "Perhaps it's practice you need, my dear. I have a few friends who'd be happy to give you some—variety. Maybe teach you a trick or two. We might try that, one night. I could watch."

Niamh stood with her back to him, staring ahead of her as if he were not even there.

"What, nothing to say to me?" He took hold of her hair again, gripping it at the nape of the neck, and wrenched her around to face him. "By God, if I'd known what a cold fish I was getting I'd never have agreed to this match, alliance or no! I should have taken that young sister of yours. Scrawny little thing, but at least she'd some life in her. You, you haven't even enough spark to answer me back. Well, go on then, get your clothes on. Make yourself beautiful, if that's not asking the impossible. I have guests to supper, and you'd better at least pretend to be civil to them."

When he had gone, Niamh sat there alone for some time, staring at her reflection in the bronze mirror that hung on the wall, her eyes blank. Then her hands took up the comb again, and she drew it through her hair just once, from the crown of her head right down to where the red-gold strands ended level with her hips. She looked across the room to where her husband's cloak hung on a peg, and beside it a belt with a dagger on it, neat in leather scabbard. There was no decision, simply the will to rise and walk over, and to take the dagger and cut, handful by handful, pull and slash, pull and slash, all the way around until her beautiful, shining hair lay about her on the tiled floor like some strange harvest of autumn. She put the knife back neatly, and then she dressed, carefully in a high-necked gown with sleeves to the wrist, a gown that revealed not a single bruise. Over her shorn locks she placed a veil of fine wool, fitted close around temples and neck, so that her hair might have been any color, any length.

"I thought, you see, I thought there was no point anymore," Niamh said. "Everything must be for a reason, or I might as well be dead. Why would I be punished unless I deserved it? If he hurts me, it is because I am worthless. Why bother with the pretense? Why try to be beautiful? Folk used to call me that once, but it was a lie. I love Ciarán more than anything in the world. And he just turned his back and left me. My own family cast me out. I don't deserve happiness, Liadan. I never did."

My mind was full of rage. If I had had a knife in my hands, and Fionn Uí Néill had been in my sight, there was not a thing could have stopped me from plunging my weapon into his heart and giving it a good twist. If I had had a mercenary or three handy, and a little bag of silver to pay them with, I would have felt a grim satisfaction in ordering his execution. But I was here at Sídhe Dubh, and Fionn was my brother's ally and Liam's. I was here with my sister, who now opened her eyes and turned to me a face so wretched, so helpless and frail, that I knew anger was of no use whatever, not at this moment. I wanted to take her by the shoulders and give her a good shake, and say, *Why didn't you stand up for yourself? Why didn't you spit in his arrogant face and give him a well-aimed kick for good measure? Or if you couldn't manage that, why not just walk away?* For I knew that if I had been in her place, I would never have stood for such treatment. I would sooner be a beggar woman scavenging by the roadway than let myself be debased thus. But somehow, in Niamh's mind, it had all been turned around. It had been neatly twisted so that she believed everything Fionn told her. Her husband said it was her fault, and so it must be. Now Niamh was all but swallowed up by the ugliness of what had been done to her. And we all bore the blame for it. The men of our household had sealed her fate when they sent her away from Sevenwaters. Even I was guilty. I could have fought against her banishment, and I had not.

"Lie down, Niamh," I said gently. "I want you to rest, even if you cannot sleep. You are safe here. This place is so well guarded, the Painted Man himself could not hope to breach its defenses. Nobody can touch you here. And I promise you, you need never go back to your husband. You will be safe. I promise, Niamh."

"How—how can you promise such a thing?" she whispered, resisting my hands as I tried to ease her down onto the pillow. "I am his wife; I must comply with his wishes. The alliance—Liam—there is no choice . . . Liadan, you said you would not tell—"

"Ssh," I said. "I will find a way. Trust me. Now rest."

"I can't," she said shakily, but she did lie down, wan cheek pillowed on one slender hand. "As soon as I close my eyes, the things come back. I cannot shut them out."

"I'll stay with you." I was hard pressed to keep back my own tears. "I'll tell you a story, or talk, or whatever you like. I'll sing to you if you want."

"I don't think so," my sister said, with a shadow of her old asperity.

"I'll just talk then. I want you to listen to my voice and think about my words. Think only of the words, see only what I speak of. Here, let me hold your hand. That's good. We're in the forest, you and me and Sean. Remember the broad path under the beech trees, where you can run and run, it seems forever? You were always ahead, always the quickest. Sean would do his best to catch you, but he never quite could, until you decided you were too old for such things. I came last, because I was always stopping to look for berries or pick up a skeleton leaf, or listen to hedgehogs snuffling in the bracken, or try to hear the voices of the tree people high overhead."

"You and your tree people," she sniffed in disbelief, but at least she was listening.

"You're running barefoot, feeling the breeze in your hair, the soft, dry leaves under your feet, running through the shafts of light where the sun slants through the branches, where it catches the green and gold of the last leaves of autumn, keeping precarious hold. And suddenly you reach the lake shore. You're warm from running and you walk on into the water, feeling its coolness lap around your ankles, the soft mud under your feet. Later on, you lie on the rocks with Sean and me, and we put our fingers in the water and watch the fish slip by, silvery bodies half concealed by the glint of sunlight on the surface of the lake. We wait for the swans to fly down to the water, one leading, the others following, gliding down in the gold of late afternoon to land swish, swish, white wings folding neatly as the water receives them. They float like great ghosts out on the ripples as dusk creeps across the sky."

I went on like this for a while, and Niamh lay quiet; but she was awake, and I saw enough of her mind to know despair was never far from the surface.

"Liadan," she said, as I paused for breath. Her eyes opened and they were anything but calm.

"What is it, Niamh?"

"You tell of times past, of what was good and simple. Those times can never come back. Oh, Liadan, I'm so ashamed. I feel so—so dirty, so worthless. I have done everything wrong."

"You don't really believe that, do you?"

She curled herself up, one arm around her body, a fist against her mouth. "It's the truth," she whispered. "I have to believe it."

There was a tap at the door. It was Aisling, come to see if all was well, for it was nearly supper time and we had put in no appearance. I spoke to her quietly, saying Niamh was very tired and asking for a little food and drink on a tray, if it was not too inconvenient. Soon after, a maidservant brought bread and meat and ale, and I took it and thanked her and shut the door firmly behind her.

Niamh would not eat or drink, but I did. I was hungry; the child was growing. I could see clearly the slight swelling of my belly now, could feel the increased heaviness of my breasts. Soon the changes would be visible to all. But Niamh did not know; perhaps nobody had thought to tell her.

"Liadan?" she said, so faintly I could hardly hear her.

"Mmm?"

"I upset Mother. I hurt her when she—when she—and I didn't even know. Oh, Liadan, how could I not see—"

"Hush," I said, struggling to hold back my own tears. "Mother loves you, Niamh. She'll always love us, no matter what happens."

"I—I wanted to talk to her; I wanted to, but I couldn't. I couldn't make myself do it. Father was so stern. He hated me for upsetting her, and—"

"Ssh. It will be all right in the end. See if it isn't." Foolish confidence, that was. How could I make it right if those who had been so strong now seemed cut adrift like leaves tossed helpless before the willful gales of Meán Fómhair? Perhaps that was part of the old evil they spoke of, something so bad and so powerful it set all awry. Still, I soothed her, and at length she lay quiet again, her fists still clenched. I remembered what Finbar had shown me, how he had filled my mind with joyful images and peaceful thoughts, to make me better. He had said I must learn to use the healing gift. Perhaps it was for no more than this: to ease my sister's rest. So I did as I had before: imagined I were Niamh, lying there rigid on the bed, trying to shut out the world. I let my mind slip into hers; but this time I kept control, so that I remained Liadan, able to find answers, able to heal.

It was not like that other night when Bran had gripped my arm fit to break it, and his mind had cried out to me like a frightened child's. But there were things I saw that I would have given much not to know. I experienced with my sister the degradation, the ridicule, the violence. Before they were wed, Fionn had seen her beauty and heard of her virtues. She had indeed once possessed both in abundance. But he had not reckoned with Ciarán and the fact that Niamh's heart, and her body, had been given already when she wed him. With a little strategy, with a little flirting and play, she might have been able to start on the right footing. She might have been able to please her husband. It is cruel for any woman to have to deceive in order to protect herself. But many have done so, no doubt, and so made their own existence at least tolerable. Not my sister. She had not been capable of the playacting required for survival. And Fionn was not a patient man. I felt the blow of his hand, and of his belt, as she had. I felt the indignity of being used when I was unwilling, and I knew her shame, although the fault was not her own.

After a while, I started to make my own presence known in her tangled thoughts. I showed her a younger Niamh: the flame-haired girl who had whirled around in her white dress and longed for a life of wild adventure. I showed her the child running fast as a deer on a carpet of fallen leaves. I showed her eyes as blue as the sky, and the warmth of the summer sun in her hair, and the look on Ciarán's face, as he gave me the little white stone, and said, *Tell her—give her this.* He loved her. Perhaps he had gone away, but he loved her. Of that I was sure. I could not show her the future, for that I could not see myself. But I bathed her mind in love and light and warmth, and her hand relaxed in mine as the candle burned lower and lower.

She was asleep, snoring gently, relaxed as a small child. Very slowly, very carefully I withdrew my mind from hers and, tucking the blanket around her bony shoulders, stood and stretched, feeling the ache of utter exhaustion in every part of my body. Finbar had spoken true; one did not perform such work without a cost. I walked unsteadily to the narrow window and looked out over the courtyard, thinking I must reassure myself that the real world was still there, for my mind was full of evil images and confused thoughts. I was drained of energy and very close to weeping.

The moon was waning, a thin crescent in a dark sky full of scudding clouds. Down in the courtyard there were torches burning, and I could see dimly the forms of the ever-present sentries on patrol, both below and high above on the walkway. All night they maintained their guard. It was enough to make you feel like a prisoner, and I wondered how Aisling and the rest of the household could stand it. I stared out into the night sky, and my mind reached beyond the stone walls of the fortress, beyond the marshes, beyond the lands to the north. I was bone weary, so tired I longed for someone to put strong arms around me, to hug me and tell me I had done my best and that everything was going to be all right. I must indeed have been exhausted to allow myself such weakness. I gazed into the dark and my mind pictured those men around their cooking fire, listening enraptured as I told the tale of Cú Chulainn and his son, Conlai, a tale of great sadness. And I thought, fianna they may be, but I would rather be there than here, that much I know. I closed my eyes and felt hot tears begin to flow down my cheeks; and before I could tell myself to stop, my inner voice cried out: *Where are you? I need you. I don't think I can manage without you.* And at that precise moment, I felt the child move for the first time inside me, a little flurry as if he were swimming, or dancing, or both. I laid a hand gently on the place where he had made himself known, smiling. *We're leaving here, Son,* I told him

silently. *First we help Niamh. I don't know how, but I have
promised, and I must do it. Then we go home. I have had
enough of walls, and gates, and locks.*

Bold words. Not that I had imagined Niamh would come
back to herself easily or quickly. If hope is gone, the future
becomes barely worth contemplating. It was as well I carried my child within my body and felt his will for life with
every fluttering movement, or I might myself have been
drawn into the pit of her despair.

The days passed, and the time came nearer when Eamonn and Fionn would return to Sídhe Dubh and I must go
home. Niamh remained insubstantial as a wraith, eating and
drinking barely enough for survival, speaking only when
the demands of basic courtesy made it essential. But I could
see small signs of change in her. She was able to sleep now,
as long as I sat by her bed holding her hand until she drifted
off; and these times on the margin of consciousness I found
to be the best for slipping into her mind and gently pushing
her thoughts toward the light.

She would not come out walking with me around the top
of the wall where the guards were, but she did come down
to the courtyard, well covered in long-sleeved gown and
matronly veil, and went with me between armory and grain
store, smithy and stables. She was very quiet. To go out
among folk seemed an ordeal for her. I read in her thoughts
how unclean she felt, how she believed they were all watching her and thinking her a slut and ugly. How they were
whispering among themselves that it was just as well, after
all, that Lord Eamonn had not wed her as they had once expected he would. Still, she walked with me and watched as
I greeted this one and that, giving my opinion on their ailments, and the exercise brought a little more color into her
pallid cheeks. On wet days we explored the inside of the
fortress instead. Sometimes Aisling went with us, but more
often than not she was occupied in kitchens or storerooms
or deep in negotiation with household steward or lawman.

She would be a good wife for Sean, a balanced, orderly complement to his bold energy.

Sídhe Dubh was indeed a strange dwelling. I wondered greatly at the character of Eamonn's ancestor who had chosen to settle here in the very center of the inhospitable marshlands. He had certainly been a man of imagination and subtlety, perhaps a little eccentric, for the place had many oddities. There were the carved pillars in the main hall, with their fanciful beasts grinning down, small dragon, sea serpent, and unicorn. And there was the construction of the fortress itself with its covered passage up from the gate, and the family's two-floored dwelling built against the inner wall. Never have I seen a house with more strange branching passageways, concealed openings, and false exits, more trapdoors and secret ways and sudden treacherous wells. I had a chance this time to discover places I had never seen before, for I had been a child when I had last visited Eamonn's home and forbidden to wander too far. In my desire to keep Niamh moving, for I knew the body must be healthy if the mind is to heal, I led my sister down the long, covered way that wound around the hill from the main gate, snaking beneath the earthen rampart and stone walls to emerge into the courtyard. This path was always torchlit and alive with shadows, and many smaller ways led off on either side. Some were lined with timbers and some with stone. These Niamh was reluctant to explore, but my curiosity had been aroused, and I went back later in the afternoon when she was sleeping. It was necessary to use some tricks I had learned from my father, which were to do with getting past guards unobserved, to achieve this. I thought it best that nobody noticed my sudden interest in possible exits from the fortress and made a decision to forbid such expeditions. I took a lantern and followed the branching ways to discover a storeroom for cheese and butter, like the caves we used for such a purpose at home. I found a small room that simply had no floor; there was, instead, a very long

drop, and when I threw in a stone, I counted to five before I
heard the splash. And farther down the same way there
were lightless cells, each holding a bench and shackles
fixed to the wall. There were no prisoners, not now. The
place was choked with cobwebs, unused for many years.
Perhaps Eamonn did not take captives. I was glad I had not
brought Niamh here, for the very walls cried out with despair; there was a dark hopelessness about the place that set
a cold hand on my spirit. I retreated quickly, vowing to myself to curb my curiosity next time. As I came up the covered way there was the slightest of sounds behind me, and a
cat shot past, streaking up from farther down that dark,
shadowy passageway with the disused cells, a black cat
moving so fast I only just had time to see that it bore in its
jaws a very large and very dead water rat. So there was a
way to the outside. A narrow way, maybe too narrow for a
person to squeeze in or out. But it was nonetheless a way. I
was tempted to go back down and investigate, but it was
close to suppertime and I did not wish to attract undue attention. *One day soon, Son,* I said silently, feeling that at
some level he understood me, *one day we're going down
there, and maybe we'll get out of this for a while. Find ourselves some space. If we're lucky we might see a bird or a
frog. I need to breathe deep. I need to see beyond stone
walls.*

I had asked Aisling already, as politely as I could, and received the answer I expected. "Don't you ever go out?" I'd
said. "Doesn't it drive you crazy being shut up all the
time?"

Aisling raised her brows at me. "People do go out," she
said, puzzled. "It's not a prison. Carts bring supplies, and
the men ride across on patrol. There's more movement
when Eamonn's at home."

"And I suppose every cart is searched from top to bottom
going in and out," I said dryly.

"Well, yes. Don't you do that at Sevenwaters?"

"Not if it's our own people."

"Eamonn says it's wiser. You can't be too careful these days. And he did say—"

She paused.

"What?" I asked, looking her in the eye.

She reached up to smooth her red curls behind her ear, looking slightly abashed. "Well, Liadan, if you must know, he said he preferred if you and Niamh did not go out while you're here. There is no reason for you to venture beyond the walls. We have everything here that you could possibly want."

"Mmm." I did not like the thought of Eamonn making rules for me, especially now that there was no possible chance of a marriage between us. Perhaps, after what had happened to me, he believed me incapable of staying out of trouble.

"Don't take me wrong, Aisling," I said. "Your hospitality is not to be faulted. But I miss Sevenwaters. I miss the forest and the openness. I don't know how you and Eamonn can live here."

"It's home," she said simply. And I remembered Eamonn saying once, *It will not be home until I see you standing in the doorway with my child in your arms.* I shivered. The goddess grant there would be chieftains at Tara with marriageable daughters, and that Eamonn would make his intentions known to them. There should be many a girl with no reluctance to warm his bed and give him an heir, once he put word about that he was looking.

Many days had passed, and the moon had shrunk to a mere sliver of light. When I got home, I would have to apply myself to sewing, for my gowns were getting uncomfortably tight over my breasts. I sat with Niamh day by day, and she failed to notice any change in my appearance. I could not tell her. How could I find the words, when she held in her poor, confused mind the guilt of not having conceived a child for Fionn after three moons, of not even succeeding in that most basic requirement of a good wife? I said to her it was early days, and not every bride bred straight away. Besides, now that she would not be going back to Tirconnell after all, surely it was better that she was not carrying Fionn's son or daughter.

"I wanted to bear Ciarán a child," she said softly. "More than anything. But the goddess did not grant it."

"Just as well," I retorted, finding it hard not to lose my temper with her. "That would really have set a stir among the Uí Néill."

"Don't joke about it, Liadan. You cannot hope to understand how it feels to love a man more than anything in the world, more than life itself. How wonderful it would be to carry that man's child within your body, even if the man himself is—is lost to you." She began to cry, very quietly. "How could you know of such things?"

"How indeed," I muttered, passing her a clean handkerchief.

"Liadan?" she asked, after a while.

"Mmm?"

"You keep saying, I need not go back to Fionn, I need not go back to Tirconnell. But where am I going?"

"I don't know yet. But I'll work something out, I promise. Trust me."

"Yes, Liadan." She spoke with a meek acquiescence that terrified me. For time was fast running out for us. The men would not stay in the south too long, with winter approaching and their own lands to attend to. By the time the moon was half full again, they would be here, and in truth I had very little by way of a plan. Niamh could not simply come home, not without explanation. So she must go somewhere else, somewhere she could be taken before Fionn returned. She must be kept in hiding, for a while at least. Later, perhaps, the truth might be told, and she could come back to

Sevenwaters. A Christian convent would be the best place, perhaps in the southwest, somewhere away from the coast and safe from the Norsemen's raids, a place where they did not know the name of Sevenwaters. There was no place where they did not know the name of Uí Néill, but maybe that part could be kept quiet. If someone could just provide sanctuary for a while, if Fionn could somehow be convinced that she was gone forever, if . . . I lost patience with myself quickly, knowing I was getting nowhere, realizing if I did not come up with a practical plan very soon, we would run out of time. It was becoming obvious I could not do this alone.

A promise was a promise and could not be broken. I thought Niamh was wrong. How could the alliance be more important to Liam or Conor or my father than Niamh's happiness? Surely her bruised body and shadowed eyes were too high a price to pay for the future support of the Uí Néill, for all their wealth and their great band of fighting men? But I had given her my word. Besides, there was more to it than the alliance. There was the secret they were all keeping from us. There was something bigger behind this that we did not understand, something so terrible it seemed to me I must act with the greatest caution lest I bring alive the evil they spoke of with hushed voices and haunted eyes.

One thing was clear to me. I had to get Niamh out before the men returned, and there was nobody in the household whose help I could enlist. They were all Eamonn's men and women, and Aisling's, and no secret would be kept from their young master and mistress. Besides, wasn't every cart searched? I thought about disguises, and abandoned the idea, knowing the close watch on all traffic in and out meant we would be immediately detected. My mind whirled with plans, each more unlikely than the last.

When it was dark of the moon, I could not light my special candle, for it still stood in my chamber at Sevenwaters. But after Niamh was sleeping, I lit another and placed it near the window, and I sat by it through the time of darkness. And now, as I drew Bran's image into my mind, he was no longer sitting under strange trees, but pacing restlessly to and fro in a more familiar setting, a lantern casting shadows on the cunningly constructed walls, the arched roof and ancient ritual stone of the great barrow that had sheltered us, so long ago it seemed. There were others there with him, and they were disputing something, and he was impatient. I felt his sense of urgency, the anxiety that drew a frown between his dark brows, the tension in his hands. But I could not hear their words. I did what I always did on those dark nights, when I knew he tried, above all things, to remain awake. I reached out to touch his mind with my own, to let him know he would never be quite alone, not now; to remind him that even for an outlaw with no past and no future, each day could be lived well. But tonight, my own dark thoughts intervened, my concern for my sister, my growing panic at not having a solution for my problem, with time so short. These things got in the way, and I could not tell if I did him any good or not. I stayed awake all night. That much I could do for him. It was not possible to see his image all the time in my thoughts, but it came to me now and then, striding out of the barrow, leaving his friends behind; standing in the darkness there, staring down at his tightly linked hands. Later, sitting cross-legged not far from where we had made our little fire with pine cones when Evan was dying and I had told him his last story. Sitting with his shaven head in his hands, and the smallest of lanterns to keep away the darkness. *I'm here,* I told him. *I'm not so far away. Just wait a little longer, and dawn will come.* But I had to work very hard to silence that other voice within me, the one that was clamoring, *Help! I need you!* Nobody could help me here at Sídhe Dubh. There seemed no way out. Unless . . . unless you were a cat, maybe.

It was worth a try, I told myself as I slipped quietly down

the covered way, just after dawn next morning. The skills I
had learned in the forest of Sevenwaters served me well. I
thought I passed by the guards unseen. I needed the lantern,
for the side tunnel was narrow and the floor an uneven jum-
ble of broken rocks. I went past the empty cells, feeling
again the cold breath of fear that lingered in their shadowy
corners. I ventured farther down, and the track became nar-
rower and steeper, and water trickled down the walls so that
I was walking in a streamlet. And then, abruptly, the water
went gurgling away underground, and the passage seemed
to end; there was an unbroken wall ahead of me, though
light still filtered in from somewhere. A dead end. But the
cat had got in. I set the lantern down and moved forward,
touching my fingertips to the wall. My shadow loomed in
front of me, huge in the lantern light. And I heard them: familiar voices, quiet, deep, so deep they were almost below
hearing. Words spoken with a slowness that seemed ancient, as if it came from the very stones themselves. They
were not, after all, fled with the coming of man; they had
merely gone deeper underground, biding their time. I stood
still, listening, awaiting their bidding.

Down.

I squatted on the ground, wondering what to look for,
what to feel for. A trapdoor? A secret way? Some sort of
sign?

Down.

Think, Liadan, I told myself, shivering. I moved along
the rock floor, following the base of the wall with my hand,
feeling for any sign, any clue as to what I must do.

Good. Good.

My hand touched something, a metal object that was
wedged under a protruding stone. My fingers curled around
it. It was a key, large, heavy, ornately wrought. I rose to my
feet. The lantern light showed me the same unbroken
stretch of rock wall before me, the same featureless walls
on either side. There was no sign whatever of a door. I lifted

the lantern high, low, examining every surface there was. I could not find the smallest sign of an opening, no crack or crevice into which this key might be fitted. My heart sank.

Go back, said the voices. *Back.*

What were they telling me, I wondered grimly as I made my reluctant way out of the underground passage and into the house again. That I must stay at Sídhe Dubh and let things take their course? That had been their advice at the place of the great barrow, and look where it had got me. Ancestors or no ancestors, I began to wonder if they knew what they were doing. The Fair Folk had told me not to heed these old voices. that they could be dangerous. Still, the Old Ones had given me a key. A key was, at least, a start.

That evening Aisling told me, very politely, that it might be better if I did not go down into those underground parts of the fortress anymore. "My master at arms is concerned about your safety," she said rather formally. I could see she was embarrassed at having to set out rules for a friend. Things had been easy between us at Sevenwaters. Indeed, sometimes we had seemed more like sisters than Niamh and I were. But here she was mistress of the house, and I sensed there was little point in argument. It shocked me that she had learned of my explorations; I had been so careful.

"I do find it difficult to be so—so cooped up," I said.

"Still, those old passages and chambers are not safe," Aisling replied firmly. "I know Eamonn would not wish you to be at any risk. Please don't go down there again."

This was an order, kindly expressed, and I knew I must accept it. My options appeared to be rapidly dwindling as time passed. It was drawing ever closer to the day when Eamonn and Fionn must return from Tara, and I had not even a shred of a practical plan. Indeed, I was beginning to doubt very much that I could keep my promise to Niamh. But, I was her sister. I could not let her return to Tirconnell and to a husband who valued her so little. I had seen the look in her eyes. I knew she meant it when she said she would kill herself rather than go on. I must get her out before they returned. Somehow, I must find a way.

I did not know, in the end, if the solution was one I discovered for myself or if the Old Ones nudged me in the right direction. Perhaps we thought alike, being of the same line. It was early morning, just after dawn, and Niamh was sleeping, curled tight under her woollen blankets, her cropped hair bright on the pillow. My nights had been increasingly restless. I lay awake pondering solutions, all of them equally impractical. I lay open-eyed, considering the risks of telling the truth to Sean or to my father or to Conor, and deciding I could not do so. My father had taught me that a promise must never be broken. Besides, I could not be sure of what they would do. There was just a possibility they might believe the alliance more important than Niamh. I could not risk telling and finding Fionn's strategic worth outweighed his disregard for my sister. So I must find my own solution. But there was no way out. What did the Old Ones expect me to do? Fly?

At dawn I rose and dressed, selecting one of my looser-cut gowns, and wondering how big my belly would have to grow before Niamh noticed the change in my appearance. Our clothes had been stored in an ancient wooden chest that was set in an alcove to the room we shared, a recess over which a tapestry hung to reduce the draft. I rummaged in the chest for a shawl, since the morning was cool, and as I stood up to wrap it around me, I felt momentarily faint. I put out my hand against the timber-lined wall of the alcove to steady myself. My fingers touched something. There was a marking on the wall, a tiny crack in the surface of the wood. It was too dark to see what it was. I fetched a candle and peered more closely. A tapestry for the draft, I thought. Where there is a draft, there must be an opening. My hand followed the crack all the way around, a square the size of a small man or woman, bending. A door. It was covered all around its margins with tiny carven marks, Ogham signs like the one my Uncle Finbar wore around his neck on an amulet. But Eamonn's ancestor was surely no druid. Were these secret signs of protection made at his bidding, or had they been crafted by an older kind, those who had dwelt in the place of the fairy fortress long before the human folk came to set their hand upon it and claim ownership of what could never rightly be theirs? The deep places belonged to the Old Ones. No upstart chieftain with a bag of silver and a few cartloads of stone for building could ever change that, try as he might to set his stamp on the landscape.

There was a keyhole. Trembling, I fetched the old key from where I had hidden it and tried it, knowing it could not fail to work. I sensed an inevitability about things now; I knew I was being led forward. I felt more fright than relief. The little door swung open, revealing a precipitous flight of stone steps spiraling downward into darkness. There was nothing for it but to pick up my skirts in one hand, and grasp the candle in the other, and step forward, hoping that Niamh would not wake before I returned.

The way was so steep and narrow I could see only the smallest distance in front of me. It was a masterpiece of construction, plunging down into the very depths of the hill, until I judged I must be below the lowest level of the house, below the courtyard, at length below even the place where the sharp rocks encircled the hill, under the fortress walls. And at last I saw light ahead, a light that was not simply the faint glow cast by my flickering candle, but an increasing brightness that was, unmistakably, the first rays of the rising sun through the mist of the marshlands. I rounded the last turn of the spiral steps and there before me, not five paces away at the end of a narrow tunnel in the rocks, was an opening to the morning. I had found the way out.

It was not much more than a crack, big enough for a girl my size to pass through, but too narrow for an armed man. Indeed, it was just as well my child had as yet scarcely be-

gun to swell my belly out, for soon enough this way would
not be possible even for me. Strange, I thought, that there
was such a chink in the impregnable armor of Sídhe Dubh,
and it was unguarded. Then I looked about me, and began
to understand. The place where I had emerged was just below the circle of pointed rocks laid around the hill. Behind
and above me, the sentries paced to and fro, to and fro atop
the high walls, apparently unaware of my presence out here
in the open. I looked in front of me, northward, and there
directly ahead was that low line of distant hills I had seen
from the ramparts. The expanse of flat ground before me
was the place of sinking bog, the place so dangerous that to
attempt to cross it was death, save for those few who knew
the way. So we could escape this far, but no farther. I
crouched quiet by the rocks, willing the guards not to see
me. There was no certainty they would bother to identify an
intruder before loosing their arrows. Behind me, the opening through which I had come was invisible, merely another
irregularity in the rocky face of the hillside. Perhaps it was
concealed by fairy arts. I had counted my steps carefully,
and noted their direction precisely, for I had no wish to be
stranded out here alone, without explanation.

I sat quiet awhile, knowing I had half a solution, but unable to grasp the remainder. It was a cool morning with
gathering clouds suggesting later rain. Down by the water
there were creatures, long-legged marsh birds, stabbing
with their beaks at strange, hopping insects. I watched them
and felt my son flex his tiny limbs. *I wish you could see
these birds,* I told him. *You'll see many birds, when we go
home to Sevenwaters. There's one called a wren. That's the
smallest and very magical. You'll find it in many tales.
You'll see an owl, and a raven, and a lark singing fit to
make you weep as it rises. You'll see the great eagle gliding
above the forest, and the swan descending to the lake, when
at last we go home.* Looking across that wasteland, I
thought about Niamh's fragility. Even if I could bring her

down here undetected, even if she were willing, what then? I did not know the way across. A boat, maybe. But there was no boat, and the patches of open water were few and far between. And we could not hope to go by day, for we would be soon spotted and brought back. Even now, I could not understand why the guards had not seen me. Their steady patrol continued high above, passing and returning. After a while I went back up, all the way up, to emerge in our chamber out of breath, with aching legs and a mind that had not yet found any answers. I shut the door and hid the key, and pulled the tapestry back into place. Niamh slept on, unaware.

Next morning I went down again. It was very early. A chill mist shrouded the marsh, and clouds veiled the first sun. Stunted bush and windswept tussock poked uneven fingers through the mantle of vapor, and there were strange creaking noises out in the bog, subtle sounds that were not made by frogs.

I shivered as I sat below the rocks and drew my woollen shawl tighter around my shoulders. There was a puzzle to solve, and I had most of the clues, but try as I might I could not put it together and make any sense of it. The Old Ones had guided me thus far. There was a way out. And I knew what time of day it would be safest. This morning I could not see three paces across the marsh before the swirling mist obscured all but the few protruding plants that somehow survived in that harsh place. At such a time pursuit would be all but impossible. Still, how could one attempt such a venture without a guide who knew the way? To try it alone would be foolish indeed. Had things been different, I might gladly have taken the risk for my sister. I might have clutched her hand and set out across the quaking bog, trusting in the oldest of forces to guide us safe, hoping to find some sanctuary before our menfolk tracked us down. But not now. My own life and Niamh's, those I might have risked, but not my son's.

* * *

Strange, how the pace of time seems to change. Now the days were speeding by, and for all her blind trust in my ability to make everything right, Niamh seemed on edge, muttering to herself by day and waking abruptly at night, shaking and weeping from some nightmare she would not speak of. And then, with the moon waxing fast, Aisling received a message. As we sat at supper over roast mutton in rosemary sauce, she passed it on.

"Good news," she said brightly, "I've heard from Eamonn. A man came in today. They have left Tara and are now quartered close by Knowth, where they meet with chieftains of the district. They will stop again at Sevenwaters and should be here in four days' time."

Niamh blanched. It was a blow, and I struggled for appropriate words.

"You'll be happy to see Eamonn again." This much at least was the truth.

"I surely will," Aisling acknowledged with a wry smile. "I can't say it has not been difficult with him away. We have reliable and skilled people here, of course, but my brother is rather particular about things, so I do have to keep a close watch on them. Besides, I'm concerned for Eamonn. He was—he was not himself those last days before they left. I am hoping to see him in brighter spirits."

I could not find a response to this and kept silent. But Niamh's words tumbled out like careless footsteps across a terrain full of traps.

"Four days! That can't be right. It is too soon. Four days, it's not enough time—"

"Don't worry, Niamh," I said, frowning into my sister's huge, expressive blue eyes, which spoke clearly of impending betrayal and tragedy. "Everything will be all right." I turned to Aisling. "Niamh hasn't been well. We might retire early, I think. She needs her sleep."

Aisling's small, freckled face was looking serious. Her eyes were on Niamh, weighing up my sister's appearance and her words.

"You should tell me, Liadan," she said carefully. "You should let me know if there is any problem. I might be able to help. Eamonn would be sure to want to help."

I doubted that very much. "Thank you, Aisling. No need to concern yourself."

Four days. The goddess help us, only four days. I spent a sleepless night contemplating the several equally impossible alternatives facing me and liking none of them. As soon as the sky began to lighten to the faint gray that presaged dawn, I was up, glad to be on my feet again, dressing in my sturdy boots and a warm gown with a heavy cloak over the top, desperate to get out of doors and away from the stone walls that now seemed to trap me and my dilemma tightly within them, an unsolvable puzzle in an unbreachable box. Before dawn broke, I slipped out through the secret door in the alcove, down the spiral stairs, and out to the stark hillside above the marsh. There I stood staring out northward. My stomach churned with nerves, anxiety made my head ache, and I was close to weeping from sheer fright at the thought of what I must try to do. For it seemed the only option was to take my sister's hand in mine and step out onto that wasteland in an act of insane faith.

A hand clapped itself efficiently across my mouth, and an arm went tightly around my chest. A voice behind me said, very softly, "Just warning you so you aren't tempted to make a noise. The guards can't see us, but they can hear us. Keep quiet. All right?"

The pressure of the arm was released. The delicately patterned hand was withdrawn. I did not need to see this hand to identify the owner of the voice. True to his reputation, the Painted Man had penetrated the defenses of Sídhe Dubh as effortlessly as a shadow.

"What, no blow on the head this time?" I inquired in a

whisper, not turning. My heart was hammering in my breast.

"Sit down." Spoken in an undertone, this was unmistakably an order. "We're in a blind spot. But it's limited. No point in going out of the way to attract attention."

I sat, and Bran moved into view, settling in the cover of the rocks three paces away from me. He wore an ancient tunic and trousers of indefinable hue, and the soles of his soft boots were coated with black mud. His face was pale, his eyes serious. He looked wonderful. He gazed at me silently, and I gazed back at him and felt a blush rise to my cheeks. A small frown appeared on his brow.

"What are you doing here?" I asked him, as my mind whirled with possibilities.

He took his time in replying; and when he did speak, it was cautiously.

"Strange," he said. "I thought I had the answers ready for anything you might say to me. But they are all fled, every one, now that you sit here by me."

"It's dangerous for you here, alone and unarmed," I said, my voice shaking. His eyes were fixed on me with an expression I had not expected to see again. "Why did you come here? There's a price on your head; you know that."

"That troubles you?" He sounded genuinely surprised.

"You were the one who changed things between us, not I." I was holding my hands clutched tight together, in case I should give in to the urge to reach out toward him. "If you think I care nothing for your safety, then you don't know me very well. Now answer my question."

"I was passing and thought you might be in trouble."

"I don't think that can be the truth. How could you know I was here? Besides, chance does not play a great part in your existence, I imagine, nor in that of the men you lead."

Bran's expression was somber. "I could tell you the truth. But you wouldn't believe me," he said simply.

"Try me. You've nothing to lose."

"You think so?"

"Brighid help us, Bran, you're in the heart of enemy territory! Why take such a foolish risk?"

"Ssh, not so loud. I'm neither alone nor unarmed. I came here to tell you to go home. I don't want you here at Sídhe Dubh. Things will come to a head between that man and me in due course. I don't want you caught in the middle."

My mouth opened and shut without a word.

"As I said, you don't believe me."

"But . . ."

"I heard a—a cry for help, that was what it seemed to be, a cry that came to me at night, when I was far away from this place. I found myself unable to disregard it and so I returned, and there was indeed news that you were here, in that man's domain. We keep a close watch on this fortress, Liadan. I've watched you come out when dawn rises and gaze around you as if you wished you could fly away. Things reached a point where I felt I should warn you."

"Nonetheless," I said cautiously, "after—after the last words we spoke to each other, it seems passing strange that you should seek me out at all. It seems stranger still that you would ask me to return home to Sevenwaters when you repudiate so utterly all those who dwell there."

"It's your safety we're discussing, not your father's character. I despise him, but that's irrelevant. Your uncle's stronghold is well guarded, and I want you back there. You must do as I tell you, Liadan. Go home. Go as soon as you can. It's not safe for you here."

"It is even less safe for you. You cannot be unaware that Eamonn has sworn to kill you if you set foot on his land or threaten what is his again. These guards will not hesitate to loose their arrows the moment you are seen. The men in green can be swift and cruel. I would not wish you to suffer the same fate as Dog did. No man should endure such an end."

I realized even as I spoke that I had said too much. Bran's eyes narrowed and he leaned closer.

"How can you know what happened to Dog?" he hissed at me. "How can you know such a thing?"

A cold shiver went though me as the images returned stark to my mind. The darkness by the roadside, the muffled sound of blows raining down, the clink of harness as they rode away. Dog's voice, wheezing in his chest: *Knife. . . .*

"I know because I was there," I said in a thread of a voice. "I know because I watched from the shadows and could not stop them. I know because . . . because . . ." My voice wobbled dangerously.

"Because what, Liadan?" asked Bran softly.

"Because he cried out for the knife at the end, and there was nobody there but me. He cried out for you to end it, but the hand that drew the knife across his throat was mine."

I heard him let out his breath, and then there was silence for quite some time. I managed to hold back my tears. I managed not to reach out my hand and touch him.

"I thought myself strong," he said eventually, looking not at me but at some point away across the mist-shrouded marshes. "I thought I could do this. But it is a test of will such as I have never yet encountered."

This made no sense to me. And time was running short.

"You're asking me to go home. I always intended that. I am only here for a visit until Eamonn returns from Tara. That will be quite soon; in four days they are expected. Then I will go back to Sevenwaters. But I cannot leave any earlier. There's my sister."

"What's to stop both you and your sister leaving today? Why wait until that man returns? If there's a problem with an escort, I will provide one. Discreetly. An effective but invisible presence."

"I'm not sure why you would think you should have any part in such a decision." I drew a deep breath. "Besides, it's not so easy. I have a—problem, a very serious problem. And there is no one I can turn to; no one I can ask for help."

There was a brief silence.

"You could ask me," he said, with extreme diffidence. Then he waited.

"This is indeed a task for the Painted Man," I conceded, "but I doubt if I could afford the price."

"You offend me," Bran snapped, but still he kept his voice down, for after all the man was a professional.

"I can't imagine why," I said. "You are a mercenary for hire, are you not? A man with no conscience? Is it not customary to discuss terms with such a man when buying his services?"

"Perhaps you should outline the task first, and we'll discuss the terms later." His tone was cool.

"I hardly know how. But I will tell it as plainly as I can, for I have very little time; my absence will soon be noted. My sister was married at midsummer. Her husband is a man of some influence."

"One of the Uí Néill."

"You know that?"

"I keep myself informed. Go on."

"She was not willingly married. Her heart was given to another man. But she went to Tirconnell. It is a bond that allies us to the northern Uí Néill, with all the strategic advantage that provides."

Bran nodded comprehension. He was scowling fiercely, his raven's mask adding to his daunting aspect.

"Her husband has—has hurt her. He has treated her cruelly. Niamh is sorely changed, a shadow of her old self. But she will not tell; I found out myself by accident, and she made me swear not to make this known to any of the family. I cannot allow her husband to take her back to Tirconnell. That way is the end for her. She would take the knife to her wrists rather than submit to him again. I know it. I—I promised her she need not go back."

"I see. And now you have four days to achieve the impossible."

"That's what it amounts to," I said in a small voice, realizing the full extent of my folly.

"What was your plan?" Bran asked.

"Half a plan was as far as I got. To bring Niamh down here early one morning when the mist was thick enough. To make our way across the marshes to the north. To beg a ride on a passing cart; somehow to get her to a place of safety."

He regarded me levelly.

"It's just as well I am here then," he said. "Where is she to be taken? For how long? What tale will be told to cover her disappearance?"

My heart was starting to thud again.

"A convent would be best. In the south, I thought, perhaps in Munster. Somewhere very safe, where my family is not known. I don't suppose you would have any such connections . . ."

"You'd be surprised. What will you tell Uí Néill? And your family?"

"Best if Fionn believes her dead. Then he will not seek her out but will look for another bride. That way the alliance need not be broken. I can hardly keep the truth from my family. I suppose I must tell them, in the end."

Bran shook his head. "You want her to disappear so there will be no pursuit. The most effective way to achieve that is to conceal the truth from all but those who need to know. Very few need to know. You should use the same story for all. For some reason—you can invent one—your sister wandered out on the marsh and lost her footing. You saw her go under. You are distraught, the husband grieves, the family mourns. Your sister is safe in her convent for as long as she wishes. Perhaps forever. What of this other man, the one you say took her heart? Will he be a part of it?"

"No. He's gone away. My family forbade that union."

"What is his name?"

"Ciarán. A druid. Why would you need to know that?"

"When you buy my services, I make the rules, and I ask the questions. Will your sister come willingly?"

"I think so. She is—damaged, frail, confused in her mind. But she wants above all to escape her husband. It is a terrible marriage, one that has come close to destroying her."

"And when this Uí Néill starts looking around for a replacement, it has not occurred to you that you yourself may be his next choice?" His tone was very severe.

I choked back nervous laughter. "You may be quite sure that will not be so," I said, as the child did a backflip in my belly.

"It would be altogether logical. If the family to which you are so doggedly loyal forced your sister into such a monstrous alliance, you can have no reason to hope they will not do the same to you."

"I would sooner beg by the road than ally myself with such a man," I told him. "It will not happen."

There was a trace of a smile. "Besides, you know how to defend yourself," he said.

"I do, and I would."

"I don't doubt it."

"Bran."

"Yes?"

"My mother is very sick. I told you. Dying. It would be cruel to tell her Niamh was dead if it were not true. I would rather not do that."

"As to that part of it, I can only advise. You are the one who must do the telling. Ask yourself, do you really want your sister to be safe? If you do, then you must be prepared to take the most difficult way."

I nodded, swallowing hard. "What would your price be for such a mission?" I asked him.

"You believe I can do this for you?"

This question took me off guard and I answered without

thinking. "Of course I believe it. I would trust you with my life, Bran. There is no other I would ask to do this for me."

"That's the price, then."

"What is?" I asked, confused.

"Trust. That's the price."

This was a conversation full of traps. I said, "I thought you did not believe in trust. You told me so once."

"That much remains unchanged. It is *your* trust that is the price for this mission. So you see, you have paid in advance."

"When will you do it?" I asked shakily, feeling tears prick the back of my eyes, dangerously close.

"I'll need two days to make some arrangements. It can't be put in place any quicker than that. Are you sure you would not prefer simply to have this Uí Néill removed from the picture? Permanently? That could be achieved with ease and more or less immediately. He would simply never return here."

I shivered. "No, thank you. I am not quite ready to burden my conscience with murder, though I did consider it, I must confess. Besides, you have enough powerful enemies. I'd rather not add to them."

There was a brief silence.

"You'd best go back in." Bran's tone was businesslike.

"I don't understand," I said unsteadily. "I don't understand why you are helping us, when you hate us so much. What is it that brings this darkness to your eyes whenever you hear my father's name? What has he done to inspire such loathing? He is a good man."

Bran's jaw tightened. "I won't speak of these things," he said. Then he rose to his feet, glancing up at the sentries.

"Yes, I know. I should go back inside." But I did not move.

"Will you give me your hand to seal this bargain?" he asked diffidently.

I held out my hand, and he took it in his own. Now, he

would not meet my eyes. As for me, I felt his touch in every corner of my body, and I fought a hard battle with myself not to throw my arms around him then and there or to say something that would reveal to him how precarious was my hold on my feelings. I reminded myself that he had the code to help him keep control. He used it well; this might have been any transaction between allies. He released my hand.

"Bring your sister down before dawn, the day after tomorrow. We'll be ready. Take no undue risks, Liadan. I want you safe. Take no chances."

"I would say the same to you if I thought you would listen," I said, turning away before he could see I was crying. How could I tell him I carried his child, the grandson of the hated Hugh of Harrowfield? How could I burden him with that? And yet, the words had been there on my lips. It was not until I had made my way inside and up to the safety of the bedchamber that I realized I had not asked him a single thing about Sean and his journey north, and whether my brother had indeed presented him with a proposition.

Chapter Ten

After that my behavior was exemplary. I made no more secret trips outside the walls, no sentries observed me venturing into unusual parts of the fortress. I helped Aisling carry out a full inspection of the brewery, and I advised the household's resident herbalist on the stocking of her stillroom shelves for winter. I did not tell Niamh exactly what was going to happen, or when, for I could not trust her to keep it quiet. Instead, I simply told her all was arranged, and she was content with that. On the surface I was calm and capable. Underneath I was stretched tight as a harpstring.

I went back over what Bran had said to me, and what he had not said, time after time. I admitted to myself that it had been his help I had wanted all along. I tried not to think of the things I had longed to say to him, and had not dared to voice. Impossible things like, *Stay with me;* and, *You will have a son before Beltaine.* Putting these thoughts from my mind as best I could, I simply thanked the Old Ones, from the depths of my heart, for bringing him to my aid when I had thought all hope lost, for somehow sending him back to me when I believed he had put me, and mine, behind him forever. What had wrought such a change was a mystery to me. I was not foolish enough to believe I might some day hold him in my arms again and hear him speak words of love. These were the thoughts of a silly, romantic girl, I said to myself severely. But I spoke to our son and told him: *He is your father. A man who is the best at what he does, always. A man you can trust with your life.*

The night before he was due to come for us, I told Niamh as much as she needed to know. That she was to get up quietly when I woke her, before dawn, and dress in the warm, dark clothes I had set out for her. That we must then leave fast and silently, going by secret ways down to the edge of the marsh. That a man would be there to guide her across and then take her to a place where she would be safe. It might be a long time before she saw me again.

"A man?" She blinked at me as she sat there in her nightdress, a little frown of puzzlement creasing her brow. "What man?"

"A friend of mine," I said. "You must not be alarmed by his appearance. He is the best protector you could possibly have."

"How did you . . . how could you . . ." Her words trailed off, but I could read the real message in her jumbled thoughts, for she was ignorant of the art of concealing what was in her mind. She was wondering how a little homebody like me could possibly know the sort of man who could be of any use to us.

"It's of no importance," I said. "What you need to remember is to keep quiet and do as I say, no matter what happens. Lives depend on it, Niamh. Then, when we get there, just follow his orders. Just do that, and you'll be away from here and safely hidden well before your husband returns with Eamonn."

"Liadan?" The tone was a child's.

"What?"

"Couldn't you come with me?"

"No, Niamh. You'll be fine on your own, believe me. I cannot come, for if both of us disappear, pursuit is certain. If such a thing happened in his house, Eamonn would follow all leads to the very end. I must stay and tell a story to cover your escape. After that, I'll go home."

"A story? What story?"

"Never mind that. Now you must sleep. You'll need all your strength in the morning."

It started well enough. After a sleepless night, I roused Niamh before dawn, and we dressed by the light of a single candle. She was painfully slow, and I did most of it for her, fastening her gown, combing her hair, putting the gray cloak around her shoulders and telling her to keep the hood on once we were out of doors, for today she did not wear a veil and the bright beacon of her hair must be concealed from view. I showed her the hidden doorway and explained once again where it led. My sister nodded gravely, with something resembling comprehension in her eyes.

"I'm ready," she said. "And—thank you, Liadan."

"Think nothing of it," I replied somewhat unsteadily. "Thank me, and my—friends, when you are safe in the house of the holy sisters. Now—"

At that moment there was a noise in the courtyard below and torches flaring. I moved silently to step up on a stool and look out our narrow window. Riders were coming up from the main entry, men in green and men with the sign of the Uí Néill blazoned on their tunics, red and white, the snake that devoured itself. There was a sound of horses' feet, of men's voices, the unbolting of doors as the household came awake. I glimpsed Eamonn, pale and serious as always, swinging down from his horse and starting to give crisp orders. I saw the upright, authoritative figure of Fionn Uí Néill among his men. Clearly there had been no stop at Sevenwaters, not for them. They had ridden straight here, and they were two days early.

Bran! was my first panicked thought as I ushered my sister under the tapestry and through the narrow opening. *Bran is here, and Eamonn is back. If Eamonn kills him, it will be my fault.* Terrible possibilities flooded my mind as we spiraled down the precipitous steps, I just below Niamh, leading her as she wailed in panic: "Liadan! Liadan, I don't think I can do this! It's so dark, and small!"

"Be quiet!" I hissed, and gripped her hand harder. "Keep your promise and do as I say." She seemed unaware of what was happening in the courtyard and I did not enlighten her; she was already near-paralyzed with fear, and her journey had barely begun. Best that she did not know how close pursuit might be.

We were very slow. *Come on, come on, Niamh.* At last we reached the foot of the steps and began to move along the short passageway.

"Careful here," I whispered. "The ground's wet. Don't slip." With any luck, nobody would look for us so early. The men would want to eat and rest first. There might still be time.

It was quiet outside. There were no voices save those of marsh birds calling as the day began to wake. A blanket of mist, sickly yellow-gray, hung above the boglands and touched the stony shore. You would think even the Painted Man could not find a way through such a heavy veil. We reached the safe spot below the frieze of pointed stones. High above us on the wall, the sentries patrolled steadily to and fro.

Then Niamh gave a little sharp squeal and I whipped a hand up across her mouth. "Ssh," I hissed. "Do you want to get us all killed? These men are here to help us."

"Oh . . . but . . . but . . ."

"Keep her quiet, can you?"

My sister's frightened eyes stared first at the man who had spoken, the man who had loomed up suddenly before her with his shaven head and patterned skin, and then at the man behind him, whose flesh was black as night and whose white teeth were bared in a ferocious grin as he greeted me with a nod. Clearly, Niamh could not decide which of them was the more fearsome.

"Bran." I drew him slightly aside, speaking in an undertone. "Eamonn is returned, not long ago, with my sister's husband. The place is full of armed men."

"I know."

"You should go now and take the utmost care. Eamonn has vowed to destroy you and would carry it out with the least excuse. Please go quickly."

He frowned at me. "Don't concern yourself with me, I am not worth it. Besides, you'll have enough to worry about."

"I do concern myself with you. Why can't you listen to good advice for once in your life?"

"Come on," called Gull softly. He had taken Niamh's hand and was leading her, gently enough, across the exposed ground to the edge of the marshland, where the fog would conceal them.

"You think me a mercenary without conscience, a man without human feelings," whispered Bran, and his fingers came up to lie against my cheek, warm and alive. "And yet you wish me to be safe. That is not consistent."

"You have a low opinion of women, and you despise my family," I replied with tears in my eyes, for his touch set off an aching deep within me that was joy and pain rolled into one. "And yet, you risk your life to come here, just so you can tell me to go home. You risk it again to save my sister. Another woman. You can hardly call that consistent."

We looked at each other, and despite myself, I felt a tear spill down my cheek.

"Don't. Don't," said Bran fiercely, and his thumb moved against my skin, as if to stem the flow.

"Thank you for coming," I whispered. "I don't know how I would have managed without you."

He said nothing, but as I looked at him I saw his eyes unshielded, deep, steady gray eyes. In them were the words he would not allow himself to speak. I put my hand up over his own.

There was a shout from above, and a twang, and an arrow whirred over our heads to land just behind Gull where he guided the stumbling Niamh down to the concealment of the mist. Gull let out a curse, and Niamh a little shriek; and then it seemed she froze in fear and would go no farther.

"Brighid help us," I muttered, and picked up my skirts, ready to run down and push her bodily to safety, the stupid girl. Bran's voice halted me.

"No," he said. "Stay here where they cannot see you. Good-bye, Liadan."

Then he turned and ran out into the path of their arrows, a plain target to draw their fire from my sister; and I stood and watched him because I had promised. I had bought his services, and that meant he made the rules. Up above on the walkway there was shouting, and I heard Eamonn's voice. The arrows began to come with speed, and they were well aimed; but the running man was swift and clever, dodging and weaving, turning around to make a quick, vulgar gesture of defiance in the direction of his attackers. He could have covered the distance in half the time; but he made sure both Gull and the struggling, terrified Niamh, whose dark hood had fallen back now to reveal clearly her cropped auburn locks, had vanished entirely into the clinging blanket of mist, before he bolted at full speed after them. The vapor swallowed them up, and they were gone.

Several things happened quite fast. Orders were given up above. Then men with swords and daggers and with spears and axes came around below the walls, running, and halted by the edge of the marsh near where I still stood motionless just below the rock barrier. Eamonn was among them, and it was he who turned first and saw me. There was no need to school my features; I imagine I already wore a convincing look of shock and fear.

"Liadan! Thank the goddess you are safe!" I could see the fury in Eamonn's eyes, scarcely masked by his relief and concern. "I thought—what happened, Liadan? Tell me quickly, we must go after these men straightaway."

"I-I—"

"It's all right, you are safe now. Take a deep breath and try to tell me." He was gripping me by the shoulders, quite hard, his hands communicating the urge to pursue, punish, and destroy.

"Niamh—Niamh is gone," I gulped. "She's gone."

"Where?"

"I—I don't know." So far I had not had to lie. I was not very good at lying. And Eamonn knew me better than many. I would have to hope his fury might blind him to any deficiencies in my story. A story that must now be told rather differently since not only Niamh but both Gull and Bran had been in clear sight before they fled.

"Across the marshlands to the north. I don't know where or why."

Eamonn scowled. "Tell me everything you know, Liadan. As quickly as you can. Every moment counts. How could you and Niamh come down here without my guards seeing you?"

"There's a hidden way. Didn't you know? A spiral staircase, a concealed door. In the alcove."

He swore under his breath. "You mean—but that way has been sealed as long as I can remember. There is no key. How could you get in?"

My hand touched the key where it lay in my pocket. It became necessary to lie. "I don't know. I woke up early this morning, and Niamh was gone. She left the secret door open, and I followed her. When I came out, she was—she was—"

"All right, Liadan," he said with grave kindness. "You need not tell that part. How many men did you see? Only two?"

I nodded mutely.

"You know what they were, I suppose?"

I nodded again.

"Why, that's what I ask myself," Eamonn muttered, pacing restlessly. "Why would he take her except in some gesture of insane defiance? What can he hope to gain by this? There's no reason to it."

I swallowed hard. "Do you think—do you think you can track them down and bring her back?" It seemed to me the mist was starting to dissipate as the sun rode higher; I could see a short way across the marsh now, the dark, sucking mud punctuated here and there by low clumps of vegetation. They were too far apart for a man to make his way by leaping from one to the next. Sooner or later he must put his foot on that black-brown spongy surface and trust it to carry his weight. A man who was unable to trust would only get over by knowing the way with total accuracy. Still, they were the best. If they said they could lead Niamh across, they could.

"Eamonn! For God's sake, what has happened? They said Niamh—" Fionn came up at a sprint, boots crunching on the rocky hillside. His hard features were set grimly, his face white.

"I regret this greatly," Eamonn said with formality, and I realized it would, indeed, reduce his status among his allies that such a slip in security could occur on his very doorstep, almost under his nose. No wonder the Painted Man had the reputation he did for sheer effrontery. "It appears she has been abducted, and there is no doubt who is responsible. My guards saw them clearly. A man with coal black skin, and another who bore an unmistakable pattern on face and arm. These are the same fianna who slaughtered my warriors before my eyes. It is fortunate my archers drove them off before Liadan, too, was taken."

"Which way?" demanded Fionn, and his expression reminded me that he was an Uí Néill and a leader of men. "I will cleave this fellow's limbs from his body when I find him! Which way?"

"You cannot go," said Eamonn bluntly. "This task is for me and those of my men who know the art of making such a crossing safely and with speed. I will do my best to bring your wife back, and I swear I will not rest until the perpetrators of this outrage are brought to justice. Now I must go, and quickly."

"Justice?" Fionn's tone was savage. "Justice is too good for them. Give me a moment alone with those scum and an axe in my hand, and I'll carve a few more pretty patterns on their outlaw hides. Don't speak to me of justice or to Niamh's sister here."

"Go inside, Liadan." Eamonn was making his way down to the marsh's edge now. Two of his men were waiting, their green tunics replaced with garments of a mud-brown shade, their riding boots with softer, more pliable footwear. They were closely hooded, and they bore dagger and throwing knife at the belt. They stood by as Eamonn stripped off his outer garments and quickly dressed in the same way. Each man bore a strong staff, taller than his own height.

"All right," said Eamonn. "I'll lead the way; stay close behind and be ready to strike at short notice. They've not so much of a start on us that we cannot make up the distance before they reach dry land. The lady will slow them. Oran, your job is to get her safe away. Once you have her, turn back and leave the rest to us. Go carefully, she'll be frightened. Conn, you'll take the black man. The other is mine."

It is no wonder women have a reputation for patience that is not shared by men. We spend so much of our time waiting.

Waiting for a child to be born. Waiting for a man to come home, from the fields, from the sea, from battle. Waiting endlessly for news. That can be the worst, as fear bites deep at the vitals and seizes the heart with chill fingers. The mind can make strange and terrible pictures while you are waiting.

Aisling was a kind girl, and I came to appreciate it through that long day. It was impossible to settle to anything. She provided mead and spiced fruits and a comfortable, private corner by a small ashwood fire, and words of sympathy. There was no need at all for me to feign distress.

"Sit down, Liadan," Aisling urged anxiously, her round, blue eyes full of concern. "Come on, sit by me. I'm sure Niamh will come back safe. Eamonn knows those tracks like the back of his hand. He's very capable. If anyone can find her, he can."

Little did she know how her words made my heart sink. "I can't help it," I said. "It's so easy to make a mistake, everyone say so, in the mist, trying to cover ground quickly—they could go off the track so easily, Aisling. How long, how long before we get a message?" My hands were shaking, and I clasped them tightly together.

"It could be awhile," Aisling said gently. "Fionn has sent his men around by the road to cut them off on the other side. Eamonn will go cautiously; there's no room for error on that path. One way or another, the outlaws will be trapped."

As we waited, Fionn paced up and down, grim faced and silent. He had opted to remain here at Sídhe Dubh, waiting for the first news, rather than ride with his men. Now he was like a caged beast, his eyes burning with anger, his hands balled into tight fists. I wondered whether he felt fear for his wife, if his spirit ached for her as mine did for Bran, knowing the men in green were close behind him with death in their eyes. Or was Fionn simply angry at the brazen theft of a prized possession, albeit one he had treated with contempt?

Time passed and there was no word. I found I could sit still no longer, and begged a respite to return to my bedchamber for a while. As I passed Fionn, he put a hand on my shoulder.

"Take heart," he said quietly. "All may yet be well."

I glanced at him, gave a nod, and walked away. There was nothing to read on his face but the look of a sorrowing husband waiting anxiously to learn if his wife lived or died. If it were not for the bruises, fading fast, there would be no evidence at all of what Niamh had endured, none but the testimony of the mind, and that I was forbidden to share. Dana help us all; what if they did not manage to get away? What if the Painted Man was not the best after all, and Eamonn caught him? It was unthinkable. If that happened, I would have no choice but to break my promise to my sister and tell the whole truth.

Trust. That's the price. I could hear Bran's voice in my head as I went into the bedchamber and closed the door behind me. There was no room for doubt. I must have faith in him. I did have faith in him. So why was my heart still hammering, why was my skin sweaty and cold, why did I feel hollow and drained, as if I had lost a part of myself?

I lay on my bed for a while, gazing at nothing, and as I grew quiet I could feel the slight movements of the child inside me. *You will be a father before Beltaine.* I had not told Bran. How could I tell him? To know this would be nothing but another burden. A man cannot be a father if he has no past and no future. A man cannot acknowledge a son who bears the blood of a family he utterly despises. Better that he did not know. Better that nobody knew whose son this was. Son of the raven. Child of the prophecy. I would not be tied to that, and nor should he. But there was Sean. You cannot keep secrets forever, not from a twin. He suspected. Soon enough, he would know. And now it was even more complicated. For whatever the bitter outcome of the chase through the marshes, it must blacken the reputation of the

Painted Man still further if he survived. Whatever happened, today's events would cut so deep that the men of my family, and the men of their alliance, could never consider dealing with the Painted Man again. Unless I told the truth. And I had promised Niamh my silence.

Poor Niamh. She would be so frightened. She would feel so alone. What if she blundered off the path in her panic? What if she froze in terror again and could not be cajoled to move? I willed myself to breathe more slowly. My mind reached out, very cautiously.

Sean?

There was no response. Perhaps I had been too cautious. *Sean? Answer me. I need you, Sean!*

There was nothing at all. I waited a long time with my mind open for his reply. So long, I almost began to think the unthinkable, knowing where he had been, knowing who he had been with. I felt doubt creeping into my mind. Trust, I told myself firmly. The price is trust.

Liadan? What's wrong?

I let my breath out in a rush. *Sean! Where are you?*

At home. Where else would I be? What's wrong?

I can't say. But it is something bad, and I can't deal with it alone. You must come here to Sídhe Dubh. Come now, Sean. Bring an escort. I—we will be coming home with you.

You'd better tell me, Liadan. Has something happened to Niamh?

Why do you ask that?

His response, when it came, was cautious. *I'm not blind, whatever you might think. Can you tell me what has happened? Shall I bring Father or Liam?*

I was shivering as I sat there and could not keep my fear from him. My every thought was shadowed with it. *No, don't bring them. Just you and a few men. I don't want Eamonn's guards riding back with us. Come quickly, Sean.*

I'm on my way. Mercifully, he asked no further ques-

tions. And by the time he got here it would be over, one way
or another.

It was nearly dusk before Eamonn returned. We were
back in the hall by then, close to the massive hearth whose
crackling fire cast gold light on the odd, carved pillars. The
eyes of the strange creatures seemed to flicker and glow as
they stared balefully down at us. There was muted noise as
serving men and women brought food and drink, and took it
away untouched. Aisling gave quiet instructions. She
looked pale and tired. Fionn sat at the table with his head in
his hands. When at last we heard a stir outside, the sentries
on the high guard posts calling and then voices in the courtyard, nobody jumped up and ran to the window to look. Instead we sat frozen, the three of us, unable after so long a
wait to believe the news could be good and unwilling to advance the inevitable moment when we must be told the
worst.

Eamonn was a man who did not lose control easily. You
had to know him well to recognize when he was angry or
upset. Even his proposal of marriage had been a model of
restraint. But now, as he came quietly into the hall and with
the slightest gesture of his hand caused the folk of his
household to vanish, it was clear that he was exhausted almost beyond endurance. His face was bleached of color,
and he looked shattered and old. Aisling sprang up to take
his arm and lead him to a seat by the fire, and he shook off
her solicitous grasp with a violent jerk of the arm. That in
itself showed how far stretched he was. Dark mud coated
his shoes and was spattered over his clothing.

"You'd better tell us," I said grimly.

Eamonn stood before the fire with his back to us, staring
into the heart of the flames.

"You have not brought my wife back." Fionn had his
voice under control; his hands were clenched. Aisling had
retreated to sit by me and was keeping her mouth shut.

Eamonn put a hand over his eyes, a hand that was not quite steady, and he said in an undertone, "The goddess help me. Who would be the bearer of such news?"

I got up and went to stand close by him, and I took his hand in both of mine. This touch he did not shake off, and he had no choice but to look at me.

"Now, Eamonn," I said, meeting his gaze as steadily as I could, though the look in his deep, brown eyes disquieted me. "Fionn waits for news of his wife and I of my sister. We know what you have to tell cannot be good, but you must tell it."

"Oh, Liadan. Oh, Liadan, I would give much not to bring you such ill tidings."

"Tell us, Eamonn."

He took a deep, shuddering breath. "It is the worst, I'm afraid. Your sister is dead. Drowned on the way across to dry land."

"But . . . but . . ."

Aisling was up in a flash, her arm around my shoulders.

"Sit down, Liadan. Come, sit down."

I trembled. There was no longer any way to tell truth from fantasy. This trap I had set for myself.

"What!" Fionn rose to his feet very slowly. "What are you telling us? How could you allow this to happen? On your own land!"

"We did everything. Sent men around by the road, your own men and mine, to block their way out. Followed behind across the bog, moving as quickly as we could. The mist was very thick, and that hampered us; but I knew they, too, would be affected by it. And Niamh would be slow, I thought, clad in a long gown and not knowing the way. They would have to talk her across, step by step.

"In that, I was right. We did catch them, but much farther across than I expected. This man is proficient at his evil works. We were closer to the far side than this when the

mist lifted just a little, and there he was. The Painted Man,
glancing back over his shoulder as he stepped from one safe
foothold to the next. He knew the way, all right. I never saw
him look down. Not once.

"I could not see far ahead, but I glimpsed Niamh's bright
hair and the gray of her cloak through the veil of mist. I
could not see the man who led her. I alerted my companions
and, taking my throwing knife from my belt, I quickened
the pace, moving up behind my quarry until there were no
more than seven paces between us. He was quite silent; he
moved soft as a deer. But up ahead, I heard Niamh's voice
as she asked a question, and a man's voice answering. I
weighed the knife in my hand, judging the distance to a certain point between that man's ribs. I knew he must be the
first to go."

Tell me. For pity's sake, tell me. I clenched my teeth together.

"I was gaining rapidly. The Painted Man had a knife at
his belt but made no sign of taking hold of it. It was almost
as if he were waiting for me to take him. I raised my knife,
poised to throw, and quick as a flash he turned and made a
subtle movement of his hand, and something small and
shiny flew by me. I heard the man behind me gave a little
grunting sound, and there was a splash as he fell, and when
I looked forward again, the Painted Man was gone. Fury
made me careless, and as I strode ahead I almost lost my
footing. I cried out after him, 'Murderer! Scum of the earth!
I will put an end to your life of destruction and waste! You
are marked for my knife, outlaw!' I heard him laugh, an
empty, heartless sound, and then Niamh gave a scream. She
had heard my voice and was struggling to get free, knowing
rescue was close at hand."

His words set a chill on my heart. I could see it as clear
as if it were right before me: Niamh, hearing her pursuer's
voice, and desperate with the fear that she might after all

not escape to freedom. Niamh panicking, there on the treacherous pathway. "Go on, Eamonn," I said, in a shaking voice.

"I don't know how much I should tell you."

"You'd better tell everything. For your own sake as much as ours."

"Out with it, man!" Fionn was less patient than I.

"Very well. Niamh screamed, 'No!' and there was the sound of a struggle ahead of me. The mist still hung low; it parted only in patches, here and there, and I could not see clearly. I moved on as fast as I could, careless of my own safety. Conn, who had been last of us three, came up behind me. But hasten as we might, we were too slow to save your sister. There was a shout from the man who had been in front, and then Niamh's voice again, 'Help me! Help!' For an instant, I saw the man's hand, black as coal, reaching out, and a flash of red, Niamh's hair as she slipped from safe footing, and I heard the sound of the—no, I will not tell that part. I saw very little, Liadan. By the time I reached the place where it had happened, there was no trace of her but the marks on the tussock where her foot had slipped and a—a patch on the surface of the mud, where she had gone under. And this."

He held out a little cord of plaited threads, gray and rose and blue, its ends bound with strips of leather. On it hung a small, white stone with a hole in it. This cord was my own handiwork, and when I saw it I felt the blood drain from my face. For this, surely, Niamh would never willingly leave behind. Never, no matter where she went, no matter what orders she was given. This little token held all she had left of her family's love and Ciarán's.

"Wh-where was this, Eamonn?" I forced the words out.

"Floating on the surface, in a small patch of open water. The cord was caught on a reed. I'm sorry, Liadan. More sorry than I can possibly tell you."

Fionn cleared his throat. "What then? What of the fianna? Were they captured?"

Eamonn stared into the fire again. "It was not long before the man showed his true colors. We moved on after them to the north, and I could hear him laughing, taunting me as he fled. 'That surprised you, didn't it?' he called back at me. 'Didn't think I'd go that far, did you?' A derisive chuckle. 'Think again, Eamonn Dubh,' he said. 'My actions are not governed by your notions of what is correct and honorable. I play only to win, and I employ whatever strategy is required. If you would catch me, you must learn I cannot be measured by the same yardstick as other men. I took the woman only to demonstrate the weakness in your defenses. Now that I've drawn it to your attention, I'm sure it will be swiftly remedied. You see, I've done you a favor.' He went on in this vein, and all the while he managed to stay just ahead of me, however I increased my speed. We drew closer to the place where we must step onto dry land to be met by Fionn's men. But the mist was still thick, and suddenly I lost sight of them. Then there was a sound to the left of the path, like the croaking of a frog; and a sound to the right, like an answer. I made my way ahead as fast as any man could go. As I reached dry ground, the mist lifted. There were Fionn's men waiting by the road, silent. But of the Painted Man and his dark-skinned companion, there was no sign. Somehow they had slipped away and out of the bog and never passed the place where the ambush was set. How they did it, I do not know, for there is no other way."

"Excuse me." Fionn turned abruptly on his heel and strode away out of the hall. His face was gray. I might have felt some sympathy for him, but I could not forget my sister's bruises. If he had lost her, it was no better than he deserved.

"I'm sorry," Eamonn said again. "Words are not adequate, Liadan. Rest assured that it will be my mission to hunt these men down and see that they receive the harshest penalty. That is scant consolation to you for such a loss."

Aisling was weeping. "Oh, poor Niamh. What a terrible way to die! I can scarcely bear to think of it. We had better send word to Sevenwaters. I will arrange a messenger . . ."

"You need not." My voice was shaking. I took a deep breath and forced myself to be calm. "Sean is already on his way; I have asked him to come."

Brother and sister looked at me and at each other, but nothing was said. It was common enough knowledge that Sean and I need not use words to reach one another, but such a skill makes even friends uneasy.

"He'll be here tomorrow," I added. "Eamonn, I have to ask you this. Are you quite sure that Niamh—that she—are you certain? After all, you did not see—could she possibly have made her way to the other side? Could you be wrong?"

Eamonn shook his head gravely. "I'm afraid not. There are no side tracks on those marshes. There is only the one way. She could not have escaped them and survived, Liadan. This will be terrible news to break to your mother."

I nodded mutely. Terrible indeed; and all the worse for the fact that I could not tell if it were true or not. It might be a long time before I knew. Meanwhile, the truths that I did know must remain concealed, and a cruel tale be told, which might be falsehood. For just in case Eamonn was wrong, just in case the Painted Man had achieved the impossible yet again and taken my sister to safety, I must keep my part of the bargain. *Trust,* I said to myself, over and over. *Trust beyond all logic. That's the price. I must be crazy.*

The next day Sean came, and we told him. He took the news quietly, having perhaps expected the worst. I conveyed to him my wish to return immediately to Sevenwaters, and I was packed and ready just after dawn the following morning. Sean refused Eamonn's offer of an escort, for, he said, the five men he had brought with him should be quite sufficient.

"It's Liadan's safety I'm thinking of," said Eamonn heavily. "This man will stop at nothing. I'd be happier if you were better protected, at least to the borders of my own land."

Sean glanced at me, brows raised.

"Thank you, Eamonn," I said, "but I don't think you need concern yourself. Surely the Painted Man will not strike again so soon. He must know you will be on the alert for him. I'm sure we will reach home quite safely."

Eamonn's hands were moving restlessly, as if itching to grasp a weapon and use it. "Your confidence surprises me, Liadan, in view of what has happened here. I will ride out with you myself, at least as far as the last settlement."

We could hardly refuse. We said our farewells to Aisling and rode away from Sídhe Dubh under a lowering, gray sky. When the time came for Eamonn to turn back, he drew me aside while Sean conferred with his men.

"I had hoped you might stay longer," Eamonn said quietly, "or let me come back to Sevenwaters with you. I bear the guilt for what has happened; I sh-should be responsible for telling them, for helping to explain—"

"Oh, no," I said. "Whoever bears the blame for this, it is not you, Eamonn. Do not add that to your burdens. You should go home now and put this behind you. You should move on." I did not like the intense, almost feverish light in his eyes.

"You are very strong," he commented, frowning. "But then, you always were. I have long admired that in you. There are few women who could speak with such courage so soon after losing a sister."

It seemed safer not to reply.

"This is good-bye, then," he said. "Please tell your parents that I wish—I so much wish . . ."

"I'll tell them," I said firmly. "Good-bye, Eamonn."

I had expected to feel relief when finally I rode away from Sídhe Dubh and its mist-shrouded marshlands, knowing I was on the road for home. But as I turned my head and caught a glimpse of Eamonn's lone figure riding back into the heart of his strange, inhospitable territory, the feeling that was strongest in me was that I had somehow abandoned him, as if I had sent him back into his own dark place. This seemed fanciful, and I tried to dismiss it; but the image remained in my mind as we rode steadily on and the terrain became more thickly wooded, rising between jagged rocks toward the margin of the forest.

Sean halted his horse suddenly and motioned to the others to do the same.

"What—" I ventured.

"Ssh!" Sean raised a hand in warning. We all sat silent. I could hear nothing but the sound of birds and the spatter of a few raindrops. After a while Sean moved his horse forward again, but slowly, plainly waiting for me to catch up.

"What?" I asked, suspecting I knew already.

"I was sure I heard something," he said, with a sidelong look at me. "It's been there awhile. As if we were being followed. But when we stopped, there was nothing. Your ears are good. Didn't you hear it?"

"Only birds calling. There can't be anyone there. We'd have seen them."

"Would we? Perhaps I should have ignored your arguments and accepted Eamonn's escort. There are few enough of us; an ambush would be a problem."

"Why would there be an ambush?" I asked, avoiding his gaze.

"Why did they take Niamh?" asked Sean. "There's no reason to any of it. Why do that just after he—"

There was a pause.

"Just after he what? You're not telling me he agreed to work for you?"

"Not exactly," said Sean carefully, "but he did say he'd

consider it; he considers all offers. He said he'd let me know when he'd worked out the price."

I was speechless. What devious game was Bran playing? Surely my brother, the son of the despised Hugh of Harrowfield, would be the last person he would wish to do business with. Such an alliance would be fraught with danger for both of them. That it had ever been seriously considered filled me with alarm.

"It would have been the turning point," Sean said, "the one factor needed to change the course of our feud with the Britons. He could have named any price; I'd have met it. So why ruin his big chance? Is the man crazy that he would do this to my sister on a—on a whim?"

"He never acts on a whim." I spoke without thinking.

Sean waited before he replied. "Liadan."

"Mmm?"

"There will be no ambush?"

"Most unlikely, I should think," I said cautiously.

"Liadan, our sister is dead, and they were seen taking her away across the marshes. There were several witnesses. Would you protect Niamh's murderer by holding back your story?"

"No, Sean."

"Tell me, Liadan. Tell me the truth. You're playing with matters more dangerous than you can know."

But I kept my shield up and would not tell. Once, as we passed along a forest path damp with the decaying fabric of autumn leaves, I sensed a presence riding beside me, though this time I heard no fairy hoofbeats. I heard the lady's voice, low and solemn, and saw without turning my head her deep, grave eyes.

You acted rashly. You let them guide you again. There must be no more errors, Liadan.

It did not seem an error to save my sister from a life of abuse. I was angry. Was nothing important to the Fair Folk but their own long schemes, which we could barely understand? Around me, my brother and his men rode on oblivious. I glanced at Sean, and back at the lady.

Your brother does not hear us. I have made him deaf to this. Now listen to me. You have been very foolish. If you could see what might come of this, you would know how wrong you are. You put your child at risk. Her blue eyes were chill. *You put the future at risk.*

What risk? I was never in danger. And I'm going back to Sevenwaters. The child will be born there. Isn't that what you wanted?

Maybe your sister is dead. She spoke coolly, as if this did not really signify a great deal. *Drowned. You might have risked all, for nothing.*

She's safe; I know it. The man who took her can be trusted.

Him? He's nothing. A tool, merely. His part in this is over, Liadan. There are only two things that need concern you now. You must not risk the alliance. Without the alliance, your uncle has not the strength to triumph. Without the Uí Néill, he cannot win back the Islands. Your foolishness nearly lost him that chance. And you must protect the child. He is our hope. No more mistakes. No more going off on your own. Do not disobey me again. Once she knows of your son, she will seek to destroy him. The boy must stay in the forest where he can be properly protected.

She? Who?

But the Lady of the Forest simply shook her head, as if the name could not be put into words, and she faded slowly until I could no longer see her. And at last we came home to Sevenwaters with our terrible news.

It was to be a long secret, held through difficult times. Times that tested my will to the utmost, as I saw my mother's shrunken features and shadowed eyes, as I endured my father's tight-lipped silences. Winter came and we were cooped up inside together more than we wished, helpless to salve one another's hurts, feeling the fabric of our family stretching and tearing apart, not knowing where to start to repair such damage. Sean and Liam argued behind closed doors. Liam spoke of vengeance; Sean now advised caution. Our strength should be held in reserve, he said, for the time when the allies would combine in a final attack on Northwoods's positions. Perhaps next summer; or if not, by autumn we would be ready. Why waste valuable men and arms pursuing the Painted Man? Besides, he was already beyond reach, so they said. Away to Gaul or even farther. Niamh was lost; no bloodletting was going to bring her back. It was an unusually restrained approach for my brother to take, and at length Liam was persuaded. We heard little from Eamonn, but I knew he would not put aside the quest for vengeance. I had seen the look in his eyes; it chilled the blood. There was death in that look, for one of them at least.

I longed to return to the secret pool in the forest, which Conor had shown me. In those still waters I might find the answers I needed so desperately. I wanted to talk to Finbar, who seemed to know so much, and pass no judgments whatever, almost as if he were a creature of instinct, not troubled by notions of right and wrong. For my secret burdened me. I must protect my sister; I would not betray Bran. But because I could not tell what I believed to be the truth, a heavy toll was taken on others I loved, and I must live daily with their sorrow. There seemed no path to tread safe from guilt and regret.

The Sight is both a gift and a curse. It is at times like these that one needs it most. But it comes and goes as it chooses and cannot be summoned by an effort of will. I did try; I tried to see Niamh, where she was, how she was, who she was with. I tried to touch Bran with my mind, but he was very far away, and it was only at dark of the moon that I felt his presence. And it was dim, faint, the merest shadow of the bond I had with Sean, who had lain next to me ten moons in our mother's womb.

I thought Sean knew. He never said; but the knowledge was there in his behavior. Why else would he talk his uncle out of revenge? Why else would he not announce to all and sundry my own link with the Painted Man? He knew, or suspected, and he understood that I intended to keep my secret even from him. But he, too, saw our parents' grief, and he found it hard not to judge me, I think.

There was one reason to be glad and to look forward. Everyone fussed, as it grew closer and closer to my time and the child grew larger. Sean joked about my increasing girth but was always there when I needed help with climbing a flight of stairs or negotiating the rough track to the settlement. For all her weakness, my mother watched me with a healer's sharp eye, prescribing doses of various pungent teas and insisting that I rest each afternoon, as the weather grew warmer with early spring and the first delicate leaves unfurled on the spreading beech trees. My father was worst of all, watching me to make sure I ate every mouthful put before me, interrogating me on how much sleep I was getting, escorting me on the slightest venture out of doors in case I overtired myself. Mother laughed at him, in that gentle way she had, saying he'd been just the same with her, both times. Then she fell silent, doubtless remembering her copper-haired firstborn, the bonny girl who had danced through the woods in her white dress.

Sevenwaters was a tight-knit community for all the vast spread of our lands, and it was hard to avoid the gossip. I found what I heard alarming. When I went to the settlement to visit the sick, which I did almost up to the end, there would always be a few folk who would stretch out a hand to touch my belly and smile shyly. "For luck, my lady," they'd mutter, or, "For good fortune, bless your heart." At first I had no idea why they would do such a thing. But I heard, eventually, the tale that they were putting about, a tale far stranger than the truth.

This tale neatly explained why I had disappeared so inexplicably and returned with a child in my belly. It explained why my father and my uncle had not sent me away in disgrace but had let me stay here at home and bear my fatherless child in the sanctuary of the great forest. The tale went that the Fair Folk had chosen me to bear this particular child so that at last the prophecy would be fulfilled and the Islands be saved. Then the lake and the forest would be safe, too. Was I not just like the girl of the old story, the daughter they called the heart of Sevenwaters? Who better than my child to fulfill the prophecy of the wise ones? And no wonder I would not name the father, for this would be a child of the Otherworld, only half mortal. Who knew what powers such a one might have? That was how they were telling it. I could have told them a few truths that would have shattered their bright vision, but I did not. Who would believe that the sheltered daughter of Sevenwaters, who had tended their ills with loving care, the reliable, domesticated Liadan, would choose to lie with an outlaw and come home with his child growing inside her? Who would believe that she would construct a web of falsehoods to protect the man who might or might not have been responsible for her sister's death? It is frightening how one lie is just the first strand in an ever-increasing fabric of untruth. And once this fabric is woven, it is very hard to unravel.

The seasons changed, and I had no news of Niamh. I had no news at all. Mother taught Janis midwifery. Bony, angular Janis seemed ageless. It was hard to believe they had once called her Fat Janis, but so both my mother and Liam had told me. The hard winters in the time of the Sorceress had taken their toll. But Janis had gentle hands, and I knew I could trust her. The babe seemed determined to lodge with his head upward; Mother said they could wait, for he still had room to turn before the end. I was quite small, and a breech birth was best avoided in any case. I was easily tired now and spent the best part of the warmer days sitting on the mossy stone seat in the herb garden, soaking up the spring sunshine and talking silently with my child.

You'll like this garden, I told him. *It smells good; and there are lots of little things. Bees, they're the ones with stripes and wings. You need to be careful of them. When it gets hotter there'll be grasshoppers. Beetles, many shapes and colors, some shiny as precious stones. Caterpillars that creep along and eat your vegetables if you aren't careful. That's why we grow garlic next to the cabbages. When Meán Fómhair comes around again, you'll be able to sit up on the grass here and watch it all.*

Sometimes I told him about his father. Only sometimes, for I did not allow myself to feed on false hopes. *He's very strong. Strong body; strong mind; strong will. But somewhere he has lost his way. I named him after Bran the Voyager, and that was more apt than I knew. For Bran Mac Feabhail, the hero of the old tale, could never come home from his long and strange journey. When he sailed back to the coast of Tirconnell and one of his crew jumped from the boat to shore, at once the man withered away as if he had been long dead. Perhaps that magical voyage had indeed taken hundreds of years, though Bran and his sailors thought they had been away only from one summer to the next. So Bran told his tale, standing on the deck of his ship as it lay alongside the jetty, and then he sailed away without ever setting foot on his home shore. Not for him a wife's welcoming arms; not for him the joy of watching a son grow.* The child gave me a purposeful kick; he had little room to move now. Maybe he was telling me something in the only way he could. *All right,* I told him, shifting uncomfortably on the stone bench. *If there is an end to his journey, we'll find it for him. He won't thank us. And you'll have to help. I can't do it alone.*

It was very close to my time. I felt quite ready; the spring flowers had emerged, pale daffodils, fairy chimes, and snowdrops, and there was a definite warmth in the air despite persistent, drizzling rain. The cherry trees wore a delicate mantle of blossom. It seemed like a good time. My attention was turned inward. I was closely tuned to every small change in my body and scarcely aware of what happened outside it. I knew Sean was away from home. He had not told me where he was going.

They turned the child around; it was almost too late to do it, and the process was uncomfortable but necessary for an easier and safer birth. After that, I told them to leave me alone, for it seemed to me it was time to give it into the hands of the goddess.

A few days later I sat in my chamber on the night when the moon was dark and looked into the flame of my candle. I had kept vigil through the lives of several such candles now; each had its small wreath of powerful herbs, and the necklace of wolf claws had encircled each, with the single black feather tucked under the leather strip. Perhaps it had helped protect him, and perhaps it had not. This particular night I was so terribly tired; my eyelids kept dropping over my eyes, and then I would wake with a start, for I must not leave him to keep vigil alone in the dark. But eventually my body got the better of my mind, and I fell asleep where I sat on my chair.

A sharp pain woke me, and when I got to my feet there was a gush of fluid down my legs. From then on, it was all pain and confusion and the hardest work I had ever done in my life. It was as well Janis was there, for my mother was quite weak and could only sit by my side letting me grip her hand, and wiping my face with damp cloths. But feeble as her body had become, her mind was still as sharp as ever; and she directed Janis and the other women with confidence and precision. Perhaps with more confidence than she felt, for she told me quietly that it seemed the child had turned again within the last few days and was now lodged firmly in position, determined to be born breech first. There was nothing to worry about, she told me firmly. I was young and healthy, and the babe did not seem overlarge. I would manage.

I must manage, I told myself. *For if I cannot push him out, I am dead and so is he. I have to manage. Let the cord not be around his neck.*

It took a long time. The candle burned on until dawn sent pink-and-orange light through the narrow window into this chamber I had once shared with my sister. One of the women made to extinguish the small flame, and I spoke to her sharply, bidding her leave it alight. That way, something of my son's father would be there in the room to witness his birth. The light increased, and so did the activity around me, and I could hear men's voices outside. At one point my mother went out, probably to reassure the Big Man, for I could imagine he was pacing restlessly, waiting for it to be over, uncomfortable that, for once, he could do nothing to help.

"It's all right to scream, lass," said Janis, somewhat later. "It's a cruel task; no one expects you to bear it in silence. Curse and weep all you want." But it seemed to me that silence meant control; and I also thought, between those arching spasms of pain, how stoical Evan the smith had been, bearing an agony surely far greater than this. For had not women been enduring this for more years than there were stars in the sky? I had a job to do, and I must just get on with it. At that point I imagined a small voice in my ear, saying, *Good. That's the way.*

Later, as the light faded to violet-gray outside, and even Janis was starting to look exhausted, my mother had them make up another tea; and when I smelled it I raised my brows, for as well as the dittany and hyssop, there was calamint and another, sharper scent I did not recognize.

"I don't need this," I said crossly. "I can do this on my own."

Mother smiled, and if she was worried she managed to hide it well. There was no sign of weariness on her neat, small features. She was pale, but these days she was always pale.

"Dusk would be a good time of day for this child to be born," she said softly. "The right time, I think. Don't forget that I am the healer, Daughter."

I scowled at her and drank, feeling another surge of pain flood through my body, and this time I could not keep quiet. This was different, stronger, more forceful, and there was an urge to push, an urge that could not be denied.

After that it was quick, almost too quick. I made a lot more noise than I wanted to; my mother told me to stop pushing, but I couldn't; someone was supporting my shoulders, and Janis was saying, "Good, good; that's it, lass." And there was one last, wrenching, impossible effort, and all of a sudden, silence.

"Quick," I heard Janis saying, and there was a flurry of movement. "Turn him upside down, that's it. Clear out his mouth. Good. Now . . ."

I was lying back, completely spent; but when I heard the first gasping wail of outrage from my son, I sat bolt upright, dashing the tears from my eyes as I reached out for him. Oh, and he was perfect. So tiny, so wrinkled and red faced, but already with a cap of brown curls plastered to his small skull with the sticky, bloody residue of birth. He was my son and Bran's. *Oh. Oh, how I wish you were here to see him. To see what a wonderful child we have made.*

"You're crying, lass," Janis said, scrubbing furtively at her own cheeks. "No need for tears. That's a fine, wee boy you have there. Smallish, but strong. He can still bellow loud enough, even after such a long struggle. A little fighter, that one."

There was a lot of cleaning up to do, as is the way with childbirth. They busied themselves around me, as my son lay, a sweet warmth, across my chest. He was quiet now, his small mouth already working in preparation for the breast, his tiny fingers clutched tight around one of mine. *Don't let go.*

Mother had been strangely silent. I thought she must be exhausted from the long night and day; but when I looked, she was still sitting there by the bed, her gaze very thoughtful as she watched the child. The women finished their work and went off to a well-earned supper, and Mother told Janis to fetch herself some ale and food and take her time about returning.

"And, Janis? Tell the Big Man he can come up, will you? Just for a little."

When all were gone, and the chamber was quiet, she spoke again. "Liadan."

"Mm—?" I was almost drifting off to sleep. The small fire warmed the room well, and a pleasant scent of lavender spread through the air; they were burning the dried flowers for their healing properties.

"I'm not sure how to say this, but it must be said. Liadan, I think I could put a name to this child's father."

"What!"

"Hush, hush. Lie down again, you'll frighten him. I may be wrong. We should wait until your father gets here. There is a very strong likeness. And Red did tell me—he told me your man is somehow connected with Harrowfield. If not for that, I might perhaps have dismissed it."

We heard the sound of booted feet taking the steps three at a time and hastening along the hall, and the door flew open.

"Liadan!" My father crossed the room in two long strides. "Sweetheart, are you all right?" And then he saw the child lying on my breast, and his mouth curved in a big, sweet, wonderful smile. It had been a long time since I had seen him smile.

"You can hold him if you like, Grandfather," I said.

And so it was that my mother told her tale, while my father stood before the fire with his grandchild in his arms, and I leaned on one elbow and drank the cup of wine with herbs that my mother had put in my hand.

"This birth," said Sorcha softly, "this birth has been so like another one I attended long ago that I cannot dismiss it as coincidence. I might have done so were not this child the image of that other, the boy I delivered on the night of Meán Geimhridh, at Harrowfield."

Father glanced at her sharply. "How could that be?" he asked. "Besides," and he looked down at the bundle that was the child, so small between his big hands, "don't all babies look the same?"

"I believe I am right," said my mother. "And I think you will come to agree with me. The labor and birth followed just the same pattern: the child determined to be born breech first, the long labor, the difficult delivery. Liadan is younger and stronger than Margery was, and a lot more determined, and so she needed less help. But it was the same."

"All breech births are difficult," I said, my heart thumping. "Who was that child?"

But Mother did not answer me. "Look at the babe," she said to Iubdan. "Look at his curling, brown hair and his gray eyes. Look at the set of his jaw and the shape of his brow. There is the seed of John's face in those features, red and wrinkled as they are. You cannot tell me you don't see it, Red."

My father moved closer to the candle, looking intently at the baby's face, and there was a sudden wail of protest.

"Here," I said, putting down my cup, and my son was returned to my arms. I stroked his back and hummed under my breath an ancient lullaby that had once sent his father to sleep, surprisingly.

"Red?"

My father gave a nod. "I see it, Jenny." Thus had he

called her ever since the time they first met, when she had
no voice to tell her real name. "And it tallies with what you
told me, Liadan, that the child's father once lived at Harrowfield. The boy would have been less a year old
when Jenny left there."

"Who—who was he?" I asked cautiously, adding up
quickly in my head and wondering if Bran could indeed be
less than one and twenty. What was it he had said? *When I
was nine years old, I determined that I was a man.* Perhaps
it could be true.

"His name was John, for his father. But they called him
Johnny."

"He does not go by that name now. Still, a name is easily
changed."

"Has your man gray eyes?"

"Yes."

"What about his hair? This child had brown, curling hair
just like your son's."

I felt a slow blush creep over my face, and I was glad
they could not see into my thoughts. "That would be right,"
I said after a little.

"Is he a Briton?" my father asked. "If so, I can understand your reluctance to reveal his identity. But you should
not forget my own origins. I have done well enough here."

"I can't say. But it is possible. Can you tell me the story,
please?"

My father frowned slightly. "Your mother's very tired."

"Then you tell it. Please, Father."

He sat down on the other side of the bed. It was dark outside now.

"I had two loyal friends at Harrowfield. There was Ben,
my young foster brother, a man quick with the sword and
quicker still with his wit. And there was John. John was my
close kinsman, my guide and sounding board, my companion in every endeavor. He was a man to whom you could
tell any secret. He was a man you would trust with your life.

John wed a girl from the south, Margery was her name. There was a deep love between them. They lost one child, and it seemed to us they might lose this one, too. But your mother was there, and so, after a very long night, he was born safely."

"There was never a child more loved and wanted than Johnny." My mother took up the tale. "Margery was so proud of him. You could see it in everything she did. She was always carrying him against her shoulder, talking to him, singing to him. She made him the most beautiful little shirts, all embroidered with tiny flowers and leaves and winged creatures. John was a reticent sort of man. But he was devoted to the two of them."

"Did—did something happen? I cannot see how the cherished infant you speak of could have become the man who fathered my child. He is not—he is not a man who was raised in love. That much I know."

"John died," said my father heavily. "He was killed, crushed in a rock fall while watching over Jenny. It was Northwoods's doing. That was a terrible thing, and Margery took the loss hard. But when I left Harrowfield, she was doing her best to raise the child alone. In my brother's household they would have been well protected."

"John's son would have grown into a fine man," Sorcha said, looking at me intently. "A fine, good man."

I nodded, feeling tears prick the back of my eyes.

My father got up. "We're tiring you," he said. "You must sleep; you must both sleep. You've done well, the two of you. My strong women." And as they turned to leave, he said to me quietly, "If my grandson is also John's grandson, that fills me with content, Daughter. John would be glad of it. I would give much to meet this child's father. I hope one day I will."

But I only nodded, and then Janis came back with food for me and I discovered I was extremely hungry.

"Wait till your milk comes in," Janis said wryly, settling

by the fire with her tankard of ale. "You'll eat like a horse then."

Later, I fell asleep with the babe at my breast; and in the window, the candle burned steadily on into another night.

Chapter Eleven

The uncles gathered. I sensed this was not solely to inspect the newborn but for a deeper, more solemn purpose. For my mother was rapidly weakening now, as if she had indeed waited only for the birth of this babe before taking her final farewell of Sevenwaters.

I was possessive of my child. There was no need for a wet-nurse: I fed him and tended to him myself; I held him and touched him and sang to him. I had a girl to help me because Father insisted on it, but she had little to do. Before my son had passed the span of one moon in this world, he had heard the tale of Bran the Voyager in its entirety. How much of it he understood, there was no way of telling.

Mother now spent most of the day lying on her bed or on a pallet set out in the sheltered garden where she could rest when the weather was fine and smell the scent of healing herbs. She liked to have little Johnny tucked in beside her so that she could stroke his soft curls and listen to the small noises he made and whisper stories to him. My father hovered, a grim-faced presence, watching over her night and day. Liam sent for Sean, who had traveled north on unspecified business.

Conor came first, with a number of his kind, white robed and silent, treading soft as forest creatures. They settled quietly into the household as if for a lengthy stay. Conor went straight to see my mother, spending some time by her bedside in private. Then he came to see me and to inspect the child.

"I hear," he observed, watching me as I bathed my son in a shallow copper bowl, "the women came close to warfare over which of them would assist at this birth. There has been much talk of this child. They were all eager to help him into the world."

"Really?" I said, gathering up the slippery form of my son and wrapping him in a cloth I had hung to warm before the fire.

"Too much talk, you think?" My uncle's eyes were more serious than his tone.

"Their tales serve to explain what they cannot, or will not, understand," I said, laying the neatly cocooned Johnny against my shoulder. "Truths that are too hard to accept."

"That is so of some tales," Conor agreed. "But not all, surely."

"Indeed no. It is as you yourself said once: The greatest tales, well told, awaken the fears and longings of the listeners. Each man hears a different story. Each is touched by it according to his inner self. The words go to the ear, but the true message travels straight to the spirit."

My uncle gave a grave nod. Then he said casually, "Why did you give your son a name for a Briton?"

I was weary of lying. Father would probably tell him that part anyway. Surely there would be no reason to make a connection.

"He is named for his father," I said, stroking my son's

damp curls and hoping Conor would leave before I had to feed the child.

"I see." He was apparently unperturbed.

"With respect," I replied, "even an archdruid does not see everything. But that is his name."

"What plans have you for the future, Liadan?"

"Plans?"

"You intend to grow old here, looking after your father and Liam in their advancing years? You wish to take her place?"

I looked at him. There was a deep gravity about his calm features; the conversation had layers of meaning I barely understood.

"Nobody could take her place," I said quietly. "We all know that."

"But you would come close," Conor replied. "Folk would respect you for it. Already they revere the child, and you have always been a favored daughter of this house."

"Favored. Yes, I know. You were very cruel to Niamh when you sent her away. Cruel and unfair."

"Our decision must have seemed thus to you," said Conor, still calm, "but believe me, there was no other choice. Some secrets can never be spoken; some truths are too terrible to be revealed. Now she is gone, and you wish to lay blame, perhaps, for her tragic fate. But her marriage was not the cause of that; and it is not enough, I think, simply to accuse your father, or Liam, or myself. There were far older things at work here."

I was furious, but could not answer him, bound as I was by promises of silence. It became very hard to maintain the shield on my thoughts. And he was trying to read me, there was no doubt of that. Subtle as his probing was, I could feel it.

"Excuse me," I said, turning my back. "I must feed the child. Perhaps I will see you later at supper, Uncle."

"He can wait a little longer, I think. He seems more interested in his fist right now. You're a strong girl, Liadan. You guard your mind with great skill. Very few can withstand me."

"I've been practicing."

"Difficult, isn't it, to contain so many secrets? I have a suggestion for you, something to think about."

I said nothing.

"Your abilities are quite—significant. Already you have an advanced mental control and an excellent grasp of logic and argument. Then there are your other gifts, which you have barely begun to exercise. Wait until the boy is a little older, weaned from the breast perhaps, able to walk. A year maybe. Then come to join us in the nemetons and bring him with you. We could use and develop your skills. You will be wasted in the domestic scene, able as you are. And Johnny—who knows what he might become, with the right training? What they say about him could be no more than the truth."

I turned to face him, gazing straight into his deep, wise eyes.

"You made Niamh's choice for her, and it was wrong, more wrong than you will ever know. Perhaps you seek to replace Ciarán, an apt pupil. A great loss to you, I imagine. But you will not order my future as you did my sister's. Johnny and I make our own choices. We need no guidance."

He seemed unoffended, despite my blunt speech, as if this were exactly what he had expected.

"Do not make up your mind so quickly," he said. "The offer remains open. The child should stay in the forest. Whatever you decide, do not forget that."

A few days later, another uncle arrived, in a style all his own. Despite the talking bird on his shoulder, and the three seamen who accompanied him, and the comely young woman by his side, Padriac still managed to make his way right to the edge of the settlement without Liam's sentries detecting his presence. Liam was quite put out, but the joy of reunion after so long soon wiped away any other feelings. Padriac's weathered skin and twinkling blue eyes, his dimpled smile and long plait of sun-bleached, brown hair drew the women's eyes, for all his six and thirty years. His female companion made brows rise and tongues wag, for she was much his junior, and her skin was the delicate golden brown of peppermint tea, and her black hair was fuzzy as sheep's wool and braided in neat, tight rows. She wore colored glass beads, white and green and red, and her dark feet were bare under a striped robe. Padriac introduced her as Samara, but he did not clarify if she was his wife or his sweetheart or merely his shipmate. Samara did not talk. She flashed her white teeth in a grin that reminded me painfully of Gull's. For still, even now, there had been no word. My sister had indeed vanished, and her rescuers with her, as surely as if they had walked off the edge of the world.

There was only one person I thought might help me, and that was the uncle who was not there. I did not know if he would come, not even to bid his sister a last farewell. Finbar was a creature of the margins, poised delicately between one world and the other. In all the long years since he had walked away from Sevenwaters into the night, not once had he come back. Not for the funeral rites of his two brothers, Diarmid and Cormack, both slain in the last great battle for the Islands. Not for my birth and Sean's, not for Niamh's. Not for the day his father died and Liam became lord of Sevenwaters. Probably he would not come now, for he could see Sorcha, and talk to her, with no need to be present by her. Such was his bond with his sister. But I wished that he would come, for I had many questions for him. If I could just know if Niamh and Bran were safe; then I might bid my mother farewell with a lighter burden on my conscience.

For if my lies had not won freedom for my sister, if my silence had not protected the man who had risked his life to help me, then I might as well have told my family the truth all along and let that be an end of it.

The house was full, and yet there was a profound quiet over Sevenwaters, as if even the woodland creatures hushed their voices, awaiting my mother's passing. At dinner, things were a little livelier. We were a strange, ill-assorted company, the druids calm and dignified, speaking quietly and eating sparingly; the seamen demonstrating a healthy capacity for our good food and, particularly, our fine ale, and keeping up a flow of banter that made the serving women blush and giggle at their work.

At the head of the table sat the uncles: Liam, serious as ever, with a weariness about his features that was something new; Conor on his right, thoughtful in his white robe; and on the left, the irrepressible Padriac and his lovely, silent companion. Padriac did most of the talking; he had many adventures to recount, and we listened appreciatively, for his stories of distant lands and the strange folk who dwelt in them took our minds off the sadness that had fallen over our household. Sean had not yet returned.

Father no longer sat with us for meals. I think he feared to lose even a moment of Mother's remaining time. As for Sorcha herself, she had accepted long ago that this spring would be her last in this life. But I could see that she was not at ease; there was one burden that she was unable to put down. I wrestled with myself in silence, sitting by her bedside one afternoon with her delicate hand in mine and my father standing in the shadows watching her.

"Red." Her voice was very soft; she was saving what strength she had, using her healer's knowledge to buy her a little more precious time.

"I'm here, Jenny."

"It won't be very long now." Her words were little more than a sigh. "Are they all here?"

My father was unable to speak.

"Sean is not yet returned, Mother." My own voice wobbled dangerously. "All of your brothers are here, all but . . ."

"All but Finbar? He will come. Sean must be home by dusk tomorrow. Tell him, Liadan."

There was a certainty in her words that silenced me. There was no point in saying, you may have longer than that. She knew. My father came to kneel by the bed, to place his big hand over hers. I had never seen him weep, but now there were traces of tears on his strong face.

"Dear heart," Sorcha said, looking up at him, her green eyes huge in her tiny, shadowed face. "It is not forever. I will still be here, somewhere in the forest. And whatever my bodily form may be, I will always hold you close."

I made to get up and leave them alone, but Mother said, "Not yet, Liadan. I must speak to you both together. It won't take long."

She was very tired; her skin had a pallid sheen, and her breathing was labored. Neither of us bid her save her breath and rest. None of the family ever told Sorcha what to do.

"There have been secrets," she said, closing her eyes briefly. "The old magic is at work here, the old sorcery that closed its evil hand on us once before. It tries to divide us, to destroy what has been so well guarded here at Sevenwaters. Perhaps not all secrets can be told. But I want to say to you, Daughter, that whatever happens, we trust you. You will always choose your own path, and to some your choices will seem wrong. But I know you will follow the way of the old truths wherever you go. I see this in you and in Sean. I have faith in you, Liadan." She looked up at Father again. "We both have faith in you."

Iubdan waited a moment before he spoke, and I wondered if, for the first time in her life, she had read him wrong. But what he said was, "Your mother's right, sweetheart. Why else have I let you make your own choices all along?"

"Now go, Liadan," Mother whispered. "Try to speak to your brother. He should hasten home."

I went down across the fields to the margin of the forest, for the house was full of sorrow and I needed trees and open air. I wanted a clear head and an uncluttered mind, not only to try to reach my brother, but to make a difficult decision. Sorcha was dying. She deserved the truth. If I told her, I must tell my father as well. They had said they trusted my choices, but surely even they would recoil in horror at the thing I had done this time. If Father went to Liam with my story, then any good my lies had done would be instantly for nothing. If she still lived, my sister might be tracked down and brought home. Perhaps they would try to return her to her well-respected husband. Then the whole truth would come out, and the alliance would be shattered. As for the Painted Man, Eamonn would hunt him down and exterminate him like some feral creature in the night; and without him his men would go back to the dispossessed, fugitive lives they had known before he gave them names and a purpose and the gift of self-respect. My son would never know his father, save in tales as some kind of monster. Then our family would indeed be destroyed. The prospect chilled my blood. And there were the Fair Folk. You must not risk the alliance, the lady had told me. One could not lightly disregard such a warning. But my mother deserved the truth, and in her own way she had asked me for it. The question was not so much did they trust me, as did I trust them? Bran had dismissed trust once as a concept without meaning. But if you could not trust, you were indeed alone, for neither friendship nor partnership, neither family nor alliance could exist without it. Without trust, we were scattered far and wide, at the mercy of the four winds with nothing to cling to.

At the edge of the forest, I sat down on the stone wall that bordered the outermost grazing field and made my mind still. This was difficult, for my thoughts were filled with urgency. *I need a sign, a clue. Why isn't Finbar here? Him I could ask without fear.*

I slowed my breathing, and let the small sounds of the forest and farm fill my mind. The rustle of spring leaves on beech and birch; the calling of birds; the creak of the mill wheel and the gentle splashing of the stream. The plaintive voices of sheep. A boy addressing his flock of geese: Get up there, stubborn creatures, or I'll give you what for; the gander's honking response. The sound of the lake water lapping the shore; the sigh of wind in the great oaks. Whispering voices high overhead that seemed to say, *Sorcha, Sorcha. Oh, little sister.*

When my mind was quite still, only then I reached out for my brother.

Sean?

I hear you, Liadan. I'm coming home. What of our mother?

Are you far away?

Not so far. Will I be too late?

You must be here before dusk tomorrow. Even the voice of the mind can weep. *Can you be here by then?*

We will be there. In his mind he put his arms around me and held me close, and I sent him back the same image. That was all.

Liadan?

This was not my brother's voice.

Uncle? My heart thumped. Where was he?

I'm here, child. Turn around.

Slowly I got up from the wall and turned to look back down the path into the forest. He was hard to see; not so much a man as another part of the pattern of light and shadow, the gray and green and brown of trunk, leaf, moss, and stone. But he stood there, barefoot on the soft earth, still clad in his ragged robes and dark, enveloping cloak. His black curls tangled around a face white as chalk. His eyes were clear, colorless, full of light.

I'm glad you are here. She asked for you.

I know. And I have come. But I think I will need your help.

I felt his fear, and knew the courage it had taken to come this far.

I will take you in. What do you need?

I fear to be—touched. I fear to be—confined, shut in. And there are dogs. If you can help with this, I can stay for long enough. Until dusk tomorrow.

"I am honored by your trust," I said aloud. "This cannot be easy."

My weakness shames me. It was indeed a long curse the Sorceress set on me. It has compensations of a sort. But I would not expose my frailties to my sister or to my brothers. It is not pity I seek, merely assistance, to be strong enough for her.

"You are very strong," I said quietly. "Another man would not have survived so long, would not have endured it."

You, too, are strong. Why do you not ask me what you wish to ask?

Because it seems—selfish.

We are all selfish. It is our nature. But you are a generous giver, Liadan. You hold those you love very safe, by any means you can. Later I will show you how to see what you long to see. Now I think we must go in.

"Uncle," I said aloud, rather diffidently.

What is it?

"Why do you reveal your fears to me when you conceal them even from your brothers?"

No man wishes to be weak. Yet my weakness is also my gift. What is commonplace in one world may be a source of terror in the other. A closed door, the baying of a hound. And yet, what is a mystery in this place becomes clear and simple in that other. It is image and reflection, reality and vision, world and Otherworld. I show you my fears because

*you can understand them. You understand because you
have the gift. You are not burdened as I am, but your spirit
recognizes the pain and the strength such knowledge
brings. You know the power of the Old Ones, how it works
still in us.*

"This gift—the Sight, the healing mind—it comes from
them, from our first ancestors? It comes from the Fomhóire
woman, Eithne?" I knew this thought for truth the instant it
came into my mind.

*It is very old. Very deep. As deep as a bottomless well, as
deep as the darkest recesses of the ocean. Like them, it
bides its time.*

I shivered.

"Come," said Finbar, trying out his voice, which was
clearly seldom used. "Let us be brave, and make ourselves
known." And we set off across the field to the house.

There was an awkward moment when folk from kitchen
and stables came out to stare, and a hound barked, and my
uncle's mind communicated to mine, without a sound, a
state of heart-hammering, mind-numbing terror, a para-
lyzed instinct for flight. I sent out a swift, silent call.

Conor? Uncle, we need you.

Folk were muttering, whispering, as we approached. A
man had his hand on the dog's collar, but it was growling
and snapping, as if some wild thing had come within reach
of its jaws. I did not know how to quiet a hound with my
mind. Beside me, Finbar froze where he stood.

"Look! That's the man with a swan's wing!" A child
spoke out, clear and innocent. "The man in the story!"

"The very same, and my own brother." A calm, authoritative voice spoke from the kitchen doorway and out
stepped my Uncle Conor, looking as if this sort of thing
were an everyday occurrence. "Away off to your work now.
There will be more visitors here before tomorrow night;
Lord Liam would be displeased to see you idle."

The crowd dispersed; the dog was led away, straining

against the hold on its collar. The moment was over. In my own breast, I could feel Finbar's breathing as it quietened, his heartbeat as it slowed. The next night and day would indeed be an ordeal for him.

"Come," said Conor quietly. "You'll want to see her straightaway. I'll take you."

"I'll talk to Liam," I said. "There are arrangements to be made. Then I must go to my son. He'll be hungry." *I will see about the dogs. Will you be all right?*

Thank you, Liadan. Later, perhaps you will show me your son.

Liam was surprisingly understanding, especially since I interrupted a meeting with his captains to speak to him. Orders went out immediately that all dogs were to be confined to kennels or kept in the stable area for the next night and day at least, and that folk were to keep themselves to themselves and leave the family alone. Liam's own wolfhounds were chained even as he spoke and led off to temporary captivity with reproachful looks on their long, whiskered faces.

"You're a good girl, Liadan," said Liam, as he returned to his meeting. From him, this was rare praise. He was not a man much given to expressions of approval. I wondered how good he would think me if I told him the truth.

"Thank you, Uncle."

It was getting late, almost dusk. There was only one day left, and I longed to be by my mother's side, sharing this last time with her. But as the wheel turns and life slips away, so also new life makes its clamoring presence known, reaching out, urgent for recognition, eager to move forward on its path. My son could not wait. He was awake and hungry, and I sent the nursemaid away to some supper and sat down to feed him. The copper bowl was ready, half filled with warm water, but the girl had not bathed him yet, knowing I loved to perform this task myself. I opened my dress and offered him the breast, and he latched on and sucked with vigor, one small fist beating gently against my flesh while his solemn, gray eyes watched me intently. I hummed under my breath, feeling that odd sense of quiet that comes with the letting down of the milk, as if some power inside bids you be still while the child drinks its fill. Later, I would take Johnny down to see my mother, if she were still awake. Now, it was her time with Finbar, and they were best left alone. She had many farewells to make, but that might be the hardest, save one.

After a while I moved Johnny across to the other side. He began a protest, then clamped his jaws on the nipple and commenced to drink again. For a small baby, he had a hearty appetite. I thought about Conor's suggestion that I might go to the nemetons. That both I, and in time my son, might join the wise ones. I considered the instructions of the Fair Folk. *No more going off on your own. The boy must stay in the forest.* In neither vision of the future was there any place for my child's father.

Johnny was asleep. There would be no bath tonight. Janis said I bathed him too much anyway; it was unnatural for a child to be so clean or spend so much time in the water. What was he, she joked, a son of Manannán mac Lir, the sea god? But I laughed off her comments. For Johnny loved the water so much, loved to float, to give himself into its warm supporting hold, to move his small limbs against its supple, changing surfaces. I could not deny him this small pleasure, and I promised him that, in the summer, we would go swimming in the lake. When he was older, I would teach him how to jump off the rocks and swim to shore, as I had done long ago with Sean and Niamh. I would show him how you could lie there with the sun warming your back and the ancient stone holding you and trail your fingers in the clear water as the silvery fish swam by. *You'll like that.*

I fastened my gown and got up, thinking to put the babe

in his cradle. But as I passed the bowl of cooling water, something flashed across its surface, evanescent as a rainbow, quickly gone. Had I really seen it? I moved closer, Johnny warm and relaxed in my arms, and stared down into the still water. I made myself quiet as a standing stone, quieter than the deepest thought.

The water was moving, shifting, as if about to boil, but there was no heat in it. I sensed the door opening and closing silently behind me, but I did not turn.

Good. So you did not need me after all.

I knew Finbar was there, in the shadows, but still I remained motionless.

The water began to swirl deosil, sunwise, as if chasing itself in circles. I felt my head swimming. Then, as abruptly as it had begun, the movement stopped. I gazed into the bowl.

The image was small, but clear. A child's hands, making patterns in sand. The picture tilted, became wider. The child was in a cave, with light filtering through from above, painting the scene in many shades of gray and blue. A cave by the sea, a place where water washed gently in and out, and you could hear the far-off cries of gulls. This was a place where many margins came together, a secret place. Within the cavern, there was a tiny, soft beach where the child sat playing quietly as a woman watched. I could not tell if this child were boy or girl. It was maybe two years old, and had a cap of dark red curls, and milk pale skin. The woman said something, and when the child looked up, I saw its eyes, which were deep and dark as ripe mulberries. The woman was so thin her bones showed through her skin. She was slender and frail as a winter birch. Her hair was a faded red-gold, hanging loose down her back. She watched the child closely, that it should not venture too near the water. And after a while, she moved to sit on the sand close by the little one, and began to add her own patterns to those already inscribed with such care. Her blue eyes were shadowed; but as she watched her small charge, her wasted features bore an expression of such joy and pride that I felt tears running down my cheeks. The woman was my sister, Niamh.

Then, suddenly, something else was there: a force, a power such as I had never before encountered. Woman and child played on, unaware. But something was pressing out against me, as if a very strong hand had been placed against my thoughts, as if a barrier had been thrown up to block my vision. *No,* said a voice. *Keep out.* And with that, the image was gone, and I was simply standing there staring foolishly into my baby's bathwater.

Shivering, I decided I did not want to let go of my son after all, and I backed away from the copper bowl and sat down in my chair, cradling Johnny warm against my shoulder as he slept on. He made small, snuffling noises, as if to reassure me. From the edge of the room, Finbar watched me.

"Did you see?" I asked him.

"I did not see as you did. But you keep your mind open to me, and so I witnessed your vision." He did not use the inner voice but spoke aloud in the soft, hesitant way he had, as if he must practice this little-used skill now he was among men again.

"What was that? It was like an iron fist, pushing me away. Like the barrier put by a—by a Sorcerer, to keep prying eyes away from his secrets. The old tales tell of such invisible walls."

"Indeed. This may be a vision best concealed from Conor, I think. I had thought it would be another, whom you would most wish to see, not your sister."

"The two are linked. What I see of the one tells me of the other, for now. But this vision was not of the present. It could not be. That was her child; I read it in her eyes. It must be a vision of what is to come."

"Or a vision of how you wish it might be."

"That's cruel," I said, choking back my tears.

"The Sight is cruel. This you know already. Will you look again?"

"I—I don't know. I don't know if I want to see."

"You're not a very good liar."

So I put Johnny in his bed and covered him with the many-colored quilt I had made and went back to look once more. Finbar made no attempt to direct me, but his silent presence gave me strength.

For a little I thought there would be nothing. The water seemed to cloud and go dark, but there was no movement. It lay still as if long untouched.

Trust. Truth. I held these words in my mind, and worked to keep out all others. *Truth. Trust.*

I closed my eyes, and when I opened them again, there was another image on the smooth surface of the water.

Tiny pictures, changing and changing. They were fighting in a strange land under a burning sun. Bran grimaced, ducking as a whirling axe flew past his head. They were in a boat, traveling swift through merciless seas. Gull held the tiller, grinning into the salt spray, and the sail creaked in the gale. Bran was bending over a man who lay sprawled on the deck, a man whose neck and shoulder were heavily wrapped in bloodstained linen.

"Can't you make more speed?" Bran shouted.

"If you want to end this voyage on the bottom of the ocean, I might manage," Gull retorted. "Fancy a life among the sea monsters?"

Then they were on shore and digging a hole under trees. They were lowering a limp form into the earth. Other men stood around, silent. The soil was shoveled in, the ground leveled efficiently.

"You should have let Liadan stay," someone said. "She'd have known what to do. She'd have saved him."

There was the sound of a blow and Bran's voice, the tone savage, "Shut your mouth!"

The water went dark again, and I thought that was all. But there was one more image to come. They were back in that place again, the place of the ancient ones, and the two of them were outside on a warm spring night, keeping watch while the others slept in the shelter of the barrow. Maybe it was now. The moon was full, and I could see their faces clearly, dark and light.

"You were unfair," Gull spoke without emphasis. "What Otter said, that was no more than the truth. You should never have let her go."

"Don't presume to offer me advice," Bran snapped. "At least I did not silence her with the knife. You know as well as I that there is no place for a woman here."

"This is different, isn't it?"

"How can it be? How could she live as we do? Besides, she is the daughter of Sevenwaters. Her father turned his back on his land and his people. For his own selfish reasons, he was not there to protect them. Ironic, isn't it? I owe to him my complete failure to be a suitable mate for his daughter. He little knew what he did when he walked away from Harrowfield."

"So you care nothing for her, is that it?"

"I don't need another lecture," Bran said wearily.

"And that's why we went racing back the moment you believed her in danger?"

There was no reply to this.

"Well?" Gull was not going to give up.

"You presume too much. There was a job to do, and we did it. That was all."

"Uh-huh. And what of the job her brother wants you to perform? You'd be crazy to agree to that. That's no less than a suicide mission."

"It would be a challenge, certainly, but not beyond me."

They were quiet for a while.

"You're fooling yourself if you think you've put this behind you," Gull said eventually.

"I don't wish you to speak of these things again," said Bran repressively. "There was nothing between me and—and the girl. She was meddlesome and sharp-tongued enough, and I was glad to see the last of her."

Gull said nothing, but I saw the flash of his white teeth in the darkness, and then the image was gone.

My knees felt weak, and I stumbled to my chair, knowing I was crying and hardly caring if my uncle saw it.

"As I said, you will not keep this man at Sevenwaters. And yet, you plan a future here for your child without knowing it. You see Johnny with his grandfather, learning to plant trees. You see yourself, teaching your son to swim in the lake of Sevenwaters. You see the child slipping into the kitchen for one of Janis's honeycakes, as we all did when we were growing up, and the world was so full of adventures there was barely time to fit them into the day. You see Conor showing the boy Ogham signs on a carven stone. The child is the key. In your thoughts, you recognize this. There is no place in his future for this man."

"How can you say that? This is his father."

"The man has served his purpose. I am sure that is what Conor would say."

I was unable to respond. Bursting with my sense of outrage and injustice, I was forced nonetheless to recognize the terrible wisdom of his words.

"It is what the Fair Folk told me, but what do you say?"

Ah. Only that there will come a point where you must make a choice. And that choice will be all your own. Do not think me heartless, Liadan. I see more than you think. I see the bond between you and this man. I see that he is your mate. How can you choose without a loss that rips out your heart?

Mother wasted none of her last night in sleep. Instead, she had Liam bring the men and women of the household to her so she could thank them and say her farewells. Many a tear was shed; many a small bunch of primroses, or single daffodil brave in white and gold was laid at her feet or by her pillow. She had had them move her to a chamber downstairs, and around the walls many candles burned, so that the space was filled with warm light. Lying small and still on her pallet, she found a kind word for each solemn visitor.

There must have been considerable pain. Both Janis and I knew what doses Sorcha had needed to take this last season to keep from crying out as the canker gnawed ever deeper into her vitals. Now, she wanted to be awake, and able to listen, and so she had taken nothing. She was indeed a strong woman, and she masked the spasms so well that few were aware of what she suffered. My father knew. His face had become an expressionless mask, save when he looked at her directly; and he was not speaking, not to me, or to Liam, or to anyone but her, unless he must. I knew he wished we would all go away and leave the two of them alone, but it was her bidding he followed.

At last these long farewells were done, and the household slept. I sat by the small fire with Johnny quiet in my arms; my father was on a stool by the bed, his long legs bent awkwardly to the side. He was wiping her face with a damp cloth. Mother's eyes were closed; she might have been asleep, save for the slight twitch of one hand as the pain struck deep.

You could tell them now. If you are ready.

I glanced at Finbar where he stood motionless, his right hand laid flat on the wall beside the window, his back turned to me as he looked out into the moonlit garden. There was no doubt of what he meant.

I'm ready. There could be no better time than this.

"Is Sean home yet?" my mother whispered.

"I'll go and see if any word has come," said Liam quietly. "Come, brothers, we should leave this small family alone awhile."

They had been grouped together, standing by the door where folk might be shepherded in and out with as little fuss as possible. Now Liam left, taking Conor and Padriac with him, but Finbar remained behind. Not for him a safe, closed chamber and blanketed bed. Not for him the temporary oblivion of strong ale. I had not seen him touch a morsel of food nor a drop of drink since he had come home.

"Mother, Father, I have something to tell you."

Sorcha opened her eyes and managed a weak smile. "That's good, Daughter. Let me . . . let me . . ."

She was short of breath, but I knew what she wanted. I made room for Johnny under the coverlet and tucked him in beside her. My father helped her curl a hand around the baby's warm body. Johnny's eyes were open, his father's gray eyes. He was growing fast, and I could see him looking, trying to make sense of the shadows and patterns of the candlelit room. By the window, Finbar did not move. I did not think I could sit down. I stood by the bed, my hands clutched tight together.

"I will not insult you by asking for your trust," I began. "Time is too short for that. You have said you have faith in me, and I must believe it. I have to tell you that I have lied to you, and hope you will listen while I explain why. It is a matter very deep, very secret, a sadness beyond tears and perhaps an ending better than we dared hope for. Your trust may be stretched to its utmost, as mine has been."

Now my father was observing me closely, his blue eyes sharp and cool. Mother lay tranquil, watching the baby.

"Go on, Liadan." Iubdan's tone was carefully neutral.

"Niamh," I said. "Niamh . . ."

Courage, Liadan.

"We all knew something was wrong when she came home. You even asked me to find out what it was. But we did not know how wrong. When we were at Sídhe Dubh, I discovered the truth. Her—her husband beat her and abused her most foully. She was already much distressed by what happened here; she believed everyone she loved had rejected her. She had hoped to make a new start with this marriage. Her husband's cruelty put paid to that. But she made me swear not to tell. She made me promise to keep it secret from all the family. Niamh was heartbroken that Ciarán had not stood by her. She was shattered when you sent her away. To be treated thus, she believed, must mean she was worthless. She would not let me tell of Fionn's abuse and cause the alliance to be broken, for that would have been yet another failure."

There was a stunned silence. Then my father said, "If this is true, and I know it must be, for you would scarcely lie about such a matter, then you should have told us. This was one promise that should have been broken."

"I'm afraid I—I could not be sure you would help. After all, you had insisted she marry Fionn. You had sent her away to Tirconnell. Your words to her were uncompromising. Sean hit her. And there was Liam and the alliance. I have never understood why she could not wed Ciarán, why you refused even to consider that match. It is unlike you to act thus without weighing the options, without assessing the arguments. It is not like you to withhold the truth. I did not understand your reasons, and so I could not risk telling."

My father was staring at me, his eyes full of hurt. "How could you believe I would condone such a thing? Allow my own daughter to be abused?"

"Hush," whispered my mother. "Let Liadan tell her story."

"I—then I . . ."

Word by word. A learning tale. Tell it slowly.

"I did not know what to do or where to seek help. Time was short, but I knew I could not let her go back to Tirconnell. I feared she would harm herself. So I asked a—a friend—to take her away, to see her safe to a place of sanctuary."

Again, a charged silence.

"I don't think I understand," said Iubdan carefully. "Was not your sister abducted by the fianna and drowned? Was not she a victim of one of their arrogant displays of pointless barbarity?"

"No, Father." My own voice was a thread of sound. "The men who took her away across the marshes did so at my request. They came to Sídhe Dubh at my bidding. They were to guide Niamh to safe ground and convey her to a Christian house of prayer, where she could remain in hiding, where she could be away from the cruelty of men."

When my father was able to speak again, he said, tight jawed, "You choose your friends poorly, it seems. It is clear they failed utterly in this venture, since they lost her before ever they touched dry ground. I hope you didn't pay them too much."

It was as if he had struck me, and this time Finbar spoke aloud.

"The tale is not told yet; it is a complex fabric with many strands. Your words wound your daughter. It has taken all of her courage to speak to you thus, and she has not been the only one to withhold the truth. You should let her finish in peace."

"Tell us, Liadan." My mother's voice was calm.

"I have—connections—that I have not spoken of. Friends, I would call them. One of these friends is the man who took Niamh from Sídhe Dubh and conveyed her to safety, to a place where she will not be hurt, where she will be treated with respect, not expected to be the Uí Néill's plaything, to a place where her family will not force her into a loveless marriage for the sake of a strategic alliance. I can give you no evidence that she is safe. I cannot tell you where she is, nor would I if I knew. But I have seen her in a vision of the Sight, and I believe that my friend has done as I bid him. The drowning, the loss in the mist—it was a sham, part of the performance designed to convince Eamonn, and later others, that she was dead, a deception to divert the hunters from their quarry. Under cover of that lie, they took my sister to safety."

A little draft stirred the candle flames. After a while my mother said very quietly, "You knew that Niamh was alive and did not tell us?"

"I'm sorry," I said miserably. "When you ask this man to undertake a mission, you follow his rules. He said she would be safer if as few people as possible knew the truth. I judged it best. And—and I don't know, exactly. I believe she is not lost. I trust the man who aided us when nobody else would."

"As I said," Father's expression was of frozen distaste, "your choice of friends seems deeply flawed. How can you possibly know if this man is telling the truth or not? Deception is his very lifeblood. Everything we have heard of him paints him as a turncoat who can be relied on only to be unreliable, changing allegiance when he will. And he is violent in the extreme, a prankster who acts on whatever insane whim takes him. I cannot believe you would trust such a man with your sister's life. Some madness must have seized you. And now you have the temerity to give your mother false hopes, now, tonight, when . . ." He fell silent, perhaps aware that my mother's shadowed eyes were turned on him.

"No, Red," she said, "don't be angry. We have no time for that. You must hear Liadan out."

I drew a deep breath, feeling Finbar's strength as he concentrated his mind on mine, not thinking for me but lending me his own courage.

"As I said, I have seen her. I have seen her alive, and happy, and with a child that was certainly her own. A vision of the future, a sure and joyful one. But even without that, I believe that she is safe. I know it in my heart because I know I can trust the man who is my son's father. It is the same man. You looked into my child's face and told me he has John's eyes. Trustworthy eyes. My son's father has the same trustworthy eyes in a face marked with the features of the raven, bold, fierce, and forbidding. He is the leader of the fianna, the one they call the Painted Man. He has done ill deeds in his life, that there is no denying. But he is also capable of great courage, strength, and loyalty. He makes few promises, but those he makes he keeps. As Conor's tale showed, even an outlaw, given the chance, can be a good and trustworthy man. This man saved your daughter. This man fathered your grandchild. He has my heart and will have it always. I would give myself to no other. Now I have told you the truth, all that I can, and I have given you my trust; for this knowledge, passed to the wrong ears, could put many lives at risk."

Well done, Liadan. Finbar gave a nod of recognition.

My parents stared at me.

"I'm silenced," said Iubdan.

Mother lifted a hand to stroke Johnny's brown curls. "So Niamh is safe. This news is a wondrous gift, Liadan. I never quite believed that she was gone . . . I think, somehow, I would have known."

"I'm sorry," said Father abruptly. "You've spoken very plainly, and I respect that. I was too harsh, perhaps. But this has caused us great pain. I did not expect that from you, Liadan."

"I'm sorry too, Father." I wanted to give him a hug, to say, it will be all right, but something in his eyes told me no, not yet. "I had two lives to protect, and both are still at risk."

"I can hardly believe that you would choose such a man."

"Do you find it hard to believe that I would choose the son of your friend John?"

"John was not an outlaw. John was not a killer for hire."

"You have been forthright in your catalog of the Painted Man's faults, Father. Yet he in turn describes you as the cause, by your relinquishment of your responsibilities at

Harrowfield, of his failure to be an adequate partner for your daughter."

Father had no reply to this.

"Red."

"What is it, Jenny?"

"This is what you must do next. You must go back, back home."

Father simply looked at her.

"You mean, back to Harrowfield?" I asked the question he would not ask.

Mother nodded. She was still looking at my father, holding him with her gaze.

"It's a mission," said Mother. "Go back and find out what happened. What became of Margery and her son. How it came about that John's boy has grown into this . . . this . . . unhappy young man."

Father stood up, turning his back on all of us. "So you think my time here is finished, is that it? That once—that when—that after this, there is no place for a Briton here at Sevenwaters? I suppose I can understand that. I suppose I may come to understand it."

Finbar, who had stayed so still and kept so silent, save for the voice of the mind, was quick enough now. In an instant, it seemed, he was by my mother's bedside and speaking aloud.

"Would you use your words to hurt Sorcha, tonight of all nights?" he asked. "Do not speak rashly, out of your own pain. She gives you this mission to ensure you do not lose yourself when she is gone." My uncle, it was clear, was not afraid of plain speaking. "She bids you go, for your daughter's sake and for your grandchild's. Seek out the truth and bring it home for them. There are wounds to be healed here, and some of them are your own."

"And . . . ," Sorcha spoke very softly, and my father was forced to turn back to hear her. I had never before seen him at such an extreme of distress, and it was hard to hold back my tears, for my tale had dealt a blow to a man already in deep pain. "And . . . you should see your brother. You will need to tell Simon that I am gone. He should know. Red. . . ."

He came to kneel by her again, and she reached up a hand to brush his cheek. He put his own fingers over hers and held them there.

"Promise me," she whispered, "promise me you'll do it and come back here safe."

He gave a stiff nod.

"Say it."

"I promise."

She sighed. "It's late, Liadan, you should be sleeping. Is Sean here yet?"

"I don't know, Mother. Shall I go and see?"

"Here," she said, "you'd better take your son. He might miss you." Her fingers moved gently against the baby's small ear, his soft hair, and then I took Johnny up in my arms, and I saw in Sorcha's eyes that she knew it was the last time she would touch him.

"Liadan, have you told Sean about this?"

"No, Mother. But he guessed. Part of it at least. He has kept faith; he has not told Liam or Fionn or Eamonn. He has not even told Aisling."

"I dislike secrets. I detest lies," my father said heavily. "We should have made all plain from the start. But it's clear this is one truth that must remain concealed for some time longer. What of Conor? Does he know any of this?"

"The only way you will get an answer to that question is to ask him," said Finbar. "And even then you may not find out what you want to know."

"Then I suppose it must remain unanswered until I return from Harrowfield," my father said. "Thus one lie begets another, and we cease to trust."

"We ceased to trust when Niamh was wed to the Uí Néill

and sent away," I responded sharply. "This tale began a long time ago."

"Longer than that," said Finbar quietly. "Oh, far longer."

I did not think I would be able to sleep. Probably none of us would sleep, except Johnny, whose infant dreams were untroubled by the shadow of parting. I carried my child along to the great hall, but it was his father I spoke to, in my mind. *I need you. I want you here. Your arms around me, your body warm against mine, to keep away the sadness. Would it make a difference if you could hear their words? If you could hear them say, "He has fulfilled his purpose," would you fight to keep us then? Or would you be afraid of what such a struggle might reveal? Perhaps you would simply turn your back and walk away.*

Then, entering the hall, I put a sharp curb on my thoughts. Sean was there, apparently but newly arrived after a hard ride into the night, for he was somewhat travel stained, and I sensed his deep weariness.

"Liadan! I was just coming. How is our mother?"

For an instant I wondered why he spoke aloud and so formally, and then I saw that Aisling was with him, unfastening her cloak, rubbing her back, her face white with exhaustion. I moved forward, masking my surprise.

"Aisling, you must be very tired. Here, sit down, let me fetch you wine—"

My words, and my feet, came to an abrupt halt.

"I suppose you did not expect us, Liadan," said Eamonn, as he stepped out of the shadows by the window. "I regret the inconvenience."

"Oh." I was gaping stupidly, caught quite unprepared. "No—I—"

"I have been in the north," Sean put in smoothly. For all his weariness, he read me well, and quickly. "I came back by Sídhe Dubh. Aisling and Eamonn were anxious to pay their respects, knowing the gravity of Mother's illness. And now I must go to her."

"She's been asking for you. She will be very happy that you have come home in time. I'll go with you—"

"No, don't trouble yourself. You should sit and rest; you look worn out. Why not put the boy down and take a cup of wine yourself?"

"I—" There was no polite way to refuse my brother's sensible suggestion. What I did not expect was that Sean would take Aisling's hand and lead her away with him, leaving me alone with Eamonn. Whatever men had accompanied them on their ride must have already retired to the kitchens and thence to a well-earned rest. The two of us were on our own, save for the sleeping child. I could think of many things I would rather be doing than talking to Eamonn at that precise moment. But he was a guest; I had no choice.

"You do look very tired, Liadan," he said gravely. "Come, sit here."

I laid Johnny down on cushions before the fire, and I sat. It was Eamonn who filled two cups from the wine jug and put one in my hand. He stood beside my chair, looking down at the still form of my son.

"So this is your child. He seems—healthy. And, after all, a son cannot choose his father."

An icy trickle of fear went down my spine. What did he mean?

"Thank you," I muttered. "He is small, but strong."

"I hope to have a word with your mother, before—I hope to speak with her in the morning. And your father. If there is time."

I nodded, my throat tight.

"I wish to make my apologies in person, to express my regrets, about—what happened to your sister. There is no way I can make amends; I acknowledge that. But I hope at least to let them know I will continue to pursue the matter to an appropriate conclusion."

"Eamonn . . ."

"What is it, Liadan?"

"It may be better simply to express your sympathy on their loss and leave it at that. My father is in some distress, and my mother is very weak. They have come to terms with Niamh's—accident. This is not the right time for vows of vengeance. It is not a time for anger."

"Anytime is the right time until I remove that scum from the face of the earth," said Eamonn tightly.

I did not want to hear him. Dark visions hovered close. Could it be that he knew this was Bran's child? How could he know? I did not want to be drawn into talk of dangerous things. Besides, it was the middle of the night, and I was too tired to be sure of keeping my thoughts, or my words, under firm enough control for this. But I did not want to sleep, in case Mother needed me. I moved from my chair to sit on the cushions laid on the floor before the hearth. Here I could put my hand on my son's small body and feel his warmth. Here I could stare into the flames and dream, for there are times when dreams are safer than the real world.

Eamonn was watching me intently. I felt it, even though my eyes were turned away.

"I would have come earlier," he said quietly, "come to see your parents; come to speak to you. I have been—away. A fruitless search, as it turned out. The man is difficult to follow, evasive and clever. All the same, he would be a fool to underestimate me. My network of informants is wide. The news they bring me can be astonishing at times, astonishing and—unpalatable." He glanced at the sleeping child, frowning. "In time I will find this outlaw. Every man has his weakness. It is simply a matter of discovering it and using it to trap him. I will find him, and he will pay in kind for his acts of savagery. He will make full and bloody reparation for what he has stolen and abased. Make no doubt of it."

I said nothing, simply stroked my son's back and took another mouthful of the wine. The last time I had been weary and had shared strong drink with a man, there had been far-reaching consequences. I must make no sign that I understood Eamonn's thinly veiled hints.

"I'm sorry, Liadan," he said, "I did not come here to speak of this."

"I know that, Eamonn. You came here to pay your respects to my mother."

There was a pause.

"Not exactly. I was due to visit you at about this time. It lacks but a few days to Beltaine."

My heart went cold. I said nothing.

"Surely you have not forgotten?"

"I—no, Eamonn; I do not forget so easily. I had thought that matter concluded the last time we spoke of it, before you rode to Tara. Surely there can be no more to be said between us on the subject?"

Eamonn was walking up and down now, as he seemed to do when he was trying to find the right words.

"Was that what you thought? You imagined I would put it all behind me, perhaps return from the south betrothed to some kinswoman of the high king? You think me weak, then, that I would give up so easily?"

I stared up at him. "I don't know what you mean," I said slowly. It sounded as if he meant—but no, that could not be so. Johnny heaved an infant sigh and settled back to sleep.

Eamonn ceased pacing and knelt down beside me, rather awkwardly. A lock of hair was falling across his eyes again, and I resisted the urge to brush it back for him.

"I don't want another wife, Liadan, I only want you—with or without your child. I want no other."

"Don't—" I started.

"No," said Eamonn firmly. "Hear me out. You have stayed here to nurse your mother, and that is admirable. You chose to bear your child alone. That showed courage. You will be the best of mothers, of that I am sure. Why you protect with your silence the man who fathered him, I cannot understand. It is shame, perhaps, that stops your tongue. That matters little now. He will be brought to account. But, forgive me, I hear your mother is slipping away fast and has little time left in this world. Niamh is gone. Sean and Aisling will soon be wed, and a new family will come into being in this household. You will be lonely and vulnerable, Liadan. You should not become the unwed sister, the household drudge living her life through others. Already you wear yourself out, trying to do everything. You need a good man to care for you, to protect and watch over you. You need a home of your own, a place where you can see your own small family grow. Marry me and all that is yours."

It was some time before I was able to speak. "How can you—how could you make such an offer, when I have a child by another man? How could you take responsibility for—for a—"

"It is unfortunate the child is a boy. Had you had a daughter, I might have brought her up as my own. Your son cannot inherit, of course. But there would be a place for him in my household. As I said, a boy does not choose his father. I might make something of him." He regarded the sleeping Johnny, frowning. "It would be an—interesting challenge." The look in his eyes frightened me.

"People would say you were crazy to make such a choice," I managed, struggling to find the words to answer. "You could have your pick of suitable young women. You must forget me and move on. You should have done so as soon as I told you."

He was sitting quite close to me now, on the floor before the fire. Eamonn had always observed the formalities. He preferred to do things the right way. But this, this had gone far beyond all rules. So he had lowered himself to sit by me and Johnny, and his brown eyes had a look in them that was close to desperation.

"When I see you thus," his voice was not much more than a whisper, "with the firelight on your hair and your hand so soft on the little one, I know there is only one choice for me. I will speak as plain as I can, and I must hope my words do not offend you. I want you in my house, waiting to put your arms around me when I come home weary from battle. I want you in my bed. I want you as my wife, my lover, and my companion. I want you to bear my ch-children. I would not fear growing old if you were by my side. There is no other woman in the world that I will have. What you have done, your error, we can—we can put that behind us. I offer you protection, security, my wealth, and my name. I offer legitimacy for your son. Don't refuse me, Liadan."

I tried to form suitable words in my head, but none would come.

"You hesitate. I will, of course, seek your father's approval again. But I do not think he will object under the circumstances."

"I—I can't—"

Eamonn looked down at his linked hands. "I have heard that you were—restless—at Sídhe Dubh, that you found its confines difficult after the freedom you have enjoyed at Sevenwaters. Too much freedom, perhaps. But I would not keep you caged, like a singing bird held against its will. I have extensive landholdings in the north. If you did not wish to settle at Sídhe Dubh, I would build a new home for you that would be more to your taste. Trees, a garden, anything you wish—with appropriate security, of course."

"Are you sure," I said carefully, "that this is not a grand gesture, an attempt to appease my family for what you see as your failure to keep my sister safe? I still cannot believe a man in your position would wish to take such a step."

These words were a mistake. His brows drew together in a ferocious scowl.

"Must I show you?"

And before I could move, his hand was on the back of my head, his fingers curling into my hair, and his mouth was on mine, and it was not the polite kiss of a man who likes to do things by the rules. By the time he was finished, my lip was bleeding.

"I'm sorry," he said curtly. "I have waited a long time for you. You promised me an answer at Beltaine. I want your answer, Liadan."

Brighid help me. Why wouldn't Sean come back? I took a deep breath and looked straight into his eyes. He knew, I think, an instant before I said it.

"I can't do it, Eamonn. It is the most generous of offers. But I'll be honest with you. I just don't feel that way about you."

"What do you mean? What way, exactly?"

This was more difficult than I could possibly have imagined. "We've known each other a long time. I respect you; I wish you well, as a friend. I want you to be content with your life. But I cannot think of you as a—" I could not manage the word, lover "—as a husband."

"Is my touch so distasteful to you? So repugnant?"

"No, Eamonn. You are a fine man, and some other woman will be glad to be your wife some day. I have no doubt of that. But this would be wrong. Wrong for you; wrong for me. Terribly wrong for my son, and for his father."

"How can you say that?" He had risen to his feet, and he began to pace again, as if he must divert his feelings into some action lest they tear him apart. "How can you remain loyal to this—this savage, when all he has done is fill your belly with his child and slink off to prey on some other innocent girl? He will never come back to you; such a man has no concept of duty or responsibility. You are well rid of him."

"Stop it, Eamonn. Don't make this any worse."

"You must listen to me, Liadan. This is a foolish decision, and indeed I wonder if you are in a fit state of mind to make it. For you are right; this is likely to be the only offer you will get, unwed and with a fatherless child. Perhaps I will be scorned for my choice, for not taking the daughter of a southern chieftain, with an impeccable pedigree and a guarantee of virginity. I care nothing for that. Where you are concerned, I have no pride left. For me, you are the only choice. Liadan, think of your family. Liam would want to see you married well and so would your father. And what of your mother? Would it not please her to hear this news be-fore—"

"Stop it! That is enough!"

"Take a little more time if you wish. You are weary, and you grieve for the loss to come. I will stay a few days, long enough for you to discuss this with your family. You may see things more clearly, when—"

"I see them clearly now," I said very quietly, and I gath-ered my son into my arms and got up from the cushions. "It grieves me to wound such a good friend, but I see there is no other way out. I must refuse your offer. I and my son, we—we belong to another man, Eamonn. Your opinion of him does not change that. Not now. Not ever. To act in de-nial of that bond would be both foolish and dangerous. Such a choice would lead to anger and heartbreak and long bitterness. I would rather be alone for the rest of my life than go that way. I am sorry. Your offer shows the greatest generosity, and I honor you for it."

"You cannot refuse," he said, his struggle for self-control harshly evident in his voice. "It was always intended that you and I—it is right that we should wed, Liadan. I know Liam will support this—"

"This is finished, Eamonn." My voice shook. "It is no-body else's business save yours and mine. I have said no. You must move on without me. Now give me your word that you will not speak of this again."

He had retreated, away from the light of the fire, and he

stood half in shadow. "I can give no such undertaking," he said in a tight voice.

"Then I will not be able to see you again save in the company of others," I said, finding the strength within me to keep my tears from falling.

He took a step toward me, and his face was chalk pale. "Don't do this, Liadan." It was as much a warning as a plea.

"Good night, Eamonn." I turned and made for the stairs, and Johnny awoke and began to wail; and without looking behind me I fled to my bedchamber. There I lit my candle and changed my son's damp wrappings. As I lay on my bed with the child at my breast, I let fall the tears I had held back; and as the candle with its whorls and spirals burned lower against the night sky, I saw again that image of the two of them locked together in some final struggle: Eamonn's hands around Bran's neck, gripping, squeezing out the last breath; Bran's knife between Eamonn's ribs, twisting ever deeper as the lifeblood flowed scarlet over the green tunic. How could I ever have thought that some day, despite all, Bran and I might be together? That he could ever be more than just a—a tool, the Fair Folk had called it, a passing mercenary who happened to father a child and then was discarded from the tale, his part in it over, his relevance ceased? He could not come back. To come close to me was death for him. Better that he had never met me for I brought him only danger and sorrow. And now the shadow stretched out, not just over him, but over my son as well. I had seen it in Eamonn's eyes. I must do as the Fair Folk bid me, and stay in the forest. I must put Bran out of my mind. For all our sakes, I must do that.

I wept and wept until my head ached and my nose ran and my pillow was soaked. But Johnny sucked on, his tiny hand stroking my flesh, his body warm and relaxed against mine, the image of trust. And as I watched him, I knew that in every dark night there was, somewhere, a small light burning that could never be quenched.

Chapter Twelve

By morning my mother was slipping in and out of consciousness. The family gathered by her bedside; the folk of household and settlement clustered in the hall and the kitchens, talking together in low voices. No work was done, save in preparation for her farewell, and that went on quietly out of doors. From time to time Liam or Conor or Padriac would disappear for a while and return later as unobtrusively as they had left. Within her chamber the atmosphere was calm. A cool, westerly breeze came in the window, bringing the scent of lilac. I had placed a bowl on the small table, with fresh sprigs of basil and marjoram, for both of these herbs have the property of giving heart in times of sorrow.

"It's as well she's drifting into her last sleep," said Janis quietly as we passed in the doorway. "The pain will be clutching hard; too hard to bear in silence. And him," she nodded toward the still figure of my father, where he sat by the bedside, "he feels it with her, every spasm. It's going to be hard for him."

"She asked him to return to Harrowfield. To see his family. She made him promise."

"Aye. She was always a wise girl, my Sorcha. She knows he'll need a purpose when she's gone. She's been his purpose since first he set foot in this house long years ago. Her shoes'll never be filled by another." She looked at me closely, her gaze sharpening. "Hurt your lip, lass? Best put a touch of salve on that; thyme's good to bring down the swelling. But I don't need to tell you."

"It's nothing," I said, and went past her into the room.

I will not dwell on that last time. My mother was unaware of much that passed, for already she had one foot on her new pathway. So she did not see the frozen look on my father's face, as if, even now, he could not believe he was going to lose her. She did not hear how Conor chanted quietly at the foot of her bed, or see how Finbar stared out the window in silence, his face as pale as the wing he bore in place of his left arm. She did not see the lines of grief on Liam's strong features or the tears in Padriac's eyes. Janis came in and out, and so did the lithe, dark-skinned woman, Samara. She was as silent and graceful as a deer, and her hands were gentle as she helped with pillows, basins, and cloths, as she lit candles and sprinkled herbs.

Sean sat opposite my father, with Mother's hand in his. And Aisling was there, her wild curls held back in a neat ribbon, her small, freckled features very solemn. From time to time she would put a reassuring hand on Sean's shoulder, and he would glance up at her with a little smile.

But Eamonn was not there. Eamonn was no longer at Sevenwaters. So much for paying his respects and making some gesture of apology to my parents for what had happened to Niamh. He had remained only long enough to rest briefly and to obtain a fresh mount, they said, and then he had ridden out again, straight back to Sídhe Dubh, leaving his men behind. Uncharacteristic, folk said. Discourteous, almost. Must have had bad news. I refrained from com-

ment. My lip ached, and the swelling was plain to see, and
my main feeling was intense relief that I need not see him
again.

When the sun was high in the sky, my mother came back
to herself. There was a brief, cruel time of coughing and
choking and fighting for breath, and she battled to hold
back her gasps of pain. It was Finbar who soothed her then,
not touching, but letting his thoughts flow into hers, blan-
keting her suffering with memories of good things, the innocent, shining things of childhood and with fair visions of
what was to come. It was no accident that he left his mind
open to me, enough for me to witness again how he used
this skill to salve and heal. He could not ease the pain of her
body, but he could give her the means to withstand it. It was
the same skill I had employed to help Niamh, but Finbar
was a master, and I sat in awe as he wove a bright tapestry
of images for her, as he made a pattern of his love to celebrate his sister's life and herald her passing.

At length she was quiet, lying back on the pillows, her
breathing easier.

"Is everything ready?" she whispered. "Have you done it
all as we planned?"

"All is prepared," said Conor gravely.

"Good. It's important. People need to say farewell.
That's one thing the Britons don't always understand." She
looked up at my father. "Red?"

He cleared his throat, unable to find his voice.

"Tell me a story," she said, soft as a little spring breeze.

My father gave one agonized look around the room, at the
silent uncles, at the hovering Janis, and Samara quietly tending the fire, at me and Sean and Aisling. "I—I don't think—"

"Come," said Sorcha, and there might have been only the
two of them in the quiet, herb-scented room, "sit here on
the bed. Put your arms around me. That's good, dear heart.
Remember that day we shared, alone on a wild shore, alone

save for the gulls and the seals, the waves and the west wind? You told me a beautiful story that day. That is the tale I love best of all."

I realized then, as never before, how strong a man my father was. He knew, as he sat there with Sorcha in his arms and told his tale with tears streaming down his face, that with each word he spoke she slipped a little farther away; that by the time his story was finished, she would be gone. He knew that he must share this most private of farewells with all of us. But his quiet voice, telling the tale, was as strong and firm as the great oaks of the forest; and his hand, stroking my mother's hair back from her temple, moved as steadily as the sun moves across the arch of the sky.

It was indeed a beautiful tale. It was the story of a lonely man who takes a mermaid for his wife; how he charms her with the music of his whistle so that she forsakes the ocean to follow him. For three years he keeps her, and she bears him two little daughters. But her longing for the world beneath the waves is too strong, and in the end he gives her up because he loves her.

There came a point in the tale when my father's voice faltered. Sorcha had given a little sigh, and her eyes had closed, and her fingers, which had clutched a fold of my father's tunic as he held her against his breast, let go their grip as her hand fell to rest against his knee. There was complete silence. It was as if the whole room, and the household, and the wild things of lake and forest all held their breath for that instant in time. Then my father took up the tale again.

"Toby's little daughters grew into fine women, and in time they took husbands for themselves; and today there are many folk in those parts with dark, tangled hair like seaweed and far-seeing eyes and a talent for swimming. But that is another story."

He hesitated again, his eyes staring straight ahead, unfocused; and I saw his hand tighten on my mother's shoulder.

"As for Toby himself," I said, knowing others must finish this tale for him, "he had thought his life would be over when he lost her. He had thought that an ending. And so it was, in its way. But as the wheel turns and returns, every ending is at the same time a beginning. So it was with him."

"Every day he would go down to sit on the rocks and gaze out westward over the water," Conor took up the narrative in his soft, expressive voice, "and sometimes, just sometimes, he would get out his little whistle and play a few notes, a fragment of a reel or the refrain from some old ballad he remembered."

Padriac was standing beside his brother; he had his arm around Samara. "He watched and watched for her," said Padriac, "but the sea folk seldom show themselves to humankind. And yet, sometimes at dusk, out in the water, he thought he could see graceful forms swimming in the half light; white arms, long, drifting hair, and splashing tails bright with jewel-like scales. He fancied he saw them gazing at him with plaintive, liquid eyes like those of his daughters, eyes with a look of the wild ocean in them."

"Then he would make his way homeward," said Liam, who had moved up on the other side, next to Sean, "and when he went indoors, instead of lighting his small lantern, he would leave his door open and let the moonlight flood into the little hut where he lived on the rocky headland. And sometimes he would sit on the steps below the door and gaze across the shining pathway, wondering how it would be to live there in the depths of the great ocean, a child of Manannán mac Lir."

"Nobody quite knew what happened to him in the end." I could hear from Sean's voice that he had been crying; but like the rest of them, he kept his tone as steady as he could. It seemed to me he had grown up quickly this last season. "Folk said he'd been seen wandering on the shore in the darkness late at night. Others told of seeing him swimming out to sea, far, far beyond the farthest stretch of safe water, and heading steadily westward. His daughters were at their grandmother's. The cottage was tidy and everything as it should be. But one day he simply wasn't there anymore."

"And they say, if you visit those parts," Finbar spoke from where he still stood by the window with his back to us, "that you'll see him, close to midnight, when the moon is full. If you go down quietly to the shore and sit very still on the tumbled boulders there, there'll be a splashing and a turmoil out in the water, and you'll see the forms of the sea people, swimming and playing close to the margin of ocean and land. Folk say Toby will be there among them, his white body touched to silver in the moonlight, and the water slipping by him as easily as it caresses the fine scales of a fish. But whether he be man or creature of the deep, nobody knows."

She was gone. We all knew it. But nobody moved. Nobody spoke. Still my father held her tight in his arms, as if he might preserve that last moment of life, as long as he stayed completely still. His lips were against her hair, and his eyes were closed.

Outside, the breeze came up, sending a gust of cool air in through the window, lifting Finbar's dark curls off his brow, stirring the snowy expanse of fine feathers at his side. And then, out in the trees, the birds began to sing again, their calls rising and blending, greeting and farewell, celebration and mourning, the voice of the forest itself as it saluted the moment of Sorcha's passing.

She had not held on until dusk. Maybe that was deliberate, for when we were able to move, when we could make ourselves move, each of us went in turn to kiss her cheek, to touch her hair, and then we went silently from the room in ones and twos and left my father alone with her. There was time for that before the sun slipped below the horizon. Time for me to reclaim Johnny from the nursemaid and feed him once more, wondering how many tears I could shed before there would be no more left. Time for Sean and Aisling to slip away quietly, and maybe seek comfort in each other's arms. Time for the uncles to retreat to the family's private chamber, share a jug or two of strong ale and exchange tales of the childhood they had shared in the forest of Sevenwaters, the six brothers and their one small sister. Now only the four of them were left.

It was as she had requested. At dusk we gathered on the lake shore in a place where a beautiful birch tree grew. There were flaming torches placed around on poles, casting a glowing light on the faces of my uncles as they stood in a circle about the tree. Liam gave a nod to Sean, and my brother went in his turn to join them.

Come, Liadan. Two silent voices summoned me, Conor's, Finbar's. I went to stand between them. The circle was almost complete.

Down by the water, where the lake laid gentle fingers on the shore, a small boat was drawn up. My Uncle Padriac, who was expert in these things, had constructed this craft with meticulous care. It was just long enough to serve its purpose. At the prow was a torch waiting to be lit, and all along the length of the boat were festooned flowers, and leaves, and feathers, and many small offerings from the forest, to see her on her way. My mother lay ready in the boat, pale and still in her white gown, on a bed of soft cushions. Samara had woven a little wreath of heather and hawthorn, of clover and marigold, and this Sorcha wore on her dark, curling hair. She looked no more than sixteen years old.

My father stood on the shore alone, gazing out over the darkening waters of the lake.

"Iubdan." Liam spoke quietly.

There was no response.

"Iubdan, it is time." Padriac's voice was louder. "You are needed here."

But my father ignored them, and the set of his shoulders was forbidding. Still, Liam was not lord of Sevenwaters for nothing. Now he stepped out of the solemn circle and walked over to the Big Man, putting a hand on his shoulder. Father moved slightly, and the hand fell away.

"Come, Iubdan, it's time to let her go. Already the sun sinks below the trees."

Father turned then, his eyes full of anguish. Gone was the control he had showed, telling her that last story. "Do it without me," he said, with a bitterness I had never heard in his voice before. "There is no place for me here. It's finished. I am not one of you, and I never will be."

Then Liam put out his hand again, very deliberately, and clasped my father by the shoulder; and this time he did not allow himself to be shaken off.

"You are our brother," he said quietly. "We need your help. Come."

So the circle was complete, and we made our farewells according to the old tradition. In an outer ring stood the druids and the men and women of the household, and from time to time they echoed Conor's solemn words. Sometimes other voices could be heard, stranger voices that whispered in the wind from the trees, and murmured in the ripples of the lake, and sang deep from the rocks and hollows of the land itself. And once, when I looked toward the place where the green sward ended and the great mysterious forms of oak and ash and beech began, complex and shadowy in the velvet twilight, I saw figures standing there, half concealed under the spreading branches. A tall woman, white faced, with a cloak of blue and a curtain of dark hair. A man crowned with bright flames, taller than any mortal. And others, jeweled, winged, half seen amid the dark tracery of leaf and twig.

The ritual completed, Conor led the way down to the water's edge; and there he cupped his hands and blew into them, quite gently, and a little flame glowed sudden and golden between his curving fingers. He walked into the water, heedless of his long robe, and put his hands to the torch that was fixed in the prow of Sorcha's little boat. The torch flared, and a bright pathway appeared before the small craft, gleaming on the inky surface of the lake. Farther up the sward, a lone piper stood ready. My spine tingled as the voice of the pipes reached out over the silent trees, the still water, on and upward into the night.

"It is time," Conor said quietly. Then each of us put a hand to the stern of the little curragh, and my father was between Liam and Conor. We gave the craft the gentlest of pushes, but it was hardly necessary, for already the water was rippling by the prow, as if the boat were anxious to be on its journey; and as it swung out from the bank and the current took it, I could see long, pale hands reaching up from beneath, guiding my mother's vessel on its way, and I could hear liquid voices, singing her name, *Sorcha, Sorcha*.

"Go safe, little owl," said Conor, in a voice I hardly recognized. And Finbar pushed back his dark cloak and spread his single wing so that the glorious expanse of shining feathers glowed rose and orange and gold in the torchlight, a brave banner of farewell. But my father stood motionless and silent, frozen by his loss as the piper's lament sang on across the forest.

I strained my eyes to keep her in sight as far as I could, for I, too, grieved, though I understood my mother was not gone, only moved on to another life, another turn of the wheel. She had wanted it thus. *Why not lie at rest in the heart of the forest where you belong?* Conor had asked. *Why not remain here at Sevenwaters*, Liam had said, *for you are the daughter of the forest?* But Padriac had said, *Let Sorcha choose*. And what she wanted most of all was to take the path of that river, to be borne along on its current, away from the lake, as she had once done long ago. For, she had said, smiling, that very waterway had deposited her, quite by chance, in the hands of a red-haired Briton, and had not he become her true love and her heart's delight? So she would choose that path again and see where it took her. I stood and stared into the darkness as the music wept and an owl cried in the night.

Folk began to disperse, heading back to the house. My father, his head bowed, shepherded by the uncles. Sean hand in hand with Aisling. Janis and her assistants hastening to make the final preparations for the feast, since a good feast, with music, is an essential part of such a farewell. I went to thank the piper. He was surely a man of near-magical skills, for that lament had echoed my innermost thoughts; its lilting melody had conjured up Sorcha's courage, her strength of spirit, and her deep love for the forest and its people.

The piper was packing his instrument away neatly in a goatskin bag. He was a thin man, dark bearded, with a little gold ring in his ear. His assistant, taller, hooded, held the bag open for him. The piper gave me a polite nod.

"I wanted to thank you," I said. "I don't know who invited you to play here, but it was a good choice. Your music comes from the heart."

"Thank you, my lady. A great teller of tales such as your mother deserves a fitting farewell."

He had stowed the pipes and now lifted the bag onto his shoulder.

"You're welcome to return to the house for food and ale," I told him. "Have you far to travel home?"

The man gave a crooked grin. "A tidy old step," he said. "The ale wouldn't go amiss. But—" He glanced at his silent companion. It was only then that I noticed, in the near darkness, the large, black bird perched on this man's shoulder, claws gripping tight, small, sharp eye fixed on me, appraising. A raven. "Seems to me," said the piper, setting off in the direction of the house as if something had been decided between the two of them without the need for words, "a drink or two wouldn't hurt. And I have to catch up with the old auntie. Can't very well visit these parts without doing that. She'd never forgive me."

"Auntie?" I queried, having to move briskly to keep up with him, for he set a fair pace. Behind us, the hooded man walked in silence. I realized, as we made our way back through the forest, that the piper was one of Janis's tribe of far-flung connections. A traveling man, Danny Walker they called him. It was a little odd. Hadn't she once said Dan was from Kerry? That surely was a long way to come, even for this.

We reached the path that led up to the main door of the keep. From within, there was a sound of voices, and lanterns burned outside to light the way.

"Your friend is welcome, too," I said to the piper, and I looked over my shoulder. The hooded man, dark bird on shoulder, had halted a few paces away. Clearly, he did not intend to follow us inside. "Will you come in?" I asked him politely.

"I think not."

I froze where I stood. Surely I had heard this voice before. Yet if it were so, it was terribly changed. Before, it had been young, passionate, and full of hurt. Now it seemed a far older man's voice and cold with restraint.

He spoke again. "Go in, Dan. Take this night to visit your kinfolk and rest yourself. I'll speak with the lady in the morning."

And with that, he turned and disappeared down the path beyond the hedge.

"He'll not come in," said Dan flatly.

I blinked. Perhaps I had imagined the whole thing. "Does he mean me?" I asked hesitantly. "The lady, he said. Myself?"

"As to that," said Dan, "you'd need to ask him. I'd be down early in the morning if I were you. He won't stay here long. Doesn't like to leave her, you understand?"

There was no chance to ask him any more. I had duties as

the lady of the house; I must offer support to all those who grieved, and share in the songs and tales with which we sent my mother on her way with honor and love. There was ale and mead and spiced cakes; music and talk and fellowship. There were smiles and tears. At length I made my way to bed, thinking the hooded stranger would be gone in the morning, and the whole thing might simply be blamed on the Sight leading me astray.

Still, I was up early and out in the herb garden, knowing it would be hard, this first day without my mother; aware I must come here and be among her special things, in the midst of her quiet domain, if I were to teach myself that life would go on without her loving presence, her gentle guiding hand. I had left Johnny with the nursemaid; it was too cold for him to be out of doors. I walked along the path, plucking a small weed here and a smaller one there, knowing I was waiting. It was barely dawn.

I sensed him just before I saw him. A cold feeling went up my spine, and I turned toward the archway. He stood immobile in the shadows, a tall figure, still cloaked and hooded in black. The bird sat on his shoulder like some creature carven in dark stone.

"Will you come in?" I asked him, still doubting the accuracy of my memory. Then he stepped forward, and slipped the hood back, revealing a pale, intense face, and the darkest of eyes, and a head of hair the deep color at the heart of a winter sunset.

"Ciarán," I breathed, "it is you. Why did you not show yourself? Conor is here; he would want to see you—will you not come inside and speak to him?"

"No." The chilling finality of his tone silenced me. The great bird reached down with a beak like a butcher's knife to adjust its plumage. Its eye was feral. "I am not come for that. No show of family spirit. I am not fool enough to believe that chasm can be bridged. I'm here to bring a message."

"What message?" I asked quietly.

"For her mother," he said. "Niamh wanted to say, I love you, forgive me. But I am come too late."

I could not speak.

"It will grieve her that I was not here in time," said Ciarán softly.

"Mother would know. It doesn't matter that it is now—after—she would still know. Is Niamh—is she well? Is she better, and safe—how did you—"

"She is well enough. Much changed." His tone was calm, but I sensed beneath it the deepest of sorrows, a burden such as no young man should have to bear. I could not read what was in his eyes. "The laughing girl who dazzled us at Imbolc is gone. She has not yet found her way. But she is safe."

"Where? Where safe? How did you—"

"Safe. *Where* is unimportant."

He had a druid's way with answers. "With you?" I asked.

Ciarán gave a sort of nod. "She needs protection. I failed her once, but that at least I can provide."

We fell silent for a while. Small birds were starting to call, harbingers of a new dawn and a new season.

"I am Niamh's sister," I said finally. "I would like to know, at least, where she is and whether she might return when the truth is known. I told my father. He understands now what an error they made when they chose a husband for her. It might be possible—could you not bring her back here and—"

His laugh startled me. The sound was dark with bitterness.

"Bring her back? How could that be?"

I said nothing, wondering at his response. Was there not some hope that things might at length be well? I did not want to believe my efforts, and Bran's, had been quite futile.

"They never told you?" asked Ciarán bleakly.

"Never told me what?" That feeling seized me again, a terror, a chill in the core of the body like a touch of darkness past or evil to come.

"The truth. Why they forbade me to wed Niamh and sent the two of us away. Why we can never return and will never wish to. How we are cursed, doubly cursed, by the keeping of secrets. They did not tell you. I suppose that is why you helped us when nobody else would. If you had known the truth, you would have spurned us."

I shrank from the cynical tone of his voice, so changed from the ardent, glowing hope with which he had once told his tale of love.

"You'd better tell me everything," I said. "My friends put themselves in great danger to help her. Tell me the truth, Ciarán. There's talk of an old evil awake, of things stirring that can harm us all. What is it? Tell me."

I went to sit on the old stone bench that stood between feathery clumps of wormwood and chamomile, and he moved closer. The bird cawed and flew up into the lilac tree, where it perched rather precariously on a slender branch.

"It was cruel," said Ciarán quietly. In the early morning light his face was ghost white. "Cruel that they kept the truth from her. No wonder she thought herself abandoned, for she did not know why I'd fled; what drove me away. She did not understand that our union was—cursed."

"Cursed?" I echoed stupidly, not knowing what he might mean.

"Forbidden. Forbidden by blood. It was not until that night, when I came to Sevenwaters with my heart beating high, prepared to do battle for my lady if it came to it, that Conor deigned to tell me, at last, who I was. All those years he'd kept it from me, a long secret never to be told. I thought myself a foundling, an infant lucky enough to be fostered by the wise ones and brought up in the haven of the forest. I dreamed of nothing more than to follow in Conor's footsteps, to dedicate myself to the ways of the brotherhood. Then I met Niamh. And it was time for the secret to be told."

In the back of my mind, somewhere, things began to make a sort of sense. A terrible, twisted, inevitable sense.

"Conor told you who you were?"

"He did. That I could never wed Niamh. That what we had done was shameful and wrong, a breaking of natural laws, an abhorrence, though it was done in innocence. Our union could never be sanctioned. For I am the son of Colum of Sevenwaters by his second wife, the Lady Oonagh. I am half brother to Conor and to Liam. Half-brother to Niamh's mother and yours. The woman who gave me birth was the Sorceress who near destroyed this family and all it held dear. So, in one blow, Conor stripped from me my love, my future, my hope of joy, and my life's purpose. Not only was I forbidden Niamh, I was as well cast out of the brotherhood, cut adrift with no star to guide me. All were quenched, every one."

"That's not what Conor said—"

"Huh! A sorceress's son can never be a druid. I carry the blood of a cursed line. Such as one as I can never aspire to the highest arts of the wise ones, the realm of light, the inspiration of pure spirit. It is beyond me and always would have been. I know that now. If I am her son, then I am a son of the shadows, condemned to walk in darkness. How he could raise me all those years and keep this from me, that I will never understand. That lie I will never forgive him."

"The Lady Oonagh's child," I breathed. "He was never accounted for in the story. Simply, he vanished from Sevenwaters when she did. When the enchantment was undone."

"Convenient." Ciarán's tone was bitter. "My father found me and brought me back. I lived in the nemetons for eighteen years, Liadan. I thought myself in every way a druid. Imagine, then, the blow the revelations of that night dealt me. And I compounded my own shame. I ran away. I abandoned Niamh to despair and abuse. The burden of that I live with every day. No matter how carefully I guard her, no matter how strong a shield I place around her, I cannot shut out what was done that night, for its legacy is lodged deep within us both."

A shield, a guard. I said carefully, "Where did you go when you left Sevenwaters that night? Conor said you went to find your past. Was it—was it your mother you sought out? Is she—?" I stopped myself. Some things, it seemed to me, were too dangerous to be spoken aloud.

"I told him." There was a darkness in Ciarán's voice. "I told Conor. I said, a man cannot escape the blood that runs in his veins. No matter whether he discovers as a child or much later, when he thinks himself a different sort of creature entirely, one perhaps who might aspire to nobility of mind, to great goodness. It matters not, for sooner or later the seed that is in us comes to fruition, that heritage we bear begins to rule us. Perhaps, if they had not told me, I might have grown old before the foul blood I bear made itself known in me and forced me to turn my back on the light. Now I do know, I told him, and I will find out just what powers this inheritance brings and how I may wield them. You may not be so ready, then, to call me brother. Then I went away, farther in spirit than in body. A perilous journey. My mother knows well the art of concealment. She did not wish to be found, not yet. But I found her. I have learned to cross the margin to that realm where she now hides herself, where she waits."

"How? How could you do such a thing?"

"It is part of the druid training, to learn to walk over and to return. A test by fire and water, by earth and air. I had endured it before, but this was different." His voice trembled. At that moment, I was able to remember he was not, after all, an old, embittered man, but a young one not so much older than myself.

"You say she waits. Waits—for what?"

Ciarán folded his arms and stared away from me up into the cold, morning sky.

"You have many questions," he said.

"It has been a long time with no news," I said quietly. "I, too, have a message. Or rather, I have something to return to my sister. I have it here. She'll be needing this, I think." I reached into the pouch at my belt and took out the necklace I had made for Niamh, the cord into which the love of her family was woven, a talisman of unbreakable strength. Ciarán took it in his hand, and his long, bony fingers touched the small white stone that still hung threaded there. For the most fleeting instant, he smiled; and I saw again the youth of Imbolc, whose look of joy and pride had shone from his intense features as he lit the fires of spring.

"She thought this lost," he said. "You have kept it well. I thank you."

"We love her." I was very close to weeping. "You don't seem to understand that. Do you have to take her away, wall her up like some princess in a tale, too precious to be seen by ordinary folk? Are we never to see her again? Never to see her child, save in visions?"

It was as if time ceased, as if breath ceased, for one still moment, and then went on.

"Child?"

There was something in that word that clutched my heart as nothing yet had done.

"I am granted a sight of these things from time to time," I told him, thinking now I had no choice but to do so. "What will be or may be. I saw Niamh with a little child, an infant with dark, red curls such as your own and eyes like ripe berries. On the sand, in a cave. It seems to me there is a path forward for the two of you. Not the path my uncle or my father would have chosen for you; not the way Conor would have had you follow, for he wanted you to return to the nemetons, whatever you may think. I don't want to believe I may never see my sister again or—"

"There are dangers such as you could scarcely dream of." His tone was hushed, edgy now. "A path I was—directed to follow. A path she—my mother—wishes me to take. She waits for my answer. She offered me much. Power such as a man can scarcely comprehend. Skills beyond the furthest art of archdruid, arts beyond the last page of the thickest grimoire of the oldest mage. I can learn from her, and I will. I will show my brother what I can do and what I can be."

"Is this a—a threat? To carry out what the Lady Oonagh could not achieve?" I was shivering and did not seem to be able to stop. In my mind was a little picture of my sister, fading and shrinking away from me.

"As for that, it will be as it must be. Niamh and I—you must understand, the past cannot be remade, whatever our dreams whisper to us. Some ills cannot be undone. And yet, when I told her the truth of it, she opened her arms to me as if there were nothing to forgive. I spit on the laws of men that lay down what we may or may not feel for each other. In all this web of sorrow and darkness, the bond between us is a single bright thread, too strong to be severed. I will keep her safe; I will pledge all that is in me to protect her. That comes first, above all. More than that I cannot say, for beyond that my path is unknown, as yet unmade. As for her family and mine, I care nothing for them; they treated us with contempt. They lost their right to her when they cast her out of Sevenwaters. Still, to you we owe a debt. To you and to the man who got her away from that place and made sure word reached me. For this reason I bring you a gift."

"What gift—" I began, but as I spoke Ciarán gave the smallest of glances at the great bird where it perched in the tree above us, and with a slight lift of the wings and a brief, intense movement of air, the raven flew neatly down and settled on my shoulder, a not inconsiderable weight. Its beak was alarmingly close to my eye, and I felt its claws through cloak and shawl and gown.

"Oh," I said, and was then quite lost for words.

"A messenger," said Ciarán. "A loan more than a gift. You may have need of him. But remember. Such a creature must be called upon only at the last extreme. Only when all else has failed and you are without aid, and body and spirit reach the end of their strength, then send him. Such a messenger should not be employed lightly."

"I see," I said, not seeing at all. What was this great creature, some sort of sorcerer's familiar? I had so many questions to ask, too many.

"It's time to go." Ciarán seemed suddenly restless, as if his mind already moved ahead of him to some distant place. "I cannot be away long."

"Still, it's quite a journey to Kerry," I said cautiously. "From one full moon to the next, and longer, would it not be?"

"That's the way Dan would prefer, by horseback or walking," Ciarán said. "But there are other ways."

"I see," I said again, my mind on old tales about druids and sorcerers. I wondered how much he had learned in those eighteen years, and how much more since last I had seen him.

"Farewell, then," he said gravely.

"I would have, you know," I blurted out, needing him to know, needing my sister to know that I was not as cold-hearted as they believed me, "even if I had been told who you were and why it was forbidden. I would still have helped her. I love her. If she is with you, despite all, perhaps that is in some way right. Perhaps, in some way, that is what's meant to be, law or no law."

Ciarán gave a nod. "One way or another, it will unfold," he said, sounding like a druid again. And as if summoned, though there had been no summons that I could detect, Dan

Walker appeared in the archway to the garden, whistling under his breath, the goatskin bag balanced neatly on his shoulder.

"We're away then?" he inquired matter-of-factly. And before I could utter another word, Ciarán moved like a shadow, and the two of them were gone. I followed, feeling the weight of the unexpected gift on my shoulder, and the clutch of its claws in my flesh. I came out onto the path and looked down beyond the hedges to the margin of the forest. But there was nobody to be seen.

Folk got used to the raven in time.

"You'd best watch that bird near the young one," Janis warned me, feeling some responsibility, perhaps, since her own nephew had been party to its arrival. "You can't trust a creature with a beak like that. And you know what they say about ravens."

But in the event, she was completely wrong. Where the baby was concerned, the bird was a model of good behavior. While Johnny slept, it perched nearby, keeping a close eye on him and holding its tongue. When he was awake and yelling for his supper, the raven had a tendency to join in, lending its powerful voice to Johnny's own, and thus assuring him of rapid attention. When I walked by the lake to admire the new cygnets or in the forest under the spreading beeches with my son cradled in my arms, the raven accompanied me, swooping like a dark shadow from one low branch to another, never far away from me and my child. I began to grow used to its constant presence. It was like a well-trained guard dog, alerting me to the approach of a wild pig or a group of woodsmen with a harsh cry of warning. I called it Fiacha, a name that has the meaning, "little raven."

As to how I might employ its services, that I could not quite grasp. Once or twice I tried to speak to the creature with my mind, but I exhausted myself to no avail. Perhaps, when the time came, I would know what to do—if the time came. There were so many rumors and portents and half-stated theories around, one was hard put to it to extricate the truth or hazard a guess as to what the future might hold. Those who had touched my pregnant belly for luck, and thought Johnny the offspring of some Otherworld being, now eyed Fiacha sidelong, and looked at me shyly and muttered about the prophecy. It was a sign, they said. My family made no effort to counter these fantasies. If people believed me the sometime consort of one of the Tuatha Dé, that at least saved explanations.

I have listened to many tales in my life, and told a few of my own. If this has taught me anything, it is that there are some occurrences that change the course of things, that make an alteration far beyond their own apparent magnitude. It is like the throwing of a tiny pebble into a pool, how it makes an ever-expanding circle of ripples, spreading right across the water's surface. The little thing was a lie, or rather a truth withheld. Conor's lie and Liam's. Even my parents had known of this secret brother. The family's lie, to one of their own. And none had told, because it was so terrible, so dangerous in some way I only half understood, that even Niamh, whose life was shattered by the effect of it, had not been allowed to know the truth. I did not think, after this, that I could quite trust any of them again. All came from that lie: true love, hopes blighted, cruelty, abuse and flight, and for Ciarán himself a descent into a kind of darkness that seemed to threaten the very fabric of our existence. For me and my family, it brought the loss of openness, the breaking of trust. Farewells too late to be spoken; partings that were forever. The lie had awoken the old evil, and now it seemed one thing after another began to deviate from its true path.

Finbar had not remained long after we sent Sorcha down the lake. Very early next morning he was gone, slipping away quietly into the forest with only myself to bid him farewell.

"You know where I am," he said. "There may come a time when you need my help. Call on me."

"Thank you." Fiacha shifted on my shoulder, his head slightly tilted, watching my uncle as he made his way down the path under the trees. "Uncle?"

"What is it, Liadan?"

"I need to tell you something. I need to tell you that I have discovered the truth about Ciarán; about who he is and why he went away. And I want to ask you something. If I wanted to know about the old evil, and what that means . . . would you tell me? Would anyone tell me? I have had so many warnings, and I hear voices that pull me one way and then another, and nobody will explain. If it's true that we are under some threat, how can we fight it if we don't understand it?"

Finbar stared at me. "You should have been my daughter, I think, for I hear my own words come from your mouth. I would have told you this myself, long ago; but Conor made us agree to silence. You'd best ask him direct. I think he will speak to you of these things now that our sister is gone. With our silence we sought to protect her from further pain, from seeing a darkness reborn that would blight our sons' and daughters' lives as it did our own. When she thwarted the Sorceress, Sorcha believed the evil gone forever; but we had not defeated it, simply given ourselves a few years' respite. Speak to Conor. Tell him your misgivings and ask him for the truth."

"I will. Thank you, Uncle. You always speak plain, and I honor you for that."

"Farewell, Liadan. Keep your light burning."

And he was gone. Later that morning, they let the dogs out.

* * *

My father left the same day, taking all of us by surprise. I had known he would keep his promise, for he was ever a man of his word. But nobody had expected so precipitate a departure, especially in view of the hazards of such a journey. Briton he might be, but he had lived among the folk of Erin for eighteen years and more, and there were no guarantees his own people would receive him well. Besides, he had first to get there, across a coastline swarming with Norsemen and a wide sea full of raiders and pirates and tricks of wind and water. For the Big Man to depart on such a venture alone spoke of a change far beyond that wrought by grief and loss. But Sean thought it made sense, of a sort.

"He'll more likely slip across unobserved and gather intelligence as he goes," said my brother. "There was a time, long ago, when this sort of thing was commonplace for him. Now he does it only because he gave his word. But he still has the skills." There was a note of pride in his voice. As for me, I did not doubt my father's ability for the task. And I knew Janis had been right. I had seen the emptiness in his eyes, and I understood that without this mission he might indeed lose himself in grief.

Father took his leave of Sean and me in the little herb garden, where the young oak he had planted for my mother in the autumn when Niamh was born now flourished to shade new generations of tender seedlings. He was plainly dressed, and had by him a very small pack, sufficient only for the most basic supplies.

"I'll go on foot," he told us. "I've a little business to attend to on the way; it needs to be done quietly. Best if I travel unseen for the most part. As for Harrowfield, we have had little news. I cannot tell what awaits me there."

"Father?" I had wished to keep my tone steady, to be strong for him. But our loss was too fresh, and my voice quavered.

"Yes, sweetheart?"

"You—you will come back, won't you?"

"That's a foolish thing to say," Sean snapped. I could tell he, too, was close to tears.

"Your brother's right, Liadan," Father said, putting his arm around me and attempting a smile. "You should not need to ask me such a question. Of course I will come back. There's work for me here, family and folk. So Liam tells me. I go now because I was bid, because I promised."

"Don't worry, Father. I'll look after everything." Sean's attempt at confidence was not unconvincing.

"Thank you, Son. Now, I must bid the two of you farewell for the time being. I know that you will be strong and courageous. I know that you will be your mother's children."

He gave me a hug, and I wept. He clasped Sean by the shoulder, and then he left us.

Not long after, Padriac gathered up his entourage and headed off westward to pay his respects to Seamus Redbeard. After that, who knew? There were always fresh horizons to be sought, new adventures to be experienced. You might, he said, spend your whole life thus and still leave plenty behind for your sons and your grandsons to cut their teeth on.

"And your daughters," I added dryly.

My uncle grinned, showing his dimples. "And your daughters," he agreed. "I hear you're a strong hand with a bow, and quick with a throwing knife, and neat on your feet with a staff. Next time I visit, I might teach you the art of sailing. You never know when you might need that."

I waited a little, choosing my time with care. The household was subdued, the loss of my mother keenly felt, the departure of my father also disturbing, for without his constant, reassuring presence folk seemed a little lost, as if the work of farm and forest and settlement could not be done with energy and spirit unless his tall figure could be

seen among them, helping to mend thatch or stack straw or
tend to the breeding cattle. Conor and his band of druids
showed no sign of leaving. I thought Liam seemed unusually withdrawn, and that Sorcha's death had hit her serious
eldest brother rather harder than anyone would have expected. It seemed to me that Conor stayed for his brother's
sake. But I suspected another motive as well. The archdruid
was often there when I worked in my garden or played with
Johnny on the grass. He would walk with me to the settlement and give the folk good advice and a blessing while I
tended to their injuries and ailments. I thought that it was
not me he watched, but Johnny. I had always trusted this
uncle, so wise, so balanced, so serenely sure. Now I could
not look at him without seeing Ciarán's shadowed eyes and
my sister's bruises. I thought about trust, and how dangerous it might prove to be if you were wrong. I thought how
perilous it was to make a choice based on trust, based on
what others told you was right. It was plain to me what
Conor wanted for me and for my son. It was the same thing
the Fair Folk wanted. Indeed, it seemed no more than common sense. Perhaps the forest was the only place my son
could be kept safe. But I could not be certain. The only
choices I could be sure of were my own.

We sat together in the garden, as Johnny lay on his blanket under the trees. There was nobody about. I was sewing,
for Johnny grew fast and was constantly in need of small
shirts and tunics. Conor sat by my side, looking down toward the lake.

"Uncle," I said cautiously, "I am not sure how to ask you
this. I have heard many allusions to an old evil, something
you thought long gone that is somehow awake again. I've
been thinking of this a great deal, especially since my
mother's passing. I remember your story, the one about Fergus and Eithne. In that tale the Fair Folk say that things will
go wrong for Sevenwaters until the Islands are regained and
the balance restored. It seems to me things are going wrong

now. What happened with Niamh was terribly wrong. I must tell you that I have discovered the reason why you forbade their marriage. I know of Ciarán's identity. But I cannot understand why you did not tell them the truth. Twice you withheld it: first from Ciarán himself, letting him grow up ignorant of who he was; and then you let Niamh believe he had deserted her, simply telling her their union was forbidden without giving the reason—that was cruel indeed. I cannot understand why you would conceal the truth thus. This has not been the way of things for us here at Sevenwaters."

"Did Finbar tell you this?" Conor's voice was calm as ever, but his hands were restless, turning a hazel twig between his fingers.

"I spoke to him of these things, yes." I could not tell him Ciarán had returned. He could not know Niamh lived, though it seemed harsh to hold back this news. In choosing to be her protector, Ciarán had indeed set my sister apart from her family. "But Finbar did not break any promises, Uncle. He told me you had bound them to silence on this matter. I have pieced the truth together from visions and—and from other things."

"I see."

"I seek an explanation from you now, if you will give one. For you warned me to keep my son here in the forest, as if he were indeed the child of the prophecy, the one who will put all to rights again. And it does appear the evil things are closing in on us. We have seen many losses here, not least the loss of trust. I understand what the Fair Folk told me, that Johnny may be the key. But he's so little." I glanced down at Johnny, who was grunting with effort as he tried to reach his toes with his fingers. "If what they say is right, then my son may have a—a momentous part to play in all of this. I'm his mother. How can I make any decisions if I have not been told the whole truth?"

Conor looked at me. "Have you told the whole truth?" he asked gravely.

I felt a blush come to my cheeks. "No, Uncle. But I do not seek to conceal an evil, only to protect those I love. And I did tell my mother the truth before the end."

He nodded, apparently satisfied by this. "I, too, sought only to protect those I cared for, Liadan. But I made a terrible error. I thought I was strong enough to undo her evil work, to counter it with a strategy of my own. But I am only human, after all; a puny piece of this game. She is beyond that, a creature of greater power than anyone realized; devious and imaginative. We thought her gone forever. We were wrong."

"Her? You mean the Lady Oonagh, don't you? The same Sorceress who turned you into swans and would have taken Sevenwaters for herself if my mother had not undone the enchantment?"

Conor sighed. "You say she would have taken it for herself. But it was not so simple. It was for her son she wanted it; it was through him that she sought to have power and influence. Her son bore her own tainted blood, the blood of a line of sorcerers; but he was also the son of Colum of Sevenwaters and had a rightful claim to the túath. With us safely out of the way, he was the heir. With him as her pawn, and by the use of her powers of sorcery, she could have swayed the destinies of kings, Liadan."

"I know you brought him up in the nemetons," I said. "Your father found him and took him from his mother, and you brought him up as a druid. I can understand that; but why didn't you tell him the truth? Why wait until it was so late that hearing it near destroyed him?"

"My father made it his quest to find Ciarán and bring him home," said Conor quietly. "Such a one as the Lady Oonagh cares little for a child of tender years. She intended, I imagine, to wait until he was old enough to be taught and then to make a sorcerer of him. So she fostered the boy with folk she deemed harmless: a childless couple in the south, who were only too glad of a bag of silver in return for the care of a small lad. Their dwelling was remote, hidden in the deep folds of a wooded valley. The Sorceress thought it safe to leave her son there awhile. She reckoned without my father's determination. So Ciarán was found and carried home to the forest. The boy was brought up in the lore, in the peace and discipline of the grove. Here, too, Lord Colum lived out the years of his old age in contemplation and study and died a good death. Ciarán was like a son to me, Liadan; a fine young man, deep, wise, perceptive, quick to learn, and strong in self-discipline. He possessed every quality one would wish for in a future leader of our kind. I was so sure, so certain I could undo her work and make of this child a man who would follow the path of light, steadfast of purpose, sure in faith, unswerving in his dedication to the mysteries. We told no one who he was. Besides myself and my father, only my sister and brothers knew of his existence. I made the choice not to reveal his origins to him. No lad should have his growing years blighted by a dark truth like that. Instead, he was simply one of us. In every way, he belonged to the wise ones."

"And yet he did not," I said. I could read Conor's distress in his eyes, although his voice was, as always, deep and sure. "For surely the son of a sorceress can never become a druid."

Conor was very pale. "I had made a terrible mistake. The boy bears his mother's blood, and in time that made itself known. I had thought I could counter it. I brought him to Sevenwaters. He longed for a glimpse of life outside the nemetons, and he had proved himself indeed worthy to assist with the ceremony of Imbolc. So safe did I believe it, I never thought he might be tempted. . . . I never thought . . . but I brought the evil down on us again. He had only to set his eyes on Niamh, and the Lady Oonagh's hand began to shape our lives once more. Through her son, she began once more to work her destructive will on the family and those we guard and protect. There was no choice, Liadan.

That night we spoke of it; Liam and I and your father. I made a decision. I made them agree to silence. We saw how Sorcha was stricken to the heart by this, how she feared for her children, that they in their turn might face the malign influence of the Sorceress. We kept it from you. We thought it best if Niamh did not know the full truth about the sin she had committed. Without that burden of guilt, we reasoned, she might better put this behind her and start anew. She made a good marriage; she was far away and safe from harm. As for Sean, nobody wished to see him rushing out, sword in hand, seeking some sort of reparation from Ciarán. Sean was to be a leader, balanced and wise like his uncle and like his father. It was best if he did not know. And if he was not to know, we could hardly tell you."

"What about Ciarán?" I asked grimly. "For it seems to me, he was worst treated of all; his whole life has been a lie."

"We told him the truth that night." Conor sounded like an old man, weary and sad. "I could offer him no less. What he and Niamh had done was an abomination, against natural law."

"They acted in innocence." My voice was shaking.

"That I acknowledge," he said gravely. "It was nonetheless forbidden and could in no way be sanctioned. It was best for Niamh to marry and start anew. As for Ciarán, he chose his own path. In that I saw his mother's influence stretching out over us once more."

I glanced up at Fiacha, who sat atop a hawthorn hedge, preening his feathers. Finally, my uncle had given me the truth. But it was blindingly clear that I would not be able to return the favor. Not now and perhaps not ever.

"Do you know where Ciarán went when he fled from Sevenwaters?" I asked cautiously. "Do you believe that the Lady Oonagh still lives, and that he sought her?"

"Some things seem too terrible to be spoken aloud. It is possible, yes. As to how he would hope to reach her, there are ways. Ciarán is adept; he might attempt such a journey without supervision, although that is unwise. I have heard nothing since he left here, Liadan."

"You sent him away, knowing he might try this?"

"I did not send him away. He could have remained with us. He was—he was an outstanding student, capable of great things; extremely skilled in all the arts of the mind and in the craft of magic. There was no need for him to leave us. Indeed, the threat posed by his ancestry could far better have been controlled within the confines of the sacred circle and of our community. He chose to go. He chose to put that behind him. I failed, Liadan. I failed him, and in the end I failed my family as well."

"You once told me," I said, "not to feel guilt since things would unfold as they must. That was a long time ago, right at the very start of this. Now I hear you saying that this is somehow your fault. Perhaps you're wrong about that. Maybe the whole thing is part of some pattern, a pattern so big that we cannot see more of it than the tiny part where we belong. That was what the Fair Folk told me, that we couldn't understand and so our choices were flawed. It seems sometimes as if we are no more than puppets that they manipulate to suit themselves. But I think we have a greater power than they are prepared to acknowledge, or why would it matter to them so much that I might take one path or another? Why would they set such store on keeping Johnny safe? Perhaps it is indeed only through small folk such as ourselves that the prophecy may be fulfilled, despite what they tell us."

"And after all," said Conor quietly, "it was through human strength and endurance that Lady Oonagh's enchantment was undone before, not by a powerful intervention of the Tuatha Dé. You are saying, then, that I may be wrong about Ciarán?"

"From what you tell me, he is neither weak nor ignorant. Despite his anger, he is surely a young man who will weigh his choices carefully and with some skill. I cannot believe that because he is her son, he must inevitably work evil in his life. To say that is to say we have no choice at all in what we do, in how we live. I don't believe that, Uncle. Perhaps we do have a short span in this world, as the Fair Folk tell us; perhaps our scope is somewhat limited. But within those limits we do have the power to change things, the power to make choices and to go where we must. If I have learned anything about myself, it is that I will not be a tool of some lord or lady and dance to their tune, not if my heart calls me onto another path. You brought Ciarán up to be balanced and wise. He bears that within him as well as the blood of the sorceress. What you imparted to him so lovingly through the long years of training has made him strong. Perhaps he is stronger than you think."

We did not speak of these things again; and at length, when summer had advanced into autumn, and Johnny could sit up by himself and move along by an odd, half-crawling, half-creeping motion, Conor departed with his silent, white-robed brethren after him. All that he said to me was, "Keep him safe, Liadan. For all our sakes, keep him safe."

Chapter Thirteen

There had been no word from Eamonn, other than an escort sent to see his sister home. For that I was profoundly grateful, for the last conversation between us was graven deep in my mind, along with the memory of his kiss. By autumn I was able to tell myself, with reasonable conviction, that he must at last have accepted no for an answer and decided to get on with his life. I was sorry if my decision had made things difficult for Sean, or for Liam, whose links with Eamonn were vital not only to their joint defenses but also to the success of any venture against Northwoods. Both had commented on Eamonn's silence. Still, it was early days yet. In time, the alliance would be as strong as ever, for was not Aisling to wed my brother next spring? That would heal many wounds.

One warm afternoon close to Meán Fómhair, when the harvest was nearly over and apples hung ripely glowing in the orchard, I took my son down to a secluded part of the lake shore. Here, the fringe of willows came almost to the water's edge, and the curve of the shoreline ensured both shelter and privacy. It was a golden day; the lake surface glittering with light, the forest starting to put on its autumn raiment, a drift of orange, scarlet, and yellow around the somber green of pines that crowned the ridge tops. As children, we had spent happy days here swimming and diving, climbing the trees, and inventing countless new games of adventure. Now, I let my son go naked on the sand, where he created strange patterns with his newly learned, half-crawling gait. And later I myself stripped to my shift and took him in the water with me, trusting that the work of the harvest would ensure we were undisturbed. Johnny grinned with delight, revealing his two new teeth, as he felt the cool water on his skin. I lifted him gently in and out with little splashes.

"This time next year, I'll teach you to swim properly," I told him. "Like a fine salmon, you'll be, or a seal maybe. Then they'll all start telling me your father was a merman or a selkie."

We played and played until he grew tired, and I put him on his little motley blanket to rest in the shade of the willows. He was not quite asleep, but seemed content to lie there awhile, gazing up at the intricate pattern of light and shadow made by the long leaves and talking quietly to himself in some infant tongue I could not quite understand. Fiacha perched in the branches nearby, watching. He had been anxious while we were in the water, flapping overhead with squawks of concern or pacing on the water's edge, where his small, neat footmarks still imprinted the sand. Now he was quiet. I went back into the water and swam, looking up to check Johnny from time to time before I ducked down under to let the coolness wash over my face, then bobbing up to flick my hair back in a spray of droplets. It was a good feeling, as if, in the strong enveloping hold of the water, I could, for a brief while, forget the complications of my life, the decisions that faced me, forget secrets and duplicity and risks, and enjoy again the innocent freedom of childhood.

At length I grew cold and began to wade back to the shore. On the little blanket, Johnny lay sleeping. He would be hungry later. I stood knee deep, wringing the water out of my hair. There was no sound, no movement, but something made me look up. The small hairs on my neck prickled, and I knew I was being watched.

Under the willows, as still as if he were himself part of the forest, a man stood. If you did not know him, you would have thought the complex pattern that marked his features was simply a trick of the light, a play of sun through willow twigs. He was dressed very plainly, in subdued gray and brown, suitable garb for a man who wishes to pass through wooded country unseen. If he bore a weapon, I could not see it. It seemed the Painted Man had found the mystic forest of Sevenwaters no more of a challenge than the marshes of Sídhe Dubh. Or perhaps he had been allowed to enter.

He made no move. Clearly, I was going to have to emerge from the water clad only in my dripping shift and somehow think of the right thing to say. I waded to shore with as much dignity as I could summon, but it is hard to feel in control of a situation when you must bend to squeeze water from your skirt, when your arms and shoulders are exposed and half your chest is bare, and your feet are covered with sand, and there is not a comb or mirror in sight. I reached the spot where my gown and shawl lay on the sward above the little beach, but he was there before me. Behind us, on the other side under the willows, the babe had not stirred.

Bran had my shawl in his hands, and he reached to put it around my shoulders. So much for choosing the right words. I could scarcely breathe, let alone say anything that made any sense. The shawl fell to the ground, and his arms went around me, and mine around him, and I felt his lips on mine, touching gently in a kiss of such sweetness that it left me close to tears. He put his hands one on each side of my face, his thumbs moving slowly against the skin of temple and cheek, as if he could not quite believe I was there in his arms. The hunger in his eyes belied the restraint of his touch.

"Oh, Liadan," he said under his breath. "Oh, Liadan."

"You're safe," I managed, as my fingers moved softly against the back of his neck, and my heart thumped rather fast. "I had not hoped—but you should not be here, Bran. Liam's men keep a watchful guard. And he still believes—I have not told him the truth about my sister and how you helped her. I owe you a great debt for what you did."

"Not so," he said quietly. "You paid, remember? Now come, let us observe the code for a little before all control is quite lost. Sit here by me."

Then he bent to pick up the shawl and put it around my shoulders.

"Now," he said, taking a deep breath, "we must sit down, three paces apart, and I will give you some news."

"I know my sister is safe," I said, sitting as he instructed. He settled on the grass nearby. "A—a messenger came on the day my mother died."

"I see. Your mother—this will have caused you sorrow."

I nodded, still finding it hard to speak, hard to breathe, hard to collect my wits at all.

"There's other news that will interest you," Bran went on. "News I came by on the way here, which may not yet have reached the ears of your uncle or your brother. Uí Néill is dead. Strangled in his sleep, as he made camp by the pass to the north. This occurred some time ago, before midsummer, I'm told. They've been keeping it quiet; there are strategic reasons for doing so. The attacker was not identified. Fled in the night, and the body not found until daybreak. Must have been a man with strong hands, who knew how to move soft in the woods."

My mind raced ahead into possibilities that terrified me. "I see," I said in a whisper.

"Could it be that there is one among your kinsmen who knew the truth? One who was not afraid to administer due punishment for what was done to your sister?"

"I think maybe Sean guessed at the truth," I said slowly. "But he has remained here at Sevenwaters since my mother died."

"Did you tell no one?"

"You sound surprised. But that was your own suggestion. Are you taken aback, that a woman could show such strength of will?"

"Indeed no. I am coming to realize I cannot classify you simply as *a woman*. In all things, you are yourself."

"Nonetheless, I did tell them the truth, eventually. My father, and Sorcha. I could not let Mother die believing Niamh had perished. I told them what you had done for me."

We sat silent, and I pondered the astounding possibility that the Big Man, nurturer of growing things, arbiter of every dispute, might have put his large hands around Fionn Uí Néill's neck and squeezed the life out of him.

"I wouldn't let it bother you," said Bran, without emphasis. "Like many another secret killing, this will probably be attributed to the band of the Painted Man. With so many ill deeds to our credit, what's one more? Your father has at least taken one step, now, to compensate for his past weakness."

I scowled at him. "Must a man kill and maim to earn your respect?"

He regarded me levelly. "A man, or a woman, must at least be able to make sound decisions and abide by them. If a man has responsibilities, he should not relinquish them on a whim. If he chooses the path of lands, and family, and community, then he must shoulder that burden for life, not toss it aside to follow any woman who dazzles him in passing."

I sighed. "I wish you could have met my mother. You'd have only needed to speak with her once to change your opinion entirely. As for my father, he made a difficult choice when he came here to be with her. He did not shirk responsibility; he simply changed one burden, as you put it, for another. She needed him, Bran. She needed him as . . ." My voice cracked, and I held back the words. *As I need you.* I would not say it.

We sat silent for a while, and then he said, "I cannot stay long. I must see your brother, for my mission is but half completed. Are there other women nearby, or are you quite alone here?"

"We're unlikely to be disturbed. Why do you ask?"

"I—I told myself I would exercise restraint when at last I saw you again, but I—"

His words were lost because suddenly our arms were around each other, and our bodies were pressed close, and the tide of pent-up desire flooded through us, for it could be held back no longer. And it was very sweet indeed to feel the hardness of his body against me and the urgent touch of his hands through the damp fabric of my shift. All faded, but those sensations. It was as if there were no man, no woman here on the shore beneath the willows, no Bran, no Liadan, simply two halves of something broken that must now, at last, inevitably be made whole again. I sighed and pulled him more tightly against me. He whispered something and moved subtly, and I gasped. Then there was a wailing from the other side of the little cove, and a cawing from the branch above, and we both went very still. The wailing increased, and we moved apart and rose, and I walked over to pick up my son in my arms as Bran stood motionless on the grass, his face very pale.

"Sorry," I said, ridiculously. "They can't wait for their dinner at this age." For my son was hungry, and cross, and there was no choice but to sit there in full view, and pull down my shift and put him to the breast. The wailing ceased instantly as he began to suckle, and the raven held its tongue, perched there above us. Fiacha had not warned me of Bran's arrival. That was a strange lapse for such an effective watch-dog.

Bran did not move. He was staring, his eyes shocked, his expression again remote, a mask.

"Clearly, you wasted no time," he observed. "Why did you not mention this before? What game were you play-ing?"

Memories of another such conversation came flooding back painfully, and tears of hurt and outrage pricked my eyes.

"What do you mean, I wasted no time?" I whispered an-grily.

"My informants usually do better. Nobody thought to tell me you were wed and with a child. I was a fool to come back here."

I was torn between insane laughter and affronted tears. How could a man with a reputation for success in the most difficult mission be so unbelievably stupid?

"I thought you came to see my brother," I said shakily.

"That was true enough. I did not lie to you. But I also thought—I also hoped—clearly my judgment was faulty. That you would ever—I cannot believe that I allowed my-self to be taken in so a second time."

"Indeed," I said, "your judgment has gone sadly awry if you would believe such a thing of me. Then I would be no better than some creature of the roadside who gives herself to any man for the asking."

Despite himself, he had moved close again, and squatted down nearby, seemingly unable to tear his eyes away from the sight of the infant feeding.

"I suppose they found you a suitable mate, as they did for your sister," he said bleakly. "At least you did not wed that man, Eamonn Dubh. I keep a close watch on him; that, at least, I would have known. What chieftain's son did your family select for you, Liadan? Did you find, once you lay with me, that you had a taste for it and could wait no longer for the marriage bed?"

"If it were not for the child, your face would bear the mark of my hand for that," I said, moving my son to the other breast. "Clearly, you have not yet learned to trust."

"How could I, after this?" he muttered.

"Your prejudices blind you to the truth," I said as calmly as I could. "Have you asked yourself why I am still here at Sevenwaters instead of with my husband?"

"I would not hazard a guess," he said bleakly. "Your family appears to follow a set of rules all its own."

"That's good, coming from you." A pox on the man; he scarcely deserved to be told the truth. How could he misread me so badly?

"You'd better tell me, Liadan. Who is he? Who is your husband?"

I took a deep breath. "I have remained here because I have no husband. Not that there was a lack of offers. I did indeed have the opportunity to wed, and I turned it down. I would not give your son another man's name."

There was complete silence, save for the small sounds the child made as he sucked and swallowed. He had become an efficient feeder and soon enough he had drunk his fill and wriggled out of my arms to go off exploring again. He crawled erratically over to Bran, planting a little starfish hand on the long, patterned fingers, examining them with apparent fascination.

"What did you say?" Bran was sitting extremely still, as if he feared to move at all, lest the world should come crashing down around him.

"I think you heard me. He is yours, Bran. I told you once I would have no other man but you, and I have never lied to you nor ever will."

"How can you be sure?"

"Since I have lain with but one man, and that only for the one night, it seems to me there is no doubt whatever. Or have you forgotten what passed between us?"

"No, Liadan." He moved his fingers just a little on the grass, and Johnny sat down suddenly, with a small sound of surprise. He gazed up at his father, his gray eyes reflecting the fascinated apprehension of Bran's. "I have not forgotten. Such a night, and such a morning, remain graven deep, no matter what follows. But this—this I cannot believe. I must be dreaming. It is surely some fantasy of the imagination."

"It did not feel much like a fantasy while I was giving birth to him," I said dryly.

He looked at me, mouth set very grim indeed. "Why didn't you tell me? How could you not tell me?"

"I came close to it, when I saw you at Sídhe Dubh. But that was not the time; and besides, it seems to me you already bear more than your share of burdens. I hesitated to add another. And yet, I did want you there. I wanted you there so much, to share that moment of joy when our son came into the world."

There was another silence. Johnny tired of the hand and crawled away onto the sandy shore. Bran watched him, and there was a look in his eyes that made my heart turn over. But when he spoke at last, his voice was under firm control.

"You know what I am. You know the life I lead. I am not a fit man to be a father or a husband. As you said yourself, I have no trade but killing. I would not see my son become another such as myself. He is better off without me, and so are you. I cannot hope to understand your kinsfolk; but I know that whatever your father's failings, your brother is a good man, well able to protect and provide for you. This should be farewell for us, Liadan. I cannot become the man you need. I am—tainted, deficient. Best that this child never knows who his father was."

I could hardly speak. "So you would replay the story of Cú Chulainn and Conlai, is that it?"

"A tale of great sadness," he said softly. "It seems to me that is exactly what this is."

The two of us sat quietly, watching the baby as he propelled himself across the sand with a determination not always matched by his control of his limbs. He would wobble on hands and knees and topple sideways, and haul himself up again.

"I was wrong, I see that," Bran observed after a while, "when I called this a burden. It is no burden, but a priceless gift. Such a gift should not be squandered on a man like myself."

"Ah," I said softly, "but gifts come unsought. Each of us accepted one the night we lay together. Your son does not judge you, and nor do I. To him you are a clean page, where anything might be written from this day on. As for me, I have never asked you to change. You are what you are. I have strong hands, Bran. Through the blackest night, I have kept watch for you. At dark of the moon, my candle has burned to light your path. You may choose to reject this gift, but I will not let go so easily. I carry you in my heart, whether you wish it or no."

He nodded. "I knew that, without understanding. There were times when I believed I saw you, there in the darkness. But I dismissed it as a weakness of the mind. Liadan, you should not tie yourself thus. You deserve better, much better: a life of honor and purpose; a man you can walk beside without shame. My world is one of danger and flight, of shadows and concealment. That will not change. I would not inflict such an existence on you, or on the—or on my son."

"If you cannot see a future in which we are together, then why did you come to see me?" I asked him straight out. "Why not simply do your business with Sean and leave as secretly as you came? You asked me once to go away with you. Perhaps you have forgotten that. You changed your mind when you learned my name. And yet, you allow my brother to pay you. What is the price for this mission? Why do you work for the son of Sevenwaters when you have rejected the daughter? It makes no sense."

"I suppose," he said wearily, "it is like the net your mother cast over Hugh of Harrowfield, which made him weak with desire so that he abandoned his duty to follow her. I find the merest thought of you makes me do, and say, things that astonish even myself. My need for you warps my judgment. I told you once that telling tales was dangerous because it makes men want what they cannot have. Since I met you, I am tormented by visions of a different existence, one in which I would not be alone. But a man like myself must remain alone. To befriend such a man, to—to commit yourself to such a man is sooner or later a death sentence. You must move on without me, Liadan."

There was a terrible ache in my heart, but I kept my tone light. "Then you think I should have married Eamonn when he asked me?" I said, brows raised. "He did ask me, several times. Even after the child was born, he wished me to be his wife and was reluctant to accept no for an answer."

"What?" He sprang to his feet in outrage. "That man would have taken my woman and my child for his own? A man whose father was a traitor of the worst kind? By the powers of hell, I should have slit his throat when I had the chance." His tone changed abruptly. "Is he supposed to be eating that?" he queried, looking at the child.

The baby had discovered a fat, squirming insect on the sand, and had managed to grasp it in his small fist. Now he was conveying the wriggling morsel toward his mouth.

"No, Johnny!" I called, and moved to free the creature from his grip and to divert him quickly with a game of mud pies while the insect made its escape.

Behind us, Bran had gone suddenly quiet. And then he said, *"What did you say?"* and it became clear to me that my mother's intuition had, once again, been exactly right.

"I called my son by his name."

"Why would you choose this name for the child?" His voice was very hesitant.

"He is named for his father, and for his father's father, a man of great integrity," I said quietly, my hands still busy forming a little castle from the damp sand. As soon as I had finished, Johnny reached out his hand and demolished my construction.

"But—how could you know this? This name—this name has been unspoken for so many years that I had almost forgotten it myself." There was a dark pain in his tone that chilled me.

"In the house of Sevenwaters, the name of John has not remained unspoken," I said gravely. "Your father was my father's dearest friend. They spent their growing years together. My father told me it gave him great joy that his grandson was also John's grandson."

"How could he know this? I do not bear my father's name. Not now. He died. He died before I could know him, killed in defense of your mother when she came to meddle in the affairs of Harrowfield and entice Lord Hugh away from his responsibilities. Perhaps my father was a good man, as you say. I never had the chance to find out."

I sighed. "Clearly, whoever told you this story had a particular slant on it. Perhaps you were too young to see that it might not be the whole truth. Who did tell you this story?"

His features went suddenly blank. "I will not speak of that."

"It might be better for you if you did speak of it," I said carefully. "You could tell me."

"Some things should remain buried. This burden is such that it cannot be shared."

"It is, perhaps, only by sharing it that its weight can be taken from your shoulders."

"I can't, Liadan."

After a while, I said, "I didn't answer your question. I'll tell you a little more of your story, the only part I do know. You see the small blanket there under the trees, where Johnny was sleeping? Bring it here."

Bran's fingers moved across the surface of the rug I had made, touching one patch and then another.

"This is . . ."

I nodded. "I took the liberty of making some adjustments to your coat, so I could wear it. This blanket holds the hearts of Johnny's family and warms his sleep with their love. My sister Niamh's rose-colored gown; my riding dress; my father's old shirt, stained from his labors on the farm. Your coat that covered me when I slept under the stars. And . . ."

His fingers had stopped and they were touching a patch of faded blue, where ancient embroidery trailed delicately across the fabric, a vine, a leaf, a tiny, winged insect. Then he turned his arm over, and there, graven with needle and inks on the inner wrist, was the selfsame creature, the very first design he had requested when he was nine years old and determined he was a man.

"This fabric comes from a gown my mother wore and treasured," I said. "She had a friend at Harrowfield, John's wife, Margery. Margery made this gown herself; she was very skilled with the needle. It was a gift to my mother, a gift of love. For when Margery's son was born, it was only my mother's skills as a midwife that saved his life. When my own Johnny was born, my mother said it was just another such labor, and the infant was so like that other that it could not be coincidence. She said, I think I could put a name to this child's father. Iubdan—Lord Hugh—agreed. I wished to give my son his father's name. I wanted to give you back your name. Your parents would not want you to hate, Bran. They owed a debt of gratitude to my mother, and she to them. They sheltered and loved her."

"You cannot know." His tone was bleak.

"I want you to tell me something. You said my brother is a good man. I believe you do not think ill of me, for all your talk of nets of enchantment, nor of my sister, whom you aided at considerable risk. But we are our father's children, Bran, and our mother's. Perhaps you should consider the possibility that Hugh of Harrowfield acted from both love and duty when he came to Sevenwaters. He did not simply walk away without providing for his people."

"You cannot understand. Best that you do not understand, that you never know."

"What happened to your mother? What happened to Margery?"

Silence. The hurt, whatever it was, lay too deep to be uncovered thus. It was well locked away.

"I will ask you one more question and let that be an end of this. What if I were in some place of danger with the child and you arranged a guard for us, Gull perhaps or Snake? What if there were an attack, and that guard was killed? Would you consider you acted unreasonably in asking him to undertake that duty?"

"He would not be killed. My men are the best. Besides, that's not the way it would be. If you and—and Johnny were at risk, I would guard you myself. I would not leave such a task to another. The question is inappropriate. I would ensure such a situation never arose. If I were—responsible for you—you would never be placed in a position of danger."

"But if it did happen?"

"My men take such risks every day," he said reluctantly. "Lives are lost, and our work goes on. For this reason we have no wives, we have no sons."

"Mmm," I said. "Well, you've broken the code at least twice now. Will you tell them when you go back?"

There was a pause.

"I will not go back until this mission is complete," he said. "And I spoke truth when I said I was here to see your brother. It grows late; I must do so and depart."

He got up, the small blanket still in his hands. Johnny was engrossed in his labors, both fists full of sand. I rose to my feet.

"It's pointless, I suppose, to ask you to come back to me safely," I said, working hard to keep my voice steady. "Perhaps it's pointless to ask you to come back at all. But I will keep my candle burning while you are gone. Please be careful."

"I must go, Liadan. Do not fear for my safety. Both your brother and I are fully aware of the risks. I—I must say farewell now. By all the powers," he said suddenly, gathering me into his arms again, "I think I would pay any price to spend tonight in your bed. You see how my judgment deserts me, when—" And he kissed me again, deeper and harder this time. It seemed to me this was a last kiss, the kiss given by a warrior who goes to battle knowing he will not return. It should have been a simple matter to step away and let him go. But my arms seemed to have a will of their own, to hold on; and his were warm and tight around my body.

"You still believe this is some spell, some woman's snare that I have laid on you against your will?" I breathed.

"How can I think otherwise? The merest touch of your hand is enough to make me forget who I am, and what I am, and what I am not."

"It's a well-known phenomenon," I told him, attempting a smile. "When a man and a woman are together, and their bodies speak one to the other . . . maybe that's all it is."

"No. This is different."

I did not contradict him for I believed his words were true. The longings of the flesh were one thing, and very powerful they were, as I had cause to know. But what was between us was infinitely stronger than that: ancient, binding, and secret. I had not forgotten those voices that called me in the place of the great barrow. *Jump.*

"Liadan," he said, with his lips against my hair.

"What is it?"

"Tell me what you want from me."

I drew an unsteady breath and pulled back just far enough to see his face. Under the raven markings, he looked very serious and, for the first time, very young; no more than the one and twenty I had found so hard to believe.

"That your spirit could be healed of its scars," I said softly. "That you could see your way. That's what I want."

For a moment, he seemed lost for words, and a small, perplexed frown creased his brow. "Your response is not what I expected. Always, you have an answer that silences me."

My fingers reached up to trace the pattern that marked his features, that circled his steady, gray eye, that defined the plane of the cheek and the strong line of the jaw. "I've been told something like that before," I said. "By my Uncle Conor. He invited me to enter the nemetons and become a druid along with my son."

"Don't go away." His response was instant, an echo of that child I had heard in my mind, screaming in the darkness. His arms tightened around me so I could scarcely breathe. *"Don't take him away."*

My heart thumped. He had frightened me. "It's all right," I said quietly. "I will keep my light burning for you. I told you that, and I will never lie to you." I rested my forehead against his chest, wondering how I could bear the moment when he would take his arms away from where they held me fast and vanish back into the forest.

"You have told me," he said very quietly, "what you want for me. But what do you want for yourself?"

I looked up into his eyes for I believed he should be able

to read the answer on my face. I would not put it into words; not now. "I'll tell you that when you come back," I said, my voice wobbling dangerously. "You are not ready to hear that answer. Now you'd better go before I give you another excuse for your argument that women turn on their tears whenever they choose, just for effect."

It was very hard to let go. But we did, and Bran knelt down next to his son on the damp sand of the little beach. Johnny looked up and said something in his incomprehensible infant language.

"Indeed," Bran replied gravely. "It was just as well, I think, that you woke when you did this afternoon. We might otherwise have made another small son or daughter to be born into a world of shadows and uncertainty." His long fingers moved very gently to touch his son's brown curls, and then he rose to his feet.

"I have no answers for you," he said, and his expression was somber. Now he was maintaining his three paces' distance, as if it were too dangerous to move close again.

Holding back my tears was becoming harder by the moment. "I have no expectations," I told him. "Wishes and hopes for the three of us, that's all."

"Good-bye, Liadan." He picked up his little pack and went away from me, walking up the sward into the shade of the willows. There he paused and turned back, looking first at Johnny and then at me; and it seemed to me the shadow was in his eyes and all around him.

"Farewell, dear heart," I whispered, and bent to pick up the damp, sandy infant, for it was long past time for us to return to the house. Still Bran stood watching, and his expression took my breath away, such a wondrous mixture it was of love and pain. Then he turned his back on us and was gone.

After that, the Sight came to visit me unbidden and with a vengeance. I believed myself strong, but it was a test such as I had never yet encountered. I understood the capricious, deceptive nature of this gift, how it did not always show literal truth, how past and present and future, how *has been* and *will be* and *may be* were jumbled together in its seemingly random visions. This was just as well, since without that knowledge I would indeed have run mad, as did some folk cursed by the same gift. It clutched at me quite without warning; and all of its images were dark ones. And even when the visions were absent, I could not escape the feeling that I was being watched; that, somehow, everything I did was under scrutiny, and being judged.

Sometimes it was quite short. I would be walking back from the cottages, my basket over my arm, and I would feel a little faint; and then, right before me, I would see the carved beasts on the pillars, and Eamonn's face, white with a desperate rage, and his hands around Bran's neck, squeezing tight. And this time, Bran's knife fell to the floor unused as the patterned fingers lost their grip, and his features grew purple and distorted, and I felt in my own chest the frantic struggle for breath, saw before my own eyes the blackness rise to take me. Or I would be sitting by the fire at home, while Johnny played on the floor with some wooden animals my father had once made for Niamh. I had not forgotten my own skills with the knife, and alongside the fat sheep and horned cow and the hen with her chickens, there were one or two I had added. A wolfhound, fierce and strong. A coiled snake. A sleek otter. There was no need for a raven: we had Fiacha, a constant, vigilant presence. I watched my son as he sat at my feet, and suddenly the creatures were alive, and one was a horse, and on it was a rider who wore on his tunic the emblem of Sevenwaters, two torcs interlinked. It was my Uncle Liam, somewhere beyond the forest, traversing a narrow way between rocky inclines. And there was a whirring noise and a thump, and with a look of mild surprise on his face my uncle toppled silently from his mount to lie motionless on the earth, a red-feathered arrow protruding from his chest. The vision faded before I could see the aftermath, and I was back in the quiet room again.

"Wooh," enunciated Johnny, practicing.

"Right; that one's a dog," I answered shakily. Liam was at home and in good health. That was one of the problems with the Sight. One might tell of what one saw and offer a warning. But there was no guarantee that would alter the course of events. One might decide to keep quiet to avoid worrying people. Then the things might happen, and there would be a terrible guilt. *If only I had told them. If only I had warned them* . . . I kept this vision to myself, for now. I did not ask Sean what mission the Painted Man undertook for him or what the price might be for such a service. I knew he would not tell me. But we were wary with one another, and it was uncomfortable. It was as if what each of us knew of Bran made us cautious, as if our separate knowledge, put together, would be in some way dangerous. Of my father, there was no word, as autumn progressed toward winter and the harvest was over. It was past time for culling stock, and root crops must be stored, and butter and cheese laid away for the cold time. There was an edginess about the household, and down in the settlement folk began to come down with a bitter, racking cough.

"Where's Iubdan when I need him?" I heard Liam muttering as he strode about the farm with a cluster of workers all asking questions at once.

The moon went through its cycle once, twice, and the nights became colder. I lit my candle, and watched my child grow. There was a chill in the air that was not simply winter's coming. I thought of the Painted Man, away somewhere beyond the farthest reaches of the forest, perhaps beyond the margins of Erin itself, carrying out some desperate, dangerous task, a suicide mission. My brother was unusually taciturn, and I could see his anxiety on his face. He and Liam had long consultations alone, and once with

Seamus Redbeard, who came and went in the space of two days. Business was afoot, and they weren't talking about it. Nobody spoke of Fionn's death. I held my tongue. But I feared for Bran, and I told myself that if I ever got the chance, next time I would have to put it to him openly. It was less than a life, to spend your life waiting; to spend your brief moments together saying farewell. I would have to present him with some sort of choice. To change his path and set his skills to another purpose, or to turn his back on me forever. And yet I thought I knew what his answer would be, and I feared to hear him say it.

Then there came a night when my visions were too many, and too dark, and I was forced to share them. Perhaps I was asleep at first, but these were more than nightmares. It was fragmented, as if my mind put together many times and places, and spun them around, and threw them back at me like poison barbs. I saw an old, old man, wandering the empty halls of Sevenwaters alone, his gnarled fingers grasping a staff of yew for support. He was mumbling to himself, *They are all gone . . . no sons, no daughters . . . How can the forest be saved if there are no children at Sevenwaters?* And I saw that this crippled ancient was my brother, Sean. The picture changed abruptly, and for an instant all was dark and I was in a tiny, confined space, my limbs cramped and folded and I could not breathe; it was hot, so hot and tight, and someone was screaming, but it was so hard to breathe, the scream was more of a whisper, *Where are you?*

My eyes opened abruptly, and I was gasping and shaking, lying on my bed at Sevenwaters, and when my terror abated I recognized that it was not entirely dark, for the small flame of the candle still glowed. My heart was hammering, and I felt cold sweat on my skin. And it was not over, for there in the quiet room I saw another vision: two people arguing, Aisling and her brother. Behind them, the carven creatures in the hall of Sídhe Dubh looked balefully on. *You can't do this!* Aisling was shouting, her eyes swollen with long weeping. *You already gave your consent! You gave your word!* Eamonn's face was cold, like that of a brithem delivering both judgment and sentence. *The alliance is no longer suitable,* he said. *The decision is made.* Aisling uttered a little wordless sound, and her face went deathly pale, and the vision changed. She was up on the guard tower, and the men had their backs turned. She was standing on the parapet in her white gown, and somebody shouted, *No!* and she took one step into space, and fell like a stone, without a sound, onto the jagged rocks far below. The Sight did not spare me a single detail. I cried out in horror, and Johnny awoke and began to wail in sympathy, and Fiacha added his distinctive voice to the general commotion.

Response was swift. First came the young nursemaid, yawning, to pick up the child and soothe him with gentle words. Then Janis, frowning, with a lantern; and Sean, quickly assessing the situation, catching the terror of my mind, for at such times it spills out unguarded. He sent the others back to bed, and I hugged my son until we were both comforted, and drank the cup of wine my brother set by me. In the window my candle burned on, for now I set it there every night, be there a sliver of moon, or a full shining orb, or a dark sky full of shadows.

"Better?" asked Sean after a while.

I drew a long shuddering breath. "I—oh, Sean—I saw—"

"Take your time," my brother advised quietly, sounding not unlike our father. "Want to tell me about it?"

"I—I don't know. It was—it was terrible, not just this, but—Sean, I don't think I can tell you this." The image was still in my mind, shattered bone, sightless eyes, bright hair and bright blood and—other things. I held a barrier around it so that he could not see into my thoughts.

"I'm worried about you, Liadan." Sean held his own wine cup between his palms and stared into the candle flame. There was a new gravity in his features; Father's absence had changed the balance of our household more than anyone expected. "These visions have disturbed you for some time, I know. Perhaps you should talk to Conor. He would come if we sent for him."

"No," I said abruptly: thinking Johnny is older now. Conor would ask me again to go into the forest with him, and I would have to find a reason for saying no. "Sean, I need you to tell me what is happening. I know it's secret; but the Sight seems to be warning me of disaster, and I fear for—for all of those close to me, and I cannot tell what warnings to give. What is this mission that the Painted Man undertakes for you? Who else knows of it? And what of Eamonn?" I would not say Aisling's name, for as soon as he heard me speak it, he would know my vision was of her, and he would get the truth out of me, a truth that might or might not come to pass. He would be bound to act on it and maybe precipitate disaster.

Sean's lips tightened. "There's no need for you to know."

"There is, Sean. Lives are at risk, and more than lives. Believe me."

"Liadan?" asked my brother.

"What?" I knew what was coming.

"This is his child, isn't it?"

There was no point in evasion now that he had finally given a voice to his suspicions. And yet he could not be told the whole truth. He could not know the other part of the tale, of Niamh and her druid and a strange flight to Kerry. I simply nodded. "Is the likeness so striking?" I asked, managing a smile.

"It will become more so with time." Sean's frown was just like Liam's. "It is too late to point out the folly of your actions, and his; too late to explain to you that this was an act of thoughtless self-indulgence. What of Eamonn? Does he know?"

"I did not tell him," I said, wishing his censure had not

such power to hurt me. "But he knows, yes. He—he hinted at spies, at covert intelligence."

"He has been acting oddly," he said, with some hesitation, after checking that the door was securely shut. "Meetings were arranged at which he should have been present and was not. I have sent messages and received no reply. It disturbs me. Even Seamus has found it difficult to reach his grandson's ear."

"Did you act with your allies' consent when you set the Painted Man this mission?" Johnny had fallen asleep again and was heavy in my arms, but his warmth was welcome, and I kept him cradled there.

"What do you think?"

"I suspect it is an arrangement between the two of you, personal and secret."

"You suspect correctly. A chance for him to prove himself. A very useful undertaking for me, with nothing to lose."

"What do you mean?" I asked, feeling suddenly cold.

"The arrangement was, if he were captured, my responsibility ended there. The risk is all his own. The man seems to have either no concern for his continued existence or a remarkable self-confidence. Maybe both."

"He is the best at what he does. But you are right; he appears to have no great will for self-preservation. That makes him a useful tool for you, I suppose."

"That sounds just a little critical, Liadan. You must not forget that we are men, and that this is war, and that such bargains are made every day. I'd have been a fool to pass up the opportunity. If he succeeds, I'll pay, and there will be more work for him."

"If he dies, how will you justify yourself to me, and to my son?" I asked him, my voice shaking.

"If he dies, it will be because he believed no mission was beyond his ability," my brother responded calmly. "He accepted this of his own free will, on his own terms."

"Sean, please. Please tell me what it is. Tell me what you

and Liam and Seamus are doing. I have had enough of secrets. I need to know this."

I think at last he recognized my desperation. No doubt
the shadow of my terrible visions still haunted my eyes.

"Very well. The mission links two elements, both of
which serve the alliance well at this point. A year ago we
were in a very strong position, from which an attack by sea
to drive Northwoods from the Islands could at last be considered again. It was the addition of Fionn's forces that
made that possible. But Fionn is dead."

"I know."

"You know? How?"

"Bran—the Painted Man—told me. I have known it for
some time. I thought it best to say nothing until the news
reached Liam and became official."

"Why would he tell you?"

"There are no secrets between us, Sean."

My brother stared at me.

"This man has come to my aid in the past. Ours was not
merely some casual encounter. His future is tied with mine
and so with yours. Perhaps you did not recognize that when
you bought his services for a mission nobody else was prepared to undertake. What are you paying him?"

"Shall I go on? Fionn died. The less said about that the
better. It is being attributed to your friend, and nobody is
bothering to advance any alternative theories. We were immediately faced with a problem. Fionn's support was inte-
gral to success in the field. In addition, the Uí Néill of
Tirconnell have maintained their ongoing dispute with their
kinsfolk in the south. There's no love lost between the high
king and Fionn's father. And Sevenwaters, and its allies,
just happen to be strategically placed right between the two.
Fionn's people kept the death quiet for a long time. Before
midsummer, it happened, less than a moon after Father departed so abruptly."

I nodded without comment.

"So on the one hand, it's vital to renew the alliance with the northern Uí Néill, but subtly, without angering the high king. Such ties are best strengthened by marriage; but Niamh is lost, and one does not offer a girl with a fatherless child, whatever her lineage, as a bride for a nobly born chieftain. Still, we've another bargaining tool: we can provide armed support, a bulwark against an attack from the south. In the future, we may be able to offer—specialist services, the kind of services in which the Painted Man excels: intelligence; subterfuge; secret entries and exits; tricks of seamanship; the masterly handling of weapons. That way your friend and I could only aid each other. Those things are for the future; for now, Liam and Seamus and I have set up a very private meeting with the Uí Néill at a secret location. We are confident of their cooperation. Eamonn's absence has been cause for concern, as I said; but Seamus will have told him that part of the plan by now, and he'll be certain to support it. He'd be a fool not to, situated as he is right by the pass to the north, in line for direct traffic out of Tirconnell."

"You have told me but half." I rose to put Johnny in his small bed and cover him with the many-colored quilt.

"Ah, the mission. I wondered at first how such men, with their highly distinctive appearance, could possibly make a success of covert ventures, of spying and infiltration. I wished to send an observer to the heart of Northwoods's camp—to Greater Island itself—to bring me accurate plans of their fortifications, to identify their weak points, to provide details of the numbers and movements of men, and information about their seagoing craft. I believed it could not be done, for the Briton has too good a network of intelligence. Most certainly, I thought so ostentatiously marked a creature had no chance of success. But I put it to him, knowing his reputation. And as you guessed, in this I acted alone. None of the allies is aware of this mission, though

Seamus knew I had such a plan under consideration. If it succeeds, I will tell them."

"You said your plan linked two elements," I said, tight-lipped. "What is the other?"

"I wanted the information, but I wanted a distraction as well. Something to take Northwoods's eye off what we were doing. Our man was to let slip, almost by accident, the news of Fionn's death; let the enemy believe our alliance with the Uí Néill broken. Feed him the news that our ability to attack is much weakened. Then, next autumn, we'd give the Briton a surprise from which he could not recover, and we would take back the Islands at last."

"And Bran agreed?"

"Not at first. He heard me out, and said he'd consider it. When he came back to me, the plan had changed. As you'll be aware, his reputation is widely known, and as a result he can go almost nowhere unrecognized. He said he would make Northwoods an offer he could not refuse. He would offer to bring information about Sevenwaters and the alliance, enough information to strengthen the Briton's grip on the Islands and present him with opportunities to attack us. The information would be false, of course. But it would be good enough to fool Northwoods, fool him for long enough for the Painted Man to gather the intelligence I need and bring it back to me before the Briton discovered the truth. Such a man as your friend is known to change his allegiance as easily as he changes his boots. He might just get away with it. If he promised more of the same, they would have good reason to let him go. When last he reported to me, he had established contact, and arrangements were in place for a small vessel to take him over in secret. And while Northwoods has been distracted by his visitor and the wealth of fascinating information he bore, we have begun to set up our new alliance and plan for the last assault."

"What cause would the Britons have to trust him?" I whispered, watching the candle flare and flicker in the draft.

"He was given enough genuine information to win them," Sean said, frowning. "The false intelligence was to be passed on after that. But I will not lie to you; I am becoming anxious. He's late to report back. There's been no word."

"Sean, I too have cause for concern. Since we are being honest with each other, I think you might wish to invite Aisling here for a while. Or go to see her, perhaps." I tried to keep my tone light, but you cannot easily hide such misgivings from a twin.

"What? What did you see?" He was suddenly white.

"I won't tell you, Sean. But it is serious. You should go and fetch her, if you can."

"I can't," he said grimly. "Not now. Liam rode out earlier tonight to discuss terms in confidence with the Uí Néill. The meeting is set for the day after tomorrow at a hidden location north of the forest. Seamus will be there; but I must remain at Sevenwaters in our uncle's absence. Liadan? Liadan, what is it?"

"You should stop him." My words came out in a strangled whisper. "You should stop Liam. Send after him and bring him back."

But I had heard the sound of death in my brother's words, and in my heart I knew we were powerless to stop it, for it was already too late.

That was the darkest of times. Grim-faced, Sean sent Liam's master of arms, Felan, away by night with urgent speed. I could read the bitter message of my brother's mind, although he did not speak it aloud. *You should have warned me.*

When Felan came back, there was no time for grieving. He gave his news in private, and when Sean gathered the household, soon after, his features were calm and pale, a picture of control. At not quite eighteen years of age, my

brother must now assume responsibility for the greatest
túath north of Tara, for its flocks and herds, its army and its
defenses and its alliances, and for all the folk who dwelt
there. And as lord of Sevenwaters, he was now custodian of
the forest. Liam had planned that it would be so in time, after careful preparation. But time had run out.

"I have the gravest of news for you," Sean said, and the
silence was complete as men at arms and serving women
and grooms and cottagers stood assembled in the hall to
hear him. The doors were bolted. "Lord Liam is dead. He
was slain by a Briton's arrow, not two days since, while riding to a secret council. My uncle was betrayed, and I will
not rest until the perpetrator is identified and dealt with."

A ripple of horror went around the room. So soon after
my mother's passing and my father's abrupt departure, this
seemed a fatal blow, one from which the household of Sevenwaters might not well recover.

"I know I have your support and the support of our allies," Sean went on, keeping his tone strong and confident.
"We will all grieve for this loss and may find it hard to set
our hands to our tasks, whether it be the harvest or the work
of the house or the bearing of arms. But my uncle would
want us to go on, to keep the defenses strong, to protect the
forest and its dwellers as our family was bound to do long
ago, and to pursue our quest to regain what the Britons took
from us. The campaign will be set back, but not forever. We
will rally and recover. We cannot mourn Lord Liam as we
would wish; we cannot send him on his way with the ceremony such a leader deserves, for these are difficult times,
and the news of this act of treachery is best kept within our
own community for now. For this reason we will bear his
body home quietly to lie within these walls for a day and a
night, and we will bury him under the oaks. In time, there
will be due ritual to remember his name and to bid him a fitting farewell. But for now, hold his image in your hearts

and minds, and keep your mouths shut. Is this understood?"

"Yes, my lord." Many voices spoke as one, and when they had taken time to express their shock and their grief, and to offer their respect and sorrow to my brother and me, every one of them went immediately back to work. The harvest resumed; women busied themselves with drying and preserving fruit, or airing linen, and Felan rode straight back out with three men clad in dark clothes, and an extra horse.

My brother had started well. Before the folk of the household he had kept his voice steady and his manner a creditable imitation of Liam's own, firmly authoritative. But later, after they had brought our uncle's body back and we had prepared him for burial and laid him to rest in the hall, surrounded by candles, that was a different matter. Downstairs, folk came in to walk past the still form of their fallen lord, to observe his stern features little softened by the sleep of death. His body was scarcely marked. Whoever had loosed this arrow had been skilled at his work. Liam's wolfhounds would not leave their master; they lay, one at his head and one at his feet, strangely silent as man or woman filed past, ashen faced, to mutter, "Go in peace, my lord," or "Safe journey, Lord Liam."

"Who'd have thought it?" Janis had said, grimly, as she poured ale for the household and scrubbed her cheeks furtively with the back of her hand. "First Sorcha and then him, scarce a season after. It's not right. Something's not right. When's the Big Man coming home?"

Johnny was with the nursemaid, and Sean and I sat together in the private room upstairs, where Niamh had tried to defy the men of the family and had been crushed. Sean was very quiet; and when I looked over at him I saw that at last, after his long day of control, he was weeping.

"I'm sorry," I said inadequately. "He was like a father to you, I know that. You've done well today, Sean. He would be proud of you."

"You should have told me before. You should have warned me or warned him. You could have prevented this, Liadan." His tone was ragged with grief, and his words hurt me deeply. "Why would you choose not to stop it? Is there some conspiracy here I cannot understand? For someone betrayed him to the Britons. Someone told them where he would be, and when, and that he would be alone."

"Stop it, Sean." My own voice was less than steady. "This is nonsense, and you know it."

"Nonsense, is it? Then tell me this. Who knew of the meeting to which Liam rode save our own allies and the Painted Man? He was given this knowledge for precisely the opposite purpose—to make sure the attention of Northwoods was diverted from the real location and intent of this council. But he was ideally placed to pass the information straight to the Britons. How can I not believe, now, that my faith in your friend has been completely misplaced? This murder surely reveals that he is no more than the trickster his reputation paints, a man who will change his allegiance at any time it suits him. My own ill-judged trust of this man has killed my uncle."

"Why would Bran do such a thing?"

Sean's lip curled. "Perhaps Edwin of Northwoods pays better than I do. The chance to remove my uncle from the picture, and at the same time to disrupt our negotiations with the Uí Néill, would have commanded a good price, I should think."

"Bran would not do that, Sean. His mission was for you. He spoke of you with nothing but respect. This is not his doing, I am sure of it."

"Such a man cannot be trusted." Sean spoke dismissively. "I was a fool to do as I did, and you were even more of a fool to be taken in by his fine words. Now our uncle is dead and the alliance in real danger. Don't you realize this could set our campaign back by years? You bear a portion of the blame for this, Liadan. I cannot believe you chose not to tell me."

I sat silent as his words fell on me like an evil rain. What Janis had said had been all too true. It wasn't right. None of it was right.

"I want Aisling," Sean said abruptly, his voice cracking as it escaped his efforts at control. "I need Aisling here. But she does not answer my messages, and I cannot ride to fetch her; I cannot leave Sevenwaters until our people recover from this blow. What did your vision show you, Liadan? What was the danger for Aisling?"

But I would not answer him, for he had hurt me too deeply.

"Liadan. Tell me."

"I won't. And I will not defend myself, except to say that you speak out of your grief, and your words wound me, for I, too, feel Liam's loss. I, too, loved him, and relied upon his strength. I should not need to tell you that the Sight does not always show true images of what is to come. If I offered a warning every time, I would create such upheaval we could scarcely live our daily lives, for we'd be always looking over our shoulders. And you are wrong about Bran. He is a trustworthy man and could not have done this. He values his friendship with me, and he would not injure his son by betraying our family to the enemy. Whoever let slip this secret, it was not the Painted Man."

"Your faith in him defies logic. It is based, perhaps, more on the desires of the body than on anything resembling common sense. You'd have done better to marry Eamonn, who could have provided some stability for you, than ally yourself to an outlaw who clearly has no respect for you or his child."

"I would never have married Eamonn. I expect I will never marry anyone. As for your arguments, you should stop laying blame without evidence and look at your security, for it does appear there is a weak link somewhere. I don't deny the fact that someone has betrayed a secret, and that this has caused our uncle's death. But it was not Bran, I know this, Sean, and you must believe me. You must look elsewhere for your informant."

"Liadan." His voice had gone quiet, as our father's sometimes did.

"What?" I asked wearily.

"Would you do something for me?"

Brighid save us. What did the boy expect, after venting his bitterness on me and turning my heart cold with his ill-chosen words of reproach?

"What is it?"

"I cannot go to Aisling. And when I send messengers to her brother, they are refused admittance. Eamonn will not speak with them. But he would not refuse you. You could make him listen. Will you go to Sídhe Dubh and talk to him? Will you see Aisling for me, and try to bring her back here?"

My heart quailed. "I don't think—"

"You could make amends thus," said my brother.

"There are no amends to be made," I snapped. "And Eamonn is the last person I want to see right now. I have no wish to go to Sídhe Dubh ever again, Sean. There is—there is ill feeling between Eamonn and myself. This would be very difficult for me. Besides, I, too, am needed here. People rely on me. And what about Johnny?"

"Please, Liadan." For a moment he sounded just like Niamh, the way she used to wheedle a favor out of me.

"I don't know. You seem to have lost your confidence in my judgment and your own. Perhaps you should send somebody else. If you believe Bran would turn against you so readily, why would I not do the same?"

"You still have faith in him, then." His tone was flat.

"He would not betray you thus, Sean. To do so would be to fail at his mission. If he has not returned, it must be because—because—" There was a flash of the Sight, and it was dark, it was so dark that at first I could not tell which way was up and which was down, and whether the walls were out there or close around me, holding me cramped up with my knees under my chin and my arms bent over my head. I tried to move and the walls were right there, so tight, so small; and it was stifling, and I could not breathe. I must make no sound, not a single whimper, or when they let me out, they would make me pay. So the voice screamed out silently inside my head, as my tears fell hot and fierce down my cheeks, and my nose ran, and I could not even sniff for fear they would hear me. *Where are you? Why did you let go?*

"Liadan," said Sean softly. "Liadan!" and I came back to myself, shivering. "You're crying," he said.

"I did not ask for the gift of the Sight," I told him shakily. "Believe me, I would give anything to have known I might prevent Liam's death. But that's not the way it works. I might have warned him, and he might have taken a different path and still have died. There's no way of knowing."

Sean nodded gravely. "I'm sorry. It is hard not to blame you. I do wonder, sometimes, if your alliance with the Painted Man has warped your judgment."

I sighed. "You are anxious about Aisling, and with good cause. I feel the same about Bran. It seems to be hard for you to understand, that I could love as you do."

"You could, perhaps, have chosen more wisely. That man can never be part of Sevenwaters. He is—feral."

"I know that, but my choice is made. Now you have sent him into great danger, for your own reasons, and you have accused him of treachery and me of weakness. And you ask me a favor."

There was a pause.

"You know what you saw. Was your vision of Aisling such that you believe her to be in immediate danger?"

I nodded reluctantly.

Sean was very pale. "I can't go there, Liadan. My people need me. Please do this, for me and for her. Eamonn will not refuse you; he could not refuse you anything. I'll provide a strong escort for you; you could leave in the morning. Take Johnny with you, and your nursemaid, if you like."

"I'll think about it," I told him, my heart going cold at the prospect of the fortress walls of Sídhe Dubh closing about me again and colder at the thought of asking Eamonn for anything at all. "It won't be tomorrow. I can't get Johnny ready in time."

"It needs to be soon."

"I know."

As I rose to retire to my bedchamber, he used the voice of the mind. *I'm sorry, Liadan. Liam was right. I'm not ready for this. But I must do it. I must shut this inside and be strong for them all. You are my sister, and I will always be here for you, whatever choices you make.*

I know that. I turned back, but he was not looking at me. He sat bent forward, and his head was in his hands. *You will be a strong and wise leader, Sean. Your children, and Aisling's, will fill these halls with laughter again.*

With those words, I was committed to do as he asked. But I feared to make this journey. I had thought I was afraid of little; but I recognized that I was afraid of Eamonn, and of his strange home in the marshes, and of the half-seen visions of evil things taking place within its stone walls. I would far rather have stayed at home with Johnny, helping the women in the kitchens, taking linctus to the ailing cottagers, secure in the heart of the forest. The Fair Folk had warned me. Conor had warned me. It was dangerous to leave.

It was not Sean's anxiety that finally persuaded me but

something far more terrifying. The moon was starting to wane, and tonight its light was veiled by heavy clouds. A strong southeasterly wind sent the sound of bending branches and rustling leaves into my quiet chamber as I prepared for bed. It was very late. The nursemaid had gone to her own rest and left Johnny with me, tucked up fast asleep under his multicolored blanket. When he woke to feed, I would take him into my own bed, for his small, warm presence was a welcome barrier against the evil thoughts that now threatened to overwhelm me. Fiacha was perched on the back of a chair, and whether he slept or woke there was no telling. I must be strong, I told myself, as I held a taper in the embers of the fire and went to light my special candle. Very strong, for others depended on that strength to keep them safe.

The candle flickered and went out. I put my hand around the wick to shield it from the draft, and held the taper close again. The wick flared briefly and died. A feeling like the touch of a cold hand went down the back of my neck. Very deliberately, I lifted the candle in its holder and moved away from the window to place it on the oaken chest by the bed. Strange shadows from the lighted taper danced across the walls.

Here there was no draft. But the patterned candle would not light. I checked the wick and tried again, and again, as a terrible fear began to take hold of me. The wick was clear; the taper burned steadily right beside it. But as soon as I moved my hand away, the candle flame guttered and died. I told myself I was being foolish, simply willing it to happen in my panic. I took a deep breath and tried again. I sat there a long time, trying and trying to make it burn, until my hands were shaking and my vision blurred with my efforts. It was dark outside; thick clouds still blanketed the moon. And I could not will the small candle to life. Tonight, this light would not shine out in the darkness.

I sat shivering on my bed with a blanket around my

shoulders, but I did not sleep, not at all that night. Johnny woke twice, and I held him and fed him and welcomed his company. But tonight, now, I wanted the Sight and it would not come. I could not even hear that child, screaming in the dark. Instead, it was I who cried out, in my mind, *Where are you? Show me. Show me.* But there was nothing as I waited, cold with misgivings, until the first pale light of dawn touched the sky.

I told the bleary-eyed nursemaid I was going out for the day and taking Johnny with me. In particular, I told her to explain, if anyone should ask, that I had taken an escort and gone on a short visit, and that I would be back in plenty of time to see my Uncle Liam laid to rest. I had no wish to be at home that day. I had business of my own.

I had already perfected a method of transporting Johnny on my trips through the forest, and now I hoisted him onto my back, tied in a strong length of sacking whose ends fastened over my shoulder and around my waist. He enjoyed this type of ride, which held him close to the warmth of my body but allowed him to see the rocks and sky and the many colors and patterns of oak and ash, birch and hazel. When he was a man, I thought, as we made our way soft-footed down a leaf-strewn path my Uncle Conor had once shown me, he would bear the memory of these shapes and hues deep within; and like all the children of Sevenwaters, he would find it hard to be long away from the forest.

I went quickly. If the Sight were to be denied me, now when I most needed to see, I must seek out what information I could by whatever means I might find. And now that my mother was gone, there was only one person I could think of who would help me without making any sort of judgment; without trying to tell me what I should do, and what I should not.

It began to rain lightly, but the great oaks sheltered us; and by the time I was scrambling up the banks of the seventh stream, where it tumbled down the rocky hillside into the calm waters of the lake, the clouds had thinned to let a weak sunlight through. Fiacha flew in short bursts, now ahead of us, now behind, keeping pace, keeping watch. There was no chance of getting cold; covering this distance so quickly, with Johnny on my back, had made sure of that. And indeed I found I had to stop and catch my breath more and more frequently. Perhaps the visitations of the Sight had weakened me, or maybe my body was not as fully recovered after my son's birth as I had thought. *Be strong, Liadan. You have to be strong.* At last I came by the clustered rowans, again bright with autumn's fruit, and slipped in under the willows. There before me was the secret spring, the small, round pool encircled by smooth stones, a place of deep quiet. I unfastened the cloth that held my son against my back. Johnny had fallen asleep, and I laid him down carefully in bracken under the trees. He did not stir. Fiacha settled on a branch nearby.

Uncle? My mind was already reaching out as I went to sit on the stones by the water. *I need your help.*

I'm here, Liadan. And he was, standing on the other side, pale face, tangled dark hair, shapeless garments not quite concealing the white swathe of wing feathers. His expression was calm, his eyes clear.

My Uncle Liam is dead, taken by a British arrow.

I know this. Conor already makes his way to Sevenwaters. But I will not go. Not this time.

Uncle, I have seen some terrible visions. I saw Liam's death, and I did not warn them until it was too late. My brother said—he said—

I know. It is very hard. There is no way to escape this guilt, Daughter. I have lived with it long years. Your brother will learn, as my own brothers did in time, that the Sight cannot be controlled; that such warnings, if given, can reap a harvest far more bitter than that of events left to their true course. Your brother is young. In time, he will be as strong as Liam was. Perhaps stronger.

I nodded. *I, too, see this, and I told him so. But I was shown another future, one in which Sean was old and quite alone. A future in which Sevenwaters was empty. Desolate. To change that pattern, I would risk much. I would challenge those who shape our course, however strong they may be.*

Finbar gave a deep chuckle, startling me. "Oh, Liadan. If my path had been different, and I had been blessed with a daughter, I would have wished for just such a one as yourself. Do you not challenge the set ways of our lives at every turn? Now come, you wish for guidance, for a vision that shows true; I see it in your eyes, and I read your urgency there. You have wept long, and I believe I can guess why."

"My candle, my little flame in the darkness—I could not light it, though I tried and tried. And there has been no word, just a terrible silence. And now the visions have ceased, and I cannot see him; I cannot hear his voice. And I saw Aisling, I saw—"

"I will help you. If truth is to be shown you, it will be here among these ancient stones. Your child sleeps sound. There is time. Come, open your mind to mine and let us look in the water together."

So we sat on the stones and felt that we were held safe, as in the strong, supporting warmth of a mother's hands. Finbar was on one side of the pool and I on the other. I let go the shields on my mind, and he did the same, and our thoughts blended and grew calm together. Time passed, perhaps a long time, perhaps not long at all, and the only sounds were the small rustling of insects in the grass and the high calling of birds overhead and the wind sighing in the willows.

The surface of the water rippled and changed. Something

bright shone there, silver flashing in the dark. I caught my breath. A drinking flask, cunningly made, its surface richly patterned with an ornate, convoluted design, its stopper fashioned of amber in the shape of a little cat, a vessel I had shared with the Painted Man on a day of death and rebirth. There was a hand, reaching to pick up the flask, to remove the stopper. The man raised the flask to his lips to drink, and it was Eamonn. The pool went dark again.

Breathe slow, Liadan. Stay calm. My uncle sent me an image of still water, of beech leaves in spring sunlight, of a child sleeping. I willed my hammering heart to slow, my mind to put fear aside. I looked in the water again.

This time the images flowed one into another, and I thought their timing true. Aisling, lying facedown on her bed, weeping and weeping until there were no tears left. A serving woman, coming into the room with a tray of food and drink, taking away another such tray, quite untouched. Locking the door. Locking my friend in. Then abruptly we were downstairs in the great hall of Sídhe Dubh. It was nighttime, for torches burned around the walls, and the stone beasts seemed ferocious, as the light flickered and played on their tiny, malign features. Staring eyes, grasping claws, pointed teeth, fiery tongues. Now I could see two men there: Eamonn, seated in a carven, oak chair, his glossy, brown hair neat on his shoulders, his features composed. Only his eyes betrayed his excitement. And Bran, the fair side of his face a mass of swollen bruising, a deep cut oozing over his eye, and a livid purple mark all around his neck, as if he had come close to death by strangling. There was a look of gloating triumph in Eamonn's brown eyes.

"Knowing your penchant for the severing of the extremities," he observed smoothly, "I've decided to start with the smallest finger and work my way gradually inward. Interesting, to see how much pain a man can bear. But perhaps a black man does not feel it as we do."

Bran's voice was quiet and level. "I will not bargain for his safety, nor he for mine."

Eamonn gave a derisive laugh. "I had not planned to allow room for negotiation. You gave me none when you butchered my men before my eyes. I thought only to keep you informed of your friend's progress. You're going to need something to occupy your mind, where you're going. Oh yes, I've plans for you. The two of you will provide me with good entertainment before the end. I'm told you have a certain distaste for enclosed spaces, a reluctance to quench lights. Who'd have thought it? The Painted Man, afraid of the dark?"

There was a brief silence.

"You disgust me," said Bran. "You're a traitor, just like your father. Did he not turn on his allies as you have done? They say he was despised and reviled on both sides of the water. No wonder Liam arranged his demise before he could do more harm. Heard that story, have you? It's a very public secret. Your own grandfather was party to it, as well as the dubious Hugh of Harrowfield. They thought to see you grow up a better man than your father. A futile hope, as it turned out. What price did you pay for the two of us, Eamonn Dubh?"

"Don't use that name." Eamonn rose and stepped toward his captive. He moved cautiously, as if constrained by some injury. There was, perhaps, a strapping around the ribs, concealed by his shirt. His hand came up and delivered a stinging blow, hard across Bran's face. I saw that Bran's hands were tightly bound, and that his ankles were hobbled together; and that for all his apparent control, this blow made him sway where he stood. "Liam is dead," Eamonn went on. "There is a new master at Sevenwaters, one who is young and untried. Their position is greatly weakened."

"Dead. How?" Bran's eyes narrowed. This, he clearly had not known.

"That need not concern you, for you will never leave here, outlaw. I will have my sport with you and the black savage you call friend, and then you will be—disposed of. You'll simply vanish without trace. Folk are saying you betrayed Sevenwaters to the Britons. Later, they will say Liam's people moved swiftly to avenge his loss and remove you permanently. Don't think to question my actions. What could a man such as yourself know of alliances and loyalties? Surely you could scarce comprehend the meaning of these terms."

"If I have no loyalties of my own," said Bran, never taking his eyes off Eamonn's face, "at least I have none to betray." He seemed to be thinking very hard indeed, as if trying to solve a puzzle.

Eamonn gave a little cough. "What has occurred is—unfortunate. But it may work to my advantage. What if my grandfather, and the Uí Néill, learned that young Sean had made a bargain with the Painted Man? What if they learned his sister had lain with an outlaw, spread her legs for him under the bushes as they camped by the wayside? The reputation of Sevenwaters might not well recover from that."

Bran held his voice level. "In time, you will regret these words. You may hold me captive now, and believe me helpless. But each foul word you speak of her brings your death a little closer."

"You are foolish if you do not understand why I paid such a high price to have you within my grasp. From the time you killed my men, I marked you for death. But once I knew it was you who had taken Liadan from me, once I knew it was your filthy hands that had touched her, I'd have paid a king's ransom. I wonder what her mother thought, hearing on her deathbed that her daughter had thrown herself away on gutter scum? Once I knew the truth, it was only a matter of time for you. I would have paid whatever it took for the satisfaction of watching you suffer and die. Feeling a little faint, are you? Your man will be in pain tonight. The touch of hot iron on a fresh wound does sting. He never cried out. Not once. Amazing fortitude."

There was no response. Bran's eyes were remote, as if he had somehow distanced himself from where he was and what he heard. Eamonn was pacing now.

"You don't like to hear me speak of Liadan, or of the child, do you? That's odd, considering the way you treated her."

"Choose your words with care."

"Huh! And you trussed up like a roasting chicken, unable to shuffle a step without falling. A man who cannot endure a moonless night without a lantern by his side; a man who fears his own dreams. Your defiance amuses me, mongrel."

"I have warned you. You tread on thin ice when you speak of her before me."

"I'll speak all I want, miscreant. This is my home, and my hall, and you are my prisoner. I'll tell you what I have long wished to tell you. You think you have some claim on the daughter of Sevenwaters because you corrupted her; because you took advantage of her innocence, and turned her against me. But she is not yours, and never has been. If she told you that, she lied to you. A woman tells the truth only when it suits her. Liadan was promised to me long since, when we were no more than children. And she's a generous girl. I knew her body, every sweet part of it, before ever you laid your ugly hands on her." He paused for effect. "Amusing, isn't it? There's really no telling if the child is yours or mine."

There was complete silence, and now Bran could no longer keep the fury from his eyes or control his ragged breathing.

"No. Oh, no," I whispered, and I caught Finbar's silent warning. *Be still, Liadan, if you would not lose this image.*

"You're lying," said Bran. His voice had lost its steadiness.

"Am I? I think you would find it difficult to prove this one way or the other. Where is your evidence?"

Bran took a deep breath and made an attempt to square

his shoulders. It seemed to me there were other bruises there that were not visible. He looked Eamonn straight in the eye.

"I need no evidence," he said quietly, his voice now under precarious control. "Liadan would not lie to me. I would trust her with my life. You cannot poison what is between us with your foul words. She is my light in the darkness, and Johnny is my pathway ahead."

Tears were streaming down my face as I watched Eamonn summoning his guards and Bran being dragged out of the hall. "Get the mongrel out of my sight." Eamonn's voice was cold. "Put him in the dark where he belongs. Let him rot there."

Then Eamonn was alone, and his face was less than calm. He poured a tankard of ale and drained it, and hurled the empty cup across the room with such violence that the metal split on the stones of the hearth. "You'll swallow those words before I'm done with you," he whispered. Darkness spread across the surface of the pool.

Breathe deeply, Liadan. I felt the comforting calm of Finbar's thoughts as he wrapped my shuddering mind in his, showing me light on water, the bright flame of oaks in autumn raiment, the torch on my mother's little curragh, a candle burning, the rays of the afternoon sun shining on the sleeping form of my small son, quiet under the willows.

Now. Better? That was very hard. What will you do?

"There's no choice," I said aloud, rubbing my wet cheeks with my sleeve. "Sean asked me to go there for Aisling. I must ride out straightaway, and when I get there, I must . . ." My mind shrank from the prospect. I could not tell Sean what I had seen. I could hear his voice now, *Such a man cannot be trusted . . . who was ideally placed to pass this information straight to the Britons?* Who would believe the word of the Painted Man over Eamonn of the Marshes? Who would accept the shadowy visions of the Sight as evidence? Sean had said, *You bear a portion of the blame for this, Liadan.* I could not tell Sean. I longed for Father to be home. He would know what to do. But Father had not returned from Harrowfield, and there had been no word, and now there was no time. I would not seek help from Conor. I knew what he would say. *That man has fulfilled his purpose. Don't waste your energy on him. The child is the key.*

"What will you do?" Finbar's clear gaze was compassionate. He did not offer any advice.

"Right now," I said, "feed the child and change him, and walk back to Sevenwaters. In the morning, I'll ride out for Sídhe Dubh and hope, when I get there, that I will know what comes next."

Finbar nodded. "I did wonder," he said, "I did wonder . . . it is a long time since I dwelt in a world of alliances and strategies and betrayals. But it did seem to me that there was something unspoken here."

"Something I might use to my advantage, if it was correct."

"Indeed. We had the same thought, then."

"It is hard to believe Eamonn capable of such treachery," I said, but in the back of my mind I saw the look in Eamonn's eyes as I refused his offer of marriage; the look of a man who sees only what he wants to see; a man who cannot bear to be defeated.

"Best tread carefully," Finbar said. "I would help more if I could. Still, you have an Otherworld messenger already." He was looking at Fiacha, where he sat perched on the low branch of a rowan, close by where Johnny now stirred among the bracken.

"I have a messenger, yes." I bent to change Johnny's damp clothing. He was awake, but quiet, for once not urgent for sustenance. It was as if the secrecy and serenity of this place had set its imprint even on his infant consciousness.

"A very powerful one. I need not ask who sent him to you."

"He came to Sevenwaters," I said, knowing that Finbar was the one person to whom it was safe to speak of this.

"Ciarán. On the night of Mother's wake. He left the bird, and he told me the truth about who he was. Uncle—"

"What's troubling you, Liadan?"

"It was a terrible thing to do, not to tell us the truth as soon as it was known that my sister and Ciarán loved one another. At least if they had done that, Niamh would have understood that Ciarán had not abandoned her without a thought. She could have held onto that in the dark times. And I might have come earlier to the understanding of the threat to my child."

"Is it Ciarán you fear, though he gave you this gift?"

"I don't know. I don't know if he is friend or foe. Ciarán said—he said his mother offered him power. That she was waiting for him to make a choice. He was very angry." I shivered. "Angry and bitter."

Finbar nodded slowly. "He's young yet. But his years of discipline must count for something. Conor would say, it will unfold as it must."

"Exactly what Ciarán said."

"Like father and son. That's the pity of it. There was good reason for our silence, Liadan, both then and earlier, when the child was brought back to the forest. None of us wished to see our half brother raised by Lady Oonagh, and turned into a weapon for our destruction. Conor sought to strengthen the boy against these influences. But the old evil is very strong. Oonagh is but one of its tools; perhaps there is a darkness within Ciarán's spirit that must always come forth, despite him, to wreak havoc among his mother's enemies. What happened was not simply chance. Each of us recognized that the thing we thought we had defeated was again alive and among us, and we doubted our strength to combat its power. Each of us felt the same terror, the awakening of a fear such as we had known but once before in our lives. To many folk, the evil thing Oonagh did to the children of Sevenwaters has become the stuff of legend, an oddity from some magical tale of long ago; yet I need but close my eyes to see her standing there before me, laughing in my face, her hair a dark flame, her eyes like poison berries, to feel myself beginning to change, to tremble with terror as my human consciousness slips away from me. I will never be the same; the path I once saw before me is shattered forever. In what happened to Niamh and to Ciarán, I saw again Lady Oonagh's cruelty and my sister's pain. The work the Sorceress wrought that day is lifelong; the fear, the guilt, the hurt of it are with us for all our days. How could one begin to share his burden with a son or daughter? How can one bear the grief of seeing it begin to blight your strong young lives? Perhaps we denied the truth, even to ourselves."

"You saw my vision; if I do not go to help him, Bran will die, and others too, and that will truly be a triumph for the powers of evil. But I'm afraid. Not for myself, but for Johnny. The Fair Folk warned me not to take him away. And there's the prophecy. Mother would not have wished me to go against that."

"You are strong. But what you attempt will be perilous, make no doubt of it."

"I don't feel strong right now." I put my son to the breast and willed my breathing slower. "I feel powerless and afraid. I fear that I will be too late."

There was a silence; then the voice of Finbar's mind, unusually tentative. *I believe I will not see you for some time, Liadan. Do not forget me. For my future is bound up with this child's. I have seen this. It's important, my dear. Don't forget. There will be many distractions.*

I won't forget. And I thank you for your help. You have a great skill in keeping these visions under control. In holding the terrors of the mind in check.

Your skill, too, is considerable. And you are learning to harness it. You are indeed a remarkable young woman. Your man spoke true when he called you a light in the darkness. Ah, now you weep again. Best shed these tears now, for after today you will have no time for weeping.

Chapter Fourteen

It would be a long ride. Once before, Sean had covered the distance in less than a day, hastening through the dark to answer my urgent call for help. But with a baby, there would be a need for stops along the way, to feed him and let him rest, and I myself would tire more quickly, bearing him on my back as I rode. A cart was unthinkable, too slow, and too hard to maneuvre and to defend on the narrow ways.

We had laid Liam to rest at dusk, under the great oaks of Sevenwaters. Discreet messages had been sent; Conor was coming, but he had been away and could not reach us in time. Padriac had moved on from Seamus Redbeard's home at Glencarnagh; perhaps he was already embarked on some new voyage to distant lands. His visits were rare; he had never wanted a part in the guardianship of lands and community. But it was sad that no brothers, no sister stood there in the fading light under the ancient trees to bid this stern chieftain farewell.

We made a fire and burned wolfbane and pine needles.

Sean spoke of our uncle's strength and courage; I of his dedication to family and túath. The people of household and settlement stood by, silent. It was a somber departure for such a great man; in time, perhaps we would be able to celebrate his life and his passing with the gathering of folk, the feasting and music he deserved. But not yet. These were dangerous times, and the news of this sudden death could not be spread indiscriminately abroad.

Afterward we took a quiet cup of ale in the kitchens around the fire. Outside, through the night air, a terrible sound rang forth, a howling of grief and abandonment that echoed the emptiness in our own hearts. This lament went on and on until my head rang with it and I could not keep back my tears. Then Sean got up and went to the door, and, looking out into the darkness, he called, "Neassa! Broc! Enough now. Inside, the pair of you!"

And after a little while, the howling ceased, and my uncle's two wolfhounds came in from the dark, their whiskery heads lowered, their tails between their legs. Sean sat down again, and the dogs went to him and settled one on his left side and one on his right. It was at that moment, I think, that my brother became lord of Sevenwaters.

Johnny and I were ready at dawn, and Sean stood on the steps to bid us farewell. I rode the strange, small horse that had once belonged to the Painted Man, and it seemed to me she showed an eagerness to be off that was more than just the anticipation of exercise and fresh air. Fiacha waited on a post nearby, his head to one side. Watching him, the horses shifted uneasily.

"I'm grateful for this, Liadan," said my brother gruffly. "Bring her back here if you can. And tell Eamonn I need to talk to him. You'll have to break the news of Liam's death. After that, he must surely see the urgent need for another council. The alliance must regroup, and swiftly. I must establish my own place, make it clear I am my own man. Ask him if he will come here and see me. But first, make sure Aisling is safe."

"I'll do what I can. Now we must go. It's a long way. Farewell, Sean. May the goddess light your path."

"Safe journey, Liadan."

A day and a night and part of the next morning it took, and every step of the way I was willing the pace to be faster, and gritting my teeth every time my son woke and wailed and we must stop yet again to tend to his needs. I bit back words of frustration as my men at arms told me Lord Sean had insisted we stop to sleep, for a while at least, and that they prepare me a proper meal. A lady could not be expected to travel rough, as a warrior might. So they set up a small shelter for me and the child, and stood guard while I lay there, open-eyed in the night, watching small clouds cross the face of the waning moon. And on the morning of the second day we rode across the causeway to Sídhe Dubh, with Fiacha flying dark-winged above us.

We had passed the outer guard posts with no great difficulty. The men there knew me and recognized my men at arms, who wore the white tunic of Sevenwaters with its symbol of interlinked torcs. They let us through with no more than a raised eyebrow as Fiacha circled, squawking. Nor were we turned back at the entry to the causeway. But one of the guards shook his head doubtfully and said, "You'll not be given admittance. He's letting nobody in, and he'll make no exceptions, not even for a lady." There was something in his tone that suggested he was not entirely comfortable with the situation. But clearly they had their orders.

So we crossed to the inner gate, the entrance to the long, curving underground way that led up to the courtyard with its high, encircling walls. As before, there were two very large guards with axes in their hands and two massive black dogs, growling.

"Identify yourselves!"

The guards stepped forward, and the dogs pulled their chains taut.

"The Lady Liadan of Sevenwaters, come to see the daughter of the house," said the leader of my escort. "We are all of that household, and I am amazed that you fail to recognize us, Garbhan, it being less than a season since last we shared a jug of ale in this very hall. Open your gates for us. The lady has come a long way and is weary."

"There's no admittance. And no exceptions."

"I'm not sure you understand." My man's voice was confident; his hand hovered by his sword hilt. "The lady is come to visit her friend. She has a small child with her, as you see. This is the sister of Sean of Sevenwaters. If there is any doubt, please send word to the Lady Aisling. I am certain she will welcome our party."

"There are no exceptions. Lord Eamonn's orders. Now take yourselves off before I loose the dogs."

The dogs appeared all too keen to be loosed, as Fiacha began to swoop down toward them, just beyond reach of their snapping jaws, and fly upward again to repeat the maneuvre, accompanied by derisive croaks of challenge. Johnny awoke and began to cry.

I edged my little horse forward. "Leave this to me," I told my men. I attempted the sort of tone Liam might have employed. "Fetch Lord Eamonn," I said. "He will see me. Tell him Liadan is here and must speak with him. Tell him I have information for him and that it's important and that I will not take no for an answer."

"I don't rightly know, my lady. Lord Eamonn's not to be disturbed, and he did say, no exceptions."

Fiacha flew past, so near to the man's face that the lethal beak came close to taking an eye out.

"Tell him."

"Yes, my lady."

We waited. Eamonn did not come down, but after a while the guard returned and the chain was unfastened and the

gates unlocked, and we rode past the slavering dogs and up
the long, curving way to the courtyard. There were many,
many guards all the way up. Enough guards, I thought
grimly, to secure the most difficult of prisoners. In my heart,
I knew Bran must be here somewhere. He must be still alive
and able to attempt an escape, or why maintain such a presence of armed men? When we emerged into the light, the
courtyard was bristling with them, and outside the entrance
to the house was Eamonn, looking stern and distant. He
stepped over to help me dismount. Johnny was wailing, and
the bird added his own distinctive voice to the din.

"Liadan," frowned Eamonn, "what are you doing here?"

"What sort of welcome is that for a friend?" I asked him.
"We are weary, and I must tend to the child."

"Why have you come here?"

My men at arms had dismounted, and were listening.

"I have news for you, Eamonn. Very important news,
which must be passed on in private. And I need to see Aisling. Perhaps you might provide my men with some ale,
and me with a quiet place to do what is needed for the child.
Then, when it is convenient, I'd like to speak with you
alone."

As he turned to give orders and to clear the small crowd
that had gathered, I saw that he did indeed move somewhat
warily, like a man not quite recovered from a serious injury,
such as a knife thrust. A serving woman came to usher me
indoors and find me a quiet corner to change and feed my
son. Food and drink were brought on a tray. There was no
sign of Aisling, and I did not ask.

Time passed. Johnny had his meal, and was quiet, and
the sun moved overhead outside the narrow windows. The
serving woman returned with two others, clucking and ad-
miring the child and offering to take him for a while, so I
could rest.

"I'd like to see Aisling," I said. "Is she here?"

"My lady's not well. I shouldn't think she'll see anyone,"

said the oldest of the women, who was holding Johnny in her arms.

"Maybe I could help," I ventured. "I have skills in healing. What seems to be the trouble?"

"Best ask Lord Eamonn."

"But—"

"Best ask him."

Reluctantly, I let them bear Johnny away to the kitchens, for he seemed content in their company, and I was indeed weary and at something of a loss. Fiacha flew after them, much to the women's alarm. With such a guard, I reasoned my son would be safe enough for now. I looked out of the window, down into the courtyard, straining for a sight of anything unusual, anything to suggest there were indeed some very special prisoners in this fortress. But apart from the presence of so many armed men, all seemed quite unremarkable.

At last Eamonn sent for me. He was in the hall, seated on his oak chair, and once the servant was dismissed, we were alone.

"Well, Liadan, please take a seat. A cup of wine, perhaps? This comes all the way from Armorica. It's rather fine. I did not expect such a visit. This is not a good time."

"Such news has no good time. My Uncle Liam is dead, slain by the Britons on the way to his meeting with the Uí Néill. Someone betrayed us, and the alliance is much weakened. Sean bid me bring you these tidings myself, and ask if I might take Aisling back with me, for he needs her support. And he wants to speak with you urgently."

"I see." His look of shocked concern seemed entirely genuine. "This is grave indeed. When did this happen?"

"A few days ago. Sean wants it kept quiet, for obvious reasons. We sent word to your grandfather, and I have come to tell you. Beyond that, it is not known. But once Northwoods chooses to make his coup public, then the enemies of the alliance may seek to move against us."

He raised his brows. "I did not think you so knowledge-able in strategies and dealings, Liadan."

"I'm learning fast," I said.

"Aisling cannot go to Sevenwaters. She is—indisposed."

"May I see her? If she is ill, I can help."

"Not this time. I'm afraid you will not be able to see her, and she most certainly cannot travel."

"Then she must be gravely ill. I'm a healer, Eamonn. You should let me tend to her. Aisling is my friend, and my brother's betrothed. You should let me help her, if I can."

"You will not remain here long enough to help. I can have no guests in the house. Aisling will recover well enough without your assistance. She has simply been—ob-stinate—and has made herself ill. You cannot see her."

I did not reply. The conversation was like some sort of game. A small risk here; a small gain there. It was hard to make strategic moves when one did not know the rules.

"Tell Sean that Aisling is unable to make the journey," he said. "Convey my sympathy to him for his loss." He rose as if to leave, and there was another awkward silence. "You will need a night's rest, I suppose, before riding home. I am surprised you brought your child with you all this way, Li-adan. Still, he appears to have weathered it well enough."

"You'll find that gutter scum have a surprising inner strength," I said quietly. "A capacity for endurance beyond the ordinary."

He took a moment to react. "What did you say?"

"I'm here to trade with you, Eamonn. I have come to buy your prisoners."

I had thought him pale, but this turned his face white as a dead man's mask.

"I—see," he said carefully. "Does your brother know of this escapade?"

"Sean is not aware of my intentions," I said, my heart be-ginning to thump. "But he knows I am here, and expects me home promptly, with or without Aisling."

"And just exactly what prisoners did you have in mind?"

"There's no need to play games with me, Eamonn. I mean the Painted Man, and another of his band whom you hold captive. I am here to deal with you for their release into my hands and our safe passage out of Sídhe Dubh."

"Deal? How, deal?"

"A bargain. I'm sure you have made many before."

He rose and began to pace to and fro, to and fro.

"You amaze me, Liadan. Even after what has happened, even after all that has passed between us, I still believed you capable of some sound judgment. That man is evil, a scourge. He should never be let loose again. And he will not be. Now tell me," and he stopped right before me and put his hands on my shoulders, and I breathed deep, willing myself not to flinch away, "how could you know he was here? How could you discover such a thing? Nobody knew."

"At least you do not pretend that he is not your captive. I suppose your sense of pride prevents that. The source of my information is confidential. But at least one other of the family of Sevenwaters knows what I know and will reveal it if harm comes to me."

"Harm? Why should I harm you? You are no threat to me and besides—no, let me avoid sentimentality. I'll put it to you plainly, Liadan. Nobody cares if this man lives or dies. You could tell the world I held him prisoner, tortured and beat him, intended to execute him. There's not a single soul would raise a finger to help him. He is an outcast, beyond hope."

"You're wrong," I said softly. "You are so wrong. Such a man can command great loyalty, as you will discover to your cost."

"Huh! The loyalty of other wretches like himself, and misguided girls who find a perverse excitement in the arms of a monster of depravity. I cannot believe you gave yourself to him when you could have—"

"When I could have had you? I'm sorry you cannot believe that, Eamonn, for it has filled your whole mind with bitterness until you cannot rightly see what you are doing, or why. This hatred is eating you up, so that you injure your family and friends, and set a dark curse on your own future. It is not too late for you to retreat. Not quite."

"If you had accepted me, my path would have been different," he said bleakly. "If you find you dislike what I have become, you have only yourself to blame."

"Your actions are your own," I said, holding back my anger. "Your choices are your own. Each of us carries a burden of guilt for decisions made or not made." I saw a little image of my Uncle Liam, lying on the track with an arrow in his chest. "You can let that rule your whole life, or you can put it behind you and move on. Only a madman lets jealousy determine the course of his existence. Only a weak man blames others for his own errors. Now, will you deal with me?"

"I cannot imagine what you think you can offer me," he said stiffly. "But I suppose a woman always has one service she can provide for a man. And there was a time, not long ago, when I might have paid much to possess your body. I would have paid with my pride, and my reputation, and everything I own. But not now. Not now that I have him in my grasp. Watching him suffer is worth infinitely more to me than a night in your bed. Though it would be interesting doing it just to make him squirm. Unfortunately, he's past that now."

"What do you mean?" I could not prevent my voice from shaking, and I thought he was aware of my alarm.

"Did you know your outlaw hero is afraid of the dark? Did you know he turns to jelly if he's shut in too long? I found that out. It took me a lot of digging to discover it. He keeps his secrets well. You'll find him not quite as you left him, I fear. As for the other one, he's looking quite untidy."

Breathe, Liadan. "I think you misunderstand what I mean when I say bargain," I told him, taking a sip of my wine, just so my hands had something to do, to still their shaking. "It is not so much a matter of what I can offer in return for their freedom. It is more a case of what you are prepared to give in order to buy my silence."

"Silence? What silence? What do you mean?"

"I have information that could be very damaging to you, Eamonn. Information that, should it reach the ears of my brother, or of Seamus, would cut you from the alliance and cause you to be looking over your shoulder for a man with a knife for the rest of your days. Information that, should it become known to the Uí Néill, would ensure you never sat at a council table with them again. And your lands are awkwardly placed. Right in the path of traffic out of Tirconnell. You should listen to me."

"I don't believe what I'm hearing." He sat down again, staring at me. "How could you possibly have any information that your brother does not already know? A girl, at home with a child, shut away in the heart of the forest? This is nothing but a bluff."

"A bluff. All right, let's try some detail. And do not forget, the band of the Painted Man is privy to many secrets and has an ear in many camps. My sources of news may be different from Sean's, but they are every bit as accurate."

"Go on," he said in a frozen voice. At that point, a man entered with a tray on which he bore another flask of wine and a platter with bread and cheese and sliced meats. He set this on a table, and Eamonn dismissed him with a jerk of the head. When the man was gone, he went to the door and slid the bolts closed.

"All right," he said. "What information?"

The sun slanted in the windows. It was past midday; two whole days since I had seen that vision of Bran being dragged from this hall, since I had heard Eamonn saying, *Put the mongrel in the dark.* Now was the moment when I must hazard all on a guess, must hope that Finbar and I had stumbled on the truth.

"I know the price you paid Northwoods," I said with hard-won steadiness. "I know it was the information you gave our enemy that caused my uncle's death. You betrayed the alliance, Eamonn. You sacrificed Liam for the sake of your own twisted desire for vengeance, because of jealous rage. And I will tell Sean, and Seamus, unless you give me what I want."

"This is outrageous!" His voice shook with shocked fury. "You can have no proof of this. I cannot imagine how you might have concocted such a tale, or who would believe you if you told it."

"I have proof. A witness of great credibility, who knows the exact purpose of my visit here. If you refuse me, your secret will soon be known, whether I return home safely or not. You'll be finished, Eamonn."

He was silent for a while. "What guarantee can you give me that this information will not become public, even if I agree to your ridiculous request?" he asked, and a small flame of hope began to burn inside me. "You might get what you want and still tell. What undertaking can you give that others will remain silent?"

"You know me better than that," I said. "Once, not so long ago, you told me I was the only woman you would ever take for your wife, or words to that effect. I think you meant it at the time. Now, I see you have lost any respect you ever had for me. But once we were friends. If I give you my word, I'll keep it. I will ensure the silence of others. But I will not put my brother at risk. I will remain silent only as long as you honor our agreement."

"I can't believe this. It is as if you have turned into some—some monster, like the man you protect. You'd better tell me your terms."

Ah, no, I thought. *It is you who are become a monster; a man who will betray, and torture, and murder, for no reason more than jealous obsession. You, whom I might once have wed.* "Very well," I said. "You will respect the alliance. You will honor your commitment to my brother in future and be honest with him and share your defenses as you did with Liam."

"And?"

"That's the long-term agreement. The instant you break it, I tell them."

"And what about the short-term?"

"First, you fetch Aisling here. My men at arms will take her back to Sevenwaters, now, this afternoon. She will remain there until spring, until she and Sean are married. She will not return here. You will attend the wedding, and smile, and give them your blessing."

"Aisling is unwell. She cannot travel."

"I'll be the judge of that. I think she will go. My men know how to convey a lady across country and look after her."

"You speak as if you do not intend to accompany her. What is the rest of this demonic bargain, Liadan?"

"I will remain here until Aisling is safely away from Sídhe Dubh. It should not take long. Then you will release these two prisoners. You will provide the three of us, and my son, with safe conduct to your borders."

He gave a hollow laugh. "You must indeed think me weak."

"I think you have enough common sense left to know when you are backed into a corner," I said carefully. "Will you do as I ask?"

"You give me very little choice. But I am not entirely without pride, though you seek to humiliate me at every turn. I will let Aisling go. I would be a fool not to agree or to refuse the first part of the bargain. I wonder if you will tire of watching me, year by year, to see if I stumble? That could grow tedious."

"I am the daughter of Sevenwaters. My brother deserves my loyalty and my support, and he will have them. Our family understands the importance of this, if yours does not."

"You should perhaps restrain your tongue. I have not yet agreed to the other part of this bargain."

"The deal is all or nothing. If you will not release the prisoners, I will make no agreement."

"I need time."

"You cannot have time. If I wished to do so, I could give my brother this news right now, while you watched. I could open my mind to his, and I could tell him. If you tried to harm me, he would know immediately. I would not hesitate."

"A pox on you, Liadan! Curse you and your sorceress's ways!"

"Will you release these men?" It was becoming harder and harder to keep control.

"Very well," he said suddenly. "Take your wretched lover and his bizarre companion. See what use they are to you after their brief but eventful sojourn in my custody. But there can be no safe conduct. There's not a man in my garrison, nor anywhere in my lands, who would convey the Painted Man to the border without sticking a knife in his back. Once outside these walls, you're on your own."

"You're saying you will let us go, so that your archers may shoot us down before we set foot on the road? That won't do. I need better than that. Do you want me to talk to my brother? Shall I call to him?"

"No. We'll play a little game, I think. When Aisling is gone, if she is able to go, I'll set you a task of hide and seek. First you find your outlaw. Then you get him out. We'll help with that, or you'll be all night at it. There'll be no 'foot on the road.' Let him go out the way he once came in, over the marshes. Don't they say no mission is beyond him? That should be easy, then. Across the hidden way, with a woman and a small child, and a man without the full use of his hands. Simple, I should think. You'll see what sort of a hero he is then. We might perhaps set you a time to achieve this. You'll need to be gone by dusk, I think. After that, we'll come down with torches and start shooting again. My men don't get much excitement these days."

"That is—evil," I whispered, staring at him. Was this the

man with whom I had once danced at Imbolc, a man I had once considered a good choice for a husband, if I had been able to teach him to smile? Was it indeed I who had changed him so completely, simply by saying no? My heart was cold. "Is not this bargain on my terms?"

"Not quite. You might decide to tell your secret now, to try to convince your brother of what you know, at a distance. You might do it, and destroy my life. But as soon as you took that step, the Painted Man would die. You would not save him that way. And your brother cares nothing for the outlaw. He is merely another piece on the board to be won or lost."

I ran my tongue over lips suddenly parched. "Very well. We have reached agreement. Now send for Aisling."

"You will not speak to my sister of this. That much must be understood."

"It's understood, Eamonn. Now send for her, and for my men at arms."

Aisling looked sick and wretched. Her small, freckled face was ashen white, and I could see the bones beneath the skin. Her eyes were purple and swollen, and her curling red hair unkempt.

"Liadan," she whispered, heedless of her brother's grim looks and of the six men at arms waiting in the hall. "Oh, Liadan, you came! Where's Sean?"

"Waiting for you at Sevenwaters," I said calmly, though I could have wept to see the state my friend was in. "Your brother has given you permission to go. These men will see you safely there. I've asked the women to pack you a little bag, and your horse is ready. You'll leave right away."

"Oh, Liadan, thank you. Oh, thank you, Eamonn!"

It was just as well, I thought, that she was at such an extreme of distress and exhaustion that it did not occur to her to ask any questions. No doubt they would come to her later when she was already on her way.

"My lady—" The leader of my guards was frowning with concern.

"These are your orders," I told him firmly. "Leave now, straightaway. Make your way back to Sevenwaters as quickly as you can; but remember the Lady Aisling has been ill, and will need to rest, as I did. Tell my brother I will come later."

"Our orders were to guard you." He sounded doubtful. "If we depart, you have no safe conduct."

"Lord Eamonn can provide what protection I need," I said. "I will remain here awhile longer. Tell my brother Lord Eamonn will be in touch. Now go, and you should be there by dusk tomorrow."

"Very well, my lady."

I climbed the steps to the place where the sentries paced. I looked out over the causeway and the long, straight track that was the only safe way out of Sídhe Dubh. I stood there watching until Aisling's auburn hair and the leather helms of the men at arms had vanished into the distance. Then I went to the kitchens and reclaimed my son and fed him. I bound him to my back again, ready for travel. Out in the courtyard, Eamonn was waiting.

"I thought I'd watch this game," he said. "But I find I haven't the stomach for it. Don't worry, my guards have instructions to let you wander about. If you need keys, or a strong man to loosen a bolt or two, just ask and they'll help you. But you enjoy this kind of thing, don't you, Liadan? I'm told you prowled about the place like a little cat in heat last time you were here. Off you go, then. There's not so long till dusk after all. Oh, and do something about that bird of yours, will you? If it swoops down on my guards just one more time, its next appearance will be on the supper table, neatly enclosed in piecrust."

We had walked across the courtyard as he spoke, and Fiacha flew over our heads to alight on the shafts of an empty cart that stood there.

"Off you go then," Eamonn repeated, as if dismissing a troublesome child.

I had no doubt where this search must be undertaken, and I feared what it might reveal. I made a rapid decision and looked direct into Fiacha's bright, knowing eye. *Go*, I told him. *Fetch help. Go now. I need help before dusk.*

He was gone, swift as an arrow from the bow, a dark streak soaring into the sky and away southward, ever southward. Then I picked up my skirts and walked down into the underground way, forward into the shadows.

It was difficult for the guards, I think. They had their orders, and they would obey them. Still they glanced at one another and muttered among themselves as I searched their underground domain, through one dark cell after another, gritting my teeth to keep back the tears, trying to still my drumming heart and quiet my breathing as I blundered into empty room after empty room.

"Where are they?" I demanded. "Tell me!" But they shuffled their boots and kept their mouths shut. The Painted Man could expect nothing from Eamonn's folk, save fear and loathing.

Behind the small cells I already knew of, there was an iron-bolted door. I asked for assistance, and a big, gray-haired man with muscles like heavy knotted cords came forward to open it for me. There were rough steps leading downward.

"I need a lantern." Johnny was wriggling on my back, now tired of the restriction to his movements. Having so recently learned to get about on his own, he was eager for fresh explorations and new adventures. I would not think of Johnny and the path across the swamp. I would think only of what came next, right now.

"Lord Eamonn said nothing about lanterns."

"I need a light. It's pitch-black down there. I could fall and break the child's neck. Would you take that story back to your wife tonight?"

Nobody moved. Grimly, I gathered my skirts and went forward down the steps. One. Two. It was so dark I could not see my hand before my face.

"Here, my lady."

Light flickered on the stone walls. The gray-haired guard was on the step behind me, a small lantern in his hand. I reached out for it.

"I'll bear it for you. You take care for the child. These steps are old and uneven."

There were ten steps, and a narrow passageway deep under the earth. It was very quiet. If rats or beetles made their home in this buried place, there was no sign of it. The dim light revealed iron rings, bolted to the cobweb-shrouded walls. At the end of the passage, another door, more of a grille, fastened with a loop of heavy chain. The place was airless, stifling.

"My lady." The guard spoke under his breath, awkwardly. "These men are outlaws, scarce worth the trouble of tossing on the midden. You should leave this, and save yourself and the child. You'll never get away across the marshes. Try it and you're as good as dead, and your babe with you. Give it up. We'd see you got home safe. None of us wants this on his conscience."

"Give me the key," I said. He put it into my hand without another word.

Beyond the grilled door was another small space, and there I found Gull. I heard his breathing just before the light revealed his dark features, now a sickly gray, his staring eyes bright with fever, his clothing ripped and stained. His wrists were locked in iron shackles above his head, so that he could not move from where he was held, sagging, against his restraints. Filthy, bloodstained rags were roughly wrapped around his hands.

I moved forward, clenching my teeth.

"Unfasten this man's hands and be quick about it!"

"Liadan," Gull croaked, as the guard reached up to the

shackles. Then he sucked in his breath as his wrists were suddenly released, and his arms fell by his sides as if there were no life left in them.

"You'll be in a lot of pain while the feeling comes back," I said, as he sank to the floor with a wheeze of agony. "But there's no time. We must get out of here. Where's Bran? Where's the chief?"

Gull moved his head from side to side, weakly, to indicate he did not know.

"You must know! Somebody must know! We have only until dusk to get away from here!"

"Can . . . walk. Can . . . go." Gull struggled to all fours, then to his knees, then stood up, swaying. "Ready . . . to go."

"That's good, Gull. That's very good. See if you can put your arm around my shoulders—watch out for the boy— that's it. I'll help you." I turned to the guard. "Tell me where he is. Please tell me. Would you see all of us die before the sun sets?"

But the man was silent, his eyes chill as he watched Gull's staggering, shivering efforts to walk. The air was thick and close around us, and each breath was a struggle. Johnny whimpered. If we left now, there would still be some daylight left. If we left now, there would be a chance to be out of sight before dusk. I might search and search until it was indeed too late and still not find him. *Put the mongrel back in the dark where he belongs.*

"Best to go back up," muttered the guard.

"Not yet," I said. "Stand still. Keep quiet." For it was there, a small cry in the darkness, a feeling of dread, a summoning of will to endure what was beyond endurance. *Where are you?* I could not tell if it was my own imagination that conjured it or if I truly heard the cry of that lost child who had haunted my thoughts since first I began to learn the truth about the Painted Man.

The voice of my mind whispered into the darkness. *I'm here. Stretch up your hand.*

Silence. Helpless, shivering silence.

Reach out your hand to me, Johnny. I will help you. Show me where you are. It was not my son to whom I spoke, my son now blessedly silent, held warm and safe against me. Gull leaned on my shoulder, and I felt the trembling control he exercised over his damaged body to remain upright, to quiet his breathing so that I could listen. *Where are you? Give me your hand. Reach up just a little farther.*

There was no sound, not that I could hear. Not in the outer world, nor in the shadowy realm of the mind. But I knew. Suddenly, I knew. I walked out through the grilled door, with Gull stumbling beside me, and the guard following with the lantern and a scowl on his face. Halfway along the dim subterranean passage, I halted.

You could hardly see it. It was very neatly fashioned, flush with the floor, the only signs of its existence the faint line around the edges, and a small depression in the stone where the trapdoor might be lifted. Eamonn's ancestor had indeed possessed an unusual and inventive mind.

"Open this trapdoor."

"It's not a job for a man on his own."

"Open it, curse you! Fetch another man if you need one. And hurry!"

They were slow, painfully slow, as I waited, shivering. *Hold on,* I told him. *I'm here. Not long now.*

The trapdoor was heavy, a solid slab of rock a handspan thick. The mechanism seemed finely tuned and expertly maintained. But it took all the strength of the two guards to lift it. At last it stood open.

"Give me the lantern," I said, and they put it into my hand. I placed it on the edge of the rectangular opening in the floor and looked in.

It was a small enough space. Just big enough to take a man who was not particularly tall, if his knees were doubled up to his chin, and his arms bent over his head. Air could get in, but not much. There would be no light. No space to move. A tomb, in which a man might stay alive for a time. How long would depend on what strength he could find deep inside himself. If you took him out occasionally, and fed him, and let him breathe before you put him back in, he might survive to entertain you for quite some time.

"Bran?" I was foolish indeed if I expected an answer. He appeared dead, his features ghastly pale, his curled-up form devoid of any movement. "Get this man out. Quickly."

They did, for their orders were to help me, up to a certain point. But nobody had ordered them to be gentle, and by the time the limp figure had been dragged from the tiny hole where they had stowed him and deposited at my feet, still curled around himself, he bore a few more bruises than before. I knelt by him, and Gull, stifling a curse, squatted beside me.

"He's alive," I said, my fingers feeling the place at the base of the neck, where the blood flowed weakly, my ear catching his faint breathing, so slow, so slow. The lantern cast little light, but I could see the bruising was extensive, and blood was encrusted on his head, where a new, soft growth of brown hair crept over the bold markings of the skin.

"Blow to the head," muttered Gull. "Deep. Hard. Came close . . . finish him. What now?"

"We get out of here," I said firmly, while my tears banked up behind my eyes and my inner voice chanted over and over, *Breathe, Liadan. Be strong. Be strong.* "Then we'll see." I turned to the guards. "Pick this man up and carry him. And don't hurt him. You've done enough damage. Take us outside."

"Damage? No such thing as enough damage for the likes of him," growled the second guard, and they were less than careful as they hoisted Bran's helpless form from the ground and bore him away up the steps, leaving us to follow as best we could. I supported Gull and carried the lantern, and at length we emerged again into the underground way, where the torches burned bright, so bright they hurt my eyes, and Gull shielded his face with one damaged hand, while silent men stood watching our halting progress.

"Our orders are to take you down to the edge and leave you."

"You'd better do it then," I told them.

Bran's body was as limp as a sack of grain, suspended between the guard who held his shoulders and the one who supported his knees. His head lolled to one side. There were bruises on bruises; no part of him seemed undamaged. What was left of his clothing was stiff with blood and filth. More entertained now there were lights and voices, Johnny babbled away cheerfully.

"Come on," I said to Gull. "Down here. You know where. Then we're on our own."

"Own," he echoed, and I wondered how much he had understood between the fever and the agony of his tortured hands. He had lost fingers from both, I could see that; how many were left, the bandages concealed. "Across," he said. "Other side."

As we stumbled down the underground way and out past the growling dogs and were led around the hill on a narrow track not far above the water's edge, I made myself consider the possibilities. If Bran came to himself and could walk . . . if Gull could find the path, and the fever did not cloud his judgment . . . if Johnny kept still and quiet, and did not distract us . . . if help came before dark, then maybe we would live and not be shot down like fugitives escaping justice. If . . . there were altogether too many ifs. It came to me as we halted on the northern side of the hill, with the sun already low in the sky and the daylight beginning to fade, that this was the reality of Bran's life and Gull's, that their whole existence was made up of moments like this, when the odds appeared impossible, and one must indeed be the best, must find solutions to the most difficult problems, and discover inside oneself a strength almost Otherworldly, in order merely to survive.

"Sure about this?" They had dropped Bran unceremoniously at my feet again, and now the big guard took a step back, speaking quietly. High above on the fortress wall, men were gathered, watching. "Not too late, even now. Leave these carrion and make your way home with your little lad."

"You'd better go." I knelt and took Bran's head on my lap. "Lord Eamonn will want to hear your report, no doubt."

"At least save the child. You can't survive such a crossing. That mongrel's near dead, and the other can't rightly walk a straight line. Try that path, and you're all gone. You could leave the boy behind. There are folks here would care for him and see him safe home."

Something flashed into my memory: my Uncle Finbar's voice, long ago, saying to me, *The child is yours. And you want the man as well . . . has it occurred to you that perhaps you cannot have both?*

"We walk this way together," I said, almost to myself, my hand moving gently over Bran's shaven skull, where the new growth of curling hair softened the fierce, ravenlike pattern. "All of us together."

The guard said no more; and soon Eamonn's men had withdrawn within the fortress walls, save for two guards with a dog, who patrolled nearby. We were left there by the edge of the dark, quaking bog: Bran sprawled helpless on the stones, I seated by him with the child still on my back, and Gull standing, staring out across the wide expanse of marshland to the distant hills in the north. He was swaying slightly.

"Snake," he muttered. "Otter. Others. Other side."

"You think they'll be there if we can get across?"

"Others. Get across." He staggered from one foot to the other and sat down suddenly. "Head. Sorry. Hands."

"I would tend to them if I could. When we get there—when we reach a place of safety, I'll be able to relieve the pain quite well for you, and give you an infusion to bring down the fever. I sent for help, but I cannot be sure that help will come, Gull. Do you understand?"

"Understand," he echoed faintly.

"We have only until dusk to get away. As soon as the sun sinks, Eamonn's archers will begin to shoot, and they will come down with torches. We have only one pathway to follow. If Bran—if the chief does not come to himself in time, I don't know what we will do."

At that moment Johnny decided to make his presence known, and there was no choice but to unfasten his bindings and open my dress to feed him. It seemed Gull was not entirely dazed by his fever, for he moved quickly enough to support Bran's head and shoulders with his knees, while I busied myself with the child. And finally, with Johnny at the breast, and the light fading to the delicate shade of fresh lavender blooms all around us, and no sound but the harsh cry of herons out on the boglands; with Bran lying still and distant as some carven warrior on a tomb, I found I could no longer hold back my tears. What had I done? Why had I thought I could ignore the warnings of the Fair Folk themselves? I had believed, somehow, that I could save these men, could make a future for them, and for myself. Now it seemed we would all perish, and Johnny as well. Him I might have protected, but for my wretched pride.

"Dying," Gull observed bleakly. "Blow to the head. Won't wake. He'd call for the knife, if he could."

"Well, he can't," I snapped, my tears forgotten. "It's not his decision. He cannot die. I won't allow it."

The small shadow of a chuckle. "Broke the code, the two of you. Wait till I tell Snake . . ." His words trailed off in a gasp of pain.

"Gull, we're going to have to try this."

"Understand. Walk. Carry. I'm strong enough."

"I don't doubt it. And you know the way, for you led my sister across once. But you are hurt and exhausted, and he will not be able to help you."

"Strong enough. Carry."

"Then we must go now, as soon as the child is fed. Dusk

is approaching fast, and it seems no help can reach us in time."

Gull gave a sort of grunt and rolled Bran onto his side. "Ready," he said. "You'll need to help. Hands, no good. Not now." For it is indeed not possible to grasp a man's arm or a fold of his clothing and hoist him onto your back when your hands are as badly damaged as Gull's were. The slightest touch made him wince with pain.

Step by step. That was the only way to do it. Take it in very small stages, and try not to think too far ahead, for to do that would make the heart fail and the last vestiges of courage die. Put Johnny in his binding and fasten him on my back, as tightly as I could. He was quiet for now. Then, bend to lift Bran's shoulders from the ground; try to help Gull to get his own shoulder underneath and lever the helpless man up. Gull's hands were quite useless. He could bend an arm around, and shove with his knees, but he could neither hold nor grip. I bit back my words. *How can you carry him? What if he slips?* Between us, we dropped him three times before, laboriously, Gull got to his knees, and then precariously to his feet, with his friend balanced across his shoulders, head on the left, legs on the right, arms dangling. Gull held his own arms hooked up behind, the mangled hands pointing stiffly skyward in their bloody wrappings. From the battlements above, there was a scatter of derisive applause.

"That's good," I said encouragingly. "That's really good, Gull. We need to go now."

Many birds were calling now, out over the wilderness; flocking to roost in whatever desolate corner of this inhospitable country they called their home. The setting sun turned the pools of open water as red as blood.

"Go now," said Gull, and we looked at each other and looked away. I saw the truth in his fever-brightened eyes. This way was death.

"I think we might share a flask of very strong drink on

the other side," I said. My words were confident; it was the tremor in my voice that gave me away.

Then Gull stepped out onto the surface of the bog, very carefully, his bare feet moving from one clump of grass to the next, right, then right again, then left. And I followed in his wake, my skirts tucked up into my belt, the child still mercifully silent. I felt cold sweat break out all over my body; I heard the quick, uneven sound of my own breathing, sensed the thudding of my heart. One step; another. We moved forward slowly; so slowly I did not dare to look behind to gauge the distance an archer might shoot with accuracy to find his target by torchlight. And then we came to a place where the clumps of vegetation were farther apart, a stride for a man, or for a long-legged woman like my sister Niamh. For me, a jump. I hesitated, as Gull moved on ahead. I could not say, *Wait,* lest I startle him and he lose his footing. *Quick, Liadan,* I told myself, *or he'll be out of sight and then* . . . I jumped, landing awkwardly, my boot sliding on the wet foliage. I put my arms out for balance and, teetering, regained my footing. Around me in the dark brown of the marsh mud, there were little sucking and plopping sounds, hungry sounds. Gull's progress was steady enough, though still very slow. A step; a pause; another step. He was bent well forward under Bran's dead weight; it must be difficult for him to see the way.

"Liadan?" His voice came back to me, strangely disembodied in the emptiness.

"I'm here."

"Nearly dark."

"I know." Later, if the clouds held back, there would be a little light. But this would be a waning moon, too faint, and too late. "We must go on as best we can."

He made no reply, but moved forward again, and I could see how his bare feet balanced on the unpredictable surface, the toes curling, the foot adjusting the set of the body's weight. I could see how, even with his hands mangled and helpless, he still kept a careful control of the burden he bore, bending to left or to right, forward or more upright, to maintain a secure stance. After dark, he would no longer be able to find the way. Then it would hardly matter what strength he had, or what skills he employed.

As the light faded, I began to feel short, sharp stabs on my hands, and on my ankles, and on my face and neck. There was a little high-pitched droning sound that came and went. Swarms of biting insects were arising from the swampy land, no doubt overjoyed to discover a large and juicy meal. Johnny began suddenly to cry, a sharp wailing of distress. There was nothing I could do to help him, and his small, panicky voice rang out unanswered over the marshes. And in the distance, I thought I heard another cry, hollow, unearthly, halfway between a scream and a song. Perhaps this voice foretold another death, as a young man at arms had once said. I told myself not to be foolish. But the sound was still there, ringing in my head, vibrating in the sickly swamp air, howling in the purple light of the dusk all around me. The wail of the banshee. Johnny was screaming in protest now. It was the first time in his short life he had cried out, and nobody had come straight away to help him with whatever he needed: dry clothes, sheltering arms, kind words, a lotion of wormwood and chamomile to take away the small, buzzing creatures that were hurting him and hurting him and would not stop.

"It's all right, Johnny," I muttered as I wobbled for balance on a ridiculously small patch of dry ground. Surely Gull didn't expect me to jump across to *there?* It was too far; it wasn't fair. I could not leap so far, not with the child on my back. If only Johnny would stop crying; if he would just stop . . . I peered ahead in the half light. On the other side of the wide, unbroken expanse of black mud, Gull had stopped walking. He was standing very still, and I sensed that he had his eyes closed. He was saying something, but I could not hear the words. It was too far. I would land in the mud halfway across, and the swamp would swallow me and my child, and it would be over. My throat was dry, my body clammy with sweat. My head throbbed. *I can't do it . . . I can't . . .* Then Gull spoke again, and I heard him. "Liadan? Still there?"

"I'm here. But I don't think I can . . ."

"Need help. Hands. Can't hold."

Dana give me strength. He must not let go; he must not. Surely we had not come so far for nothing.

"I'm coming," I called, and jumped, willing my body across the impossible space. I landed a little short of the larger islet of dry ground where Gull stood, my feet sinking down into soft mud, my body sprawling forward on the grassy ground. I gripped the foliage hard as I felt the voracious clutch of the bog around my legs, tugging me down. Johnny was sobbing in shuddering gasps, telling me his small tale of woe, that the world was suddenly different, and that he wanted me to make it better, right now please. My face screwed up with effort as my hands grasped and clawed on the wet leaves, and then, with a decidedly unpleasant sound, the clinging mud released me. I crawled away from the edge and got to my feet beside Gull. The light was almost gone; I could barely see his face before me.

"Put your hands up," he whispered, and his voice betrayed the pain I could no longer read on his features in the darkness. "Take the weight for me. Not long. Rest. Hands."

I stood behind him and reached up to put my own hands against Bran's limp form. Then Gull attempted to unhook his arms from where they were bent up to hold his friend secure on his shoulders, but the cramp was so bad, he was hard put to move them at all. Still stoical, he bit back a scream of pain as he brought his bandaged hands slowly down. Now that we were standing still, Johnny seemed to anticipate a swift response to his protest, and his voice grew louder and more insistent.

Gull staggered sideways and regained his footing. All I could do to help him was make sure Bran did not fall from where he lay balanced; we would never get him up again, for one error on this small, safe patch of ground would send him rolling down into the sucking mud.

"We can't go on, can we?" I asked Gull bluntly.

"Go on." He tried to flex his fingers and sucked in his breath. Bent his elbows experimentally, with a groan. "Go on . . . no choice. What else?"

"We can't see the way. And there's a limit to how long you can hold him."

"Can't stay. Men. Torches. Go . . . other side."

But it was dark, and we could not go.

"Perhaps you should put him down." My heart was cold, but I forced myself to say it, although it seemed as good as admitting we had failed. Going on was pointless. If Gull collapsed, which appeared more likely by the moment, the men were both gone. And that would be the end for Johnny and me. Without Gull to guide us, we could go neither forward nor back.

"Can't put down. Never . . . up again."

"All right. Let me think for a little. Perhaps there is an answer."

"Men . . . torches," repeated Gull in a voice now barely audible.

"They would not cross in the dark to pursue us." Eamonn had said only, *We will light torches,* and *We will shoot.* Nothing about coming after us. "Would they?"

"Listen," said Gull. And now, between Johnny's sobs, between the strange gurgling song of the swamp and the strident croaking of frogs and the endless buzzing of the blood-sucking insects, I could hear men's voices, distant enough, but coming ever closer. Peering back in the darkness, I thought I could see lights, moving slowly toward us over the inky surface.

"Put him down," I said heavily, "for we can go no farther." At least, if we must die, I would do so with my arms around the two of them, Johnny and his father, and with the best of friends by me. There it was again, an eerie counterpoint to the little sounds of night: that distant, mourning wail that turned the spirit to ice.

"Strong," Gull whispered. "Strong. Stand. Carry." And he lifted his arms again, and stretched them up to support the other man's body. On my back, Johnny fell suddenly silent.

"Sorry," I choked. "Of course I will not give up. How could I think of such a thing? Our mission is but half completed."

Then all at once there was another sound, a harsh cry, and this time it came from the other side, in front of us. A squawking, cawing sort of cry. The voice of a raven. My heart lurched.

"Maybe help has come," I said through dry lips. "Maybe help has come at last."

Now we could see, northward across the marshland, a small, dancing ball of light, an odd, flickering shape that seemed to be flying swift toward us and calling out in Fiacha's voice as it came. Nearer and nearer, above the dark surface, this apparition moved, and as it came close I heard a rustling and creaking in its path, as if the very bog itself were changing as it passed. Gull stood beside me, mute. As for Johnny, he was quiet now, but his fists maintained a tight grip on my hair. There had been altogether too much jumping and bouncing around, those little hands told me, and I had better make sure there was no more.

Gull exclaimed softly in a foreign tongue, and I spoke under my breath. *Dana, mother of the earth, hold us safe in your hand.* For as we watched, we saw that the light was like a burning torch in the shape of a flying raven, not so much a bird as an Otherworld fire in the semblance of a bird. And as this light passed over the bog, strange plants rose out of the mud, long branched, strong tendriled, and wove themselves together with clinging fronds and tangling twigs to form a narrow pathway above the surface; a pathway that led ahead of us, straight to the north, straight to the low hills and to safety. The light, which might or might not have been Fiacha, hovered above, showing us the way.

I cleared my throat. "Just as well you didn't put him down," I said. "Come on."

"On," said Gull, and stepped onto the delicate-looking tangle of foliage, scarce two handspans wide. It creaked under his weight, but held firm. I moved after him, and Johnny made a sound of protest. I began to sing to him, quite softly, so as not to distract Gull, who must still move with great caution, for there was a considerable way to go, and he must support his burden and maintain a straight path. I sang the old lullaby, a song so ancient that nobody could remember what the words meant. This language might still be known somewhere: perhaps amidst the standing stones with their cryptic markings, that had looked on in silence as I lay with Bran in the rain and made this child. Perhaps in the hearts of the oldest oaks that grew in the deep, secret places of the forest of Sevenwaters. I sang, and Johnny was quiet, and we moved steadily on to the north. The ball of light flew from one side to the other, sometimes behind, sometimes in front, always keeping pace. It was Fiacha all right. Once, I looked back, for the voices of Eamonn's men could still be heard somewhere in the darkness. And I saw that in our wake, where we had walked across a narrow, safe pathway of twisted growth, now there was no path, only a line of bubbles on the surface of the mud. And in time the voices behind us faded, and the lights disappeared, and we were alone in the night with our strange guide.

Aid had come, as I had been told it would, when we were at the extreme of need, when our own strength was all but exhausted and we had run out of solutions. I was bone weary and my head throbbed, but now I allowed my mind to consider, cautiously, what must be done when we reached dry land. Gull had said Bran was too far gone to wake. He had said the chief would ask for the knife if he could. If I were to refuse this, it must be with good reason. I had got it wrong with Evan and had prolonged his suffering. This time, if I said I could heal him, I must do it. I must bring him back.

"Other side," said Gull, up ahead of me. The cawing,

flapping ball of brightness that was Fiacha was in front of him, and Gull's figure was silhouetted against the light, bent over, his poor hands still helplessly pointed upward, and the unconscious man held firm by his friend's broad shoulders and supporting arms. These men had such strength, such powers of endurance, it was no wonder simple folk believed them to be something more than mortal. They shared a bond of brotherhood, a loyalty that meant your own life was of little consequence when your comrade was in trouble. This they had without ever acknowledging it, even to themselves.

"Yes," I replied. "We must keep on until we reach the other side. And hope there will be help close at hand, for Eamonn's men can still use the road, and may do so now."

"No," said Gull. "Other side. Look."

Startled, I looked up and forward, and felt my parched lips stretch into a grin, and my eyes fill with tears. Not ten strides ahead of us there was a bank sloping upward, and at the top a line of scrubby bushes growing, and somebody was standing there with a lantern. We had reached the other side, the four of us. We had done it.

Chapter Fifteen

It was hard, at the last, to maintain the careful pace along the narrow, mysterious way; hard not to give in to the sudden tide of elation that swept through body and spirit and made one want to run forward, laughing with relief. But Gull walked steadily on, each pace calculated precisely, and I came after, step by step, for the burdens we bore were precious and must not be let go until we were sure, quite sure, that it was safe.

The figure with the lantern stood very still. A tall man robed and hooded in black. After what Gull had said, I had hoped some of them would be close by: Otter or Snake or Spider; with luck a few of them, and horses. We made our slow way across the last patch of swamp, and I could hear the woven pathway sinking back into the mud behind me as I went. None would use this way again. And at last I saw Gull step onto dry land and stagger a few paces up the bank. He bent to roll Bran off his shoulders onto the earth, and I walked forward until I was next to him and looked up.

Fiacha flew, a bright ball of flames, to alight on the shoulder of the tall, hooded figure; and the moment he landed, the light was gone, and he was an ordinary raven again, if any raven can be considered ordinary.

"Well," said Ciarán gravely. "You are here, and he still lives. This was bravely done." He glanced at Gull and then back at me. "There's help close at hand."

"Th-thank you," I stammered, my fingers touching Bran's brow, feeling how cold he was, sensing how little time was left. "Fiacha found you then. I did not expect that you yourself would come. The four of us owe our lives to you."

"Fiacha. That's apt."

"Why did you help us?" I asked him. "Why did you do this? Doesn't it go against what she—what your mother would want?"

He regarded me levelly, with something of the look of my Uncle Conor. "We owe you a debt, Niamh and I. Now it is repaid in part, at least. As for the bird, I am his custodian; but he makes his own choices."

"You didn't answer."

"Let us call for help. This man is close to death. You must move him before it is too late." He gave a short, piercing whistle, and Fiacha a croak. "You must work fast if you are to save him."

"I know. How did you do this? How did you—?" I gestured back toward the swamp, where there was now no trace of any pathway.

"A druid's skills lie in manipulating what is already there," Ciarán said. "Wind, rain, earth, fire. They lie in understanding the margins between world and Otherworld; they lie in the wisdom of growing things. What I have done tonight is not so much. Tricks learned in the nemetons, no more. There has been no high magic here. But I am no longer a druid; and Conor will realize, one day, that his teaching was only the beginning for me. He will discover, in time, exactly what I can do."

"You are his brother," I whispered.

"If he had chosen to tell me that when first he began to teach me, things might have been different. Now it means nothing."

"Are you telling me you intend to follow the Lady Oonagh's path? A descent into evil, for the sake of power? And yet you guard Niamh like a treasure; you came to save me and—and the child."

His stern features were softened by the most fleeting of smiles. Up the bank, there were men's voices, and the flare of a torch.

"My mother thinks me a suitable tool for her purpose," he said quietly. "And indeed, she has much to teach me. Conor himself instilled in me a thirst for learning. Besides, what is this but a great game of strategy? Now your men are here, and I must go. Niamh cannot be left for long."

There was a lump in my throat. He was my last link with my sister, and I sensed a very long farewell. "I wish you well," I said. "I wish you what joys are possible. And—and that you should not choose the pathway to darkness."

"I am pledged to guard your sister before all else."

"Tell Niamh I hold her in my heart," I said softly, not at all sure he would even tell her he had been here or that he had seen me and my son.

Ciarán's voice was very grave. I thought he spoke now almost against his better judgment. "I hesitate to say it," he said, "but if you wish to keep your child safe, I think you should take him away. As far as you can go. There are those who would do much to ensure he might never grow to be a man and a leader. Still, the two of you do not appear to be lacking in protectors."

As he spoke, there came through the bushes a number of men, men with strange, exotic markings on the skin of their faces and limbs and bodies, men clad in outlandish garb made from wolfskins and feathers and metal, with helms that gave them the semblance of Otherworld creatures, half human, half beast. I felt a stupid grin of relief spreading across my face as I sat with Bran's head on my lap and Gull slumped beside me on the ground. And when I looked back toward Ciarán, he was gone.

"Sweet Jesus!" It was Snake, he of the skin garment and the patterns on wrist and brow. "What happened to him?" He squatted down by Bran, his fingers reaching to touch the crusted wound to the head. "Deep blow; days old. You know what he'd say."

There was a murmur from the men who encircled us in the darkness.

"Ask her," Gull said weakly. "Ask Liadan."

Snake turned his fierce, bright gaze on me. "Think you can save him?" he queried. The men went very quiet.

Now that I was sitting down, I felt extremely weak and terribly tired. Snake's voice seemed to come from a long distance, and my own sounded strange.

"Of course I can," I said, my tone of certainty entirely feigned. "But we must hurry. We must get him to safety first. Off Eamonn's lands. I want to go to that place where we camped before. You know where I mean. The place of the standing stones. Where you can go underground."

Snake nodded. "Quite a ride," he said.

"I know. But we should go there. And Gull needs help, too. His hands are badly hurt. And—"

Johnny began to cry again, softly this time, as if to say, *Why isn't anybody listening to me? I'm tired and wet and hungry, and I did tell you before.*

There was another murmur of voices, and someone let out a low whistle.

"A child!" Snake exclaimed under his breath. "Yours? You came across there with a child on your back?"

"My son."

Another whistle.

"Where's his father then?" asked someone rather boldly from the back of the group.

"None of your business," snapped a voice I recognized as Spider's.

"This is his father," I told them, thinking they had better know the truth now, to save complications. "And like to die, if we are not on our way soon. There's very little time. You'd better strap the chief up to one of your stronger men, so he is not jolted too much. Is there a horse for me?"

For a moment, they did not move. I had stunned them into silence. Then Snake began to rap out orders. Spider, his long fingers gentle, came over to touch the baby's small head and offer to carry him for me.

"Thank you," I said, "but he's used to me, and he's tired and scared. Later maybe."

I had thought I had enough strength left to ride. But when two men came to lift Bran up, very carefully, and Otter took my hand to help me to my feet, my knees gave way and my head spun, and there seemed to be many-colored stars dancing before my eyes. Then there was a brief dispute about who would convey me and my child before him, until Snake, who appeared to be in charge, nominated Spider, and Spider, grinning, lifted us onto his tall horse and sprang up behind.

It was a long and weary journey. We stopped twice, in concealed places among rocks, and after a rest and food and plenty of attention, Johnny grew calm again, as if our perilous adventure were merely another slight variation in his daily routine. *He is his father's son,* I thought with some bitterness, and the tale of Cú Chulainn and Conlai came back to me. It would be up to me to ensure that our own tale did not follow such a pattern.

Bran was borne behind Otter, tied to his back as we had once done with Evan the smith. When we stopped, I had them prop him up against a tree trunk, and I made them fill a cup and try to get some water into him. I could have wept to see him lolling there so helpless. I knew quite well what he would say if he could see himself. *This man has no fur-*

ther use, he would say. I watched the fierce-eyed Snake carefully wiping away the crusted blood from the deep head wound, and the hard-bitten Otter tucking a warm cloak around the chief's sprawled limbs, and I sent a silent plea to Díancécht, the great healer of the Tuatha Dé Danann. *Give me the strength to achieve this task. Give me the skill. I cannot lose him. I will not.*

Gull could not ride. He sat before a large, silent man they called Wolf, on a large, silent black horse. When we paused to rest, I examined his wounded hands. I could not do much without my healer's bag, without herbs and ointments and instruments, without clean bandages and time. But I told Snake, quietly, what things I would need when we reached our destination; and he replied that anything I required would be found, one way or another. I thought it best not to inquire too closely as to quite what this meant.

Gull had lost three fingers from one hand and two from the other. The wounds had been cauterized cleanly; still my heart was cold at the thought that this was Eamonn's doing, Eamonn whom I might once have wed. It did not matter who had struck the blow, him or another. It was his mind that had conceived this cruel punishment.

"Barbaric," I muttered as I wound a strip of cloth, torn from my shift, around Gull's hand. "An act of insane vengeance." But in the back of my mind, I heard Eamonn's voice, bleak as winter. *If you dislike what I have become, you have only yourself to blame.* A shiver ran through me.

"Put me in mind of the smith," said Gull. "When the chief cut off his arm and you sealed it with a hot blade. Came close to fainting right away. Same sort of thing, this."

"You endured a great deal for him."

"What about you? You're an exceptional woman, Liadan. No wonder he broke the code for you."

"Surely he must have broken that particular rule before. A man of his years cannot be quite so strong in self-denial," I observed, tucking the ends of the bandage neatly in place.

"Known him since he was little more than a lad. Never seen him go with a woman. Not once. Self-control. Important to him. Maybe too important. With you it was different. You stood up to him. Moment he saw you, it was only a matter of time."

I did not reply, but I wondered greatly. Could it be that for Bran, too, that night of enchantment we had shared had been the first time? Surely not. These things were different for a man. A man thought less of it than a woman did, and besides, a man like him would hardly be short of opportunities. I found I was blushing and turned my face away from Gull.

"Liadan?" His voice was soft. "We're all with you, lass. We can't afford to lose the chief. Without him, we're nothing."

"You've been so strong." My voice betrayed my weariness. "Without you, I'd have given up."

"You wouldn't, you know." His tone changed suddenly. "Want you to tell me."

"Tell you what?" But I knew what was coming.

"What are my chances? How much is this going to hold me back? No trade but combat, you understand. If I can't fight, if I can't get out of a tight spot, or into one if I need to, I'm finished. Tell me the truth. How does it look?"

"Why were you there anyway? I thought it was supposed to be a one-man mission."

"You knew that? Yes, he went on his own, and chose not to give us any useful information, the fool. You'd think he wanted Northwoods to finish him off. Next we heard, he was on his way back to Erin in a little boat sailed by men in green. Knew that was unlikely to be part of the plan. I tried to be a hero. Rescue mission. I was even more fool than he was. Nearly came off, though. Eamonn was just a little too clever for us, played us off one against the other. This is the result. Now tell me."

"You'll be able to draw a bow, left handed. You'll have to

teach yourself again. You'll be able to ride, if you keep exercising your hands while they heal. You will not be able to wield a sword or scale steep walls, or use your fingers to choke the life out of a man. But you will be able to teach others the skills of combat. And you can learn to be a healer. I would teach you myself. This band needs such a one."

"I thought maybe you . . ." he began, and fell silent.

"That depends," I said. "It depends on him. On what he wants."

Gull was quiet for a while, gazing at his bandaged hands. "What would the chief say? How would he rate my usefulness?"

"He'll think you worth keeping, I imagine. Especially after I tell him how you saved me and his child. How you bore him across the marshes on your back."

Gull looked at me very directly. "It was you who saved us," he said softly. "But for your courage, we would have died in Eamonn's dungeons. Are you sure? Are you sure you can bring him back?"

"It was you who would not let me give up hope out there," I whispered.

We went by concealed ways, as once before, and if from time to time a man or two rode away alone, to rejoin the group some time later bearing a small bag or bundle they had not had before, nobody was asking any questions. It was close to dawn when we reached the place of the great barrow and dismounted under the tall beeches that sheltered its low entrance. Spider helped me down. Johnny had ridden the last part of the journey on the back of a young man they called Rat, and seemed none the worse for it, his gray eyes intent as he looked at the changing shapes and colors around him and tried to make sense of it all.

"Right," said Snake, as men departed without need for

orders, to tend to horses, and set a watch, and make a cooking fire. "Where do you want the chief? Inside, for shelter?"

"No," I said, glancing at the tiny, strange faces on the lintel of the ancient doorway. "Not in there. You know how he—best use the barrow for your men, since many can sleep there safe and dry. Can they make a small shelter for us under the trees, perhaps at the other end near the water? Dry, and private, but somewhere he can see the sky when he wakes. I'll need a little fire and lanterns for later; and I suppose a watch must be kept. I'll need a man to help me."

"We'll take it in turns." They were unstrapping Bran now, lowering him gently from Otter's horse, while Otter himself flexed his limbs and stretched his back, and got down with some caution.

"Herbs," I said. "I need someone to gather them. I must make a poultice for the head wound, and a healing tea. Gull can use both as well. I'll need self-heal. And herb of grace, that will still be in bloom, and I know it grows here. If you can find wild thyme and calamint, I will break the leaves into a small bowl and set it by him. These herbs help dispel sorrow; we must remind him of the good things he chooses to relinquish if he will not return to us."

Snake nodded. He issued quick orders, and the men transferred Bran to a board, and bore him off to the other end of the barrow. Horses were led away, supplies unpacked. A quiet orderliness was apparent as the men went about their business. I heard Johnny's small voice, the words incomprehensible, the tone confident.

"I should attend to my son," I said, thinking whoever had him had better know what babies could or could not eat, and where they might or might not be safe. "Those insect bites—there is a wash that can be made up, with figwort—"

"He'll do well enough," grinned Snake. "Rat comes from a big family; he'll make a good nursemaid for you. I'll tell him about the figwort. You go down and explain what you want for the chief. Then you'd better rest, and the child with you. Long ride, for a girl."

"It was. It seems a lifetime since I left Sevenwaters. We owe you a great deal. How did you know when to come, Snake, and where?"

"Knew where they were, him and Gull. We watch that place, Sídhe Dubh, watch it constantly, ever since Eamonn turned his back on a friend once before. He had an ally in the north, known to the chief, a man who'd done us a few favors from time to time, given us shelter and safe passage when nobody else would. This fellow had a solid agreement with Eamonn over a stretch of land, or he thought he did. Paid for it in fine cattle, bargain sealed. Then one night the men in green came down on his outpost and burnt it to the ground with the guards still in it. What made it worse was that one of them had his family there, wife, small daughters, paying a visit. Burnt to death, the lot of them. When the chief heard that, he said it just went to show, sons always turn out like their fathers. Old Eamonn, this one's father, he sold out his allies to the Britons."

"I know."

"You would, I suppose. Anyway, Eamonn's neighbor called us in to help, and we did. Accounted for his troop in a manner designed to put fear into him. The chief couldn't resist his own little touch, severed hand and so on. Came off a man long dead, you understand. Effective, but not pretty. It's the chief's way."

"But," I could not avoid saying, "the tales they tell of you, of the chief and all of you—they attribute acts of cruelty every bit as bad as this to the band of the Painted Man. How can you judge Eamonn if you do the same yourself?"

Snake frowned. "We're professionals," he said eventually. "We don't kill women and children. We don't make mistakes and burn the innocent along with the enemy. Besides, you can't believe the tales. If we were responsible for everything they pin on us, we'd have to be in fifty places at once. Ask Rat what he thinks of Eamonn Dubh. It was his mother and little sisters died in that fire."

I looked over to the place where the fire now sent a long plume of smoke into the early morning air, down the hill a little. Rat sat with Johnny on his knee, his fingers busy with some sort of game that had my son bouncing up and down with excitement. The child's fair skin was dotted with angry pink swellings where the marsh insects had attacked him; Rat's tricks diverted the small hands from rubbing these spots and worsening the itch. I could see how this young man got his name. His eyes were set close together over a long, sharp nose, and his teeth were uneven in a wide, smiling mouth.

"He's a good lad, Rat," said Snake. "Learns fast, for all his foolish looks. Now go to the chief and leave young Johnny with us awhile. We'll call you when breakfast's ready."

"You didn't answer the question. How did you know when to come?"

"Got a message. Red-haired fellow, had a very strange look about him. We were already close at hand, knowing they were in there but not how to get them out, since Eamonn had strengthened his defenses. Fellow told us to go down by the track and wait under cover for a signal. Not long after, there you were. Like magic."

"Indeed," I agreed, and then I forced my weary body to move and went down to the other end of the barrow, where the smooth rocks overlooked the still pool. Where the standing stones, carven with signs so old even a druid could not interpret their meaning, were mute guardians of the deep mysteries of the earth. And as I walked by them I thought I heard a voice saying, *Good. Good.* This was no place of the Tuatha Dé, with their gods and goddesses, their dazzling beauty and terrifying power. It was a place far older and darker. A place of the Old Ones who had been my own ancestors, if the tale of the outlaw Fergus and his Fomhóire bride were to be believed. I believed it. I felt it within me as I touched a hand to the stones of the great barrow. There was a slow vibration from deep inside the earth, and it said again, *Good.*

So little time. So little time to bring him back to himself before he perished from his wounds or from despair or from simple thirst. Bran could not drink. The men had made a shelter by the rocks, canvas stretched to form a roof, the front open so you could look out over the serene pool or watch the little fire that burned between stones. He lay there motionless on a low pallet.

"You need to watch the child with that fire," one man warned. "We built it high, just in case."

But as it was, I'd no need to worry about Johnny. They brought him to me to be fed and to sleep; and I tucked him up on the bed of bracken they had made, and covered him with a rug made from a fox's pelt. His own little blanket, sewn with such love, had been left behind in Sídhe Dubh. As for his waking time, I would glimpse my son in the arms of one or another big leather-clad nursemaid, or perhaps cradled in a neat hammock or borne high on broad shoulders, or sitting by Rat on the leaf-strewn ground, holding a piece of crust in one hand and exercising his fine new teeth. The insect bites subsided; someone had indeed found figwort. Rat informed me the child was very advanced for his age, and I agreed with him. I accepted that Johnny had suddenly acquired more uncles than any lad might possibly need, and I left them to it, though not without regret. He was so small, and so fearless.

As for Bran, I dared not let the others know how scared I was. I had poulticed the head wound, so that he wore a neat bandage around the skull over the fast-growing curls. It was Gull who helped me, refusing to go and rest; Snake, too, hovered nearby. We sat Bran upright, and held his head up, and put a moistened sponge to his lips. But the liquid ran down his chin and onto the blanket, as if he had lost the will to help himself.

"How long can he go without water?" asked Gull.

"One more day, maybe." I tried to disguise my distress, but my shaking voice betrayed me. I could see how the flesh had fallen away from Bran's cheeks, leaving the bones stark and prominent under the boldly patterned skin. I could feel how skeletal his fingers were, how frail his wrist, where the small image of a winged insect stood out on the dry, pallid skin. I could hear how faint and slow his breathing rasped. How long Bran had been held in that cramped, underground tomb, Gull could not say, for he had lost count of the days while they were in Sídhe Dubh.

"I need you to do something for me," I told Snake, who stood at the foot of the pallet.

"Anything."

"I want you to send someone out and try to find my father. He is Iubdan of Sevenwaters, but he was once called Hugh of Harrowfield, a Briton. He's a very tall man, strongly built, with red hair. Hard to miss. He traveled across the water, midsummer last, and is overdue to return to Sevenwaters. He could be on his way back; should be, if the news from home reached him. I know that if he's to be found, your men can do it. They'll need to make haste."

"Consider it done."

"Thank you," I said. "Later, I want the men gathered here. We must—we must try to call the chief back. Somehow, we must make him understand that he can't go yet; that he's needed here."

"I'll fetch them. Ask us for any help you need, Liadan. You mustn't wear yourself out. Let us be strong for you."

I touched his wrist gently, where the bracelet of painted snakes wove its way around his well-muscled arm. "You already are, Snake, you and the rest of them."

* * *

I kept my misgivings to myself. I had no doubt this was the task Finbar had once spoken of, a task of healing that would stretch my skills to their limit. But Bran lay as if lifeless, gone deep within, as if he had fled of his own will to that tiny, dark prison where Eamonn had confined him, almost as if he believed that that was where he belonged. As I watched the sun rise in the sky and steady and pass over, I knew he was slipping away from me. He had once said of himself, *Fit to live only in the darkness*, and *Go back in your box, cur.* So at the last extreme, that was exactly what he had done. He carried his prison inside himself, and the door was bolted. To find it and unlock it meant making a path through dark memories, secrets he had told me were best left buried.

Still, I was not alone. Perhaps we might summon the strength to call him back, all those of us who loved him. That would be the first step. As for the second, I could not take that without guidance, for it was a task to make the boldest heart quail.

Snake was gone; Gull kept watch by Bran's side. I went out to sit on the rocks above the pool where once Bran and I had lain in each other's arms, heedless of the rain. I looked into the dark water with a feeling of growing certainty, and I called silently to my Uncle Finbar.

Uncle? I am here, and I have something to ask you.

Here, under the standing stones, the response was instant, though dim, an image barely visible on the surface, hardly a picture of a man, more a trick of the light that made you think there might, just possibly, be someone there.

Liadan, you are safe then.

I'm safe. But he is not, not yet. He is gone far inside himself, and I need to know if I am right, if I can find him again. I believe this is the task you spoke of, and I will do it. But it scares me, Uncle. I fear what I will discover.

The man in the water nodded gravely. *Be warned, Daughter. He will use all his strength against you, and his strength is formidable. He will fight you every step of the way. It's a cruel task, for you must unfasten the bindings of his heart and lay it bare. There's great pain there, a pain he does not want to share with you. There is a frozen child who hides within a prison of lost dreams. Find him, take him by the hand, and lead him forth from that dark place.*

I was chilled to the bone. He spoke like a voice from another world.

I will do it.

If I could help you, I would, child. But this is your task. And you must begin now. The longer you delay, the farther he flees from you, until there is no way back.

The water rippled, and he was gone.

I called Snake, and he joined me by Gull in the shelter.

"Right," I told them. "I think there are two parts to it. There's a summoning to bring him out from where he's hiding. Then there's a healing, a putting together so he will stay with us. The first part, you all help me with. I'll do the second part alone."

"Not a lot of time," Gull commented quietly.

"I know that. It must be finished by dawn, or he'll escape us. You should call the men now, and I'll explain it to them."

"Liadan," said Snake awkwardly, "You know he'd hate this."

"What do you want me to do? Leave him to die of thirst; let him perish alone and wandering in some place we cannot see? Or maybe help him on his way with a little sharp knife? Is that what you think I should do?"

"There's not a man here would say that, except the chief himself. If he could stand outside himself and see this, he'd be the first one to draw the blade across his throat. We're all behind you, Liadan. None of us wants to be the one who has to explain this to him when he comes back, that's all."

"I will explain it to him. Now go, fetch the men."

We sat by Bran's side, waiting. He had not stirred; his face was pale and calm, as if sleeping. There was no outward sign he lived, save the slight, slow rise and fall of his breathing. His fingers were limp and cold, and I tucked the blanket over them, still gripping his hand in mine. I wondered if somewhere, deep down, he could feel that I had not let go.

The men came in ones and twos, soft footed despite their heavy boots. Most were armed. All wore the strange raiment of their calling, the skins and feathers and decorations that were their pride and identity. All were solemn. They gathered around the pallet, sitting, crouching, standing in silence. Not quite the full complement; even at such a time, the watch must be maintained.

"Very well," I said. "He can hear us, make no doubt of it. He has a head wound, a bad one; but men have recovered from worse, and he is very strong, you know that. But he cannot swallow, and a man does not last long without water. We must bring him out of this sleep."

"What if he doesn't want to come out?" This was the big, dark-bearded fellow, Wolf. I had not heard him speak before; his voice was guttural, heavily accented.

"That's just it," I said. "He thinks it not worth returning to us. We must persuade him otherwise. He needs to know how you value him; he needs to be reminded what good things he has done for you, and what it means to you. He must be made to recognize what he has given, and what he *can* give. Only you can do that."

They looked at one another and moved uneasily.

"We're fighting men," said Rat, who stood holding Johnny against his shoulder and patting his back, "not bards nor scholars."

Another man spoke apologetically. "Can't think what we'd say."

"You remember the tales I told you?"

There were nods and half smiles.

"Well then, it's just like that, only shorter. Each of you tells a little tale, a tale of the Painted Man. We'll do it in

turn. And with our tales, we call him back. Simple, really."
I caught Gull looking at me quizzically, and I suspected he
knew my brisk confidence was totally assumed. Underneath, I was cold with the fear that we might fail. Their
faces began to brighten with hope.

"That's good," said one man admiringly. "Fancy thinking
of that. You're a rare one. Can I go first?"

"Surely."

The tales were many and varied. Some were poignant,
some funny, some the stuff of high tragedy. There was the
story of how Bran had saved Dog from the longships, and
how, said Snake, even though poor Dog was dead now, he'd
certainly returned the favor; for if Dog hadn't hit me on the
head that day in Littlefolds, I'd never have met the Painted
Man and there would have been no Johnny. And, Snake
added, now that the chief had me and his lad, he'd have to
be a complete fool not to want to wake up. There were tales
from the south and tales from the north, tales from Cymru
and Britain and Armorica. There were tales told by Norsemen and Ulstermen and Gauls. All sorts. But they had one
thread in common. In every tale, the Painted Man had
reached out his hand to an outcast, a man with no place to
go in the world, and welcomed him to a band of comrades,
a code, and a purpose. Gull whispered his, a story of blood
and loss, of anguish and despair.

"You called me back to life when I sought to end it. It
was your hand stayed mine when I would have given in to
the darkness. Now I step into your path. I bid you halt and
return to us. Your work is not finished. We need you, friend.
Now it is my turn to call *you* back."

We had woven our net of words all afternoon. It was a
fine, strong net, like the men who made it. Now dusk was
coming on.

"Listen to Gull," I said, holding back tears. "Listen to us
all." I had told them Bran could hear. Now I doubted the
truth of that for, try as I might, I could not sense the small-

est spark of thought in him, the weakest fragment of vision in his mind. If he were not already gone, he had the most powerful of barriers in place.

"Bran," I said softly, my fingers moving against the sunken flesh of his cheek, "we love you. We are your friends. We are your family. Come out. Come back from that dark place. Walk out from the shadows, dear one."

Gull made a little movement with his bandaged hand, and then one by one the men came forward to touch Bran's arm, or grip his shoulder, and here or there I saw a surreptitious wiping away of tears.

When they all had gone but Gull and Rat, I took Johnny in my arms and went out by the fire to feed him, and allowed myself to weep. As I sat there, Snake came back with Wolf, and they changed Bran's clothing and sponged his body. While they worked they talked, cheerful, practical talk about an armorer in the north who had developed a new process for tempering iron and what a fine, precise type of sword he was making and what price might be negotiated for such a superior kind of weapon. I knew their talk was for the chief, and I recognized their efforts. But I was weary, weary to the point of sickness, and sad beyond measuring: and I closed my eyes where I sat. Then, unbidden, a nightmare was on me, walls closing in, utter darkness, no sense of time or space, no sound but the thumping heart and labored breathing, and I was scared, I was scared Uncle would beat me again, I could feel the stinging pain in my back and my legs from last time, I could feel the ache in my arms from when he made me hold the rock up over my head . . . I'd been weak, and I'd dropped it, and if the belt hurt it was my own fault because you only got punished if you were not strong enough . . . my nose ran and I sniffed without thinking, and my heart raced . . . no sound, that was the rule, no sound or there was trouble . . . it was hard not to cry when you had wet yourself and you were hot and thirsty and scared and nobody came . . . when all you could do was count up to ten, over and over again . . . when you waited and waited for her to come back for you because maybe, just maybe, if you were brave enough, she would still come, even now . . .

I came to myself abruptly, my head throbbing, my heart thumping. The terror was real, as if I were there in that small, dark space myself, and I blinked and forced myself to breathe slower, forced my eyes to see the still water of the pool and the soft willows gray-blue in the twilight. I felt the warm weight of the baby in my arms.

"Liadan?" Gull was beside me, his features near-invisible in the fading light. "All right?"

I nodded. "Yes. He's there, Gull. Not far away. There just below the surface and too frightened, or somehow too ashamed, to come out. He heard us; I know it."

"How can you know?" Gull asked, his voice full of wonder.

"I—I hear his thoughts. Share his memories and feelings, when he lets me in. It's a gift, and a curse. It might help me to reach him, help me to unlock whatever barrier this is that he's built around him. But I need to know. I need to understand what makes him hide like this. I think—I think, whatever it was, it happened when he was very young. When he was quite small. Did he ever tell you . . . ?"

"Not him. Lives by the code. No past, no future. He never said a thing. Seems to me the man was born old. I wish I could help."

"Never mind," I said, my heart sinking. "I must just do my best to reach him. I'll need to be alone tonight. I'll put Johnny to bed in the shelter, then you should leave us. All of you."

"I'll stand watch out here."

"Oh, Gull, with those hands you should be in an infirmary, in good care. You take too much on yourself. At least get some sleep."

"What about you? You can't go on forever." He put his hand on my shoulder. "We'd look after you, you know. If he—we'd look after you and the boy."

"Stop it!" My voice rang out harshly. "Don't say that! He's going to live. I'll have no words of defeat here."

There was a brief silence. Then Gull said, "Made for each other. Incapable of failure, the two of you. No doubt the lad'll grow up to be a great leader. How could he not? Now, I'll have them fetch you a bite to eat; then we'll do as you say. But there'll need to be a guard. Can't hurt, since not one of us will sleep tonight."

I had thought to send them all away to the barrow so that we were alone in the place of our destiny, by the dark pool under the moonless sky. There were old things stirring; I felt their presence in the shadows, and knew this was a night of changing. I had thought that in the darkness Bran might reach out to me as once before, and I might seize his hand and hold on until morning.

But this was not a place for lone acts of desperation; this was a place of fellowship. Snake brought food and ale and insisted I stay out by the fire to eat it. And when I was seated on a flat stone, with a bowl of stew on my knee, others came out of the night to stand around me silent. I looked at young Rat anew, since hearing his own tale. The fire set by Eamonn's men had done him a great wrong. Spider and Otter were not there; they had been absent all day.

"Got something to ask you," said Snake diffidently.

"What?"

"Say you work wonders, and he comes out of this. Wakes up sudden, saying where am I? How do you think he can live with what's happened? And what about you and the child? He wants you. You want him. But he'd never agree to keep you here with us; no life for a lady, nor for a little lad. He'd never risk you that way. And he'll never give it up. It's all he knows; the only way he can justify going on. You planning to fix him up and ride away off home again? That'd be a cruel ending for all parties, that would."

"You ask me that seriously?"

"Maybe not. Can't see you doing such a thing. But you

know how he is. He won't let you stay. Pack you off home and then go and get himself killed as soon as he can. That'd be my prediction."

There was a silence. Gull glanced at me, and at Snake, and it seemed as if he wanted to speak but would not.

"What is it, Gull?" I asked him.

"I've been thinking," he said cautiously.

"Come on then, out with it." Snake's attention was caught immediately. "If you've got a plan, let's hear it. Time's short."

"A plan. It's hardly that. A notion, no more. Kept on going through my head all the way across that godforsaken swamp. Once I thought of it, it stayed there and got bigger. I know we can't go back and live in the world again, farmers, fishermen, and so on. But we do have skills: seamanship, tracking by stealth, all kinds of combat. We know how to plan a raid and execute it faultlessly. We know how to get in and out of places in ways nobody else even thought of. We've our own methods of solving problems and of getting information. There's many a chieftain, both in this country and over the water, would pay in fine cattle and silver pieces to have his men taught such skills."

Once again, Gull had astonished me. Wolf was listening round eyed.

"Where?" asked Snake bluntly. "There's not a corner of Erin where we're welcome for more than a night or two. Settle down, and before you know it some lordling we've offended comes in with his henchmen to torch our camp and butcher us in the night. We've always got to be two steps ahead. Always on the move. Even this place isn't safe; not for long."

I cleared my throat. "Bran told me once—he said to me, he had resources. He had a place. Where is that place?"

"Know nothing about that," said Snake. "Not the settling type, our chief." He and Wolf both looked at Gull.

"No need to keep secrets from Liadan," Gull said quietly. "She's one of us."

After a moment Snake nodded, and Wolf gave a grunt of agreement.

Gull turned back to me. "The chief told you then," he said, glancing over at the man lying motionless in the open shelter.

"He did. A long time ago. What kind of place is it, Gull?"

"An island. North. It's a wild, inhospitable place. Easy to guard. Not so easy to reach. Beautiful, in its way. You could build a camp there. Folk could come and be taught."

"Like that island in the story," said Snake absently, his mind clearly racing ahead of his words. "The island of that warrior woman, you know? What was her name? And you'd be there as well, you and the boy. Like the tale."

"I'll tell you now, I have no intention of imitating the exploits of Scáthach, or of her daughter," I said dryly. "But you are right. Whatever unfolds, I intend to stay by him."

"What chieftain would pay good silver to such as us?" Rat asked. "What about our reputation? These lords must be careful of their alliances. There's not a one of them would place any trust in such a venture." Despite his words, his eyes shone with hope.

"As to that," I said slowly, "I think it is possible your enterprise might, in time, be accepted. All you need is a start. The patronage of a highly regarded leader. Perhaps also some additional resources; that could be discussed. My brother could give you both."

"Your brother?" Gull raised his brows. "The lord of Sevenwaters? He would deal openly with such as us?"

I nodded. "I believe so. My brother once spoke of trading in specialized services. Certainly he understands the value of what you can offer. It was on my brother's mission that Bran was taken prisoner this time. Sean owes me a favor for that, and for another—transaction I carried out for him. I believe he will agree."

Snake gave a low whistle.

"You might consider broadening your scope," I went on.

My mind was warming to the idea. "An army needs surgeons and healers, astrologers and navigators, as well as warriors. And men must learn that there is more to life than killing and destruction. I have no wish to be the only woman on this island."

"Women?" Wolf's tone was awed. "There would be women there?"

"I see no reason why not," I said. "Half of the world is made up of women." The men looked over at Bran and at one another.

"Work to do," said Snake, getting to his feet. "Thinking. Planning. I'll go and put it to the rest of the lads. What a turnaround. But who's going to ask him?"

"Perhaps you should draw straws," I said.

The men were already deep in debate as they walked back to the main camp, leaving me alone with Gull. The bright mood of enthusiasm faded abruptly; before there could be any contemplation of a future, tonight's battle must be won.

"Gull," I said, "this is dark of the moon."

He nodded without speaking.

"If I cannot reach him tonight, it is all over. Best leave me alone now. No lights. Let the fire die."

"If you're sure."

"I am sure. I promise I will call if I need you. But keep the others away. No interruptions or I may lose him."

He took the lantern and moved down beyond the fire, leaving me in darkness. Johnny slept. I put my arm across Bran and laid my head beside his on the pallet, my face close to his own. His breathing was shallow, with an interminable pause before each inward gasp. At each turning point something still drove him to that effort of will. I closed my eyes and slowed my own breathing, so that we shared the rise and fall . . . in . . . out . . . life . . . death . . . and I willed myself back down the path of time, through the secret byways and crooked paths of memory. I reached with all the strength of my mind to find him in that twisting labyrinth. And at last, now, through veils of shadow, through layers of darkness, he began to let me through.

No air, can't breathe, heart thudding, blood running swift, out of control, out of control . . . one and two and three, four and five and six . . . how long, how long before the next time . . . how long before it is light again . . . do not seek to find this man, here in the box, in the dark . . . he's long gone . . . long gone . . .

The thoughts faded and were lost. I reached out further, deeper into the shadows. *Tell me. Tell me.* It was as if my own mind flowed into his and became a part of him, while my body was a shell, untenanted. *Show me.*

Story. Tell me a story. Long tale, many nights. There was a boy who set out on a crooked pathway . . . he thought he knew where he was going . . . four, five, six . . . but he was lost, lost in the dark, and nobody came . . . he was wandering and falling . . . falling away down . . .

I will hold your hand, no matter where you go; no matter what you are, I told him. *I will never let go of what I love, not until the end of time and beyond. Look up, dear heart. Look up and follow the light. Come out to me.*

Dog, with his guts spilled. Evan, so strong and in the end so helpless. Gull shut up in that place with a butcher. These men followed him, and their reward was suffering and death. They followed him into the shadow . . . so many lost . . . a crushing burden . . . count them . . . count the stones in Sídhe Dubh, the layers of darkness over his head, weighing him down . . . gutter scum, unworthy of hope . . . flee from him, for his touch is death . . . his love is a curse . . .

If you will count, count the stars, dear one. How many stars in the sky, looking down on us as we lie in each other's arms and taste joy? How many gleaming fish in the lake where I splash our son in the water and hear his shrieks of glee ring out in the clear air? A fine little salmon you made, that night in the rain. How many times does the heart beat,

*how fast does the blood run when at last we touch, and touch
again, and breathe the same desperate, longing breath?
Count those things, for they are the stuff of life and of hope.*

*Hope . . . this man is forbidden hope. Touch this man,
and he will draw you down into the box beside him, into the
darkness. Words spin by like dry leaves, whispering into
emptiness . . . he cannot hear them . . .*

He was leaving me again, escaping my grasp, fleeing
down the long, dark way to his place of hiding, deep within.
How could I follow? How could I find him, once the shadows concealed him again? I summoned all my strength, and
reached after him. *The story. Tell me. A boy. A man. He went
on a journey. Tell me his tale.*

When it came, it was tenuous indeed, a little thread of
thought. But it was a tale: his own tale.

*Tell . . . tell the story . . . there's a man, and they finish
beating him, and someone in green puts him in the hole in
the ground and shuts the door. It's dark. It's too dark, and
small. But he must go on, because . . . because . . . he can't
think why, but he must. He knows how to go on; he's done
this before. He's done it before over and over. Counting, to
keep the other things out; counting, one, two, three . . .
There's a child, and he's being jostled up and down in her
arms, and he doesn't like it. She's crying and running, and
that makes him cry too. Then she says, "It's all right,
Johnny. Now crouch down small and keep very quiet. It's
not for long, sweetheart. I'll come back for you as soon as I
can. Don't be frightened; just keep really still and quiet, no
matter what you hear." She puts him in a hole in the ground,
and shuts the door. Thumb in mouth, hand over head, knees
up, heart thumping. One, two, three, he counts as he hears
the crashing and screaming outside, as he smells the burning and the blood. Four, five, six. Over and over he repeats
the numbers, a talisman of protection. One, two, three . . .
one, two, three . . . So dark. So long. Too long. And then—
and then . . .*

The thoughts wavered and were gone. I felt as weary as if I had fought a battle; my head throbbed, my hands shook, my eyes were full of tears. I lifted Bran's cold hand to my lips.

"All right," I whispered shakily. "It's a start." But I could make little sense of it. Had his mother abandoned him long years ago? The Margery my mother had spoken of with such love and respect? How could that be?

Show me more, I begged with the voice of the mind and tried to let him feel, without words, that whatever his past had been, we loved and needed him now. Such a message I could have passed to Sean, or Conor, or Finbar in a flash. I might have reached such a one as my father or Niamh or even Gull with a little more difficulty, though they would have felt no more than a lightening, a sense of well-being, and would not have known what I did. I had worked thus with my sister at Sídhe Dubh, when despair came close to overwhelming her. But wounded though he was, Bran was a man of immensely strong will, and he was fighting against me as Finbar had predicted. And already I was exhausted from my efforts.

Come out!

My heart thumped. The Old Ones were come to help me. Their voices called from the depths of the earth, soft and strong.

Come forth from the darkness. Would you leave your son fatherless, your woman alone and grieving? Would you cast your men adrift without purpose? Come out and answer this challenge.

"Do not heed them."

I jerked upright, clutching Bran's hand convulsively. This was a different voice, and its owner stood eerily lit at the foot of the pallet. It was the Lady of the Forest, her face a gleam of white in the darkness, her cloak midnight dark save for its sheen of blue. The flame-haired lord stood behind her, his light dimmed to an eldritch glow. Their ex-

pressions were stern; their eyes cool. I trembled to see them
here, remembering their fury when I had refused them.
Bran lay by me quite helpless, and my little son was here,
with only me to defend him.

"Do not heed these voices," the lady said again, "they
lead you astray. They are old and confused, an ancient,
twisted people of the rocks and wells. There is no meaning
to their words."

"Forgive me," I said, shivering, "I think they are my own
ancestors, for the folk of Sevenwaters are descended from a
mortal man and a woman of the Fomhóire. Those you call
twisted seek only to aid my task. Time is short. If you are
not come to help, then I must ask you to leave us alone."

The lord's brows rose to extravagant heights. He made as
if to speak, but she stopped him.

"Liadan," she said, and there was a sorrow in her voice,
"this man is dying. You will not call him back. It is cruel to
hold him thus. Let him go. He longs to be released. The
man is damaged and broken, no fit mate for a daughter of
Sevenwaters. He cannot protect the child. Let him go and
bring the boy back to the forest."

I clenched my teeth and kept my silence.

"Heed us, girl." As the lord spoke, small sparks arose
from his hair and from his robe, so that he was haloed with
golden light. It touched Bran's wan features with a ghastly
semblance of health. "Dark forces stretch out toward your
child. There are those who would do anything to prevent his
survival. We can keep him safe. We can ensure he grows
strong in body and spirit, fit for the task that lies ahead. You
must bring him back. Or . . ."

I saw the seed of an idea forming in those changeable
eyes, and quick as a flash I sprang up and snatched the
sleeping Johnny from his nest of bracken to hold him tight
in my arms.

"You're not taking him!" I spat, as alarm and fury surged
through me. "Fair Folk or no Fair Folk, you won't steal my

son and leave me with some changeling! And you won't dismiss his father either. They are mine, the two of them, and I'm keeping them both. I'm not a fool. I know the danger. I know about Lady Oonagh and—and—"

I went back to the pallet, where I could stretch my arms around my small family, where I could make a strong wall of love to hold the three of us together. "We'll be safe. We'll keep each other safe," I said defiantly. "I know it. We have many protectors here. As for the prophecy, if it's to come about, it will come about whatever I may do. It will unfold as it must."

As I spoke, there was a thickening of the air, a darkening of a night already profound in its blackness. A chill ran through me that was beyond cold, a freezing clutch deep in the bone. There was another presence here; one that now stood by the pallet, watching. In the darkness I thought I could detect a flowing robe and a deep hood, and within that hood, where a face might be, nothing more than ancient bone with blank holes for eyes.

"You may choose to defy us," said the lady gravely. "But you cannot deny *her*. If she comes for him, he must go. It is his time. She will take him from you, however strong your hold. Let go, Liadan. Release this broken spirit from the fetters of life. It is not love, but selfish cruelty, to hold him thus. The dark one waits. She will give him the rest he craves."

I gritted my teeth, and blinked back my tears. My voice, when I found it, was a tiny whisper. "Not true. He can't go. We need him here. I can hold on. I can."

The dark figure shifted, and I glimpsed a hand outstretched, a hand that was no more than bone and sinew.

"Go away," I breathed, "all of you. Leave this place now. I care nothing for who you are or what you are. I defy your powers and your demands. I am a healer; my mother taught me her craft with love and discipline. This man will not die, not while I hold him in my arms. While I warm his heart with my own, he will not leave me. You cannot take him. He's mine."

And when the hooded one would not go, but lingered there, beckoning with her skeletal fingers, I began to sing. I sang very softly, as if I were lulling a child to sleep. Over and over I hummed my small tune, and my fingers stroked the new growth of hair on the patterned skull of my fallen warrior, and I gazed into the dark and spoke defiance with my weary eyes. *He's mine. You can't have him.*

"Fool of a girl," muttered the bright-haired lord. "Wretch of a mortal. That so much should rest on *them*."

But the lady stood and watched me, considering. I wondered why they did not simply use their magical powers to make me give up my son, or to rob Bran of his last breath, or indeed to drive every Briton from the Islands if that was what they wanted. Johnny gave a little sleepy cough and a sigh.

"As you say, child," said the lady. "It will unfold. Your choice may determine whether it unfolds at great cost, with blood and darkness. Your vision is so short you cannot see who may be trusted, and so your decisions are flawed. But it is your own choice, not ours. Our time is nearly at an end; it is your kind that will guide the course of events and influence the turn of the tide. Whatever happens, we will fade and conceal ourselves, as the Old Ones did. We will be little more than a memory for the sons and daughters of your children's children. The pathway you set here will be a long one, Liadan. We cannot choose for you."

Awake. The voice of the earth called, sang, groaned deep with the weight of ages. *Awake now, warrior.*

Tears filled my eyes, and I whispered my response. "I will wake him. Trust me." I turned back to the tall beings who stood before me in the darkness. "For me there is but one choice," I said steadfastly.

"Your son's blood will be on your hands." The fiery lord's voice shook with a fury beyond mortal rage, a noise like thunder; yet the sleeping babe did not stir. "You want too much. You want more than you can have." He faded, until all that I could see of him was a faint outline in little sparks.

"It's a long tale," said the Lady of the Forest. "We thought it would be simpler. But the pattern is branching. We did not think the children would leave the forest. Your sister was corrupted. You are simply stubborn. There's too much of your father in you. So we must wait longer than we anticipated. But you will see its unfolding, Liadan. You will see what you have wrought tonight."

I wept as she too faded away, wept because I knew what I must do and because her words gave voice to a terrible fear and a gnawing guilt that I had tried to ignore since I rode out to Sídhe Dubh, since I first sensed Bran was in trouble and needed me. What if I was wrong? What if my pigheadedness brought death for my son and unleashed evil on the folk of Sevenwaters once more? Who was I to defy the warnings of the Fair Folk themselves?

I felt something. The smallest twitch against my hand where it clutched Bran's, as if his fingers tried, weakly, to curl around mine. Had I imagined it? Now his hand was limp and still again. Perhaps it was Johnny who had moved, tucked snug now next to his father on the pallet. But I was sure, I was almost sure of what I had felt. I could not give up. I would not. I must start again, right now, for time was passing swiftly, and I thought Bran's breathing slower and shallower than before, the breath of a man who walks steadily down his final pathway. The hooded one had retreated, but I sensed she still waited, out there in the darkness. Perhaps she could be patient, for in the end would she not take all?

"Help me," I whispered, and the voices came back, deep and sure. *Come out from the shadows, warrior. A mission awaits you. Walk forth from the darkness.* I closed my eyes once more.

Tell . . . tell the tale . . . there's a boy, bigger now. He's got a lot of bruises from the beatings. It's because he's no good, gutter scum, that he must be punished. Uncle says so. When Uncle gets really angry, he shuts the boy in the box. In the box it's dark. And small, smaller all the time as he grows. He learns to be quiet. He counts in his head. He learns not to cry, not to sniff, not to move, until the lid opens and light streams in, blinding and fierce. They drag him out, cramped and stinking, for more punishment.

There's a woman. The man beats her, too, and they do the thing, the grunting, pushing, sweaty thing. Uncle makes him watch. Uncle makes him watch a lot of things. The boy tells himself he will never do that. It's a dark thing, mindless, animal, dark as the terror of the box. Do that and he will be Uncle himself.

There's a dog, for a bit. The dog wanders in one cold night and decides to stay. It's mangy, stark ribbed, wild-eyed. The boy sleeps warm that winter, curled by the dog in the straw of the outhouse. By day the dog follows him, padding quiet in his shadow.

One fine spring morning Uncle beats the dog for killing chickens, and the boy holds it as it dies. As the boy buries the dog, he makes a vow. When I am a man, he swears, next winter or the one after, I will do what must be done here and move on. I will move on and never look behind me.

I felt tears rolling down my cheeks to dampen the linen beneath Bran's head and mine. *Hold on, dear one.* Could he hear the voice of my mind through the shadows that beset him? *I'm here beside you, with my arm around you. We need you here, Bran. Come back to us. This dark dream is over.*

And faintly, so faintly, I thought I sensed a response, like a sigh, a breath, a fragment of thought.

. . . Liadan . . . don't go . . .

Then there was sudden light, out by the smothered fire, and the sound of footsteps, and Bran was gone, his inner voice abruptly silenced, the tenuous link instantly broken. I sprang up, furious, and staggered out of the shelter, for I had not realized how my efforts had exhausted me, nor how long I had sat there unmoving. It must be well into the night. How dared they disturb us? I had given strict instructions. How dared they do this?

"I told you!" I snapped as Gull came up toward me. "I told you not to come here tonight. What are these men doing?"

"Sorry," Gull said ruefully. There was something in his voice that made me wait for more. "Thought you'd want to be interrupted for this."

Down by the remnants of the small fire four men were standing. One of the men was Snake, and one of them was Spider, I could see from the long, thin legs and the awkward way he gestured with his hands, and there was broad-shouldered, barrel-chested Otter, and a tall man with hair as red as an autumn sunset. As I walked forward this man turned toward me, and it was my father.

I ran to him and he hugged me close, and I soaked his shirt front with my tears, and the other men watched us in silence, until Gull said diffidently, "We'll go, if you want."

"It might be best," I sniffed. "I—I have to thank you for carrying out my mission so quickly and so successfully. I did not hope—"

"Not so difficult," said Otter gruffly. "Iubdan here was on his way back already. Waylaid him, that's all. Heavy hand with a staff, your father's got, excuse me for mentioning it." He was rubbing the back of his head cautiously.

"I must speak with you alone, Liadan," said my father. "You know, I suppose, that Liam is gone. We must return home to Sevenwaters in the morning."

"What do you mean, *we?*" demanded Snake incautiously.

"Liadan can't go." Gull's tone was level, final. "We need her here."

"With respect," said my father very quietly, in the tone men had learned to fear, "that will be up to my daughter and to me. I hope you will extend us the courtesy of a little time together in private."

"The chief's dying," said Snake, his eyes like slits as he looked my father up and down, perhaps weighing his age against his size. "He needs her, she can't go."

I stepped between them and took each by a sleeve. "Enough," I said, with what firmness I could muster. "I need my father to help me now. As for the other matter, I will give you my answer at dawn. Now go."

"You sure?" queried Snake under his breath.

"You heard Liadan," said Gull. "Now move. Do as she says."

Within moments my father and I were alone.

"Well," Iubdan said, lowering his tall form to sit on the rocks and stretching out his booted legs before him. "I didn't expect to find you here. What am I to do with you, Liadan? You seem to have developed a taste for breaking rules and flouting conventions. Don't you understand the danger you are in here?"

"Forget that for now," I replied tersely. "There's a far more pressing matter to be attended to."

"What can be more pressing than the need for us to get back to Sevenwaters, with Liam slain and Sean alone, with our neighbors gathering and jostling for advantage? We should be there, not here with this rabble."

"I know you must go home," I said quietly, "Sean needs you more than he realizes. He faces a great challenge and must be supported. And—and he needs level heads about him, men of experience who can judge which allies may be trusted and which must be watched. You must go soon. But I have a terrible task here, Father, and I, too, need your help. Snake spoke the truth: Bran is dying. He has come close to abandoning hope altogether, for he believes himself not worth saving. He clings by the merest thread. I need your help to keep that thread intact, until I can grasp his hand and bring him back. Mother sent you across the water to find truth for us. I need to know what truth you discovered. I need you to tell me now, quickly."

"I understand your urgency, Liadan; I recognize the bond you share with this man, and the trust you place in him. And I know your judgment is sound. Still, you expect quite a leap of faith from me, Daughter. Are not these the very same outlaws who snatched your sister away and came so close to losing her? True, they have treated me with unexpected courtesy. To hear them speak of you, one would imagine you a creature part queen, part goddess. But why won't they tell me anything about how you came to be here, so far from home, and so soon after the loss of your uncle? How can I not fear for your safety?"

"These men would lay down their lives for me and for my son, every one of them. We are safe here, Father."

"Your son? Johnny, too, is here? But—"

"Please, Father. Please tell me what you have discovered. I need to know what happened to Bran; what happened to his mother. Did you learn Margery's story?"

"I did, Daughter, and a sad and twisted tale that turned out to be. I pursued it through the settlements of Harrowfield, back through eighteen years I followed it. I cannot tell you the full tale, but in the village of Elvington, which lies over the hills from Harrowfield, I uncovered a part of it long kept secret."

"Tell me. No, better still, come with me to sit by his side and tell the two of us. He—he believes his mother left him, that she abandoned him. That is a deep wound his spirit has carried all these years. But my mother told me Margery loved her son, and I cannot believe she left him willingly."

"Tell you both?" Father looked perplexed, as we went to stand by the still, gray-faced figure in the shelter. "How can he hear us? Surely this man has lost any awareness of the world around him. Surely he is beyond saving. Your love, perhaps, makes you expect miracles. But miracles are rare, sweetheart. I have seen men like this before—"

"Stop it!" I cried. "Stop it! If you have only defeat and death to tell, you might as well not have come here at all! I need your help, not your words of doom. Now tell us your tale." I took up Bran's patterned hand in mine and held it against my cheek.

Father was staring at me, his blue eyes very bright. "I've noticed," he said, "the way men move to obey you without question here in his encampment of outlaws. Indeed, they speak your name with a respect verging on awe. Yet the situation perplexes me. No man wants to see his daughter in such circumstances. You must forgive my plain words. I speak thus because I hate to see you hurt. Your mother's judgment was without fault. I never told her what to do. Your own choices are—difficult for me to accept. But I made you a promise once, and I intend to keep it though it's costing me dear to see you thus."

"Tell the tale."

"Very well. It's a tale of ill chance, of lost opportunities; a tale that does indeed give strength to this man's argument that I myself bear some responsibility for what he has become. For that, I can make amends. The past I cannot alter; that tale is already written. It began in the year when Margery's son was three years old, and she traveled with friends to Elvington for the winter fair."

I listened to his quiet, measured voice. Outside, Gull had returned to keep vigil by the fire, a dark figure in the deeper blackness of the moonless night. Beyond the circle of light, shadows gathered under the tall beech trees and between the ancient stones and across the unruffled surface of the dark pool. Somewhere out there, a hooded presence waited, silent and still as if she were herself no more than shadow.

"You know already," said my father, "how my friend and kinsman John was killed in my service, crushed in a rock fall, while guarding your mother. I set him that task, but it was Richard of Northwoods who ordered the killing. Margery took her husband's loss very hard. They were devoted to each other, and to be robbed of her man when their son was still no more than an infant was cruel indeed. She became withdrawn and quiet, and it was only her small Johnny who gave her the strength to carry on. In him she saw the future John had been denied; in him she saw her own purpose.

"Her child was the focus of all her attention, for a time, while the wound of her loss was still fresh. As you know, I left Harrowfield myself within a year of John's death, while Margery was still in mourning. In time she was persuaded by her friends that it would be good for her to venture forth a little and be seen. So in the winter when Johnny was three years old, she traveled with a small party from Harrowfield to Elvington for the Yuletide fair. Not such a very long ride. It can be done quite easily in a day, or more gradually with a stop overnight. That was what they did, since the child traveled with them and tired more easily.

"It is here that the story begins to grow confused. My brother told me the party was ambushed by raiders somewhere in the hills above Elvington. Who these attackers were, or what their purpose, remains unsure. Perhaps they were Pictish tribesmen from over the border, come for sheep. When a group of well-dressed folk rode across their path, it must have seemed an opportunity too good to miss. Later that day, a shepherd found the travelers' bodies lying by the track, near one of the isolated cottages; every man and woman slaughtered. But not the child. He was not accounted for, although they did search. It was odd. The notion that the Picts might have taken him, as slave or hostage, was soon dismissed. He was simply too young, too much trouble for men on the move. But no small body was found. Wild dogs, they decided eventually. Wild dogs had carried him off somewhere, as they might a rabbit or fawn. There was no point in looking any farther. The news came back to my brother, and with regret he accepted it. It was a sad end for Margery, who had come to Harrowfield as a new bride with such hopes.

"That might, indeed, have been the end of the tale. Six

years passed. John's and Margery's names faded into the history of Harrowfield, as did indeed my own: Lord Hugh, who had once been master of the estate and who had abandoned them for a green-eyed sorceress from over the water, a witch whose brothers were half man, half beast. So the years went by. My brother married. The work of Harrowfield continued. Edwin laid claim to Northwoods and began to build its strength again.

"And then, at the folkmoot, where a leader passes judgment in matters of dispute or wrongdoing, my brother Simon was presented with a bizarre case. There was, at first, no reason to believe it part of the same tale. A man had been murdered at an isolated cottage in the hills above Elvington, a cruel and vicious fellow loathed and feared by neighbors and village folk alike. It was like an execution, neatly done with a small, precisely placed wound straight to the heart, the instrument of death a narrow, toothed knife, an implement more commonly used for boning fowl. It had been awhile before anyone found the body. Nobody liked to go out there. Rory could be a monster when he'd a drop of ale in him, prone to violent rages, and with altogether too much of an eye for the young girls. When Simon told me the man's name, I remembered him well enough. He'd been up before me on serious charges, accused of raping the daughter of a local miller and getting her with child. He didn't care for the penalty I set him; I never heard such an ugly tirade of threats and curses. I ordered substantial reparation paid to the girl's family, and I banished him from my lands for five years. It seems he chose to return as soon as he heard I was gone. And now he was dead. He'd no wife; not by that time. She'd simply disappeared, and folk said, no wonder. He used to beat her, and the theory was, one time he'd gone too far and had to dispose of her quietly. Nobody asked. Nobody dared. So who killed him? Who'd attempt such a thing, let alone carry it out so efficiently? Many wished him dead, but all feared to do it. There was nobody; nobody but the child."

I should have guessed this was the next part of it, for Bran had told me. *I will do what has to be done here and move on.* "Tell me about the child," I said.

"There was a boy," said my father. "Some folk said he was Rory's son and some that he was a foundling, somebody's bastard, a brat nobody wanted, who had wandered into the cottage one day and been allowed to stay. An extra pair of hands. Nobody could remember when he came there. They couldn't recall Rory's woman with a baby, not her. They just spoke of seeing this scrawny little wretch of a boy, all over bruises. Like a ghost he was, but no weakling. The lads would tease him, and he'd turn on them like some feral creature; and in time they learned to fear him and to leave him alone.

"So here was Rory with a tidy little wound to the heart and not a trace of the boy to be found. The people of Elvington presented it to my brother in the formal setting of the moot. What was to be done? Was the murderer to be pursued? And what about Rory's cottage, and his chickens? Who would get those?

"Simon ordered inquiries to be made. He had never been close to John, himself, and had hardly known Margery. But they were kin; and if the boy lived, he should be found. It was not so much a matter of bringing him to justice, for Rory's loss was a blessing to the folk of Elvington. It was more a matter of seeking out the truth and righting past wrongs. There was a search, and they turned Rory's cottage and outhouses upside down doing it. Not much there. The man drank away any profit he made on his chickens. But they did find something odd, and it began to awaken more memories among the locals. Under the floor of the outhouse there was a little root cellar, dug into the earth and shored up roughly with boards. And when one or two of the village folk saw that, they began to recall things from the odd time they'd been up there for a laying hen or a few eggs."

I nodded. "They used to shut him in there for punishment," I said.

My father stared at me. "How could you know that?"

"He told me. Not in words. He showed me. You said he was beyond any awareness of the world. But you're wrong. His mind still races. It is flooded with evil memories. He was imprisoned, not so long ago, in a small, dark space. Now he seems trapped there forever if I cannot lead him out. I have used my ability to see what he sees, to link my thoughts with his own. This way I hope to reach him before it is too late. Now tell me, what did folk say about this discovery?"

"You take my breath away, Liadan. This, surely, is a gift far greater than even Conor can summon, a perilous gift."

"Tell me, Father."

"They started to remember. Times when the lad was nowhere to be seen, and Rory had told them a mongrel was best kept in his box until he learned to obey. Times when they'd been at the door and heard small sounds from beneath the floor, a slight movement, a tiny scratching. A rat, said Rory. One of them had seen it, had seen Rory's woman get the child out of there, shaking, shivering, silent, his clothing soiled from where he'd relieved himself. Filthy pig, she'd said, and slapped his face. The strange thing was, he didn't utter a word. No tears. No attempt to protect himself either. Just stood there and waited until she'd finished. That made her angry, and she hit harder. People didn't like going up there; they didn't like what they saw. But nobody would protest. Terrified of Rory. Besides, they said, what happened in a man's own home was nobody else's business."

"How did they find out who the child was?"

"Ah, the search revealed that. Hidden away within the cottage was an item that made it quite plain." He reached into his pocket and took out something small and soft, made of a fine strong fabric with a silky finish to it. He unfolded it on the blankets between us, so that it lay across Bran's heart. There was not much light, but I could see traces of fine embroidery, leaves, flowers, little winged insects. "There's no doubt who this belonged to," said my father. "She'd a fine hand with the needle, had Margery. You'll have seen such patterns on the blue gown your mother wore . . ." His voice trailed off, for that wound was still fresh.

"Indeed," I said softly.

"Margery's people were beekeepers in the south," he said. "This was her small pouch, where she kept her valuables. She'd have had a little silver for the fair. That was gone, of course; Rory squandered whatever came his way. He couldn't sell this, nor its contents; they were a clear sign of her identity, and all knew she had met her end in those parts. It's unbelievable that Rory knew who the boy was and chose to keep it secret. He would have known as soon as the search took place; perhaps he himself joined in, alongside my brother's men. Why didn't he bring the child out and have him conveyed home to Harrowfield? But Rory chose to let them believe the tale about wild dogs. For some reason he decided to keep the boy. Such men relish what power they have. I suppose he found this small slave amusing. Rory knew the child was my kin, and he had nothing but hatred and resentment for me after what I had done to him. That, no doubt, is the source of this man's bitterness toward me. He'd have grown up hearing nothing but ill of me and mine."

"What was in the pouch?" I asked him.

My father passed me a small metal object, on a fine chain. I held it in my hand, feeling rather than seeing the locket, silver I thought, chased with delicate patterns around an enamelled center.

"What's inside this?"

"Two locks of hair. One brown and curling, the other fair and silk fine. The first is John's; the second belonged to their daughter who died soon after birth. The locket was a gift from John when they first knew she was with child—a gift of hope. Margery wore it always. They little imagined it would become a symbol of death and loss. How it came to be in Rory's cottage, nobody knows."

"Ah," I said, "but he remembers, and so I know."

"How can he remember? He was barely three years old."

"Her voice. Her hands. She hid him in the root cellar. I suppose they were close by this cottage that stands alone in the hills when they came under attack. To go inside, to try to hide, would be pointless; the Picts are no respecters of property, and would have flushed them out by fire or simply hacked their way in. But she could conceal the child for long enough. She bade him be still and quiet as she lowered him down into the tiny, dark space under the floor. He did as she told him, though he didn't like the dark or the strange sounds coming from outside. I suppose she tucked her precious things in with him—the purse, the silver pieces, the locket that held the love of those she had lost. Then she went outside and ran to divert their attention, the way a mother bird flutters and dips her wing and draws the hunting beast away from the nest where her young wait helpless. So she died, and the child kept silent. Kept faith, though the time stretched on and on. He waited and waited, and at length his small prison was opened. But the hands that came to release him were not his mother's. They were the hands of a monster; and it was then the darkness truly engulfed him."

My father nodded gravely. "I cannot but believe you, for this fits neatly with the tale folk tell. I asked my brother why did people not question the appearance of a child so suddenly, where another had disappeared. But there were no good answers to be had in Elvington. It seemed the child was kept hidden for a considerable time. Folk heard crying, sometimes. Instead of arousing their curiosity, it had the opposite effect. They're a superstitious breed in those parts. Said it was a ghost, the ghost of the child taken by wild beasts. That kept people away. Later, when the boy came to be seen around the cottage and in the village, nobody thought it might be the same lad. They said the brat didn't seem like the son of gentlefolk."

"They let him be beaten and abused all those years, and nobody did a thing about it."

"It requires great courage to interfere in the affairs of a man such as Rory. Big, strong, vicious, a man with a reputation. All feared him. Simon knew nothing of this at the time. Had he known, he might perhaps have taken some action to intervene. But he had his own problems. I feel the responsibility for this, Liadan, feel it as a heavy weight. That John's son was subjected to such cruelty so close to home, is unforgivable. And so, you see, your man was right when he blamed me. If he has become an outcast, he may well lay the responsibility at my feet. I could not have prevented his mother's death. But I could have protected him."

"The past cannot be rewritten, Father."

"That's true. But the future can be shaped—if he survives."

"He will survive. He need only recognize that once he was loved, that once he was the child of a man and woman of great integrity who would have given anything to see him grow up safe and happy and make something of his life. He need only see that, and he will be set free."

"I cannot believe that he has heard us."

"You will need to tell it to him again. You will need to tell him what this means to you. Perhaps he hears. At least, our words fill the silence. What of the next part of the story?"

"Rory was killed. Nobody wept for him. All they wanted was the cottage, and the chickens. Did the boy kill him?"

"He administered punishment. Efficiently, as with everything he does. He waited until he was a man, and then he took control and walked away from the nightmare. But it was still there, seared like a brand on his spirit. Even now he carries it with him."

"A man? Was he not barely nine years old?"

I nodded. "Old enough to walk his own path. Why wasn't your brother able to find out what had become of him after that?"

"He tried, but his resources were limited. Simon was beset with difficulties. Edwin had taken a firm grip on Northwoods by then, and the feud was alive again. My defection, as they saw it, certainly made it no easier for Harrowfield to remain neutral. And Simon was not trained to run the estate as I was. He had to learn quickly. Elaine helped him a great deal; she has more of a head for it than he ever will. But folk remember. I was not forgiven for what I did, and the demands on my brother were heavy. Even now, these long years later, his path is less than smooth."

"What do you mean?"

"He took the news of Sorcha's death very hard. Although he has a wife and his people's respect, his heart always belonged to your mother. The whole of that tale has never been told and never will be. I thought him close to despair. He asked me to stay, but clearly that was not possible. I fear for him, Liadan. Harrowfield has no heirs, and Edwin of Northwoods watches closely."

"No heirs?"

"They have no sons. The closest of the blood are myself and Sean. And—this man." He glanced down at Bran's hollow-cheeked face.

"Your words disturb me, Father. Would you go back? Would you lay claim to Harrowfield again?"

"My brother needs help. He needs someone with a strong hand and a clear head; someone who can reestablish his defenses, and make it plain to Northwoods that Harrowfield is not for the taking. Had Liam lived, my path would have been plain. But I cannot leave Sean to deal with the affairs of Sevenwaters alone. He is young yet and overhasty, for all his strengths. In time he will be a fine and capable leader, but for now he needs my help to rebuild his alliances and establish his place. We must start again with the Uí Néill. My first duty is with my son. Nor have I forgotten my daughters. I wish to see you safe and settled. And Niamh, I did not do well by her, and I must be sure her future is in good hands."

"But what of your brother? Might not Harrowfield be lost if you wait? If Edwin moved to grasp Simon's holdings, our campaign for the Islands would surely be doomed."

"Indeed. It is a dilemma, for it would be folly for me, or for Sean, to try to hold estates on both sides of the water. But there is another possibility." He was looking at the unconscious man again.

"Bran?" I whispered, shocked. "That's—it's unthinkable, surely."

"I would suspect," said Iubdan evenly, "that for a man such as this, nothing is unthinkable and nothing impossible. Isn't that what they say about him?"

"Yes, but—"

"This man is my kinsman's son; he was born in the valley. He is, to all accounts, both strong and resourceful, if somewhat misguided. It could be argued that Harrowfield is his destiny, Liadan, and yours."

"He has so much to come to terms with; he could not be faced with that, not yet."

"You think he would lack the courage to return there, to the place of his nightmare? That does not tally with the leader his men speak of with such respect, a man who rises to every challenge. It does not tally with the love and loyalty you give him."

I swallowed. His words both terrified and enthralled me. This was a mission: a bright future. But first, the fetters of the past must be broken.

"Father," I said, "I need to be alone now, alone with Bran. Gull will find you a place to rest. Just tell me one more thing."

"What is it, Daughter?"

"Tell me quickly, give me a picture of John and Margery, before these horrors overwhelmed them. How it was with them and their little son."

"John thought Margery the finest thing in the world. The

most precious. Saw her on her father's farm, gathering honey. Brought her north with him. The love between them shone bright from the first. He was a man of few words; some called him taciturn. But you could see it in his eyes when he watched her. You could see it in the way they touched one another. She lost one child soon after birth, and they grieved together. Then Johnny was born, and lived. John was so proud. He was not ashamed to play with his small son, to throw him up in the air, and catch him in strong hands as the child squealed with excitement. There was a fire in the house once, and I'll never forget John's expression as he raced upstairs to rescue his son, nor the look in Margery's eyes as the two of them came out safe. Margery watched over the child and loved him. Folk said he was very quick to learn. Early to crawl, early to walk, early to form words. Margery was teaching him to count. She'd put a row of white stones out on the floor and play a little game: one, two, three. There was never a child raised with such love, Liadan."

"Thank you, Father," I said. "It is these things, perhaps, that have guided him through the shadows thus far. Tonight, I will tell him this. Now you should go."

"This man is indeed fortunate, as I was," said my father quietly. "To gain the love of such a woman is a priceless gift. I hope he understands its value."

"We have both received such a gift, he and I," I said.

"I've one more small tale to tell, and then I will do as you bid. There was something Margery said, something she told me before I left Harrowfield. Her son was born on Midwinter Day, just before dawn. I have good cause to remember that. She said, a child born at midwinter comes into the world on the shortest day of the year. From that point on, the days stretch out. And so a child born at midwinter walks always toward the light, all his life. The child was there, in her arms, when she told me this. Remember that, Johnny, she said to him. Sorcha, also, was a midwinter child, and for her this small prophecy was surely true. But it seems this man has forgotten and seeks out only the darkness."

"It seems so. That is the surface. Deep inside, there is a small light that still burns. Tonight I will find it."

"You are very certain."

"Third rule of combat. Never doubt yourself. Now be off with you, for time runs short."

"Liadan."

"What is it?"

"You make this seem so simple."

"The world is simple, I think, in its essence: Life, death, love, hate. Desire, fulfillment. Magic. That, perhaps, is the only complicated part."

He frowned. "You seek to heal his wounds, to reach him, and somehow change his vision of the past. That is danger-ous, Liadan. Besides, did you not say yourself, the past can-not be rewritten?"

"I know the dangers. I am armed against them. Armed with love, Father. I do not seek to make these wounds van-ish as if they had never been. I know he will always bear the scars. I cannot make his path grow broad and straight. It will always twist and turn and offer new difficulties. But I can take his hand and walk by his side."

Chapter Sixteen

Gull had put out the fire and quenched his lantern. I suspected both he and my father stood guard not far off in
the blackness. Shivering in the autumn air, I took off my
boots, gown, shift, smallclothes. Then I slipped under the blankets and lay down next to Bran. On his other side, Johnny slept
on, a small, warm presence tucked close to his father. The
darkness was profound, blotting out all signs, all landmarks.
Up, down, left, right, all were gone. You could not tell if the
walls were out there or right beside you, shutting you in tight.

Closer, breathed the ancient voices. *Closer.* So I entwined my body with Bran's, flesh on naked flesh, and I
clasped my arms tight around him. I could feel his heart
beating against mine; my breath kept pace with his own.
That's better, the voices seemed to murmur. *Stay close.
Don't let go. Tonight there is no light but you.*

And this time I heard him straightaway, almost as if he
had been waiting for me.

. . . dark . . . too dark . . . one, two, three . . . too dark . . .

Tonight is dark of the moon. There have been such nights before. This one is different. I am here with you.

. . . too dark . . . can't . . . too long . . .

She said she would come back for you, but she couldn't come back, Johnny. She couldn't come, though she wanted to more than anything. I have come for you instead. Did you ever ask why didn't she come?

His heart began to race, and I stroked his skin with the tips of my fingers and willed us both to stay calm. His mind was full of images of darkness: hurt, pain, pictures half complete, distorted, jumbled together; knife, blood, screams, hands letting go. Death. Loss.

. . . she never came back . . . she never came . . .

She loved you. She gave her life so that you would be safe. She did not abandon you, Johnny.

. . . gutter scum . . . slattern's mongrel . . . my own mother didn't want me . . . scarce fit for the midden . . .

Those are lies. Let me show you. Take me back, Bran. Take me back before.

There is no before. She left me. Be very quiet, Johnny . . . quiet as a little mouse, sweetheart, no matter what you hear . . . wait for me . . . I will come back for you as soon as I can . . . her hands, pushing me down, down where it's dark. Her hands letting go. Shutting the door. She never came back. That is all there is. There is nothing else.

Ah, but I have come for you. She could not, but she loved you and wished you safe. Take my hand, Bran. I'm very close. Stretch out your hand to me.

Outside the shelter, around the pool, the trees rustled, but there was no wind.

. . . it's dark. I can't see you . . .

Take me back before. Do it, Bran, do it.

I told you, there is nothing before that. Her hands, letting go . . . nothing more.

Who taught you to count, one, two, three, all the way to ten? A clever child. A child like your own son, eager for knowledge, thirsty for adventure. Who set out the white stones for you and taught you numbers?

. . . one, two, three, four . . . her fingers pointing, her nails scrubbed clean, her hands small and fine . . . I reach ten, and she claps her hands. I look up, pleased with myself, and she's smiling. Her hair is like sunshine; her eyes full of brightness. Good, Johnny, good. What a clever boy! Shall we do it again? Let's put our little pigs in two rows; that's right. Now the farmer's going to count them, half to go to market, half to fatten up for the winter. How many in this row . . . one, two, three . . . but she went away . . . she let me go . . .

She would never have left you willingly. She hid you, and then she gave her life for you. Didn't you hear the story my father told? Your mother was the bravest of women. She wanted a life of joy and purpose for her small, midwinter son; she wished him to walk ever toward the light. As for your father, his pride in you shone from his face as he held you high in his strong hands . . . you're going up, up into the sky . . . going up so high, knowing those hands will always catch you.

. . . I cannot . . . I . . .

Always, he would catch you. Every time. His eyes were as gray and steady as your own, and as true. Go back, Johnny. Go back before.

Up, up, and down. Up, up and down. Flying up in the sky. Falling into his hands. He smiles. Curling hair, weathered face. Eyes alight with pride. I shriek with excitement. No more, son, he grins. You'll wear me out. One last time, up, up and down. Then arms around me, warm, strong. I put my head on his shoulder, thumb in mouth. Good. Safe.

I felt a drop of water on my face, warm in the chill of the night. But it was not I who was weeping. I dared not lift my head to look. I dared not move away from where I lay pressed close against him, lest I destroy something as fragile as a single filament of cobweb. I drew a deep breath and felt the weight of utter exhaustion descend on me, near overwhelming. Around us the whole grove was stirring, foliage rustling, twigs cracking, water rippling; the very stones seemed to cry out in the blackness of the night.

"Help me," I whispered into the dark. And I hummed a little of the old tune, just the refrain with its small arch of melody. The strange wind gusted over the top of the barrow, releasing a powerful voice, a deep sound that lay on the margins of hearing, a cry older than the oldest memory of humankind. Ringing from the great mound, sounding from the depths of the earth, vibrating forth from the standing stones, a call that could not be ignored.

Come out, warrior! A mission lies before you, a mission lifelong, whose challenges are many, whose rewards are beyond measure. Come forth now and show us true courage. Show us true strength of spirit, as once you did, long years ago. For the strength of the child is the strength of the man. The child and the man are one.

The cry ceased, and the rustling died down to a hush, a profound silence of deep anticipation. Something was expected of me, I could feel it, something more. Bran lay as still as before. Outwardly, nothing had changed, but for the slow tears that trickled down his face and onto mine, so that we shared the same grief for good folk whose lives had been cut short, the same sorrow for lost opportunities. I had to do something, but I was tired, so tired I thought I could sleep forever, tucked up warm with my man and my son, the deep, innocent sleep of a little child . . . but no, I must not give in to that. It was near dawn, and I did not have him, not yet. The silence was complete, save for the tiny whisper in my mind. *Do it.* But what? What? If he had not awoken to that ancient clarion call, what could I say that could possibly be more compelling? I had done everything and still he did not stir. My father had said, you make this seem so simple. But it wasn't, it was the hardest thing I had ever done . . . and yet perhaps, after all, the answer was very simple indeed.

Come, Johnny. In my mind, I held out my hand, and reached down to the child crouched in the small, dark space. He would not look up at me; his fingers covered his eyes, as if, while he blocked out the light, he would himself remain invisible. *Take my hand, Johnny. There are ten steps up, see? But maybe you do not know how to count to ten. You do? Then we'll walk up one at a time, and count them as we go. When we get to the top, the night will be over. Take my hand, Johnny. Reach up just a little farther. Yes. Yes, that's good. Good boy. Now count. One, two, three . . . four, five . . . well done . . . six, seven . . . eight . . . not far now . . . you can do this . . . nine . . . ten . . . good, dear heart. Very good . . .*

The voices of the Old Ones echoed mine, deep, sonorous, wise. *Good. Good.* Then, suddenly and totally, weariness overtook me. I fell into a deep slumber, and I dreamed a wonderful dream in which I lay here by Bran's side and felt the salt tears on his cheeks, a dream in which he stirred and put his arm around me, and touched his lips to my temple, and was himself again. In my dream I wound my arms around his neck and felt his body warm and alive against my own, and I told him I loved him, and he said yes, he knew that.

Abruptly, I was awake, and it was light, not the soft light of early dawn but later, much later, the full brightness of morning. How could I have allowed myself to fall asleep, how could I? I reached out, and my hand touched the small, sleeping form of my son, cocooned in the blanket as the two of us lay on the pallet together. Had I half woken and fed him and slumbered again unaware? How could I do such a thing? I reached out farther. Bran was gone. My throat went dry, and chill fingers clutched at my heart. He could not have woken and got up. That was impossible after so long without food and water; he would be too weak. That meant—that could only mean . . . I sat up and remembered belatedly that I was completely naked. I reached for my gown, where I had dropped it by the pallet last night. My hands were shaking. I could not find it nor my shift. There was an old shirt there, which would cover me to the knees, and I dragged this over my head, and stumbled out of the shelter. Three men were seated by the newly kindled fire: Gull, Snake, and my father. Their heads turned as one toward me.

"Where—what—?" was the best I could manage.

My father read my expression quickly and got up to take my hands in his and to speak reassuringly. "All's well, Liadan," he said. "Take a deep breath now. He is awake and in his right mind. You're as pale as a ghost, Daughter. Here, sit by us a little."

"I—I—where?"

"Not far, we're keeping an eye on him. Down yonder." Gull jerked his head toward the far end of the pool away from the barrow.

"He wouldn't let us wake you," said Snake apologetically. "Not in the best of moods, is the chief, as we predicted. But he's alive. You've done it."

"He is up, and walking?" I could not believe it. He had been near death. Surely this was some cruel dream. "He shouldn't be out of bed. How could you let him—?"

"Gave us no choice. Near bit our heads off. But he's had plenty of water, and as I said, he's being watched. Best left alone for now."

"Fetching outfit," remarked Gull, looking me up and down.

I blushed. "Where are my clothes?"

"Somewhere being spruced up for you. We'll find you some fresh ones. You'll be needing them."

"I must go—I must—"

"Maybe not yet," said Gull. "Gave us orders. Leave him alone. Later, maybe."

My father cleared his throat. "I've spoken with him at some length, Liadan. I told the story as you bid me. You should perhaps heed these men's advice and give him time."

"I don't think so," I said, and I walked away under the beeches in my bare feet and my ill-fitting shirt; down to the northern end of the pool where a great tree had fallen long ago. Now its massive trunk was overgrown with fine mosses, and its cracks and crevices, its small, shadowy passages held the lairs and hiding places of a myriad of tiny creatures.

I suppose I had not really believed it, not quite, until I saw him, seated on the rocks beyond this tree with his back to me and an obstinacy in the set of the shoulders that I recognized well enough. He wore his old clothes of indefinable color, and they hung on him like the garments of a far larger man. He was looking down, and in his hands he turned the little silver locket over and over. I longed to run forward, to wrap my arms around him and reassure myself that this was real and not some false vision. But I went cautiously, my bare feet making no sound. Still, this man was an expert at what he did. He spoke without turning, halting me when I was ten paces away. His voice was tightly controlled.

"Your father leaves this morning. You'd best pack up and go with him. Best for you. Best for the child. There's nothing for you here."

It took every scrap of will I had not to burst into tears, not to give him the opportunity, again, to tell me a woman cried when it suited her, just to get what she wanted. It took every bit of restraint I could muster not to walk up and slap him on the cheek, and point out to him that while I might not want gratitude, I did not expect to be dismissed like a hireling whose task is complete. I had learned a lot since first I met him. I had learned that the most evasive, the most difficult quarry must be taken with care and patience and subtlety.

"I—I remember you told me once," I said, holding my voice as steady as I could, "that you would not lie to me. Did my father happen to mention a promise he made me?"

There was a long pause before he replied.

"Don't make this more difficult for the two of us, Liadan," he said, and as I came close, I could see how his hands were trembling where they held the locket.

"Did he?"

"Yes."

"Very well. So you know that this choice will be my own and not my father's."

"How can there be a choice? It is no more than common sense that you should leave me. What future can there be for . . . for . . ."

I came up to him and moved to stand before him, three paces away. If anyone were to break the code this time, it would not be me.

"Look at me, Bran," I said. "Look at me, and tell me you want me to go. Tell me the truth."

But he stared down at his hands and would not. "You must indeed think me weak," he muttered. "After this, I will forfeit any respect."

And despite all his efforts, I could see the mark of a tear on his face, gleaming on the patterned side, where he had not been able to hold it back.

"I wish I could dry these tears," I said softly. "I wish I could make this better for you, but I don't know how."

There was the tiniest silence; a heartbeat of time, while the trees and rocks and the very currents of air seemed to hold their breath. Then he reached out his hand, blindly, and took my arm, and pulled me toward him. I stood there with his head against my breast and my arms wrapped around his shoulders, as he set free the rest of the tears he had held back for so long.

"There, Bran. It's all right. It's all right now. Weep, dear heart."

It was a long time, or a short time. Who can say? The men left us undisturbed, and the tall beeches looked on in silence, and the sun climbed higher in a cool autumn sky. It is not such a terrible thing for a grown man to weep. Not when he has eighteen years of grief and sorrow within him; not when at last, after such a long and painful journey, he has found the truth. Eventually he was done, and I used a corner of my disreputable attire to wipe his face for him and said, rather severely, "You should not even be out of bed. Did you have anything to eat this morning, or were you too busy giving orders?"

I moved to seat myself by him on the rocks, close by, so that our bodies touched.

"It was indeed wondrous to wake," he said shakily, "and find you lying there beside me, and not a stitch of clothing between us. Both wondrous and frustrating since I was so weak all I could do was look at you. Even now, I can scarce lift my arm to put it around you, let alone take advantage of this interesting garment you wear. I suspect there is little between it and yourself."

"Ah," I said, and felt a blush rise to my cheeks. "You're acquiring a sense of humor. I like that. There will be other mornings."

"How can there be, Liadan? How can there be time for us? You cannot live among the men, traveling by stealth, always looking over your shoulder, outcast, pursued. I could never subject you, or him, to that risk. The decision lies outside what you or I might want for ourselves. Your safety must be the first consideration. Besides, how could you stay with me after what has happened? I allowed myself to be taken by—that man; I allowed Gull to be maimed, and you to endure the most appalling treatment, you and my son. Now I am reduced to a shivering, weeping shadow of a man. What must you think of me?"

"I have not changed my opinion of you since last we met," I said steadily.

"What are you saying, Liadan?" Still he stared at the ground and would not meet my eyes. I slipped off the rock where we sat and went to kneel before him, giving him no choice but to look at me. I put my hands around his, and the silver locket was held, protected, by the two of us.

"Remember," I said quietly, "you asked me back at Sevenwaters what I wanted for myself? I said you were not ready to hear it. Do you think you are ready now? How much do you remember of what has happened here?"

"Enough. Enough to know we walked through years, not days. Enough to know you were there beside me. It is this that makes it so hard. I should order you to go and let that be an end of it. I know what is right. But—but I find that this time it is, after all, beyond me to bid you farewell. I hold my mother's love in my hand here and know love endures beyond death. That a heart once given is given forever."

I nodded, with tears dangerously close. "She hid her most cherished things," I said. "This locket, with the tokens of her lost ones. Her small purse, bearing the symbols of who she was and whence she came. And her little son. She gave her life for you. John gave his life in the service of his friend and kinsman. That is the truth."

He nodded soberly. "I have been wrong about some things. You will not hear me recognizing Hugh of Harrowfield as a hero, but I find the man has some good points. He was very straight with me. I respect that. He is more like you than I could have imagined."

"He's known for his honesty."

"Liadan."

I looked into his eyes. His face was starkly pale, his features drained, exhausted. But the eyes were giving me another message entirely. They were hungry.

"I haven't answered, have I? Haven't told you what I want? Do I need to say it, Bran?"

He nodded, without saying a word.

"I told you I had not changed my opinion of you, not since you came to me at Sevenwaters and we so nearly forgot the rest of the world for a time. What has happened these last days is a part of our journey together. Together we suffer and endure and change and walk forward again, hand in hand. I think you strong beyond belief; at times too strong for your own good. I see in you a leader, a man of vision and daring. I see a man who is still afraid to love, and to laugh; but who is learning both now that he knows the truth about himself. I see the only man I would have for my husband and the father of my children. You and no other, Bran."

He lifted his hand and reached out to touch my cheek, very carefully, as if he must learn how to do this again, now that everything had changed.

"This is a—a proposal of marriage?" he asked me, and there was the very smallest trace of a smile at the corner of his mouth, something I had never seen before.

"I suppose so," I said, blushing again. "And, as you see, I'm doing it properly, on my knees."

"Hmm. This would, however, be a partnership of equals you're offering, I imagine?"

"Undoubtedly."

"I cannot speak the words. I cannot bring myself to refuse you. And yet, how can I accept? You ask the impossible." His face was bleak again. "You ask me to subject those I love best to a life of danger and flight. How can I agree to such a thing?"

"Ah," I said, "I would not have told you this, not yet; but you give me no choice. It seems there is a place for you—

for us—in Britain, at Harrowfield. A place and a mission. So my father tells me. His brother's hold on the estate weakens; Edwin of Northwoods watches closely, thinking to broaden his own domain. My father cannot return there to help them, but you could go. It need not be now; but it is something to consider. This is your father's land, Bran; these are your father's people. You scorned Lord Hugh once for turning his back on Harrowfield to follow his heart. Now he gives you the chance to do what he cannot: to help Simon strengthen and unite these good folk once more."

There was a lengthy silence, and I began to regret my words. Perhaps I had been right before. Perhaps it was too soon to tell him.

"Hugh of Harrowfield would trust me with this?" Bran asked softly.

I looked into his eyes. There was no mistaking the light newkindled there, a flame of hope and purpose.

"He would trust John's son," I said. "And so, in time, would the folk of Harrowfield, when you proved yourself."

"You would do this? You would come with me, all the way to Britain? Live among foreigners, away from your family?"

"I would not be away from my family, Bran. Wherever the three of us travel, that is home. Besides, you forget. I am half Briton myself. Simon of Harrowfield is my uncle; these folk are both mine and yours."

He gave a little nod; his hand tightened on mine. "I can scarce believe this," he said. "And yet I do believe it. My mind already jumps to what can be done and how we will achieve it. I fear to return there; it is a place of darkness and terror. And yet I long to return and make things right again. I long to prove what seemed impossible: that I can be my father's son."

His words made me want to weep; I was still bone weary from the night before and from changes that came so fast I could scarce keep up with them.

"The men," Bran said suddenly. "What about the men? Where will they go? I cannot leave them alone, without a place and a purpose."

"Well, now," I said, "it may be these men are more resourceful than you think. Let's go up to the fire. Can you stand? Walk, with my help? Good. Use my shoulder for support. Go on, do it. Nobody expects you to exhibit godlike strength, excepting maybe yourself. That head wound alone was enough to kill a man. You've been starved for days, and you're all over bruises. I want to see you drinking some water and eating a little porridge. Your men have a proposition to put before you, one that will interest you and answer many of your concerns. They have kept watch for their chief most faithfully, Bran. You might perhaps manage a kind word or two. And I must bid my father farewell, for he is needed at home. Later, we will speak with him further of these things."

"I—" He stood swaying, chalk faced, like a ghost of himself.

"Come, dear heart. Lean on me and let us walk this path together."

They knew him very well. And so neither Gull nor Snake nor any of the others sprang up to offer support as we walked slowly and carefully toward the fire. Nobody made any fuss or any comment. But there was a place to sit for the two of us, and water to drink, as well as ale, and plain oaten porridge in earthenware bowls. My father was still there, but he was dressed for departure.

"You have something to tell me, I understand," Bran said, with a forbidding scowl on his face, once he was seated. Around us many men were gathered, all of them, I thought, except the few who kept obligatory watch on the perimeters of the camp. There was an air of deep expectancy about them, but this was soon shattered by the arrival of Rat, bearing my wailing son.

"You'd better go on without me," I said, taking the child into my arms and rising to my feet. "This is men's business, I suppose."

"You belong here," Bran said quietly. "We will wait for you." He turned back to look at Gull, with his bandaged hands; at Snake, whose patterned features bore the pallor of more than one sleepless night; at Otter and Spider, who had ridden out on a mission; at big, grim Wolf and at young Rat, guardian of what was smallest and most precious. "I've got a few things to say to you all," he began.

As I fed Johnny in the shelter, I watched these men, and I hoped they would not speak of Eamonn and of what he had done. It was clear my father had not yet learned the truth; and indeed, he must be kept in ignorance of it. The balance would indeed be delicate now between the partners of the alliance, and I must lose no time in telling Bran what bargain I had struck with his enemy to secure his release.

Johnny was soon finished and wriggling on my lap, ready for more adventures. I set him on the ground, observing that his clothing had changed somewhat from the neat shirt and leggings in which he had traveled out from Sevenwaters. It seemed so long ago, it was as if the whole world had changed since that day. Someone had been busy with the needle, and now my son wore a small jacket of deerskin, and boots of the same soft hide, neatly sewn with narrow strips of leather. A kind of tunic went underneath the jacket, covering him down to the boot tops. Its fabric was woven in stripes, blue, brown, a deep red. A fine cloth; someone had sacrificed a garment of his own for this small masterpiece to be created. Johnny began to creep out of the shelter, and I plucked him up in my arms and ventured forth.

"I'll take him for a while," said my father as I came up. "You will not wish me to be present, I imagine, for your planning."

"You should stay, I think." As I spoke, I glanced questioningly at Bran. "For this plan, if it goes ahead, will involve my brother, and so yourself. You should know of it."

Bran's scowl deepened.

"She's right," Gull said. "Either this goes ahead with the help of Sevenwaters, or things stay as they are. There's no risk in telling him."

"I'm not liking the sound of this," said Bran. "Come on then, out with it." His tone was fierce; but when I went to sit by him, and slipped my hand into his, I could feel his trembling and knew the control he must exert to appear as he did. His scowl gave a clear message. *I am the Painted Man. Think me weak at your peril.*

So they told him. They laid it out before him, as my father sat on the ground with his grandson between his legs, playing a little game with twigs and leaves. One after another, they spoke. It had been well rehearsed. Gull outlined the bare bones of the plan. Snake elaborated a little. There were no emotive arguments; no talk of women and settling down. Simply a neat structure of logic, of advantages to be gained and profits made, and of how certain problems might be overcome. Otter came next. He could have known of the plan only since his return last night, but he set out full details of how the venture would be paid for and how my brother might be involved, and of how gains could be shared among all after the costs of running the establishment were covered. Of how, in time, Sean's investment could be repaid, in silver or cattle or services.

Bran had not said a single word, and his expression gave nothing away. As for my father, it was as well he sat a little apart, watching Johnny, for I could see the shocked look on his face and how he struggled to remain quiet.

"There's a matter of accommodation." Now it was the turn of big Wolf, usually a man of very few words. "I'm told there's a croft or two on this island, and some stone walls to keep the sheep from the cliffs. We'll need more.

Simple, low, built for wild weather. I've some skill in building. I could teach the rest of you. We'd set it up thus—" He squatted down and began to draw with a stick on the earth, and all watched him with deep concentration. ". . . thatch, well tied . . . practice yard . . ."

I was weary again, and I laid my head on Bran's shoulder, almost without thinking. His hand tightened on mine, and I caught my father's glance. Already it held the shadow of another farewell.

They finished. There was a silence in which nobody seemed to wish to speak first. It was Iubdan who broke it.

"You wish me to put this—proposition—to my son when I return to Sevenwaters? You are aware, I suppose, that Sean has come to the leadership of his túath but recently and bears a heavy load for one so young?"

Bran gave a nod. "Lord Liam was a strong leader, a man of balance. No doubt he'll be missed in these parts. But your son has the ability to do better, in time. He has vision. There's no need for you to speak to him of this. I must consider it first. If I decide to go ahead with it, I'll set up a meeting. I've information for Sean, information he sent me to gather."

"I could, I suppose, take it back for him," my father said. His tone was less than enthusiastic.

Bran frowned. "Such intelligence is best not shared, unless strictly necessary. The risk is minimized if one man tells it direct to the other. I'll meet with Sean when the time's right."

Someone whistled softly. And Gull said incredulously, "You're telling us the mission was a success after everything? That you got what he needed? That you kept it to yourself, even when—"

"No mission is too difficult for the Painted Man," I put in quickly. "I'm surprised you don't know that by now."

"Back to work now, the lot of you," said Snake, getting to his feet. "There's much to think about and to consider.

The chief will give us his answer when he's ready. Go and prepare Iubdan's horse, and those of you who are escorting him, check your weapons and supplies. He needs to be away."

"Here," said Rat, crouching down by my father, and reaching out his hands to Johnny. "I'll take him now." He picked up the child, and Johnny's small arms went trustingly around his neck.

My father got up. "Very well," he said, in a distant sort of tone, and he put out his big hand to touch his grandson's cheek, gently. Then Rat was off, jogging away to the main encampment with his small friend bouncing and squealing excitedly in his arms. The men dispersed, all but Gull, for when he made to follow them, Bran took him by the arm and said, "No. You stay."

So there we were, the four of us by the small fire, with so many words unspoken between us, it was hard to know where to begin. Eventually, Bran looked up at my father and spoke quietly.

"Liadan has told me of your proposition for Harrowfield. There is much that can be done there, I think. Alliances rebuilt; borders secured; defenses strengthened."

"You may wish to take time to consider it," my father said cautiously. "Such a role is somewhat alien to you, I expect. But you are my kinsman, and Simon's; you have a valid claim to be involved with the estate, and an ability that seems beyond dispute."

"There is no need to consider," Bran said. "We accept the challenge. For the immediate future, I want Liadan and my son safe away from these parts. We will ride north and may be gone for some time. My men must be settled and established in their new endeavor; that will not be a simple matter. Once that is done, we will go to Harrowfield: Liadan and I, and Johnny. I must speak plain to you. It is not for Lord Hugh that I agree to this, but for my father and my mother and for the place that gave me birth. I wish to lay some things to rest; thus can it be done and a new beginning made."

Father's blue eyes were cool. But the little inclination of his head was an acknowledgment of Bran's strength; I could tell he was both surprised and impressed.

"Good," he said. "I will ensure Simon is advised, discreetly, of what we intend. The news will hearten him. I am a little uneasy about the immediate future. I would ask you to undertake to keep my daughter safe, and my grandson. But such a question seems inappropriate here."

I felt Bran's hand tense in mine, heard his sharp, indrawn breath.

"It is quite appropriate, Father," I said. "As I have told you, these men are skilled in such things. You trust my judgment, do you not?"

"Liadan's well protected with us," put in Gull, and he, too, was angry, "safer than ever she'd be in the houses of some you call friends."

"What do you mean?"

"Nothing, Father. Gull simply refers to the ability of these men to pass unseen, to avoid detection, and to employ unusual methods of defense. You must not be concerned for me. I had never thought I would go far away from Sevenwaters, but this is the right choice, the only choice."

"You would take my daughter from me, then," Iubdan said, watching Bran closely.

Bran looked back at him, his gray eyes steady and clear. "I take no more than is freely given," he said.

"You'd best be off," said Gull. "It's a fair ride. Our men will escort you as far as your borders."

"There's no need." Father's tone was cool. "I am not yet so advanced in years that I cannot defend myself or despatch an enemy."

"So we've heard," said Bran. "Nonetheless, there are dangers you may not know of. Who knows what traps may await a solitary traveler? My men will accompany you."

"I'd like a word with my daughter alone," said Iubdan, unsmiling, "if that's allowable."

Bran released my hand. "Liadan makes her own decisions," he said. "As my wife, she will continue to do so."

Gull's brows rose, but he said nothing.

I walked down to the water's edge with my father, watching as he picked up a smooth white stone and skipped it across the water, one, two, three.

"Will this work, do you think?" he asked. "A school for warriors? A home for the outlawed?"

"That's up to him. It will be modified, no doubt, amended and improved to suit his own ideas. It is a new path for him; he has many changes to come to terms with."

"He needs you. They need you. That much I comprehend. Your choice still shocks me. I think I made an error in watching you grow. You are so like your mother in every way that I did not expect surprises from you. I never really thought you would leave the forest. But then, I once made such a choice myself, against all the rules. And you are my daughter as well as hers. That you will in time return to my home, to Harrowfield, fills me with pride and hope. I wish I could watch my brother's face when first he sees you. But I cannot imagine Sevenwaters with both your mother and yourself gone. It will be as if the heart of the place is stilled."

"Conor, no doubt, would agree with you. But the heart of the forest beats very strong and very slow, Father. It would take far more than this loss to halt its rhythm."

"I have other concerns. There are secrets here that puzzle and disturb me, veiled references, a part of the tale that is untold."

"It must remain untold, Father. I, too, am bound by a promise."

"You told me Niamh survived and was taken to a place of safety. She's my daughter, Liadan. I spoke of righting wrongs. There is a wrong there that must be attended to, I believe. I would welcome Niamh back home. If you are able to tell me where she is, you should do so. Your mother wished, very much, that we might make amends."

"I'm sorry," I said quietly. "I have an idea where she might be, but I can't tell you. Only that I know she is safe and well looked after. She doesn't want to see us, Father. She doesn't want to come back."

"I lose you all then," he said flatly. "Niamh, and Sorcha, and you. And the little one as well."

"There will be a tribe of children at Sevenwaters in a few years. And you will see me from time to time, and Johnny; I'll make sure of that. You'll be busy, Father, too busy for sorrow and regrets. Now you must go home to Sean and Aisling and give them your support. The three of you must work hard to keep Sevenwaters strong. You will hear from us in due course. And wish Sean well from me."

"I will, sweetheart."

"Father."

"What is it?"

"I couldn't have done this without you. However far I travel, I'll never forget that I am your daughter. I will always be proud of that."

Then they called him, and he hugged me, quickly and hard, and was gone, a tall, flame-haired figure striding away to the camp, where men waited with horses. I stood by the pool, gazing across its silvery surface, and as I looked, an image appeared, a reflection in the still waters: a stately white swan, floating there with folded wings. A reflection with no reality, for on the surface there was nothing, not a single bird swam on that mirror-calm water. I blinked and rubbed my eyes. The image remained, feathers like a midwinter snowdrift, graceful arching neck, eyes colorless as clear water, deep, so deep.

You've done very well, Liadan. It was my Uncle Finbar's voice. *You are a master at this, and I salute you.*

It is you who are the master. You showed me this skill.

I could not have done what you did; challenged the dark one and pulled a man back from the brink of death. Your strength amazes me. Your courage astonishes me. I will watch your path, and his, with interest. Don't forget me, Liadan. You'll need me later. The child will need me.

A sudden chill passed over me. *What do you mean? What do you see?*

But out in the water, the beautiful inverted form of the swan fragmented and spread across the surface and was gone.

Three days later we were ready to move on. I had had to be very strict and make sure Bran ate and drank and rested, for if I had left him to go his own way, he would have tried to force his damaged body to be its old self again immediately, with disastrous results. However, he wasted not an instant. When obliged to rest, he would still be planning, and giving orders, and chafing to be up and active again. As for the nights, although my inclination was quite otherwise, I slept apart from him, sharing the bed of bracken with my son, and Bran made no comment. I had been bold that night, bold enough to strip naked and warm his flesh with my own. Now I felt a little awkward, for what was between us was new and fragile, and there were many men about. Besides, it seemed to me some things must wait until he had regained his strength.

Plans were made. The band was to split into three groups. There was work to be done. Otter's group was to go south on a mission unspecified. Snake's group was headed northwest, toward Tirconnell. Our own group was to ride north to the place under consideration and have a look at it before the final decision would be made. Wolf would assess the difficulty of access for men with building materials. Gull would see what skills were available locally and judge what reception might be given to such a venture. At an appointed time, the others would meet up with us, and the future of the band would be determined. He'd make no decisions in a hurry, Bran told the men. Too much was riding on it.

I'd had to work hard to stop him rushing off south the moment he thought himself fit to get up on a horse, seeking vengeance in blood. I'd had to explain the bargain I had made to get him and Gull out of Sídhe Dubh. How I'd promised silence for their release.

"A promise made to such a man is nothing," he said, tight-lipped. "After what he did to you, death is too good for him. If I do not despatch him, your father or brother surely will when they learn the truth."

"They won't," I said. "Not from me, and not from you or Gull or any of these men. This tale cannot be told. I gave Eamonn my word that we would keep silent and with good reason. He may be a turncoat, a man who can be blinded to what is right by his own desires and his own lust for power. But nobody can deny that he is a strong leader. He's wealthy, influential, and clever. And he has no heirs, not yet. If he were gone, it would lay his estates open to a struggle for control that would plunge the alliance into disarray and confusion. Seamus Redbeard is old, and his child is an infant. There would be claimants from everywhere. It would be a bloodbath. Better if Eamonn remains. We need only continue to watch him." My deeper misgivings I would not tell him. For I recalled the warnings of the Fair Folk, and Ciarán's own words. Somewhere out there was someone who would stop at nothing to prevent my child from growing to a man. Someone who, for her own reasons, did not want the prophecy to be fulfilled. I had seen the look on Bran's face as he watched his small son sleeping, or borne high on Rat's shoulders, looking about him with bright-eyed intelligence. I had seen Bran's hard features alight with a wonder new discovered, and I knew I could not tell him.

"You cannot have any faith in Eamonn Dubh," he said, frowning. "Might not he turn against your brother at any time?"

I smiled. "I don't think so. My brother weds Eamonn's sister in spring. I've ensured that will happen. And Eamonn knows I am watching him. I drove a hard enough bargain for my silence and yours."

"I see," said Bran slowly. "You are a dangerous woman, Liadan, a strategist of some subtlety. But you frustrate me. There will always be an itch in my hands for this man's neck. If ever I meet him face-to-face, I cannot answer for what I might do."

"Where we're going, you'll be too busy to give it a moment's thought," I told him.

"You assume we're going ahead with this venture, then."

"I know you could not bring yourself to deny the men their dream."

He looked at me, and that little attempt at a smile played about his severe mouth again. "I see I can have no secrets from you," he said. "I had only to see the light in their eyes, and hear the hope in their voices, to know what choice must be made. But I could not tell them so, not then. Such a tactic would have appeared weak. Besides, this waiting is a good test for them. It forces them to assess every aspect of the project, to sound out the strengths and weaknesses, and to address the problems."

"I know," I said.

Planning was complete, and there was but a day to our departure. It was morning under the great beeches, now quite bare against a pale sky. The weather was fair, though cold. With luck, we would cover the distance quickly, even with a babe among us. This last day was for final consultations among the leaders of each group, and for packing up the camp and erasing all trace of our presence once again. That process would alter once the venture went ahead. These men would have to become accustomed to waking in their own beds, to women's faces at their fireside, to settling. It would be an end to the pattern of flight and constant change. Hard for them, but not so hard, maybe, if they put their minds to it. I thought about Evan's woman, Biddy, with her two boys. Maybe she was still waiting, somewhere in Britain, for her man to come back for her. She'd sounded a strong, capable woman. They'd need a few like her. I thought I might mention that later.

I sat by the pool with Johnny on my lap, dreaming a little as I threw tiny pebbles into the water. Johnny liked the plop-plop they made and seemed content to sit quiet, watching. Behind me in the encampment, the work of the day unfolded with the customary order and discipline. It felt very strange to know that tomorrow I would ride away and never go back to the forest save as a visitor; that, in time, I would live on my father's estate and raise my son among Britons. I hoped my mother would not have thought this a betrayal. I hoped the Fair Folk had been wrong about what it would mean.

Best go now.

The old voice startled me; I had not thought to hear those ancient ones speak again now that Bran was saved and our path set.

We are going, I said silently, *in the morning. We will not return here.*

Go now. Go. It was slow and deep, as always, but this time the words were a warning.

Now? You mean—now, straight away? But why?

I was foolish to ask maybe. In an instant, the Sight was on me, and there was a young warrior fighting, and I thought it was Bran until I saw the features plain of any pattern save the most subtle of markings on the brow and around one eye, the merest hint of a raven mask. He was injured; I saw the pallor and heard the rasping breath. He lunged forward, and in one swift movement his opponent dashed the sword from his hand, and I saw in the young warrior's eyes that he recognized his death right before him. His eyes were gray and steady; his expression without fear. I clasped my arms tight around the child on my lap, and he gave a squeal of protest. The vision changed, and there was a girl, a girl crying, her whole body racked with sobbing; her two hands up over her face in a futile effort to contain her grief. Her curling hair was a deep red, her skin pale as new milk. As she wailed her anguish, a fire arose around her, its crackling flames hungry, consuming; and I had a strange sense that it was her very cries that whipped this fire to ever greater fury. Then, abruptly, the vision was gone.

Best leave now, said the voice once more, and was silent.

Such a warning cannot go unheeded. I sought out Bran and told him, not everything I had seen, but that the Sight had shown me our departure must be immediate. They were well practiced. Before the sun began to sink in the west, we were gone, riding off in our three separate directions with silent efficiency. My own band traveled north, going by secret ways. We stopped when it grew dark, for Bran insisted the child and I should sleep. We camped under rocks, partway up a hill. I fed Johnny; Bran and Wolf stood guard; Rat made a small fire and prepared food. Gull was settling the horses, for he insisted on doing his share of work, damaged hands or not.

After a while Bran came back up the hill to crouch down beside me. Johnny had finished drinking; I held him against my shoulder as he fell asleep.

"I'm sorry," I said quietly, "to disrupt your plans. We could have stayed another day, probably. The Sight does not always show true; and these voices can be misleading."

"Maybe not," said Bran, in a strange tone. "Come out here; I want to show you something."

I followed him out to a place on the rocks where there was a long view back to the south. In daylight, I imagined, one might be able to see as far as the great forest of Seven-waters itself. Now all was dark, all but a certain place, not so very far behind us, where a huge fire blazed.

"Strange, is it not?" Bran observed. "A lightning strike, maybe? But the sky is clear; no sign of storm. And there's been rain; trees and bushes and the very grasses do not burn thus, with a consuming heat, save in time of great drought. See how this fire moves and takes all in its path? Yet the night is still. Passing strange."

"It's there, isn't it?" I whispered, shivering. "In that place where we were?"

Bran put his arm around me rather cautiously, as if he were still learning what he might allow himself to do.

"But for you, we'd all have been in its path tonight," he said. "Your gift is a powerful one. You saw my death once. Do you remember that?"

"Yes."

"It seems to me that you have prevented that; that you have held back death; that you have changed the course of events. Not much scares me, Liadan. I've trained myself to face whatever comes. But this scares me."

"It frightens me, too. It leaves me open to—to many influences, to voices I would sooner not hear, to contrary visions. It can be very hard to know when I should heed them and when to go my own way. And yet, I would not be without it. But for this gift, I could not have brought you back."

He did not reply, and the silence drew out so long I began to be worried.

"Bran?" I asked softly.

"I wonder," he said hesitantly, "I did wonder if perhaps you—if maybe you regretted that. Had second thoughts, I mean. Now that you have seen—now that you know these things about me, things I have never told anyone . . . I am not the man you once thought me to be. I did think maybe . . ." He ran out of words.

"Why?" He had astonished me. "Why would you believe

such a thing, that I would not want you, that I might love you any less because of that? I have told you; you are the only man in the world I want by my side. Nothing will ever change that. I cannot make it any clearer."

"Then——" He stopped himself again.

"Then what, dear heart?"

"Why would you . . ." he spoke so quietly I strained to hear. "Why would you wish to sleep apart, why shun my bed, after that night, that longest of nights when I woke and found you there beside me, a gift of such precious worth it wiped away a lifetime of shadows? I ache to feel that moment again and this time, to hold you close, and touch you, and——I have no words for this, Liadan."

Perhaps it was just as well it was dark. I was laughing and crying at the same time and could hardly think what to say to him.

"If I were not holding the child," I said shakily, "I would show you this instant how my body burns for yours. It seems to me you have a short memory. I recall an afternoon by the lake of Sevenwaters when it was only our son's intervention that brought the two of us to our senses. As for these last days, I thought only to spare your health. You have been through a severe trial. You are still bruised in body and mind. I did not wish to——to demand more than you might——"

I sensed a ferocious scowl in the darkness. "You thought me incapable? Was that it?"

"I——well, I . . . I am a healer, after all, and it is only common sense——"

He stopped my words with a kiss, a firm, no-nonsense sort of kiss. It was briefer than I wished; Johnny was between us and in danger of being squashed.

"Liadan?"

"Mmm?"

"Will you share my bed tonight?"

I felt a blush rise to my cheeks. "More than likely," I told him.

The goddess blessed us, I think. Someone looked kindly on us that night, for Johnny fell asleep and never woke until morning; and the others took themselves off and arranged a watch, and we heard not a whisper from the three of them. As for me and my man, we lay closely entwined under the shelter of the rocks, and we showed no more restraint than we had that afternoon by the lake, for it had been a long time. We clung and gasped and wept in our need for each other, until at last we slept, exhausted, sharing a blanket under the great bowl of stars. At dawn we woke from the sweet warmth of shared sleep, and neither of us stirred save to touch softly, and brush lips against flesh and whisper little words, until we heard Rat busy with the fire, and Gull making some comment about where we might have got to.

"There will be other mornings," I said quietly.

"Until now, I don't think I ever really believed that." Bran was getting up, reluctantly, covering his finely decorated body with the plain traveling clothes he favored. I watched unabashed, marveling at how lucky I was.

"We must believe it," I said, and at that moment Johnny awoke and began to call insistently for his breakfast. "We must believe in a future, for him, for these men, and for ourselves. Surely love is strong enough to build that upon." I think it was for the Fair Folk I spoke, more than for us. But if they heard me, they gave no sign of it. I had made my decision. I had changed the course of things. If that meant I would never hear from them again, so be it.

So we rode away northward, without any fuss, a quiet, orderly band of travelers dressed in clothing that would draw no attention, a man whose face was a study in light and shade, whose features bore the bold, fierce pattern of the raven, and were at the same time fair and young. Which side you saw depended simply on how you chose to look at him. A woman with dark hair plaited down her back and strange, green eyes. A black man with odd-looking hands, and a gull's feather in his braided hair. A youth bearing a child, and a large, silent fellow on a large, silent horse. Ever northward we rode, to the rugged coast that looks out toward Alba, home of warrior women. Behind us the land of Ulster awoke to the morning, an autumn sun hazy bright over soft green valley, and sparkling lake, and the dark loveliness of the great forest of Sevenwaters. Behind us a fire burned out, and a plume of gray smoke marked the site of its destructive force, a force Otherworldly in its precision and its fury. Perhaps the Sorceress believed us dead, perished in its furnace. But we turned our backs to it and rode steadily away, and as we rode I heard it in my head once more, though the place of the barrow was far behind us now, the deep, humming sound of the west wind as it moved over the top of the ancient mound and passed across the narrow aperture left there for the mysterious piercing entrance of the midwinter sun. It was like the sonorous, ancient note of a great instrument; a salute of recognition and of farewell. *Well done, Daughter,* breathed the voices of my ancestors. *Oh, bravely done.*

Look for

Child
of the
Prophecy

by Juliet Marillier

Now available from Tor Books

Every summer they came. By earth and sky, by sun and stone I counted the days. I'd climb up to the circle and sit there quiet with my back to the warmth of the rock I called Sentinel, and see the rabbits come out in the fading light to nibble at what sparse pickings might be found on the barren hillside. The sun sank in the west, a ball of orange fire diving beyond the hills into the unseen depths of the ocean. Its dying light caught the shapes of the dolmens and stretched their strange shadows out across the stony ground before me. I'd been here every summer since first I saw the travelers come, and I'd learned to read the signs. Each day the setting sun threw the dark pointed shapes a little further across the hilltop to the north. When the biggest shadow came right to my toes, here where I sat in the very center of the circle, it was time. Tomorrow I could go and watch by the track, for they'd be here.

There was a pattern to it. There were patterns to everything, if you knew how to look. My father taught me that.

The real skill lay in staying outside them, in not letting yourself be caught up in them. It was a mistake to think you belonged. Such as we were could never belong. That, too, I learned from him.

I'd wait there by the track, behind a juniper bush, still as a child made of stone. There'd be a sound of hooves, and the creak of wheels turning. Then I'd see one or two of the lads on ponies, riding up ahead, keeping an eye out for any trouble. By the time they came up the hill and passed by me where I hid, they'd relaxed their guard and were joking and laughing, for they were close to camp and a summer of good fishing and relative ease, a time for mending things and making things. The season they spent here at the bay was the closest they ever came to settling down.

Then there'd be a cart or two, the old men and women sitting up on top, the smaller children perched on the load or running alongside. Danny Walker would be driving one pair of horses, his wife Peg the other. The rest of the folk would walk behind, their scarves and shawls and neckerchiefs bright splashes of color in the dun and gray of the landscape, for it was barren enough up here, even in the warmth of early summer. I'd watch and wait unseen, never stirring. And last, there was the string of ponies, and the younger lads leading them or riding alongside. That was the best moment of the summer: the first glimpse I got of Darragh, sitting small and proud on his sturdy gray. He'd be pale after the winter up north, and frowning as he watched his charges, always alert lest one of them should make a bolt for freedom. They'd a mind to go their own way, these hill ponies, until they were properly broken. This string would be trained over the warmer season, and sold when the traveling folk went north again.

Not by so much as a twitch of a finger or a blink of an eyelid would I let on that I was there. But Darragh would know. His brown eyes would look sideways, twinkling, and he'd flash a grin that nobody saw, nobody but me where I hid by the track. Then the travelers would pass on and be gone down to the cove and their summer encampment, and I'd be away home, scuttling across the hill and down over the neck of the land to the Honeycomb, which was where we lived, my father and I.

Father didn't much like me to go out. But he did not lay down any restrictions. It was more effective, he said, for me to set my own rules. The craft was a hard taskmaster. I would discover soon enough that it left no time for friends, no time for play, no time for swimming or fishing or jumping off the rocks as the other children did. There was much to learn. And when Father was too busy to teach me, I must spend my time practicing my skills. The only rules were the unspoken ones. Besides, I couldn't wander far, not with my foot the way it was.

I understood that for our kind the craft was all that really mattered. But Darragh made his way into my life uninvited and once he was there he became my summer companion and my best friend; my only friend, to tell the truth. I was frightened of the other children and could hardly imagine joining them in their boisterous games. They in their turn avoided me. Maybe it was fear, and maybe it was something else. I knew I was cleverer than they were. I knew I could do what I liked to them, if I chose to. And yet, when I looked at my reflection in the water, and thought of the boys and girls I'd seen running along the sand shouting to one another, and fishing from the rocks, and mending nets alongside their fathers and mothers, I wished with all my heart that I was one of them, and not myself. I wished I was one of the traveler girls, with a red scarf and a shawl with a long fringe to it, so I could perch up high on the cart and ride away in autumn time to the far distant lands of the north.

We had a place, a secret place, halfway down the hill behind big boulders and looking out to the southwest. Below us the steep, rocky promontory of the Honeycomb jutted into the sea. Inside it was a complex network of caves and chambers and concealed ways, a suitable home for a man such as my father. Behind us the slope stretched up and up to the flattened top of the hill, where the stone circle stood, and then down again to the cart track. Beyond that was the land of Kerry, and farther still were places whose names I did not know. But Darragh knew, and Darragh told me as he stacked driftwood neatly for a fire, and hunted for flint and tinder while I got out a little jar of dried herbs for tea. He told me of lakes and forests, of wild crags and gentle misty valleys. He described how the Norsemen, whose raids on our coast were so feared, had settled here and there and married Irish women, and bred children who were neither one thing nor the other. With a gleam of excitement in his brown eyes, he spoke of the great horse fair up north. He got so caught up in this, his thin hands gesturing, his voice bright with enthusiasm, that he forgot he was supposed to be lighting the little fire. So I did it myself, pointing at the sticks with my first finger, summoning the flame. The driftwood burst instantly alight, and our small pan of water began to heat. Darragh fell silent.

"Go on," I said. "Did the old man buy the pony or not?" But Darragh was frowning at me, his dark brows drawn together in disapproval. "You shouldn't do that," he said.

"What?"

"Light the fire like that. Using sorcerer's tricks. Not when you don't need to. What's wrong with flint and tinder? I would have done it."

"Why bother? My way's quicker." I was casting a handful of the dry leaves into the pot to brew. The smell of the herbs arose freshly in the cool air of the hillside.

"You shouldn't do it. Not when there's no need." He was unable to explain any farther, but his flood of words had dried up abruptly, and we brewed our tea and sat there drinking it together in silence as the sea birds wheeled and screamed overhead.

The summers were full of such days. When he wasn't needed to work with the horses or help around the camp, Darragh would come to find me, and we explored the rocky hillsides, the clifftop paths, the hidden bays and secret caves together. He taught me to fish with a single line and a steady hand. I taught him to read what day it was from the way the shadows moved up on the hilltop. When it rained, as it had a way of doing even in summer, we'd sit together in the shelter of a little cave, down at the bottom of the land bridge that joined the Honeycomb to the shore, a place that was almost underground but not quite, for the daylight filtered through from above and washed the tiny patch of fine sand to a delicate shade of gray-blue. In this place I always felt safe. In this place sky and earth and sea met and touched and parted again, and the sound of the wavelets lapping the subterranean beach was like a sigh, at once greeting and farewell. Darragh never told me if he liked my secret cave or not. He'd simply come down with me, and sit by me, and when the rain was over, he'd slip away with never a word.

There was a wild grass that grew on the hillside there, a strong, supple plant with a silky sheen to its pale green stems. We called it rat-tails, though it probably had some other name. Peg and her daughters were expert basketweavers, and made use of this grass for their finer and prettier efforts, the sort that might be sold to a lady for gathering flowers maybe, rather than for carrying vegetables or a heavy load of firewood.

Darragh, too, could weave, his long fingers fast and nimble. Once summer we were up by the standing stones, late in the afternoon, sitting with our backs to the Sentinel and looking out over the bay and the far promontory, and beyond to the western sea. Clouds were gathering, and the air had a touch of chill to it. Today I could not read the shadows, but I knew it was drawing close to summer's end, and another parting. I was sad, and cross with myself for being sad, and I was trying not to think about another winter of hard work and cold, lonely days. I stared at the stony ground and thought about the year, and how it turned around like a serpent biting its own tail, how it rolled on like a relentless wheel. The good times would come again, and after them the bad times.

Darragh had a fistful of rat-tails, and he was twisting them deftly and whistling under his breath. Darragh was never sad. He'd no time for it; for him, life was an adventure, with always a new door to open. Besides, he could go away if he wanted to. He didn't have lessons to learn and skills to perfect, as I did.

I glared at the pebbles on the ground. Around and around, that was my existence, endlessly repeating, a cycle from which there was no escape. Around and around. Fixed and unchangeable. I watched the pebbles as they shuddered and rolled; as they moved obediently on the ground before me.

"Fainne?" Darragh was frowning at me, and at the shifting stones on the earth in front of me.

"What?" My concentration was broken. The stones stopped moving. Now they lay in a perfect circle.

"Here," he said. "Hold out your hand."

I did as be bid me, puzzled, and he slipped a little ring of woven rat-tails on my finger, so cunningly made that it seemed without any joint or fastening.

"What's this for?" I asked him, turning the silky, springy circle of grass around and around. He was looking away over the bay again, watching the small curraghs come in from fishing.

"So you don't forget me," he said, offhand.

"Don't be silly," I said. "Why would I forget you?"

"You might," said Darragh, turning back toward me. He gestured toward the neat circle of tiny stones.

"You might get caught up in other things." I was hurt. "I wouldn't. I never would."

Darragh gave a sigh and shrugged his shoulders. "You're only little. You don't know. Winter's a long time, Fainne. And—and you need keeping an eye on."

"I do not!" I retorted instantly, jumping up from where I sat. Who did he think he was, talking as if he was my big brother? "I can look after myself quite well, thank you. And now I'm going home."

"I'll walk with you."

"You don't have to."

"I'll walk with you. Better still, I'll race you. Just as far as the junipers down there. Come on."

I stood stolid, scowling at him.

"I'll give you a head start," coaxed Darragh. "I'll count to ten."

I made no move.

"Twenty, then. Go on, off you go." He smiled, a broad, irresistible smile.

I ran, if you could call my awkward, limping gait a run. With my skirt caught up in one hand, I made reasonable speed, though the steep, pebbly surface required some caution. I was only halfway to the junipers when I heard his soft, quick footsteps right behind me. No race could have been less equal, and both of us knew it. He could have covered the ground in a quarter of the time it took me. But somehow, the way it worked out, the two of us reached the bushes at exactly the same moment.

"All right, sorcerer's daughter," said Darragh, grinning. "Now we walk and catch our breath. It'll be a better day tomorrow."

How old was I then? Six, maybe, and he a year or two older? I had the little ring on my finger the day the traveling folk packed up and moved out again; the day I had to wave goodbye and start waiting. It was all right for him. He had places to go and things to do, and he was eager to get on his pony and be off. Still, he made time to say farewell, up on the hillside above the camp, for he knew I would not come near where the folk gathered to load their carts and make ready for the journey. I was numb with shyness, quite unable to bear the stares of the boys and girls or to form an answer to Peg's shrewd, kindly questions. My father was down there, a tall, cloaked figure talking to Danny Walker, giving him messages to deliver, commissions to fulfill. Around them, the folk left a wide, empty circle.

"Well then," said Darragh.

"Well then," I echoed, trying for the same tone of nonchalance, and failing miserably.

"Goodbye, Curly," he said, reaching out to tug gently at a lock of my long hair, which was the same deep russet as my father's. "I'll see you next summer. Keep out of trouble, now, until I come back." Every time he went away he said this; always just the same.

As for me, I had no words at all.